Martyn Gregory is one of Britain's leading investigative journalists who specialises in revealing the activities of British-based multi-national companies. Many of his television investigations have made headline news.

In 1995 Gregory reported, produced and directed 'The Torture Trail', a ground-breaking exposure of British Aerospace and other companies involved in the trade in electro-shock batons – weapons that can be used for torture. The film was made for Channel 4's *Dispatches*, and it won British television journalism's highest honour – the Royal Television Society's award for the 'best home current affairs documentary'. The film also won Amnesty International's 'best documentary' award in 1995, and Tony Blair MP, the leader of the British Labour party, presented the Campaign for Freedom of Information's 1996 'media' award to Gregory for his 'brilliant achievement' in exposing the British torture trade.

In 1995 Martyn Gregory became the first journalist ever to successfully sue the British government for libel. Government ministers, led by the then President of the Board of Trade, Michael Heseltine, accused Gregory of fabricating the evidence he used to make 'The Torture Trail'. After he sued the Department of Trade and Industry, the government made an 'unreserved apology' to Gregory in the High Court; it admitted that the programme was 'properly researched', and paid him substantial damages and costs.

Gregory's 1996 follow-up *Dispatches* film, 'Back on the Torture Trail', which exposed continuing British complicity in the torture trade, was described by John Pilger as, 'a stunning piece of work . . . the best and bravest investigation on television, anywhere, for a very long time'.

Between 1992 and 1996, Gregory made several widely hailed

films that exposed dirty-tricks campaigns by British Airways against its British rivals. His 1992 *This Week* film, 'Violating Virgin', first revealed British Airways' dirty-tricks campaign against Richard Branson and Virgin Atlantic, and ignited the conflict between the two airlines. His subsequent investigations for *World in Action*, ITN and the BBC's *Newsnight* and *Forty Minutes* programmes have revealed dramatic new evidence of British Airways' dirty-tricks campaigns.

As a freelance journalist Gregory has written for the *Guardian*, the *Independent* and *The Times*, as well as contributing articles for the Royal Institute of International Affairs at Chatham House. As a television journalist he has worked for the BBC, where he was a producer/reporter for six years in news and current affairs, and for Granada TV, Thames TV and ITN.

He now runs his own production company, Martyn Gregory Films, in London where he lives.

DIRTY TRICKS

British Airways'
secret war against
Virgin Atlantic

Martyn Gregory

WARNER BOOKS

A *Warner* Book

First published in Great Britain in 1994
by Little, Brown and Company
This updated edition published in 1996 by Warner Books

Copyright © 1994, 1996 by Martyn Gregory

A CIP catalogue record for this book
is available from the British Library

ISBN 0 7515 1063 7

Typeset in Palatino by M Rules
Printed and bound in Great Britain by
Clays Ltd, St Ives plc

Warner Books
A Division of
Little, Brown and Company (UK)
Brettenham House
Lancaster Place
London WC2E 7EN

To John Harrison
(1946–1994)

My friend and former BBC colleague, John Harrison, died in South Africa in March 1994 as he reported on the elections that brought Nelson Mandela to the presidency of a free South Africa. Fred Harrison paid this tribute to his brother at his memorial service in London: 'John died in the pursuit of journalistic excellence. He would never compromise, and he never ceased to explore the outer edges of what is possible . . . When he died, John was in the process of returning to society the riches of the talents he had acquired. That was his gift.'

John was an inspiration to me. I was devastated to learn of his death the day after *Dirty Tricks* was first published. This poem was written by Fergal Keane, one of John's BBC colleagues in South Africa. It expresses my feelings of loss far better than I am capable of doing.

> Dead. So hard to say that word, to believe it.
> So I will choose not to. Rather I imagine that
> any moment now you will come rolling in the door,
> a ship of life, bound for the shores of promise.
>
> Dear, lost friend, we will harbour your memory,
> we will bind our loss in the warm currents of
> your laughter, we will search the African sky
> for your wild blazing star.
>
> In the long term, the picture will become less clear,
> we will all of us drift into other lives;
> but your voice will endure, singing out to us
> between the spaces in the wind, always free,
> always John.

Fergal Keane

Contents

Acknowledgements

I am sure that most authors owe a debt of gratitude to those who are closest. I am certainly no exception. I have been very touched by the support and the understanding that my friends have extended to me while I wrote this book.

To find the peace I needed to write, I spent the summer of 1993 in the South of France – 'Aux Deux Soeurs', in the lee of the Baux de Provence. Shortly after I arrived I broke my leg on the tennis court. There was little excuse not to write after that, but I know what an immense burden I placed upon those with whom I stayed. Were it not for the kindness and the support of the friends who came to look after me, I would not have been able to write. Greg Ainger, Patsy Newey and their son 'little John' spent ten days nursing me, cooking for me and providing wonderful company when the day's writing was over. Kevin Loader and Philippa Langdale first took me to hospital, and without Caroline and Laurent Delanney I would probably still be in France! I know my car would be.

All of you, as well as my hosts in Provence, Carolyn Wood and her small son Jack, helped me in ways that I know you will remember, and I will most certainly never forget.

I wrote the additional material for the paperback in the first half of 1996, and I want to thank my friends and colleagues at my new

TV production company, Martyn Gregory Films, for their support and understanding. Running the company and making films while writing this book has not been easy, but Julian Bellamy, Peter Dumont, Julia Stroud, Victoria English, Chris Martin and Eliane Drakopoulos have helped to make it possible.

This book arose from two investigations into Virgin Atlantic's dirty-tricks allegations against British Airways. The first was 'Violating Virgin?' for *This Week* in February 1992 and the second was 'BA's Virgin Soldiers' for *World in Action* in April 1993. I have also drawn on information I gathered while I directed a film for the BBC about the collapse of Laker Airways. 'A Case of Corporate Murder', in the BBC's *40 Minutes* series, revealed how Sir Freddie Laker, the pioneer of cheap transatlantic flying, was put out of business by BA and a cartel of international carriers, assisted by Mrs Thatcher's government which was desperate to privatise BA.

Successful television is always the result of teamwork, and I have been extremely fortunate to have worked with talented collaborators. Michael Chrisman helped me to produce the *This Week* and the *World in Action* films and it is difficult to imagine a more dedicated and discreet colleague. You will recognise some of the revelations in these pages as being your own, Michael. Richard Lindley brought thirty years of reporting experience and a proper scepticism to the *This Week* film, which strengthened it enormously.

I would like to thank the former editor of the *Sunday Times* 'Insight' team, Nick Rufford, for allowing me access to his files and to his research. Nick covered the dirty-tricks story with distinction for his newspaper and this book is enhanced by his contribution to it.

In Frank Haysom at Thames TV and George Jesse Turner and Howard Sommers at Granada TV, I found three most pleasant people and three of the best cameramen I have worked with. Paul Woolwich, the former editor of Thames TV's *This Week*, Charles Tremayne, the executive producer of Granada TV's *World in Action*, and ITN's former head of programmes, David Mannion, all showed resolve and editorial courage. I would like to express my gratitude to them, and to their television companies, for supporting my journalism when under enormous pressure not to do so.

After the hardback edition of this book was published, I broke the extraordinary story of John Gorman for the BBC's *Newsnight* and the *Guardian*. Gorman is a BA shareholder who complained to the airline after he swallowed glass in a complimentary drink on a flight to New York, and then found himself the victim of a vicious dirty-tricks campaign. Gorman claims the campaign has been mounted by BA and the Metropolitan Police at Heathrow, and my investigation into the affair forms the last chapter of this edition, 'The Virgin Stooge'. I would particularly like to thank my *Newsnight* producer, Dee McIntosh, for her enormous determination and commitment in extremely trying circumstances. I would also like to thank the editor of *Newsnight*, Peter Horrocks, for commissioning two films on the Gorman affair, and for robustly and intelligently overseeing them, and *Newsnight*'s brilliant cameramen/journalists Ian Pritchard and 'Sir Francis' Considine. The first *Newsnight* film was transmitted in August 1994.

Karen Beedle cheerfully dedicated much unremunerated time and effort to helping me research the hardback edition of the book, and Eliane Drakopoulos provided invaluable research assistance as I prepared the paperback edition. ITN's Angela Fryer helped me open a very important door, and Jill Samuels' contribution to my investigation into the collapse of Laker Airways and the subsequent litigation was enormous.

I am particularly indebted to those who took time out of their own busy lives to read early drafts of the manuscript. My brother, Adrian, read it, as did Trish Powell and Miff Stourton and Mr Mustard. Caroline Delanney travelled from France to read it and to provide detailed and sympathetic criticism. Kevin Loader read the manuscript twice, and Julia Madonna's detailed scrutiny helped me to eradicate many errors. All of you helped me to improve the book, and I am really grateful to you.

This paperback edition is dedicated to my friend and former BBC colleague, John Harrison, who died in the week that *Dirty Tricks* was first published in March 1994. My sympathy goes to his wife, Penny, and their two sons, as well as to Joan Thirkettle's children, Daisy and Michael. Another distinguished TV news reporter, Joan passed away in the spring of 1996. I got to know Joan as she specialised in Virgin-related stories, and because she doggedly reported the unravelling dirty-tricks saga for ITN, where we briefly became colleagues in 1993. One of her finest moments is recounted in Chapter 13 when she confronted Lord King as he stepped down from the chairmanship of BA.

I would also like to remember Andrew Nitch-Smith, the brilliant solicitor who worked for Denton Hall. Andrew was one of Tiny Rowland's lawyers, and he helped me throughout my investigations into the activities of the Fayed brothers and Brian Basham. The last time I saw him was at the launch of *Dirty Tricks* in March 1994. He died shortly afterwards, still only in his early forties, of a massive heart attack, leaving his wife, Marian, and their three young children.

I would like to thank my agent, Hilary Rubinstein, and the editorial and production staff at Little, Brown. Editorial director Alan Samson had the faith to commission this book, and has lent encouragement and experience, enthusiasm and understanding to the project ever since. My script editor, James Woodall, wrestled with the inadequacies of my prose, and desk editor, Helga Houghton, worked furiously hard to produce both editions of the book. Picture researcher Linda Silverman searched long and hard to find the best pictures.

Richard Branson agreed to be interviewed, and to allow me access to the daily diary of events that he kept throughout the dirty-tricks affair. He also asked his staff to co-operate with my investigations. Thank you all for your help and your cheerful immunity to my plague of calls!

Since my first phone call to British Airways' press office in February 1992, well before any legal action between the two airlines was started, I have yet to be granted one formal, on-the-record interview with any member of British Airways' staff about any of the matters referred to in this book. In the course of my investigations into the dirty-tricks affair for Thames TV, Granada TV, ITN, the BBC, the *Independent* and the *Guardian*, BA's press officers have treated my calls with civility, but they have been under progressively strict instructions not to co-operate. Occasionally short faxes are emitted by the press office at moments of great pressure, but they are invariably unenlightening.

I would, therefore, particularly like to thank those past and present members of BA who urged me to write this book, and who
defied their management's edicts in order to assist me with interviews and documents.

When I approached Lord King, Sir Colin Marshall and Robert
Ayling to invite them, and several of their senior managers and
employees, to give their version of events, I was referred to BA's
external lawyers – in New York. I duly phoned them but we
have yet to meet. I was also referred to another brick in BA's
stonewall, Sir Tim Bell, one of Mrs Thatcher's former public relations advisers.

Following the collapse of BA's defence in the 'dirty-tricks'
libel case in January 1993, Sir Tim was hired to interpose himself
between British Airways and those trying to investigate the airline's activities in relation to Virgin Atlantic or Air Europe. To do
this he employs familiar tricks of the PR trade: flattery, charm,
intimidation, threats of legal action, and prodigious economy
with the truth.

When Sir Tim was told by a colleague that I was writing this
book he exploded in a fit of rage. 'That despicable man!' he cried,
before lapsing into a tirade of abuse. I regard Sir Tim's description
of me as an enormous compliment – it certainly encouraged me to
carry on writing when my enthusiasm flagged. Although the
activities of a number of public relations men are described in this
book, I would like to dedicate the revelations in the pages that follow to you, Sir Tim.

From 'that despicable man',

Martyn Gregory
London,
July 1996

Preface

Although I did not realise it at the time, I started this book on the day I first met Richard Branson: 8 January 1992. At the time I was working as a producer-director on the ITV current affairs programme *This Week*. Following a pre-Christmas flurry of press coverage I had been asked to look into Branson's claims that British Airways was running a dirty-tricks campaign against his airline.

I arrived early for our meeting at Branson's Holland Park home in West London, which at that time doubled as his office. He was standing outside the house with a group of Virgin Atlantic stewardesses in their distinctive scarlet uniforms. I wondered what was going on. I watched from the other side of the tree-lined street as Branson and his stewardesses suddenly threw their arms to the sky. 'Across the pond for £99! Only on Virgin Atlantic! Roll up! Roll up!' cried Branson.

I rebuked myself for not realising that I had stumbled on a Branson photo-opportunity. Branson and his group of hostesses posed in front of a cardboard Virgin tail-fin with the details of his winter saver to New York plastered all over it. A small cluster of cameramen dutifully recorded the event. After a short interview with a television reporter, I was amused to see Branson manoeuvre the cardboard tail-fin rather awkwardly up the steps to his front door and disappear inside with it.

I waited for a few moments before knocking on his door. I viewed the prospect of making a film about Virgin Atlantic's quarrel with British Airways with mixed feelings. I had spent much of the previous year filming in the Gulf and the Middle East, first in Israel and Kuwait during the war, and then in the Lebanon just before the British hostages were released. A spat between two British airlines seemed tame in comparison, and I was sceptical about what little I had read of Branson's claims in the papers. Given his well-chronicled ability to use himself to publicise anything bearing the name 'Virgin', I needed to be convinced that his 'dirty-tricks' allegations against BA warranted attention.

I remembered the dramatic day in 1985 when Richard Branson's transatlantic power-boat sank just short of its destination. I was a junior producer in BBC news. The first reports of Branson's potentially fatal accident reached the newsroom just after the *Six O'Clock News* ended. A series of newsflashes updated viewers on Branson's fate, and a heated debate developed over whether the story should lead the *Nine O'Clock News*. The South African Prime Minister, P.W. Botha, was due to address his parliament in Cape Town that evening: teams of BBC people were expecting to report a speech announcing the end of apartheid. So what should lead the late news bulletin? The historic end of apartheid, or the disappearance of a self-publicist in a boating accident?

I backed the minority P.W. Botha faction, but was relieved when the issue was resolved by the course of events before transmission. The *Nine O'Clock News* led with a report that Branson had been fished out of the Atlantic alive; later, Botha had failed to cross the Rubicon. 'British hero rescued from the cruel sea' was a much better lead than 'apartheid to continue'. Reservations about the genuine news value of stories involving Branson remained a dilemma, however, and I was keenly aware of it as I climbed the steps to his front door.

Branson was wrestling with the cardboard Virgin tail-fin in his spacious hall as I entered. We spent the morning talking about his claims against BA. He was joined by Will Whitehorn, a fresh-faced Scot who had been his personal press officer for the past few years, and I was joined by my colleague, Michael Chrisman, a taciturn New Yorker who was *This Week*'s associate producer.

I was surprised by Branson. He had returned tanned but clearly not relaxed from his Christmas holiday on Necker, his Caribbean island. For hours he pored over notes he had scribbled in battered diaries detailing his claims. Frequently interrupted by Whitehorn, Branson outlined Virgin's case as best he could.

Whitehorn couldn't stop talking and Branson sometimes found it difficult to start as he struggled to read his own notes. He constantly dragged his hands though his wiry fair hair, cupping his chin in his hands as he tried to read his own handwriting. Fleetingly he appeared to me to be more like the distraught figure in Munch's classic frieze, 'The Scream', than the familiar chat-show guest. The photo-opportunity grin had been left in the porch with the cardboard Virgin tail-fin.

Branson and Whitehorn told us extraordinary stories of private detectives, stolen passengers, shredded documents. They told us of a mysterious American who once worked for BA, and a 'dodgy PR man' with the improbable name of Basham who, they claimed, had been hired by Lord King to trash Virgin Atlantic in the press. They eventually produced a typed list of allegations against Lord King's airline, headed 'BA's dirty tricks'.

Just before we left Branson said: 'I am quite convinced that Lord King is trying to drive Virgin Atlantic out of business. There is absolutely no doubt in my mind.'

We left Holland Park with a bundle of documents and much food for thought. I was impressed by Branson and Whitehorn's sincerity, but Chrisman and I needed to do our own research. Branson's list of allegations sounded more like the ingredients for a novel than a plausible explanation of a plot to ground his airline.

Eventually, we established what we thought were interesting questions for BA to answer. We asked Lord King to take part. He refused. Before transmission, I received a letter from the head of BA's legal department, Mervyn Walker. Walker accused me of

falling into the trap of being used as a vehicle for Richard

Branson's propaganda, which sets out to contrive controversy with British Airways to create publicity for himself
and his company and to inflict serious damage on the reputation of British Airways.

We are not prepared to be provoked into playing Mr
Branson's futile game and, therefore, must decline to take
part in interviews on this occasion.

I was surprised that the legal director had been instructed to write
to me, and startled at the ferocity of his response to our request to
interview Lord King. I wondered how he had come to his conclusion that I had fallen for Richard Branson's propaganda.
Nonetheless, we made a point of including extracts from Walker's
letter in the programme when it was transmitted on 27 February
1992.

The next day, BA's in-house weekly newspaper, *BA News*,
reproduced Walker's letter to me almost in its entire form under
the front-page headline, 'Branson "Dirty Tricks" Claim
Unfounded'. Lord King repeated similar sentiments in a letter to
viewers who had written to BA to complain about the allegations
contained in the programme. Three weeks later, Richard Branson
sued BA for libel on the basis of both the *BA News* article and
Lord King's letter.

'King was effectively calling me a liar, so I sued him,' said
Branson, who had never previously issued a writ on his own
behalf.

Another three weeks passed, and King countersued Branson, also
for libel. It was spring 1992. The dirty-tricks affair became *sub judice*
and, for the rest of the year, the story all but disappeared from public view. Both King and Branson ploughed millions into hiring the
best lawyers they could find to prosecute each other in what was
immediately dubbed 'the mother of all libel battles' in the press. At
stake were the reputations of two of the best-known products of
Mrs Thatcher's 'enterprise culture'. Both had become household
names because of their airlines – King for the transformation of
British Airways, Branson for the creation of Virgin Atlantic.

On 11 January 1993, the dirty-tricks affair exploded back into
public consciousness.

Lord King and British Airways paid Richard Branson and Virgin Atlantic £610,000 in damages, the largest libel sum ever paid in British history.[1] In addition, BA paid the entire cost of the libel action – estimated at £4.5 million. Lord King and his airline also apologised to Richard Branson for perpetrating a series of activities which gave Virgin Atlantic's chairman 'reasonable grounds for serious concern'.

What everyone else by now referred to as 'dirty tricks' BA preferred to call 'disreputable business practices'. The airline admitted in the High Court that these included passenger poaching, document shredding, and obtaining access to computer information about Virgin Atlantic. In addition BA admitted trying to plant 'hostile and discreditable' stories about Virgin and Richard Branson in the press. Because it was the publication of Mervyn Walker's letter to me that had sparked the libel battle, BA also acknowledged in the High Court statement that my film had 'independently investigated the dispute'.

British Airways insisted, however, in the High Court statement that 'the directors of British Airways were not party to any concerted campaign against Richard Branson and Virgin Atlantic'. In a subsequent elaboration of the airline's position, BA stated that 'the regrettable conduct . . . was confined to a relatively small number of unconnected incidents involving a small number of employees'.

Under enormous pressure from the airline's institutional investors and the non-executive directors on BA's board, Lord King and the chief executive, Sir Colin Marshall, were required to sign pledges affirming that they had not 'implemented or authorised' any of the 'disreputable business practices' that the airline had apologised for in court. The chairman of BA's non-executive directors, Sir Michael Angus, who was also President of the Confederation of British Industry at the time, went further. In a statement, he claimed that Sir Colin Marshall 'did not know' about any of these 'disreputable activities'.

It was difficult to find many outside the BA boardroom who

---

[1] Others have been awarded more, but no one has been paid more.

believed this. The board, however, was satisfied with the directors' pledges. Lord King stepped down as chairman and the board appointed him president. The chief executive, Sir Colin Marshall, was promoted to chairman, a post which he now combines with that of chief executive. Robert Ayling, formerly the director of the marketing and operations department, was also promoted to become group managing director.

By caving in, British Airways had avoided a trial that was scheduled to last three months, but Lord King and his airline could not avoid a wave of criticism from all quarters of business and political opinion in Britain. For the airline that had awarded itself the title of 'The World's Favourite Airline' after its privatisation in 1987, the fallout from the dirty-tricks affair was a public relations disaster of unparalleled proportions.

No criticism of BA was more savage than that of *The Times*' columnist Bernard Levin. So disturbed by the affair was he that he devoted two entire articles to it. Levin detected

> a stench so relentless that I have found myself unable to sleep . . . The stench is made up of several sub-stenches, including self-exculpation, blame-shifting, cowardice, knavery, crocodile tears and a miasma in which anything can be lost and no doubt has been.
>
> Lord King presided over an enterprise that would have had the mafia saluting, while his fetcher and carrier, Sir Colin Marshall, trotted behind him.

Levin concluded his second article by posing the following questions: 'Who instigated? Who knew? Who denied? Who covered up? These are the four crucial questions that must be answered.'

An even more fundamental question should be added to Levin's list: 'Why did BA do it in the first place?'

This book is my attempt to answer all of these questions.

BA's Management Tree

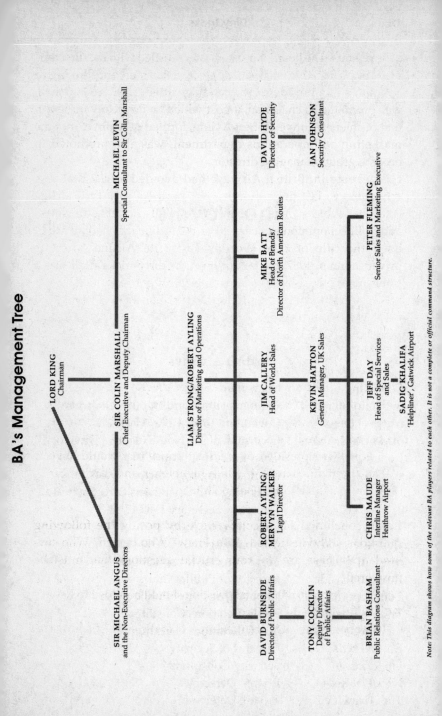

LORD KING
Chairman

SIR MICHAEL ANGUS
and the Non-Executive Directors

SIR COLIN MARSHALL
Chief Executive and Deputy Chairman

MICHAEL LEVIN
Special Consultant to Sir Colin Marshall

LIAM STRONG/ROBERT AYLING
Director of Marketing and Operations

DAVID HYDE
Director of Security

IAN JOHNSON
Security Consultant

MIKE BATT
Head of Brands/
Director of North American Routes

JIM CALLERY
Head of World Sales

PETER FLEMING
Senior Sales and Marketing Executive

KEVIN HATTON
General Manager, UK Sales

JEFF DAY
Head of Special Services
and Sales

SADIG KHALIFA
'Helpliner', Gatwick Airport

**ROBERT AYLING/
MERVYN WALKER**
Legal Director

CHRIS MAUDE
Interline Manager
Heathrow Airport

DAVID BURNSIDE
Director of Public Affairs

TONY COCKLIN
Deputy Director
of Public Affairs

BRIAN BASHAM
Public Relations Consultant

Note: This diagram shows how some of the relevant BA players related to each other. It is not a complete or official command structure.

The Players

British Airways

Lord King	Chairman
Sir Colin Marshall	Chief Executive and Deputy Chairman
Michael Levin	Consultant to Sir Colin Marshall
Sir Michael Angus	Chairman of the Non-Executive Directors
Robert Ayling	Chief Executive from 1995
	Group Managing Director 1993–5
	Marketing and Operations Director 1991/2
	Company Secretary 1987–1991
	Legal Director 1985–1991
Gail Redwood	Company Secretary 1991–4
Mervyn Walker	Legal Director from October 1991
David Burnside	Director of Public Affairs
Tony Cocklin	Deputy Director of Public Affairs
Brian Basham	Public Relations Consultant
Sir Tim Bell	Public Relations Consultant
David Hyde	Director of Security
Ian Johnson	Security Consultant
Nick Del Rosso	Private Detective
Tom Crowley	Private Detective

Liam Strong	Marketing and Operations Director until September 1991
Mike Batt	Head of Brands & Vice-President, North America
Jim Callery	Head of World Sales
Kevin Hatton	General Manager, UK Sales
Peter Fleming	Senior Executive, Sales and Marketing
Sue Hollis	London Sales Manager
John Scaife	Business Analysis Unit
David Noyes	General Manager, Telephone Sales
Chris Maude	Interline Sales Manager, Heathrow
Yvonne Fletcher	Interline Sales Executive, Gatwick
Jeff Day	Head of Gatwick 'Helpliners'
Sadig Khalifa	'Helpliner', Gatwick Airport
Dick Eberhart	US Vice-President, Commercial Affairs
David Williams	Head of Sales, Southern California (Los Angeles)
Wendy Partridge	Customer Relations Executive
John Turnbull	UK Solicitor, Linklaters & Paines
John Dickey	US Attorney, Sullivan & Cromwell, USA

Virgin Atlantic

Richard Branson	Chairman
Will Whitehorn	Press Officer
Gerrard Tyrrell	Solicitor, Harbottle & Lewis

Others

Margaret Thatcher	British Prime Minister, 1979–1990
Malcolm Rifkind	Secretary of State for Transport, 1990–1992
Sir Freddie Laker	Chairman, Laker Airways
Harry Goodman	Chairman, Air Europe
John Gorman	BA Shareholder and Complainant
Yvonne Parsons	
Caroline Mickler	} Virgin Atlantic Passengers
Dr James Sorrentino	

1

Dangerous Games

West London. Late March 1992

John Reilly drove his white transit van to the junction of the A40 and the Edgware Road in West London. He parked under the flyover and switched off the engine. He glanced up and noticed people making their way into the vast Metropole Hotel. The engine ticked quietly as it cooled. Reilly sat silently.

After about fifteen minutes, a darkly clad figure on a motor scooter appeared on the other side of the road. Reilly recognised the silhouette of the Territorial SAS officer against the headlights of the oncoming traffic. The man waited for a break in the traffic before bringing his bike over to Reilly's side of the road. Reilly wound down the window as the man removed his crash helmet to reveal closely cropped, dark hair.

'How did it go?' the man asked.

'No problem,' replied Reilly as he stretched to retrieve a large envelope from behind the passenger seat. He passed it through the window.

As his contact melted into the darkness, Reilly started his van and headed home down the A40.

John Reilly had joined the swelling ranks of Britain's 'private investigators' as the clammy tentacles of the recession began to grip Britain in the late 1980s. A thin, ginger-haired man with a wispy beard and waxen complexion, Reilly lived a parasitic existence. As the recession began, the private detective hunted debtors, bankrupts and unfaithful partners. Most of his clients were solicitors and suspicious spouses who were keen to remain anonymous. They used him as a 'circuit-breaker' or 'cut-out' to isolate them from their dirty work.

Reilly advertised his services in the Yellow Pages under 'Metropolitan Private Investigations – Discreet Inquiries Undertaken'. He worked from a small, cluttered house in Teddington which he shared with his wife and mother-in-law. Reilly had drifted into private detective work without any formal qualifications or experience. A former wedding photographer, he had started his undercover existence by conducting 'static' surveillance, a mind-numbingly tedious occupation, involving sitting for hours in a car, or sometimes under a hedge, waiting to photograph 'suspects'. Reilly progressed to private investigations, and worked out of a tar-paper shed at the bottom of his garden. The shed doubled as a dark room.

In the middle of March 1992, detailed instructions had been left on Reilly's answerphone for an assignment on his patch. Reilly always preferred working from a recorded message. The circuit-breaker kept all his taped instructions until he had been paid to ensure that he was not cut out of his commission. The voice on the answerphone told Reilly to steal sacks of rubbish from an address in Teddington. As normal with 'rubbish runs', Reilly would have to sift through the garbage once he had stolen it. In this case, the client asked him to recover all the documents he found in the rubbish bags.

Even though 'rubbish runs' were Reilly's stock-in-trade, he had never quite got used to the stench of the kitchen waste and disposable nappies he often encountered. The smell made him want to vomit. At least he didn't have too far to go on this occasion – the Teddington address the voice had left on the answerphone was less than a mile from where he lived.

In the early hours of the morning, Reilly drove his white transit van towards his target's home. Dressed in the dark pullover and jeans he normally wore for rubbish runs, he drew up to the address in Teddington Park. Leaving the engine running, he slipped out of the van and made for the bin-bags. He tip-toed up the gravel path trying to make as little noise as possible. The bags were to the right of the front door. He stooped down, picked up two of them and carried them quickly back to the van. As he crept up the drive a second time, the low growl of a dog disturbed the silence. Reilly doubled back quickly towards his van with another sack over his shoulder, hoping the animal would not start barking.

Reilly heaved the three sacks into the back of the van. The dog started barking as Reilly clambered back into the driver's seat. He threw the engine into gear and accelerated away. The job had taken him less than three minutes.

Reilly's heart pounded as he drove. The barking dog worried him. When he was clear of the house, he pulled the van into the side of the road. Slipping quickly into a different jacket and pulling a baseball hat firmly down over his head, he walked back to the scene. He was concerned that the incident might have caused a disturbance, and that he might have been spotted. He walked past the house twice, searching for any sign of a commotion, any indication that he had been spotted. Nothing stirred.

The following morning, Reilly braced himself before inspecting the contents of the sacks. As normal, he emptied the garbage onto a plastic sheet in his garden. Sifting through the trash, he carefully separated out documents, magazines, credit-card slips, train tickets, letters and even tiny scraps with scribbled notes or phone numbers from the rest of the trash. As he uncreased an envelope Reilly became aware for the first time that the owner of the rubbish was a Mr Roger Eglin. The name meant nothing to him.

When Reilly went back into his house there was a message waiting for him on his answerphone. It was the voice again. It instructed him to repeat his rubbish run the following week.

The next day John Reilly's wife woke him at seven o'clock. A policeman was at the front door. Detective Constable Johnnie Elfed from Twickenham CID told Reilly that some rubbish sacks had been removed from outside a house in Teddington in rather odd circumstances. The gaunt young policeman asked if he could step inside and discuss it. John Reilly looked at him in astonishment.

Oxford. 14 March 1992

Richard Branson sensed a trap. He had just taken a call from Frank Kane, a reporter on the *Sunday Telegraph*. Quoting an anonymous but 'reliable' source, Kane told Branson that the source claimed Virgin Atlantic had employed private detectives to spy on British Airways in its 'dirty-tricks' war with the national carrier. Kane said the source had told him that agents working for Virgin were bugging the telephones of key members of the British Airways board of directors as part of a highly sophisticated undercover campaign against BA.

Branson interrupted the reporter frequently to check names and details. He jotted all the claims down in his diary.

Virgin has employed private investigators to spy on BA.

The investigators are called International Investigations – IGI.

[Virgin] has been tapping BA people's phones for the last six months.

The detectives were employed for Virgin by Goldman Sachs [a merchant bank used by Virgin].

As he replaced the receiver Branson noticed his hand was shaking. Virgin's chairman had good reason to be shocked at what Frank Kane's source had told him. Branson didn't tell Kane that only two days earlier he had, indeed, been listening to an illicit recording of a phone call between two of the most senior members of the British Airways board, Sir Colin Marshall, and his powerful right-hand man, Robert Ayling. Marshall and Ayling were considered throughout the airline industry to be the second and third most influential men at BA after Lord King.

The tape had arrived anonymously at Virgin Atlantic's Crawley headquarters the previous week in a brown jiffy bag. After marketing manager Chris Moss had listened to it, he immediately alerted Branson. Two days later, the *Sunday Telegraph* was tipped off about an alleged Virgin undercover operation against BA involving phone tapping.

Richard Branson and his lawyer, Gerrard Tyrrell, spent the

remainder of an extremely tense Saturday trying to get the *Sunday Telegraph* not to run the story. The newspaper was bombarded by calls from Branson's weekend retreat in Oxfordshire and from the London-based Tyrrell. Branson finally received an undertaking that the story would not run after Tyrrell threatened the paper with instant legal action if they printed the allegations.

Now, a relieved Branson tried to recall every detail of the very mysterious forty-eight hours that had just elapsed.

The tape had arrived in an envelope addressed simply to 'Virgin Atlantic'. Like other miscellaneous mail, it found its way into Chris Moss's in-tray. There it remained for nearly a week. Assuming it was one of the thousands of unsolicited music tapes for Richard Branson as chairman of Virgin Music, Moss finally slotted it into his office tape player as he opened the rest of his correspondence.

Hearing two men calling each other 'Colin' and 'Bob' on his speakers, Moss thought someone was playing a practical joke and carried on sorting his mail. Then he heard the two men discussing the letter Branson had written to BA the previous week, and a television programme about the dirty-tricks affair. He studied the jiffy bag for clues as to who had sent it. The smudged postmark revealed that it had been sent on 4 March from London NW2. There was nothing at all to indicate the identity of the sender.

Moss swiftly decided the tape was not a hoax and drove immediately from Crawley to his boss's home in London's Holland Park. Sitting in Branson's front room surrounded by dozens of model aeroplanes and pictures of Branson's family, the two men listened intently to the tape with growing astonishment.

It began routinely. Sir Colin Marshall and Robert Ayling were discussing a management conference they had attended at Chewton Glen, a sumptuous hotel set in wooded grounds in the New Forest in Hampshire.

Marshall's voice sounded tinny, as though he were speaking on a mobile phone. Between crackles of static and 'data bursts' – barely audible squeaks carrying billing information – Branson could make out their conversation clearly. They were talking about him.

'I think the whole thing is just scandalous and now we've got this two-page letter from him, I gather,' said the chief executive.

'Yes, it came in addressed to you on Friday and was copied to the rest of the board and I've got my copy,' said Ayling.

'It was copied to the rest of the board, was it?' asked Marshall.

'Yeah.'

'Oh. The chairman was complaining last night that he hadn't received his copy.'

'No, it's copied to the rest of the board,' confirmed Ayling.

Branson knew immediately what the two men were talking about. The letter Marshall and Ayling were discussing was his ultimatum. He had written to Marshall threatening to take BA to court unless it stopped trying to put Virgin Atlantic out of business by a series of 'dirty tricks'. Branson had aimed his latest salvo at the chief executive because his relationship with his rival chairman, Lord King, had deteriorated to such an extent that the two men no longer communicated.

For over a year Branson had been complaining that BA had been targeting his routes by slashing its fares, that it had been attempting to block Virgin Atlantic's access to new routes and that it had withdrawn co-operation on safety training and engineering matters. He had also complained loudly over reports that some of his passengers were being lured onto BA flights in Britain and the USA by BA hit squads.

Branson claimed that his plans to expand Virgin Atlantic had been plagued by a BA-inspired smear campaign against himself and the airline in the press and in the City. He had proved to his own satisfaction that the rumours were being spread by Lord King and two of his key public relations men, David Burnside and Brian Basham. Branson knew that in over twenty years in business none of his ventures had had to endure such negative press coverage. And neither had he.

Branson had addressed his ultimatum to Marshall because he thought the chief executive might act as an honest broker between himself and Lord King. The illicit tape disabused Branson of that notion very swiftly. Branson listened as Marshall appeared to welcome the idea of Virgin taking legal action against BA.

'I mean, it may be a good thing if he [Branson] starts suing us because that will at least tie the thing down in some sort of controlled process.'

Ayling replied: 'Well, anyway, I guess we'll have to put our best thinking-caps on for tomorrow and decide how we should reply to this – the reply will clearly be a public document.'

'We always assumed, wrongly as it's turned out, that the story would die because it would run out of steam,' Marshall said.

'One possible approach would be for you to write him [Branson] a letter, um . . . sort of more in sorrow than in anger and say, look . . . you've been complaining, and every time you make these complaints they are looked into. You, the chief executive of the company, now formally invite him to set out in specific detail exactly what each allegation is and exactly on the basis of what evidence each allegation is made.

'But don't say you are going to answer them because, um . . . you know, I don't think you want to . . .' concluded Ayling.

'I *bet* they bloody well don't want to answer,' muttered Branson under his breath.

Moss stopped the tape and looked at Branson. He was not sure whether his boss wanted to continue. He appeared ill at ease. Branson signalled to Moss to carry on.

The conversation turned to BA's ambitious global-expansion programme. The carrier had its sights on a small German airline called Delta. It planned to use the acquisition to get a toehold in Germany and start to challenge Lufthansa, the giant state-run airline. Delta had an impressive reputation among business travellers. BA had money to spend and it appeared from the tape that Ayling had been stalking the carrier for weeks.

'It [Delta] makes about a million quid a year at the moment,' he told Marshall. 'Anyway he [Delta's owner] wants about ten million sterling for it.'

'And the idea is that we would buy . . .' began Marshall before Ayling interjected.

'We would buy Delta totally.'

'I see,' said Marshall. 'It is certainly very interesting.'

Then Ayling lowered his voice. Moss turned up the volume of the tape recorder. Branson's living room suddenly filled with Ayling's whisper.

'I think we mustn't tell anyone, Colin . . . I mean, the chairman has from time to time asked me about Germany. I have been very cagey about it. I have not given away any names or what is going on.'

Ayling appeared to be very anxious that King should not find out details of the Delta plan and he asked Marshall not to breathe a word to King.

'Right, I agree,' said Marshall.

Ayling continued: 'I want a proposition to take to the board on Friday. Even if we pay a bit over the odds, you know, if it gives you a position to start up within continental Europe, it is worth the investment. And it would be a terrific immediate counter to some of this bad publicity.'

'I could not agree more,' said Marshall.

'Which is what I feel,' concurred Ayling.

'Yeah, it's excellent,' said Marshall.

Branson turned to Moss: 'This is unbelievable. Marshall and Ayling seem to be planning to spend £10 million to buy an airline simply to distract attention from their campaign against us. And it sounds like they're doing it behind King's back!'

Industry gossip had it that BA's board had been badly divided since privatisation. To eavesdrop on two of the most senior members of BA's board plotting behind their chairman's back was rare insight.

The taped conversation tailed off into a discussion about an Institute of Travel Management dinner at which Ayling had encountered Branson when he gatecrashed the pre-dinner reception.

'I was rather upset about it,' Ayling confessed. 'There he was, large as life, but he didn't stay for the dinner.'

As the two men chuckled, Branson lost interest in what they were saying. He walked to the French windows and stared out into his garden, hands plunged into his trouser pockets. Moss turned off the tape recorder. Branson was trying to make sense of what he had just heard.

Less than a week beforehand, he had made the most difficult decision of his business career. He sold Virgin Music, the company he had built up from scratch to become the biggest private record company in the world, to Thorn EMI. The sale made him a billionaire. It also made him very sad, temporarily. After breaking the news to his staff, he burst into tears and ran out of the company's offices into Ladbroke Grove and headed towards Holland Park.

At the Tube station a newspaper hoarding brought him up short: 'Branson sells Virgin for £560 million'. His brief wallow in self-pity ended abruptly as he mentally rewrote the headline: 'Man gets £560 million and bursts into tears'. 'What a prat!' he thought, and walked quietly back home contemplating how the largest equity transaction to an individual in British corporate history might help him boost his struggling airline.

What Branson had never said in public was that he had sold Virgin Music to save Virgin Atlantic. The airline bug had bitten him very deeply, and he frequently described the carrier he founded in 1984 as the love of his life. By the spring of 1992, however, exactly a year after the Gulf War had wrought havoc with the airline industry, coupled with the worst recession since the Second World War, Virgin Atlantic stood on the brink. It survived only because of the strength of the other Virgin companies and Branson's devotion to it.

When Branson came to believe that the British Airways dirty-tricks campaign had undermined the airline to such an extent that its existence was threatened, he sold Virgin Music. To his family and his very close friends, he confided that he had done so to 'flick a V-sign at BA and show them they weren't going to mess around with my airline'.

Branson knew there were those within his companies who thought his devotion to Virgin Atlantic had become a dangerous obsession which could threaten the whole Virgin Group.

In 1984, Branson made a point of hiring seasoned professionals to run the trendy airline. As it grew, Branson recruited solid managerial expertise to compensate for his own lack of experience in the industry. Senior managers came from Laker Airways, British Caledonian, as well as BA itself, to raise the fledgling airline to maturity. Now some of them were cautioning him against squaring up to British Airways. Privately, some thought that Branson and his young press officer, Will Whitehorn, had severely miscalculated their tactics against BA.

Branson appointed the twenty-seven-year-old Whitehorn as Virgin's corporate affairs director in 1987 shortly after the Stock Market crash. An Aberdeen University graduate, he made a good initial impression with his handling of Virgin's PR as Branson bought the Virgin Group back from the Stock Market in 1988. However, Whitehorn's previous experience of the airline industry was limited to a short spell as a British Airways helicopter crewman immediately after leaving university. By pure chance, when Branson launched Virgin Atlantic in 1984, Whitehorn sold some of the airline's first tickets working behind the counter at Thomas Cook, where he was then working as a graduate trainee.

At the beginning of 1991, it was Whitehorn who took a call which first warned Virgin that private investigators had been hired by BA to undermine the airline. Whitehorn later met the caller in a smoky bar in the bowels of Waterloo Station. In clipped tones, a white South African private detective warned Whitehorn that Kroll, the heavy-duty corporate investigators based in New York, had been hired by BA to work against Virgin.

Branson and Whitehorn laughed the suggestion off at the time, but were forced to reconsider their attitude after several senior members of the airline's staff had their cars broken into. Even more disturbingly, a series of anonymous phone calls warned

Branson that private detectives hired by BA were shadowing *him*.

By spring 1992, Branson was worried that although he and Whitehorn had had some success in throwing BA on the defensive, nobody appeared to take his dirty-tricks allegations very seriously. A recent television documentary challenged him either to 'put up or shut up' about them. Very few of the specialist transport or aviation correspondents in the press or broadcasting gave his case much credence, and the trade press was hostile. The *Travel Trade Gazette* described his claims as 'mainly nonsense', the *Sunday Telegraph* concluded its examination of the dispute with the observation that there was 'not a whiff of dirty tricks' in the BA camp. The *Sun* asked, 'Where's the writ, Richard?'

Although descended from generations of judges and barristers, Branson abhorred the idea of sorting disputes out in court, viewing such cases as a waste of time, money and effort, particularly his own. Few situations in the fluid and highly litigious world of pop music were not better sorted out in person than in court. By the middle of March 1992, however, he felt his credibility was at stake: within his own airline, in the media and, perhaps most importantly if Virgin Atlantic were to survive, with British Airways. Everything could depend on his next move.

Chris Moss eventually broke the long silence.

'What shall we do? Shall we leak it to the press?' he asked.

'No,' said Branson emphatically, as he continued to stare out into the garden. He turned to look at Moss. 'Send it to Colin Marshall.'

'I beg your pardon?' asked the marketing man.

'Just do as I say,' said Branson quietly.

Speedbird House, British Airways Headquarters.
16 March 1992

Sir Colin Marshall's jaw dropped as he listened to the tape that Richard Branson had sent him. Marshall is renowned for his almost robotic ability to control his responses; but when Mervyn Walker, the airline's newly appointed legal director, played the tape, he became visibly disconcerted.

Marshall had no difficulty in remembering the conversation with his colleague, Robert Ayling. Now, just over a fortnight later, he had the uncomfortable experience of sitting in his office in BA's tightly guarded Heathrow headquarters listening to their words being played back to him on tape. He was baffled. He was also alarmed. Richard Branson would now know how he and Ayling were planning to respond to his dirty-tricks accusations. This was potentially damaging from BA's point of view, as the airline had been locked in private talks with Virgin Atlantic to try and achieve a resolution of the dispute since the *This Week* programme aired two weeks earlier. Branson would now know that while his lawyers were talking to BA's lawyers, Marshall himself was untroubled by the thought of a court battle with Virgin. However, BA's chief executive could be sure that Branson did not know why he was so relaxed about the prospect of taking on Virgin Atlantic in the courts.

Several weeks earlier, Marshall instructed David Hyde, his head of security and a member of BA's board of management, to conduct a discreet probe into what most board members saw as a Branson publicity blitz against 'The World's Favourite Airline'. The investigation was codenamed 'Covent Garden'. It had already produced some fascinating results: behind Branson's protestations and his air of injured innocence, it seemed the entrepreneur was himself playing an undercover game. Furthermore, there was evidence that Branson was profiting from the leak of confidential information from BA.

At the end of 1991 Branson wrote a highly publicised 'open letter' to the non-executive directors of BA which showed a degree of knowledge of the inner workings of BA. The *Sunday Times*, the *Guardian* and *The Times* all ran articles that accused BA of pulling a variety of dirty tricks against Virgin Atlantic which were suspiciously well informed. Lord King, David Burnside and Brian Basham were singled out for attack – the three suspected they were being personally targeted. Branson's campaign reached its climax at the end of February 1992 when *This Week* broadcast Branson's claims that King, Burnside and Basham were behind a plot to smear him.

David Hyde analysed the mysterious tape in great detail and

returned to BA's chief executive. In a written report, the Covent Garden team explained how the mysterious tape fitted into the pattern of Branson's offensive against BA.

> Our latest findings indicate that the tape recording, the television programme and the articles in the *Sunday Times* are part of a well-orchestrated, generously funded, often illegally conducted and ultimately personally controlled exercise by Richard Branson to, legitimately or otherwise, discredit British Airways, its main board members, policies and personnel.

The written report also concluded that Branson was employing no less than five private investigative agencies against BA. One part of the operation was being masterminded by John Thornton at Goldman Sachs, who had deployed a team of up to forty people on the case. According to Hyde, Thornton had also subcontracted some tasks to IGI, an American-based investigative agency whose British operation was based in London. IGI's job was to dig for dirt on BA and run a 'hostile' campaign against the airline aimed at destabilising the company and key members of its board. Hyde even thought it was 'probable' that Marshall and several other members of BA's board were under surveillance by agents working for Branson. Hyde calculated that the operation was costing Branson up to £400,000 per week. It had probably been going on since the end of 1991.

Marshall asked Hyde if his team were certain.

'One hundred per cent,' Hyde replied.

'And you know that Goldman Sachs are involved.'

'That's been confirmed.'

'So what do you make of the tape?' Marshall asked.

'It's Branson flexing his muscles,' replied Hyde.

The probe Hyde had organised seemed to offer an explanation for the battering that BA had received at Branson's hands in the past six months. However, the tape, and Branson's apparent resolve to take his campaign to court, posed a dilemma of corporate and personal dimensions for BA's chief executive.

Ever since Branson first complained publicly about BA's dirty tricks at the end of 1991, Sir Colin Marshall had taken personal charge of BA's response. He authorised a series of blanket denials of all Virgin Atlantic's charges to the press, to television and to Branson himself. Within twenty-four hours of Branson's first formal complaint, Marshall responded with a stinging rebuke:

> Your suggestions that BA is involved in a deliberate attempt to damage your business and seeks to compete other than through normal promotional and marketing efforts are wholly without foundation . . .
>
> Would it not be better if you were to devote your undoubted energies to more constructive purposes?

Because Marshall had formulated BA's tough response to Branson, it was widely assumed he was confident of the outcome of the dispute. By spring 1992, Sir Colin was more firmly in control of the day-to-day running of BA than at any stage during his nine-year stint as chief executive. Lord King was in the autumn of his mercurial business career, and his grip on the airline's affairs was slowly weakening. King planned to cede the executive chairmanship to his chief executive in the summer, and Marshall hoped finally to succeed King as overall chairman of BA, as well as chief executive, the following year.

King recruited Marshall in 1983 after a long search, but it was an open secret within BA and throughout the industry that the two men had never been close. In 1988 there were press reports that Sir Colin tried to organise a boardroom coup against King. After King cleared out almost the entire BA board in the mid-1980s, he and Marshall competed to fill key BA posts with their own men to bolster their positions. Many senior managers and executives could be identified by their political allegiances – a King man or a Marshall man.

Whatever their differences, King and Marshall had little difficulty in agreeing on Richard Branson. King had long disliked the former hippy, with his baggy jumpers and his fleet of second-hand jumbos. Sir Colin Marshall had been one of the first to warn how much commercial damage Virgin Atlantic could inflict upon the national carrier if it were allowed to grow unchecked, and he had led BA's efforts to prevent that happening. Although Branson still had only eight planes he was now inflicting serious damage on British Airways' public image, apparently relishing his own role as the plucky David battling the monopolistic Goliath trying to blow him out of the skies.

Marshall re-read Branson's letter, sent with the tape, which concluded by threatening to take BA to court. Branson would sue BA unless Lord King publicly apologised to him for the dirty-tricks campaign before 18 March. Marshall knew there was about as much chance of King doing that as joining Branson on one of his fabled balloon trips. However, if Branson did carry out his threat, Virgin Atlantic would be the first British airline to take BA to court since Laker a decade earlier. The implications for BA as it continued to seek an American partner could be substantial and Marshall needed to contemplate his strategy very carefully indeed.

BA had initially scorned Sir Freddie Laker and his airline's liquidators when they took action under America's anti-trust laws alleging that BA had conspired with a cartel of others to put Laker out of business. After three gruelling years in the US courts, during which BA faced both criminal and civil investigations, BA engineered an out-of-court settlement. Although BA never admitted it tried to drive Laker out of business, it contributed the lion's share of the multimillion-dollar settlement that a cartel of major airlines agreed to pay to Laker Airways' liquidators. After months of tortuous transatlantic negotiations which dominated his early years at BA, Marshall himself had sat opposite Sir Freddie at BA headquarters in 1985 to witness him finally signing off on the deal only minutes before the midnight deadline. The Laker case was widely estimated to have delayed the privatisation of BA by at least two years.

In his letter, Branson claimed that he had no knowledge of where the recording came from. He concluded: 'Someone is playing mighty dangerous games.'

Marshall decided to call Branson's bluff. He ignored the 18 March deadline. He was becoming increasingly certain that it was Branson who was playing the 'dangerous games'. David Hyde's Covent Garden operation not only indicated that there was an undercover element to Branson's campaign against BA, it also held the promise of further revelations about the unconventional entrepreneur's activities.

In addition to the evidence already unearthed by Covent Garden, a series of mysterious and still unexplained incidents had occurred. Both Lord King and Sir Colin Marshall thought it possible their phones were being bugged. The PR men, Burnside and Basham, had also reported that their phone calls had been cut in peculiar circumstances. The car of a senior member of the BA board, Sir Francis Kennedy, had been broken into and his briefcase stolen. Operation Covent Garden was on the trail of the private detectives BA believed were responsible. No one had yet been positively identified, but Marshall and Hyde were confident that it would only be a matter of time before Branson's undercover operation would be exposed.

Twickenham Police Station. 28 March 1992

John Reilly sat opposite Detective Johnnie Elfed at Twickenham police station. His pale eyes stared blankly at the policeman. It was not yet eight o'clock in the morning.

'I can't believe I'm writing this down,' said the detective as he took Reilly's statement. 'Two bloody bin-bags!'

'Why *are* you writing it down?' asked the investigator.

'Orders from upstairs,' said DC Elfed, rolling his eyes to the ceiling. 'They say this is a sensitive one.'

'Why?'

'Search me.'

'You're not going to charge me, are you?'

'I honestly don't know ,' replied DC Elfed.

After giving a statement, in which he admitted stealing the bin-bags, Reilly was released on police bail without being charged. The police told him that a decision would be taken after the General Election in a couple of weeks' time. Reilly still had no idea who Roger Eglin was, or why his rubbish was deemed to be 'sensitive'.

Two weeks later, as John Major was celebrating his election victory, John Reilly picked up a copy of the fortnightly satirical magazine, *Private Eye*. To his amazement it included a reference to his arrest. The short article revealed that Roger Eglin, whose rubbish he had stolen, was a senior journalist on the *Sunday Times*. Reilly was even more confused after he had read the article.

> Quite who would want to steal anything from grey man Eglin's bins remains a mystery. What could he have to hide?
>
> A clue is the fact that Eglin is something of an aeroplane fanatic, and when he was [*Sunday Times*] business news editor he was one of the recipients of phone calls made by a British Airways mole called Robert.
>
> The mole has also been feeding Richard Branson with information, hence the bearded teenager's allegations of a dirty-tricks campaign against his airline. The fact that quite the reverse is the case seems to have been overlooked, but wouldn't Branson find it just dandy if John Riley [*sic*] claimed that he was working for British Airways?

Reilly was completely baffled. The policeman who had arrested him had referred to his case as a 'sensitive' one, but Reilly found it difficult to believe that his nocturnal rubbish collection could be linked to the 'dirty tricks' dispute between the 'The World's Favourite Airline' and Virgin Atlantic. *Had* he been working for British Airways? *Was* the reverse the case?

When Reilly returned to Twickenham police station on 13 April, he was formally charged with the theft of Roger Eglin's rubbish. However, no one at the station was able to tell him why the matter was being taken so seriously nor, indeed, for whom he might have ultimately been working.

The following day British Airways announced that it was responding to Richard Branson's libel suit against Lord King and BA by countersuing Virgin Atlantic Airways and its chairman for libel. In a statement, Mervyn Walker said that BA's claim was based on the 'untrue and defamatory allegations made by Virgin and Richard Branson that British Airways has conducted a campaign of "dirty tricks" against them'.

The most bitterly fought battle in the history of British commercial aviation was heading for the High Court.

2

The Hunters and the Poacher

By the end of the 1980s it was difficult to think of two British businessmen who had better captured the *Zeitgeist* of the Thatcher decade than John King and Richard Branson. For many the chairman of British Airways became the ultimate Thatcherite business hero, and the chairman of Virgin Atlantic the best-known entrepreneur of the Thatcher generation. It was richly ironic, therefore, that as the 1990s opened the two men were preparing to go to war in the High Court.

Neither John King nor Richard Branson had needed Thatcherism to make money. King made himself a multimillionaire in ball-bearings while Mrs Thatcher was still an opposition MP. By the time she became Prime Minister, Richard Branson had made himself a multimillionaire by selling records. However, it was during the 1980s, as both men took to the skies, that the thirty-something child of the 60s, with his shaggy hair and perpetual grin, and the sixty-something engineer, with his Havana cigar and a manner to match his name, became household names: King for the transformation of British Airways, Branson for the creation of Virgin Atlantic.

Knighted by Britain's last Labour Prime Minister, Jim Callaghan, Sir John King was ennobled by Mrs Thatcher in 1983, two years after he accepted her invitation to prepare the state-owned airline for privatisation. The honours were but a prelude to King's eventual status as an icon in Thatcherism's hall of fame. Lord King of Wartnaby stripped the overmanaged, overmanned, dispute-ridden, publicly owned state monolith to the bone before conjuring its rebirth as the jewel in crown of Mrs Thatcher's privatisation programme. When King took over in 1981, BA was losing £140 million a year and was popularly known throughout Britain as 'Bloody Awful'. By 1989 the airline's shareholders were celebrating a pre-tax profit of £268 million and a dividend of 7.75p per share. King did not feel the need to blush when he boasted that he had created 'The World's Favourite Airline'. Mrs Thatcher wrote in her memoirs that she was 'especially pleased' with the BA privatisation.

In a decade when self-made men stalked the corridors of power, Lord King sat contentedly at the right hand of the seat of power itself. King was 'One of us'. Related by marriage to the Queen, Wartnaby walked with kings, hunted with hounds and holidayed with the Reagans. In the decade of the social climber, John King was one of its most distinguished mountaineers and Margaret Thatcher provided him with the oxygen to strike for the summit. By the end of the 1980s the past was most certainly another country for a man who had left school at the age of twelve to start work on the factory floor.

'In my mind, I've always lived in the world I live in now,' Lord King told *The Times* in 1990 as the Thatcher era drew to a close.

Lord King came to inhabit his new world at a time of life when most men are contemplating retirement. Mrs Thatcher's personal invitation was decisive.

'I knew her . . . I had worked for her in the political arena, and so that suggestion is not too far from the truth,' Lord King recalled. Elevated to the chairmanship at the age of sixty-three, King would also coyly admit that he was seduced by his 'romance' with British Airways.

Richard Branson's courtship with Virgin Airways, meanwhile, was very short indeed. Rapidly consummated after being attracted by no more than an idea in need of his cash in 1984, Branson's relationship with Virgin Atlantic blossomed into a passionate affair which came to dominate his business life. Branson boasted that while British Airways liked to call itself 'The World's Favourite Airline', he would build up the world's 'best' airline which would eventually fly to the twelve most lucrative destinations in the world.

Most aviation analysts predicted that his one-plane airline would not last more than a year. Branson said it would. Many commentators suggested he would inevitably follow the pioneer of cut-price air travel, Sir Freddie Laker, into bankruptcy. Branson said he wouldn't. British Airways taunted him by saying he was 'Too old to rock and roll, and too young to fly'. Branson told them to get stuffed.

As Virgin Music grew into the largest private record company in the world and Virgin Atlantic flew through uncharted skies, its bearded pilot came to epitomise the entrepreneurial spirit of the Thatcher years. The man who dressed up as Biggles to launch his airline became synonymous with taking risks, and succeeding – or at least getting away with them. His enthusiasm for an idea, whether in business or in pursuit of improbable records on land and sea, often seemed to rise in inverse proportion to its chances of success.

In less than five years Richard Branson became the first to fly across both the Atlantic and Pacific Oceans in a hot-air balloon, and he completed the fastest ever crossing of the Atlantic Ocean in a powerboat. All three world record-breaking adventures nearly cost him his life. Twice he was fished out of the Atlantic Ocean by rescue teams and, after his transpacific balloon bid was blown unexpectedly off course, he survived a violent crash in the frozen wastes of Canada. The world-record bids brought Branson and Virgin more publicity than Virgin's advertising budget could contemplate buying, and the image that endured was one of adventure. In the process the entrepreneur, whose biography is subtitled 'Adventure Capitalist', spawned a much broader, if less powerful, constituency than Lord King's.

When Branson launched Virgin Atlantic in 1984, he was known only to those who took a close interest in the fortunes of his Virgin Music record company. Branson's biographer, Mick Brown, observed that by 1984 the teeth, the sweater and the houseboat, 'the components to the Branson myth', were fixed in the public imagination. Less than ten years later a poll of British teenagers showed that Branson 'the myth', as well as Virgin 'the airline', had taken wing – Branson was voted Britain's most popular role model. Unusually in the annual survey, Branson came top of the poll amongst not only teenagers but also their parents – he was the role model that the children who were questioned wanted to emulate, and that their parents wanted them to grow up to become.

'Branson has done the impossible – twice,' said a youth psychologist commenting on the results. 'He's a role model on which young people and their parents see eye to eye. There's an F-factor to Branson which appeals to young people: he's got fame, fortune and fun.'

Lord King's reputation was based on an entirely different set of criteria: power, politics and a predatory instinct that was evident to both his admirers and detractors. His friends found King the man in King the huntsman. One of King's oldest friends, Lord White, described him as 'The bravest fellow I've ever seen in the hunting field'. 'Self-made King, he's always in for the kill,' eulogised the *Daily Mail* as the profiles of Mrs Thatcher's favourite Lord flowed during his transformation of the national carrier into a model of Thatcherite rectitude. As the master first of the Badsworth and then the Belvoir hunts, bloodsports simultaneously satisfied King's predatory instincts and helped him to acquire the patina of a well-established countryman. As his wealth and his estates grew, King indulged his outdoor passions at his Scottish retreat. However, the image of King in his 'Saturday country' of the Vale of Belvoir, his massive hands clasped tightly about the reins of a straining steed, was the one in which both friends and enemies found the soul of Mrs Thatcher's huntsman.

King felt justified in employing brutal tactics when he became chairman of British Airways. BA had become a national joke since it was formed in 1974 by an amalgamation of British European Airways and the British Overseas Airways Corporation. When King took over, not only was the airline losing £140 million a year, but its staff was represented by seventeen different unions, many of whom had played their part in the 1979 'Winter of Discontent' that had done so much to propel Mrs Thatcher into Downing Street, and send Labour to the political wilderness for a generation.

Blood flowed from the boardroom downwards as King ruthlessly imposed his view that he had to change the people running the airline rather than their attitudes. He had no interest in persuading those who espoused the old consensus of the error of their ways. King chaired BA board meetings as if they were trials and he the judge, jury and executioner. Sometimes King appeared not to be listening to a word that was said as his pale blue eyes peered unblinkingly at a board member he had placed in the dock.

Within two years King had removed nine of the fourteen members of the BA board and replaced them with his own appointees. Out went the standard-bearers of the old consensus on public ownership, and in came King's men. BA's new chairman did not believe that persuasion was a virtue. When King was appointed, Roy Watts was BA's chief executive. Watts liked to recall a story with which the new chairman regaled his colleagues.

John tells a story about a farmer who had a troublesome mule. The farmer called a man in to help him train it. All the man did to help was to hit the mule over the head with a block of wood.

The farmer asked, 'What are you doing that for?'

The man replied, 'I am trying to attract his attention.'

King himself had no difficulty in justifying the methods he employed to attract the attention of the bloated national carrier: 'It was imperative that we shake off the public-sector philosophy if we were to compete with the 160 or more airlines that were in our marketplace around the world. [BA] had become a self-serving organisation rather than reacting to the demands of the marketplace. There were so many departments and divisions and operations which were not required 365 days of the year.'

As King rebuilt the board in his own image, he made sweeping cuts throughout the airline. By the time BA was ready for privatisation in 1987 it employed 22,000 fewer staff than it had in 1979 and flew 62 fewer routes. King paid for the redundancies by selling off £250 million-worth of BA's surplus assets, including dozens of aircraft and a million square feet of office space in London. The criticism he attracted after allocating such a large sum to redundancies helped soften his image as a Thatcherite axeman:

'You tell me the amount of money needed to say to a man, "By the way, you no longer have a job",' King retorted to his critics. 'The staff were sensible, and it was quite nice for a lot of people who wanted to retire anyway. I have been criticised for being ruthless at the time, but you must be careful of that word because it means without compassion. I believe that the amount of compassion that we showed was quite considerable.'

A supporter remembered the reaction to King within the airline: 'He stood British Airways on its head. The management used to say, "These are the routes, these are the aircraft, let's get some passengers." Now they are saying, "There are the people who want to fly, let's organise the airline to cater for them."'

King was convinced that many of the managers he had inherited at BA were not up to the task of winning new passengers or catering for their needs. Without passengers there would be no profits. Without profits there would be no privatisation. King reserved particular contempt for trade unionists, and a certain category of managers he discovered at BA that he witheringly described as 'balcony bosses'.

'The managers used to appear on balconies and look down on the staff, before hurrying back to their offices,' King recalled. 'Trade-union dominance, taxation and control of pay had destroyed the confidence of management to manage.'

King first walked on to a factory floor in the 1930s when he was in his early teens. A private soldier's son, he left school without any educational qualifications at all. By the time he left his teens King was running his own business, seizing upon a gap in the market to supply components for Rolls Royce aeroengines.

Immediately after the Second World War, King laid the foundation stone of the Pollard engineering company on a patch of derelict land in Ferrybridge in Yorkshire. It was a symbolic moment. Employing direct labour to build the plant, and importing engineers from the Midlands to train local workers, Pollard was soon turning out millions of ball-bearings – 'one of the most basic things you can make,' says King. In his prime as chairman of British Airways, King would still proudly recall the ball-bearing

empire he built from the Ferrybridge wasteland, 'where they were
virtually in clogs and shawls' when he arrived in 1948. Before he
sold the Pollard Ball & Roller Bearing company, as it became
known, in 1968, it had become an international company with fac-
tories on three continents. King's own status as one of Britain's
leading industrialists had also been firmly established. Pollard
was sold for nearly £10 million, of which £3 million went to King.

In 1972 King became chairman of Babcock International, the
large engineering corporation. Within a very short space of time
Babcock was a much smaller engineering corporation as King
slashed the workforce from 40,000 to 24,000. However, it also
became a highly profitable outfit and, as King drove it forward
into lucrative overseas markets, his triumph at Babcock forged his
reputation for turning round lame-duck companies.

King savoured money, and relished the contacts his growing
success brought him. Homes in Scotland and Leicestershire, and
a Mayfair flat in London, were amongst the trappings. Through
his second wife, the Honourable Isabel Monckton, the youngest
daughter of the Eighth Viscount Galway, he came to boast of
ties with the Royal Family. His wife taught Prince Charles gar-
dening, and King was said to keep pictures of himself with
young royals in his desk at BA. King's gruff charm, pugnacity
and fondness for Havana cigars gave him the appearance of the
classic, self-made millionaire. But he never lost his sensitivity
about his humble origins: 'There are some things people don't
need to know. I hate rags-to-riches stories and I hate being asked
personal questions.'

Such transparent evasiveness and a highly selective entry in
Who's Who, which omits his date and place of birth, acted as a
magnet for those who wished to probe further. In 1990 the
Independent did just that. The newspaper found that elderly resi-
dents in the leafy Surrey village of Dunsfold where King was
brought up retained some uncharitable memories.

'John King has kept a secret about this village, and this village
has kept a secret about him,' remembered an elderly contemporary, Nellie Stenning. 'He was known as Jack King in those days.
He was the school dunce. At everything. Everyone knows that.
When some of his aeroplanes go over here making a clatter I

sometimes open a window and shout up at them, "Curse you, Jack King".'

The resentment the newspaper discovered appeared to stem from the war years. John King was twenty-one when war broke out, and half a century later villagers bitterly remembered the flash young man about town. While the men of Dunsfold were fighting Hitler, King 'the dunce' dressed in Savile Row suits and ostentatiously drove the first Daimler Automatic to be manufactured through Guildford, 'with a dolly bird to make a splash'.

A seventy-six-year-old former machine-shop foreman recalled how the young King earned his nickname: 'We used to call him the "Clamping Stay King". He could turn out the clamping stays but he was never properly trained as an engineer, so he couldn't set the machine up properly to do the job.'

King's response to the *Independent* article was to remove all of BA's advertising from the newspaper.

His mission at British Airways was as political as it was commercial. His unscripted mission was to prepare BA for privatisation at a time when denationalising the command elements of the British economy was a concealed Thatcherite passion. The Conservatives had scarcely mentioned the subject in their 1979 election manifesto, but with Mrs Thatcher's Falklands triumph being accompanied by the disintegration of the Labour Party, the Conservatives revealed their privatisation plans for British Airways in their 1983 manifesto. When BA was finally floated in February 1987, King had transformed the company's prospects to the extent that the share offer was oversubscribed eleven times.

As the Tories stalked the national carrier it was important for King to be in charge of the operation. Britannia had once ruled the waves; if a privatised British Airways was to rule the skies for Britain and for 'free enterprise', it was critical that 'one of us' was in the cockpit. And it was essential to King that 'one of us' was in Downing Street.

As soon as he was appointed chairman, King commissioned headhunters to look for a new chief executive. He wanted someone to shake up the day-to-day management of the airline while he mapped out strategy. For over a year the headhunters scoured the airline industry on both sides of the Atlantic. King needed someone with experience of managing, making money and working phenomenally hard. He needed the right courtier.

In 1983, after nearly two years of searching, King sprung a surprise. He announced the appointment as chief executive of a forty-nine-year-old businessman who, like King, had never worked in the airline industry.

King poached Colin Marshall from Sears, the giant footwear and retail chain whose British flagship store, Selfridges, is in Oxford Street. Like King, the Edgware-born Marshall had not been to university and had started his working career at the foot of the ladder – as a cadet purser with Orient Steamship. Marshall forged his reputation in the cut-throat world of the American car-rental game, and became one of the very few British executives to attain boardroom status in the United States.

Like King, Marshall relished making money and he demanded a high price for his services. Marshall's appointment as chief executive was delayed partly by a wrangle over his salary. Press reports at the time related how Lord King had to seek a Downing Street meeting with Mrs Thatcher in order to clear Colin Marshall's salary. King argued that he needed the freedom to pay Marshall the private-sector rate. With Mrs Thatcher's consent Marshall joined BA at the beginning of 1983 on a salary of £88,000 – more than twice Lord King's. For both men the promise of privatisation was the lure, uncorking the prospect of much larger salaries and generous share options.

In 1989, at BA's third Annual General Meeting, shareholders learnt that King and Marshall had awarded themselves pay increases of 116%. This took the chairman's salary to £385,000 and his chief executive's to £252,568. King imperiously brushed aside challengers from the floor of the AGM who complained that BA's staff were having to make do with only 6%.

Turning to Marshall, he gestured, 'I'm rather keen to keep him. He could get more.'

Sir Colin Marshall nodded silently.

He was knighted in 1987 for his role in privatising British Airways. More than anyone else Marshall was responsible for the transformation of BA's drab, state-owned image. In the first two years of his tenure, he authorised the expenditure of £120 million on revamping the airline's image which he described as the 'care-worn, rather dated image of an airline that offered an inadequate service to its customers'. To make a clean break with BA's unhappy past, Marshall spent the money on designing a new livery for the planes and new uniforms for the staff.

Marshall and the concept of 'service' became synonymous at BA as the chief executive taught the airline's managers the tricks he had learnt from two decades in American management. Observably mid-Atlantic in bearing, Marshall was distinctly American in method.

'Management must be seen in the trenches,' he declared as he rolled up his own shirtsleeves and brought Lord King's bosses down from their balconies.

'We're Number 2 – We Try Harder' was the motto of the Avis car-hire company that Marshall joined in the 1960s. It also became his personal slogan as he transformed the company's European operation. When Marshall joined Avis in 1964, it had only six cars for hire in Europe. He left having become company chairman and expanding the European fleet to 12,000 cars. Marshall became renowned for appearing unexpectedly at far-flung parts of the Avis empire to visit his staff. Sometimes he would serve behind the counter himself dressed in the celebrated red coat of the counter staff. When Marshall joined BA, the dynamic workaholic touched down unexpectedly on distant runways all over the world as he carried King's word to the four corners of BA's global network.

Marshall developed a reputation for meticulous attention to detail. During meetings, he would test the airline's junior managers on esoteric points. On one occasion, he was told that the carpets on Concorde had been shrunk by shampooing.

'By how much have they shrunk?' Marshall demanded. 'By how many millimetres?'

Another senior marketing man recalls his first encounter with Colin Marshall.

'The first thing he asked me was why there were only three cheeses available on Concorde on his flight from New York the previous day!'

Under the slogan 'Putting People First' Marshall taught BA's staff how to be more responsive to the demands of the travelling public. Marshall was particularly concerned that BA should target the millions of business travellers who had deserted the airline in droves in the late 1970s, when British Airways was a by-word for inefficiency and appalling service. Marshall campaigned to convince the staff who had survived King's cutbacks that they were salesmen for the new-look airline.

'In the service industry, you are selling an intangible sensation. If people are left with a positive feeling, they'll talk about it. If they talk about it, you'll get very good exposure that comes free of cost and is much more believable than any other form of publicity.'

American-style working breakfasts, confidence-boosting sessions, Saturday management conferences and snatched lunches were all part of the Marshall formula to get BA's staff to try harder. No one could accuse the chief executive of not doing so himself. He averaged a fifteen-to-eighteen-hour day, and one of the few criticisms of him in his early days at BA was that he tried *too* hard, and took on too much. This never bothered Lord King.

In Colin Marshall, King found a suitable foil for his own buccaneering, blustering style. While King relished hobnobbing with royalty, and rubbing shoulders with Cabinet ministers and fellow members of the House of Lords, Marshall understated his power. He preferred to spend his rare breaks playing tennis or grabbing a skiing holiday with his family who had followed the itinerant executive's zigzag progress across the Atlantic and back.

To King's evident delight, Marshall adopted a deferential manner towards him, addressing him not by his name but as 'chairman'. To his colleagues, Marshall did not come across as a warm man.

'Colin was a really cold fish when he arrived. The sort of guy you suspect shakes hands with his wife when he gets home every night,' said one.

King knew that with Marshall as his right-hand man he would be in little danger of being overshadowed in the publicity stakes or usurped in a boardroom coup. It was not that Marshall lacked ambition but, fifteen years younger than his chairman, he could afford to bide his time.

Shortly after King installed Marshall to market BA out of the doldrums, Mrs Thatcher won the 1983 General Election. With the prospect of privatisation secure, King recognised that politicians' perceptions of BA would be as important as those of business-men. Formerly friendless, BA would need to proselytise its changing image with the travelling public and also in Whitehall, Westminster and Fleet Street, a constituency sometimes described as the 'greater Whitehall' in the aviation industry. In the decade of the bid, the counterbid and the takeover, King was determined to ensure that, as the airline approached privatisation, it had the best advertising and the best public relations that money could buy.

To advertise the new BA, King hired Saatchi & Saatchi, then run by the two brothers, Charles and Maurice, and Tim Bell. In his biography of Margaret Thatcher, Hugo Young describes how 'In a nice union of Thatcherite stars, King, the favourite businessman, and Saatchi & Saatchi, the favourite advertising agency, projected British Airways as the world's favourite airline and propelled it eventually into the private sector.' King believed public relations was as vital as advertising:

> Those companies that have survived have mostly learnt that living in the public eye is not an option they have the luxury of rejecting. The reason is simple self-preservation. Today, there is literally no quoted company in Britain that is immune from the possibility of takeover.
>
> Companies that habitually treat media with disdain are apt to learn too late that when the enemy is at the gates they need all the well-informed friends they can get.

King appointed David Burnside, a thirty-three-year-old Ulsterman, to mastermind his public relations effort in 1984. Politically the two men were soulmates. Both admired Mrs Thatcher, and it is doubtful if either would have joined BA were privatisation not on the agenda. Indeed, Burnside came very close to joining the Conservative and Unionist Party itself in 1984 as deputy director of communications to Tony Shrimsley. Shrimsley was dying of cancer, and it was made clear to Burnside that he would succeed when his boss was forced to give up work.

The Tory Party chairman, John Selwyn Gummer, had been impressed by Burnside's lobbying on behalf of Walter Goldsmith's economically 'dry' Institute of Directors in the early 1980s, when Burnside was director of the Institute's public relations operation. Burnside lobbied successfully for the economic arguments of the 'dry' right in opposition to the 'wet' CBI.

When Lord King asked the City editor of the *Sunday Telegraph*, Ian Watson, for a recommendation for the post of director of BA's public affairs department, Watson suggested Burnside. Just before the Tories lured Burnside to Central Office, King swooped and got his man. It was to be the start of a long and mutually beneficial relationship between Lord King's British Airways and the *Sunday Telegraph*, and David Burnside and Ian Watson.

Burnside learnt his politics on the streets of Belfast as a passionate activist in the cause of Ulster's union with Great Britain. A Protestant, he admired the success of the Ulster workers' strike in 1974 which brought down the power-sharing executive set up under the Sunningdale agreement. After leaving Queen's University, Belfast, where he was chairman of the university's Conservative and Unionist Association, he worked as a press officer for William Craig's hardline Vanguard Unionist Party for two years between 1975 and 1977. Appointed to the executive of Craig's party in 1975, Burnside was amongst the first to call upon Protestants to take up arms against what he saw as the 'threat of communism' – in the form of the IRA.

Writing in a 1975 edition of the *Ulster Defender*, published by the Londonderry Command of the Ulster Defence Association, David Burnside declared:

> If Ulster is to be defended against Communism, then either the present authorities must fulfil their constitutional role of maintaining order and defending the law, or the people will have to take steps to defend themselves.

The poorly cyclostyled *Ulster Defender* included a five-page pull-out by a fellow contributor writing under the *nom de guerre* of 'The Armourer'. The Armourer's article included detailed pictures of Armalite machine guns ('It looks tinny, it feels like a toy. But the

Armalite is a lethal and accurate weapon') as well as pictures explaining how to load and dismantle AK47 and Bushmaster machine guns.

The Armourer's article foreshadowed the rise of Protestant terrorism:

> Protestants are not asleep . . . their paramilitaries are getting stronger with very day that passes. Their determination to destroy Ulster's enemies has been proved in the past and there is just a chance that they too will acquire some of these arms for the defence of their country, religion and heritage.

When Burnside's article appeared, he was serving as a private in the 10th Battalion of the Ulster Defence Regiment, then part of the British Army. He was formally warned that if, as a part-time private, he continued to write articles which incited armed insurrection, and which were highly critical of the army he was supposed to be serving, he would be dismissed. He did and he was.

Normally departures from the UDR were kept secret to protect the identity of those who were prepared to run the risk of serving the Crown in Ulster. In Burnside's case, he chose to court publicity by appealing against the decision and the hearing was reported in Belfast newspapers. Burnside's appeal was rejected and his military career was terminated. In 1992 the Ulster Defence Association was banned by the British government after a series of bloody Protestant terrorist atrocities.

Emerging as high-flying public relations operator in the late 1970s and early 1980s, Burnside did little to hide his strong Protestant beliefs. He continued to commute weekly to London from the family farm in Ballymoney, and enjoyed marching with the Orangemen when his busy schedule permitted. In 1982 he stood unsuccessfully in the Ulster Assembly elections for North Antrim. Burnside actively opposed the Anglo-Irish agreement after it was signed in 1985; he joined the Friends of the Union, the ginger group formed by Mrs Thatcher's parliamentary private secretary, Ian Gow, when he resigned his post in protest at the agreement.

Journalists who spent time with King and Burnside remarked

that both men 'would love to have fought a war'. King epitomised success and power; 'The King of Ambition Fulfilled', ran one headline. Burnside radiated danger beneath his cultivated exterior. Because of his background, and his rather menacing approach to those he disapproved of, Burnside became known among journalists, and throughout the airline industry, as 'the Irish kneecapper' after he joined BA.

However distasteful some found his methods, Burnside's effectiveness as a PR operator was beyond dispute. Lord King and the Ulsterman, who was young enough to be his son, built one of the most effective lobbying machines in Britain. As a result British Airways was regularly given the highest rating of any British company for its communications by parliamentarians and captains of industry; Burnside became widely regarded as the most powerful in-house PR director in Britain. He was given a budget of £5 million, and he spearheaded the efforts of a department of forty permanent staff in London and overseas, supported by scores of agencies in nearly 100 countries that BA flies to.

Burnside reflected his master's voice so accurately that King gave him enormous scope to speak to the media on his behalf. Over the years thousands of stories quoting a 'senior BA executive', or 'it is thought that Lord King . . .' emanated from Burnside's lips. When King promoted Burnside to BA's board of management it was in recognition of his status as one of the brightest stars in BA's firmament. Burnside's finely tuned political antennae enabled him to keep the ear not only of Lord King but also of Sir Colin Marshall. Both men spoke to him daily as he established himself as the media's most important point of contact with British Airways.

Unusually for a public relations man, Burnside understood the power of silence. Journalists accustomed to gushing overtures from PR people with reams of handouts and handfuls of press-packs would find themselves tumbling into the black holes of Burnside's silence when they asked for, say, an interview with the chairman. Burnside would consider the request and evaluate its author in complete silence before pronouncing. His verdict would be based on his assessment of the likely 'dividend' for BA.

Another unusual tendency the PR man exhibited was a personal fondness for the limelight. In the four-part BBC 'Airline' series, Burnside popped up in several of the episodes himself. In one sequence Burnside was filmed telling a silent Sir Colin Marshall what BA's line should be. In further illustrations of Burnside's cosy relationship with both King and Marshall, viewers saw Burnside at the Kremlin, Burnside on board Concorde, Burnside briefing the chairman, Burnside phoning Marshall in New York, and Burnside 'pressing the flesh' with King at the Conservative Party Conference, rarely more than a few feet away from his Lordship's shoulder.

In one interview, Burnside described negative coverage of BA as 'crap'. Those who wrote such 'crap' or refused, as King put it, to 'see the light', were harshly dealt with. Paul Maurice of the *Daily Mail* was excommunicated by King after he wrote a series of articles questioning BA's safety record. A letter from Burnside informed him that Lord King and Sir Colin Marshall agreed that he should no longer be invited to BA's press conferences, that they would refuse all interview requests from him and that he would not be invited on any press trips. Unable to fulfil his duties as an aviation correspondent, Maurice became a radio presenter at BBC Radio Lincoln.

By contrast, those who were enraptured by Lord King's charisma and his success at turning British Airways around found themselves warmly embraced by Burnside and his multimillion-pound PR act. The 'Airline' television series captured the moment perfectly in 1989. The BBC filmed BA's chairman heading a delegation on board a special Concorde flight to Moscow. Basking in the glow of BA's revived fortunes were leading representatives of the airline's fan club – a selection of Fleet Street's finest, paid for by BA, and a clutch of politicians who claimed they were paying for themselves. As Concorde headed for the Soviet capital, the BBC asked one of BA's passengers for his opinion of King as chairman. The passenger was the former chairman of the Conservative Party, Cecil Parkinson, then Mrs Thatcher's energy secretary. His verdict was unequivocal:

'I think he's been outstandingly successful. He took over a very unprofitable, heavily overmanned airline, which wasn't exactly a byword for quality and service, and if you go anywhere in the world now, British Airways is admired, it makes money, its staff is contented, it's efficient, so I think he's done a very good job.'

As Parkinson oozed, the camera pulled back to reveal that the
seat next to the secretary of state was occupied by Lord King. BA's
chairman was purring contentedly with no obvious hint of embarrassment. King had appointed Parkinson to the board of Babcock
International Engineering after the MP had resigned from the
Cabinet in disgrace in 1983 following his affair with his secretary,
Sarah Keays. Once restored to the Cabinet, Parkinson had to resign
from King's board but the minister had lost none of his affection
for his former chairman.

'I've known John for a number of years, he's never asked me, as
a minister, for a favour, he wouldn't dream of presuming on a
friendship in that way. Now, I think if he's your friend, he's your
friend, and he doesn't care whether you're a member of the staff of
British Airways, a stewardess on the airline or a minister from the
government. If he's your friend, he's your friend and he's a very
straightforward person.'

Two weeks after the interview was recorded, Mrs Thatcher
appointed Cecil Parkinson secretary of state for transport, with
direct Cabinet responsibility for British Airways.

King judged the continuing support of Thatcher's government
vital to his ambition of transforming BA into a world force capable
of taking on the American and European megacarriers. Because
BA had to compete with foreign carriers that continued to be heavily subsidised by their governments, King argued that BA needed
maximum political and regulatory support from the British government to strengthen its competitive position and reward its new
shareholders. It was a theme that was as appropriate to BA's dislike of domestic competition as it was relevant to the airline's
ambition to become a serious player on the world stage. King used
the language of 'free enterprise' and 'competition' but, in reality,
he favoured eliminating domestic opposition, rather than competing with it, in order to maintain BA's virtual monopoly of the
British market. King fiercely opposed any concessions to BA's
domestic rivals, and argued that granting licences and routes to
them was to strengthen the weak at the expense of weakening the
strong.

King knew from the moment he was appointed that Number 10
stood four square behind the project, and that his work at BA was

umbilically connected to Mrs Thatcher's vision of 'enterprise culture'. Dramatic evidence of Mrs Thatcher's resolve came during the anti-trust suit that Laker Airways' liquidators took against British Airways and other major airlines for their role in bringing down Laker Airways in 1982.

Laker's demise was precipitated when Mrs Thatcher's first government permitted PanAm, and a group of other major airlines including Lufthansa and TWA, as well as British Airways and British Caledonian, to slash their fares in unison by up to 66% on Laker's routes in the autumn of 1981 .

When the transport minister, Iain Sproat, phoned Laker to tell him that he was going to approve the fare cuts on 16 October 1981, Sir Freddie told the minister his airline would go out of business in three months. Laker vividly remembers his feelings, when the government gave the go-ahead to the fare cuts,

'I wasn't against lower prices, but this was an obvious "get Laker" ploy. The prices were predatory because it was impossible for the major airlines to make a profit on such low fares – their prices were below cost. They were running their flights on my routes at a loss to put me out of business.'

Three months and two weeks after Sproat's phone call to Sir Freddie, the Midland Bank ordered Laker Airways to call in the receivers. Laker's crash induced a rare display of indecision in Margaret Thatcher. On the day that Laker went under, she called senior ministers and civil servants to her room in the House of Commons to contemplate an intervention to save Sir Freddie. The Chancellor, Geoffrey Howe, joined Iain Sproat and Ray Colgate of the CAA who remembers the meeting vividly: 'The Prime Minister was very indecisive. She said, "I can't bear to think of all my passengers being stranded abroad. My passengers! My poor passengers! Can't we put in £5 million, put a ring fence round it, and that would be the end of the story?"'

Colgate replied that the government would be committing itself to an open-ended situation, and would probably have to put more money in within months. The Prime Minister was immediately alive to the dangers:

'She said "Oh dear! An open-ended situation! I couldn't wish that on my poor taxpayers".'

Caught between her concerns for her 'poor passengers' and her 'poor taxpayers', Thatcher decided to spare the taxpayers and forbade a cash injection to try to save Laker. 'Most important was her reluctance to use taxpayers' money to support the symbol of free enterprise', recalls Colgate, 'because that would sully the symbol.'

Ironically, on the day Laker crashed, the government gave Lord King £53 million of taxpayers' money to help finance BA's redundancy programme. According to Colgate, 'The need for the redundancy payments was attributed by some in part to the impact of Laker's low fares policies.'

With no competition from Laker Airways, transatlantic fares soared back towards their pre-Laker levels. The major airlines, including BA, once again began harvesting the yields from the transatlantic routes that they had enjoyed before Laker started Skytrain. In 1977, the cheapest transatlantic fare was £196. After Skytrain offered its first fare of £59, the major transatlantic carriers slashed their prices on Laker's routes to match and, eventually, undercut him. Weeks after Laker Airways crashed, the cheapest fare was £136 and, by 1983, the cheapest fare was £175.

Prompted by Sir Freddie's lawyer, Bob Beckman, the liquidators of Laker Airways, Touche Ross, started a billion-pound lawsuit in Washington. It alleged conspiracy and violation of anti-trust laws against the cartel of international airlines who had slashed their fares in unison: British Airways and British Caledonian, TWA, PanAm, Lufthansa, Swiss Air, the Dutch carrier KLM, the Belgian carrier Sabena, Scandinavian Airline System (SAS), and the tiny French carrier Union de Transports Aeriens (UTA). The American aircraft manufacturer, McDonnell Douglas, was also named as a defendant.

Once the Touche Ross suit had been filed, the American government independently instituted a criminal investigation into Laker's allegations of price-fixing. The Chief of the Transportation Section of the Anti-Trust Division of the Department of Justice, Elliott Seiden, described the case as one of the most important of his career. 'The nature of the violation was very serious . . . unauthorised price-fixing is considered in the United States to be one of the most serious anti-trust violations that can be committed, so when you combine . . . the importance of the industry and the significance of the violation . . . this made it a matter of great importance to the United States.'

For eighteen months Seiden led a team of lawyers and economists as they investigated the conspiracy and price-fixing allegations. A Federal Grand Jury was set up to take evidence on the price-fixing charges, and Sir Freddie Laker made a well-received appearance before it. On behalf of BA, the Thatcher government opposed Seiden's probe, and the liquidator's civil suit, at every turn. In 1983 the government invoked the Protection of Trading Interests Act to prevent BA, and BCal, giving evidence in the USA. The Conservative administration argued that the American courts had no right to try the case. However, in June 1984, the House of Lords unanimously voted in favour of Touche Ross being able to proceed with the case.

Mrs Thatcher and her Cabinet colleagues became even more concerned in the autumn when it became clear that the Department of Justice was preparing to prosecute British Airways on the price-fixing charges. Four BA executives were to be indicted, and Lord King's airline would be the only defendant in the criminal proceedings. If found guilty, the executives in question faced jail sentences, and BA faced substantial fines.

Seiden recalls the Justice Department's anger at the Thatcher government's attempts to prevent the case being heard in the States. 'We believed that what we were doing was right and appropriate, and that the British government was inappropriately interfering with the legitimate law-enforcement activities of the US government. There was a clash of principle, and the most difficult thing to sort out is when there's a clash of principles'.

The imminent indictment of BA put privatisation as well as principles at stake. It was clear at Heathrow, and in Downing Street, that privatisation could not proceed until the criminal and the civil aspects of the anti-trust litigation had been resolved. With outstanding charges of economic crime against one of Britain's most popular entrepreneurs and his cut-price airline, British Airways could not be privatised. Indeed, the prospectus for the sale could not be drawn up due to the uncertainty surrounding the outcome of the Laker cases. If British Airways lost either of them, the whole privatisation process, certainly under Lord King and his new regime at British Airways, would be in jeopardy. Seiden recalls: 'It became clear that this investigation and its possible outcome could negatively impact the ability to privatise British Airways. This appeared to be a very important part of Mrs Thatcher's economic reform plan.'

Seiden was right. Mrs Thatcher was determined that the privatisation of BA should not be jeopardised. Having failed to halt Touche Ross in Britain, she tore into Reagan's administration with a ferocity that shook those she encountered. Her demand was simple: the Justice Department's probe should be halted. According to Duncan Campbell-Smith's authoritative account of the BA/Laker litigation, 'The Struggle for Take-Off', the American ambassador to London, Charles Price, retreated 'quite shaken from a private audience at Number Ten'. *The Times* reported that the Prime Minister was becoming 'almost obsessive with the American government's attitude'. The Laker liquidator, Christopher Morris, remembers the determination with which Thatcher tried to sabotage the Laker case: 'I don't think the reigning monarch was brought into it, but virtually everybody else was.' One of Morris's American attorneys, Michael Nussbaum, remembers Thatcher's intervention vividly: 'It was my understanding that Maggie called her friend Ronnie and said, "We wouldn't take it very kindly if you indicted our national airline or its executives"'.

Thatcher's determination to kill Laker's case involved much more than a phone call to the President. Her first objective was to derail Seiden's criminal investigation. If BA had been found guilty of price-fixing in Washington, the liquidator's civil suit would have become a formality. After the trebling of damages, BA could have faced a fine of a billion and a half dollars, more than enough to get Laker back in the air again and effectively bankrupt BA.

Thatcher dispatched the Attorney General, Sir Michael Havers, to Washington to raise the Laker case with the President. Christopher Morris recalls: 'Havers actually travelled to America as a tourist, and went to the back door of the White House to see Ronald Reagan and to take him a letter from Mrs Thatcher.'

After Havers' mission, Thatcher took up the case personally with Reagan, and, in November 1984, Reagan submitted. The President summoned officials from the Department of Justice, the State

Department and the National Security Council to the Oval Office, and informed them that the Grand Jury would be disbanded, and the investigation would be terminated. Reagan cited foreign policy and defence considerations as the reasons for his decision.

Seiden was aware that Reagan needed Thatcher's active support in the Strategic Arms Limitation Talks [SALT], and for his embryonic plans for America's Strategic Defense Initiative, which became known as 'Star Wars'. 'The President was scheduled to meet with Mrs Thatcher at Camp David in December, and they were to have important discussions leading up to the resumption of SALT talks with the Soviet Union in early 1985,' Seiden recalls, 'so we presumed that the President was weighing law-enforcement interests on the one hand, and issues of national security and defence on the other. Justice might have been denied to Freddie Laker, but it was certainly advanced in the case of humanity.'

Reagan's virtually unprecedented breach of the separation of executive and judicial powers made front page news in the USA: the press reported that the President's decision followed consultations at 'the very highest level', but gave no hint of the horse-trading that preceded it. In her memoirs Lady Thatcher recalls, 'I regarded the *quid pro quo* for my strong public support of the President as being the right to be direct with him and members of his administration in private.'

In February 1985 Thatcher went to Washington to be direct with Reagan again on behalf of BA. Lord King sat contentedly in the audience as Mrs Thatcher became the first British Prime Minister to address both houses of the US Congress since Winston Churchill. After Reagan cancelled the criminal investigation into the Laker case, Thatcher made a point of giving SDI strong support in her address.

As soon as the photo-opportunities were over, Thatcher was in private talks with Reagan. With the criminal investigation terminated, the Prime Minister turned her attention to Touche Ross's civil suit on behalf of the creditors of Laker Airways: the privatisation of British Airways had been postponed indefinitely until the suit was resolved. British and American officials were struck by Thatcher's insistence upon discussing the unresolved civil suit before the multitude of world issues that confronted Britain and

America at that time. On this occasion the target of Thatcher's attack was the refusal of the American government's Export-Import Bank to come to an out-of-court settlement with BA over the Laker case. Exim was one of Laker's largest creditors with an exposure of $153 million, and it was threatening to pursue its anti-trust case in the courts. When Mrs Thatcher arrived in Washington she received a half-hour briefing on the increasingly complex issues involved in Laker's civil case against British Airways and the other defendants.

The head of the British government's legal team, Bill Park of the solicitors, Linklaters & Paines, recalls that Mrs Thatcher grasped the details very quickly. 'She got it absolutely right, and said "Thank you for the explanation; what a pity the President won't understand a word of it!"'

Park recalls that when Thatcher raised the Laker case with Reagan, the two leaders were alone. '. . . It was considered so important between them that they discussed it without any aides present. There was no one else present at all.'

There is no record of whether or not Reagan did understand what Thatcher said to him on the Laker case, but the British team struck an unexpected difficulty soon after the meeting. 'The difficulty we had was that Margaret Thatcher came back and said, "Everything's sorted out. He will take the appropriate steps",' recalls Park, 'but when Reagan went back to his team they said, "Well, Mr President, what did you arrange?" He replied, "I don't know. I've forgotten!"

'It was absolutely devastating when you'd spent three weeks setting the thing up to find that it had come to nothing because Reagan couldn't remember what he'd agreed to do!'

Reagan's administration eventually prevailed upon Exim to go along with BA's efforts to settle Laker's liquidators' case out of court. In July 1985, three and a half years after Laker's crash, BA joined the other defendants in paying Laker and his creditors, including the Exim bank, substantial compensation. The effect of the Thatcher/Reagan pressure to resolve Exim's position resulted in the bank announcing that it recovered more from the liquidation than the $153 million it was owed when Laker Airways defaulted. The bank recovered $136 million from the sale of

Laker's planes, and $25 million from the settlement fund which Park and BA organised on behalf of the defendants. The precise details of the fund were never officially disclosed, but $69 million is the most reliable estimate. BA paid approximately half of the total, which satisfied all of Laker's creditors from individual passengers to major investors. In return for relinquishing his own claims against BA, Sir Freddie himself was awarded $8 million.

In a statement announcing its payments to the creditors, and to Sir Freddie, Colin Marshall said, 'Our payment bears no admission of guilt on behalf of British Airways . . . to drive Laker out of business or to breach US anti-trust laws'. Now the path to privatisation really was clear.

Sir Freddie was shocked when I revealed to him the details of how Thatcher's manoeuvres had prompted Reagan's intervention nearly ten years later. I told him in 1994 during an interview for 'A Case of Corporate Murder', an investigation into the collapse of Laker Airways for the BBC's *40 Minutes* programme. Laker denounced the Prime Minister who had hailed his pioneering achievements at the Conservative Party conference only months before his airline crashed: 'It is unbelievable. It stinks. It is deplorable that the privatisation of British Airways, important as that was, should be put before the destruction of an industry. British Airways is now a bigger monopoly than it was before.

'I think it's another reason why politicians should not be involved in industry. Politicians are not very good at being legislators and they're terrible managers of businesses.'

For the remainder of his chairmanship at British Airways, Lord King particularly treasured a photograph of himself with Ronald Reagan on holiday on the President's ranch. BA's chairman loved America, and would sometimes begin speeches there with a tribute that President Reagan himself might have delivered:

'It is always a pleasure to be once more in the land of the free, the home of the brave.'

British Caledonian joined BA in contributing to the Laker settlement fund. However, Britain's largest independent airline was also on its way to becoming another victim on the altar of the Thatcher-King drive to privatisation, and their determination to ensure that BA's shareholders would invest in a company that continued to enjoy a virtual monopoly of British commercial aviation.

Sir Adam Thomson's entire fleet, which bore the proud symbol of a rampant lion, was bought by British Airways in 1987 for £250 million after a titanic tussle with the Swedish airline, Scandinavian Airlines System. As SAS's boss, Helge Lindberg, left London, having failed to grasp the prize that once seemed his, he commented ruefully: 'Such a price is too high for BCal. It makes it clear to us that BA is paying the price for keeping its monopoly.'

BA's bid to keep its 'monopoly' had been given an enormous boost three years earlier when the Conservative government rejected the CAA's recommendation that the strengthening of a second-force carrier would be in the best interests of competition and the consumer.

The CAA recommended that some of BA's routes be redistributed, and that a strong second-force carrier would increase consumer choice and lead to greater competition. King opposed the CAA proposals with one of the most effective lobbies in British political history. He organised mass demonstrations by BA's staff against the proposals, marches on Downing Street to hand in petitions, the mass lunching of Tory MPs in the Savoy Hotel and the arm-twisting of MPs and civil servants in the corridors of power with which he was so familiar. Sir Adam Thomson recalled: 'Lord King was fighting to keep his state-owned inheritance intact for prospective investors. I was fighting for opportunities for growth and expansion so far denied by the said state ownership.'

To a government more committed to privatisation than competition, there was ultimately no contest, and its subsequent decision not to legislate to ensure competition in the domestic airline industry became one of the defining moments of a turbulent decade in British commercial aviation. Although BCal managed to soldier on until 1987, Sir Adam Thomson believed its fate had been effectively determined in 1984 when the government capitulated to BA and ignored the CAA's recommendation. In Thomson's view, BCal was 'grievously wounded by the stab in the back administered by a conniving cabinet in the latter months of 1984. The *coup de grâce* was delivered as it tried to lift itself up to stand, free, on its own two feet by the same politicians at the end of 1987.'

The CAA was said to be 'disappointed' by the government's decision to ignore its 1984 recommendation. King was triumphant, and as he and Sir Colin Marshall manoeuvred BA into position to swallow the airline's most important domestic competitor in the mid-1980s, Sir Adam Thomson's airline once again felt the full force of the BA lobby as King outflanked SAS to gobble up BCal. The queue of Conservative MPs supporting King's newly privatised airline in its bid to repel SAS was led by Norman Tebbit. The former Trade Secretary urged his countrymen to 'repel the Viking invader at all costs', as Helge Lindberg and Jan Carlzon tried to buy into BCal at the end of 1987.

After the CAA accepted a BCal-SAS proposal, which would have given the Swedish airline part ownership and provided for operational collaboration, BA applied to revoke all of BCal's route licences on the grounds that the airline would be controlled by foreign interests. Sir Adam Thomson described BA's tactic as 'a move of absolute petulance', but he was powerless to keep BCal in the air when King and Marshall put together a shut-out bid of £250 million for the airline's entire shareholding. It was almost double what King had put on the table at one stage in the negotiations, and an indication of how keen he was to maintain BA's virtual monopoly of the domestic airline industry. The Monopolies and Mergers Commission allowed BA to take over the BCal routes only after King agreed to give some of them up to other British airlines; but BA's strategic objective was achieved as the national carrier took over its most important domestic rival.

Ironically, some of Thomson's planes ended up in storage in the Mojave Desert in California when BA could no longer afford to keep its whole fleet in the air at the beginning of the 1990s. The aeroplane graveyard had filled up rapidly with planes from all over the world towards the end of the 1980s as worldwide recession, and the deregulation of American commercial aviation, caused scores of airlines to go bankrupt. The swelling aero-morgue served to underline that only the fittest would survive. Billions of dollars worth of planes waited to be dismantled, sold for scrap and turned into Coke cans, if no one could afford to return them to the sky. The Lockheed jets, that once bore the lion of British Caledonian, lay there in King's colours. The planes were a symbolic reminder to those who wanted to challenge King that, if forced to choose between the interests of BA's shareholders and the interests of the consumer, the newly created pride of Mrs Thatcher's shareholding democracy would win out.

On 22 June 1984 Virgin Atlantic's first flight soared above the countryside of southern England as it took off from Gatwick Airport. Piloting the 'Maiden Voyager' were two of the world's most famous cricketers, Viv Richards and Ian Botham, and Richard Branson. At least that's what the plane full of Branson's family, friends and assorted celebrities thought when a pre-recorded video of the 'captain' and 'first officer' flashed onto the plane's in-flight screens shortly after take-off.

Branson launched Virgin Atlantic by promising to put fun into flying – a novel idea in an industry that often appeared to present the experience of flying as something that had to be endured. As Branson lobbied the Civil Aviation Authority for permission to fly to the States, consciously and proudly following in the footsteps of Freddie Laker, he claimed that there were 250,000 people who would fly to New York 'if the price was right'.

The concept of what Richard Branson describes as a 'high-quality, value-for-money airline' was born sixteen years after the teenage entrepreneur had started his business career from a public phone box.

'Hello, my name is Richard Branson, I'm eighteen and I run a magazine that's doing something really useful for young people.'

This was Branson's selling pitch as he canvassed for contributors and advertising for his first business venture in 1968 – *Student* magazine. The awkward, toothy youngster – a product of Stowe public school and an impeccable upper-middle-class background – was swept along in the tide of the late 1960s. The teenage Branson did many of the things hippies were supposed to do – growing his hair, demonstrating against injustice throughout the world, and exploring the opportunities of the era of free love and mind-bending drugs as enthusiastically as any of his contemporaries. But before the 1960s generation had taken off its caftans and stubbed out its joints, Branson was already involved in a distinctly non-hippie activity: he started making 'bread' – dismissive hippie-speak for money, necessary for subsistence but otherwise useless.

When the fortunes of *Student* magazine nose-dived, Branson started selling records by mail order to help prop it up. By 1971 Virgin Music had begun to blossom and, two years later, the company expanded into a record label, a recording studio and music-publishing operation. Branson recalls how the process that he refers to as 'synergy' worked at Virgin:

> From the mail-order business we went into retailing records, from the retailing of records we went into record production, through the setting up of the Virgin record label. We soon found that it was possible to negotiate music-publishing rights as well as record rights with the same band, so we set up the music-publishing company. Once we got past the very early stages, we realised that we were spending an awful lot of money on recording costs, so we got into the recording-studio business. When music videos became a necessary part of marketing records, we didn't just make them and waste them, we began to distribute them ourselves. This got us into the video-distribution business and it was a natural move to begin to acquire other products for video distribution.

Mike Oldfield's *Tubular Bells* made Virgin its first million. Branson left the musical judgments to others while he specialised in making the deals with the artistes.

As hippies became the dinosaurs of the pop-music scene, Branson reinvented Virgin Music's image by signing the iconoclastic punk group, the Sex Pistols, whose loathing for long hair and anything to do with hippiedom was one of the major parts of their appeal. 'Never Mind the Bollocks, this is the Sex Pistols' was Virgin Music's first punk record and it became a landmark in the company's progress to glory. Branson delighted in trying to outmanoeuvre the group's maverick manager, Malcolm McLaren, as much as he revelled in their anarchic music. As the Queen celebrated her twenty-fifth anniversary on the British throne, the Sex Pistols' record 'God Save the Queen' ('It's a fascist regime') provided the theme tune to the 'Stuff the Jubilee' movement; the BBC ban on the record ensured that it reached the top of the charts in the month of the Jubilee itself.

As records became 'product' and the revolution in pop music became an 'industry' in the 1980s, Virgin's synergy sustained Branson's empire. Virgin artists made records in Virgin studios to be sold in Virgin record shops. Books about Virgin artists were published by Virgin and sold in Virgin shops, and Virgin films were made about the Virgin singers, the Virgin artists and Virgin's chairman: very simple; very profitable; very Virgin.

Branson was not only the deal-maker, he was the catalyst, the inspiration and the motivator. Part of Branson's success in building the Virgin music and publishing business lay in his ability to delegate tasks to the right people, and knowing the limits of his own abilities. In the next fifteen years the company that Branson named Virgin – 'because we were novices in business' – signed Peter Gabriel, Phil Collins, Maxi Priest, Paula Abdul, Lenny Kravitz, Janet Jackson and, finally, the Rolling Stones.

Branson formed over a hundred more companies bearing the Virgin imprimatur. As a multimillionaire, he also became a natural target for people with hare-brained schemes who thought they only needed his money to get them off the ground. Most of the projects he received were unworkable. Patents and plans were returned with polite letters of refusal. However, as he sat huddled by the warmth of a winter fire in his Oxfordshire country home in 1984, one particular proposal aroused his curiosity.

A bundle of papers had been sent to him by Randolph Fields, a lawyer and self-styled entrepreneur. Fields had set up, on paper, an airline called British Atlantic and applied for a licence to fly from Gatwick to New York on a frequency left vacant by the collapse of Laker Airways two years earlier. What Fields' airline lacked was an aircraft, and that required Branson's money.

By the end of the weekend, the idea of adding an airline to his empire had begun to grow on Branson. The people who bought Virgin records tended to be young. Many of them travelled. They followed the hippie trails to India, they rode the Magic Bus, they explored America hitchhiking, or on a Greyhound bus. A Virgin cut-price airline would allow them to cross the Atlantic cheaply.

There was another factor. The idea of an airline appealed to the restless side of Branson's nature. Nobody in Branson's company could doubt that they were in the presence of a fidget, a corporate Peter Pan drawn inexorably to a new challenge. It was all very well being a millionaire, but Branson had been one for over a decade. His restlessness required new horizons, and once he decided that Virgin would take flight, no one was going to stop him. Typically, he decided to back Fields' idea on the weekend that he read his proposal.

'I think you're a megalomaniac, Richard. I don't want to know. This is the beginning of the end of our relationship.'

Firm and prophetic words from Branson's second cousin, Simon Draper, with whom he founded Virgin Music. Virgin's other co-founder, Ken Berry, was similarly sceptical. Both men's views were swept aside by Branson. He did, after all, own 85% of the company. However, Branson promised his two friends and business partners that the airline would never be allowed to jeopardise the record company and that he would stick to one of the golden rules they had established at Virgin: 'Have a way out'. He calculated that if he hired a Boeing 747 over ten years, he could 'walk away' or bail out of the airline business at a cost of no more than £2 million. As Virgin's record sales were booming in the mid-1980s Branson reckoned he could take the risk and 'protect the downside' if it all went wrong.

The commercial aviation establishment tried to block Branson's airline from the outset. British Caledonian opposed Virgin's application to fly across the Atlantic. A lawyer representing BCal remarked at the Civil Aviation Authority hearing that Branson would need 'a lot of groups on *Top of the Pops*' to run an airline. It was not a good argument: Virgin Music's profit in 1983 was £11.4 million, more than twice British Caledonian's. A large chunk of the profits were due to Virgin Music's latest phenomenon, Boy George and his band, Culture Club. Because Branson financed the airline with the profits from the huge worldwide sales of their records, Virgin Atlantic was popularly dubbed 'the airline that Boy George built' after the Civil Aviation Authority awarded Branson's and Fields' airline the Gatwick-Newark licence it had refused Fields the previous year.

Following three months of frantic activity that Branson describes as the hardest of his life, Virgin Atlantic was ready for take-off. Recognising that what he knew about running an airline could be written on the back of a boarding pass, Branson hired people who had experience of flying and who shared his commitment to the concept of Virgin Atlantic – many were ex-Laker Airways and, as the airline grew, some were BA refuseniks. Two key ex-Laker exec-utives who helped launch Virgin Atlantic were Roy Gardner, who later became managing director, and David Tait, whom Branson sent to New York in March 1984 with a simple instruction: 'Set up an airline. We'll be sending you a 747 a day in three months' time.' Tait has run Virgin Atlantic's US operation ever since.

As 'Maiden Voyager' sped down the Gatwick runway for the first time in June 1984, the only blemish on the white plane was the dis-tinctive scarlet logo. 'Shady Lady' and 'Maiden Japan' soon followed and, by 1985, Virgin passengers could buy Virgin holi-days. In 1986, Virgin Mail Service started delivering mail as the airline's network of routes expanded. Branson's synergy was alive and flying in the 1980s.

For the launch of each new Virgin Atlantic route Branson invited a posse of camera crews, photographers and reporters to accompany his family and key members of the airline's staff involved in founding each route. It was the start of a love affair with the media that would endure for years to come. The promot-ers hired to publicise the launch of Virgin Atlantic had little to do. It was Branson the press wanted to talk to, as the once diffident entrepreneur became his airline's best advert. Kitted out in a brown leather aviator's helmet, Branson was reborn as Biggles.

As Virgin Atlantic took flight, Branson's image metamorphosed from a relatively obscure record-company boss to one of the best-known faces in Britain. Within two years he started winning awards for his communications skills. The self-deprecating, some-times rather nervous but accessible persona that Branson presented was a refreshing change from the normal PR hoops that journalists have to leap through, and the lists of questions they have to submit in advance. Sometimes he even asked journalists what they thought he should say.

Branson's openness contrasted vividly with the crabby Lord King, and helped him to build his reputation amongst journalists who dealt with him. This approach also robbed hostile newspapers of the 'tycoon exposed' genre of stories that brought down many in the airline industry and beyond. As Branson's dispute with British Airways deepened, his approach would be repaid many times over.

Branson spoke openly about topics that others would have tried to hide: his experimentation with drugs, the failure of his first marriage, and his two brushes with the law. The more serious was a 'bust' in 1971, when he was caught pulling a fast one on the Customs and Excise by selling records in his first Virgin shop that he claimed he had bought to export. He spent a night in the cells and agreed to pay a fine of more than £50,000 over three years; charges were dropped and he escaped a criminal record. The night the barrister's son spent locked up had a far greater corrective impact than the fine. 'A night spent in the cells with just a filthy blanket and one drink, and you learn never to do it again,' he recalls.

Earlier the same year Branson had been convicted of poaching on private land in Suffolk after being caught shooting pheasants. The gamekeepers hauled him in front of the landowner and the police insisted on prosecuting him. The fine was nominal. Twenty years later, as Branson took to the skies which King the huntsman considered to be his own, the image of the poacher seemed peculiarly apt.

Branson was delighted that more than any other airline, Virgin Atlantic initially inherited Freddie Laker's mantle of cheap-and-cheerful flying. Before his first flight in June 1984, Branson asked Laker if he could name his first plane after the pioneering entrepreneur. A disillusioned Sir Freddie said he thought it was rather too close to his airline's 1982 crash to be appropriate. However, the trailblazer was generous with his advice. He told Branson to aim not only for the cheap-and-cheerful 'bring your own sandwiches' Magic Bus, but also the lucrative business-class market.

'I paid close attention to the mistakes which appeared to have caused the failure, as well as what might be done to avoid repeating them. For example, we would obviously need to protect ourselves against currency fluctuations. We should go for carrying freight as well as passengers, and that would mean using 747s instead of DC10s. By concentrating too exclusively on offering a discount, price-led service, Laker had made himself very vulnerable to price cutting by the big carriers. And by the time they introduced a business class – two months before the collapse – it was too late. So we decided to have a unique, high-quality business class to complement a competitive and good economy class.'

Branson performed a delicate juggling act as he tried to appeal to business travellers without alienating the cheap-and-cheerful end of the market. He began to plug Virgin's 'Upper Class' – 'first-class service at business-class prices' – using a range of new incentives. Free limousines were laid on to ferry passengers to and from airport terminals on both sides of the Atlantic at both ends of the journey. Sleeper seats were redesigned for greater comfort. There was an improved menu that passengers could select from when they felt hungry, not when the food trolley arrived. Individual video screens – the world's first on commercial airliners – were introduced so passengers could select their own entertainment. Because he put fewer seats in his jumbos there was sixteen inches' more legroom than British Airways offered in its equivalent service. There was also a free economy ticket for every Upper Class ticket purchased.

When Branson introduced his Upper Class innovations from 1988–9, Virgin passenger loads initially fell. However, the airline's yields increased and soon a third of Virgin Atlantic's income was generated by business-class passengers. Branson's up-market strategy put him on a collision course with British Airways, who realised he was not only attracting economy-class passengers who were being squeezed out of the end of its planes, but was also aiming for the business end of the market. Since privatisation, BA had spent millions on securing the loyalty of exactly the kind of passenger Branson was trying to win over. It had already launched Club Europe and Club World in 1988 at a cost of £25 million. Marshall's next aim was to carve out a larger share of the lucrative first-class passenger market. He was frank about his plan to achieve it.

'There are no indications of major growth in the first-class market, so our objective is to take business from other airlines by offering the highest standard of passenger service in the world.'

In 1989, Marshall unveiled a £24 million facelift for BA's first-class service. It had taken years to plan and was expected to increase by a fifth the 250,000 passengers flying first class with BA each year.

Branson's personal enjoyment in owning and running an airline, while attempting to create a product that would one day fulfil his ambition of creating the best airline in the world, was transparent from the moment he welcomed the first passengers onto Virgin Atlantic's inaugural flight to New York. Even when there are no television crews or profile-writers, Branson's staff frequently welcome him on board his own planes; normally he's in economy class or amusing the flight crew as they while away the hours on automatic pilot.

Superficially many of Branson's business attitudes remain those of an archetypal small businessman made big – very big. Although he sold Virgin Music in 1992 for $1 billion, the cornerstone of Branson's business philosophy is that 'small is beautiful', and he espouses many attitudes associated with small business. His Virgin Atlantic staff are not, for example, represented by trade unions.

'That would be an admission of defeat because then I would have to create personnel departments and lose contact with my staff.' Branson values his staff more highly than any other component of his business. 'They are the front line. To passengers phoning in to book an airline ticket or buying a record in a Megastore, the Virgin staff they deal with ARE Virgin and much more important than the people who run the company. And if, as chairman of the company, I can't spend a moment talking to the switchboard operator who answers the phone when I call the air-line, I wouldn't be doing my job.'

For Branson, his preoccupation with his staff's well-being makes good business sense. 'Unlike many British companies, our philosophy has always been to put our staff first, customers second and shareholders third. As a result 99% of the key people have stayed with the company . . . With a loyal, happy staff, a company can achieve anything. If our hostesses and stewards are enjoying the job, then our customers will enjoy flying with us. So putting staff first effectively puts customers first also – and because customers are happy, our shareholders benefit . . .'

All the members of Virgin Atlantic's staff are given Branson's home phone number and his Holland Park address. They are encouraged to write to him with ideas, problems or suggestions. If a Virgin plane is over one and a half hours late anywhere in the world, staff are under instructions to let him know immediately.

When Branson himself is on board a Virgin flight he serves drinks from the trolley and spends hours on passenger patrol, chatting to his customers. When his energy permits him to take his seat, Branson immediately starts scribbling notes on ideas and innovations that have cropped up in conversation with his staff and his passengers. After the visitors' book, in which Upper Class passengers are invited to comment on their flights, has been passed round, Branson grabs it and reads every comment.

'It's like being the owner of a small club. The owner can pay attention to detail. It's easy to introduce new ideas and to change things that don't work.'

Out went the live entertainers on board and in came personal videos, Virgin fun packs, children's entertainment, masseuses and manicurists for business travellers. The theme remained the same – flying should be fun.

Conventional airline marketing wisdom holds that successful airlines base their strategy on the 'four Ps' – Product, Price, Promotion, and Placing. With Virgin Atlantic's low-cost base, young staff and attractive product, Branson was confident that he could produce something which would attract passengers. However, as Sir Freddie Laker and Sir Adam Thomson discovered before him, there is a fifth 'P' – for politics – that determines not only an airline's success but also its survival

Despite the moves towards deregulation of the skies in the USA and Europe, governments remain integrally involved in the decision-making process of all airlines, particularly in Britain. Airlines have to compete according to carefully worked out rules determined by governments and their agencies – civil servants and government-appointed regulators act as umpires.

At the most basic level, governments determine safety and engineering standards and fashion the commercial environment within which their country's airlines are obliged to operate. Airspace is sovereign, and governments also have the right to determine who flies into and out of their airspace, when they can do it and where they can land.

Inter-governmental talks are regularly held to grant licences for routes and to establish the frequency of flights by one nation's airlines into another nation's airspace. Such talks create the shape of a country's airline industry, and governments then distribute the routes, the slots and the frequencies between those who want to fly. Politics holds the key, and politics, with a large and a small 'p', is where Branson's touch has been known to desert him.

Branson was initiated into active politics, with a very large 'P', by Vanessa Redgrave's Workers' Revolutionary Party in 1968. He never joined, but marched shoulder to shoulder with the actress as a fellow traveller to the American Embassy in Grosvenor Square in protest at the war in Vietnam.

Branson's progress has not, however, been a simple and familiar retreat from youthful ideals to the warm embrace of capitalism. Despite the repeated and strenuous efforts of the Conservative Party to claim the most successful entrepreneur of his generation as its own, Branson has resisted their entreaties. Throughout the 1980s he received scores of requests from Conservative Central Office to contribute to the party's barren coffers. Branson declined. He believes it is wrong in principle for businesses to donate money to political parties.

He resolutely refused to endorse the Conservative manifesto throughout the Thatcher decade. When John Major started the 1992 General Election campaign trailing Labour in the opinion polls, Central Office placed Richard Branson at the top of its 'celebrity supporters' list which it released to the press in a bid to boost its sagging campaign. Branson was livid as he had specifically stated he would not join the list. He phoned the Tory Party chairman, Chris Patten, and demanded his name be instantly removed.

Were Branson an active politician he would probably have been described as a Tory 'wet' in the 1980s – attracted by Thatcherite economics but repelled by its social insensitivity. In a different age he might have been a one-nation Tory. His belief that there is such a thing as society, and that businesses have a role to play in it, leads him to distinctly non-Thatcherite views on many issues, and to espouse an eclectic mixture of principles and causes that has included the fight against AIDS, Parents against Tobacco, health care and gay rights.

Despite his huge wealth, Branson has consistently refused to sell his gay London nightclub, Heaven. For Branson it is a matter of principle which he has stuck to, despite siren voices warning him of potential dangers. Calls for him to sell the club reached a crescendo when he floated Virgin on the Stock Exchange for eighteen months in the late 1980s. He refused point blank.

'I think many gay people have a bloody miserable time in many ways, and now there is this terrible disease [AIDS] that is wiping many of them out. If I can run a club where gays can have a good time, then I think that's worthwhile. It will be the last place I sell.'

Racism appals Branson and he refused to apply for a licence to fly on British Airways' most profitable single route – to South Africa – until Nelson Mandela was released from prison in 1990. The temptation of applying to fly to Johannesburg should not be underestimated. Since 1946 BA (formerly as BOAC) and South African Airlines have enjoyed a duopoly on the route, and have kept prices artificially high for generations. As a state-owned airline and as a privatised company, BA flew continuously to South Africa in defiance of international sanctions against apartheid. The London–Johannesburg route returns an annual profit of £30 million for BA, making it the most profitable single route per passenger in the world.

Although Branson was not destined to become 'one of us', he did nonetheless become personally associated with Mrs Thatcher in the mid-1980s. After he broke the transatlantic speedboat record in 1986, Branson asked Mrs Thatcher to join him on a celebratory trip up the Thames in Challenger II and, despite warnings from his closest colleagues at Virgin, he accepted an invitation to chair UK 2000 in 1986. The scheme was initiated by the then Environment Secretary, Kenneth Baker, with the ostensible objectives of providing employment for Britain's growing army of young unemployed and simultaneously improving the environment.

Branson accepted after consulting senior members of the opposition parties, and after Baker had given him an assurance that the scheme would be run in a strictly non-partisan fashion. UK 2000 was immediately and predictably condemned from the outset by non-Conservatives, who charged that it was hypocritical to tackle the symptoms of the government's anti-inflation policy rather than the chief cause – Mrs Thatcher's monetarist strategy.

The worst fears of Branson's advisers came to pass when Mrs Thatcher decided to hijack UK 2000 by declaring that its objective was to 'Tidy Up Britain'. The first Branson knew about the change of emphasis was during a visit to the Scilly Isles to thank the islanders for their help with his Challenger transatlantic bid. A photographer from the *Sun*, acting on a tip-off from Number 10, arrived unexpectedly in a helicopter with a broom for Richard Branson. The photographer handed Branson the broom, took his picture and congratulated him on becoming the new 'Minister for Litter'.

The summer that followed was uncomfortable for Branson. As the 'Minister for Litter', Virgin's chairman became associated with one of the most memorable and ludicrous photo-opportunities of the decade – Mrs Thatcher trying to stab errant items of litter in a park during a light gale with one hand while the other clutched her handbag. As one who knew a thing or two about photo-opportunities, Branson winced with the nation. As some of his Virgin colleagues had warned him, the desire to 'do something really useful' can be even more difficult to fulfil in politics than in business.

Branson can now afford a wry smile but, at the time, he became too closely identified with Mrs Thatcher for his own liking, and there was a price to pay in credibility. Elvis Costello and other progressive rock acts, for example, refused to have anything to do with Branson or Virgin as a result.

It was Branson's brief emergence into the international political arena, after Saddam Hussein invaded Kuwait at the beginning of August 1990, that precipitated the chain of events that would eventually lead to his High Court confrontation with Lord King.

The month before the Iraqi invasion of Kuwait, Branson celebrated his fortieth birthday. The event induced an unexpected bout of self-doubt. As the head of a multimillion-pound empire with worldwide interests Branson had recently married Joan

Templeman, his longstanding partner and the mother of his two children, Holly and Sam. He was internationally fêted as one of the outstanding businessmen of his generation. However, he was still driven by unfulfilled ambition to make a larger and more important contribution. He was even considering selling Virgin Music in order to devote himself to charitable projects that would fulfil his adolescent yearning to 'do something useful'.

Saddam Hussein's invasion of Kuwait, and the imprisonment of scores of British people as 'human shield' hostages, gave Branson the opportunity to do just that: get them home. Live Aid had been a big moment in a decade not previously noted for its altruism, and Branson set about attempting to extricate the hostages from Iraq with a Geldof-like sense of purpose and drive. He had unexpectedly found the chance to express his entrepreneurial talents in the cause of helping people in trouble rather than making another million.

At the request of Queen Nohr of Jordan, who phoned him at home a month after the invasion, he also started relief flights to provide essential supplies for the thousands of refugees who had spilled out from Iraq into Jordan. After intensive negotiations with the British and Iraqi governments, Branson flew with a volunteer Virgin crew to pluck the hostages from Baghdad, and ran into a barrage of criticism for his trouble. One member of a Gulf relatives' support group accused him of 'a sick publicity stunt'.

Branson was badly wounded by the criticism. When he had had time to reflect upon the episode he told his biographer, Mick Brown: 'If I go out to promote one of my companies, to make lots of money, I never get criticised for that. But if anybody tries to do anything positive they get criticised. It was the same for Bob Geldof.'

As Branson's soul-searching continued he wrote in his diary:

What are my motives for doing this? Is there any truth in the jibes? [In July] I was at an all-time low: I seemed to have run out of a purpose for life; I'd just turned forty and was seeking new challenges. I was even considering selling up everything except the airline, getting smaller and concentrating on one business venture, but also to have the time to use my business skills to concentrate on issues where I felt I could help. I thought I could get more satisfaction in this way.

Do I need recognition for this? I don't think so. In order to campaign on many issues you need to use yourself. The situation with the refugees has now been arrested, and by not speaking out it might not have been. How often can one use the press in this way in one small country like England without losing one's appeal to the public? It should be a hint that if one was doing it for personal glory then one wouldn't be able to do it at all.

King Hussein and Queen Nohr subsequently invited Branson to Jordan to witness the distribution of the aid he had helped to raise, and thanked him warmly for his action. So did many of the families of the hostages that he had flown out of the Gulf.

The sight of Edward Heath and Richard Branson accompanying the Baghdad hostages on a Virgin plane produced very mixed feelings in 10 Downing Street, and at BA. Lord King was unspeakably angry. Not only had Virgin usurped BA's historic role of coming to the government's aid in times of national crisis, Branson was also flying home some of BA's own staff and passengers who had been held when their flight landed just after Saddam invaded Kuwait. In King's eyes Branson's walk-on role in Middle Eastern and Gulf diplomacy was 'doing something really useful' once too often. BA's chairman had failed to recognise Branson as an enemy until Virgin's airlifts started. Baggy jumpers, second hand jumbos and a perpetual grin did not gain access to any of Lord King's clubs, but now Branson appeared to be following BA's chairman into the heart of the British establishment.

King reportedly stormed into Whitehall, and demanded to know if Virgin had become 'part of the Foreign Office?' Returning to BA, he summoned Marshall and Burnside to urgent meetings. 'Do something about Branson', seethed BA's leader.

By the autumn of 1990 the poacher found himself firmly in the hunter's sights.

3

The Braces and the 'Grinning Pullover'

Lord King was particularly enraged by Virgin Atlantic's Gulf exploits because British Airways had been unsuccessfully trying to 'do something about Richard Branson' and his tiny airline long before Saddam Hussein invaded Kuwait. In 1988, one of British Airways' most influential voices had warned Lord King and Sir Colin Marshall in a confidential report that,

> while Virgin is not a major competitor, it is a continuous thorn in our side and will have to be carefully watched if not tackled head on.

The author was an American, Michael Levin. Marshall had hired Levin as soon as he took up the post of chief executive in 1983 and, by the end of the decade, he was widely held to be the third most powerful man at British Airways. Marshall held Levin in the highest possible regard, describing him as 'a brilliant man, a workaholic and a great ideas man'. The American's report on Virgin Atlantic was written when it posed no commercial threat whatsoever to British Airways.

> If Virgin Atlantic stood still and only continued to operate its two routes with its two Boeing aircraft, I guess that BA

would not have to concern itself too greatly, having a world-wide network and a revenue turnover approximately fifty times greater than Virgin's.

Levin pointed out in his 1988 paper, however, that after British Airways had swallowed British Caledonian earlier the same year, Branson was planning to expand Virgin Atlantic rapidly and could soon pose a major threat on BA's long-haul routes. Levin noted that Virgin had quickly snapped up some of British Caledonian's most profitable routes – to New York's JFK, Los Angeles and Tokyo – and had filed applications with the CAA to fly to Hong Kong, Melbourne, Perth, Sydney, Adelaide and Singapore. While Virgin Atlantic was most popularly charac-terised as being a flea to BA's elephant, Levin warned BA that it ignored at its peril the company whose chairman relished the motto 'small is beautiful'.

> Let us not neglect our own backyard and ignore the potential threat from within . . . BA is in danger of falling into the trap of complacency and seeing Virgin Atlantic coming up on our blind side.

Colin Marshall first met Michael Levin in the USA while his own reputation as one of Britain's high-flying businessmen was taking off at Avis. BA's future chief executive became entranced by the mercurial New Yorker who regaled him with stories of a life of adventure.

A talented linguist, Levin graduated from Harvard during the Second World War. He counted French and German amongst his second languages, as well as Russian and a smattering of other Slavic tongues. The young graduate was recruited by the Office of Strategic Services (a forerunner of the Central Intelligence Agency) and became one of the first Americans to enter the concentration camps in Germany at the end of the war. He took responsibility for interrogating Nazis as they were rounded up.

Returning to civilian life he dabbled in music journalism and wrote for a weekly jazz magazine, *Downbeat*, before becoming a radio and television producer. In 1952 Levin drew on his experience in television to mastermind General Eisenhower's advertising campaign for the White House. He later set up his own advertising agency before moving into teaching in Massachusetts.

In the early 1970s Levin settled down in California as principal management consultant at the Stanford Research Institute. He advised companies ranging from Rockwell to Sun Oil to Avis, where he met Marshall.

Levin immediately struck a chord with Marshall. Both men shared the view that companies stagnate and decline unless they are in a state of perpetual change. Levin described the vast corporations he advised as 'lethargies' in need of being woken. To wake them up, Levin himself would play the role of catalyst. While Marshall 'kept the polish on the product', Levin's role was to shake up the management.

Before joining BA neither Marshall nor Levin had ever worked in commercial aviation, and their careers at the airline were intertwined.

'Levin was Marshall's creature,' remembered one former colleague.

'What do you mean?' contradicted another. 'Marshall was Levin's creature !'

'Levin was welded to Marshall,' a third colleague recalled.

Marshall placed Levin in an office adjacent to his own at Speedbird House with an interconnecting door. BA's chief executive paid him $100,000 a year for his services, substantially more than Lord King's salary before BA was privatised. Levin enjoyed the reputation of influencing Marshall's thinking more deeply than anyone else, and together they set about awakening the vast state-owned monopoly from its particular 'lethargy'.

When Mrs Thatcher's election victory in spring 1983 assured the privatisation of British Airways, King and Marshall's overwhelming priority was to prepare for flotation. Marshall made Levin the head of a 'special task force'. Its role was to evaluate the operation and performance of the entire airline and its vast bureaucracy. Levin made no secret of how appalled he was at what he found. One former colleague remembers how he dealt with the problem.

'The place was flooded with middle-manager do-nothings whom Colin Marshall couldn't fire. Mike Levin thought they were completely useless. So he got them to do things that he knew they would find totally unacceptable, like cleaning the planes before they took off every morning! Shortly afterwards they started leaving.'

Sir Colin Marshall remembers the assault on Lord King's detested 'balcony bosses' only slightly differently:

'Junior staff became quite accustomed to the sight of senior managers climbing aboard aircraft at six o'clock in the morning to make sure cabins were spotless before the first service of the day took off.'

As Levin cast a critical eye over the disastrously managed state airline, his own, rather mysterious, reputation began to grow. Few who encountered the chief executive's secretive guru expressed neutral opinions about him. Some of his junior colleagues were as enthralled as their chief executive. They remembered his 'visionary qualities', and how he had the ability to sit through a whole meeting in silence, and then dazzle the assembled executives and managers with a pinpoint résumé of what had been discussed and how a problem should be tackled.

A more sceptical executive recalls: 'He was like a Maharishi to those guys. They used to sit at his feet and just lap it all up. Sessions in Levin's offices were a bizarre mixture of therapy and theory.'

So powerful was Levin's hold over Marshall that rumours grew at BA that the American was employing lessons in psychological warfare learnt while working for the CIA in Vietnam. Like many other rumours about Levin this was entirely untrue. They would probably not have been spread had Levin himself not given them credence. His family denies that he worked for the CIA and says he did not even go to Vietnam. However, the colourful rumours reflect the closeness of Marshall and Levin's relationship in the eyes of those who worked with them, and indicate how proud Levin was of his Svengali image.

As Marshall's marketing revolution swept through BA, Levin's reputation as the chief executive's hatchet man grew. The perpetual revolution that Levin and Marshall instigated in the higher echelons of BA was aimed at clearing out dead wood. However, it also led to a large exodus of talented managers, many of whom went on to prosper with other airlines and in different industries. One such former executive described Levin as 'totally unprincipled and completely immoral', while another assessed him as 'a brilliant catalyst, an average analyst and a poor manager'.

Even some of those who respected Levin were envious of the empire he and Marshall built at their Heathrow base, and the growing influence of the man who wrote all the chief executive's speeches. Levin rarely left Heathrow and Lord King, who ruled his kingdom from BA's West End offices in Enserch House in St James's Square, once claimed never to have met him. The animosity between the two, fuelled by King's distrust of intellectuals, was unmistakable to those who knew Levin in the 1980s.

'Levin loathed King. He thought he was the most pompous and useless thing that had ever come along, but he would never have said so publicly. It would have been bad for the airline and bad for Colin.'

It was perhaps inevitable that as Marshall's relationship with King began to disintegrate, Levin's role at BA began to emerge into public view. After the successful flotation in 1987, the chairman and his chief executive sometimes seemed to be pursuing their own agendas and Levin was central to the execution of Marshall's. The chief executive believed that building strong alliances with other international carriers was crucial to BA's ambition to become a megacarrier capable of competing with the American and European global carriers.

Together Marshall and Levin steered BA to the brink of a $750-million deal with United Airlines in 1989. This would have secured a 15% stake for BA in the vast American carrier. However, the deal collapsed acrimoniously in October 1989. By the time it did there was open speculation in the British press that King was actually quite pleased that 'Marshall's deal' had fallen through. Levin was cited in reports as 'a prime source of tension' between the chairman and the chief executive as their pursuit of divergent agendas became clear.

When Marshall asked Levin to turn his attention to Virgin Atlantic, there was no doubt the chief executive would examine closely the results of his work. One of the reports Michael Levin produced ran to thirty pages and it had a quasi-academic feel to it. He quoted liberally from works by marketing theorists such as Kotler, Mintzberg and Weichmann, and borrowed heavily from Mick Brown's biography of Branson in an effort to help BA understand how its tiny rival and its chairman ticked. 'Virgin is Branson,' was one of Levin's less original conclusions.

Some of Levin's other observations were more tenuous, influenced by substantial doses of the theoretical marketing psychobabble for which he was renowned at BA:

> . . . from childhood [Branson] was driven by a need for achievement and independence and had faced 'role deterioration', a disruption in his life, from where he set out on his own, and in moments of crisis, not seeking security but going on into deeper insecurities. These are also reflected in Mintzberg's description of the chief characteristics of the entrepreneurial mode of strategy-making.

Some of the report was more comprehensible. In a phrase that quickly entered BA's vocabulary, Levin described Branson as 'the grinning pullover', who benefited from his image as a self-made man and who was also perceived by 'the British' to be an underdog in competition with BA. Apart from his colourful turns of phrase, there was little new in this part of Levin's report, but he was the first senior figure at BA to warn how much potential damage Virgin Atlantic could inflict.

Levin cited internal BA research which consistently found that passengers preferred flying with Virgin Atlantic to flying with British Airways. He stressed that by targeting his popular product at a 'niche' in the market, Branson had the potential to deprive BA of substantial amounts of revenue. Levin concluded his report on Virgin with the recommendation that the tiny airline should be tackled 'head on'.

Marshall's response to Levin's promptings was swift. As Branson prepared to launch his new services on the old British Caledonian routes, Marshall decided to challenge Virgin Atlantic on its oldest and most profitable route, to New York's second airport, Newark. BA's daily service to Newark would start in March 1990.

Because Virgin Atlantic was barred from flying from Heathrow, Richard Branson had successfully concentrated on developing the Gatwick-to-Newark route as an alternative gateway to New York. The ploy had worked. British businessmen looking to America developed a liking for the convenient airport south of the New Jersey Turnpike as American companies spilled out from New York. As well as boosting Virgin's profits, the Gatwick–Newark route helped to change the airline's image from a small, leisure-orientated carrier to one that was becoming renowned for its business-class service. 'Yuppies' swiftly became a term of abuse on both sides of the Atlantic, but for international airlines they were a key source of revenue and Branson was beginning to attract them as well as 'the scruffy rich'.

As Marshall's men prepared to launch BA's Heathrow–Newark service, Virgin Atlantic won the *Business Traveller* magazine's award for 'Best Business Class – Long Haul' for the second year running and *Executive Travel* magazine's 'Best Transatlantic Carrier' for the first time.

To sell tickets on BA's new route across the Atlantic, Marshall looked to another North American saviour, Jim Callery. Marshall had appointed Jim Callery as head of world sales after the Laker settlement had cleared the way for privatisation: the American was with Amtrak when Marshall recruited him, and before that he had spent many years with TWA.

To many of his sales force, Jim Callery epitomised the ultra-competitive culture that had developed within BA under Lord King and Sir Colin Marshall – hard selling, and equally hard-ball politics. If Marshall believed that to fly was to serve Lord King, Callery had no embarrassment about flying to serve the Lord Himself. A devout Catholic, Callery believed his workforce should turn their own lives into a mission to sell BA.

'A good Christian is one who sells a product that has integrity,' Callery told the BBC in 1989. The fixed smile and the Messianic gleam Callery wore as he expanded on this particular article of faith was familiar to the BA sales force, a quarter of whom Callery sacked when he arrived at the airline in 1986.

Pronouncements like these and Callery's evangelical approach to selling swiftly won him the title of the 'Reverend Jim' below stairs at BA.

'Callery would sack you because he genuinely believed God told him to,' recalled one former BA saleswoman who had suffered just such a divine intervention.

The 'Reverend Jim' himself describes his relation with the Almighty rather differently.

'I have a value system that is very deeply religious and the God I follow said, "I came to serve and not to be served", so if you believe that, then service is the most honourable profession anyone could be in.'

One former member of the Reverend Jim's 'congregation' remembers the sales department's cheerleader:

'His commitment to BA is total. He's very much a happy-clappy, born-again sort. In my dreams I used to have this image of him patrolling the Heathrow check-in area in open-toed sandals. He would be banging a tambourine and singing "Onward Christian Soldiers". The soldiers in question would be dressed in BA uniforms marching to the war against other carriers!'

Callery didn't hide his contempt for shirkers in BA's sales force. He believed most of them inhabited what he acidly described as the 'comfort zone'.

'The ones in the comfort zone worry me the most because they are the ones who will do enough to satisfy an acceptable level of performance but never reach high enough in case next year you come back and ask for more. We must commit to a level of performance that is just excellent. I hope no one will associate me with being an autocratic general but I am demanding. When people sign on, I do expect them to perform.'

The BBC airline documentary caught Callery bawling out the general manager of his UK sales department, Kevin Hatton, in front of the nation for failing to reach the Holy Grail of the monthly revenue target.

'The promise that you made you've not delivered,' Callery hissed menacingly at the fraught-looking Hatton, never allowing an icy smile to leave his face.

When the Reverend Jim launched BA's 'Selling to The World'

campaign, he defined the national carrier's sales objectives in an
appropriately revivalist 'Mission Statement':

> The generation of maximum profitable revenue across the
> worldwide British Airways network through the identifica-
> tion and exploitation of every sales opportunity by a
> professionally committed, results-orientated sales force, *clos-
> ing out anyone or anything that attempts to interfere with the
> delivery of that revenue*. [My italics.]

By 1990 Virgin Atlantic was BA's only British competitor on long-
haul routes 'interfering' with the delivery of its revenue. The
Reverend Jim and his sales team set about 'closing out' Branson
with zeal.

As Callery got to work on launching BA's Newark service,
Marshall also acted on some of Michael Levin's other recommendations. Recognising how different Virgin Atlantic's product was
from those of BA's other competitors, Levin urged Marshall to
watch Branson's operation like a hawk. '. . . We cannot afford to
become complacent about the potential problems an airline such
as Virgin Atlantic can cause us,' Levin told Marshall, urging him
above all to gather 'any information, indicators, and significant
intelligence . . . about this airline'.

Marshall delegated this task to the massive marketing and operations department. In 1989 the marketing and sales departments
were merged with the operations department to form marketing
and operations – the heart of BA's competitive effort. The first
director of marketing and operations was Liam Strong, one of
Colin Marshall's appointees. Strong's department would have
overall responsibility for launching the Newark route.

Marshall had recruited Strong, an Ulsterman, from Reckitt and
Colman. Many BA-watchers immediately put Strong on their
shortlists as a possible successor to Sir Colin himself. A good-
looking, fair-haired man, Strong's boyish smile disguised an
ambitious operator prone to arrogance; he came to BA with a
reputation as a dynamic manager with the capacity to act swiftly
to sort problems out.

Helping Strong to devise BA's strategy to counter Virgin was the head of marketing, Mike Batt. A former Mars Bar salesman, he had one unusual advantage over his colleagues: he had briefly been one of Virgin Atlantic's most senior managers. Branson's airline had poached Batt from BA at the end of 1989.

After less than a week at Virgin, Batt phoned Colin Marshall and asked for his old job back. He told Marshall that the job he had been recruited to do at Virgin Atlantic was not the one he ended up doing. The chief executive welcomed his marketing man back without hesitation.

Richard Branson remains baffled by his sudden departure.

'It was all very mysterious. I was in Japan at the time preparing for the transpacific balloon trip and he left before I returned. He didn't really have time to get his feet under the table, but he did have time to meet every head of department at Virgin Atlantic and get a good briefing from each one.'

Batt's unexpected reappearance at BA caused mixed feelings. He had developed a reputation for being something of a chameleon as he worked his way towards the top of the BA management tree, exhibiting an ability to change colour to suit the priorities of the moment. Some of his colleagues were not as impressed by Batt as they thought he was by himself.

'Mike is rather like a cushion,' said one. 'He tends to resemble the shape of the last person who sat on him.'

Batt the businessman epitomised the new generation of executives who swept all before them in the 1980s at BA. Like King he came from a working-class background and, like so many who prospered at BA during the Marshall and Levin era, he knew little about airlines but appeared to know everything about 'brand marketing'. He brought a down-to-earth approach to his work:

'There always has been a mystique and a romance about aviation, but in terms of the principles involved of satisfying your customer there's no difference between selling airline seats and chocolate bars.'

To some within BA, Batt the 'brand man' epitomised the age of designer marketing and constant repackaging.

'Mike Batt is obsessed by status, career progress, and consumerism. If the word yuppie had not already been invented by the 1980s, it would have been invented to describe him,' said one colleague.

Once reinstated in his former capacity as the head of BA's marketing department, Batt briefed Liam Strong on Virgin Atlantic's 'sloppy' management. Keen to demonstrate to BA that his flirtation with Virgin was an aberration, Batt tackled the task of devising tactics to counter his former employer's inroads into BA's transatlantic traffic with renewed vigour.

In the build-up to the launch of BA's own Newark service, Batt advised Strong to study Branson's operation in the most minute detail – attempting to find out precisely how many people travelled on Virgin's flights and what the specific yields were from each of his flights. Batt urged Strong to place particular emphasis on an analysis of the lucrative business-class market.

An initial probe into Branson's operation was carried out by John Scaife, in BA's business analysis unit. Scaife's task was to assess how BA could best attack Branson's operation, using the in-built marketing and sales advantages that its massive global operation and dominance afforded. BA also had access to the most powerful marketing tool available to any airline: a computer reservation system (CRS).

BA's CRS is known throughout the industry as BABS – the British Airways Booking System. BABS holds the details not only of BA's bookings and flight details, but also those of other airlines. The vast expense of setting up and running a CRS is prohibitive for smaller airlines and, as the importance of CRSs grew during the 1970s and 1980s, small British airlines and their handling agents began to rent space on BABS. Virgin Atlantic and British Midland were two of the airlines that did this.

As John Scaife prepared his first analysis of Virgin's operation for Strong and Batt, he secretly accessed Virgin's computerised departure control system (DCS), to establish how many passengers were flying to Newark.

Virgin Atlantic's handling agent at the time was Ogden Allied, one of many who rented space on BABS. Before every Virgin flight departs, Ogden is obliged to place key information into BABS on the departure control system – how many passengers boarded, in which class of seats they are sitting and, eventually, the weight of the plane. The DCS also records the departure time of all flights.

Equipped with such information, Scaife was able to prepare a detailed analysis of each Virgin Atlantic route. BA could calculate how much money Branson was making on each flight, which of his ticket deals and marketing ploys were working, and which were not, and even if his planes left on time.

Some of these statistics are published routinely six months later by the CAA, and are available for general inspection. However, to have them at hand almost instantly provided BA's marketing and sales strategists with a significant competitive advantage as they priced their product on Virgin's existing routes, and plotted their challenge on the Newark route. The marketing and operations department could work out very precisely where they needed to pitch their prices to hurt Branson's passenger loads and how they could attack his all-important 'yield'.

Strong, Callery and Batt were kept reliably informed about Virgin's week-by-week performance on all its US routes. As Scaife peered into the computer at the beginning of 1990, he marked the papers on Virgin that contained information accessed from its rival departure control system 'Strictly Confidential'. They were then circulated to Strong and his colleagues in BA's Heathrow fortress as well as to Kevin Hatton's UK sales team in Buckingham Palace Road, and their counterparts in BA's New York headquarters.

Scaife's work was fed into a special task force, known as the 'Virgin Project'. Set up by Liam Strong at the beginning of 1990, its brief was to examine how best to tackle Virgin's product – a much wider brief than simple number-crunching. What Michael Levin had described as 'Virgin's distinctive flying experience' was now threatening something that the most sophisticated computer could not recognise: BA's brand image.

If Revenue was God for Callery, Image was God for Batt and his marketeers. Revenue and Image were Gods at whose altars their masters prayed – both King and Marshall attributed BA's turn-around in the late 1980s to 'brand management'. The brand-management creed holds that a product or service has intrinsic value for the consumer. In the 1980s this was embodied in the concept of 'lifestyle'. In an age when marketing men liked to believe that products and people moved fast, Batt the 'brand man', who had once devoted his life to packaging and repackaging 'fast-moving consumer goods,' set his sights on repackaging the fastest moving and most perishable product of them all: aeroplane seats.

In the seminal BA advertising campaign of the time, a yuppie in a hurry, suitably attired in late 1980s braces, was filmed boarding a BA 'Red Eye' in New York. The yuppie is pictured savouring his flight, sleeping soundly, and arriving fresh for a breakfast meeting in London – or possibly a dawn raid on one of the world's Stock Exchanges. The yuppie naturally shows no sign of jetlag as he breezes into his boardroom meeting – courtesy of The World's Favourite Airline.

The yuppie in the ad looked very much like the people in BA who created and paid for it. But as BA's men in braces approached the drawing board for their campaign against Virgin, Virgin's computer data was telling them that the Red Eye market was increasingly Branson's; the 'Grinning Pullover' was no longer relying upon the 'scruffy rich', he too was attracting boys in braces.

Virgin responded to BA's Red Eye campaign with a characteristic mixture of facetiousness and flair. In Virgin's TV ad a female executive is seen making her way on board a Virgin flight, and enjoying the Virgin service provided for her by a male flight attendant. As he turns away having served her with a complimentary drink, she turns to check out the shape of his bottom – a suggestion from Joan Branson – before settling down to sleep in her voluminous Upper Class seat.

As she slips into her Virgin limousine in New York, a familiar tune wafts into the advert as a line of executives who have flown with 'another' carrier watch the Virgin passenger with envy as they queue for a taxi. The singer asks, 'Don't it turn your red eyes green?' to the well-known Crystal Gale song, 'Don't it make your brown eyes blue?' As the Virgin limo glides into New York, the red eyes of the 'other' carrier's passengers turn green. 'Let Virgin seduce you,' whispers the familiar voice of Frank Muir at the end of the ad.

The marketing problem Virgin posed BA was simple: according to all of BA's internal market research, passengers thought Richard

Branson had a better product. A BA marketing man explained the dilemma:

'Kudos was slipping away rapidly as well as revenue. BA had an excellent product, and the boys in braces had come to think of yuppies as their passengers. But gradually the reality dawned that Branson had an even better image and a much better brand, mainly due to the way he handled himself and his fame and the way he was marketing his product. And his Virgin hostesses were much sexier!'

John Scaife was appointed as secretary to Liam Strong's 'Virgin Project', which considered many different ways of recasting BA's brand image to combat Branson's. Strong brought in representatives from the sales department, capacity management and market development to join Scaife. The group discussed the possibility of 'route-specific branding' – creating a special identity for BA flights that were head-to-head with Virgin's – and 'in-flight themed entertainment' as counters to Virgin Atlantic's.

The Virgin Project was hamstrung by BA's size. Branson's 'small is beautiful' philosophy enabled him to respond very rapidly, and relatively cheaply, to innovative ideas he thought would appeal to the niche of the market he was hoping to corner. This was not an option for BA. The airline's massive size brought problems of its own as it sought to tweak its 'marketing mix'. Countering rivals was a complex and potentially very expensive task. As an example, Mike Batt estimated that to put one extra chocolate on the food tray on all BA's domestic flights would cost £1 million a year. To provide passengers with a toothbrush, toothpaste and cologne to freshen up with on the same range of flights would cost between £10 million and £12 million.

The Virgin Project considered whether continuing to target Virgin's routes to try and lure Branson's passengers with discounted tickets and better deals was wise. The major dilemma the group faced was how to lure the braces back from Branson without appearing to be attacking Virgin. Quite apart from leaving BA open to accusations of anti-competitive behaviour, some members of the group felt that there was a danger that by targeting Virgin, the importance of BA's Lilliputian rival would be unnecessarily enhanced. The Virgin Group told Strong that BA would

play straight into Branson's hands if it appeared so worried by
him that a custom-made product was deemed necessary to
counter Virgin Atlantic. Ultimately, Scaife's group concluded, the
best that BA could hope to achieve would be to contain Virgin's
expansion and protect its own market share.

This was not what either Marshall or Strong wanted to hear.
Strong didn't think the Virgin Project's ideas were radical enough
and told Scaife and his team to get back to the drawing board.

BA launched its Newark service with business-class fares that
were slightly higher than Virgin's. Its Club Class fare was £1,061,
compared to Virgin's £889 mid-week, and £939 weekend, Upper
Class fares. In the back of the plane, BA offered economy returns
ranging from £269 to £335 depending on the season, substantiaily
more than Virgin's £209 to £279 fare band.[1]

A month after the launch of its Gatwick–Newark service, British
Airways found out that its first attempt to tackle Virgin Atlantic
head on – by targeting Branson's most lucrative route – had
started to backfire.

At the end of April, when John Scaife accessed Virgin's passenger figures from the computer, he was startled to find that far
from damaging Virgin's passenger loads, BA's new service to
Newark appeared to have stimulated demand for *both* of
Branson's New York routes. Virgin Atlantic had actually sold
more seats on its flights to both New York airports, Newark and
Kennedy, in the month following BA's Newark launch than it had
done in March. Scaife alerted BA management in London and
New York. BA typically gives its routes up to three years to 'bed
down' before assessing their performance, but stimulating
Branson's business was not exactly what it intended.

The heat was turned on the departments responsible – in BA-
speak, this is known as 'downward pressure'. Nowhere was this
phenomenon more evident than in the UK sales department which
had been responsible for developing the marketing plan for the
Gatwick-Newark launch since late 1989. UK sales generate nearly
half of all BA's annual revenue, and, by the summer of 1990,

---

[1] Figures from the CAA.

according to the Reverend Jim's criteria, Virgin Atlantic was 'interfering with the delivery of BA's revenue'. As Branson launched his Los Angeles service in May with his customary rash of photo-opportunities, Callery started pressuring Kevin Hatton to get his sales team to 'do something about him'.

On a sunny June morning, a large red Volvo swung into Buckingham Palace Road. It was one of the complimentary limousines Virgin Atlantic provides to take its Upper Class passengers to Gatwick Airport. The car stopped outside the unattractive, window-dominated building that BA's UK marketing and sales department shares with Victoria Coach Station. The Virgin chauffeur politely showed two of BA's most senior salesmen into the limousine: Kevin Hatton, and Martin George, Hatton's new marketing manager.

Some members of Hatton's staff laughed openly as they peered out of their office windows and watched their grey-haired boss scuttling into the Virgin limo, as if he didn't want his team to see him. 'It's all right for some,' was one of the drier observations. Sampling the opposition's product is standard airline practice, but it is rarely carried out by senior management. Hatton's staff attributed this rare personal excursion into field research by their boss to downward pressure from the Reverend Jim.

As the limousine slid off, Hatton's staff returned to their desks. Some in Liam Strong's marketing and operations department, such as Peter Fleming,[1] a senior marketing executive, were bemused by the airline's preoccupation with Virgin Atlantic.

Fleming had spent all of his working life in the British airline industry since leaving Keele University in 1981. At British Caledonian he worked his way through the passenger services department before transferring to commercial planning and finally to marketing. When BCal merged with BA in 1988, the national carrier recruited the bright young graduate to the sales and marketing department at Buckingham Palace Road.

---

[1] 'Peter Fleming' is not the BA executive's real name. BA knows who he is but he does not wish to court publicity.

Peter Fleming noticed BA's obsession with Branson and his air-line a few weeks before Hatton's excursion on Virgin Atlantic. Fleming had attended one of the airline's quarterly summits at Speedbird House to determine which routes the company should bid for, and which ones it should develop. These influential sessions map out schedules for up to two years ahead. Participants fly in from BA posts all over the world. Fleming represented Liam Strong's department at the summit with his colleague, Nigel Bishop.

One of the longest discussions that took place at the meeting concerned BA's flights to Australia, and whether BA should start two services a day (a 'double-daily'). Neither the UK nor Australian sales teams felt a need for extra capacity on the route. One of Fleming's specific responsibilities was to analyse BA's rev-enue on flights to Australia and, on the basis of his analysis, he argued that if BA increased its service from twelve to thirteen flights a week, the planes would be at best half full.

Fleming was surprised to find his argument countered by the 'Virgin factor'. Others pointed out that Virgin had announced it would start a new service to Australia if it could get the slots. Fleming's objection to flying half-empty planes half-way across the world at enormous cost to BA was opposed by those who argued that BA should grab the slots while it could, as a defensive measure against Branson's threatened expansion. Opponents argued that not only should BA increase its flights to use up its existing slots, it should also bid for fourteen slots to blot Virgin out of the picture completely. The Virgin factor won the day, and to Fleming's surprise the meeting decided to bid for slots for flights that BA's sales teams were convinced they could not sell seats on.

'It struck me at the time,' says Fleming, 'that it was anti-competitive behaviour and, from BA's point of view, counter-productive. We weren't making much profit on the route with a daily service, so we certainly weren't going to make *any* if BA had to bear the cost of running a double-daily on one of the most expensive routes in the world. The decision seemed to me to be taken with the sole aim of stopping Branson getting on to a lucra-tive long-haul route, and keeping the BA-Qantas monopoly of the route intact.'

One of the documents prepared for the Speedbird House

summit contains a detailed analysis of BA's competitors on the 'Kangaroo Route' from Qantas and Air New Zealand, to Singapore Airlines and the giant American carriers. The document assesses the threat they pose to BA's profits. It concludes:

> The greatest new threat to BA in Australia would obviously come from Virgin who, if their development plans succeed, could start a ferocious price war throughout the whole region and throw the market into instability.

The document frankly admits that BA was bidding for more slots than it needed to block Branson:

> . . . . we have contracted for fourteen services by 1991 in an effort to keep Virgin from Australia . . .

Michael Levin's Virgin report had warned Sir Colin Marshall of Branson's push east:

> These routes are also in BA's strongest areas, giving head-to-head competition in hard-currency markets. Virgin's expansion into the Far East and to Australasia in the future shows their recognition of the market desire for more exotic leisure locations and the future of the Pacific Rim as tomorrow's cash-cow.

Peter Fleming recalls the impact that adhering to Levin's advice had on the sales department:

'It gradually began to dawn on us that the normal business criteria we would apply to decision-making were suspended when it came to Virgin, and that the pressure to damage Branson must be coming from much higher up in the airline. The Reverend Jim would normally resist very strongly bidding for capacity we could not sell, as this was bound to make the figures at the end of the year look very bad for the route in question.'

As Branson started helping out in the Gulf, King's outburst at the government became the stuff of BA legend. The chairman's apoplexy infected the airline's conventional decision-making criteria, and BA's publicly stated competitive ethics dissolved rapidly. Under mounting pressure himself to do more about Branson than simply targeting his routes with bargain basement fares, Sir Colin Marshall asked Liam Strong's Virgin Group to establish quickly how Branson's relief flights were affecting the configuration of his tiny fleet.

Scaife swiftly updated his bosses on the Virgin passenger loads for the month that Branson ran his relief flights to Jordan. Apparently aware of the sensitivity of the data he was accessing, Scaife wrote 'Highly Confidential' at the top of his analysis, as he had done on other computer-gained documents. Apart from the obvious legal implications of using another carrier's computer information, BA would have attracted dreadful publicity if it were to be revealed that the national carrier was secretly plotting against a British rival that was planning to bring its own passengers and staff to safety. The document was dated 28/9/90, the end of the month in which Richard Branson started his relief flights.

VIRGIN: RECENT PERFORMANCE

I understand that Sir Colin Marshall has expressed interest in Virgin's recent traffic performance, and their current fleet configuration.

Although we have not been able to gain access to their actual passenger uplifts since the beginning of May, we can still access their booked loads immediately prior to departure, and by inferring likely no-show rates we can get a reliable estimate of their actual loads.

Data captured in the last weeks suggest the following results . . .

Scaife then produced a list of figures 'captured' from the computer for Sir Colin, detailing the most up-to-date Virgin passenger numbers, in both Upper Class and economy. In brackets were BA's own figures. The 'seat factor' figure represents the percentage of seats filled in the respective cabins.

New York [Kennedy]	Upper Class		Economy	
Seat Factor	57	(54)	83	(94)
Average Passengers per Flight	28	(19)	251	(179)

New York [Newark]	Upper Class		Economy	
Seat Factor	71	(70)	89	(82)
Average Passengers per Flight	31	(25)	270	(152)

These were disappointing figures for BA. For months it had targeted Virgin's flights with cheap ticket deals and flooded selected travel agents with tens of thousand of heavily discounted tickets. Scaife's figures showed Marshall and Strong that Virgin was also outstripping BA in economy class to Miami, and running neck and neck in both cabins to Los Angeles. The only head-to-head route where BA enjoyed a substantial advantage over Virgin was the Japanese run which Virgin had only flown for a year, and was only permitted to fly four times a week.

Tokyo	Upper Class		Economy	
Seat Factor	25	(86)	67	(94)
Average Passengers per Flight	36	(70)	201	(250)

Scaife stressed to Strong and Callery that the information he could access from BABS was limited. He could only get hold of Virgin's booked loads, not the number of passengers who actually boarded the planes. Without this more detailed information he could not accurately analyse the most crucial factor: Virgin's yields. For that, much more detailed information was needed. BA needed to know not only how many passengers booked, but also how many passengers boarded the planes, in which part of the planes they sat, the prices they paid for the tickets, and the punctuality of the service. Once the precise 'traffic pattern' was established, Virgin's routes could be properly assessed, and attacked.

As it contemplated the last decade of the century, British Airways was keenly aware that its own future and the whole shape of the world's airline industry would be determined by computer power. At the beginning of the 1990s, the airline was spending £150 million annually on computers – the equivalent of buying two new jumbo jets. Sir Colin Marshall liked to describe information technology as 'inseparable from the operation of The World's Favourite Airline' that, in 1989–90, carried over 25 million passengers to 164 destinations in 75 countries.

> With an average of one flight departure every two minutes with two or three classes, 70,000 passengers each day and a mass of historical data to analyse, we have employed the most sophisticated forecasting and decision support systems imaginable to help make us the most profitable airline in the world. This is the strategic use of technology.

By the start of the 1990s it had also become the airline's biggest intangible asset. BA was aware that the strategic use of computer technology proved to be the key to survival for American Airlines and United Airlines during the 1980s as President Reagan's government deregulated the skies. Both airlines possessed powerful computer systems of their own. PanAm and TWA did not and, by the end of the decade, were limping towards takeover.

The hero of American Airlines' survival and transition to the megacarrier status BA craved was SABRE – the world's most powerful computer reservations system. It holds the details of every schedule in the world, and over ten million airfares. It takes nearly half of all bookings in the USA. Located in Tulsa, Oklahoma, SABRE is protected by security arrangements that would grace a nuclear installation. The president of American Airlines, Bob Crandall, once quipped to a reporter that if he was forced to choose between American Airlines and its computer reservation system, SABRE, he would sell the airline.

Computer power can easily turn into computer abuse. Because of their power and scope, and their potential to distort markets, CRSs were investigated by British Members of Parliament in an inquiry that lasted from 1987 to 1988.

The inquiry was triggered by the increasing use of computer reservations systems as marketing tools following American deregulation. The CRSs held the key not only to flight reservations but also to distributing an airline's product. With vastly superior American CRSs, like SABRE, poised to enter the British and

European markets, the potential for anti-competitive abuse would multiply rapidly. The MPs took evidence for months from regulators, the representatives of computer reservations systems and a cross-section of the travel industry.

A high-powered BA delegation warned the MPs: 'It is not in the interests of the consumers or the industry to encourage some of the practices prevalent in the United States' CRS business.'

The BA team was led by Luke Mayhew, the head of distribution and marketing systems, and he was accompanied by his senior project manager, David Noyes. Roger Maynard, then vice-president commercial affairs, North America, and subsequently promoted to become head of BA's corporate strategy department, completed the delegation. Maynard had first-hand knowledge of the USA's anti-trust laws. Maynard was a former civil servant who had been deeply involved in the British government's attempts to abort the Laker anti-trust case in America. The former air attaché at the British Embassy in Washington joined BA after President Reagan had saved BA from the possibility of criminal proceedings for its alleged role in killing Laker Airways.

The BA team stated that by the late 1980s two-thirds of British Airways' business came through BABS. The carrier predicted that, by 1992, its control over its own bookings would be weakened to the extent that the same amount of business would come through third-party systems like SABRE. The terms and conditions under which such systems were allowed to operate were thus of paramount importance to BA as it pushed towards megacarrier status.

In evidence given to the parliamentary committee, the BA delegation said the potential abuse of CRSs in the new, deregulated aviation industry of the future troubled the airline deeply: 'We firmly believe that there should be no competitive advantage to an airline on the basis of whether it owns or does not own a CRS,' said Mayhew.

The transport committee's final report addressed itself specifically to the concerns over the anti-competitive abuse of commercial information stored on CRSs:

The CRS-owner can track the effect of price changes, see approximately how many of its rivals' seats are assigned to a given discount-fare classification, how much full-fare business it attracts compared to rivals, and monitor changes in market share . . . It can even see how loyal its own frequent flyers are.

Pertinently, in relation to BA's probe into Virgin's computer data, the transport committee acknowledged:

While an airline has access to commercial data about its competitors . . . an imbalance in competitive advantage will occur.

BA was aware, therefore, that as it set about using the information that Virgin Atlantic had placed in confidence on BABS, it was breaching the undertakings it had given to the House of Commons. Indeed, the man responsible for organising the extraction of the Virgin data from the computer for Sir Colin Marshall was David Noyes, one of the BA delegation that had given the House of Commons transport committee such pious assurances about BA's conduct. The airline knew that 'capturing' Virgin's data drew it into the twilight zone between sharp practice and anti-competitive behaviour. BA also knew better than the MPs the truth of the MPs' verdict that

The misuse to which a CRS-owner puts privileged information is one which is difficult to prove and to regulate . . .

As British Airways staff started accessing even more detailed information about Virgin Atlantic, the airline could be reasonably certain that the commitments it made to the House of Commons' transport committee would not be exposed, and almost entirely certain that Richard Branson would not find out.

In September 1990, a small group of BA sales staff was ushered into a conference room at Gatwick Airport. As the last person took her seat, Jeff Day, the head of special sales and services, locked the door.

'You must not discuss what we talk about today with anyone in BA,' he began, 'and certainly not with anyone from another airline.

When you go home you must not discuss this meeting with your families. When you go to the pub you mustn't tell your friends.'

Day was addressing members of BA's Helpline team. 'BA doesn't make its money by helping old biddies to the gate.'

Some of them glanced at each other, uncertain what their boss was going to say next. Up until that point, helping elderly passengers to their flights was precisely what the Helpliners had been doing.

Dressed smartly in their BA uniforms, white carnations in their lapels, the Helpliners were familiar figures in Gatwick's two terminals. Formally known as 'meeters and greeters', and colloquially as 'a high-class tart service', part of their role was to help passengers experiencing difficulties transferring between flights. Intrigued, Day's audience listened carefully.

'Those days are gone. What you will be doing from now on is to get as much information about other airlines as you can, particularly Virgin Atlantic . We want to know exactly how many people get on Branson's flights, how many in economy, how many in business class. If there's a delay, we want to know by how long and why the delay occurred. He's always boasting about his service and the number of awards he's won, but there's not much point in having a good service if the planes are late, is there?

'If a plane goes technical [develops a technical fault] we want to know why. If he has a security alert, we want to know about it.'

The Helpline chief added that BA's sales department in London was also keen to get any information the team could glean about Dan Air and Air Europe flights. Both BA's other independent British rivals were based at Gatwick. By the summer of 1990 a quarter of all flights into and out of Gatwick were Air Europe's, making it the dominant carrier at London's second airport: it had become Britain's second largest scheduled carrier.

Some of the Helpliners were surprised. Intelligence gathering was not part of their job description, but Day's request seemed harmless enough. With war looming in the Gulf and the recession playing havoc with the industry, no one in the Reverend Jim's sales force needed reminding that the line between making a profit and making a loss was an extremely fine one.

Then Day lowered his voice. He told the Helpliners that they could obtain most of the information about Virgin, and the other two British carriers, by extracting it from BA's own computer reservation system, BABS.

The Helpliners now understood why they were meeting behind closed doors. One of Day's team was forty-one-year-old Sadig Khalifa. The youthful-looking Libyan had worked for British airlines since 1974 when he joined British Caledonian in Tripoli. Khalifa and his family moved to Britain and, when BCal was taken over, Khalifa joined BA. Khalifa then worked as a check-in agent at Gatwick before joining the Helpliners in 1989.

Day moved over to a computer terminal and showed Khalifa and his colleagues how to use BABS to get the information London required. Khalifa remembers his lesson well:

'Day showed us how we could get Virgin's flight details by tapping into the computer with our regular BA code and calling up the Virgin flight numbers. We could see the number of passengers booked on to each flight, the number who actually boarded in both Upper Class and economy, as well as the departure times.'

Virgin Atlantic's handling agent, Ogden Allied, put the details of the flights that it was responsible for on BABS. Thus the Helpliners could access this highly sensitive information directly from BABS without the knowledge of any of Branson's staff.

The Helpliners' base was Room 1278, a small, windowless room, airside in Gatwick's North Terminal. BA was so concerned to keep the operation secret that a special combination lock was installed. The code was given only to the Helpliners.

One of the Helpliners would act as a 'base-man', coordinating each daily shift, while the other members of the team came into the room on a rota basis throughout the day. A kettle with tea and coffee was provided so that the Helpliners could make themselves drinks without having to leave the room. Information on Air Europe and Dan Air was collated along with Virgin Atlantic's details. Khalifa and his colleagues wrote out the details of their rivals' flights in longhand on exercise paper. At the end of each shift their work would be placed in plain brown envelopes marked 'Virgin', 'Air Europe' and 'Dan Air', and locked in supervisor Jenny Sutton's drawer. The Helpliners were instructed to destroy all other references to Virgin and never to remove anything from the office. The following day Sutton sent the brown envelopes to Barbara Cassani in the Reverend Jim's sales department in Buckingham Palace Road for analysis.

Day stressed to the Helpliners that they must never leave the office with any of their findings, and that all references to Virgin must be destroyed at the end of each shift.

'BA were interested in Air Europe's and Dan Air's performance,' Khalifa remembers, 'but we were told that Virgin was the top priority.'

Some Helpliners rebelled. One, Liz Gormali, felt it was immoral to obtain confidential information about BA's rivals in the way Day had instructed her to do. Gormali had once worked for Dan Air's handling agent, Gatwick Handling, and she was well aware that airlines placed such information on the computer in the strictest confidence.

Sadig Khalifa and his colleagues covered for Gormali to prevent her being victimised by management, or being accused of languishing in the Reverend Jim's 'comfort zone'.

'Liz could well have lost her job if she had refused to do what she was told to, so we took it in turns to fill in for her. We would arrange to swop with her when it was her turn to go into the locked room and sit at the computer,' Khalifa recalls.

When the Helpline team had difficulty getting information, they attempted ingenious alternative methods. As Ogden Allied was required to have a complete record of all Virgin's flight details, Khalifa was detailed to try and hack directly into Ogden's computers in the South Terminal.

'Airlines rent the gates from which their flights leave and as soon as the flight takes off the gate is deserted. So I and a colleague approached a Virgin gate and tried to hack into Ogden's terminal to get the exact breakdown of the flight that had just left.

'My colleague stood guard by the moving walkways, keeping a lookout while I tried to get into the computer terminal. We were very obvious in our BA uniforms, and we had no pretext for being there, as all BA's Gatwick flights leave from the North Terminal. No one spotted us but, unfortunately, Ogden had protected their terminal by issuing swipe cards to their staff and we couldn't get into it.'

Undaunted, the Helpliners started impersonating the staff of rival airlines to try and con the information out of their handling agents. This technique was essential to obtain Dan Air's passenger and flight details. Unlike Ogden, Gatwick Handling did not place its information on BABS, so the BA unit couldn't get hold of it. When Khalifa and his colleagues needed Dan Air information, they phoned Gatwick Handling and impersonated their rival's staff. When Ogden did not put all the information BA required about Virgin Atlantic or Air Europe on BABS, the Helpliners compensated in the same way.

'It was very easy to do,' Khalifa later recalled. 'One way or another we managed to monitor every flight that went out of Gatwick.'

'From the moment Branson started his Gulf relief flights Virgin became public enemy numero uno', recalls Peter Fleming. 'I personally thought that Branson had done a good job by helping to get British people out of a tight spot, but within BA there was fierce resentment. People felt that King was right to complain, and that Branson was trying to take over our role as national carrier.'

By the end of September BA's senior management was briefing its departmental heads on BA's counter-Virgin strategy. Kevin Hatton, whose own research trip on Virgin had caused his staff so much amusement, told his managers that BA had set up a special unit to discredit Richard Branson. Fleming was briefed by his colleague Nigel Bishop after his meeting with Hatton:

'I thought the notion of targeting the chairman of a rival company in this way was offensive. I'm sure it wasn't Kevin Hatton's idea. Such a policy would have been determined at a much higher level. Nonetheless, hating Virgin became the order of the day.'

Fleming felt unable to take issue with his superiors on the matter, thinking it would certainly blight his career. He was, however, beginning to question the ethos that the American marketing men and the boys in braces were establishing at BA in deference to Lord King.

'It reminded me of a tribe of silver-backed apes with King as the dominant male. Most of the key players were male and spent much of their time engaged in willy-stretching competitions. At the first sight of an interloper on BA's territory they would screech and thump their chests in response, taking their lead from the dominant male. If King thumped his chest and said "Hate Branson", then that's exactly what they would do, each trying to out-thump the other and screech louder than his peers.'

In November 1990, Branson started his bid to extend his so far limited encroachments into King's territory in earnest. He applied to the CAA for slots to bolster Virgin's service to Tokyo and, even more significantly, he started lobbying the Transport Secretary, Cecil Parkinson, to allow Virgin to fly from Heathrow Airport. Branson saw both decisions as critical to the future of his fledgling airline. So did BA. Both King and Branson knew that all the independent British airlines that had attempted to compete from Gatwick against scheduled services from Heathrow had failed, and that both Air Europe and Dan Air were in difficulties.

In applying to increase his service to Japan, Branson was asking the CAA to transfer slots from one British carrier to another at a foreign airport for the first time. He had flown four services a week to Tokyo's Narita Airport since 1989 but the most exciting prize of all still eluded him: a daily flight to Japan. The prospect became a serious one in May 1990, when Japan agreed to increase British airlines' quota of flights into Tokyo from seventeen to twenty-one a week, after lengthy inter-governmental negotiations. The deal would be effective from November 1990.

However, Branson had a problem. Although the Japanese government had agreed to four more flights a week, the Narita Airport authorities in Tokyo keep a very tight control on take-off and landing slots, and they refused to issue more slots to British airlines on the grounds that the airport was full.

As a result Branson turned his attention to lobbying the CAA in a bid to get the authority to redistribute Britain's existing slots. The CAA had full powers to modify or cancel any airline's licences at any time, but it had never redistributed BA's existing slots in the manner that Branson was proposing. Effectively, he was asking the British government to take slots away from BA, a possibility that Lord King most certainly never envisaged when the state-run airline was privatised. BA gave every appearance of regarding its slots and its routes as its own in perpetuity. Lord King instructed his legal director, Robert Ayling, to mount a vigorous lobby of the CAA to prevent Branson getting the extra slots and, even more importantly, to stop him flying from Heathrow.

Allowing Virgin Atlantic to fly from Heathrow would represent an historic decision that would need government approval. Under the traffic distribution rules introduced in 1977, no airline could operate international services from Heathrow that was not already doing so. It was claimed that the traffic distribution rules would ease congestion at Heathrow, and encourage the development of Gatwick as London's second airport, although Heathrow was much less crowded then than it is today. It was also a means of boosting BA when it was owned by the state, as it was the only British airline that qualified. Following privatisation, and acutely aware that Laker Airways and British Caledonian had perished at Gatwick, Branson said the rules belonged to another age. In putting his case to the CAA, he argued that if the government's objective of creating 'a number of efficient and profitable airlines strong enough to compete with each other and foreign airlines' was to be achieved, the traffic distribution rules simply had to be changed. He told the CAA:

'When passenger preference for Heathrow condemns a Gatwick operator to disastrous losses, and while BA at Heathrow can over-price massively without regulatory or market constraints, no British airline will ever become strong enough to compete effec-tively. BA's monopoly-bred bulk is currently and continuously reinforced by the traffic distribution rules.'

Branson's rhetoric sprang from a cold assessment of commercial reality, and his experience of trying to run Virgin Atlantic from what some describe as 'the Gatwick ghetto'. Aviation experts cal-culate that moving the same flight at the same price from Gatwick to Heathrow will produce between 10% and 25% more revenue – 15% is the average figure accepted in the industry. Flights that BA have switched from Gatwick to Heathrow have been known to yield up to 70% more revenue.

Furthermore, the busiest international airport in the world has superb interlining potential for airlines that are allowed to use it –

a crucial bonus for an airline like Virgin Atlantic which does not have a domestic or European network to feed passengers onto its long-haul flights. Even more significantly, a third of all passengers using Heathrow are premium passengers – business- or first-class passengers. A comparison of destinations served by both airports reveals that for every passenger travelling through Gatwick on business, eight travel through Heathrow. A further bonus is the boost Heathrow gives to airlines' cargo capacity – the longer runways at Heathrow allow larger planes to carry more freight. With BA retaining the massive domination of take-off and landing slots it was given at privatisation, and with no long-haul British competition, Branson argued it was hard for the national carrier *not* to make a profit.

As Branson started his public lobbying, he was considering another offensive against BA. Virgin Atlantic's chairman had no idea of the extent of BA's growing obsession with his airline, but he claimed that the national carrier had been targeting his flights with large fare cuts for several months, and using its Heathrow base to 'dump' cheap tickets at Gatwick in a bid to undercut Virgin Atlantic. What BA described as vigorous competition was predatory, anti-competitive pricing to Branson, umbilically linked to BA's Heathrow-based dominance.

'BA was clearly abusing its dominant market position. Lord King could afford to make substantial losses on our Gatwick routes while keeping his prices sky high on his other routes. Thus BA could subsidise the losses on the routes where it competed with us by abusing its near-monopoly position on other routes.'

With the outcome of his bid to enter Heathrow by no means certain, Branson went to Brussels with his economic adviser, Hugh Welburn, to visit the European Commission's competition commissioner, Sir Leon Brittan. The Virgin delegation's mission was to see if Virgin Atlantic had a case under the Treaty of Rome's competition laws. After the meeting, Richard Branson was sufficiently encouraged to instruct his lawyers to start drafting a complaint about BA's anti-competitive behaviour against his airline.

Branson's consultations with the EC were reported in the press at the end of 1990 and, at the beginning of 1991, rumours that Branson was planning action in the European courts reached

British Airways. They triggered immediate panic in BA's sales force.

Sales chief Kevin Hatton ordered his staff to destroy all documents relating to Virgin that might be considered anti-competitive, and to make sure there was nothing incriminating about Air Europe or Dan Air left in the files either. Sales and marketing staff started combing their files for any reference to Virgin.

Any documents they found were placed in black bin-liners and removed for shredding. Fleming and another senior marketing executive, Peter George, were asked several times if they had purged their files of references to Virgin.

Fleming and George were both involved in analysing Virgin's financial performance – Fleming on the Tokyo route and George on the key transatlantic routes. George had devised the UK sales' marketing plan to target Virgin Atlantic's Upper Class market to Newark. He had also been involved in the project organised by Barbara Cassani to assess Virgin's 'punctuality' at Gatwick. Cassani had been a recipient of the Helpliners' secretly accessed computer information.

'Peter George went through his files with great gusto,' Fleming recalls. 'He was particularly keen to make sure that I had got rid of the minutes of one particular meeting, which I assumed was the one which referred to the setting-up of the unit to discredit Richard Branson. I had never been given that set of minutes, but Peter hovered over my desk making sure I'd got rid of everything.'

It was a day of frantic activity. 'People were shredding anything they could find with the name "Virgin" on it. The operation was organised by Martin George, who had sampled the Virgin flight with Kevin Hatton the previous year. His secretary came round asking us how we were getting on. Even apparently harmless documents like the "Virgin Competitor of the Month" filofax inserts found their way into the black bin liners.'

The filofax inserts were specially produced for the sales force with details of key competitors. In September 1990 Virgin was dubbed 'Competitor of the Month'. The insert listed details of the carrier's computer systems but did not include specific instructions about how to access its data.

Nigel Bishop, who had briefed Fleming on the anti-Virgin unit and accompanied him to the Speedbird House summit at which it was decided to block Virgin's bid for Australia slots, found half a dozen dubious documents and sent them off to the shredder. In BA-speak, the documents were 'liable to be misconstrued' as anti-competitive.

Not everyone was sure what should be shredded. Hatton was surprised to be interrupted at a conference at Speedbird House while the shredding was in full swing. One of his sales managers was so worried about the anti-competitive implications of some of the Virgin documents she had discovered that she had thought it worth pulling him out of his meeting. Hatton told her to destroy them all.

Liam Strong's enormous department was the focus of the shredding in Britain, and a parallel operation was conducted in the USA. Sammy Gershwin[1] walked into his office in BA's Los Angeles sales bureau and was surprised to see a team of sales staff going through the filing cabinets.

'It was a bit curious to see them looking through the files in a concerted effort. I asked them what they were up to and they said, "We're looking for references to Virgin Atlantic." I wasn't too surprised because staff had been asked at the end of 1990 to go though files, find any references to Virgin and get rid of them.'

However, in a ten-year career with BA, Gershwin had never witnessed anything similar to the destruction of the Virgin documents.

'This was unique. I'd never heard of an instruction given like this before. This was the first time I'd ever heard of this happening within the company.'

Although Branson was threatening to take BA to the European courts, BA's American operation was acutely aware of its possible exposure to anti-trust action. The memory of Freddie Laker was still fresh in BA's corporate psyche. In London, Fleming found BA's panic telling:

'British Airways has a strict document-control policy to enable it to get rid of the vast mass of paperwork the organisation generates. This is well known and widely adhered to. But singling out papers

---

[1] 'Sammy Gershwin' is not the real name of the BA employee.

relating to a particular rival in this way struck me as highly irreg-
ular. I'd never witnessed anything like this before.

'At the end of the operation Martin George stood in the middle
of the open-plan office in his shirtsleeves and asked if we had
finished.'

The braces' first attempt to tackle the grinning pullover had
ended in shreds. Documents 'liable to be misconstrued' were
destroyed from the West Coast of America to BA's London headquarters. But BA had scented blood. The hunter would not to be
denied another shot at the poacher.

4

Tokyo Storm Warning

Richard Branson ascended slowly above Mount Tajachiko in Japan in the largest hot-air balloon ever made. 'Pacific Flyer' was twice the height of Nelson's column and larger than the Albert Hall. The Virgin logo was plastered in vast letters over the side of the balloon. Hundreds of white doves were released as Branson and the internationally renowned balloonist, Per Lindstrand, floated into the skies, suspended in a tiny capsule.

The two men were starting their bid to become the first to fly across the Pacific Ocean by balloon. Only a month earlier a Japanese balloonist, Fumio Niwa, had died trying to beat Branson and Lindstrand to the record. Niwa's helium balloon had ditched in the Pacific, and he died of exposure before the Japanese rescue services could get to him.

Although they had waited nearly eighteen months for their second attempt at a transpacific balloon crossing, Branson and Lindstrand had decided to abandon it completely if war broke out in the Gulf before they could take off. The publicity value of the trip had become negligible as the world watched the count-down to the first strikes on Iraq. Despite his determination to break another world record, Branson thought it would be tasteless to be ballooning while the allies were bombing. Having waited for ten days for the correct wind conditions, Pacific Flyer finally took off at 0500 hours, 15 January 1991.

The balloonists were soon out of radio contact. Branson wrote in his diary that he had no idea if the passing of the allies' deadline to Saddam Hussein had resulted in war.

By the time Branson took off, the spirit of adventure was coursing through his veins. As he made his way towards the vast balloon, he had been told that Virgin Atlantic would be allowed to expand its Tokyo service. Branson raised both fists in the air in his familiar gesture of celebration as he stepped into the capsule: he heard that the Civil Aviation Authority had awarded him four of BA's slots to fly into Tokyo's Narita Airport. It was an unprecedented move and, as Branson soared away, Lord King and Sir Colin Marshall awoke to read the news in the morning papers.

BA was furious. David Burnside issued an immediate press release describing the move as a 'slap in the face for the customer . . . We don't believe the CAA has acted in the interests of the travelling public.' King announced that BA would appeal to the government to reverse the CAA's decision.

Pending the approval of John Major's new Secretary of State for Transport, Malcolm Rifkind, the CAA's decision was a landmark for Virgin Atlantic. In a display of brinkmanship at the CAA hearing on the Tokyo slots on 3 January, Branson had threatened to withdraw altogether from the London–Tokyo route unless he could fly daily.

'A daily service is essential if we are to offer real competition to the customer,' he told the tribunal.

Now, two weeks later, Branson had his eyes set very firmly on a much more important goal than the survival of his airline: his own. A technical fault had caused Branson mistakenly to jettison half of the remaining fuel supply into the Pacific Ocean. It was impossible to turn back, but to cross the ocean before the remaining fuel ran out would require the Pacific Flyer to travel faster than any balloon had ever travelled before.

On the other side of the globe, someone was taking a special interest in Branson's progress through the stratosphere. Brian Basham instructed his chauffeur to turn up the radio in his Mercedes as he was being driven through the City of London.

Although all the news bulletins were dominated by reports of the allied bombing of Iraq, Basham's ears pricked up as he heard the last headline mention Branson's ballooning odyssey.

Brian Basham had been recruited as a public relations consultant to British Airways in 1985. In the run-up to privatisation, he won the BA account for his company, Broad Street Associates. In spite of his longstanding loyalty to his client, he admitted to a professional admiration for Branson's ability to capture headlines even in the least promising of circumstances.

'He's a brilliant publicist, the best in the business. I have astonishing admiration [for him]. He's a very, very great marketing man. He's created one of the world's best brands.'

The dark green Mercedes drew to a halt outside London's Savoy Hotel. With the engine off, Basham sat silently in the back seat waiting for the latest report on the progress of Branson and Per Lindstrand as they hurtled towards possible destruction.

Basham had distinct reasons to monitor Branson's celestial progress. Ever since Branson had captured headlines around the world the previous autumn with his relief flights to Jordan and Iraq, Basham's conversations with British Airways had been dominated by one topic: Virgin Atlantic and its unconventional chairman.

Basham reported directly to BA's public affairs director, David Burnside, who had the ear of both the chairman and the chief executive. However, after the CAA's Tokyo recommendation compounded the outrage BA felt over Branson's exploits in the Gulf, Burnside began to find that his normally envied position could be a disadvantage. Basham recalls that both masters were filling Burnside's ears with the same message:

'David Burnside was coming under a huge amount of pressure to counter the publicity which Branson was building up . . . to hit back against Branson. Colin Marshall has every day's press coverage read out to him about seven o'clock every morning. He gets up very early and is in the office very early. And he would react very strongly every morning to anything on Branson . . .'

The pressure to 'do something' about Branson was then transmitted to Basham.

'David Burnside would generally telephone me first thing in

the morning and ask me what was to be done or how we could respond.'

As Basham contemplated what advice to give BA, he tried to understand why British Airways were worried about such a tiny airline. Basham had built his twenty-year career in public relations by attempting first to understand problems from his client's point of view before offering advice on strategy and tactics. Basham noted that King and Marshall were needled by Branson in slightly different ways. BA's chairman never recovered from the indignity of seeing his rival chairman personally retrieve BA staff and passengers from Baghdad in a rented jumbo.

'And it went deeper than that,' says Basham. 'Lord King was particularly angry at what he called the "scurrilous allegations" which Branson made against him . . . which were reported [to him] in conversations with personal friends and with journalists, who told him, David Burnside and me of the remarks which Branson had made but which they chose not to publish.

'It was a fear, a real fear of Branson which I couldn't really understand.'

Basham observed that the chief executive's concerns about Branson were more commercially based. Marshall was convinced that Branson was misrepresenting the size of his operation, pulling an old trick that he had used successfully when he founded *Student* magazine.

'Sir Colin Marshall was angry because he thought Branson portrayed his own business as bigger than it was.'

It was evident to Basham that, by the beginning of 1991, Marshall regarded the Tokyo decision as vindication of Michael Levin's warnings that Branson could become a serious commercial menace to BA.

'He's a man under such tight control that he's almost robotic . . . But he also gets very angry. Richard Branson made him extremely angry and, much more than King, Colin saw Branson as a real threat.'

The CAA's Tokyo decision prompted Marshall to write a forthright letter to *The Times*:

British Airways' entitlement to slots at Narita exists by virtue of many years' operation and investment in the market. We object to the confiscation of that entitlement without compensation.

King and Marshall considered they had good reason to be angry. At its flotation in 1987, the value of BA was in its extensive network of routes, flights and landing slots. These assets represented the bricks and mortar of what British Airways was offering to shareholders, just as much as the airline's fleet of aircraft and its commercial property. Stock Market analysts referred to BA's underlying strength to talk up the sale. The 125p share price took account of these hidden assets. BA's privatisation prospectus contained a letter from John Moore, then Transport Secretary, assuring would-be investors:

The government has no intention of promoting further route transfers.

King insisted that he had received reassurances when BA was privatised that there would be no arbitrary changes in its routes or in regulatory policies. BA's chairman considered that by planning to strip BA of its four Tokyo slots, the government had also robbed BA's shareholders. A former BA executive remembers King's anger:

'King was furious, and he had every right to be. It was like taking 200 square feet of retail space from Harrods and giving it to a rival. Do you think Harrods would be happy?'

Notwithstanding a long working relationship, as well as a personal friendship, it was Basham's turn to feel the downward pressure from Burnside. The Ulsterman warned Basham what failure to 'do something about Branson' would mean:

'David Burnside . . . said that he wouldn't be able to protect us as an agency in holding the British Airways account. We would lose it if we couldn't do something about Branson.'

Burnside's warning came at a sensitive time for Basham. He had just founded a new company, Warwick Corporate, after the disintegration of Broad Street Associates. He had endured an acrimonious split with his former partners, John Coyle and Alan Parker, and was very keen to take former Broad Street clients to

Warwick. Basham's longstanding link with Lord King and David Burnside ensured that he took the BA account with him to Warwick but, as one of the most influential public relations operators of his generation, Basham was aware that the pressure was on to deliver.

Broad Street had grown fat on City takeover fever. Basham was one of the PR men who rewrote the rules of corporate PR, turning himself into a roving ambassador for his clients. He prowled the City, often clutching a mobile phone in each hand, as the shares bonanza of the 1980s fanned the fires of mergers and acquisitions. PR men who could help their clients seduce bankers, analysts and stockbrokers could earn massive fees. With vast sums of money available to the armies of negotiators, bankers, lawyers and advisors who represented the 'raiders' as well as the 'defenders' in takeover bids, Basham's achievement was to help make PR an integral and lucrative part of the process.

He specialised in 'hostile' takeovers, developing his own brand of what he calls 'pro-active' PR, and what many on the receiving end describe as 'negative' or 'crisis' PR. Dubbed the 'Streetfighter' for his uncompromising tactics in an uncompromising decade, Basham was known as the toughest on the block.

He was also renowned for his charm, his ruthlessness and his flamboyant lifestyle. Regularly seen being chauffeur-driven through the City receiving phone calls and faxes in a car that bristled like a hedgehog with aerials, he entertained a stream of clients, stockbrokers and editors of the City pages at his own table in the Savoy hotel. His party trick was to bite chunks out of wine glasses at the end of an evening.

In 1986 Broad Street earned over £3 million in fees and the company was valued at nearly £25 million. Its founder made himself a millionaire and bought homes in London, in the country, and in Spain. He spent a small fortune on expensive cars and motorbikes. Before the stock market crash in 1987 Broad Street spent tens of thousands of pounds on a massive party in the Docklands to celebrate the company's success and Basham's forty-fourth birthday. Hundreds of Basham's clients and friends made their way by riverboat to celebrate his achievements as they enjoyed a fun fair and danced into the early hours. They applauded vigorously as the PR man cut an enormous birthday cake. As the 1980s roared for Basham, it must all have seemed a world away from his humble childhood as a butcher's son. But it was not. Just over the Thames from Basham's extravagant birthday party was his birthplace, the South London suburb of Catford.

Basham entered financial PR through journalism. Having failed to become a trainee journalist, he eventually got on to the City pages of *The Times*, having started as a copy boy in the *Daily Mail*'s City office. Basham swiftly got to know the movers and shakers in the City, and witnessed at first hand how closely City journalists and public relations people often work. Recognising that he had a facility for figures as well as for charming colleagues, he abandoned journalism for a career in public relations. After a spell with John Addey Associates, the well-known City PR firm, he formed Broad Street in 1976.

By the time the PR world gathered to celebrate Basham's forty-fourth birthday, his list of clients read like a *Who's Who* of new money. They included Ernest Saunders of Guinness, the Saatchi brothers and Mohamed Fayed. The arriviste Egyptian was a natural target for Basham, as he actively sought clients who had as keen an interest as he did in breaking the City's dated concepts of 'old money'. The Fayed brothers' ambition was to buy the House of Fraser and its flagship, Harrods.

The Egyptian brothers indisputably had access to a great deal of money. However, before the Office of Fair Trading, and Norman Tebbit at the Department of Trade and Industry, would give the Fayeds the go-ahead to purchase, the government had to be sure that the Fayeds were who they said they were, and that they had the money to fund the purchase.

Before the government could be persuaded, the City had to be convinced. Some of the City's best known banks, Kleinwort Benson, the Royal Bank of Scotland, Morgan Grenfell, Lazards, SG Warburg, and Cazenove, as well as two of its most distinguished law firms, Linklaters & Paines and Herbert Smith, formed a distinguished and highly critical audience that needed to be convinced. Brian Basham persuaded the Fayeds that he was the man for the job.

Before Basham embarked upon his Herculean task, the Fayeds' unremarkable family background underwent a mysterious transformation. The schoolteacher's sons from the ghettos of Alexandria in Northern Egypt were introduced to the press as 'members of an old-established Egyptian family who for more than 100 years were shipowners, landowners and industrialists in Egypt'. It was true that the Fayeds owned two roll-on roll-off Mediterranean cargo ferries. It was *not* true that they were 'leading shipowners in the liner trade', as their press handouts stated.

With Basham's help, and in the face of fierce opposition from Tiny Rowland's Lonhro, the Fayeds managed to con the British government, the City of London, influential sections of the British press, and the shareholders of the House of Fraser that they were men of independent means, 'Egyptian Anglophiles', descended from an ancient line of wealthy Pharaohs. The prize in the dirtiest takeover battle of a dirty decade was ownership of Harrods. The public relations strategy was Brian Basham's.

A selection of Conservative-leaning British newspapers that were relishing the Thatcherite boom of the mid-1980s as much as Basham was, played a key role in his strategy. Knowing how important the financial pages of the press were in winning City opinion, Basham introduced the Fayeds to selected journalists who did not peer too closely into the fog of PR fantasy he had helped create around the brothers.

The *Sunday Telegraph*'s Ian Watson, a mutual friend of both Brian Basham and David Burnside, was one of a number of reporters who was persuaded of the Fayeds' wealth and heritage. As Basham encouraged scribes to clamber on board the Fayed bandwagon, he actively encouraged them to suspend disbelief. Sumptuous press receptions were arranged and, for the select few, there were weekends at the Ritz hotel in Paris which the Fayeds bought in 1979. Basham's simultaneous pampering of the press and the Fayeds paid handsome dividends: the Egyptian *inconnus* became one of Broad Street's main clients and, in March 1985, Norman Tebbit gave the Fayeds permission to bid for the House of Fraser.

Those that challenged the Fayed fantasy were issued with writs or worse. When ITV's *This Week* made its way to the ghettos of Alexandria in 1989 to visit the Fayeds' real birthplace, the camera team was beaten up by a gang of thugs in the pay of the Fayeds.

Mohamed Fayed chuckled about the assault in his Park Lane headquarters when he heard about it.

The Harrods victory established Basham's reputation as a 'hidden persuader' of distinction, and won the grudging respect of his opponents who recognised the importance of his invisible role. One of Lonrho's lawyers, Andrew Nitch-Smith of the City firm Denton Hall, was keenly aware of his presence.

'Like any good public relations man, Brian Basham played a hidden role. I don't know of anyone at Lonhro who ever met him. He operated by opening doors behind the scenes, setting up the meetings, organising the lunches, putting the Fayeds together with the right members of the press. He knew who would be susceptible to particularly unpleasant allegations about Mr Rowland, and just how to plant them in the press or in the ear of a Member of Parliament. He operated by appealing to the lowest common denominator, which in the Fayeds' case was positively subterranean.'

Five years after the Fayeds bought the House of Fraser, the Department of Trade's inspectors belatedly exposed their deception. The inspectors concluded that they had told many lies, even to the extent of providing the DTI with false birth certificates. But, by 1990, the Fayeds could afford to lose the battle with the DTI inspectors as they had already won the war for Harrods.

The DTI inspectors highlighted Basham's 'seriously misleading press releases' but, in reality, they had only touched upon one aspect of what Basham himself describes as his 'tawdry trade'. 'Trashing Tiny' was the other key element in the Fayeds' strategy. Basham won frequent mentions in dispatches, private dispatches, in a war where the Egyptian generals struck campaign medals for their soldiers' abilities to, as they put it, 'fuck Tiny'.

A key quality Basham offered his clients was discretion, whether polishing their image *or* trashing their opponents. Until the 700-page DTI report revealed some of his activities, Basham's ability to work off the record and to leave no fingerprints appealed to clients who, like the Fayeds, had something to hide. In the press Basham was described as a 'lethal' operator, and the 'King of unconventional activities'.

Basham robustly defends his role in the takeover, insisting that he included only information he received from the Fayeds and their bankers, Kleinwort Benson, in his press releases. He points out that Rowland tried unsuccessfully to sue him on two occasions, and proudly displays the motions to strike him out of the legal actions on his office wall at Warwick Corporate. 'Everyone got paid, no one got hurt', is Basham's verdict on a battle in which Lonhro is widely thought to have lost £50 million and ended with Rowland's capitulation to the Fayeds in 1993.

David Burnside hired Basham in November 1984, at an annual fee of £80,000, to help BA prepare for its flotation. Basham remembers Broad Street's first task for the national carrier:

'Because there were no quoted airline companies [in Britain], the level of knowledge among potential investors was very low. I approached this task in my usual way, which is to apply proper research techniques.

'I was involved at all stages during the flotation. I helped devise the strategy and I advised on determining the price at which the company was floated. I argued for a low price to ensure a successful flotation. We brought the government round to our point of view, lowering their financial sights considerably.'

Basham became a familiar figure at BA's AGMs, and also won mentions in dispatches during BA's fierce campaign to take over British Caledonian. He remembers how he and Burnside moved against SAS's president, Jan Carlzon:

'David and I did a whistle-stop tour of all the Scandinavian countries. We touched down in each one and held airport press conferences. We exposed SAS to the "daylight test" by pointing out to the press in each country the difference between what Carlzon was saying to the British press, and what he was saying to his own people.'

Burnside and Basham also made certain the Scandinavian press understood that the xenophobia Norman Tebbit was whipping up in Britain against SAS's bid for BCal reflected Lord King's utter determination to keep the Scandinavians out.

'I remember addressing the press conferences in Churchillian tones,' remembers Basham with a smile, 'and telling the journalists that SAS could be sure that we would fight them on the runways and in the corridors of power, that we would oppose their applications for every licence, every route and every slot.'

The Scandinavians were startled by Burnside and Basham's version of 'negative PR'. *'Blitzkrieg'* was how a leading Swedish newspaper described the impact Lord King's emissaries made in a single-word headline on the front page.

Three years after BA successfully fended off the Scandinavian challenge by swallowing BCal, Virgin Atlantic replaced Sir Adam Thomson's airline as BA's main domestic competitor on the long-haul routes.

Basham was not impressed by Lord King's public stance towards Virgin and its unconventional owner. Basham told BA as diplomatically as he could that, in his view, its handling of Branson was amateurish. Lord King was playing into Branson's hands by reacting irritably to gossip about what Branson had supposedly said, and was thus providing journalists with welcome copy. Burnside shared Basham's view that King should not be seen to be engaged in hand-to-hand combat with Branson in the columns of the press. Both PR men thought such encounters made it far too easy for Branson to play the David-and-Goliath card.

Aware of the high regard in which Lord King held Basham's advice, Burnside arranged a special meeting at the beginning of 1991 with BA's chairman. To Basham fell the extremely delicate task of giving his lordship PR therapy for his Branson disorder.

'On the question of Branson, I remember saying to Lord King, "If I were you I would never let the name of Richard Branson pass my lips, even at a private dinner party. Wipe his name from your mind. Every time you mention Branson's name, even your friends gossip to other friends, telling them how angry you are. This comes to the ears of the press, who discuss it further, and some of them find it interesting enough to write about. The only effect of that is to irritate you further; it gives Branson satisfaction and moreover serves to put him on the same level as you, which is not only an insult to you but a *dis*service to British Airways." I told the chairman that he should be positively "sniffy" about Branson.'

Richard Branson and Per Lindstrand managed to make it across the Pacific Ocean in their balloon and successfully broke the transpacific record. Their lives had, quite literally, been suspended by a thread after they lost most of their fuel, and they had crash-landed in the icy wastes of Canada. Having survived the landing, they nearly froze to death before being rescued.

Invigorated by his adventure and delighted to be alive, Branson announced that he intended to submit a formal complaint to the EC about BA's anti-competitive activities. He had no idea that the rumours of his action in Europe had already provoked the mass shredding operation at BA. Branson said the complaint would highlight the predatory discounts being offered by BA on Virgin Atlantic's routes, the refusal of BA to cooperate with Virgin on cabin-crew training and safety matters, and Virgin's maintenance complaints against BA.

Among the reporters waiting for Branson on his triumphant return from Japan was Roger Beam from Thames TV. He was due to interview Branson for a documentary about the simmering row with BA. Beam's programme, the regional current-affairs show, *Thames Reports*, was preparing a programme, 'The Virgin File', based on the airline's proposed submission to the European Commission.

Branson raised the stakes even higher by announcing that Virgin intended to sue BA over alleged shoddy servicing which had grounded a Virgin jumbo in 1989. Will Whitehorn's press release claimed the delay had grounded the plane for three weeks during peak time in summer, and Virgin wanted £4 million in compensation.

If Branson and Whitehorn intended to enrage King and Marshall, their timing could not have been better. Virgin's threats of legal action in Britain and Europe added insult to the injury of the CAA's Tokyo recommendations. Branson's offensive also came as the national carrier started to experience the first serious downturn in its fortunes since privatisation.

BA had reported a loss of £1 million a week since Saddam Hussein's invasion of Kuwait six months earlier. Revenue on some routes was down by 50% as millions of passengers simply disappeared. After fighting started in the Gulf, the proportion of seats filled dropped to 45% across BA's fleet. Lord King regarded the break-even point as 65%. Stock Market forecasts of BA's profits were very gloomy. Some analysts were predicting that the air-line's record 1990 pre-tax profit of £345 million would be cut by more than half because of the serious losses in the second half of the year. As Branson announced he would be complaining to the EC, BA's shares fell back to a new low of 125p – their precise value when the airline was privatised four years beforehand. The last thing BA needed was a blast of negative publicity from Branson and Virgin.

On 29 January, the day Thames TV's 'The Virgin File' was due to air, Sir Colin Marshall summoned David Burnside to determine how BA should respond to Branson. King and Marshall had refused invitations to participate in the programme, and BA even considered taking out an injunction to try and prevent it being broadcast. From the chairman and chief executive there was silence; from Burnside there came a bitter press release which abandoned the statesman-like tone that BA usually adopted:

VIRGIN'S INTERESTS ARE NOT IN THE CUSTOMERS' INTERESTS

Mr Branson has clearly decided to launch an onslaught against British Airways and all its interests.

This is very unfortunate. He would be better employed concentrating on his own customer service standards and competing fairly with British Airways.

Behind every slick and picturesque PR image there is a substance of reality and the general public should be under no illusion as to what that reality is.

Deciding not to dignify any of Branson's specific allegations by commenting on them in detail, Burnside attacked Branson's motives in language that took journalists by surprise. BA's tone had suddenly become more like the last gasp of a company about to be swallowed in a hostile takeover bid. Burnside was sarcastic:

Mr Branson might, for example, concentrate on publishing Virgin's punctuality and reliability record, and the very high level of recurring customer complaints. His interests are not in the customers' interests. The right course of action for

> British Airways, in these circumstances, is to respond not in
> public but before the appropriate authorities.

A Press Association reporter thought the press release so unusual
that he passed it to Richard Branson as he sat in Channel 4's
London headquarters. Branson was attending a press viewing of
Across the Fiery Sky, an instant film of his transpacific drama. The
reporter interrupted Branson as he watched the moment when he
and Lindstrand jettisoned most of their fuel into the Pacific Ocean.

Branson read it in baffled silence.

'I was particularly upset by the fact that the press release attacked
me personally. BA seemed to be suggesting that there was something sinister and unpleasant lurking behind my own image.'

The claims about Virgin Atlantic also disturbed him. He was
proud of the reputation Virgin Atlantic's service had won in the
face of tough competition. Because he encourages Virgin passengers to write to him personally should they have complaints about
any aspect of Virgin Atlantic's service, he knew that the allegations
about 'recurring customer complaints' were untrue.

'We had just won a clutch of "Airline of the Year" and "Best
Transatlantic Carrier" awards in head-to-head competition with
all the major airlines in the world. We wouldn't have got anywhere near that if passengers were constantly moaning about the
service. Which they weren't.'

Branson ignored legal opinion that the accusations were serious
enough to warrant suing BA for libel.

'I thought suing BA would be a waste of my time and my
money, even though I had been told that I had a good case. I
thought it would be much better to try and sort it out personally
with Lord King.'

Branson had only ever met King once before, at an airline function. Virgin's chairman had lightheartedly suggested that King
might like to join him as ballast on his next balloon adventure.
King had jokingly offered to sponsor the trip. It was a good-
natured exchange which held the promise of future rapport. Still
blithely unaware of the contempt in which Lord King really held
him, Branson hoped that writing personally to his rival chairman
might ease the poor atmosphere that was developing between the

two airlines, even if it would not resolve the issues he had listed in his draft complaint to the EC. Branson sought to evoke the businessman in King:

> I am writing to put on record to you that I resent the level of personal abuse your people at British Airways have recently resorted to. I have no idea at what level within BA the current campaign has been authorised.
>
> As chairman of a small independent airline I have behaved no differently than you would have done in my place . . .
>
> We have sought remedies through the CAA, the Department of Transport, the EC and the High Court when appropriate. We have not at any stage made offensive personal remarks about you or Sir Colin Marshall. I would expect the same courtesy from your company.

Lord King's reply to Richard Branson showed that he remained the master of the calculated snub:

> Dear Richard,
>
> As I said to the *Sunday Telegraph*, 'I run my airline, Richard Branson runs his. Best of luck to him.' I do not wish and do not intend to say anything more on the subject.
>
> Yours,
>
> John King

By the time the exchange took place Lord King had further reason to be riled by Branson. At the end of January, shortly after the CAA's Tokyo verdict, another crucial decision went against BA to Virgin Atlantic's direct benefit. The CAA announced that it would be recommending to the government that the 1977 traffic distribution rules be repealed, effectively deregulating Heathrow.

For BA this meant that the world's biggest airline, American Airlines, and another American megacarrier, United Airlines, would now be preparing to fly from its home base, replacing the increasingly feeble PanAm and TWA. In last-ditch bids to avoid bankruptcy, PanAm and TWA had announced they would be selling their transatlantic routes to American and United.

For King this meant that two more barons of the sky would be striding the runways at Heathrow. American Airlines' boss Bob Crandall, universally regarded as one of the most outstanding executives in the USA, would be arriving with more than 600 planes at his disposal, and his omnipotent SABRE computer. Stephen Wolf of United Airlines would be joining him and, to King's further chagrin, Branson and his second-hand jumbos had escaped from the Gatwick ghetto BA had lobbied so hard to keep them in.

Branson lost no time in capitalising upon the CAA's recommendation. Branson announced that he hoped to capture 30% of the transatlantic market by 1995. By transferring some of his flights from Gatwick he claimed he could cut his prices by 15%.

The grinning pullover had arrived in the big league.

As with the Tokyo decision, British Airways announced it would lodge an appeal against the Heathrow decision with the Department of Transport, which had finally to approve the CAA's recommendations.

Although David Burnside started to crank up BA's battle-weary lobby machine again, both he and Lord King knew that the political tide was no longer flowing so strongly in their direction. They petitioned with less confidence than at any time since King became chairman.

Margaret Thatcher and Cecil Parkinson had both been unceremoniously dumped by the Conservative Party at the end of November 1990, as the government plummeted in the opinion polls and a General Election loomed. John Major replaced Parkinson with Malcolm Rifkind as Transport Secretary. Altogether less 'clubbable' than King's erstwhile business partner, Rifkind would have the final say on the Tokyo slots. Few at British Airways could envisage the new Secretary of State for Transport overturning the CAA's Heathrow recommendation. As the whole of Europe moved slowly towards liberalising airline regulations and reducing the role of government, BA judged it unlikely that John Major's government would stick its neck out to protect BA's 'grandfather rights' at Heathrow, which effectively barred any new airline from using London's main airport.

So while BA went through the motions of complaining to

Malcolm Rifkind, it started planning in earnest to meet the challenges of the American carriers and Virgin Atlantic, BA's first ever British long-haul rival at Heathrow. 'Doing something about Branson' now took on a new meaning. The key was to stop him expanding. If he couldn't raise the money to expand, then he wouldn't be able to 'cherry pick' more of BA's lucrative routes. Under the banner of 'Mission Atlantic', BA would try to 'inhibit Branson's ability to compete'.

The public affairs department and its highly paid auxiliary would be expected to play a full part in attempting to stifle Branson. Brian Basham was in no doubt what BA meant by trying to 'inhibit Branson's ability to compete':

'If British Airways had been able to put him out of business they'd have been very happy to do so.'

Basham recalls that neither he nor David Burnside was able to shake the chief executive's view that Virgin was under-capitalised, poorly managed and, therefore, vulnerable.

'David became quite exercised about this, and he talked to me about what we should do.'

Basham suggested a way forward to Burnside which he hoped would please his client, as well as helping to relieve the pressure on himself and BA's director of public affairs. He proposed that his new company, Warwick Corporate, should produce a report for British Airways on Virgin Atlantic, analysing the strengths and weaknesses of the airline and its owner.

'I told him the company should stop thrashing about and set up an organised inquiry.'

Basham argued that BA should get 'back to the brickwork' before Virgin could be effectively attacked, a characteristic opening move from the master of 'crisis PR'. Basham contended that BA's assumptions about Virgin Atlantic should be based on a rigorous analysis of his financial affairs. Branson's airline should be exposed to the 'daylight test' that many of his other clients had found useful in their takeover battles throughout the 1980s. Basham argued that however annoyed King and Marshall might be, the only way to take Branson apart was on the basis of detailed financial research and analysis. This, argued Basham, was how to prevent Branson gaining the finance he needed to expand the airline, and fulfil his boast of winning a 30% share of the transatlantic market by 1995. If the government and the CAA would not listen to BA's arguments, perhaps those investors Branson would be approaching to finance his expansion would be more receptive. Going 'back to the brickwork' should be British Airways' first step.

'The stated objective was to unravel the complexities of Virgin's business and how it had developed since he had taken the business back into private ownership. One reason for wanting to do this was to discover whether or not the stories and gossip that we [Burnside and Basham] were getting from BA were true – for example that Branson was under-capitalised and poorly managed – and whether he was truly in a position to be able to afford all those ambitions which he had talked about in the press.'

Basham and Burnside also saw the report as a shield against Lord King and Sir Colin Marshall, as well as a weapon of attack in BA's bid to stop Branson's threatened expansion.

'David and I had a subsidiary objective . . . if we could tell management that we were producing a report, and in particular tell this to Colin Marshall and Lord King, the relentless pressure upon David, and from David to me, to plant unsubstantiated stories in the press would cease until the report was finished.'

Burnside agreed with Basham's proposal to make the report wide ranging. It would not only analyse Virgin Atlantic, but also Branson's entire group of Virgin companies. Branson's personal background, his strengths and his weaknesses would also be examined. Both PR men thought this idea would appeal to Sir Colin Marshall, who had authorised a similar probe into the affairs of Air Europe shortly after BA was privatised in 1987. At that time the Gatwick-based carrier and its flamboyant chairman, Harry Goodman, appeared to represent the biggest domestic threat to British Airways. 'We're going to take on the fat cats of Europe,' Goodman boasted as he expanded his airline in the late 1980s to take advantage of the anticipated deregulation of Europe's airways in 1992. Like Laker a decade earlier, Goodman was threatening to break the European cartel's stranglehold on commercial aviation.

Like Branson, Goodman had just taken Air Europe's parent company, the International Leisure Group, into private owner-ship in order to expand it more rapidly. By May 1987, Air Europe was on its way to becoming a fully fledged, scheduled airline when it won licences to fly to eight new European destinations.

International Leisure Group was Britain's largest travel company after the Thomson group. It incorporated Intasun, Club 18-30, Global, Coach Europe and Drive Europe. ILG's travel oper-ations enabled Goodman to boast millions of 'captive passengers', and provided a synergy similar to Branson's.

'We're never empty . . . we will always have more passengers than aircraft seats,' boasted Goodman.

Like Branson, Goodman had also learnt some of the lessons of Laker's experience and he was turning his attentions increasingly to the business-class market as well as the holiday and leisure segment. By spring 1988 Goodman had announced he would be doubling the size of his fleet by spending £750 million on thirty new Boeing jets. When the Civil Aviation Authority granted him the right to fly from London to Brussels and Paris – the latter the busiest route in the world – at the expense of British Airways, Goodman was able to proclaim, 'We are now the second-force airline.'

Air Europe replaced British Caledonian as Britain's second car-rier when British Airways successfully completed its takeover of Sir Adam Thomson's airline in 1988. As BA battled to convince the government that its acquisition of British Caledonian need not be referred to the Monopolies and Mergers Commission, Goodman showed a Branson-like capacity to tweak Lord King's tail. He announced in the summer of 1987 that Air Europe would bid for British Caledonian, and put himself at the head of the consortium of British airlines that opposed the merger with BA.

But was Air Europe a British airline? Was Goodman having to rely on foreign funds to finance his heady expansion plans? BA had heard rumours that Goodman's parent company was actually controlled by foreign investors. If it was, then Air Europe's status as a British carrier could be challenged.

Sir Colin Marshall authorised a very discreet probe into Harry Goodman's affairs. Using Brian Basham's Broad Street company as a circuit-breaker, BA commissioned the New York-based detective agency, Kroll, to investigate. Kroll are corporate investigators much feared by those whose affairs they look into. Their brief from BA was to establish if Hudson Place Investments, the vehicle used by Goodman to take ILG into private ownership, was actually controlled by foreign investors. Kroll scoured the world for evidence of Goodman's ultimate 'beneficial owners'.

BA was understandably sensitive about using a foreign-based detective agency against one of its domestic rivals. Normally BA's legal or commercial analysts would undertake such work but, on this occasion, the airline appeared keen to leave no fingerprints; so it arranged for Brian Basham to organise the investigation.

Kroll's Air Europe probe was commissioned through Burnside's public affairs department, which subcontracted the work to Basham's Broad Street company. Laundering the work through Broad Street in this fashion meant that BA, Kroll and, indeed, Broad Street could deny the link between BA and the private detectives if questioned. All three companies subsequently did.

Basham presented his invoice to Burnside for signature. Because the probe cost £17,500, exceeding Burnside's £10,000 authorisation limit, Burnside obtained Sir Colin Marshall's signature before the balance could be released to Broad Street.

Michael Levin, meanwhile, was busy probing Air Europe's affairs at the same time as Kroll. Levin was particularly interested in Goodman's extra-curricular activities. Senior BA executives and managers were invited into the suite of offices that Levin shared with Marshall, and grilled about Goodman's personal life.

Shortly after Kroll and Levin got to work on Air Europe, the first of a string of highly damaging stories about Goodman started to appear in the tabloid press. As he proclaimed Air Europe 'Britain's second largest scheduled carrier', in spring 1988, *The People* splashed, 'Blackmail threat to holiday chief'. This story painted Goodman as the victim of a blackmail threat, but included references to his previous drug convictions.

Some of the tabloid stories about Goodman's private life were true. However, by the end of 1989, Goodman became convinced that a stream of false rumours and innuendos about Air Europe's financial health was emanating from British Airways. Goodman calculated that the smears cost Air Europe £15 million in net cash outflow in the last six months of 1989, and he seriously contemplated suing the national carrier. He decided not to on the grounds that the prospects for both the airline and the travel group were extremely good at that time.

'We had made a profit of £13 million in the previous year and we were looking to the future with real confidence. ILG had a 20% share of the travel market which gave us a massive passenger base of two million. We thought we could ride the whispering campaign. Although the airline was growing rapidly, we were still small in comparison with BA, and I didn't want to tie up the entire management in a protracted legal battle. I thought we would be better off building the airline.

'Despite the substantial evidence we had gathered to show that BA was behind the whispering campaign, I still found it difficult to believe that BA would *really* stoop to such tactics. BA was the national carrier and in a sense we all looked up to them.

'Another factor was political. The feedback from our lobbyist in the House of Commons made it clear that the government would regard it as "unhelpful" if we sued Lord King, and that our future licence and route applications would not be looked at sympathetically if we took British Airways to court.'

Just over a year later, at the start of 1991, the Gulf crisis damaged Goodman's prospects of survival more seriously than any rumour campaign could hope to do. The word on the streets patrolled by Burnside and Basham was that both Dan Air and Air Europe were looking rocky and might not survive the war. The views of pessimists in the City were backed up by the Reverend Jim Callery's computer analysts, who were secretly accessing Air Europe's computer information as well as Virgin Atlantic's. Peter Fleming was preparing weekly reports for his boss Kevin Hatton.

'I was asked to access BABS to obtain details of Air Europe's load factors at Gatwick. There was a great deal of interest within BA at the time as to how Air Europe was performing and what revenues it was making, and I submitted results on a weekly basis in a written form to Kevin Hatton and, occasionally, did a spreadsheet report. It was obvious that the business market was fairly weak at Air Europe, and it was possible to work out that it was not in good shape.

'A detailed report on Air Europe was also requested by Kevin Hatton from one of my colleagues which went into great detail as to the nature of the airline, how it was financed and who the personalities were, as well as the normal competitive information my unit was supposed to handle.'

Three years after they organised Kroll's probe into Air Europe for Sir Colin Marshall, David Burnside and Brian Basham once again sat in Enserch House, BA's suite of executive offices in St James's Square.

'David asked me to produce a budget for the report on Virgin. I came to the conclusion that we could not produce the first phase of the report for less than £50,000,' recalls Basham.

Burnside once again required Sir Colin Marshall's approval for such a major outlay, as his own authorisation limit was still only £10,000. He found the chief executive responded well. Although he was unaware of the convergence of opinions, Basham's proposal to produce a report reinforced Michael Levin's advice to the chief executive. Levin had recommended: 'Branson's companies should be studied for any indications of a shift in priorities or evidence of weaknesses that could represent market opportunities. Confusion between strategic and operational issues that could pull down the organisation are frequent problems of entrepreneurial firms.' Michael Levin also warned Marshall that 'BA is in danger of falling into the trap of complacency, and Virgin Atlantic is coming up on the blind side.'

Despite the massive efforts BA's marketing, sales and operations departments had put into countering the Branson threat, the grinning pullover had come up on the blind side so swiftly that he was now set to launch both his expanded Tokyo service and a major assault on BA's transatlantic market. Perhaps if Burnside's public affairs department could harness Basham's distinctive talents, the PR men could succeed where the marketing and sales people had failed. Marshall gave Burnside the go-ahead to pay Basham to expose Virgin to his 'daylight test'.

As Basham searched for a codename for his project he quipped: 'When you think of Virgins, you think of Barbara Cartland, not Richard Branson!'

Basham codenamed his work 'Operation Barbara'.

5

Mission Atlantic v. Virgin Atlantic

John King sat in the House of Lords underneath a painting of the Battle of Trafalgar. Clad in ermine, his mood matched the grey, gun-metal skies that shrouded the Palace of Westminster. In hushed tones BA's chairman confided to the *Financial Times*:

'The situation is very serious indeed. It is not just the recession and the Gulf War. It's also the uncertainties over the whole regulatory framework . . . these uncertainties may force us to reconsider our overall strategy.'

Lord King was speaking as allied bombers pulverised Iraq. Much of the world sat transfixed by the first video war in history and tried to come to terms with the concepts of 'surgical strikes' and 'smart' bombs.

King had already decided to sack 5,000 BA staff and halt the airline's £2-billion spending programme. New recruitment was frozen, overtime halted, and some staff were offered unpaid leave or shorter working hours. After nearly half a century BA had stopped flying to Ireland entirely, and reduced the frequency of its flights to many areas of the world. Some of Lord King's planes were flown to the Mojave Desert in California to be placed in silent, suspended animation until the recession passed. He lamented:

'Our major markets, including the US, have experienced dramatic collapses in traffic. Revenue fell more sharply in January than in any previous month in our history. It is unlikely any major international carrier suffered more in the Gulf War than British Airways.'

As soon as the Gulf War ended, Lord King rallied his remaining staff. In a conscious attempt to seize the mood of the times and to identify the airline with Britain's contribution to the triumph in the Gulf, BA called its troops to arms under the banner of 'Mission Atlantic'. In sub-Churchillian tones, King warned that BA had to face 'the most supreme challenge' in its history, as it sought to overcome the legacy of the Gulf War and the challenge posed by the opening up of Heathrow.

'The Gulf War is over . . . but ours is not!' cried Liam Strong, BA's marketing and operations boss to a mass meeting of his sales and marketing teams as he prepared them for their role in the 'war'. 'The battlefield will be Europe,' Strong continued. Blood-curdling exhortation was mixed with crude characterisation in an effort to spur staff to rush to the barricades in BA's defence.

'The dogfight is on!' snarled *Cabin Crew News* in one of Mission Atlantic's less subtle offerings. The flight crews' circular portrayed the two American carriers as pit bull terriers. The dogs were swathed in Stars and Stripes, baying for BA's blood. BA itself was characterised as a British bulldog with a Union Jack for a necker-chief, bravely holding the line against the combined threat of the Americans and Virgin:

> It will be some consolation for you to know that we've got a few British Bulldogs of our own! Its been a rough, tough world out there for some time now, and we are not short of our own sharp characters who are well used to mixing it with the best of them.

In the laboured canine analogy, Virgin Atlantic was portrayed as 'the Jack Russell of the pack'. Branson's Jack Russell is pictured in the begging position with a large packet of Mates condoms by its side. Underlying the leaden humour and schoolboy cartoons was a serious message:

> . . . He's cleverly snapping around at the dinner table,

picking up only the tastiest morsels thrown to him by the
government, such as Heathrow, Tokyo and our prime US
routes.

Unless we all fully understand and appreciate the implications of this new competitive situation, our very
livelihoods could be in jeopardy.

With thousands of jobs being cut, few at BA needed reminding of
the seriousness of the situation. The imminent arrival of real
domestic competition at Heathrow was something Lord King and
Sir Colin Marshall had every reason to fear. BA had effortlessly
dominated the transatlantic routes in the absence of domestic competition, with its main challenge coming only from the badly
weakened TWA and PanAm.

American Airlines paid TWA $445 million for three of its prime
transatlantic routes out of Heathrow. American is the biggest airline in the world: it claims that every minute of the day four of its
planes take off from an airport somewhere in the world en route to
over 200 destinations.

The pioneer aviator Charles Lindbergh made the first flight
from St Louis to Chicago for the company that was to become one
of the formative influences upon the history of commercial aviation. American Airlines expanded to employ nearly 100,000 staff
and generate a turnover of nearly $13 billion by 1991. It was the
first airline to reward its frequent fliers for their loyalty when it
introduced the AAdvantage scheme in 1981. Within a decade it
had more than twenty million members.

When the Chicago-based United Airlines bought most of
PanAm's transatlantic routes, its chairman, Stephen Wolf, heralded the acquisition as 'an historic changing of the guard at
Heathrow . . . dramatically altering the face of transatlantic air
service'. BA and United almost came to terms in the 1989 deal
masterminded by Sir Colin Marshall and Michael Levin, but after
that fell apart Wolf decided to challenge Lord King on his home
ground. Neither American giant was immune to the effects of
the recession and Lord King knew both would be fighting as
hard as they could to establish themselves on the runways of the
world's busiest international airport. The summer of 1991

promised to be the longest and hottest in Heathrow's, and BA's, history.

British Airways appeared to be certain only that its North Atlantic revenue would drop. The official theme for Mission Atlantic was 'preserving our business'. Mission Atlantic itself seemed a particularly appropriate banner for men like sales boss Jim Callery, with his distinctive mixture of fundamentalist fervour and military assignation. The Reverend Jim believed that Virgin Atlantic would pose a particular threat to his sales team at Heathrow and, before long, his Christian soldiers were bible-bashing in characteristic fashion.

'Get your heads up!' cried Callery's UK sales boss, Kevin Hatton, like a football manager giving his team a half-time pep talk. 'You're lying down and letting Branson kick you in the balls! We've got to fight back!

'We've been in this game since God was a lad – it's our market, not theirs. You are the ones who should be controlling the park – they are the Virgins!'

Hatton's audience from the marketing and sales department listened in silence, unsure quite what to make of their leader's unusual cascade of mixed metaphor and exhortation. One thing appeared certain to all who listened to Hatton's sermon: no one involved in Mission Atlantic would be spending much time in the Reverend Jim's 'comfort zone'.

An important distinction developed between what BA's representatives said in public, and the airline's private calculations. Public utterances from Lord King and Sir Colin Marshall downwards tended to be variations on a simple theme: BA only had 250 planes in comparison with the 1,500 that the two American megacarriers could put in the sky. By comparison Virgin had only eight planes and thus didn't count. David Burnside briefed his staff in public affairs to play down the significance of Virgin Atlantic and Branson to any enquiries from the media. In line with Lord King's policy, he instructed his press officers to tell the media that BA's real competition was from the world's megacarriers. The tactic had worked very satisfactorily during BA's takeover of British Caledonian, and had superficial plausibility in Virgin Atlantic's case.

It was, however, extremely misleading to suggest that Virgin did not present a serious challenge to BA. The American carriers' global status was beyond question, but their size was only partially relevant. Only a tiny fraction of American and United's planes would be allowed to fly from Heathrow, on the routes they had bought from TWA and PanAm, after the redistribution of slots and landing rights had taken place. American, for example, would be allowed only nine flights a day out of Heathrow.

A more relevant analysis of the comparative potential threat to BA posed by the Heathrow débutants is provided in the breakdown of the weekly number of seats offered by each carrier.

BA	278 transatlantic flights with	83,000 seats available
American	168 flights	35,000 seats
United	122 flights	30,000 seats
Virgin	89 flights	30,000 seats[1]

Although Virgin had fewer flights, Branson's jumbos enabled him to carry more passengers per flight than his rivals, who used smaller planes as well as jumbos.

By themselves these figures do not portray the full threat Virgin posed to BA's profits. Ever since Virgin Atlantic's first flight in 1984, it had consistently and persistently filled more of its seats per flight than any of its rivals. The measurement used by airlines is 'seat factor', which means the percentage of seats filled on every flight. So not only was Virgin offering a comparable number of seats across the Atlantic to the two American carriers; if it kept up its record, Virgin would also fill more seats than its rivals due to its higher seat factor.

Another factor in Virgin's favour was its much lower cost base, which meant it could afford to offer cheaper fares than BA and still make a profit. This was something of which Sir Colin Marshall had been painfully conscious as Virgin started its expansion. In a revealing article in *BA News* in 1989, the chief executive wrote:

---

[1] Source: *Management Today*, November 1991.

We now face a situation where many of our newer British competitors have costs at least 20% lower than ours. That means they can operate a flight for a fifth less than we can. If we had to charge a typical fare of £100 to make a profit, they could charge £80 and still make the same profit.

By admitting that BA's costs were at least 25% higher than Virgin's Marshall was also illustrating just how potentially vulnerable BA was to Branson's challenge at Heathrow. Given the strength of Virgin Atlantic's brand, it was potentially, therefore, in a much stronger position to chisel into BA's market share, and its profits, than either of the American carriers, particularly as its reputation amongst business travellers was growing rapidly. BA knew that it was in the business-class market that its 'War on the Atlantic' would be fought.

BA claimed a massive 40% market share on transatlantic flights out of Heathrow, and industry analysts estimate that the airline enjoyed an average profit margin of 15%. As a result, BA's transatlantic flights produced nearly 95% of BA's overall profit in 1990. Out of a total profit of £167 million for the year, the transatlantic route network made no less than £158 million. BA's turnover for 1990 was £4.9 billion, of which £1.6 billion was generated by the Atlantic routes.

American and United would survive and prosper, irrespective of how they fared at Heathrow Airport. For Virgin, by contrast, the move to Heathrow was a matter of necessity and survival. It did not escape Lord King's notice that virtually all of Virgin's profits came from transatlantic flights from Gatwick, and that by splitting his airline's operation Branson had committed himself to converting his Heathrow toehold into a foothold, and then into his base within five years. Few at BA believed Branson's boast that he would win 30% of transatlantic traffic by 1995, but Lord King believed it would be far better if he were not given the opportunity in the first place.

Accordingly, David Burnside and Brian Basham moved Operation Barbara into full swing. At a time when the national carrier's fortunes were at their lowest ebb since privatisation, it seemed to be a fair assumption that even Branson would find it hard to persuade investors that a tiny airline was a safe place to invest money. The prospects of 'doing something about Branson' might never be better.

Basham's team at Warwick Corporate was trawling through mountains of press cuttings about Branson, and inspecting the accounts of over 100 companies registered in the name of the Virgin Group at Companies' House.

'We went through four or five years of press cuttings to try to build a picture of his business. The rate of [Branson's] activity would have made ICI's hair stand on end,' remembers Basham. 'British Airways' view that this was a one-man business was clearly given the lie by the huge activity rate. But it did seem to demonstrate that he was going from one thing to another a great deal, which made us doubt at one stage that he would make a complete run of the airline. He seemed to have a terrifically low boredom threshold.'

BA gave Basham every assistance as he coordinated the investigation. The airline sent much of the research it had undertaken on Virgin since the mid-1980s to Basham's Clerkenwell Green offices. BA had been studying Virgin Atlantic since 1986 when Branson's airline flew only two routes out of Gatwick: to New York, and to Maastricht, long before the Dutch city gave its name to the European Treaty. In the days before Michael Levin turned his, and Sir Colin Marshall's, attention to the potential threat that Virgin Atlantic could pose BA, a four-person 'Adopt-a-Competitor' team studied Virgin in a bid to pick up tips from an innovatory rival.

Included in the crates of material from BA was Michael Levin's 1988 report which had influenced Sir Colin Marshall's view of Branson's challenge so profoundly. The intensive analyses of Virgin Atlantic's operation which Liam Strong's marketing and operations department had undertaken were handed over to Basham's team, including the latest information extracted from Virgin's computer systems. These figures gave the up-to-date breakdown of Branson's passenger loads, the mix of economy and Upper Class passengers, and the punctuality of his flights. From the figures it was possible to work out Branson's yield in precise detail and thus analyse his performance more closely than by using publicly available statistics.

Relevant BA departments were instructed to assist Basham in any way they could. Derek Stevens, BA's chief financial officer and one of the airline's five executive directors, told his staff to undertake an analysis of Virgin's up-to-date accounts and pass them onto David Burnside to be fed through to Basham.

Ken Cook, a retired BA marketing executive, was the link between BA and the Warwick Corporate team. His job was to ferret out items of information on Virgin Atlantic for Basham from BA's large back-catalogue of research which had been generated by several different BA departments.

BA was not, however, proposing to pay Basham £50,000 for a cuttings job, or for reheating BA's competitor-unit reports. Basham knew King was not interested in prompting an academic debate about the merits and demerits of Virgin Atlantic. 'Inhibiting Branson's ability to compete' meant blowing Branson out of the sky. His Lordship was still glowing with fury at the loss of the Tokyo flights and the Heathrow decision. Much more important to BA was the excavation of Branson's past in a bid to find long-buried skeletons.

Basham tried unsuccessfully to interview Randolph Fields, the co-founder of Virgin Atlantic, whose subsequent fall-out with Branson had been acrimonious and well chronicled. Fields said he didn't want to know.

Basham knew that Branson's ownership of the gay nightclub, Heaven, was a topic that exercised Lord King considerably. BA's chairman had never quite been able to come to terms with the idea of Branson aspiring to run an airline, as well as owning a nightclub for people he described as 'queers'. After lunching at British Aerospace with Sir Ray Lygo, King passed on a rumour to Basham that dustmen from Westminster Council refused to collect rubbish bags from outside Heaven on the grounds that some of them contained hypodermic syringes with needles infected with the AIDS virus. King instructed Basham to circulate the story. The PR man claims he refused – he thought it was a 'bloody mad' request – but he knew that the chairman would be looking to him to develop the Heaven angle in his report.

Basham sought out the former *Sunday Times* journalist, Dominic Prince, in his quest to expose Heaven to his 'daylight test'. Basham knew Prince combined a colourful career as a City journalist with freelance work for the investigative agency, Kroll. Prince was later to find fame of sorts in the *Sun*. In the summer of 1992, as the controversy about Cabinet Minister David Mellor's extra-marital affair with the actress Antonia de Sancha turned into a national debate over public office and private morals, it was revealed that Prince, described by the *Sun* as a 'Mellor lookalike', had also had a brief relationship with de Sancha. He described to the newspaper how the actress enjoyed sucking his toe. His account subsequently inspired the *Sun*'s 'From Toe Job to No Job' headline when Mellor eventually quit the Cabinet.

When Prince met Brian Basham for dinner in February 1991 the chunky journalist had just left the *Sunday Times*, and was heading for a brief spell with the *Independent*. They had known each other for years, and when Basham mentioned that he was on Branson's case, Prince said he had some interesting information to give him. On the phone Prince had said that a friend of his had been 'shocked' by what he had seen at Heaven. When they met, Prince told Basham that KAS, the security consultants, had recommended to Branson that Heaven be closed down but the advice had been ignored. He also gave Basham a copy of an article he had written about Heaven but which had not been published. The article was little more than notes, and it contained no response from Virgin or Branson. However, it was potentially highly damaging: it claimed that KAS found 'someone was on the take' at Heaven, there was 'trouble with the bouncers', 'drug dealing', and 'the club was being used as a soliciting area for male prostitutes. Homosexual MPs and well-known public figures used to frequent its premises'; 'the fire risk' was said to be 'appalling'. The article claimed that David Stirling (who founded KAS) told Branson about the findings on his wedding day, but that Virgin's chairman turned down KAS's recommendation to close the club.

The months of downward pressure on BA's public affairs department to deflate Branson had also yielded other fascinating scraps of information about the airline's methods of operation. In Basham's increasingly urgent bid to puncture what BA saw as Branson's balloon of self-publicity, some of these hitherto unconsidered trifles became newly meaningful.

Basham recalled that he and Burnside wasted no time in debriefing BA's head of central marketing, Mike Batt, after he returned from his brief spell as Virgin Atlantic's joint managing director, and before he started to mastermind the American end of BA's offensive against Virgin.

On the night he left Virgin Atlantic, Batt was sitting in the BA boardroom being quizzed over dinner by Burnside and Basham about Virgin. Although he had been with the airline less than a week, and had not met Richard Branson, Batt had made a point of debriefing many of its senior managers. Batt told Burnside and Basham that Virgin was so badly managed that he thought a major accident in the air was inevitable. Batt said his main reason for leaving was that he thought the airline would not stand up to the sort of inquiry that would inevitably take place after a disaster.

The first draft of Operation Barbara was ready by the beginning of March. Burnside and Basham sat in BA's Enserch House offices, reviewing Operation Barbara and rehearsing their presentation for Lord King and Sir Colin Marshall. At Burnside's suggestion, Basham had produced a series of easy-to-read presentation slides summarising the main points of his report for BA's chairman.

'David said the old boy was less keen than ever on reading in great detail. The more comprehensible I could make the presentation, the better it would go down.'

Ironically for Basham, he had just become the victim of the sort of negative press coverage that he and Burnside were cooking up for Richard Branson. The previous weekend, the *Daily Mail* devoted three full pages to the 'Basham phenomenon' under the headline, 'The Rise and Fall of the Candyfloss Man'. The paper reported that the six million shares in Basham's Broad Street company, worth nearly £25 million at one stage, were now worth so little that they could not be cashed. The *Mail* devoted thousands of words to charting the decline of Basham the 'Eighties Man . . . The boy from Catford was the high-flying image-maker City tycoons needed and feared – until he began to believe in his own invulnerability.'

While the article described the younger Basham as 'the budding genius of the business world', it relished the task of

chronicling the subsequent decline of his Broad Street empire and
the dissolution of his first marriage. Former colleagues and
friends, as well as anonymous rivals, were liberally quoted as they
inserted a colourful array of knives between Basham's shoulder-
blades. The article illustrated Basham's 'fall' by juxtaposing a
photograph of the smiling PR man at his 1987 Docklands celebration party with a contemporary snap of a furtive-looking Basham
turning away from the photographer's lens. The *Mail* savoured its
observation that '. . . this morning no amount of Basham hyperbole
can mask his own desperate predicament'.

As he fought to get Warwick Corporate off the ground, and
take as many former Broad Street clients with him as he could
muster, this was the sort of publicity that Basham could have done
without. Basham hoped the *Mail*'s concluding thought would
prove prophetic: 'Some people say he will be high-rolling again
before the year is out.'

Satisfying British Airways' desire to see the back of Richard
Branson and Virgin Atlantic would not be a bad start for Warwick
Corporate, Basham mused, as he sent Burnside his new company's
first ever invoice. Basham charged BA £46,000 for his report
including VAT, deeming it wise to bring the project in marginally
under the projected £50,000. In a private note to Burnside that
accompanied the invoice, he scribbled: 'Note the invoice number
[BA/91/01]. It could become a collector's item.'

It would.

Basham submitted his invoice to BA for Operation Barbara on
Friday 8 March, the end of a week in which the landscape of
British commercial aviation changed dramatically. Branson had no
idea that Lord King had put Burnside and Basham on his case, but
he knew that the first week of March provided a vivid microcosm
of both the potential and the peril of trying to run an independent
British airline.

On the Wednesday Malcolm Rifkind rejected BA's appeal
against Virgin Atlantic and the two American megacarriers being
allowed into Heathrow. Although Rifkind's confirmation of the
CAA's January recommendation was anticipated, the breach of
BA's fortress Heathrow was a sweet moment for Virgin Atlantic's
chairman. Branson wrote immediately to Rifkind:

Dear Malcolm,

Thank you for being brave over Heathrow. Having seen the way some Conservative MPs attacked your decision I've come to realise the power of BA's lobbying. Although to date we have resisted lobbying MPs we have decided to find one or two MPs who are pro-competition to try to redress the balance in the House somewhat and hopefully who reflect public opinion better. Hopefully next time you make such a decision you won't feel so lonely!

In the meantime, I promise that we will put the investment and time into building Virgin Atlantic into a true alternative to British Airways.

Thank you for putting us on a slightly more level playing field.

Kind regards,
    Richard Branson

The CAA announcement forty-eight hours later that it had thrown out BA's appeal against Virgin Atlantic's new Tokyo slots caused Branson's cup to overflow:

'I am completely and utterly delighted. Until this month no government in fifty years has encouraged competition in the airline business.'

Once the CAA's recommendations on Heathrow and Tokyo were confirmed, Lord King was unable to contain his anger with John Major's government any longer. In a furious interview in the City section of the *Observer*, edited by his son-in-law, Melvyn Marckus, King laid serious charges at Malcolm Rifkind's door:

If I had been told by the government that this would happen at the time of privatisation, I would have felt compelled to refer to it in BA's prospectus.

King accused John Major's government of betraying its principles and the thousands of investors whom Mrs Thatcher had encouraged to buy BA shares at the time of privatisation. He also made some extraordinary claims about the impact of the Tokyo slots decision on British Airways:

That is £250 million of the revenue lost to our public share-holders that will go straight into Richard Branson's private pocket.

As Branson read Lord King's outburst he jotted a note in his diary: 'Lord of the Lies and Lord of the Flies. Does The Lord Tell the Truth and Nothing but the Truth?'

Next to this observation Branson jotted a comment to the effect that BA appeared to have something in common with the Soviet Union: 'both . . . seem to be having problems adjusting to a free-market economy'.

At the Civil Aviation Authority hearing, BA stated the Tokyo decision could cost the airline £10 million. Whatever was King on about? Branson started drafting yet another reply to King's dissembling.

Virgin Atlantic had benefited from the political climate of the age. The government was sufficiently committed to realising the rhetoric of its competition policy to loosen slightly BA's iron grip on British aviation. However, as the champagne corks popped in Virgin Atlantic's Crawley headquarters, rumours were spreading through the town's airline community that another independent airline, Air Europe, was in grave trouble.

On the day Richard Branson heard he could fly from Heathrow, Harry Goodman was summoned to an emergency board meeting of the International Leisure Group. Crisis talks had been going on all week to attempt to save Air Europe's floundering parent company. ILG's major shareholder, Werner Rey, had been forced to pump £40 million into the group during the Gulf War to prevent a breach in the terms of the loans which underpinned the company. Goodman left the meeting having received assurances that the consortium of major banks, headed by Citicorp, would continue to back Britain's 'second-force' carrier, and its enormous leisure and travel division.

Goodman was accompanied to the meeting by a doctor. When he left he returned to the Humana Wellington Hospital in St John's Wood, where he had been receiving treatment for the previous ten days. Goodman was lucky to be alive. He had been feeling dreadful for weeks.

'I put my symptoms down to the phenomenal stress of trying to keep Air Europe in the sky, and the travel and leisure group together in the worst economic conditions in aviation history.' Goodman was almost fatally wrong.

Driving home from his local golf club at the end of February, Goodman blacked out at the wheel of his car. In the crash that followed he escaped with two broken ribs. Doctors discovered, however, that he was diabetic and that had caused his blackout: 'The doctors told me that I had been incredibly lucky. They said if I hadn't had the crash, my condition wouldn't have been diagnosed and I could have been dead in two days.'

His airline was, however, in a terminal condition. Thirty-six hours later he flicked on breakfast television, from his hospital bed, and learnt that the administrators had been called in and his sixty-plane fleet was grounded. Six thousand people lost their jobs as the vast travel and leisure consortium folded overnight. Citicorp called in their £350 million loan as ILG was 'in technical breach' of the conditions attached to the loan. The fax from Citicorp's lawyers arrived at two in the morning: the massive onslaught on Europe's scheduled services that Goodman had planned for 1992 was stillborn. Like Laker Airways, Air Europe had fallen at the hurdle of Europe.

'I was in a state of total shock,' recalls Goodman, 'utter disbelief. I can still think of no other comparable example of where a business ILG's size was put into receivership because of a "technical breach".'

The demise of Air Europe left those within BA who had plotted to bring the airline down with mixed feelings. Senior management wore expressions of barely suppressed glee, but amongst the Helpliners at Gatwick Airport there was some sadness. Some of the Helpliners had been accessing Air Europe's confidential computer information; now they watched Air Europe's staff walk away from their check-in desks for the last time. Many of them were in tears. With the deep cuts in BA's own workforce, the Helpliners knew that as Air Europe's pilots and cabin crews arrived to find their planes grounded, many would never fly again or work in the airline industry in any capacity. Sadig Khalifa remembers feeling a sense of guilt as well as responsibility:

'We wondered if we had had anything to do with it. It was hard to say, but a number of us started questioning what we had been asked to do, and what the information might have been used for further up the line in BA.

'A couple of weeks later BA closed the Helpline down saying now it could get the information on Virgin from other sources.'

At the Victoria headquarters of the UK sales team there were celebrations at the passing of another independent British rival. Peter Fleming, part of the Liam Strong team that accessed Air Europe's computers, had just left BA but he kept in touch with his former colleagues:

'I'm afraid to say that the collapse of Air Europe was regarded as a bit of a success from the management point of view. People were delighted to see the back of another airline. They seemed to get a buzz from the fact that other airlines just couldn't survive in the marketplace.'

The speed of Air Europe's demise horrified Richard Branson and the staff of his much smaller airline and travel group. Like Goodman, Branson had bought his company back from the City in order to expand it rapidly. If he needed any reminder of how fickle banks and investors can be, the demise of Air Europe provided it.

On the day Air Europe went under, Branson answered a knock at the door in Holland Park.

'Good morning, Mr Branson, my name is Sidney Shore from Lloyds Bank.'

Branson's heart sank immediately. Lloyds were Virgin Atlantic's principal bankers.

Shore had spent the week in crisis talks with all of Britain's independent airlines. The impact of the Gulf War had played havoc with their finances. On the Monday he had been in talks with Air Europe to whom Lloyds had made a £100-million loan; on the Wednesday Shore was in similar talks with Dan Air. Today was Friday, Air Europe was dead and he wanted to see Richard Branson in person.

'Sidney Shore said Lloyds were in a panic. With oil prices still spiralling and no Japanese or Americans flying anywhere, he assumed we must also be in trouble, as we only fly to Japan and the USA.

'He was also worried about the escalating public hostilities with

BA. Lloyds were not keen on two of their customers scrapping in such a public fashion. I told him there was not much we could do about that as we hadn't started the fight! But his main worry was about our finances.'

Branson was able to calm Shore. Virgin Atlantic's parent company, Voyager Travel, was set to declare a profit of £8.5 million on a turnover of £209 million to the year ending July 1990 – the month before the Iraqi invasion of Kuwait. Since then, Branson was able to tell Shore, Virgin Atlantic had survived the Gulf crisis much better than he had feared. The airline had suffered only a 2% dip in the number of passengers flying during the crisis. Assuring the Lloyds man that he would correct whatever negatives there were in Virgin's performance by 'creating the best airline in the world', Branson sent a relieved banker on his way.

Shortly afterwards Shore dropped Branson a note to reassure him of Lloyds' continuing support.

> My visit portended more than it warranted. I had had a dreadful week with Air Europe and Dan Air. I overreacted. There was not a sudden change in the bank's attitude to you & I'm sorry if I caused you any distress.

Richard Branson's reply began:

> Dear Sidney . . . If things had been going badly for Virgin Atlantic, I would hate to have seen your face!

Despite Virgin Atlantic's robust performance during the Gulf War, Branson felt the mantle of investor confidence being tugged from his shoulders.

'At the end of the Gulf War everyone assumed that we should be in trouble. Lord King had announced that the Gulf War had hit BA's revenue badly, and said he was about to spend millions making thousands of his staff redundant. Air Europe had gone down and Dan Air had almost gone the same way. If you are an independent airline it only takes one bad year and you're out of business. Laker was profitable for thirty-five out of the thirty-six years he was flying.

'If we were going to survive I knew we would have to expand to meet the opportunities that the Heathrow and Tokyo decisions gave us.'

Branson turned to the former Secretary for Trade and Industry, Lord Young, for help in trying to raise the money he needed to expand Virgin Atlantic. David Young had been one of Mrs Thatcher's most treasured allies. The Prime Minister once famously said of him, 'Others bring me problems, but David brings me solutions.' Branson had struck up a good relationship with Lord Young when he was in Mrs Thatcher's government, and the minister had joined him on Virgin Atlantic's inaugural flight to Tokyo in May 1989. Since leaving government Lord Young had eschewed involvement in politics and he joined the board of Salomon Brothers, the merchant bank. Over lunch at the bank in late March, Young introduced Branson to Fraser Marcus, the head of Salomons' transportation department. Young and Marcus said Salomons would be happy to try and raise the equity for him. Marcus recalls the advice he gave to Branson in their opening talks:

'There was clearly scope to interest a potential investor after the Tokyo and Heathrow decisions in favour of Virgin. Successful airlines are focused airlines. With Richard Branson's stated ambition to fly business-class passengers to the twelve most profitable destinations in the world, and with no requirement to finance unprofitable routes, Virgin looked a good proposition. He had already proved he could put an excellent product in the sky. We told him that the problem he would face would be the illiquidity of the investment – the airline is a private company with no ready exit for investors' finance. There would be limited sources of finance available for such a specific form of investment.

'The other main problem we spoke of was regulatory. In reality the airline industry remains heavily regulated, very difficult to break into. Branson had yet to win the licences and the slots he needed to expand, and he didn't need Salomons to tell him that British Airways would oppose him every step of the way.'

David Burnside and Brian Basham eased themselves into deep green leather armchairs in front of Lord King's huge mahogany desk on 19 March, two days after the chairman's explosion in the

Observer. King's departure from their advice to wipe his mind of
Richard Branson only two days beforehand left Brian Basham feeling uneasy about BA's approach:

'I thought King had got the wrong target in his press outburst.
Publicly, BA should have been attacking the government, possibly
pressing for a judicial review of the Tokyo decision. Branson had
only done what any businessman would have done in his position.
It was the government who had handed BA's routes over to him.'

King's world was everywhere before Burnside and Basham –
photographs of King with his wife, Isabel, and his wife with her
cousin, the Queen. Family photos and paintings of hunting scenes
fought for prominence with bronze busts of the King family pug
and models of Concorde. Pictures of King with the Pope, King
with the Reagans, and King with George Bush stared at the two PR
men as they shuffled though their papers. On the chairman's desk
there was a photograph of the former Prime Minister, Mrs
Thatcher, and one of his close friend and fellow BA board member,
Lord White. A champagne cooler nestled in the corner of the room.

King puffed deeply on an afternoon Havana as he started to
inspect Basham's report. He had just returned from lunch at
Greens in Westminster.

Basham explained to King how Branson's tendency to run all
his businesses short of cash had persisted from his earliest ventures in journalism and the music business. He showed the
characteristics of a poker player, possibly a compulsive gambler:

> His method of operation was to run his companies very
> short of cash, but then to use the strength of the brand to
> refund the business. He had two weaknesses in that. First of
> all, he was running out of bits to sell and every time he did
> sell something he lost more control. Secondly he had sold
> minority interests, which restricted his flexibility.
>
> A lot of his ability to be able to refinance his business
> relied very much on his personal image, the free-wheeling
> former hippie. That's his biggest bankable asset, no question
> about it.

However, it was Branson's image, Basham argued, that could be his downfall. Under 'Vulnerabilities' Basham listed possible weaknesses: Tax arrangements; Hypocrisy; Sensitivity to criticism; Alienates press; Cash weaknesses; Erratic commercial behaviour. Amongst Basham's recommendations were suggestions that BA should 'Bring [Virgin's] cash-flow analysis up to date', examine Virgin Atlantic's 'Future financing needs', and 'Explore personal arrangements'. Basham drew King's attention to his rival chairman's tax position:

> If you accept that his image is all important, then one of the things we felt could damage [him] were things like his tax arrangements. I mean, here was a man who seemed to have no great regard for money and dressed in a certain style and that sort of thing. And we felt that his tax arrangements demonstrated a certain personal hypocrisy.

In an appendix, Basham included a 1990 report by the *Sunday Times* 'Insight' team entitled 'The Artful Dodgers'. The article probed the offshore tax arrangements of a number of well-known businessmen, including Richard Branson.

It showed that Branson had avoided £18 million in tax when he sold 25% of Virgin Music to Fujisankei by selling shares held in trusts set up in the Channel Islands. The tax – 40% of Branson's profit on the £46 million sale – would normally have been payable to the British government. The existence of Branson's tax shelter had until then been buried in the small print of a prospectus issued in advance of Virgin's Stock Market flotation. Unhappy at the disclosure, and at the implication that he was a tax dodger when he had done nothing to contravene British law, Branson instructed his lawyers, Harbottle & Lewis, to bombard the paper with faxed threats. To Basham, Branson's behaviour indicated how highly he valued his public image and demonstrated a recognition of the potential damage to Virgin companies if it was tarnished:

> He showed extreme sensitivity to criticism. This was very important. We felt that if these things [his tax arrangements] were to cause his image to suffer, then his method of operation – running his company very short of cash – could

become a real problem, because he wouldn't be able to pull
the rabbit out of the hat in terms of refinancing.

Without actually accusing Branson of being a tax dodger, Basham
noted in his 'Personal Profile' of Virgin's chairman:

> Following Polly Peck–Asil Nadir, the Special Office of the
> Inland Revenue is looking at offshore trusts where the bene-
> ficial ownership is felt to be in the UK.

In analysing Branson's business style, Basham steered clear of
libel. He opted instead for suggestive appraisal. He described
Branson's approach to business as 'irrational and experimental',
detecting 'obsessive tendencies' which had led to the 'erratic and
spontaneous' strategic development of the Virgin Group and the
airline.

Three paragraphs of the report were devoted to Branson's gay
London nightclub, Heaven. The review by the security consultants, KAS, that Dominic Prince had told Basham about was
mentioned.

> KAS discovered indications (but no hard evidence) of fraud
> and other problems with the police, bouncers, fire risk, drug
> dealing, homosexuals and male prostitutes. KAS recom-
> mended closing the club and re-opening with new staff.
> Branson vetoed the move.

Dominic Prince's article on Heaven was attached to the report as
'Appendix VII'.

Both Basham and Burnside knew that King would be looking
for mention of the AIDS story, as he was the source of it. Mindful
of his own advice to BA that the company should be prepared to
see anything eventually appearing in print, Basham had watered
the anecdote down. However, the text did not require the reader
to possess much imagination to realise what the relevant paragraph meant:

> There have been suggestions that Westminster Council

would not remove rubbish bags from the club on the grounds that they contained infected sharp objects.

Similarly, Mike Batt's damaging observations about Virgin's aeroplanes 'falling out of the sky' were not mentioned. Perhaps remembering the DTI inspectors' pointed criticism of the fictitious press releases about the Fayeds' family history, Basham stuck firmly to his own advice and excluded the more spicy allegations. If need be, these could be imparted over lunch at the Savoy or a quiet drink at Annabel's nightclub.

The PR dimension of BA's campaign against Branson and Virgin crystallised in Lord King's office that March afternoon under a cloud of blue cigar smoke. Mrs Thatcher's low-born Lord sat plotting Branson's downfall with two of his most loyal courtiers, a butcher's son from Catford and a Protestant farmer's son from Ballymoney: the Streetfighter and the Kneecapper. The three self-made men were bound by an awareness of and sensitivity to their own backgrounds, and enormous pride in the progress that had brought them to prominence at British Airways. The BA trio felt it safe to assume that Branson, the most celebrated self-made businessman in Britain, would be equally sensitive about his own background. He had, after all, created Virgin in his own image. Basham recalled, 'It is one of the great ironies of the clash between BA and Virgin that King came from extremely humble stock and Branson, who was so often portrayed as the David fighting King's Goliath, is a solid upper middle-class boy.'

The strategy the BA trio devised was to paint Virgin as a dangerously overstretched airline, headed by an irrational eccentric who indulged in a range of physically and morally dangerous pursuits. This combination of defects could cause investors to lose confidence in Branson just as they had in Harry Goodman. The PR strategy would complement the schemes of the marketing and sales departments.

Sir Colin Marshall's office contacted Basham to make sure the chief executive received his briefing on Operation Barbara before an important meeting with Malcolm Rifkind on 26 March. Marshall was due to lead a BA delegation to the ministry to present the airline's business plans for the short and medium term.

The government routinely consults with British airlines as it prepares to negotiate aviation treaties with foreign governments and licensing authorities. BA was still reeling from the impact of the Gulf War and struggling to adjust to the arrival of John Major. The chief executive's first formal encounter with the new transport secretary and his most senior civil servants thus assumed heightened significance.

It threatened to be an awkward affair. The *Observer* article that had reported Lord King's fury ten days beforehand had appeared under an unambiguous headline: 'Rifkind Blamed for BA Crisis'. The Tokyo decision, coming days after Rifkind confirmed that Virgin Atlantic and the American carriers would be allowed into Heathrow, led directly to Lord King's eruptions in the press.

> The tragedy is [Lord King told the *Sunday Times*] that they were allowed in at all.

He publicly blamed Rifkind and his team for bowing to pressure from the American government and mishandling the negotiations. To say that King disliked Rifkind would be a considerable overestimation of the warmth of his feelings.

> Transport policy — what transport policy? [King raged in the *Observer*] It seems that every time we build up profitable routes, someone comes along and says, 'I'll have some of that', and the government obliges.

Rifkind had flatly rejected all of Lord King's arguments against the expansion of Virgin's Tokyo operation on the grounds that the deal the government had negotiated with the Japanese was good for Great Britain plc, and did negligible harm to BA. Sir Colin Marshall's task, therefore, was not made any easier by his chairman's cantankerous public outbursts.

Brian Basham presented his report to Sir Colin Marshall at 11.15 on 26 March 1991 at Speedbird House, only hours before the meeting with Malcolm Rifkind. Marshall had signed Basham's £46,000 invoice for Operation Barbara, but Basham knew that Marshall would be looking not only for value for money, but also for something that Burnside's embattled in-house PR team could not provide.

'It was very difficult to have any sort of conversation with Colin at that time without the name of Branson cropping up,' recalls Basham. 'Colin's a pretty hard businessman, commerce is a pretty tough game, and Colin is one of the toughest players. Like King, he wanted to see Richard Branson stopped.'

Basham specifically tailored the presentation of his report to Marshall's preconceptions about Virgin and Branson, some of which the PR man believed were in fact wide of the mark.

The first page of Operation Barbara attempted to disabuse Marshall of three 'popular *misconceptions* about Virgin': 'Virgin is small', 'Virgin's management is of low quality' and 'Virgin is financially weak'. Basham pointed out that in reality the combined value of the Virgin Group of companies was nearly £1 billion, and that its management had proved to be resourceful and fast-reacting to changing situations. Basham also noted that joint ventures had been used to finance the organic development of the group.

However, he stressed to Marshall, as he had to King, that the Branson companies were cash-hungry and that failure to find suitable partners was his most obvious potential source of weakness.

> Japanese loss of confidence for any reason could and probably would cut off his cash lifeline and could lead to disaster.

The similarities between Michael Levin's 1989 report for Marshall on Virgin and Basham's Operation Barbara were striking. Both concluded that the core strength of Branson's companies was in the brand. The brand was built on Branson's image as a free-wheeling hippie. Destroy the image, and you put Branson out of business.

Sir Colin Marshall was not, however, entirely satisfied by Basham's report. Basham recalls his reaction:

'Colin said that he found my report helpful but that it didn't go far enough. He saw Branson as a major threat to BA, but he believed there were further weaknesses that should be probed. He said he thought the report should have been more hard-hitting.

'I told him that it was far better to produce a balanced report that would be recognised as such by serious journalists. I would then have a better chance of guiding them to the conclusions BA wanted them to reach.'

Basham told Marshall that with Lord King's authority he had already started briefing the *Sunday Telegraph* and the *Observer* on his findings.

Despite his reservations, Marshall slipped a copy of Operation Barbara into his briefcase as he set off for his meeting with the men from the ministry in Marsham Street. Accompanying Marshall was BA's legal director, Robert Ayling.

Throughout the airline industry, Ayling's knowledge and experience of the Whitehall machine is acknowledged as being without equal, for very good reasons. His recruitment to BA from the civil service to become legal director in 1985 was one of the shrewdest appointments that King and Marshall made as they steered the airline towards privatisation. As an under-secretary in the Department of Trade, Ayling had drafted the bill to privatise British Airways, and he had become head of the Department's aviation law branch. On the night of 4 February 1982, Ayling was summoned to advise Margaret Thatcher at the meeting in her House of Commons office at which she decided not to try and save Laker Airways, with a cash injection. Ironically, the personable civil servant owed his transfer to British Airways to the subsequent anti-trust suit that Laker's liquidators brought against BA. Ayling became the British government's special advisor in its battle to scupper the Laker suit. His immediate boss on the Laker case, Bill Park, who eventually masterminded the settlement of Laker's civil suit on the government's behalf, described Ayling as 'a first class lawyer with political antennae'.

According to Park, one of Ayling's key roles was to keep Mrs Thatcher and her cabinet briefed on developments in the government's bid to defeat the Laker liquidator's case in the USA. In this capacity Ayling impressed Colin Marshall as well as the British government's opponents in the Laker camp. Sir Freddie Laker's lawyer, Bob Beckman, recalls, 'Robert Ayling was a highly respected civil servant, brilliant in my opinion. He was the brains behind the British government's efforts to destroy Laker's case in America.'

Bill Park remembers discussing Ayling's recruitment to BA with Marshall on Concorde during one of their many trips to the States to fight Laker's claims, 'Marshall said to me, "I want Ayling and you will get him for me." And so I had to set to work to arrange for Robert to go to British Airways, which he did.'

After Mrs Thatcher persuaded President Reagan to halt the criminal investigation into BA's efforts to undermine Laker Airways at the end of 1984, Marshall plucked Ayling from the civil service. Appointed BA's legal director in 1985, his primary task was to oversee the legal aspects of the privatisation process he had drafted for Mrs Thatcher's government. In 1987 Ayling was appointed company secretary. Thus he came to occupy a unique position in both the aviation industry and its folklore; BA's legal director and company secretary was reaping the rewards of his endeavours as a mandarin.

The winter of 1991, however, was a difficult one for Ayling, to whom Marshall looked to dovetail BA's political lobbying against Virgin with Basham's streetfighting mission. Ayling unsuccessfully masterminded British Airways' representations to the Civil Aviation Authority over the Tokyo slots. Ayling told Basham he was convinced that Branson timed his publicity salvos to coincide with CAA hearings and to disadvantage BA at key moments.

'Robert's view was that Branson's use of publicity was very commercial and very cynical . . . his activities all amounted to a cynical campaign to discredit BA [and] to discredit Lord King – even perhaps split the BA board.

'Like Marshall, Ayling believed Branson wanted to make Virgin look more powerful and larger than it was, to influence the authorities and in particular to influence the CAA and Malcolm Rifkind.'

As Marshall and Ayling led BA's lobby through the corridors of power, they opted for a low-key approach in trying to undermine Virgin Atlantic, a foil to their chairman's bombast.

At the meeting with the Secretary of State on 26 March, Marshall and Ayling pursued the Mission Atlantic strategy of de-emphasising Virgin's importance in public. The BA duo railed mightily against the two American megacarriers' being allowed into Heathrow. 'BA's main competition comes from foreign airlines,' they told the government delegation, demonstrating their point with a slide on an overhead projector illustrating BA's 'Declining Real Yield'.

They pointed out the unfairness of the Civil Aviation Authority's recent decisions, and drew Rifkind's attention to the enormous subsidies that other countries' national carriers were receiving from their governments. In the main presentation session, Marshall stressed BA's publicly held policy that it had no wish to constrict Virgin Atlantic's growth. The BA delegation did, however, elaborate on its concerns that Richard Branson was seeking to expand into a recession. A source at the meeting confirmed that Marshall and Ayling went further than Basham was going in his press briefings by telling the government team that Virgin had failed to find sufficient financial support in Britain, and was thus hoping to raise equity finance in Japan. Sir Colin Marshall did not have to point out the parallels with Air Europe to a Secretary of State who had spent the previous month resisting calls to intervene to save Harry Goodman's mainly Swiss-owned airline. BA's chief executive restricted himself to expressing the hope to Rifkind that the CAA would investigate Virgin Atlantic's financial arrangements properly, as it had apparently failed to do in the case of Air Europe. BA had, of course, known for more than three years that Air Europe was substantially owned by foreign interests after its discreetly commissioned Kroll probe. According to the same source at the meeting, BA did not reveal to the secretary of state that it had been employing Kroll to probe Air Europe, or that Brian Basham was working on Virgin.

Over tea and biscuits, BA amplified its 'concerns' about Virgin. Ever since Virgin had started flights to Japan in 1989, BA had been suggesting to the government that the carrier might not grow to maturity, gently questioning the wisdom of government negotiating an increase in slots to allow a competitor with an uncertain future to expand. BA's argument was that if Virgin *did* follow the path of Laker, British Caledonian and Air Europe, the valuable slots might eventually be lost to carriers from other countries. BA cloaked its anxiety for its own profit margins with 'concern' for passengers who might be deprived of services should Virgin go under.

Two aspects of Marshall and Ayling's lobbying tactics are worthy of comment. The first is that their claim that Virgin Atlantic had failed to attract support in the UK financial markets was not true. Richard Branson did not start actively to look for an equity partner until September 1991, and when he did a number of British investors expressed interest. BA's aim appeared to be to sow seeds of doubt in the minds of the men from the ministry which would then be nurtured by Operation Barbara in the months that followed.

The second is the BA team's insidious references to Air Europe, in the context of Virgin's need to attract foreign investment. This was another way of attempting to undermine Rifkind's confidence in Virgin Atlantic. BA told the minister that Virgin had 'yet to prove its fitness' to take up the US routes it had won permission to fly on.

Emboldened by the demise of Air Europe earlier in the month, BA felt confident in spreading rumours about Virgin's financial position at the highest level in Whitehall at a time when major uncertainty surrounded the future of all independent British airlines. Air Europe had gone down, Dan Air had just avoided the same fate, and Virgin Atlantic was being forced to look for foreign investment, BA told the government.

Underlying BA's routine curtsies to the political pieties of the age – 'it will be the customer who suffers', 'we don't want to stifle Virgin's growth' – was a clear message to the minister: British investors won't back independent British airlines, so why should you? Particularly if backing Virgin means weakening BA . . . Furthermore if you continue to support the redistribution of BA's assets to Virgin – its routes and its flights – you might eventually be called upon to intervene when Branson follows Goodman into liquidation. If you don't, then Great Britain plc will be the loser when Branson's routes are redistributed.

Lord King's rumour-mongering in the City, Marshall and Ayling's astute political footwork, and Basham's streetfighting were items on the same agenda: to discredit Richard Branson and Virgin Atlantic, and prevent him from expanding his airline to take more of BA's profits. The BA men used different vocabularies but their language was the same.

Basham made straight for City journalists from the broadsheet newspapers he had cultivated in the course of his twenty-year career in financial PR. He supplied Melvyn Marckus, the City editor of the *Observer*, with a copy of his report over breakfast at the Berkeley Hotel. Marckus, who is Lord King's son-in-law, had known Basham for two decades.

BA's chairman became a director of the *Sunday Telegraph* in 1990, and Basham made sure that Lord King's paper also received Operation Barbara. Basham himself had a firm relationship with the paper, but it was one that had damaged the reputation of the most established of the Conservative Sunday newspapers.

During Basham's generalship of the Fayed brothers' campaign for Harrods, the *Sunday Telegraph* was one of the papers that had been taken in by the brothers' fantasies. The paper's then City editor, Ian Watson, had later been cited by the DTI inspectors as having fallen for Brian Basham's 'seriously misleading press releases', a process that was apparently assisted by the Fayeds' lavish hospitality budget. Despite Watson's departure to edit Robert Maxwell's *European*, BA's links with the *Sunday Telegraph* remained strong. Brian Basham retained close contact with the City desk editor, John Jay, and one of his reporters, Frank Kane.

Basham was delighted at Jay and Kane's response to his report on Branson and Virgin. 'Frank and John came to the same conclusion as we had. Virgin was vulnerable and the government was unwise to support him to the detriment of British Airways and its shareholders.'

The *Sunday Telegraph*'s printing presses rolled on 31 March with a dramatic headline emblazoned across the City pages:

VIRGIN HEADING FOR STORMY SKIES

Underneath the headline were 1,500 words from Frank Kane. The first sentence set the tone:

> The international airline industry is littered with corporate wreckage – the hulks of carriers which thought they had identified a niche market ignored by the established giants of the skies.

Kane summoned the ghosts of Laker, British Caledonian and the recently deceased Air Europe before posing 'the crucial question' facing Branson's efforts to expand Virgin Atlantic: 'Can he finance this expansion without suffering the same fate as so many of his predecessors?'

Basham was delighted. Over breakfast in his Suffolk cottage, BA's PR man reflected on the success of a textbook operation from his own manual of pro-active PR. He also felt confident the *Sunday Telegraph* article might take some of the heat off himself and Burnside.

In preparing his report, Kane spoke to Branson at some length and his article was peppered with quotations from Virgin's chairman. Kane gave weight to Branson's extraordinary business career, but also asked searching questions about his capacity to expand Virgin and, crucially, from BA's point of view, Branson's personal vulnerability.

There was no clue as to who had inspired the article. It quoted Basham's report obliquely, referring to it as 'research on Virgin's aggregated operations', but gave no hint that the work had been conducted by BA and its PR man.

> A study of Voyager's accounts for 1989 reveals short-term debt of £30 million, long-term debt of £62.9 million, and equity of £22.75 million, giving a traditionally calculated gearing figure of more than 400%.

Sunday Telegraph readers might have been forgiven for thinking that their correspondent had been burning the midnight oil at Companies' House examining Virgin's accounts. In fact the figure came straight from BA: Kane had copied the figures from Basham's report.

(Lawyers representing Kane wrote to me threatening to sue me over this account of how Kane wrote his article. They said it was 'untrue and gravely defamatory of Mr Kane'. They insisted that Kane had independently researched Virgin's accounts. John Jay wrote in similar terms in the *Sunday Telegraph*. The editor of the paper, Charles Moore, refused to give me the opportunity to respond, and refused to print a letter I sent to him. Indeed, Jay told his readers that it was *he* who had inspired Kane's article – contradicting both Basham's (taped) and Kane's (verbal) original accounts of how it came to be written. When I interviewed Kane about his article, his first response was, 'Oh! you mean the Operation Barbara article?'

I replied to Kane's lawyers by challenging Kane to produce the independent company searches he and Jay subsequently claimed that the *Sunday Telegraph* had undertaken – either the documents, or the receipts for the searches. At the time of writing, seven months later, I have heard nothing further from either Kane or his lawyers. Thus my original account of how an article based on Basham's Operation Barbara report and briefing came to appear in the *Sunday Telegraph* remains unaltered from the first edition.)

Kane also repeated some of the Basham-inspired hints about Branson's personal vulnerability:

> There is another danger, too. What Branson is selling to the Japanese and other potential partners is, in essence, Branson himself – the daredevil entrepreneur, equally at home as he moves from his Heaven nightclub in London to a high-altitude balloon over the Pacific to the boardroom of a £1 billion group of companies. What happens if, literally, the balloon bursts?

Kane had faithfully reflected BA's agenda. As Basham knew from a lifetime's plying what he describes as his 'tawdry trade', once an article is printed it goes straight to cuttings libraries and data bases throughout the world. Kane's was the first entry in what BA hoped would become an archive of anti-Virgin material, capable of deterring investors from advancing Branson the money he was seeking. Basham remembers, 'I thought Frank had written a very fair story. It shed a great deal of light on Branson's business because my report was a seminal one – the first to be written about Branson's business after he took it private.'

Basham's pleasure at seeing so much of Operation Barbara published in the City pages of a serious right-wing newspaper so soon after Marshall's meeting with Malcolm Rifkind was short-lived. The following day Burnside called him to say that Marshall had complained during their morning phone briefing that the article had not gone far enough. Marshall used the same phrase that he had used when he discussed Operation Barbara with Basham himself: it was not 'hard-hitting enough'.

Virgin Atlantic's Heathrow launch was now less than three months away. Basham and Burnside knew they would be in for a long, hot summer. So would Richard Branson.

6

The Battle for Heathrow

Richard Branson crouched in the back of a windowless transit van as it made its way out of London. Over one eye he wore a black patch. A parrot perched on his shoulder. His pirate's costume was completed with a hat featuring a skull and crossbones, and a peg-leg. The van came to a halt at the entrance to Heathrow Airport by the huge model of Concorde. It was dawn on 1 July 1991.

From the back of the transit, Branson peered through the driver's window. At a signal from Virgin's marketing director, Chris Moss, a small team of workmen ran towards the model of Concorde – the symbol that tells anyone arriving at Heathrow's Terminals 1, 2 or 3 that the busiest airport in the world is the home of British Airways. Within ninety seconds, the workmen had slipped a made-to-measure silk sock emblazoned with the Virgin logo over the Concorde's tail-fin. Hastily erected sign-boards proclaimed Heathrow as 'Virgin Territory', obscuring BA's familiar advertising logo, 'The World's Favourite Airline'. Virgin was fleetingly colonising BA's most potent virility symbol for that most highly treasured of all Branson activities: a photo-opportunity.

On cue Branson emerged from the white van. Shepherded by Will Whitehorn, a media posse simultaneously clambered out of a second van. As Branson posed unselfconsciously, the cameras seized their moment. By lunchtime a picture of Branson's pirate claiming 'Virgin Territory' was splashed across London's *Evening Standard.*

After the CAA's decision which gave Virgin Atlantic its extra flights to Tokyo, Lord King had described Branson as a 'pirate' who was stealing his routes. To mark Virgin Atlantic's historic launch from Heathrow, Branson the Poacher became Branson the Pirate for the day. Taking Lord King at his word he stole the Hunter's Concorde for a publicity stunt.

By the time Heathrow security, and an agitated team from BA, arrived on the scene, the Virgin party and its media entourage had vanished. Many weeks after the images of Branson's 'Concorde moment' had found their way around the world, BA lodged a formal complaint about a 'serious breach of security' at the Concorde Supersite.

The Concorde stunt was typical Branson: an original idea, meticulously executed which also succeeded in its intention of getting right up British Airways' nose. A senior BA executive remembers the fury the pirate stunt caused:

'It just wasn't the way serious people were supposed to behave! Proper businessmen are supposed to spend their time looking after their airlines, not farting about in fancy dress and floating around in balloons.'

For Branson there was a serious purpose: Virgin Atlantic's private market research indicated that the airline was still unknown to 50% of business travellers. Virgin's unconventional arrival at Heathrow looked like a prank but the publicity was priceless. In contrast to the months of behind-the-scenes hand-wringing and brainstorming at BA, as it sought to tweak the ingredients of the marketing mix to lure passengers back, Virgin's recipe had a familiar main ingredient.

There was Richard Branson dressed as a pirate, Richard Branson at the check-in desk, Richard Branson personally welcoming each passenger on board Virgin's inaugural flight from Heathrow, Richard Branson being interviewed, Richard Branson being photographed and Richard Branson hosting an all-day party for his staff and thousands of corporate guests at Terminal 3. Any reservations Branson had about continuing to use himself to market his airline after the criticism he had endured during the Gulf relief flights had been swept away.

'Today is the second most exciting day in the history of Virgin,' he proclaimed. 'The first was when we launched the airline in 1984.'

Heathrow had never seen anything like it. While rock bands played in an enormous marquee, a funfair entertained the children. Many younger members of BA's staff slipped out of their uniforms and joined the party after work. Lord King declined Branson's invitation.

For his Heathrow service, Branson matched BA's business-class fares to Tokyo and across the Atlantic, and undercut King in economy class: Virgin offered a return economy fare of £229; the cheapest BA ticket was between £269 and £279. [1]

Two weeks later, thunderous applause erupted in London's Barbican Theatre. On stage was Lord King, addressing British Airways' Annual General Meeting. In his speech BA's chairman railed once more against the government's decision to 'confiscate four of our slots each week at Tokyo's Narita Airport and open up Heathrow to all comers'. King warned his shareholders that 'continued liberalisation of the airline industry could mean the UK will become an insignificant bit player on the aviation scene'.

Asked by a shareholder how much money BA intended to give to the Conservative Party in the coming financial year, King was unequivocal: 'No further political contributions will be made in the current financial year.'

BA's hard-pressed shareholders rose to applaud a gesture that marked a sea-change in British Airways' increasingly fraught relationship with the party that had enabled them all to buy a stake in the airline. In the previous two years, British Airways had made an annual donation to the Conservatives of £40,000 and in 1989 King had promised to increase the sum in time for the next election. Now, with the Conservative Party facing an election within the year and reporting a deficit of £5 million, Mrs Thatcher's favourite Lord had cut BA's financial ties with the government led by John Major.

---

[1] Figures from the CAA.

King also announced that job losses at BA could reach 7,000 in 1991. Partly because the airline had to finance so many redundancies, its profits had nosedived from £345 million to £130 million, a much worse figure than predicted. Any remaining doubts that BA faced its most serious crisis since privatisation were dispelled when King and Marshall both announced they would be taking pay cuts of over £100,000 each.

Having raged against the government, the American airlines and Richard Branson since the beginning of the year, King used the annual gathering of shareholders to show that he'd finally had enough. And John Major's transport secretary had clearly had enough of King. In a stinging riposte to BA's chairman, Malcolm Rifkind flatly rejected BA's complaints as mere whinges:

'No airline has a legal right to a landing or take-off slot. Rather, airlines have permission and this must be subject to the public interest.' Rifkind left King in no doubt what the future criterion for aviation policy would be. 'What is best for the travelling public, and if this conflicts with the interests of any individual airline, the former will take priority.'

Richard Branson was in Milan opening a Virgin Megastore when he heard about Lord King's outburst:

'I thought it was bloody childish and proved that BA just saw their donations to the Conservative Party as being in return for political favours.'

Branson was exasperated at BA's behaviour. That summer the Heathrow slot-scheduling committee was chaired by a British Airways' representative, Peter Morrisroe. (The committee is chaired by different airlines on a rota basis.) Virgin Atlantic applied for eighty-six take-off and landing slots; Branson was appalled when Morrisroe's committee offered him only twenty-eight .

'It basically meant that we couldn't fly on the routes we had been given permission to fly on,' he recalled.

Furthermore the committee had given Virgin Atlantic slots to fly from Heathrow at impossible times, as Branson recorded in his diary:

They gave us four flights to New York's Newark Airport, but

no flights back. Completely hopeless. They gave us only one flight to Los Angeles at the wrong time and only two to Miami, also at the wrong times.

When Virgin Atlantic's negotiator on the committee, Paul Griffiths, challenged Morrisroe, the BA man assured him Virgin Atlantic would get its slots in the autumn. Branson was furious.

'Airlines make all their money in the summer season, as BA knows very well, and this was just an attempt to stop us starting proper services on time on 1 July.'

Morrisroe told Griffiths: 'You had a perfectly good operation out of Gatwick – it was your decision to come to Heathrow.'

Richard Branson recalled that BA had tried to pull an identical stunt in 1984 when Virgin Atlantic won its first ever route at Gatwick. The equivalent Gatwick committee was also chaired by BA and it granted Virgin Atlantic its first slot (to New York) at 0200. 'It's a bit like being invited to take part in a Grand Prix and then finding that there's no place for you on the grid!' Branson wrote later.

In reality, British Airways had resigned itself to seeing Branson on the runways of Heathrow, Gatwick, North America and Japan for as long as the government continued to back him. Or until he went out of business. Although King would continue to bluster against government policy and Rifkind in particular, BA had in fact given up hope of getting its routes or its passengers back from Branson.

While King's verbal salvos captured the headlines and Burnside's press department continued to parrot the company line that the real threat came 'from the American megacarriers', BA was quietly bringing the second arm of a well-planned pincer movement into play against Virgin Atlantic.

Sir Colin Marshall and his route planners defined all of Richard Branson's transatlantic routes as 'core' routes. In BA-speak, 'core' routes are to be 'defended at all costs', on the grounds that if BA lost business on them, the airline would suffer long-term corporate damage. Defining a destination as a 'core route' places it at the top of BA's priority list. Below 'core routes' are 'important' routes, which the company tries to make profitable, and 'tactical' routes which the airline operates only if they are profitable.

By the summer of 1991 Virgin Atlantic had achieved a unique status in the eyes of Lord King and Sir Colin Marshall. All Branson's North Atlantic routes (New York JFK, Newark, Boston, Miami and Los Angeles) were defined as core routes, a view taken of no other airline's flights. Furthermore, all of the transatlantic routes Branson had applied for a licence to fly on, or announced his intention to fly on (San Francisco, Washington, Chicago), were so defined too. BA's decision to 'defend', in other words to attack, all of Branson's actual and potential routes was an indication of the seriousness with which the airline took his challenge. It was also a tribute to the entrepreneur's acuity in selecting some of BA's fattest routes on which to compete. In 1990, BA's Tokyo service and its transatlantic flights from Heathrow to New York's Kennedy Airport, including the Concorde service, Newark, San Francisco and Orlando accounted for 85% of its long-haul operating profit. If Branson had his way, he would soon be flying on all of them. In another move, BA started to discuss whether it should mount extra flights on the routes Branson had won permission to use, by taking up all the available slots.

The department under the most pressure to attack Virgin was Liam Strong's marketing, sales and operations department. It had experienced a torrid time in the build-up to the battle of Heathrow. Just after BA had dedicated Mission Atlantic, a poll for the consumer magazine *Which?* found that while British Airways called itself the 'The World's Favourite Airline', Virgin Atlantic was Britain's favourite airline.

The Consumer Association quizzed 35,000 airline passengers and Virgin Atlantic swept the board, winning high marks for catering, comfort and service. Over half of those who replied said they would definitely recommend Virgin to a friend; less than half said the same of BA. Branson's airline was rated as giving above-average value for money, Lord King's below-average value.

To compound BA's misery, the *Which?* survey divided the world's top fifty airlines into four divisions: Virgin was the only British airline in division one, while BA limped along in the middle of division three. In the same *Which?* survey in 1989, both airlines had been in division two.

Liam Strong read the *Which?* report with alarm and immediately convened yet another special task force to work on countering the Virgin threat. For Strong's 'Virgin Project II' he brought together a high-powered team under the Reverend Jim Callery's head of marketing, Tim Shepherd-Smith. The hastily assembled group worked outside the Mission Atlantic structure, and it was given the specific task of countering the Virgin threat. The group was chaired by Mark Ralf from service delivery. The other members were Sue Moore, general manager of marketing development, Kay Foster from service development and Roger Davies from corporate strategy. Strong told Shepherd-Smith that he thought BA should take Branson's threat very seriously indeed.

Monitoring Virgin's performance swiftly became an obsession in the marketing department. Members of BA staff from the marketing department and beyond were sent on Virgin flights, and told to assess the quality of every aspect of Virgin's service. From check-in to touch-down, the performance of the Virgin crews was scrutinised and the quality of the food and the in-flight entertainment were carefully noted. Some zealous BA reporters even noted how comfortable the Virgin hostesses appeared to be in their uniforms, and drew diagrams showing how the meals and refreshments were displayed on the trays. Others provided a minute-by-minute log of their flights and scrutinised the cabin crews' performance, awarding them marks out of ten.

Within a month Shepherd-Smith was able to circulate BA's senior management with the first fruits of Virgin Project II's deliberations. Entitled simply 'Virgin', the report was divided into two main sections, 'Summary of the Threat' and 'Current Activities to Address the Threat'.

BA's service delivery standards department worked out exactly how Virgin Atlantic made its money in the previous year. The official IATA (International Air Transport Association) passenger breakdowns were now available, and they were supplemented by the more detailed figures BA had been extracting from the computer over the previous year. Notes taken at the group's meetings acknowledge that it was getting the exact breakdown, or 'mix', of passengers unofficially – in other words, from the computer.

The Virgin Project II correctly identified the Gatwick–Newark route as by far Branson's most profitable, accounting for 33% of revenue in 1989–90, despite the launch of BA's new service.

The second section of the paper, 'Current Activities to Address the Threat', details some of the ideas that BA had come up with to counter Virgin's service. Had he been able to read the paper at the time, Branson would have been flattered to know that imitating Virgin's introduction of personal videos was one proposed aim of the Club World Class development due in 1993.

'Additional activities' to counter Virgin included both above- and below-the-belt proposals. The broad thrust of the paper was to target Branson's flights by picking the best crews to provide the best service, and concentrating new product development and enhancement on routes where BA flew head-to-head with Virgin.

However, nestling amongst the list of suggestions was the novel one that BA should 'refuse to carry Virgin passengers when Virgin cancels a flight'. The group had identified one of Virgin's key potential weaknesses. Because Branson had so few planes, it was often difficult to replace an aircraft that had developed a fault. In such cases Virgin would try to place its passengers on other air-lines' flights, and BA would more often than not be the beneficiary as it flies to all of Virgin's destinations. While BA would lose extra revenue by refusing to fly Virgin passengers, the Virgin Project II reasoned that this unusual departure from airline custom and practice could seriously damage Virgin's reputation for dealing efficiently with cancellations.

Equipped with his team's recommendations for action against Branson, Liam Strong prepared himself for Sir Colin Marshall's monthly review of his marketing and operations department's progress. Nothing, however, had prepared the summit of marke-teers, salesmen and operations managers for a presentation by Tony Cook from the marketplace performance department of BA's corporate strategy division. The centrepiece of Cook's contribution was the quarterly *TAPS – Transatlantic Passenger Survey* – con-ducted by IATA. Its quarterly results are always eagerly anticipated.

TAPS provided BA with its most important qualitative infor-mation about its own performance in relation to other airlines. While Jeff Day's Helpliner unit at Gatwick was able to provide BA with instant, if 'unofficial', quantitative data on Virgin Atlantic, Air Europe and Dan Air flights by accessing their computers and impersonating their staff, *TAPS* is the most important indicator of the qualitative mix, and the best guide BA has as to how its brand is faring in the marketplace. This particular *TAPS* was conducted among the thirteen major airlines flying across the Atlantic during the first quarter of 1991, during the Gulf War. Its verdict was crushing for the teams of BA marketeers who were trying to match the appeal of Virgin's brand.

> Virgin reigned supreme in business class . . . for the eighth consecutive quarter they are ranked the top carrier.

After the presentation, the chief executive flicked quietly through Cook's summary. No one wanted to break the uncomfortable silence that had descended on the meeting. After British Caledonian had been swallowed in 1988, no one at BA thought that barely three years later, another British carrier would be competing on the long-haul routes and winning so handsomely.

Virgin was also voted best economy-class carrier, but it was the size of Virgin's lead over BA in business class that appeared to shock Marshall. Virgin Atlantic was the top-ranked transatlantic carrier in no less than seventeen of the twenty-one categories, and second in two of the remaining four. Overall, passengers put Virgin top of both business and economy class with BA coming sixth and seventh respectively. And not only did *TAPS* give Virgin a remarkable overall rating, it also painted a demoralisingly poor picture of what passengers thought of BA. BA's assessment of *TAPS* concluded:

> This quarter has been fairly disappointing for British Airways as Club World has failed to consolidate on the improvements noted last quarter, and the launch of World Traveller has done little to improve our overall position in economy . . . there is little evidence of improvement in the eyes of the passengers.

BA's chief executive was incredulous. Marshall could not believe

that Branson was wiping the floor with BA in almost every department, and ordered Liam Strong to get his Virgin team to conduct
an urgent inquisition into the reliability of the figures.

After a flurry of activity, BA's market-research boffins advised
Marshall and Strong that the results were the most reliable indicator available; they had found nothing to suggest the findings
were inaccurate. Strong informed Marshall that he would take
appropriate action.

Michael Levin's warnings to BA had been spot-on. Despite BA's
best efforts, the 'Grinning Pullover' had come up on the blind side
and outflanked the boys in braces. It was now time to tackle
Branson 'head on', as Marshall's mentor warned might one day be
necessary.

The banner of Mission Atlantic provided the cloak under which
a whole range of activities designed to damage Virgin Atlantic
took place. King and Marshall's troops were sent into battle on the
'core routes' to achieve victory 'at all costs'. Their collective aim
was to undermine Virgin and Branson's financial, personal and
corporate integrity, prevent him flying on any more routes,
swamp his existing routes with excess capacity, and flood the
market with discount fares. Aided by British Airways' vast and
ever-increasing computer fire-power, raiding parties from the
sales force were mustered to target the most profitable of Virgin's
corporate accounts, to identify Upper Class Virgin passengers and
to steal them from travel agents, and from airport terminals, as
they prepared to board Virgin Atlantic planes. Few of the BA
troops on the front line knew the overall plan – foot soldiers rarely
do – or the ultimate objective: to blow Richard Branson out of the
sky. To make sure that no one outside BA pieced together the
plan, strict instructions were issued that all evidence of activities
that took place in the twilight zone should be destroyed.

BA's policy was born, in part, out of desperation. The airline's
revenue continued to nosedive. Following Mrs Thatcher's departure
from Downing Street, and the furious exchanges over the Heathrow
and Tokyo decisions, Lord King and Sir Colin Marshall had given
up hope of getting BA's slots or its passengers back with the help of
the government. BA's free-market and pro-competition rhetoric had
no more meaning in the summer of 1991 than when the airline used

it in relation to Laker, British Caledonian or Air Europe. 'Competition' in the domestic market still meant eliminating BA's competition rather than competing with it, and the only way to achieve this goal on the North Atlantic routes would be to put Virgin Atlantic out of business. Both King and Marshall knew that if Branson flopped at Heathrow, his airline would go under. If he succeeded he would become far more than the 'thorn in our side' Michael Levin had identified only three years beforehand.

When Lord King removed BA's funds from the Tory Party, Will Whitehorn's reaction was to the point.

'He just turned to me', Branson recalls, 'and said, only half jokingly, "This is war".'

Neither Branson nor his press chief knew how right he was. Mission Atlantic's troops had been on manoeuvres all summer and, by the time Lord King addressed his shareholders, BA's 'War on the Atlantic' had already entered its third week. And as hostilities began, some very strange things were starting to happen to some of Virgin's passengers.

Yvonne Parsons found herself in New York on 18 July. As the operations director for a London-based international data-base company, she was on one of her regular swings through the Americas. She had started her punishing schedule by flying to Buenos Aires on BA at the end of June. Now she was looking forward to going home. She was booked on Virgin's night flight out of Newark to Gatwick the following day.

As Parsons sat in her company's New York office putting the final touches to her business, the phone rang:

'Hi, it's Bonnie from Virgin Atlantic here. I'm sorry, but our flight out of Newark tomorrow could be delayed. If you wish, I can book you on the daytime British Airways flight to make sure you get back on schedule.'

'Are you sure there's going to be a delay?' Ms Parsons inquired.

'Pretty sure,' replied Bonnie. 'And if you do decide to transfer, we'll get you into BA first class.'

Parsons couldn't afford to lose her last day in New York. With over twenty Virgin Atlantic flights already under her belt in 1991, she knew the transatlantic timetable backwards. She remembered that Virgin also flew out of Kennedy Airport at night. Parsons decided to risk being delayed and she declined the upgrade to BA first class.

The following day Parsons phoned Virgin Atlantic in New York to check on the possible delay.

'There's no delay, madam,' she was reassured. 'And, Ms Parsons, we have no record of any of our agents phoning you.'

Yvonne Parsons was perplexed but thought no more about the matter.

As Parsons' Virgin limousine took her through the Sussex countryside to her home in Shoreham-on-Sea on 19 July, another of the company's limousines was making its way through heavy London traffic to Heathrow Airport.

Inside was Darren Costin, his band and several boxes of musical equipment. Costin and his fellow musicians were late for their flight to LA for a recording session. They tumbled out of their Virgin limo and rushed towards Virgin's Upper Class check-in desk. There were only forty minutes left before departure. The band, their instrument cases plastered in Virgin stickers, epitomised Branson's success in attracting 'the scruffy rich'.

As Costin checked in he realised he had left his camera in the limo.

'Oh shit!' he cried, and hurtled back to the limousine. As he ran, he noticed a man and a woman were running beside him, one on each shoulder. Both were in British Airways uniform.

'Good morning!' cried the male BA jogger. 'Have you ever considered travelling on another airline?'

'No,' replied Costin, 'at the moment I'm considering that I'm just about to miss my flight!'

The trio jogged on.

'We notice that you have been travelling with Virgin quite frequently.'

'I'm being watched, am I? Spooky.'

The BA reps paused for breath at the exit to Terminal 3. They watched as Costin retrieved his camera from the Virgin limousine. As he sped back into Terminal 3 again they took up the pace:

'BA can offer you a business class seat at an economy fare.'

Costin stopped. Panting, with one hand on his hip and the other clutching the camera now dangling from his neck, he replied, 'Thanks, but no thanks.'

Costin rejoined the band at the Virgin check-in desk. BA's hunters had lost their quarry.

Costin was most probably approached by one of a family of aggressive BA switch-selling teams conceived by Mission Atlantic in the early months of 1991. The idea had emerged from the Reverend Jim Callery's world sales department.

BA told its staff that United Airlines regularly attempted to switch-sell passengers to their own flights in the USA through programmes with the inelegant acronyms of TORQUE (Try Our Real Quality United Experience) and HUG (Help Us Grow). With United due to fly from Heathrow in the summer, BA started recruiting teams to try the same thing; Virgin Atlantic would be the first British airline to be targeted in what Jim Callery called 'Protecting Our Business'.

As with much of the rhetoric surrounding the language of Mission Atlantic, the phrase had a double meaning. To Virgin Atlantic 'Protecting Our Business' quickly came to mean 'Stealing Our Passengers'.

BA's sales department set the mobile teams a target of over £1 million in their first financial year. The Heathrow teams were designed to roam the terminals 'hunting', 'poaching' or 'prospecting' for passengers. Their job specifications required an ability to use the computer systems on which BA and its rivals placed their sensitive booking details. With airside passes the poachers could roam throughout the Heathrow terminals seeking their prey in the baggage halls and arrivals terminals – for transferring passengers – as well as at the piers and gates.

In the language of the 'War on the Atlantic', BA tried to build a highly trained team whose 'interface with the competition' took place behind enemy lines 'in the heart of enemy territory'.

The teams were led by Chris Maude, a marketing and sales manager in the customer services department. To the intense annoyance of BA's management, the team swiftly became known as 'Maude's Marauders', after BA's *Cabin Crew News* coined the phrase. Maude told his bosses he was furious.

'I will obviously try to limit the damage but we must squash this nickname at every opportunity. Part of the learning curve of now being in an aggressive, competitive marketplace.'

BA was worried that if its sales agents were seen to be switch-selling passengers from other carriers, the exercise would backfire. Exposure of the switch-selling would undermine the good relationships they were simultaneously trying to build with the carriers whose passengers they were stealing.

'We won't last five minutes in Terminal 3 if we are *seen* as aggressive,' Maude warned his colleagues. 'We would be accused of poaching . . . it would make the staff's role undo-able.'

Maude clearly felt he needed highly skilled staff to perform the clandestine activities required of his teams. Maude set about recruiting his Mission Atlantic agents from experienced BA staff with at least two years 'passenger contact experience' behind them, as well as 'good communication and interpersonal skills'. Sensitivity would be required from agents, who would have to establish good personal rapport with the ground staff of other airlines while attempting to steal their passengers when the opportunity arose.

The Marauders were told to hunt revenue for BA in a number of different ways. When other airlines' flights were seriously delayed, cancelled or overbooked, the Marauders offered seats on a BA flight – this would bring extra revenue to BA and help the airlines with disrupted flights out of difficulties. In airline jargon, the Marauders were trying to establish BA as their rivals' 'preferred alternative carrier'; passengers lured to BA when rivals' flights were cancelled provided 'disruption revenue' for the sales teams.

The Marauders' predatory work was clandestine: Mission Atlantic agents would sidle up to passengers travelling with competitors to try and devour their business by switch-selling them to BA. The Marauders did not waste their energies on bargain-basement ticket-holders who had bought non-transferable tickets from bucket-shops. Instead, the powerful BABS computer was brought into play to aid the switch-sellers and make sure the Marauders targeted only high-yield, business-class passengers.

Static Marauders would use BABS to find the computer records of BA's and rivals' flights to try and establish the target passengers' itineraries. The Marauders' task would then be to identify the travellers from their baggage tags, incoming flight number or, in the case of Virgin, limousine drop-off point – and try to persuade the passenger to switch to British Airways.

Internal correspondence between the Marauders identified the best places to poach passengers – normally out of sight of the airlines the travellers held tickets for.

The Marauders were dressed in BA uniform, which gave them instant authority with passengers and helped them to gain their confidence before they started the hard-sell. The Marauders were also equipped with radio links to increase the speed of poaching and reduce the visibility of the operation. If an agent succeeded in making a switch-sale, the passenger's ticket could be automatically 'endorsed' without the need to go to the relevant ticket desk in another part of the terminal. Once the Marauders had latched on to a sale in this way, the passenger's name, address and contact numbers would be entered into the computer so the passenger could be tracked in future.

If necessary, a range of bribes and incentives, such as ticket upgrades, would be available if the targeted passenger needed persuading to abandon Virgin Atlantic or one of the American carriers. The switch-sellers described the money they gained for BA in this way as 'endorsed revenue'.

While BA's Marauders moved into action against Virgin and the Americans at Heathrow, the airline kept a sharp lookout for any rival that tried to switch-sell its own passengers away from BA.

On the first day of United Airline's operations at Heathrow on 3 April 1991, some BA staff claimed that United representatives were trying to do just that, in Terminal 1. They were told to alert Robert Ayling's legal department immediately if they came across any further evidence of American airlines importing their hard-sell techniques to Heathrow. Publicly, BA expressed outrage at such activities. An edition of *Mission Atlantic News*, an internal BA bulletin, in the summer of 1991 caught the mood of self-righteous indignation:

. . . As an indication of the sort of tactics we may be up against, we are told that in the States it seems to be acceptable practice for airlines to poach passengers directly from other carriers' check-in and reservation queues!

By the time Virgin Atlantic launched from Heathrow, BA had not only set up covert teams to ape the switch-selling it claimed to be shocked by, it had also devised other methods of trying to steal Virgin passengers before they got anywhere near their terminals.

Caroline Mickler works for Copyright Promotions Ltd in London and she frequently flies abroad on business. At the beginning of July she booked a round trip to Tokyo Narita. She was to fly out on BA but asked her travel agent to book her back on Virgin. She thought she would try out Virgin's much trumpeted new Tokyo–Heathrow service. The day after Costin's experience with BA's mobile sales team at Heathrow, Caroline Mickler was called by British Airways.

'Hello. It's John Danks here from British Airways Latitudes Club. I am phoning to let you know that we have a special offer on at the moment. If you change your return flight from Virgin to BA and join our Latitudes Club, we will give you two free return tickets to Paris.'

Mickler instructed her travel agent to re-book her return flight on BA, and Danks said he would put the tickets and a Latitudes application form in the post.

The increased competition between British airlines at Heathrow had brought unexpected dividends for Mickler. She became one of the early beneficiaries of 'Operation Switch-Sell'. As Branson posed as a pirate for the cameras by the briefly 'Virginised' model of Concorde, teams of BA telemarketing agents were starting a massive switch-selling campaign designed to steal his newly-won Heathrow passengers to the Far East and across the Atlantic.

Mickler's 'switching' had been done by a BA telephone sales agent working for the 'Latitudes Far East Campaign'. BA's Latitudes Club was one of the key innovations the airline intro-duced to meet the challenge of the new American carriers at Heathrow. One of the key reasons for American Airlines' success in becoming a megacarrier was its pioneering frequent-flyer scheme, American Advantage. Since its introduction in the early

1970s, AAdvantage had been copied by airlines all over the world. Most airlines now have similar frequent-flyer schemes to reward regular travellers, and to try and retain their loyalty. When passengers have totted up a certain number of 'airmiles' they can trade them in for upgrades, free tickets and related travel facilities, such as car-hire or hotel accommodation. Virgin Atlantic runs Virgin Freeway along similar lines. Airmiles accumulated by Virgin passengers can be traded in for free flights or exchanged for other benefits from other parts of the Virgin empire. Such schemes are very popular with passengers who travel regularly at their company's expense – they don't have to pay for their tickets but they do reap the benefits that frequent-flyer schemes bring, as in the case of Caroline Mickler. BA's marketing experts argued strongly that BA should introduce a similar scheme or risk business travellers deserting in droves when American started flying out of Heathrow.

The key problem BA faced with Virgin was the strength of its brand. As a result the Reverend Jim had sent his sales teams into action in a bid to compensate for the failure of the boys in braces to develop a brand image to challenge Branson's.

His staff remember the Reverend Jim as a galleon in full sail in the summer of 1991, clerical robes flowing as he swept around Speedbird House urging his sales teams into battle. Revenue was falling and the comfort zone had become a dangerous area to be caught lounging around in.

'Cascade to your selling teams!' cried the American as he swept through the offices of BA's Heathrow HQ. 'Does making money turn you on?!' he screamed at one of his sales team who left the airline shortly afterwards, distinctly unaroused by the prospect of making it with the Reverend Jim. Many others suffered Callery's bizarre mixture of hard-sell and TV-style evangelism in silence.

The approach the Reverend Jim's telephone switch-sellers were told to adopt appeared to be: 'If you can't beat Branson's product, try and bribe his passengers'.

The stated purpose of the sales department's phone-bashing campaign was to persuade passengers, particularly those flying first or business class, to join the Latitudes Club. The actual purpose was to take them from Virgin Atlantic and other carriers.

Membership of the Latitudes Club was free. Two schemes that started on the day of Virgin Atlantic's Heathrow launch had been very carefully thought out; between them they covered all Virgin Atlantic's destinations to Japan and North America. Passengers who switched to BA from any of Branson's flights were rewarded with lashings of bonus airmiles. Virgin's Tokyo passengers could win *triple* airmiles by switching to BA, as could passengers to Miami, Boston, and New York's JFK and Newark airports.

Virgin passengers who switched to BA to fly to LA could win up to six times the normal allocation of airmiles. Thus a business traveller who flew first class to LA at his company's expense on BA would be rewarded with 1,350 airmiles (as opposed to the normal 225) – more than enough for two return tickets to Paris. A club-class ticket would yield 900 airmiles (150) and an economy ticket 450 (75).

The bonus Latitudes airmiles were powerful weapons in the hands of BA's telephone switch-sellers as they played their part in the 'defence' of BA's 'core routes'. The telemarketing teams did, however, experience some difficulty in getting hold of rival airlines' passengers.

Many of the contacts that Callery's teams required for passengers flying out with BA and back with Virgin could be obtained from BABS. Travel agents either put their own contact numbers, or that of the passenger, straight onto the computer. Virgin's Upper Class passengers have to give the airline contact numbers and addresses so the drivers of the complimentary limousines know where to pick them up, and so that they can be advised of any changes to their schedule.

Encouraged to 'Smile-As-You-Dial', the Reverend Jim's telemarketing teams were urged to get on first-name terms with passengers once they finally got through to them before starting their switch-selling pitch or offering Latitudes membership. In doing so, BA's publicly stated competitive ethics regarding the use of computer information simply dissolved.

The man Jim Callery appointed to head his switch-selling effort was David Noyes, BA's general manager for telephone sales in the UK. Noyes had been part of the BA delegation which gave evidence to the House of Commons' 1988 transport committee looking into the uses and abuses of computer reservations systems. After their exhaustive hearings, the MPs' first recommendation was that 'customer information belongs to the travel agent and should not be accessed by the CRS owner'.

The MPs also noted that travel agents as well as airlines were concerned by the potential abuse of computer reservation systems:

> [agents] are concerned about security of customer information which may be stored on the CRS . . . This abuse is something system designers can and should prevent.

The BA delegation of which Noyes was a part nodded in agreement. At that time BA was extremely concerned about the computer power the American airline industry was just about to unleash.

'No competitive advantage should accrue to the owner of a computer reservation system,' stated the BA delegation emphatically.

Now, under pressure from Marshall and King to strike back at Branson, Noyes and his team of telemarketing sales agents abandoned the airline's pledges to Parliament. Not only did BA use information from its own CRS to try and pinch Branson's passengers, it also spent a great deal of time devising methods of extracting information about its rivals' passengers from travel agents when their details were not available from the computer.

BA spent the summer preparing carefully worded scripts to help the Latitudes telemarketing agents wheedle passenger contact numbers out of the travel agents who had taken the bookings. The agents first had to employ another new entry into the Mission Atlantic dictionary of double-speak, 'flight-firming'.

Callery's smiling diallers read from prepared scripts:

> It is important that I speak to Mr/Mrs/Ms . . . to check that he/she will definitely be travelling with us . . .

This was not true. 'Flight-firming' was not part of the telephone teams' written brief. It was a ruse to try to get the contact phone numbers for passengers whose flight-plans included a non-BA sector.

If the travel agent did not surrender the contact number, the agents' prepared scripts told them to say that BA wanted to get in contact with the passengers in question to offer membership of Latitudes. If the travel agents still resisted, the BA telesales teams were told to close the conversation politely. What the travel agents were never told was that once in contact with passengers, like Caroline Mickler, the telesales team would try and switch-sell the passenger's non-BA sector to BA.

The Latitudes team reported to Graham Stokes, a commercial manager in the telephone sales department. Like Chris Maude's mobile Marauders, Stokes was aware his operation lay somewhere between what rival carriers would regard as sharp practice and illegality. With its massive domination of the domestic airline market, middle managers like Maude and Stokes had both had the dangers of infringing US anti-trust laws drummed into them regularly by BA.

That BA was aware of the potential legal problems it could run into with switch-selling was clearly demonstrated shortly after the assault on Branson's routes started in earnest at the beginning of July. A BA passenger told a member of the telemarketing team that he had been the subject of an attempted switch-sell by American Airlines. Graham Stokes immediately got in touch with Robert Ayling's legal department. He was told to try and secretly record the telephone conversation the next time contact was made with the passenger. Unfortunately for BA he did not return the call.

Unusually for a woman who took twenty-six Virgin Atlantic flights in 1991, Yvonne Parsons flew to New York on BA at the end of September. She was travelling with her boss to Kennedy Airport, so she went along with his preference for BA. For the return leg, on 27 September, she made sure her office booked her on Virgin Atlantic.

On 26 September, Parsons got a call in her company's New York office from Virgin reservations to say that the airline couldn't guarantee the non-smoking seat her office had booked for her. Parsons was irritated. She is an asthmatic and she had never had any problem getting an Upper Class non-smoking seat before.

The Virgin rep announced himself as Larry. 'We can get you on

BA's flight to Heathrow, Ms Parsons, and put you in First Class. We can also offer you triple airmiles on the BA Latitudes scheme.'

Parsons refused the offer and asked to be wait-listed on both the Virgin flights. Larry said he would call her back.

As she put the phone down it crossed Parsons' mind that it was rather odd for Virgin to be offering BA airmiles. She thought no more about it until the following day when she phoned Virgin to check if she had got her non-smoking seat. To her astonishment she experienced the same blank response from the Virgin reservations office as she had received in July.

'There's no one here called Larry, Ms Parsons, and we have no record of a call to you advising you of a problem. We have you confirmed in non-smoking on tomorrow's flight out of Newark to Gatwick.'

After being messed around by Branson's airline twice in less than three months, Parsons was cross.

'Virgin are usually very efficient but after two identical mix-ups I wondered what was happening to them. They were fine at 35,000 feet but a shambles on the ground.'

This was exactly the impression BA had been trying to create since Virgin's move to Heathrow.

In early August, Will Whitehorn was sitting in Virgin's cramped Campden Hill Road office one sweltering morning when his assistant, Mo Foster, put a call through to him from the *Daily Telegraph*.

'Hi, Will! It's Damien McCrystal here, from the *Telegraph* City desk. Sorry to bother you but I've picked up a lead that a lot of your flights out of Heathrow were late leaving last month. Naturally there's some interest here after your spectacular launch and so on.'

'I'm pretty certain we weren't any later than anyone else, Damien. I'll check it out and get back to you. By the way, where did you pick this one up from?'

'Well, you know I can't really tell you that, Will,' replied McCrystal.

'I bet it was BA, wasn't it?' inquired Whitehorn.

'No comment. Well . . . put it this way, it came as a result of a lunch, and the lunch wasn't with Virgin!'

Whitehorn's suspicions were well founded. The story had come directly from BA. David Burnside's number two, Tony Cocklin, discovered that the computer print-out was showing that Virgin Atlantic's punctuality in the first month of its Heathrow operation was dreadful. The figures indicated that it was the worst of *all* the airlines operating out of Heathrow in July. Airlines officially have to wait six months until they know their rivals' punctuality figures, when IATA publishes them. Placing the story at the beginning of 1992 would have done nothing to alleviate the pressure on the public affairs operation in the summer of 1991, so Cocklin gave the details to Brian Basham to do with as he saw fit.

Over lunch at the Savoy Grill, Basham then gave the *Daily Telegraph*'s City editor, Neil Collins, the delayed-departures story. It was passed on to Damien McCrystal to chase.

Whitehorn immediately checked the *Daily Telegraph*'s claims about the airline's punctuality. The summer of 1991 was chaotic at Heathrow. International air traffic was only just beginning to get back to normal after the Gulf War, and the disruption caused by the introduction of several new airlines. Whitehorn established the take-off times of every Virgin flight out of Heathrow in July and found that the potentially damaging story was untrue. In common with other airlines, there were delays, but Virgin's overall performance was about average for the month. Whitehorn was quite pleased, considering Virgin had never flown from Heathrow before. He phoned McCrystal and read him the figures.

McCrystal jotted them down. As they flatly contradicted BA's claims, he phoned Basham again and challenged him to stand his story up in the light of Whitehorn's evidence. Basham, in turn, went to his source.

'I went back to Burnside at BA and asked for more details. Tony Cocklin gave me a complete breakdown of every airline's departure time from Heathrow that week. Branson was far and away bottom,' Basham recalled. He was on the point of giving the print-out to the *Daily Telegraph*. However, as he prepared to fax the figures to McCrystal, he got a call from Burnside.

'David told me that I shouldn't give the detailed breakdown to the *Telegraph* under any circumstances. He'd just discovered that the information had come out of the computer, and that we shouldn't have it.'

Basham was now in a quandary. He had been told to try and place the story by BA, he had excited the *Telegraph*'s interest, but now was unable to back the story up: very embarrassing. Basham was forced to return empty-handed to McCrystal. The *Telegraph* dropped the story on the grounds that the only evidence available – Whitehorn's – contradicted BA's claims.

The public affairs department was at the start of its learning curve on how best to handle sensitive computer data. At Virgin, both Branson and Whitehorn breathed a sigh of relief when they heard that the departure-times story would not be in the paper. Although both suspected that BA was behind the false rumour, they had no proof. The journalists on the *Telegraph* would not reveal their sources, despite coming under pressure from Virgin to do so.

For Burnside, Cocklin and Basham, the departure-times incident was worrying. Burnside had assured BA's board, and its senior management, at their annual retreat before the AGM that the departure-times story would soon be running in the press. The botched attempt to get it into the *Telegraph* reflected badly on public affairs and Brian Basham. Virgin Project I and Virgin Project II, as well as Mission Atlantic, had all identified the media as one of the key ways to hit back at Branson. By the late summer, Burnside had nothing very substantial to show for his efforts.

The public affairs department's strenuous efforts against Branson were, however, gradually being noticed by other BA departments. Because much of the anti-Virgin plotting took place at the very highest level, at Lord King's offices at Enserch House and in Sir Colin's suite at Speedbird House – outside the regular structure of Mission Atlantic – only those who needed to know did know. Generals don't make a habit of keeping their troops informed on every detail of strategy, particularly when they are hoping to take their enemy by surprise.

However, in the summer of 1991 eyebrows were raised throughout BA when it was discovered how earnestly the public affairs department was attacking Virgin. A massive internal review of the national carrier's overall competitor-monitoring activities took place. Scores of the airline's managers and executives were interviewed, as well as representatives of major companies outside the airline industry, such as Ford, Guinness, Unilever and GEC. The object of the review was to establish if BA would compete better with its rivals throughout the world by creating a central competitor unit.

It was a summer of relentless interviewing and study. The review eventually concluded that there was 'general dissatisfaction with BA's current competitor-monitoring and appraisal processes' – finding them badly coordinated, and discovering areas of duplication, particularly with regard to Virgin Atlantic.

Considerable resources were being devoted to competitor monitoring. Few managers interviewed outside Burnside's department knew it was involved in the monitoring of competitors at all, until Burnside himself and Cocklin were interviewed as part of the review. Their interviews revealed BA's hidden Virgin agenda. Although 'The World's Favourite Airline' was just about to take on American and United in its own back yard, BA's tiny British competitor dominated the conversations.

Cocklin said he had already set up a competitor project on Virgin in the public affairs department. Its task was to draw together as much publicly and privately available information about Virgin as possible. This enabled Burnside and himself to brief King and Marshall on competitive strategies, and also to pre-empt, as well as to respond to, press stories on Virgin. Both Burnside and Cocklin suggested that pro-active PR against Branson was called for, and stressed that they needed much more information from other departments about his performance if this was to be achieved. Burnside said he was particularly keen not to give up his direct line to King and Marshall on competitive issues.

In the measured tones that internal BA communications are prone to adopt, the review recorded its 'considerable surprise' at these activities.

Cocklin told the review panel that he needed to know more about Virgin's punctuality, load factors and customer service standards so that he and Burnside could better advise Lord King and Sir Colin Marshall on how BA's anti-Virgin strategy should proceed. By the summer Cocklin was getting the information he required on Virgin from the all-seeing eyes of the computers in the marketing and operations department.

The irony of the botched attempt to place the *Telegraph* story was that when the official IATA figures were released six months later, they showed that Virgin's record *was* average for the month. Whitehorn was able to disprove the unsubstantiated claims BA gave Basham simply by going through Virgin's own records. The BA computer had got it wrong.

BABS is not capable of registering when a plane takes off, only when it pushes back from its stand. Virgin planes *were* late pushing back but not taking off, which is the key criterion by which passengers judge an airline's performance. Apparently, more seasoned operators push back as soon as they can to achieve a good computer rating for their departure record, and to save money – airlines cease paying for the hire of their 'gates' as soon as they push back. Such tactics explain why passengers often have to endure long waits between pushback and take-off.

The public affairs department's fumbling was not appreciated by members of BA's most senior management. Burnside found himself coming under pressure to explain why the departure-times story did not appear as he promised it would. It *was* rather difficult to explain.

Shortly after the *Telegraph* decided to drop the late-departures story, Burnside and Basham sat in conference in Enserch House. Robert Ayling sauntered into the room. Remembering Burnside's promises to publicise the late departure of Virgin's planes the previous month, he teased the two of them.

'Well, well . . . the world's two greatest PR men and you can't get a simple story about Branson being late out of Heathrow into the papers. Whatever has become of you?'

'Fuck off, Bob!' retorted Burnside. 'You know bloody well we got those figures out of the computer and that Brian can't give them straight to the press.'

'You give me the clearance and I'll get the story in the press tomorrow,' added Basham.

'I don't think that would be a very good idea,' Ayling replied sheepishly, before retreating from Burnside's lair.

Within BA itself the rumour-mill had moved up a gear. To

complement Lord King's grumpy muck-spreading in the City, and the airline's pressure on Basham to plant anti-Virgin stories, BA had its own in-house computer gossip sheet, which had the unlikely acronym of CIDER. CIDER provided its readers with a chatty update on the latest developments in other carriers, and inevitably Virgin featured prominently during 1991.

The computer screens from which it could be accessed reminded BA staff that CIDER was 'strictly confidential' and for 'internal use only'. BA staff were encouraged to make contributions of their own to CIDER. All they had to do was to 'press the F6 key'. With the 'internal use only' disclaimer, CIDER became a very good way of circulating gossip about Virgin. The information contained on it was often unsourced and unchecked – the F6 key was, after all, open to anyone.

As Lord King's fury with Branson rose, CIDER reported:

> Virgin's costs cannot fail to rise . . . the fleet will also have to expand and this will involve further financial outlay and commitment with no immediate return on investment.
>
> Virgin has serious ambitions for long-haul expansion, but there is a real danger of it overstretching itself . . . with route and fleet expansion being a drain on resources, Virgin is going to be increasingly more dependent on the North Atlantic for its profits for the next couple of years. Any downturn could therefore very quickly prove disastrous to Virgin.

In September 1991, another report revealed: 'Virgin To Lay Off Cabin Crew'. Claiming the rumour came from Gatwick, CIDER also claimed that Branson had pulled out of a deal to obtain an extra 747. All these claims came from an anonymous source but anyone with access to the BA computer could read them. None of them was true but the claims soon started working their way through to the grassroots of the airline community at Gatwick and Heathrow. From there, they spread round the world.

A week after the unsourced CIDER rumours about Virgin, a small figure clad in black leather dodged through London's morning rush-hour traffic on a motorbike. Brian Basham had

abandoned his chauffeur-driven limousine after hearing traffic
bulletins warning of severe hold-ups on the Westway, out of
London. He was determined not to be late for a crucial appointment with Robert Ayling. Sir Colin Marshall had just promoted
Ayling to head of marketing and operations in the wake of Liam
Strong's departure. Strong had left to take up the post of chief
executive at Sears – the retail group Colin Marshall left to join BA
in 1983.

Both in their mid-forties, Strong and Ayling had been tipped as
potential successors to the fifty-seven-year-old Marshall as chief
executive. The former civil servant who had joined BA in 1985
with no previous business experience was now the third most
powerful man in BA, and the favourite to succeed Sir Colin if
and when he slipped into Lord King's shoes. Ayling joined the
board and took responsibility for the marketing, sales and operations departments, and thus for guiding Mission Atlantic. Until a
successor as legal director was appointed, he retained his legal
brief.

Possibly hoping that the frictions of the summer might be eased,
David Burnside had suggested to Ayling that he should have a
detailed discussion with Basham about Operation Barbara. Ayling
was working hard on BA's case against Branson's application for
another of BA's slots at Tokyo, so Virgin could fly daily to the
Japanese capital. After BA's failure to stop Branson expanding at
the beginning of the year, to say nothing of Lord King's volcanic
reaction, the symbolic importance of Branson's application could
not be underestimated.

Basham arrived slightly late for the meeting, and Ayling was
surprised to spot BA's leading PR consultant making his way
through Speedbird House security with a crash helmet under
his arm.

Ayling was familiar with Basham's report, and the two men
discussed the apparent weaknesses of Branson's corporate structure and the progress of Basham's 'daylight test'. The word in the
City was that Branson had now started his search for an equity
partner in earnest. With the CAA hearing due shortly, BA was
concerned to continue to present as negative a picture as possible
of Virgin's capabilities of filling the slots it was bidding for.

Both men were convinced that the redistribution of BA's slots, post-privatisation, was wrong in principle and that BA should spare no effort to ensure it did not happen in practice.

After thirty minutes the meeting drew to a close. Basham told Ayling how he was busy briefing selected journalists on his report. The PR man argued that he had no problem about telling them that he had produced the report for BA. Ayling disagreed, and before Basham left the room, Ayling warned him not to brief the report on the record:

'Robert sucked his teeth and said no, I shouldn't do it.'

As Richard Branson started his bid to expand Virgin Atlantic yet further, BA's hidden persuader remained quietly and anonymously 'off the record'.

7

Branson's Black October

Richard Branson was drying his hair after a lunchtime swim in the basement of his Holland Park home when he got upstairs to his office. Autumn sunlight streamed through the huge windows and flooded the end of the huge oak table where his notes and correspondence were scattered. As Branson eased himself into the straight-backed wooden armchair from which he works, a note from Emma Dona, one of his assistants, caught his eye. She had taken a call from a journalist who wanted to talk to him and she had transcribed what the journalist said.

'Had a telephone call from somebody who wanted to spread some malicious gossip – from a large corporation, you can guess who. Tell Richard he doesn't need me to tell him who it is.'

'I certainly don't,' thought Branson and carried on drying his hair.

'Malicious gossip', indeed; he had no concrete proof, but he was becoming convinced that British Airways was at the root of it.

Another Frank Kane article in the *Sunday Telegraph* on the eve of Virgin's Heathrow launch carried the headline, 'Virgin heads for Heathrow Dogfight'. Indeed, the dogfight had already started in the City pages of the national press. Since the Heathrow launch on 1 July, Will Whitehorn's operation in Campden Hill Road had been inundated by a stream of negative calls from journalists. The

Daily Telegraph's query about Virgin Atlantic's punctuality marked the start of a series of inquiries from City desks and the trade press. Whitehorn noted that an alarmingly high proportion of journalists were chasing negative leads about Branson himself. They were also phoning up with inquiries about the airline's reliability, its performance in the air and, increasingly, the state of its finances.

'There was a level of press interest in Virgin Atlantic greater than I had ever previously encountered,' recalled Branson. 'Not even the launch of the airline in 1984, or the flotation of the Virgin Group, generated as many calls.'

As Branson tried to pilot Virgin Atlantic out of the recession and the potentially catastrophic impact of the Gulf War, the City rumour-mill was in full swing. It particularly irked Branson that this coincided with his decision to expand Virgin Atlantic. In September he had formally agreed terms with Lord Young's merchant bank, Salomons. Fraser Marcus and his team had been commissioned to sell a 20% equity stake in Virgin Atlantic. Branson hoped Salomons would be able to raise £50 million from the sale.

Branson knew it was inevitable that when investors were invited to purchase a sizeable equity stake in his airline, questions would be asked about not only Virgin Atlantic but the Virgin Group as a whole. The problem was that, as Marcus and his team at Salomons started to get the prospectus together, they found that the damaging rumours about the health of Virgin Atlantic's finances were taking root. Other contacts backed Salomons' observations. Some sources said the rumours were coming direct from Lord King and BA.

Branson knew by the beginning of October that the future of the Virgin Group was now firmly on the agenda of the City pages of the serious newspapers. On 2 October, the *Guardian* devoted a whole page of its influential finance and economics section to an article highly critical of the group. 'Will Richard Branson's Balloon Burst?' ran the headline, with two sub-headings: '. . . behind the man with the Midas touch, there is a picture of a highly indebted and not-very-profitable conglomerate', and 'The melody lingers but it won't meet investment needs'. The picture the *Guardian* used was of an uncharacteristically forlorn-looking Branson gazing at a model of a Virgin 747. The conclusion of the article was unequivocal:

> The Branson balloon appears to be pursuing a dangerous path to the stratosphere . . . [and] Mr Branson's balloon journeys are unfortunate models for any business to follow.

Branson found it hard to imagine a more damaging or badly timed article. He got the *Guardian* to give him space to defend his companies the following week against what he saw a 'grossly distorted analysis'. The *Guardian* also printed an apology, but Branson was annoyed at having to undergo what he saw as ill-informed public scrutiny.

The fun of being in the airline business was beginning to have its down side. When Branson picked up the 'World's Best Business Class' award for the fourth year running at the *Business Traveller* awards ceremony, he also picked up the presenter of the award – Ivana Trump, the estranged wife of billionaire property developer Donald Trump. In a moment of exuberance, Branson turned her upside down, ensuring that pictures of himself and the inverted billionaire's wife featured in much of the tabloid press the following day. Ivana Trump quipped: 'I'm sure glad I wasn't wearing my G-string today!'

At the lunch that followed the presentation of the awards, Ivana Trump sat next to Lord King. Within hours Virgin received a faxed complaint from Trump about Richard Branson's behaviour. Branson was convinced King had put her up to it; he responded by placing adverts in the press highlighting the 'Best Business Class' award, with the punchline 'Virgin turns up Trumps again!'

Branson even took to including a set-piece joke about his deteriorating relationship with Lord King whenever he made a formal speech:

'Lord King came to my office the other day and asked to see me. My secretary told him that I was dead, so he went away. The following day he called again and asked to see me. Once again he was told I was dead. He called for a third time the next day and asked to see me. For the third time my secretary said I was dead and asked Lord King why he kept coming round asking to see me. Lord King replied, "I know he's dead, but I just like to hear you say it!"'

Beneath the banter, Branson was worried about the impact of the rumours on Virgin Atlantic's prospects. When he read his assistant's note, he was not surprised to read that the 'malicious gossip' was coming from 'a large corporation'. He was, however, surprised to discover that the message was from Chris Hutchins, a gossip columnist on the *Today* newspaper. Branson had not seen or heard anything from Hutchins for a couple of years, but he vividly remembered the last time they spoke – or failed to speak.

'Arise Sir Richard', the *Today* front page bellowed in 1989. Underneath Chris Hutchins' byline was the revelation that the Queen had decided to knight Branson. It wasn't true. Furthermore, Hutchins wrote the story without speaking to Branson or his office.

Branson continued to receive mail addressed to 'Sir Richard Branson'. Others had suffered far worse indignities in the figment of tabloid imagination, and the incident hadn't bothered Branson. However, Hutchins' failure to perform the most basic of journalistic functions – checking facts – had not done much for Branson's view of him. But as he reread the message, any reservations Branson held about Hutchins' professional abilities were overcome by his concern to get to the bottom of the rumour campaign. Maybe the gossip columnist had picked up some tittle-tattle.

Branson dialled Hutchins' number.

'Richard, first of all I want you to know that I've done Alcoholics Anonymous,' Hutchins began. 'I'm clean, so you can take what I say seriously.'

Hutchins had had a serious alcohol and drug problem for years, which had damaged his career. His personal plight became widely known among journalists and by many of his contacts, hence the self-deprecating introduction. He continued:

'I had a call from Brian Basham. He's a BA PR man. He is to Lord King what Tim Bell is to Hanson. I know Basham's wife Eileen quite well, as she used to work for me here at the paper. She phoned me first to say that Brian has a good story about "Branson and drugs".

'Anyway, when I rang Basham, he said he had been doing a

detailed study for BA on Virgin's operations. He said BA wanted
to stop Virgin getting any bigger. It wanted to stop Virgin getting
refinancing from Japan. Basically, BA was looking for a scandal
story. Basham mentioned Heaven, and suggested I check out the
drug position there. He told me I should also look at the recent
piece in the *Guardian* on your cash position.

'He *also* told me that BA didn't want to be seen to have your
blood on its hands.'

Branson was shocked. He found it difficult to take in everything Hutchins was saying to him. He had never heard of Brian
Basham. Other journalists he had quizzed about the origins of the
rumours always refused to reveal their sources.

Branson's instant reaction was to suggest that Hutchins should
turn the tables and investigate BA. Maybe this would be a way of
flushing out the rumour-mongering. Hutchins parried that idea. It
was one thing to tip Richard Branson off about rumour-mongering,
it was another to start investigating the 'World's Favourite Airline'.
After all, it was Basham's wife who had given him the tip-off.
Hutchins knew that gossip columns don't flourish by blowing contacts. Hutchins also had personal reasons to be grateful to the
Bashams. When he was in the grip of alcoholism, Eileen was kind
to him. She covered for him at work on *Today* newspaper and
helped him gain admittance to a clinic for treatment.

At the end of the conversation with Branson, Hutchins said that
the most he could do would be to put the idea of investigating BA
to his editor, Martin Dunn. Under pressure from Branson he also
agreed to drop in at Holland Park the following day with detailed
notes he had taken while he was speaking to Basham.

As soon as he had finished speaking to Hutchins, Branson
phoned Will Whitehorn.

'Chris Hutchins!' Whitehorn roared with laughter. 'He's the
bloke that did that "Arise Sir Richard" story about you in 1989. I
wouldn't trust him at all.'

Despite his jocularity, Whitehorn had much less charitable
memories than Branson about *Today*'s 'Arise Sir Richard' fantasy.
Branson's press officer was woken at midnight by the Press
Association soon after the early edition of *Today* hit the streets. He
had to spend the next forty-eight hours flatly denying the story to

a host of callers from all over the world. Whitehorn eventually extracted an apology from the editor of *Today*, but the incident damaged the relationship between Virgin and the newspaper.

'Well, I don't know if Hutchins thinks he owes us one,' Branson continued, 'but he's just phoned up to tell me who's behind BA's rumour campaign against us.'

'Really?' Whitehorn listened with renewed interest.

Whitehorn was by now fed up with having to deny fictitious rumours about Virgin Atlantic. He had just finished reassuring *The Times*' veteran aviation correspondent, Harvey Elliott, that Virgin Atlantic was not on the point of announcing massive redundancies.

'Have you ever heard of a PR man called Bingham?' Branson asked Whitehorn.

'Who?'

Branson looked down at his notebook. 'Brian . . . Bingham or is it . . . Basham?'

'Brian Basham? Yes, I certainly have,' replied Whitehorn.

'Well, Hutchins claims BA is employing Bash-am to bash us!', Branson joked weakly.

'Oh, Christ!' said Whitehorn. 'BA aren't using him, are they?'

'Apparently so,' replied Branson, who then started to relate his conversation with Hutchins.

Whitehorn began to feel ill. He had worked in financial PR in the mid-1980s with Lombard Communications. At the time Basham and his Broad Street company were in their prime. Whitehorn was well aware of Brian Basham's reputation, remembering him as a legend in the world of financial PR, renowned both for his roguish charm and unscrupulous methods of operation. And now he was on Branson's case.

Two hours later Richard Branson was in Will Whitehorn's car heading for London Weekend Television for an appearance on Clive Anderson's Channel 4 chat show. Branson and Whitehorn talked incessantly, often simultaneously, sometimes getting on each other's nerves as they wrestled with the Hutchins development. If what Hutchins was saying was true, much of the last few months began to fit into place. Could Basham really be the hidden hand behind BA's campaign?

Branson had been working since four o'clock that morning. He had preempted the dawn chorus to present an early-morning chat show on the London Broadcasting Corporation (LBC), standing in for Angela Rippon. By the time Branson started his television interview with Clive Anderson in the evening he was feeling low and was quite unable to respond to the teasing barrister. Hutchins' phrase about BA not wanting to be seen to have 'his blood on their hands' was pounding through his brain. Towards the end of the interview Anderson had Branson on the ropes, digging him gently in the ribs about British Airways. Branson snapped. Seizing a glass of water from the table between the two of them, he poured it over Anderson's head.

Whitehorn was watching the recording from the gallery.

'I think that was the moment when I realised just how the dirty-tricks affair was getting to Richard. Of course, no one in the studio had any idea of what was really on his mind. Anderson and the audience just assumed it was one of his less funny pranks. But I was in the gallery watching his face closely on a TV monitor and there was anger etched in his expression.'

After light hospitality and routine apologies, an unusually sombre Branson made his way to Whitehorn's South London home where the two chewed on the situation and slices of takeaway pizza.

The following morning Branson was up at four o'clock again to stand in for Angela Rippon. Shortly after he returned home, Chris Hutchins turned up. He sat, somewhat apologetically, on one of Branson's enormous sofas as he elaborated on his conversation with Basham.

'I smelt a rat when Eileen phoned me. I didn't believe Basham when he said that he was doing nothing but studying Virgin's finances. Basham's company went bust earlier this year, but Lord King is still paying him well.' Hutchins handed Branson a print-out from his computer. 'I don't suppose I'll get any more upgrades on BA flights after this, but what the hell,' he said.

The computer had recorded the time the call began – 13.40 on 24 October. Branson read the transcript.

Brian Basham: 'Have you been talking to my good lady wife about the Heaven story? . . . Well, the fact of the matter is that you can apparently buy anything down there in the way of drugs. Personally I'm not interested in what goes on at Heaven; what I am interested in is how Branson runs his operation. Needless to say, my clients British Airways are very interested in that [since] he won the two Japan slots.'

Basham paused to confirm their conversation is off the record.

'I take it that all this is just between the two of us?'

After Hutchins assured him that it was, Basham continued.

'I'm taking a really good look at his [Branson's] cash position. He's always run very tight with his money to the point of getting into trouble, then he refinances. For example, he sold some stores to W. H. Smith. Now he's getting Japanese investors. It is a dangerous way to operate but all right as long as your reputation is intact. He'd be in real danger if a story came out exposing what goes on at Heaven. It would certainly inhibit his reputation.'

Hutchins then noted what Basham said when he asked the PR man why he didn't investigate Heaven himself.

'I have no intention of . . . I don't want to put Branson out of business. In fact, looking at it from my clients' interest, the last thing they want is to be seen having Richard Branson's blood on their hands.'

Changing tack, Basham then turned the conversation to the story Lord King had urged him to spread about Heaven.

'There's a huge heap of rubbish outside the British Aerospace office in the Strand which backs on to Heaven. When Admiral Sir Ray Lygo wanted it cleared, his office manager called Westminster Council. They said their people wouldn't touch it because of all the needles. It is not there now.

'Eileen knows I've got a major interest in Mr Branson. There was a huge piece in the *Guardian* on Branson, analysing his finances and the roller-coaster way he operates. I'm not saying I had anything to do with it. He refinances periodically; at the moment he must be bleeding with all these fare cuts. I would be interested to hear how you get on with your inquiries.'

Branson was trembling slightly when he finished reading the print-out. He had known roughly what to expect after his call to Hutchins the previous day, but seeing the journalist's notes in black and white was unnerving. It was the first time he had encountered a professional PR assassin at work. He was the target, Virgin the intended victim.

Although Branson was unsettled, he had planned his response carefully before Hutchins arrived. He devised a scheme which required the journalist's cooperation. During their first phone call, Hutchins told Branson that he was due to meet the PR man for a more detailed briefing at the Savoy hotel the following week. Before Hutchins left Holland Park, Branson persuaded him to try and record the meeting. Branson explained to Hutchins why he needed positive proof of what BA was up to, and the planned encounter at the Savoy would be an ideal opportunity. At first Hutchins resisted, but he eventually succumbed. The trap was set.

Branson detailed Whitehorn to find out everything he could about Basham. Branson himself wanted to know more about the man who was out to get him and his airline, as well as Basham's boss, David Burnside, whom the cuttings referred to as 'Britain's most powerful in-house PR director'.

Richard Branson phoned the chairman of British Midland, Sir Michael Bishop, to ask if he had encountered BA's director of public affairs. Bishop most certainly had. He told Branson:

'Burnside is a very sinister and unpleasant man.' Bishop was aware of Burnside's political activities in Ulster, as well as his formidable reputation as a tough public relations operator. 'He's a media kneecapper,' added Bishop, 'and he tosses BA freebies around like confetti.'

The cuttings Whitehorn dug out on Basham were also salutary.

Basham's star appeared to be in the ascendant once again. The *Daily Telegraph* had spotted his distinctive green Range Rover, with its faxes and its phones, dropping him at the Savoy. Only ten days before Hutchins' call, he had featured prominently in a *Sunday Times* article entitled 'Spotlight on the Hidden Persuaders'. The article had listed Basham as 'one of the main players in financial PR'. He retained his tag as 'the streetfighter of the PR gang' and, in addition to BA, he listed Lord Hanson as one of his clients.

The report had been prompted by a private letter from Lord Hanson criticising one of his other PR consultants, Sir Tim Bell, for his handling of the press in the battle with ICI. The letter from Hanson found its way on to the front page of the *Observer*. Bell and Basham had both been hired to work for Hanson, but Bell suspected Brian Basham of leaking the letter. Basham denied it.

After hours of furious phone-bashing, Whitehorn also established that one of Basham's closest contacts was the *Sunday Telegraph*'s Frank Kane, who had been the journalistic scourge of Virgin for the past few months. Branson was intrigued by the press cuttings. His interest in the journalist who had plied him with more negative questions than any other through the summer was heightened still further when Kane phoned him shortly after Chris Hutchins left Holland Park.

Kane started quizzing Branson about a letter he had written to his staff that had been leaked to the *Sunday Telegraph*. When Branson demanded to know how Kane had got hold of it, Kane refused to tell him. He said it had come in a brown paper envelope.

Branson had written the letter to his staff in late September. In it, he summarised the prospects for Virgin Atlantic in the wake of the Gulf War. He expressed his confidence in Virgin Atlantic's future, but also announced cost-cutting measures. He reminded them that all airlines had suffered in the past nine months:

> The Gulf War, when the Japanese stopped flying for months, subsequent spiralling fuel prices, the recession, the added competition and so on. The losses for the industry as a whole have been astronomical.

Branson warned his staff:

Our loads have been good but our yields have slipped quite
considerably. The initial forecast for the next twelve months
has given us cause for concern and, therefore, we have taken
some immediate measures to counterbalance it.

Kane quizzed Branson on the cost-cutting measures to which the
letter referred. Then he went on to ask if it were true Branson was
planning wage freezes, recruitment freezes, overtime bans, laying
off of engineering staff and merging flights.

'I hear you are definitely combining routes,' said Kane. 'I am
also told that if you keep your eight 747s going through the winter you will lose £50 million . . .'

As Kane rattled through his list of questions and allegations,
and gave what Branson thought was a ludicrous interpretation of
his staff letter, the newspaper article lying on the table caught his
eye. A picture of Brian Basham on his car phone stared at Branson
with the headline, 'Spotlight on the Hidden Persuaders'.
Everything was beginning to make a little more sense.

Branson terminated the conversation with a terse response.
'You are a BA puppet, Frank. I don't know why I bother to return
your calls because it never makes any difference to what you
write.'

Kane was not the only reporter who had got hold of the story
about Branson's letter, as Whitehorn vividly remembers:

'We got call after call. I had every Sunday newspaper on and
three dailies with variations on the same theme. The kind of allegations that were being thrown at me were that we'd laid off
engineers, which I knew to be untrue, that we'd laid off cabin
crew, which I knew to be untrue, that we were having to combine
flights, which I knew to be untrue. There was a long list, and they
seemed to be coming from one source. I know that when a number
of newspapers phone with an almost identical story that there is a
concerted campaign. It doesn't just "happen". Life is not like that.
People don't sit in different editorial offices in different parts of the
country, let alone the same city, and suddenly think, "Oh, Richard
Branson has sent a letter to his staff this week, let's find out what
was in the letter, let's find out what might be happening at Virgin
to support the downside of that letter." It was concerted and

somebody was organising it. I knew in my heart where it was coming from, but I had no evidence.'

The following Sunday Branson started to read Kane's article in the *Sunday Telegraph* with some relief. The report was balanced in content and neutral in tone. On this occasion, his conversation with Kane did seem to have made a difference to what he had written. Branson had used the exchange to let him know that Salomons were handling the airline's equity sale and this had given the reporter his headline, 'Young helping Branson to raise £50m'. Branson could find little to object to until he read 'Branson has been trying to sell equity in the business since March.'

Fraser Marcus at Salomons also spotted that line. Both men knew it was not true – Virgin and Salomons had only agreed their deal in September, and the merchant bank was still in the process of getting the airline's prospectus together to present to potential investors. The American banker remembers his reaction:

'I was very perplexed by that line in Kane's article. It was only one line in one newspaper but it made us look really stupid. The last thing we needed was potential investors thinking we were offering them shop-soiled goods that others had passed up.

'We try to make each of our prospective clients feel special, the "only girl at the dance syndrome", if you like. If they think we've been trying to hawk merchandise around town for half a year before coming to them they lose interest very quickly.

'Frank Kane spoke to me several times before he wrote the article and I told him that we hadn't even *started* to look for equity partners. He seemed to have a very good inside source but he gave me the impression he knew the answers before he asked the questions.'

Branson was furious. As he contemplated the possible impact of the article on the equity bid, Hutchins phoned to confirm he would be meeting Basham on the Monday as planned. At the BA man's request, however, the venue had been changed. Basham said he wanted to give Hutchins a report he had prepared on Virgin, and said he didn't want to be *seen* handing it over at the Savoy. Instead Basham had invited Hutchins to his North London home. Branson was becoming intensely curious about Basham. Why didn't he want to be *seen* to be handing over the document?

Hutchins said he would do his best to tape the conversation, but
surprised Branson by asking if he could borrow a tape recorder
with a small microphone. He said *Today* didn't have any available.
Branson told him to speak to Will Whitehorn.

By now Branson was beginning to share some of Whitehorn's
reservations about Hutchins' mission. Whitehorn wasn't sure
Hutchins was capable of carrying out his undercover operation
satisfactorily. Both men even thought it was even possible they
were being set up by BA. But as they talked through the possibilities they agreed that something had to be done. *The Times* as well
as the *Sunday Telegraph* had been handed a copy of Branson's staff
letter, and although coverage in both of the weekend papers had
been reasonably balanced, the articles had prompted another rash
of enquiries about Virgin's finances. Chasing the *Sunday Telegraph*
lead, the *Daily Telegraph* had been on to Whitehorn on Sunday
morning with a familiar refrain, 'We hear rumours you're losing
money hand over fist . . .'

The trickle of calls from journalists about Virgin Atlantic turned
into a flood. Whitehorn fielded calls from the *Evening Standard*
and the *Guardian* who wanted to know if the rumours about
Virgin Atlantic's finances were true. Reporters from the trade
press called to see if Branson would be giving a press conference
about his airline's troubles. Both men knew that something had to
be done. At the end of a dreadful month, the gossip columnist's
improbable mission appeared the best option available – in fact,
the only option.

Branson did, however, run a check on Hutchins. He phoned the
editor of *Today*, Martin Dunn, to make sure he had given his bless-
ing to the project, and to establish this was not a BA set-up. Dunn
confirmed that Hutchins had his support.

The following morning found Whitehorn in Tottenham Court
Road buying a small tape recorder for Chris Hutchins. He caught
Hutchins at *Today*'s Wapping office just before he left for his meeting with Basham. Whitehorn showed him briefly how to work the
tape recorder and wished him well.

As Hutchins left, Whitehorn introduced himself to Martin
Dunn. Branson's press man was leaving nothing to chance. The
editor assured Whitehorn that if Hutchins returned with

something interesting, he would put an investigative reporter on the story.

As Hutchins made his way to his North London rendezvous with Basham, he carried the hopes of Virgin Atlantic with him. Branson's staff noticed him pacing silently and nervously around his sitting room that morning, unaware of what was preoccupying him.

Eileen Basham greeted Hutchins when he arrived at 11.30. The two journalists hadn't seen much of each other since they worked on Hutchins' gossip column and there was much to catch up on. Eileen prepared tea and apologised for Brian's absence, explaining that he would arrive soon.

Under Hutchins' suit, the miniature cassette recorder was taping their idle chatter. Hutchins became increasingly conscious of a very faint whirring inside his breast pocket. He began to sweat slightly as he contemplated what might happen if the tape ended and the machine made a click as it turned itself off. Because he had only just got hold of the recorder before he left the office, he was completely unfamiliar with its characteristics.

Basham entered, full of apologies for being late, and the two men chatted for a few minutes about the demise of Basham's Broad Street Associates and the birth of Warwick Corporate. Hutchins brought him to the point of the meeting as quickly as he could. He was painfully aware that his host's late appearance had used up valuable recording time.

'There are some things that I need to clarify in order to get this story right. First of all, to go straight to the heart of it, have we got anything on Branson?'

Basham picked up a copy of the report he had prepared for BA and smoothed it open

'I did some research . . .' he began, modestly, and then launched into his familiar 'spin' on Operation Barbara. He had been pushing the report for the past six months and the patter was practised.

'The pattern with Branson is that he has lots of schemes going on, some of them big capital eaters. His whole world is based on *Tubular Bells*, I mean, you know more about the music business than I do, so you know [that]. He got cash and he immediately borrowed. Business is not about profit, it's about cash, cash availability. It's about whether you've got enough cash to pay your overheads, and at the end of the day whether you've got enough cash left over. Profit doesn't matter.

'What [Branson] does, he runs his cashflow close to the wire all the time, and just before he runs out of cash, he refinances. He'll sell some record shops in Japan, he'll sell some shops to W. H. Smith, and if you look at the weekend press, Frank Kane in the *Sunday Telegraph* [says] he's trying to raise £20 million.'

Basham paused before carrying on to allow Hutchins to catch up with his note-taking. Hutchins could think only of the tape recorder and how superfluous his notes really were. Basham continued.

'Branson has two things which could really drag him down. One of them is his physical courage, if you like, in ballooning, which is a very, very dangerous occupation. Even with safeguards and everything, if you are up at whatever he is, 80,000 feet, right up in the fringes of the atmosphere in a balloon, it's dangerous. Lots of things could go wrong. And if he got into trouble, I believe the business would collapse, because it's his charm and his magic that pulls the cash into the business.

'There is also what I call "moral danger", if you like, which really focuses on Heaven. And if he's got Heaven, I can't believe that there aren't other things.'

Hutchins interjected: 'Why, what's wrong with Heaven?'

'Nothing wrong with Heaven,' Basham said quickly. 'Nothing wrong with Heaven at all. It's a gay nightclub. For Lord King to own Heaven would be bizarre, right? For Branson to own Heaven, if he wants to become a serious businessman, is bizarre, and leads him into danger. It not only leads him into danger, it leads the business into danger. Can you imagine a hypothetical case: Salomons get a prospectus together, and they are just in the middle of a float, and Heaven is raided? Charges are pressed against the ownership. Right? Not inconceivable.'

Basham enunciated the syllables in the last sentence very deliberately so Hutchins couldn't miss the point: 'NOT IN-CON-CEIV-ABLE'. Hutchins felt he was witnessing a well-rehearsed performance.

'Especially if there are lots of drugs involved. And that is where I think he is bound to run amiss. I think he has got some problems and he does run his business very riskily.'

Basham interrupted his briefing to phone his office. The copy of the Operation Barbara report he had brought home was lacking a vital appendix.

'Hello there, sorry to bother you, I'm just in the middle of a meeting. Thank you very much for getting the document together. It's very useful . . . There's one thing missing from it which is quite crucial, which is that original report that our friend did on Heaven. I want it because it talks about the war between the bouncers. Could you fax it to my home . . .? Thanks very much.'

Basham was referring to the unpublished article about Heaven by Dominic Prince. Before ringing off, Basham asked his office to call Frank Kane to see if the *Sunday Telegraph* journalist could get a copy of the Branson letter he had written about over the weekend.

Hutchins started questioning Basham about the government's controversial decision to allow Virgin Atlantic to expand its service to Tokyo. BA's PR man warmed to his theme:

'I try and look at my clients' business through their eyes. So when I see Branson getting routes from British Airways, I think it's scandalous. I think it is scandalous for two reasons: first of all, I think he runs a dicky business, just dicky. Bits of it are good, but I think it's dicky . . . I wouldn't care to invest in that business with my money.

'What King understands is that anybody who runs a business like Branson is taking a big risk on going bust – this is Freddie Laker all over again.'

Basham's second reason reflected Robert Ayling's implacable opposition to the expansion of Branson's Japanese routes, which the two men had discussed at Speedbird House the previous month.

'I think that for the government to give these routes, which are really big assets . . . to a businessman is bad news, scandalous. To take those routes away from a business which has been privatised, where you've got lots and lots of . . . shareholders . . . and take it away from all those private shareholders and to give it to somebody who's got . . . a privately run business is, I think, doubly scandalous.'

Basham took Hutchins through a list of Virgin Atlantic's senior management team before pausing to dwell on Mike Batt, the former joint managing director of Virgin Atlantic, now back in the BA fold.

'Mike Batt was taken into Virgin to take over from Richard Branson. Anyway, he worked for one week and resigned. I took him out to dinner and asked what happened. He said well, actually, the business is appallingly run.

'He said one day, without doubt, an aircraft is going to fall out of the sky – because aircraft always fall out of the sky, you know. *Must* happen. If an inquiry takes place, someone is going to swing, because the procedures and the way the business is run are appalling.'

As Basham drew the meeting to a close, he sought undertakings from Hutchins.

'I have a couple of concerns. First of all, I don't want to be involved in this at all. Secondly, I mustn't have *BA* involved in this at all. I mean, all the good I might have done by saying: here is Virgin, good and bad . . . would be entirely wiped out if it looked as though BA were in any way running some sort of campaign against Virgin, which they are not. All right? We've got to be terribly careful . . . Hutchins asked if Lord King would object to anti-Branson stories appearing. 'No!' replied Basham emphatically. 'If you blow Branson out, it doesn't bother me as long as neither BA nor I are associated with it.'

Basham escorted Hutchins to the door. He showed the reporter some scrape marks on the front door where someone had broken into the house. 'I really must get this place swept for bugs again,' he joked as Hutchins stepped outside.

As Hutchins walked away from the house he waved to Eileen, who had appeared at a window. Inside his breast pocket, his tape recorder was still turning.

The following afternoon, the tape recorder that Will Whitehorn had bought for Hutchins lay on Richard Branson's oak table in

Holland Park. Beside it was a copy of Brian Basham's report for BA on Virgin Atlantic.

Branson sat with his knees hunched up under his chin. He listened intently as the tape recorder emitted almost inaudible, squeaky noises. Hutchins had completed his mission and was sitting at the side of the table, nervously studying Branson's reactions. It was, however, very difficult to hear what had been recorded on the tape. It was possible only to make out the sound of two men with very similar-sounding voices, chatting quietly to each other. Their conversation was interspersed by long pauses during which nothing appeared to have been recorded. Branson grimaced with frustration. From time to time phrases emerged which caused Branson to stop the tape, wind it backwards a little way, and replay it.

After a while, his attention wandered and he started leafing through Basham's report. He called Whitehorn round from his nearby office in Campden Hill Road and asked him to try listening to the tape.

Shortly afterwards Whitehorn was in Virgin's Town House Studios in Shepherd's Bush listening to Hutchins' tape again. This time, the contents boomed over enormous six-foot speakers. The Town House audio engineers fiddled determinedly with a vast range of brightly coloured knobs in an attempt to remove the interference. Every time Hutchins had shifted position, the sensitive microphone seemed to have moved – it sounded like men hacking frantically through a jungle of dried wood.

Like Branson, Whitehorn had found the past few months exceptionally stressful and he arrived at the studio with the tape feeling very nervous. The Basham trap had been sprung but had he been caught? The studio staff soothed the chain-smoking Whitehorn with cans of cold beer. The sound quality was poor and very distorted but, as the minuscule tape moved silently in the sound deck, the voice of Brian Basham finally crackled clearly through the speakers:

'If you blow Branson out, it doesn't bother me, as long as neither BA nor I are associated with it . . .'

Whitehorn punched the air.

That night Branson and Whitehorn played the enhanced tape to themselves over and over again, scarcely able to believe what they were hearing. Together they scoured every word of the Basham report, picking it to pieces.

'I don't know how much BA paid Basham for this,' Branson remarked to Whitehorn, 'but I hope it didn't take much more than an afternoon.'

Branson was alternately furious that BA should be paying Basham to trowel lies amongst gossip columnists, and ecstatic that his scheme had worked.

'It had taken me some months to realise what they were up to. Listening to Basham on the tape was unreal. What he was saying was an utter disgrace. Up until that point I had never come across that sort of trashing PR. I had naïvely thought that PR men were supposed to promote their own company and its products, not smear the opposition.

'But when I heard the tape I also knew we'd caught BA with its pants down, and I was convinced by the end of that day that we now had the means to stop them.'

Two days later Brian Basham was enjoying a pheasant shoot on Viscount Althorp's estate. He was entirely unaware that his discussion with Chris Hutchins had been recorded, or that Richard Branson was busy having its contents transcribed by one of his personal secretaries.

He sauntered back to his Range Rover chatting to his shooting partners with a couple of pheasants dangling over his arm. His chauffeur approached him with a list of calls that he had taken on the carphone. Several of them were from Nick Rufford on the *Sunday Times*. Basham had met Rufford briefly at BA's lavish reception at the Conservative Party conference in Blackpool earlier in the month, but had never had any professional dealings with him.

When Basham returned the call, Rufford explained that he was putting together an analysis of Virgin Atlantic for the coming Sunday in the light of the on-going debate on the airline's future. He was keen to get the BA perspective on Branson. Basham said it wouldn't be possible to meet until the following week as he had no gaps in his schedule. After Rufford hassled him and stressed his deadline could not be moved, Basham relented and agreed to a short meeting at the Savoy Hotel on the Friday evening. He said he wouldn't be able to stay long, as David Burnside had invited him to British Airways' annual public relations get-together at the Hilton that evening. Once a year, representatives from BA's worldwide web of PR men and women are flown into London for a week-end conference to assess performance and plot strategy. Basham was keen not be late. One of the highlights of the evening was to be the presentation of a BA Gold Service Award to Ken Cook, the veteran marketing man who had funnelled BA's internal research on Virgin Atlantic to Brian Basham's Operation Barbara team.

Basham strode briskly into the familiar surroundings of the Savoy Hotel shortly before eight o'clock. One or two members of the hotel staff greeted the familiar figure as he trotted down the steps of the sumptuous foyer and shook hands with Rufford. Basham apologised to the reporter for being late and for having to leave shortly. To compensate, he summarised his client's main arguments against Branson as the two men sipped their cocktails.

Basham kicked off with the story he had told Hutchins about Virgin's sloppy management and the danger to the company if one of Branson's planes 'fell out of the sky'. Once again it was sourced to Mike Batt, BA's senior vice-president for sales and marketing in the USA. Basham said that if such a disaster occurred, Virgin did not have the resources or the organisational capacity to deal with it.

'My wife is going to the States; there is no way I would let her fly Virgin,' Basham told Rufford. He shook his head. 'Every bone in my body tells me that Branson is a flake.' Then, in hushed tones, BA's PR man made the startling suggestion that Virgin was on the brink of bankruptcy. He said Branson was having to pay for his planes' fuel in cash because of Virgin's low credit rating. When Rufford asked if Basham knew anything about Branson's September letter to his staff, quoted in the *Sunday Telegraph* the previous week, Basham said he would arrange for it to be leaked to him. 'I will get the industry intelligence boys on to it.'

An hour and a half later the letter arrived at the *Sunday Times'* Wapping offices in a plain brown envelope. The 'industry intelligence boy' responsible for sending the letter to Rufford was Frank Kane, the first journalist to receive the letter. Basham had simply

phoned Kane and told him to bike it to the rival Sunday newspaper.

The week before the public relations team started circulating
Branson's private letter to journalists, Tony Cocklin had sent it to
members of BA's board. Sir Colin Marshall, Robert Ayling and
financial director Derek Stevens, as well as BA's head of corporate
strategy, Roger Maynard, got copies. Two of BA's most senior
anti-Virgin strategists, the Reverend Jim Callery and Mike Batt,
were also sent it.

As Rufford checked through the details of his story he phoned
Basham again. Rufford took the precaution of taping the call to
satisfy the *Sunday Times* lawyers if they challenged details in his
story.

Unaware that the conversation was being recorded, Basham
regaled Rufford with a list of independent British airlines that had
gone bust, apparently to illustrate how vulnerable independent
airlines are to a recession.

'[This list] is extraordinary: Channel Airways, World Wide
Aviation, British Eagle, Scottish European, Air Safari, Southern
Airways, Laker Airways, Air Europe, British Caledonian,
Highland Express, Donaldson, Scimitar, Senator, Victor,
Westwood Aviation, Scillonian, Air Charter, Air Link, Lloyd
International, Paramount and Novair . . . These are all companies
that come off the top of the head . . .'

In fact the list came from the back of an envelope: Basham and
Cocklin had scribbled the names down over drinks at the Tory
Party conference. Basham then repeated the rumour about Branson's fuel situation which had originated from the 'competitor
monitoring' activities in BA's public affairs department.

'The question of the fuel is something we can't verify . . . but it's
something which a number of people I've spoken to have heard
and they think it's Shell. We think he's having to pay up front for
fuel.'

When Rufford put Basham's allegations to Whitehorn, Branson's
press man was livid. The 'cash for fuel' claim incensed him.

'That's a very damaging lie. I bloody well hope you're not going
to print that because if that sort of thing gets into print about a
small airline it can be fatal – belly-up in months.'

As Rufford began to read Basham's list of independent airlines that had gone bust, Whitehorn interrupted him: 'I'll call Richard and get you a quote right away.'

Branson was disturbed to hear that Basham was on the loose again, and particularly worried by the 'cash for fuel' rumour. It costs tens of thousands of pounds to fill a jumbo with fuel before each flight, and credit facilities with fuel companies are a vital component of any airline's financial arrangements. He found it hard to imagine a more damaging notion than rumours of his staff staggering to departure gates across the world with suitcases stuffed with banknotes before Shell would agree to fill his planes up with fuel.

He also knew that the British airline industry would instantly assume Virgin Atlantic was on the brink of collapse if the story surfaced in a newspaper. Sir Freddie Laker had told him that similar rumours had helped to undermine Laker Airways, and he knew Harry Goodman had also complained that BA circulated unfounded gossip about Air Europe before it crashed. Despite some success in dealing with the knocking stories since the autumn, Branson knew the tag of 'the second Freddie Laker' was becoming increasingly difficult to shake off.

Having checked with Shell that BA's claims were unfounded, Rufford tracked Basham down on his way back from Twickenham, where he had been watching the Rugby World Cup Final between England and Australia. He told Basham that 'Insight' were now putting together a rather different story – that the fuel story was untrue, and the 'Insight' team had, therefore, done an article about his attempts to smear Branson and Virgin on behalf of BA.

Basham was furious. He slammed his car phone into its socket and instructed his chauffeur to drive to King's Cross to buy an early edition of the *Sunday Times*.

'It was bad enough that Rufford had double-crossed me but then he had the cheek to phone me up and gloat about it!'

Richard Branson read the article at his Oxfordshire home on 3 November. Headlined 'Branson accuses BA of Dirty Tricks', the article for the first time publicly identified Brian Basham with BA's PR offensive against Virgin. 'Insight' reported that BA's PR man had arranged for the Branson letter, leaked to the *Sunday*

Telegraph the previous week, to be sent to the *Sunday Times* within hours, and that other journalists had received copies of a confidential report on Branson and Virgin prepared by Basham. Branson was quoted saying that he had a list of 100 specific complaints against BA which he was, once again, thinking of taking to the European Commission. To Branson's relief the article omitted any reference to Basham's 'cash for fuel' claim.

A footnote to the 'Insight' article drew Branson's attention to an article in the business section, 'Branson's Pickle'. The author, Andrew Davidson, had interviewed Branson, but it was clear to Virgin's chairman that he had also been briefed by Basham; the same journalist had written the article which identified Basham as a 'hidden persuader' only two weeks earlier. By now the full transcript of Basham's chat with Chris Hutchins had been completed, and it had become the filter through which Branson analysed everything he now saw in print.

'Branson's Pickle' cited anonymous critics who 'believe Branson may be overreaching himself and could easily end up as the next Freddie Laker'. The article warned that 'anything that dents Virgin's image could cripple his [Branson's] chances of success' in trying to raise fresh money for the airline and bidding for new slots to Japan and South Africa. Despite denials from Branson, BA's agenda was continuing to crystallise in the business and City pages.

The 'Insight' team's exposure of Basham, however, could hardly have been published at a more embarrassing time for Burnside as he hosted BA's annual jamboree at the Hilton, surrounded by his staff from all over the world.

'I told you not to deal with pond life,' the Ulsterman barked at Basham.

Burnside himself had been briefly quoted in the 'Insight' article. Publicly adhering to the 'sniffy' attitude that he and Basham had urged upon Lord King in his dealings with Branson, Burnside's comment belied the enormous pressure he had been under for the past year:

'We run our business. We are not interested in others.'

By sheer coincidence Burnside had invited Andrew Neil, the editor of the *Sunday Times*, to address BA's PR conference at lunchtime. Basham remonstrated with Neil as soon as he arrived. He said he was particularly annoyed that Nick Rufford had taped him, and told Neil that he had been misrepresented in the paper. Neil rebuffed him and said there was no question of the paper issuing a retraction.

Burnside told Neil he had a thick file on Branson and Virgin. 'I asked him to let me have it', recalls Neil, ' but I never heard any more from him. Both Burnside and Basham were rather sheepish about the "Insight" story, and were not keen to make an issue out of it.'

In the afternoon Burnside brought Basham more bad news. *Today* was planning to run a front-page story on BA's 'dirty tricks' the following morning,

'I think you'd better get on the case, Brian.'

Basham grabbed a nearby phone. His mind flashed back to Chris Hutchins' visit to his home at the beginning of the week. As he leafed rapidly through his diary, searching for the number of *Today*, his recollections of their encounter raced through his mind.

He remembered giving Hutchins a copy of Operation Barbara to take away, and a photocopy of the article on Heaven nightclub but, as he waited for the phone to be answered, Basham found it difficult to think of anything that had occurred between him and Hutchins that might warrant a front-page story. After a twenty-year career in public relations, Basham felt he had a pretty good idea of what made a tabloid splash. Anyway, Hutchins was supposed to write titbits in the gossip column.

As soon as Hutchins came to the phone, Basham knew that something was badly wrong. He sounded guilt-stricken and evasive when Basham pressed him about the following morning's story.

'Hutchins told me the story was out of his hands. He told me that *Today* was going to run a story on "dirty tricks" in which I would feature. I told him that I thought he was behaving pretty treacherously.

'He sounded close to tears at one stage. He said he was fed up with being in the middle of everything and that he was merely a pawn. I told him he was a worm.'

Basham still had no idea that Hutchins had taped him. In the course of a dramatic Sunday afternoon, he and Burnside

bombarded *Today* with menacing phone calls as they mounted a
fierce rearguard action to stop the paper running the story.

In Oxfordshire, Branson's hopes that BA's 'hidden persuader'
was on the brink of being completely exposed were rising steadily.
The newspaper faxed him its front-page story for the following
day. Hutchins had written the article with one of the paper's
investigative reporters, Bob Graham, and the article was peppered
with quotes from Hutchins' tape of Basham's briefing. *Today*
wanted Branson to see the copy, to confirm that his own quotes
were accurate.

As Branson read through the article, Basham struck lucky. He
contacted Roy Greenslade, who was at that time working as an
associate editor on *Today*, and explained his side of the story.
According to Basham, Greenslade said:

'If I have anything to do with it, a story like that will not run in
this newspaper.'

Greenslade says he simply gave Basham an assurance that the
story would not be run without him being given the chance to
respond. Greenslade and *Today*'s editor, Martin Dunn, both had
reservations about basing a story simply on the tape. As the newspaper pondered whether to run the story, it was approached by
both sides: Burnside phoned Greenslade at home in a state of great
agitation, and Branson spoke to Martin Dunn. Greenslade remembers feeling that Branson's own eagerness to see the story in print
was a factor which caused *Today* to hesitate.

'We felt that Branson was trying to use us. He was so desperate
to see the story in the paper. He said he had a dossier of information on BA's "dirty tricks" but we hadn't seen it, and we felt
reluctant to rush into print on the basis of the Hutchins tape alone.'

Today's reservations, coupled with British Airways' fierce opposition, led to the front-page story being scrapped at the very last
moment, and then being dropped from the paper altogether.
Branson was disappointed. *Today* was the first paper to get positive proof of what BA was up to, albeit with his active assistance.
He was partly comforted by the thought that it would be better to
get the story in a more influential newspaper – the small *Today*
tabloid has a circulation of only 500,000. He thought the *Sunday
Times* was fine as far as it went, but the Basham tape was, for

Branson, the clincher, and it had not seen the light of day. The 'Insight' article stirred interest in the airline industry, but little sympathy. The outpouring of editorial support Branson hoped for failed to materialise. In fact the reverse occurred. The *Travel Trade Gazette* devoted its editorial column to Branson's claims under the heading 'Virgin's Troubles Are a Drop in the Ocean'. Its verdict was that his allegations were 'mostly nonsense'. Seasoned aviation correspondents and travel writers regarded Branson's claims with scepticism. There was an almost universal feeling that British Airways would not stoop to the depths to which he was claiming the company had descended. Branson was frustrated.

'The "Insight" headline read "Branson Accuses BA of 'Dirty Tricks'". The "Insight" team had discovered what BA and Basham were up to, and I thought the *Sunday Times* should stick its neck out and say this is wrong and BA shouldn't be doing it. I didn't see why I should have to do the accusing. It was plain to anyone who read the article that BA was telling lies about Virgin.'

Will Whitehorn watched Branson's frustration grow.

'Richard had already had the trial. He had been the judge, the jury and the executioner. In his own mind BA was guilty and he was astonished that, as journalists started to discover what King and his people were up to, it wasn't splashed across the front page of every newspaper in the land.'

Branson and Whitehorn now embarked upon a long march to gain credibility for their 'dirty tricks' claims. To do so, they knew they would have to break the iron grip in which BA had held the aviation lobby since its privatisation.

8

Breakfast in America

On 14 November 1991, New York City woke up in its usual noisy fashion. Yellow cabs bounced along the potholed streets through clouds of steam as traffic marshals gave their morning performances. The smell of coffee and bagels greeted businessmen leaving Park Avenue as they filtered into the Regency hotel to 'do' breakfast. Inside, a solid shift of New York's movers and shakers monopolised the tables. Waiters moved apologetically along a queue of the hotel's guests, offering them small slices of melon as they waited for tables to become vacant.

Anonymous in the sea of power breakfasters were Sir Colin Marshall and his old friend Michael Levin, BA's former marketing guru.

The seventy-year-old American's controversial BA career had ended in disgrace when his reputation as a philanderer caught up with him. In 1986 one of BA's New York operations managers, Marie Ring, filed a suit against Marshall's chief consultant, accusing him of ruining her career after she refused to sleep with him. It was not the first time Levin had been accused of sexual harassment. BA finally settled Ring's $5 million suit out of court in 1989, and Levin was fired. Marshall was unable to save his friend and BA never disclosed the amount of money it paid to Ring, but the chief executive publicly defended Levin, claiming 'it was never proved'.

Levin returned to New York feeling that BA had betrayed him, and he severed most of his links with the airline. However, he did keep in touch with his friend Colin Marshall, for whom he claimed he did some consultancy work after BA terminated his contract. The two old soldiers were veterans of many campaigns and they had much to talk about.

The architect of BA's anti-Virgin policy had continued to dabble in BA's affairs from his Manhattan base, keeping in touch with Marshall and old allies on the chief executive's wing of BA's political spectrum. As the two men shared breakfast, Levin told Marshall that he had been contacted by an investigative reporter who was probing Richard Branson's 'dirty-tricks' claims.

Today's Bob Graham established very early in his inquiries that many roads led to Levin. In the wake of the paper's debacle over the Hutchins tape, Graham phoned the former marketing supremo from London several times in the week before he was due to meet Marshall for breakfast. Graham had been warned by some of Levin's former colleagues in BA that the American taped all his calls, so the reporter did the same. Graham was fascinated by the insight Levin had into BA's operation and particularly by his comments on the phone.

'John King and David Burnside are the men you are interested in. Burnside does things that have no place in a company like British Airways. I do know Sir Colin is not aware of what is going on there. Burnside is in a very peculiar position. There is not an ethical bone in his body. Some of the things he is involved in are very unethical. I can't say if his Lordship knows about all of them.'

When Bob Graham asked Levin if he would do a full, on-the-record interview on the subject, Levin replied that he would have to clear it with Marshall. Over their breakfast on Park Avenue, Marshall asked his mentor to do no such thing. 'Marshall Aide Slams King in Dirty Tricks Row' would not have done Sir Colin's cause any good at all, particularly when the aide in question was the progenitor of BA's obsession with Virgin. It would have been impossible to guarantee which way the story would play.

Marshall told Levin, however, that he was troubled by the recent exposure of the PR campaign against Branson, and the vituperative politics that were continuing to infest the BA board. As the breakfast drew to a close, Levin acceded to Marshall's request to come over to London for Christmas and the New Year. He also agreed not to give Bob Graham an interview. He phoned the reporter immediately after his breakfast with Marshall and said that as he was still engaged in consultancy work for BA, he would not be able to speak on the record.

When Marshall returned to London he was sufficiently concerned about Graham's contact with Levin to get BA's press office to try and find out what the reporter was up to. Significantly, he did not ask David Burnside to check the reporter out, but another senior member of the public affairs department, Peter Jones. Nor did Marshall tell either King or Burnside about his continuing contact with Levin, and he did not warn either of them that Levin was still meddling in BA's internal politics.

Levin's conversations with Bob Graham had a significant impact on Richard Branson's view of who was responsible for the campaign against him. When Graham phoned him to get his reaction to Levin's claims, Branson jotted down Graham's résumé of what he had been told by Marshall's consultant.

> [The Anti-Virgin] group was set up at King's instigation. Burnside ran it. No boundaries were set – legal or not. Two other senior members of BA . . . were involved. Levin [was] told that Basham was part of the plan.
> I know people do things – unethical – outside the law. Especially David Burnside.

Today did not publish the result of Graham's investigation, but his conversation with Levin, of whom Branson had never previously heard, shaped Virgin's view of who at BA was driving the campaign against the airline. After learning of Levin's disclosures, and having listened to the tape of Basham in action, Branson saw King, Burnside and Basham as the hostile wing of BA, and Marshall as the potentially honest broker between himself and King. Graham relayed to Branson Levin's claim that Marshall was 'not aware of what was going on'.

Branson's Holland Park home and office became the epicentre for the dirty-tricks crisis in late 1991. To the casual visitor the house was a monument to his life's work, with pictures of his family taking pride of place in the vast living room amongst a growing collection of awards for Virgin Atlantic. A bevy of secretaries and assistants moved discreetly around the lower floors organising Branson's diary, and receiving a stream of callers from the record company and other parts of the Virgin empire. Beneath the relaxed atmosphere, however, there was mounting tension and anxiety as Branson's luxurious base continued to be bombarded with inquiries about the future of the airline and the entire Virgin Group.

Branson's most chilling conversation in this period was with Peter Smith, the former group managing director of the International Leisure Group, Air Europe's parent company. Smith warned him that Air Europe had had to endure a BA-inspired rumour campaign in 1989 when the company was in robust financial health.

Like Virgin Atlantic, Air Europe was taken into private ownership not long before BA's campaign started. Like Virgin Atlantic, Air Europe was attempting to get an ambitious expansion plan off the ground when it was hit by a barrage of rumours about its financial well-being. As Smith sketched in the details of the Air Europe experience, Branson grabbed a fresh black notebook and started scribbling.

In the summer of 1989, Air Europe's chairman, Harry Goodman, had received an anonymous letter from two BA pilots. Using the names 'Bob' and 'Harry' they wrote in urgent tones of 'a very real threat to discredit Air Europe by rumour'. The letter claimed that the rumour campaign was to be instigated by Jeremy Butler, then BA's general manager for flight-crew training, and Colin Barnes, then director of BA's flight crews. There was a serious worldwide shortage of pilots in 1989, and the letter claimed that the whispering campaign would be designed to dissuade pilots from joining Harry Goodman's expanding fleet. 'Harry' and 'Bob' claimed the real objective was to call Air Europe's financial credibility into question and to make sure the rumours were leaked to the press.

Only days after the anonymous letter was received, the rumours started. Air Europe's staff heard that the airline's pilots would be laid off, that orders for planes had been cancelled and that the company faced a financial crisis. At the time, none of these whispers was true. The company was heading for a pre-tax profit of £13 million in 1989. When Smith added that within a week Air Europe's press office, in response to inquiries from the local radio station, was having to deny that the airline couldn't pay its fuel bills, Branson stiffened. A week earlier, one of BA's PR men had been sitting in the Savoy telling the *Sunday Times* exactly the same story about Virgin.

Smith told Branson that within a month of Goodman's receiving the anonymous tip-off, he had been forced to call an emergency meeting of his staff at Manchester and Gatwick Airports to deny the rumours. Smith set up a special task force under the airline's legal director, John de Vial, to monitor the rumours.

Air Europe staff who attended the mass meetings were asked to report any further rumours to de Vial's group. However, even as the task force was being set up, and the airline's staff alerted, the rumours were having a devastating effect.

By the end of July 1989, Air Europe executives were forced to clear their diaries to hold a crisis meeting with their bankers and with key suppliers. The company's ambitious expansion plans were under serious threat. Peter Smith recalled an urgent trip to Seattle in late July to reassure the company's plane supplier, Boeing, that the rumours had no substance. Another supplier, Fokker, also needed reassurance.

As part of its expansion scheme, Air Europe was due to move into new headquarters in Crawley in October 1989. Two months before the move British Telecom told Air Europe it had postponed the installation of its new £300,000 telephone-reservation system. BT had accepted the order months before but, on the eve of the installation, it had instituted a formal credit check on the airline.

Goodman and Smith were furious. They started an immediate investigation. They swiftly established from BT that the postponement was a direct result of the rumours it heard about Air Europe's financial health. The BT executive responsible for the Air Europe account was summoned to a meeting at Crawley. He admitted that the rumours had come from BA. The executive was in a position to know, because he handled the telephone accounts of both airlines.

What the BT man did not know was that Goodman's chief of security had bugged the meeting. Goodman and his senior management had become so worried about the rumour campaign that they had all their calls taped as well.

Having established from John de Vial's task force that BA's rumour campaign had reached Air Europe's staff, its suppliers and its banks, Goodman wrote to Lord King and asked him to put a stop to it. Lord King's secretary replied that he was on holiday.

Several weeks later British Airways' legal director Robert Ayling replied formally on behalf of the company. He rejected Air Europe's suggestions that BA was rumour-mongering, and categorically denied a dirty-tricks campaign.

Smith told Branson that by the end of 1989, Air Europe faced a very tough decision. De Vial's dirty-tricks monitoring unit had by then accumulated a bulging 'black book' of statements and affidavits from pilots, managers and executives, as well as the BT tape. ILG estimated that by the end of 1989 the rumour campaign had cost it £15 million in cash outflow. The airline experienced a noticeable tightening of credit in many areas. Overseas airports started asking for deposits for take-off and landing, and fuel suppliers wanted money in advance before planes were refuelled. Smith said that after much heart-searching, Goodman decided to accept Ayling's assurances, and stepped back from taking legal action against the national carrier. He hoped that his lawyers' letter to Lord King would be a shot across BA's bows. Just over a year later, ILG went bankrupt.

Smith told Branson: 'Not suing BA could have been our fatal mistake. Air Europe got into serious difficulties in 1990–91, when the recession began really to bite, and the Gulf War took an enormous toll on our passengers. But by then our financial credibility had been severely damaged by BA's 1989 rumour campaign, and the negotiations with our backers became far more difficult. For the second time in as many years we were going to them and asking them to back us. In the middle of the worst recession in aviation history, that was once too often.'

Branson recalled the visit he had received from Sidney Shore from Lloyds Bank on the day that Air Europe went down. Smith's account of the role BA had played in eroding confidence in Air

Europe and ILG preyed on Branson's mind constantly that November.

'I don't think I have ever seen Richard so depressed,' recalls Will Whitehorn. 'He very rarely lets anything get on top of him, but I really thought he might just jack the airline business in and concentrate on Virgin Music.'

Branson himself was acutely aware of the promise he had made to Simon Draper and Ken Berry when he launched the airline in 1984: Virgin Atlantic would never be allowed to bring the rest of the group down. With BA's assault in full cry, Branson felt that his promise was in jeopardy.

'Confidence is the most important thing in any business. It is so difficult to explain to people who are not involved in commerce just how vital confidence is, particularly in a recession. It sounds absurd to say that the Virgin Group would have collapsed when the record company was worth over half a billion, but once confidence had started to slip away from Virgin Atlantic, anything could have happened.'

Branson's diary in that period reflects his torment. His daily notes from his conversations with journalists, with his suppliers and with his colleagues in Virgin Atlantic are speckled with phrases and jottings that would lead a psychiatrist to diagnose immediate paranoia – unless the observations happened to be true.

[On BA] An organisation set up to discredit me . . . a file in the chief executive's safe about me . . . Destroyed all papers on Virgin . . . Evidence dirty-tricks department set up during the Gulf War . . .

[On Brian Basham] He handed over a further document on Heaven . . . they [BA] didn't want to be *SEEN* to [be] having Richard Branson's blood in their hands . . . If a scandal story appeared Virgin would have difficulty getting finances for expansion . . . He must be bleeding with all those fare cuts . . .

[On surveillance] BA tap their own employees' phones at home . . . the actual company investigating me is ASI Investigators . . . Will Whitehorn had had his car broken into . . . again . . .

[On the sources who contacted him] Have to remain unnamed . . .

[On 'More BA Tricks'] ringing some of our passengers direct trying to persuade them to switch from Virgin to BA . . .

On Brian Basham's rumour that Virgin Atlantic's credit rating was so low that it was being forced to pay for its fuel in cash, he wrote:

This may be the only time in my life that I am so speech-less . . . in my utter contempt . . . no comment seems the only thing to say.

There are many decent people in BA who would be aghast if they knew fully what was going on.

In November, Branson got a break. One of the 'decent people' in BA wrote to him. The senior marketing executive, Peter Fleming, had left BA in spring 1991. The former British Caledonian man had never felt quite at home at BA, and he was particularly offended by the campaign he witnessed against Branson and Virgin in the last twelve months of his three-year spell with the national carrier. Having left one small airline which had been swallowed by BA, Fleming was appalled to witness the tactics BA was employing against its remaining British competitors. He accepted a voluntary redundancy package as BA embarked upon another round of what it likes to describe as 'downsizing', but which its staff understand as cutbacks.

When Fleming left BA he wrote to Virgin Atlantic's marketing director, Chris Moss, outlining some of BA's anti-competitive activities against Virgin. Moss drew his chairman's attention to the letter but Branson did not pursue the matter. When Fleming wrote again in early November detailing how his former department had plotted against Virgin Atlantic, Branson was on the phone immediately, quizzing him in detail about his letter.

Fleming had a revealing list: the slot-blocking ruses to keep Virgin off lucrative routes; the targeting of Virgin passengers by the BA sales force; the schemes to nobble travel agents; the setting-up of a task force to undermine Branson's image and his airline;

and, eventually, the mass shredding of the documents these activities generated.

Fleming's testimony gave Branson and Whitehorn something to get their teeth into – evidence that Basham was not a lone BA shark who had strayed into Virgin waters.

Towards the end of October Branson had stumbled across another worrying clue. As he studied the Upper Class travellers' suggestions book on Virgin Atlantic's Newark flight, he came across an intriguing comment from a businesswoman, Marcia Borne:

> You obviously have BA worried! I received a call asking why
> I booked on a Virgin Atlantic flight today rather than BA.
> Good job! Good luck!

Marcia Borne was a personnel manager with Procter and Gamble in New York who normally flew BA on her quarterly trips to the UK from the USA. On this occasion she had decided to fly with Virgin to try Branson's service out. She told Branson she was 'stunned' to get a call from BA asking her why she had changed carrier for her return leg:

'The guy from BA said, "If you change your mind, let us know and we can change your ticket." It didn't bother me until I started checking around to find out why my itinerary was so public. The more I thought about it the more it bothered me. I didn't know there was a big computer in the skies which told everybody else where I was going to be. I was a bit upset.'

So was Richard Branson. His suspicions that BA were getting into Virgin's computers had been aroused by Peter Fleming. Fleming had confessed to Branson that he had personally accessed Air Europe's confidential flight information, and was in no doubt that his colleagues were doing the same to Virgin. The difficulty was establishing a link between the theory and the practice. Branson had initially thought BA might simply be accessing travel agents' computer booking systems.

As fresh scraps of information made their way to Virgin, Whitehorn and Branson had no hesitation in recruiting the media to their cause. They remorselessly fed new leads to sympathetic journalists in the quality press, as well as to *Today*, which continued to resist Branson's entreaties to publish the transcript of the Basham–Hutchins tape. In their desperation, Whitehorn and Branson then tried to build up an alternative lobby on the dirty-tricks story to counterbalance the network of 'Basham's boys' who, in their eyes, were headed by Frank Kane and his editor, John Jay, on the *Sunday Telegraph*.

Whitehorn put the *Guardian* in touch with Marcia Borne, and gave the paper details of Fleming's shredding allegations and Brian Basham's report, all of which the paper subsequently included in a full-page article: encouraging coverage for Virgin Atlantic, but from BA there was a stony silence.

These new discoveries made Branson further aware of the effect the smear campaign was having on his plans to expand Virgin Atlantic. As Fraser Marcus and his team put the final touches to Virgin Atlantic's equity prospectus at Salomons, they started talking to potential investors, ranging from the Sultan of Brunei to the Prudential Insurance Company. The response was not encouraging. Even companies that were in successful partnership with other parts of the Virgin Group could not be tempted even to talk about investing in the airline.

'The biggest single factor we encountered at this time was the fear of what BA might do to Virgin,' recalls Marcus. 'Some companies were influenced by the press suggestions that Branson was destined to become the second Freddie Laker. Others simply did not want to invest in a tiny airline that was squaring up to the national carrier. In the eyes of most investors there could only be one winner.'

This was a view that found an echo in Virgin Atlantic itself, where some felt Branson was getting the dirty-tricks issue out of proportion. No one challenged Branson directly, but privately some directors wondered whether Whitehorn and Branson hadn't become obsessed with BA. Branson sensed their reservations.

He convened a council of war at Holland Park. Present were his most senior advisors, including both Virgin Atlantic's joint managing directors, Roy Gardner and Syd Pennington. Gardner had joined Virgin Atlantic even before Branson. The airline's founder, Randolph Fields, recruited the former Laker Airways' executive as the putative airline's technical director before he approached Branson to finance its launch. Pennington had only joined Virgin Atlantic the previous year after spending more than twenty years with Marks and Spencer.

For months, Branson had kept Virgin Atlantic's lawyers, Harbottle & Lewis, aware of each new discovery that he and Whitehorn made. At the Holland Park summit, Harbottles were represented by two of the firm's partners, Colin Howes, Branson's closest legal advisor since he founded Virgin Atlantic, and Gerrard Tyrrell, a thirty-four-year-old litigation specialist. Both men had worked with Branson for nearly a decade; Howes specialised in commercial matters for the airline and Tyrrell was the veteran of dozens of litigation battles arising mainly from Virgin Music. At Tyrrell's suggestion the barrister, Jonathan Crystal, was also invited to attend.

The Virgin team debated how to plot a course through uncharted territory. Challenging BA's campaign against the airline was eating up an increasing amount of Branson's time, and it had become almost a full-time occupation for Whitehorn and his assistant, Mo Foster, in Campden Hill Road. The airline's Crawley headquarters had also started receiving a steady stream of disturbing rumours that questioned Virgin Atlantic's future and indicated that Basham was not working alone. The 'cash for fuel' rumour had been picked up by Les McKinty, a Virgin Atlantic manager who had been told by a BA employee that Virgin was being refused credit for aviation fuel. Another Virgin Atlantic employee, Joe Barron, told Branson that his father had been told that Virgin was making cash payments for fuel at Heathrow. Barron senior worked for BA.

Mike Scoates, Virgin's head of operations at Heathrow, discovered that an alarming message was being displayed on BA check-in computers around the world. The instruction, 'Do not accept Virgin Atlantic coupons', appeared to be a breach of airline protocol under which flight tickets are transferable between airlines. Scoates said his opposite number at BA, Chris Maude, had assured him that the computer message was the result of 'unauthorised action by junior staff'.

Branson was convinced by the time of his meeting that the

catalogue of incidents must indicate that the campaign against Virgin had been sanctioned at the highest level within BA. However, convincing those who spent their lives running the airline of the wisdom of tackling BA publicly was not a straightforward task.

Everyone present was aware that while the public skirmishes between the company and BA sometimes gave the impression that BA and Virgin were slugging it out on relatively equal terms, BA's dominance of the British airline industry was awesome. Its omnipotence daunted some of Virgin Atlantic's seasoned executives, who warned Richard Branson that a prolonged dispute with BA might cause severe problems in key areas.

While Branson and Whitehorn had borne the brunt of challenging BA's smear campaign, life for many members of Virgin Atlantic had become much more difficult as the exchanges with BA grew steadily more acrimonious. Virgin Atlantic's engineers, for example, expressed concern that an even more public clash with BA could lead to complete non-cooperation by their BA counterparts. With Virgin's eight jumbos strung out between the West Coast of America and Tokyo, BA could create enormous problems for the airline if the traditional goodwill between engineers was suspended entirely. Already some Virgin crews and ground staff were reporting that routine courtesies had been suspended.

There was renewed suspicion that BA was employing private detectives to probe Branson's affairs. His personal secretary, Penni Pike, took a call in the autumn from an anonymous male who told her to 'tell Richard Branson BA have put the private detectives on him'. The man slammed his phone down without giving his name.

The former Air Europe executive, Peter Smith, who had already described the effects of BA's whispering campaign against Air Europe so vividly, also mentioned in passing that he believed that the New York-based investigation agency, Kroll Associates, had been hired to probe Air Europe's affairs. Neither Harry Goodman nor Peter Smith was able to prove it, but the suspicion lingered months after Air Europe's crash.

In February 1991, just before Air Europe went down, and

shortly after Burnside had started attacking Branson in his press releases, a private detective, Frank Dobson, phoned Whitehorn. Dobson told him that Kroll was working for BA against Branson. When Dobson refused to give more details over the phone, Whitehorn arranged to meet him.

Whitehorn was accompanied to the meeting by Gerrard Tyrrell from Harbottles two weeks later on a snowy February morning. The two men made their way to the downstairs bar at Waterloo Station that Dobson had selected as the rendezvous point. The burly private detective repeated his claim that BA was employing Kroll. He said he was '100%' certain of the source that had given him the information. He described how Kroll specialised in corporate investigations, and outlined the surveillance and bugging techniques he believed their agents used. Dobson claimed he knew of several journalists who worked for Kroll, including Dominic Prince. Dobson alleged that Prince had told his contact that Kroll had been hired by BA to find 'dirt' on Virgin.

When the two Virgin men emerged from the smoky bar they both burst out laughing. 'It was far too much like a film to be real,' Tyrrell remembers. In a record of the meeting he wrote as soon as he returned to his office, the meticulous lawyer recorded, 'It was difficult to work out if Dobson was genuinely trying to help or whether in fact he was fishing for business or, indeed, whether or not he was a plant.'

Dobson phoned Whitehorn a week later.

'I told Dobson that we were not thinking of instituting any proceedings against BA because there was no evidence to support what he had told us. I also said I had discussed the matter with Richard, who had stressed that Virgin wanted nothing to do with private detectives.

'Even after the turmoil of the summer and the autumn it never occurred to me to link Frank Dobson to BA until we started hearing fresh rumours about private detectives working against us, and got hold of Basham's report on Virgin.'

Whitehorn was disconcerted to read that Basham claimed in his report that Frank Dobson was one of Branson's key advisors. The report claimed that he was a wealthy 'Rhodesian expatriate', who used to work for the white South African government's notorious

Bureau of State Security (BOSS). Basham's report claimed that Dobson's present company, Fintra Associates, was working 'in direct competition to Kroll'.

Whitehorn remembered that Dobson had claimed at the Waterloo meeting that Dominic Prince worked for Kroll. The Basham report had an article by Prince on Heaven attached to it. Could Dobson have been right? *Were* Kroll working against Virgin? Or perhaps BA had been trying to set Branson up by planting Dobson in Virgin's ranks as a double agent? What seemed too corny to contemplate in a smoky Waterloo Station bar at the start of the year now appeared to be riddled with meaning and significance.

After everyone at the Holland Park summit had chipped in, Branson swept their doubts and uncertainties aside.

'By this stage I'd really got the bit between my teeth. I just wanted to get it out into the open. I understood what people were saying about the dangers of a prolonged dispute, but I thought the quickest way to stop BA was to get everything out in the open.'

At Jonathan Crystal's suggestion, Branson decided to write a letter to British Airways in a bid to bring the affair formally out into the open. The letter was drafted by Crystal, for reasons Branson remembers very clearly:

'I didn't want to take legal action, but I did want the letter to be drafted by a lawyer because we intended to release it to the media.

'Jonathan told us we should state openly and honestly what we believed to be the case, but that we shouldn't overstate it or leave ourselves open to legal action by BA.'

The other decision Branson made was to write not to Lord King but to the chairman of British Airways' non-executive directors, Sir Michael Angus.

When Branson's letter arrived at Speedbird House on 11 December, the row that had been simmering between the two airlines finally boiled over in public. Branson addressed his open letter of complaint about BA's dirty-tricks to the 'Non-Executives' Chairman, Sir Michael Angus', and copied it to 'Lord White of Hull, The Hon. Charles Price II, Sir Francis Kennedy KCMB CBE, and Michael Davies'. Angus very swiftly passed his copy to the chief executive.

As he scanned Branson's letter, Sir Colin Marshall asked his secretary to call an urgent meeting of BA's most senior legal minds to help him prepare an instant response. Marshall read Branson's opening paragraph.

> In January 1991 British Airways was required to transfer four slots per week at Tokyo to Virgin. Six months later, Virgin was allowed to start operating from Heathrow. It is as if these decisions by regulators to enable Virgin to expand have engendered such fear and anger that normal and acceptable standards of commercial behaviour have been abandoned by British Airways.

The letter cited the *Guardian*'s allegations of 'an anti-Virgin unit', and the document shredding. It also mentioned the anecdotal evidence that British Airways were employing private detectives to spy on Virgin:

> Bizarre incidents have been taking place recently more suitable for an episode of Dick Tracy than the airline industry . . .

Branson attached an eight-page appendix which invited BA's non-executives to investigate a cat's-cradle of dirty-tricks accusations. He cited the two examples of passenger poaching he had discovered – Marcia Borne and (without referring to her by name) Caroline Mickler – and the ticket-endorsement dispute that Mike Scoates, his Heathrow manager, had brought to his attention.

The main thrust of Virgin's epistle, however, was directed at Brian Basham's activities, his rumour-mongering at the Savoy and his role in leaking Branson's private letter to Virgin Atlantic's staff. Branson referred to the PR man's briefing of Chris Hutchins, but did not reveal to BA that he had a tape of the encounter. He did tell them he had obtained Basham's report on Virgin.

> The 'report' would be a joke if it were not half-plausible in its presentation. It reflects the style of a private-placing document and appears to be a strange mixture of fact and

inaccuracy which combine to create a most damaging impression.

Branson had no idea at this stage that Sir Colin Marshall had paid £46,000 for the document, or that it had been specifically authorised by the chief executive and the chairman of British Airways. He also had no idea that his private letter to his staff had been studied by members of BA's board, and its anti-Virgin schemers, before Basham had been given permission to leak it to the press.

In his letter Branson did, however, put his finger on some of the key questions that would come to dominate the dispute between the two airlines.

> Who has authorised Mr Basham to conduct himself in this way? What expenditure has been incurred in relation to his activities? Are the shareholders aware of this activity? Who amongst the senior management (including Lord King, Sir Colin Marshall and Mr Burnside) knows of these activities?

Before closing his letter, Branson reminded BA of the role it played in grounding Laker Airways and the humiliation it suffered in the American courts as a result.

> I would have thought that British Airways' experience of trying to eliminate the competitive threat posed by Laker Airways was sufficient deterrent against trying to do the same to others. I am sure you remember the impact upon BA of its actions towards Laker Airways.
>
> BA's privatisation plans were disrupted, the directors in the United States were threatened with criminal prosecution, there was a huge waste of management time, BA attracted considerable adverse publicity, millions of dollars were spent in legal expenses and BA made the biggest single contribution to the massive settlement fund.
>
> As directors of a high-profile privatised industry . . . I ask you in the interests of the reputation of British Airways as Britain's flag carrier . . . to address the issues and matters

raised in this letter and respond as a matter of first importance and urgency.

Marshall was riled by the public nature of Branson's attack. Although Virgin Atlantic's chairman stated in his letter that his complaints should be 'dealt with internally within BA', his intention in releasing the 'open letter' to the press was clearly to generate maximum publicity, and thus rob BA of the chance of dealing with the matter quietly or internally .

No one at BA could be convinced that the timing of Branson's salvo was unconnected to the CAA's decision to turn down his request for another Tokyo slot the previous day – least of all Robert Ayling, who had masterminded BA's successful defence against Branson's case.

Although Ayling had finished his stint as legal director and company secretary in the autumn, Marshall still drew heavily on his experience and guidance as his young successor, Mervyn Walker, found his feet. Educated at Oxford University, the thirty-two-year-old Walker was appointed legal director when Ayling was promoted to replace Liam Strong; Walker had joined BA in 1986.

On the night of 11 December 1991, Ayling and Walker stayed with the chief executive until they were all satisfied that the denial of Richard Branson's allegations would be suitably emphatic. Marshall decided that he would add his authority as chief executive by replying to Branson personally, even though Virgin Atlantic's chairman had written to Sir Michael Angus.

Having masterminded the British government's response in the Laker anti-trust action when he was at the Department of Trade, Ayling knew that Branson's complaint was on a much smaller scale. The Laker case had lasted three years, and had eventually generated nearly a million documents in evidence. Branson gave no hint that he possessed a remotely comparable volume of evidence, and showed no appetite for a legal battle to which his small airline would have to devote enormous resources. It was doubtful if *any* small airline would possess the resources or commitment to embark upon the enormous step of challenging BA in the courts, certainly not without better evidence than Branson appeared to possess thus far.

Virgin's charges bore closer similarity to Air Europe's 1989 complaint about BA's rumour-mongering than to the Laker case. On that occasion an emphatic denial by Robert Ayling had served BA well. Aware of the difficulty not only of proving his case, but of the financial and political risks of taking on the national carrier in the courts, Harry Goodman had shied away from the legal option. Fifteen months later the banks shied away from the International Leisure Group, and Air Europe went bust.

The distinction between Goodman and Branson was that Virgin Atlantic's chairman had created a significant head of steam in the media, and had started to catch the airline industry's attention: Air Europe's complaints had created only minor ripples in the trade press. BA, therefore had to move swiftly to prevent Branson's widely publicised allegations gaining credence with a government publicly committed to the concept of competition in the airline industry. BA's external lawyers, Linklaters & Paines, were summoned to give their opinion of the legal implications of Branson's charges. Bill Allen and Michael Cutting of Linklaters spent the evening studying the Branson allegations. After a series of telephone conferences between Marshall and Ayling and Linklaters, Marshall decided that he would reply to Branson as well as Sir Michael Angus. Mervyn Walker was given the task of drafting their two replies.

The following day Marshall and Angus approved and signed the replies Walker drafted, both were then faxed to Branson.

Marshall wrote:

> Your suggestions that British Airways is involved in a deliberate attempt to damage your business, and seeks to compete other than through normal marketing and promotional efforts, are wholly without foundation.
>
> This is not the first time that unjustified allegations against British Airways have been made by your company. Would it not be better if you were to devote your undoubted energies to more constructive purposes?

The reply from the chairman of BA's non-executive directors was equally pithy. Angus told Branson it would be 'wholly inappropriate' for the non-executives to carry out an investigation on behalf of a third party. He concluded that 'the proper course of action is for any such allegation to be addressed to the Company'.

Marshall's tactic of harmonising BA's simultaneous replies to Virgin's chairman ensured that BA maintained a united front, and Branson's hope of glimpsing daylight between the executive and non-executive directors of BA was made to look naïve. By lunchtime the following day, the early edition of London's *Evening Standard* was leading with Branson's 'astonishing attack' on BA.

David Burnside's press officers maintained a holding pattern in response to an avalanche of media enquiries until Sir Colin and Sir Michael had signed BA's feisty replies. Burnside's press strategy was simple – Branson's claim that Virgin was the victim of an attack by BA was not true. In fact, the reverse was the case; BA was the victim of a publicity attack by Branson. Basham, meanwhile, was instructed not to respond personally to the allegations that Branson had made against him in the letter.

Burnside was convinced that the release to the press of Branson's letter to Angus would erode the credibility of his case. His press officers responded as they had earlier in the year when Branson had threatened to make a complaint about BA to the EC: they claimed his case was groundless, and that he was merely seeking publicity at BA's expense.

Taking Sir Michael Angus's reply literally, and disappointed that his allegations were dismissed so lightly, Branson wrote again to Sir Colin a few days later. He asked BA's chief executive to take a serious look at his points. After all, reasoned Branson, Marshall had a reputation for paying almost unhealthy attention to detail, and he was known throughout the industry as a control freak. Branson had spent weeks deciding precisely what should be in the letter. The eight-page epistle distilled nearly eighteen months of *angst*. Marshall could hardly have had time to read the allegations properly, let alone investigate them.

Again Branson was to be disappointed. On 17 December, Sir Colin replied in perfunctory fashion, concluding: 'I see nothing to be gained from further correspondence'.

The Holland Park summit had agreed a two-pronged strategy; if BA didn't respond satisfactorily to the open letter, Virgin would campaign through the media on the basis of the dirty-tricks accusation contained in it. Whitehorn was given the task of taking on the mass battalions of the BA public affairs department and its responsive cohorts in the fourth estate.

'The 11 December letter helped my job a great deal,' Whitehorn recalls, 'in the sense that journalists became more wary of repeating Burnside's and Basham's feeds from BA. It gave me on-the-record ammunition to fight back with. From that time on I could say "Look, what you are saying is a pack of lies and I know where you're getting your information from."

'I think the letter also took BA by surprise in that we highlighted some of the lies that were being told about our own company. I don't think many companies would have done that, particularly in a recession and in the middle of trying to get an equity bid off the ground.'

As Whitehorn started his media campaign to floodlight Virgin Atlantic's complaints against BA, Branson made another attempt to sort matters out with Lord King, face to face.

Somewhat to his surprise Branson had been invited to the *Sunday Telegraph*'s Christmas party by the paper's City editor, John Jay. Hoping that Lord King would be there nibbling mince pies, Branson set off to join 'Basham's boys', as he and Whitehorn had taken to calling Jay and Frank Kane. Ever the optimist, Branson made his way to the party at a pub close to the paper's offices. 'I hoped that we might let bygones be bygones and call the whole thing off.'

Branson exchanged festive pleasantries with Lord King, but to his disappointment, BA's chairman showed no interest in discussing the dramatic exchanges between their two companies. Within minutes of being introduced, King turned his back on him and started chatting to other guests.

Branson spoke briefly to Kane. In his letter to BA's non-executives, he had highlighted Kane's erroneous October report about the stalled equity bid as being amongst the most damaging 'spoiling tactics' he suspected Lord King's airline of inspiring. After assuring the worried reporter that he had not been personally named in the letter to the non-executives, a rather crestfallen Branson abandoned his seasonal mission and caught a taxi home.

As he bounced around in the back of the cab, he knew that the
dirty-tricks affair had passed the point of no return. Public humiliation would be the only retreat possible if the allegations did not
stick. The price of retreat could ground Virgin Atlantic. Branson
knew that the airline was only just breaking even and that it was
only the strength of the other parts of the Virgin Group – the music
and leisure divisions – that was keeping his dream in the sky.

By making his dispute with BA so public, he had raised the
stakes by further complicating Salomons' chances of being able to
sell the 20% stake in the airline. Fraser Marcus warned him that
after the 'dirty tricks' open letter, a new factor entered the minds
of potential investors.

'Not only had serious concerns been raised in investors' minds
by the stream of negative publicity about Virgin's finances, there
was now the prospect of a battle royal with BA,' recalls Marcus.
'There weren't that many people who would back an airline as it
was just about to square up to BA. Certainly not with the £50 million Richard wanted.'

Salomons had also warned Branson that their task was being
further complicated because the allegations of anti-competitive
behaviour that he had been making for over a year against BA
remained unproven.

Only one BA board member gave Branson any reason to hope
that his letter might have had an impact within BA. Michael Davis,
one of BA's non-executive directors and a long-standing friend of
Branson's father Ted, made a call to Virgin Atlantic's chairman.
Davis assured him that his complaints were being looked into.
Branson's diary records that Davis said his 11 December letter
would be 'like an iceberg', by which Branson understood that
much would go on beneath the surface. In that respect, Davis was
right.

Lord King and Sir Colin Marshall's top priority was to establish
whether Branson had a legal case against BA. There was no doubt
that Branson was upset at Virgin Atlantic's experience of the sharp
end of the Mission Atlantic campaign, and particularly by
Basham's Operation Barbara report, but BA needed to establish
whether anything he raised would stand up in a court of law.
Colin Marshall asked Linklaters & Paines to assist Mervyn Walker

in his task of assessing BA's legal exposure. In the meantime, the campaign against Virgin Atlantic would continue.

'To be honest, no one at BA took his allegations very seriously. We didn't think we'd done anything wrong,' Brian Basham remembers.

Since the spring, the PR man's work had been integral to BA's strategy of trying to deny Branson the opportunity to expand Virgin Atlantic. It was embarrassing to BA that Basham's uncharacteristic gaffe in the Savoy had been exposed in the *Sunday Times*, but this did not lead to a revision of strategy by Lord King or Sir Colin Marshall. Burnside had rebuked his friend and colleague for dealing with 'pond life', but Basham was instructed to continue as before, if a touch more circumspectly.

King and Marshall remained determined that Branson should not achieve his ambitious expansion plan, and that Operation Barbara should continue to try and stop it. Marshall had not considered Basham's report on Virgin and Branson was worth the £46,000 he had paid for it, but the PR man's briefings were proving priceless. The negative coverage of Branson and Virgin was dovetailing neatly with the uncertainties he and Robert Ayling were trying to place in the minds of the government and its civil servants at the Ministry of Transport and the CAA – the 'Greater Whitehall'.

Basham's achievement was not simply to place a string of stories hostile to Branson in supine newspapers such as the *Sunday Telegraph*. He had created a ripple effect, which was influencing the coverage of the entire group of Virgin companies more profoundly than at any time in their history . By Christmas 1991, nine months after he first presented Operation Barbara to Lord King and Sir Colin Marshall, Basham could point to an expanding cuttings file that had severely unsettled Branson and Virgin Atlantic. Even more importantly, the word in the City was that Branson's equity bid was now in trouble.

From Sir Colin Marshall's point of view it was politically convenient that Burnside and Basham's work was attracting Branson's attention as well as that of the press. It was clear from his letter that Branson assumed it was the King-and-Burnside axis that was inspiring the BA campaign against him. With Levin drawing Branson's attention towards his political enemies at BA, Marshall could let matters take their course, without excessive danger to his own position.

For the man who would be King, his breakfast conversation with Michael Levin in New York was a turning-point in the dirty-tricks affair. For Levin it was the end of the affair altogether. The day before he was due to leave New York for London to see Marshall, the seventy-year-old was diagnosed by his doctor as having cancer. In the early hours of Christmas morning Levin had an emergency operation for bowel cancer. Although his doctors declared it a success, he suffered a heart attack on 6 January 1992 and died.

Levin had performed his last service for Sir Colin Marshall. The shock his family experienced at his death was compounded when they found out that he had died in New York. He had not told them that he had been admitted to hospital. Levin's immediate family had assumed he was in England with BA's chief executive, as he said he would be. Mysterious to the last, Levin had told them that he was going to London 'to help Colin out' as he was in trouble.

When Levin's possessions were handed back to his family, three letters from the 'office of the BA duty mole' were found in his jacket. The 'duty mole' was not identified, but the correspondence contained spicy BA gossip, and it had been sent to Levin from Sir Colin Marshall's office. The chief executive and Levin exchanged BA gossip regularly. Levin's family recall that he received daily faxes from Colin Marshall's office until his death, and continued to write some of his speeches.

Perhaps conscious of the flak he had taken at BA over his close-ness to Levin, Marshall did not attend his old friend's funeral in New York. Unaware of the sensitivity of Levin's relationship with Marshall, the American's family was very disappointed. Marshall's guru was dead. But he would not be forgotten.

9

Barbarians at the
Departure Gate

Speedbird House. January 1992

'This is not the time for the faint-hearted! In UK sales we are doing everything short of breaking arms and legs in order to grab every passenger possible . . . no matter how we do it.

'One passenger per flight is the difference between success and failure, so every passenger counts and we must steal every one that we can!'

The Reverend Jim Callery beamed with pleasure as he listened to his London sales manager, Sue Hollis, rallying the troops. He had deputed one of his most effective evangelists to spread Mission Atlantic's message to a high-powered meeting of BA's departmental heads and their senior managers.

'We are going to miss our target for the year by so little. If only people realised how many opportunities there are to switch-sell,' Hollis continued.

Her audience included Kevin Hatton, the UK sales boss, who was in danger of not delivering on yet another revenue 'promise' to the Reverend Jim, and David Noyes, who had run the telemarketing teams of switch-sellers since the summer. Hollis's audience was under a three-line whip from Callery. He had instructed them to attend the meeting to 'lend your help to our number 1 priority of bringing in the revenue'.

However, by the beginning of 1992, the Reverend Jim's sales teams were in serious danger of not attaining the Holy Grail – the annual revenue target was slipping from their grasp. As a result Hatton and Callery had converted many of their missionaries into evangelists of BA's new age of switch-selling. Earlier in the year BA was so concerned that United Airlines was trying to switch BA passengers that it immediately alerted Robert Ayling's legal department. Now Ayling was in charge of the marketing and sales department himself, and BA's War on the Atlantic spawned switch-selling teams on both sides of the Atlantic.

'In December we missed our Premium Push target to the North Atlantic by one passenger per flight! That's all! Only one passenger per flight! We were so close, but we didn't get the ball between the posts!' The prospects for January looked no better. 'It looks as if we're going to lose out again, particularly on the North Atlantic, by a ridiculous target of one a flight yet again!'

Hollis appealed to other BA departments to release staff when they weren't required, to help the sales teams with their 'punter-pinching' operations. She wondered out loud if pilots could help to switch-sell in their breaks between flights. No effort was to be spared in the desperate bid to close the revenue gap. The switch-sellers were to target all the airlines flying across the Atlantic but Virgin was the main threat. If the one-passenger-per-flight was to be found, the chances were it would be a Virgin passenger.

Six months after Virgin, United and American had started their Heathrow services, BA estimated it would lose a total of £100 million revenue in a full year. Virgin was winning a larger share of the market than the two American carriers, putting it in second place behind BA over the Atlantic. On the New York routes, for example, the market-share figures were:

BA	41%
Virgin	18%
American	17%
United	15%

To Los Angeles, BA continued to dominate, but Virgin had more than doubled its 1990 market share of 12% by moving from Gatwick:

BA	46%
Virgin	26%
United	16%
American	13%[1]

Of BA's projected revenue loss of £100 million, Callery's department calculated that Virgin would be responsible for £33 million. As he contemplated the early results of BA's Atlantic War, the Director of its North American routes, Mike Batt, sighed, 'Damage limitation is the name of the game.'

Although BA's own market-share figures were holding up well, the threat that Virgin Atlantic posed to the Reverend Jim's annual revenue target was demonstrably larger than it ever had been before.

Sue Hollis described the ploys that sales had developed to boost the efforts of Maude's Marauders at Heathrow. She described how her sales teams had been scouring the top London travel agencies organising seminars on switch-selling. The teams would get the agents to find the details of business- or first-class passengers booked on other airlines, Upper Class in the case of Virgin, on their computer screens. The BA reps would show the agents how the national carrier could provide a flight at a very similar time, and promise travellers who switched lashings of bonus airmiles through the Latitudes scheme. If the agent agreed to switch a passenger during the presentation, BA rewarded the agent with a £5 Marks and Spencer gift voucher on the spot.

Another ploy involved teams from the sales-support division of BA. They had been told to tell travel agents that they would only

---

[1] Source: Virgin, MIS & CAA. The figures are rounded up and exclude the clutch of 5th-freedom carriers who land in London en route across the Atlantic and vice versa.

wait-list their passengers for BA flights that were full if the agent would agree to switch-sell a passenger to BA while they were on the phone.

The device of 'flight firming' was still being used by 'Pinch the Punter' operatives as a ploy to switch-sell passengers flying one way with BA and the other with a rival.

'Desperation Boulevard!' whispered one of Hollis's audience to her neighbour. 'I think the Reverend Jim has got a Mad Mullah on his hands!' came the hushed response. BA personnel attending such revivalist sessions had learnt to be careful what they said and how they looked. The Reverend Jim took a dim view of challenges to his orthodoxy and, as Hollis ranted, the hard-sell fundamentalist scoured the assembled congregation for 'negative body language'.

Branson's 11 December letter to BA had not caused the airline to rethink its switch-selling strategy. Robert Ayling appeared untroubled by the concept of punter-pinching, and had continued to fund the introduction of new switch-selling teams at Gatwick in the closing weeks of 1991. Ayling worked closely with Sir Colin Marshall to prepare BA's rapid response to Branson's complaints about the evidence he had collected of BA's passenger-poaching activities. Marshall and Ayling told Branson publicly that nothing other than 'normal marketing and promotional efforts' were being used against Virgin.

Ayling knew, however, that one of his key responsibilities in his new role as director of marketing and operations was to ensure that BA not only competed fairly in the increasingly cut-throat marketplace that had developed since the end of the Gulf War, but was also *seen* to be competing fairly. As the former head of the British government's aviation law branch, and with his first-hand experience of handling the Laker case, no one at BA was better versed in the dangers of anti-competitive activity than he.

After helping Sir Colin Marshall to compose BA's response to Branson's letter, Ayling wrote to all the managers who answered to him, as well as BA's policy group. Ayling stressed the criteria they should adopt in deciding what might constitute anti-competitive behaviour:

> A good rule-of-thumb test is whether the Company would
> be embarrassed by public disclosure of any action which
> might adversely affect a competitor . . .

Surprisingly, Ayling's interpretation of his role to ensure BA competed fairly appeared to be 'make sure you don't get caught'.
Ayling was later to claim that he knew nothing about the switch-
selling activities of his sales teams until Branson's letter to BA.
When he did find out what was going on, there is no evidence that
he asked his managers to stop poaching Virgin's passengers, or
any of the other activities Branson complained of. On the contrary,
his letter to his departmental heads conveyed a straightforward
message: carry on poaching.

Indeed, as 1992 opened, a new Gatwick-based team of switch-
sellers from Ayling's department was activated to complement
the work of Maude's Marauders at Heathrow. To convey a less
confrontational image of switch-selling, Chris Maude christened
the new teams 'Interline Sales', to belie their 'punter-pinching'
activities. The Interliners task, however, was identical to the
Marauders' – to steal passengers from rival airlines while appearing to be carrying out routine terminal sales duties.

The Gatwick team was led by sales and transfer supervisor,
Denise Fletcher, who had spent four months recruiting and training the agents in preparation for the team's pre-Christmas launch.
She became an 'Interline Sales' executive while she ran the team,
and she reported to Jeff Day. Day was an old hand at Gatwick who
had organised the undercover element of the Helpline team's
work as it extracted information on Virgin and Air Europe from
BABS. The veteran Helpline campaigner, responsible for the view
that 'BA doesn't make its money by helping old biddies to the
gate', was now to be placed in charge of BA's efforts to intercept its
rivals' passengers before they got anywhere near the departure
gate.

Heathrow was BA's home ground. The airline viewed much of
Gatwick as opposition territory, the traditional home of Britain's
independent airlines who, before Virgin Atlantic, had never managed to breach BA's Heathrow fortress. 'Interliners' conveyed a
less confrontational posture but the team's objectives were

identical – to capture maximum revenue from competitors.

The teams of passenger-poachers worked out the most efficient ways of targeting their rivals' passengers through BA's computer reservation system. Only the high-yield business- or first-class passengers were of interest to Robert Ayling's teams in their daily trawl of BABS to find switch-selling targets. They used the passenger name records (PNRs) held on BABS to find details of passengers whose bookings showed that, either before or after their BA flight, they would be using another carrier.

Another reason BABS was such a powerful tool for British Airways was that some travel agents placed bookings with other airlines directly onto BABS. Thus Ayling's Interliners could target passengers for switch-selling who were not flying on BA at all. By doing this they could approach passengers without travel agents being aware and kicking up a fuss about their commissions, and without rival airlines knowing BA had been accessing their bookings information.

In the case of Virgin Atlantic, BABS provided another benefit for BA. Virgin Atlantic bookings throughout the world are placed on the massive SHARES computer in South Carolina. Because the SHARES system crashes on average two or three times a year, Virgin Atlantic downloads the information about all its flights to BABS twenty-four hours before each one departs. This meant Maude's Marauders and Ayling's Interliners could obtain the names and, in the case of business customers using the limousine service, the contact numbers of all Virgin Atlantic's Upper Class passengers from their own computer.

It was clear to BA from Branson's letter that he had no idea that the random examples of passenger-poaching he had discovered had occurred as a result of such a sophisticated operation. To make sure Branson remained in ignorance, fierce internal memos were circulated warning of the potential dangers to BA of these activities being exposed. To reinforce the warnings, the Reverend Jim's sales department installed extra shredders so that documents 'liable to be misconstrued' could be disposed of appropriately.

As the Interliners set to work at Gatwick, their highly confidential reports to management were marked 'PLEASE READ AND

DESTROY'. Ayling instructed his department not to do anything that would embarrass BA were it later to become the subject of 'public disclosure'. If the reports were destroyed they couldn't embarrass BA. In what BA describes as its management system of 'devolved accountability', this meant that the Interliners were responsible for not getting caught.

All Denise Fletcher's weekly reports to Jeff Day and her superiors were marked 'Highly Confidential'. They summarised the amount of revenue her team had captured for BA, as well as intelligence on Virgin and other airlines.

The bulletins from Ayling's Interliners reveal how important Virgin had become to the efforts of the Reverend Jim's hit squads to reach their revenue targets. An internal memo dated 12 January 1992 reveals that of a total of £133,000 in 'endorsed revenue' claimed by the switch-sellers, passengers poached from Virgin accounted for £47,810, more than twice as much as any other carrier, and over a third of the total. Punters 'pinched' from United Airlines yielded £8,847 and American Airlines a mere £810.

When Branson returned from his Christmas and New Year break in the Caribbean, he opened a letter from a businessman in Liverpool. Geoffrey Luce wrote to Branson complaining about being badly treated by BA staff at Gatwick, and he highlighted 'their scurrilous and disgraceful comments regarding Virgin'.

Geoffrey Luce's teenage son, John, had been due to fly Virgin Upper Class to Miami on his way to the Cayman Islands shortly before Christmas. Virgin phoned to advise the Luce family that the 11.15 flight to Miami was delayed, and offered to transfer John to a BA flight to make sure that he got to Miami in time to catch his connecting flight to the Cayman Islands. The Luces readily accepted the offer, and father and son made their way to Gatwick to catch the BA flight. When they arrived at the BA check-in desk with John's ticket, seat number and reservation reference, the clerk told them he had been given instructions not to accept Virgin passengers on BA flights without validation. When a supervisor was called she confirmed that this was the case and informed the Luces that they could get validation from the Virgin shop in London.

Geoffrey Luce, a seasoned traveller himself, pointed out that the transfer had only been organised at the last minute, and that he did not want his young son to have to stop over in Miami overnight if he took the delayed Virgin flight. He was astounded by the reaction of the BA supervisor.

'I was told in front of others, "We are in competition with Virgin. We do not like them, they do not pay us when we carry their passengers and we do not like Virgin passengers."'

The Luces trooped off to the Virgin check-in and John boarded the delayed Virgin flight. Geoffrey Luce wrote to Branson to thank Virgin's cabin crew for taking care of his son during his overnight stay in Miami, and to express outrage at BA's behaviour.

'I am sixty-two years old, have had a heart attack, a by-pass, and a stroke and recovered from all of this. I do not bother to argue with people like BA staff, since I refuse to drop to their level . . . But to suggest cheating, lies and downright dishonesty are your [Virgin's] behaviour model is a disgrace . . . I do not believe that line managers say these things off the cuff and it reflects some-thing of the arrogance and officious behaviour practised by senior management.'

Branson noted that the incident Geoffrey Luce complained about occurred on 11 December, the day he sent his letter to Sir Michael Angus and the non-executives.

While relationships with BA continued to deteriorate, Branson took encouragement from his airline's growing reputation amongst business travellers. With an expanded Tokyo service now in place, and 30,000 Virgin seats a week available over the Atlantic, both airlines were monitoring the response of premium passen-gers at the top end of the market very carefully. In 1991 Virgin Atlantic had been declared 'Top Transatlantic Airline' by the *Travel Trade Gazette*, 'Best Transatlantic Airline' by *Travel News* and 'Best Business-Class Long-Haul Carrier' by *Business Traveller*. Richard Branson's airline had also been voted 'Airline of the Year' and 'Best Transatlantic Carrier' by the readers of *Executive Travel* magazine for the first time in a poll dominated by BA since its privatisation.

The first travel awards of 1992 were due to be presented at a lavish ceremony at the Dorchester hotel in London's Park Lane, at the end of January. BA and Virgin Atlantic representatives gathered with the international airline industry to discover who had won the *Executive Travel* magazine awards for 1992. The significance of the annual awards is considerable because *Executive Travel* magazine conducts its poll exclusively amongst the industry's most valued travellers – business- and first-class passengers. After a year of bitter controversy which had started with Branson threatening to take British Airways to the European Commission and ended with his pre-Christmas dirty-tricks broadside, the 1992 awards ceremony had added spice.

Branson not only brought his senior management team, including Syd Pennington, Roy Gardner and Chris Moss, but also his mother, Eve, who sat expectantly in a black trouser suit and gold trim alongside the great and the good of the British airline industry. Robert Ayling and David Burnside headed a low-key BA delegation. Because the poll's organisers alert the winners of each category in advance to make sure they turn up to collect their awards, seasoned observers thought Lord King's absence for the first time in most people's memory was significant. And so it proved.

Virgin Atlantic swept the board. Nine times during the evening Virgin representatives made their way to the podium to be presented with awards by Prince Edward. (Virgin was only eligible for thirteen categories.) Virgin not only won 'Airline of the Year' for the second year in succession; *Executive Travel*'s premium passengers had also voted Richard Branson's eight-plane operation 'Best Transatlantic Carrier', 'Best Long-Haul Carrier', and 'Best Business-Class Carrier'. In addition, Virgin won 'Best In-Flight Entertainment' for the third year in a row, 'Best Food and Wine', and 'Best Ground and Check-In Staff'.

The editor of *Executive Travel*, Mike Toynbee, sang the airline's praises.

'Not only has Virgin come of age, it has been praised for all the elements frequent travellers name as their priorities.

'Richard Branson has proved what he has always maintained: a small airline which takes the trouble to research what makes flying enjoyable, and trains its staff to anticipate passenger needs, can be more than a match for established carriers.'

As Toynbee's eulogy continued, Ayling looked down at his feet. At the end of the evening, Branson himself strode purposefully forward to receive the 'Airline of the Year' award. Flanked by a group of Virgin stewardesses, he waved the gold model aeroplane above his head as he encouraged the knot of photographers to snap away;

'Go on then!' he cried, relishing the moment.

Branson's laid-back demeanour and ready smile hide an exceptionally competitive nature. This was a moment of real pride for him only seven and a half years after Virgin's first flight. No airline in the history of the awards had ever won so many categories. Branson was in his element as the hundreds of airline luminaries applauded him warmly. They chuckled as Branson announced he had a special present for His Royal Highness. Jane Breedon made her way onto the stage and started massaging Prince Edward's shoulders. Virgin Atlantic's first masseuse was Branson's latest innovation for Upper Class passengers.

Away from the spotlight in the Dorchester Hotel's ballroom, one man was not applauding. David Burnside watched motionless as Branson celebrated – a canapé in one hand and half a glass of wine in the other. His heavily lidded eyes had wandered towards some of Branson's air stewardesses who were clutching their airline's awards. The flight attendants laughed as Branson announced that Virgin would now be protesting to the Advertising Standards Authiority about BA's use of the slogan, 'The World's Favourite Airline'.

'We have been told that BA awarded themselves this title on the basis of their passenger volume, not their quality. That's rather like saying that passengers prefer British Rail's service to the Orient Express or that the M25 is The World's Favourite Motorway!'

BA's director of public affairs was not amused. To Burnside's obvious surprise, Branson joined his group at the reception that followed the presentation ceremony. He made polite, inconsequential conversation with Burnside, tilting his head slightly in an unsuccessful bid to try and read Burnside's lapel badge which had slipped to an awkward angle on his suit jacket.

As Branson made his way out of the Dorchester to a celebration party for his staff, he asked Whitehorn:

'Who was that bloke with the strong Irish accent?'

'That was bloody Burnside!' giggled Whitehorn.

As the Virgin contingent departed for a night of revelry, Burnside became engrossed in deep conversation with Robert Ayling who was himself still holding one of the few awards BA had won that night: 'Best In-Flight Wine'.

Burnside's cultivated exterior in Branson's presence disguised his concern about BA's campaign against Virgin. Too much had gone wrong in the past three months. The spotlight was beginning to fall on himself and Brian Basham far too often for his liking. While BA's vice-like grip on the aviation lobby remained largely intact, BA's public relations operation was beginning to make the news, not mould it. During a *Times* investigation into Branson's dirty-tricks claims earlier in the month, Burnside had instructed his press officers to tell the paper's reporters he was 'unavailable' for comment. Burnside told the journalist working on the investigation, Tony Dawe, 'We'll have to do something about you.'

The negative publicity the dirty-tricks affair was yielding had shaken BA – it was bad for the airline's image, and bad for Burnside and Tony Cocklin in the public affairs department. BA's image as a flagship British enterprise which conducted business in a gentlemanly and honourable fashion was starting to wobble. BA was delighted when the press started to ask before Christmas if Richard Branson would become a second Freddie Laker or Harry Goodman, but dismayed when the spectre of its own role in Laker's demise re-emerged in the New Year. The millions of pounds it had spent on upmarket advertising was being dissipated by the spate of dirty-tricks allegations. The public affairs department's £5 million budget to help BA cultivate 'editorial support' to complement the airline's vast advertising campaigns was beginning to look frayed. Suddenly at the centre of a growing crisis, Burnside was able to provide few answers to the many questions he was being asked.

Burnside found it difficult to believe that Branson was beginning to turn the tables on BA without external assistance. While

Burnside and Basham were acknowledged masters of 'negative PR', Branson and Whitehorn had no track record in conflictual PR at all. If Branson was hiring professionals to bolster his efforts, they shouldn't be hard to find, reasoned Burnside. His own suspicions had already been alerted.

Just before Christmas Burnside's long-serving secretary, Diane Marshall, received a mysterious call from an anonymous male. The caller claimed he could provide information about how sensitive information was being leaked from BA's electronic mail system in London and New York. The caller said he worked for 'Whitehall Security Services' but would not leave a number.

British Airways took the call seriously enough to launch an initial investigation which succeeded in establishing contact with 'Whitehall Security Services'. The organisation denied making the December call to Burnside's office but BA's head of security, David Hyde, was not convinced, and neither were Lord King and Sir Colin Marshall.

After a series of high-level meetings, King and Marshall charged Burnside and Hyde with masterminding a highly sensitive, undercover mission, codenamed 'Operation Covent Garden'. Its objective was to regain the initiative for British Airways, and to undermine Branson's fight back. Covent Garden would be contracted out, like Brian Basham's Operation Barbara. The man chosen to lead the undercover operation was another close friend of Lord King's, 'security consultant', Ian Johnson.

British Airways first turned to Ian Johnson in 1986 when security was on every Western airline's agenda. President Reagan had just bombed Tripoli, Libya's capital, in retaliation for alleged terrorist attacks on American military personnel. Reagan had secured Mrs Thatcher's approval for some of the US warplanes to take off from bases in Britain. Intelligence experts predicted that a Western airline was a likely target for Libyan retaliation. Two years later a bomb, possibly placed by Libyan agents, destroyed PanAm flight 103 over the Scottish town of Lockerbie.

As airlines throughout Britain and the USA tightened their security procedures, British intelligence told King that BA was an obvious and symbolic target for terrorist attack. Lord King's family link with the Royal Family, and the friendship with the Prime Minister and her husband that King boasted of publicly, increased the threat still further.

Johnson himself emerged from the royal security network – he was once in charge of Prince Charles' personal security. A former member of the Army Intelligence Corps, Johnson had been stationed in the Middle and Far East, and Cyprus. A fluent German speaker, he also became an expert on Arab terrorist groups, and learnt to speak colloquial Arabic. He is a member of the Institute of Investigators. King instantly took to Johnson's disciplined approach. His company had just carried out a security 'audit' for the BBC, in which he carefully and systematically assessed the threat to each of the Corporation's scores of properties.

Johnson's ability to mix in the highest circles also impressed King, no mean social mountaineer himself. The former army man had highly placed contacts and clients; among them were reputed to be members of the Saudi Royal Family whom Johnson got to know while working as general manager of a large private security company in the Middle East. Johnson's smooth charm and social skills were matched only by his reputation for being tight-lipped about his clients' business. 'Johnson was a clam,' said Basham.

King was particularly concerned about security arrangements at BA's first ever general meeting of British Airways' shareholders following privatisation in 1987. It was to be staged in a blaze of publicity at the Albert Hall. The location, chosen in anticipation of a high proportion of BA's new shareholders attending, posed a potentially serious security problem with the warren of passages beneath the platform providing a bomber's paradise.

Hired by BA, Johnson energetically secured the Albert Hall AGM against terrorist attack. Acting on King's personal authority, he set up secure zones which only pass-carriers could enter. Even some dismayed members of BA's in-house security staff found themselves excluded. When the meeting went off without a hitch, Johnson was called upon for other security work. King offered him a job at BA. Johnson declined on the grounds that he could make more money if BA contracted out its security requirements.

King agreed, and Johnson launched Ian Johnson Associates on the back of a BA contract.

Johnson conducted periodic sweeps of BA's offices for electronic bugs, and organised 'close personal protection' – security-speak for bodyguards – for some members of BA's board. Johnson accompanied King on trips to Northern Ireland and to Conservative Party conferences. The BA Chairman even asked Johnson to help install a burglar-alarm system on his estate in Strathnaver in Scotland. Delighted with the results, King recommended Johnson to Marshall, who was considering fitting alarms to his London home in Montpelier Square.

Johnson works from Walnut Tree Cottage, which nestles discreetly in the tiny Surrey village of Seale, just outside Farnham. Behind false garage doors, annexed to the rustic dwelling, are the modern, computerised offices of Ian Johnson Associates, International Security Management Consultants.

The cottage's clever architectural disguise has prompted visitors to compare Johnson's hi-tech control room to Tracy Island, home of the characters in the *Thunderbirds* TV series. Like the fictional Tracy family, Johnson prefers to keep his operation out of the public gaze. Among his clients are top names in commerce and industry for whom confidentiality is paramount. Saatchi and Saatchi, Hanson, Thames Water and the BBC are amongst the household names that have used his services. Discretion is Johnson's byword. Inquiries to the company from the media are politely but firmly rebuffed.

Villagers in Seale remember Lord King visiting Johnson at home in Walnut Tree Cottage as their professional relationship blossomed into friendship. King reciprocated by inviting Johnson to his club, White's, where they could be seen playing backgammon together. A keen tennis player and golfer, with an athletic build and military disposition, Johnson impressed his clients with an easy manner, although he irritated some members at White's by using his mobile phone while drinking with Lord King.

David Hyde called Ian Johnson to Speedbird House to brief him on the requirements for Operation Covent Garden. Hyde himself is described by his colleagues at the airline as a solid BA yeoman with a background in engineering. He gave Johnson two tasks: to identify and locate the mole who was suspected of leaking information from within BA, and to find out who was working for Branson. Johnson was given a copy of Basham's Operation Barbara, and a further briefing by David Burnside on BA's overall offensive against Virgin Atlantic.

Johnson recognised immediately that his relatively small operation in Walnut Tree Cottage would have to be bolstered if he was not only to track down a mole in the vast airline, but also penetrate what King and Burnside suspected could be a sophisticated operation being run against them by Branson. So he recruited two private detectives who had worked with him in the past, Nick Del Rosso and Tom Crowley. Nicknamed 'The Likely Lads' by Johnson, the two gumshoes cut very different figures. Former Metropolitan Police officer Del Rosso is an enormous, lumpy man with fair, tightly curled hair. The softly spoken detective was in the CID for many years, investigating 'heavy' cases of murder and rape. He took up private investigations after his career in the Metropolitan Police came to an end.

Like Del Rosso, Crowley is a quietly spoken man but the similarities between the two end there. A whippet-thin former customs investigator, he specialised in fraud investigations and undercover surveillance when working for Her Majesty's Customs and Excise. Crowley crops his dark hair, and prefers jeans and casual jackets to Del Rosso's business suits.

When Johnson approached Crowley and Del Rosso, they were both working for Carratu International, one of the largest firms of private investigators in Britain, with offices in Cheam in Surrey and in Chancery Lane, London.

At the time, Carratu International was chaired by Vince Carratu, a former Scotland Yard detective and an expert in exposing fraud and counterfeiting scams. A small, energetic man, Carratu is regarded as an elder statesman among private investigators. Since he founded his company in the early 1960s, it had established its reputation for undercover work and, by the early 1990s, boasted a growing 'corporate investigations' unit. Carratu International specialised in breaking up counterfeiting rings: the Gillette razor blade company and Chanel perfume hired Carratu to expose forgers who were illegally copying their products. In the USA, Carratu had been hired by the prosecution in the highly publicised Klaus Von Bulow case, in which Von Bulow was accused of poisoning his wife.

As Vince Carratu prepared to hand over the running of his company to his son, Paul, he was regarded as the *eminence grise* of the undercover world. The British Airways' contract seemed the perfect opportunity for Ian Johnson Associates and Carratu International to start working together, as Crowley and Del Rosso were known to both companies.

According to one source at Carratu, Ian Johnson stressed that total secrecy must be observed at all times.

'We were not allowed to mention British Airways' name in any reports. We could not register the job in their name and reports had to be delivered by hand to Ian Johnson.

'Johnson also said we must do absolutely nothing to upset Richard Branson or bring ourselves to his attention. He had publicly accused British Airways of hiring private detectives to work against him. If he found out what we were doing it could have been catastrophic for BA.'

Johnson also told Carratu that Lord King would pay for the work via an account based in Jersey, so that BA's involvement in the project could not be traced back to the airline.

Johnson set about his task with characteristic military zeal. He assigned alpha-numeric codes to the members of BA's board of directors and board of management who were most closely involved in Operation Covent Garden, as well as Brian Basham and his own team. Johnson reasoned that if documents did fall into the wrong hands, no one would be able to understand what they meant.

David Hyde was C1. Sir Colin Marshall was C2. David Burnside was S1 and Brian Basham was S2. Johnson's core team of Del Rosso and Crowley were R1 and R2.

At £100 per hour, Johnson's team did not come cheap so, with Sir Colin Marshall's authority, Hyde placed an initial above-the-line spending limit of £15,000 on Covent Garden, hoping for an early result. Before long specialist counter-espionage technicians were crawling all over BA's Enserch House and Speedbird House communications systems. One of the 'sweepers' was Mervyn Finch, a former soldier in the Royal Corps of Signals and a specialist in electronic warfare, who had learned his trade in the Lebanon and Cyprus. For weeks, Finch painstakingly searched table lamps, wall sockets and items of furniture for tiny microphones or transmitters. He used highly sophisticated equipment and applied the skills he had learned intercepting enemy radio transmissions and jamming enemy frequencies. Finch described his contribution to Operation Covent Garden as 'a ball-breaking job'.

Johnson also called on another highly trained specialist, Jimmy Stokes, to test for telephone bugs. Stokes was based at British Telecom's Investigations Unit in Hemel Hempstead in Hertfordshire. The Unit maintained a longstanding arrangement with the Home Office after privatisation to execute telephone tapping warrants for MI5. Johnson's man, therefore, was one of only a handful of top experts in call-tracing and 'listening on the line' in Britain. Stokes' exceptional skills earned him top rates as a private consultant, and the nickname 'The Technician'.

Stokes swept the offices and regularly checked seals that had been placed over electrical and telephone sockets. The seals were sophisticated anti-tampering devices of the type used by intelligence services. They carried a tiny BA aircraft logo which showed up when a light of specified wavelength shone from a special torch. Invisible to the naked eye, the logo was broken if any attempt was made to remove the socket cover to plant a listening device. Like Finch, 'The Technician' found nothing.

Another of Covent Garden's early activities was an internal 'security audit'. One theory was that the mole might be intercepting sensitive material discarded by BA's senior executives on its way to the shredder, and passing it to the media or directly to Branson. The airline operates a 'red bag' system, whereby material for shredding is placed in red nylon bags which are collected nightly and removed from Speedbird House and Enserch House for destruction by an outside contractor. The 'security audit' drew a blank as well.

The activities of Johnson's team were kept a closely guarded secret within BA. Monthly payments were submerged in Hyde's security budget. Johnson initially kept Hyde and Marshall informed of progress on a 'need to know' basis. Lord King was briefed over Scotch and backgammon at White's.

Exactly a week after Virgin Atlantic's triumph at the Dorchester Hotel ceremony, Richard Branson walked through the aeroplane graveyard in the Mojave Desert. The unblinking sun was the only visible object in the blue Californian sky. In the thin air, all Branson could see were abandoned aeroplanes. Some were in suspended animation, some were already dead and being dismembered in an adjacent scrapyard. Others were being embalmed.

A dozen PanAm 747s, with their distinctive pale blue globe motifs, stood in a straight line stretching for over half a mile. Particularly poignant were seven Lockheed 10–11s in British Airways' livery. The enormous planes stood silently as a single technician drained the remaining oil from their engines, and sealed their orifices with silver foil. Branson scratched his beard as he reflected that the capacity of his entire fleet was not much larger than that of BA's slumbering giants. These were some of the planes Lord King was itching to get back in the air.

Branson had driven to the Mojave graveyard in the foothills of the Sierra Nevada mountain range that morning from Los Angeles with the team from *This Week*. I had telephoned Branson in the middle of January to tell him that after investigating his accusations against BA, we wanted to make a film about the dispute.

The first person we interviewed was Peter Fleming, who confirmed what he told Branson, and revealed new details about the close interest the marketing and sales department at BA had taken in Air Europe. As the crash of ILG had resulted in the loss of 6,000 jobs, as well as the demise of Air Europe, we started looking into it. We held a series of secret meetings with former Air Europe executives who told us that although they had little concrete proof, they were certain that Branson was now experiencing the sort of smear campaign against Virgin their airline had had to endure. All the executives had now moved on to other careers and none would agree to be named.

The vast tentacles of BA's patronage and power stretch well beyond the aviation industry. We were told that a 'black book' of evidence existed about BA's dirty tricks against Air Europe, and in particular Harry Goodman. When we approached the International Leisure Group's administrators, KPMG Peat Marwick, they refused to cooperate, as did ILG's solicitors, so we concentrated on the Virgin story.

There was enormous scepticism amongst the aviation lobby and the trade press about Virgin's claims. MPs we spoke to gave the dirty-tricks claims very short shrift. However, the more closely we examined Branson's claims, and spoke to the sources he and Whitehorn cited, the more interesting the story became. We became convinced that there was something important struggling to get out, particularly in America. Many journalists we spoke to were personally committed to one side or the other – mainly BA – or worked for papers that were committed to trumpeting Lord King's achievements in privatising BA for political reasons.

A number of journalists told me that they thought the dirty-tricks story was fascinating, but that they could not investigate it because their editors were committed to BA, either through political inclination or the lure of BA freebies. Having no links in the aviation industry was a positive advantage to us. *This Week* was very unlikely to make another film about the topic, so we didn't really care whom we offended as long as we got the story right.

We made certain that our programme manager at Thames TV bought and paid for our tickets to Los Angeles before we stepped on board our Virgin flight to start filming Branson and his Virgin team. One of *This Week*'s most seasoned reporters, Richard Lindley, a veteran of the BBC's *Panorama* as well as of ITN, had joined our investigation, and we flew with Branson to the West Coast of America to explore some interesting leads in the USA, and to interview Branson himself. To our surprise, Branson was a reluctant participant in the film, despite his obvious desire for it to be made.

Branson's confidence appeared to have slipped badly since our first encounter with him at the beginning of January. According to those closest to him, he was withdrawn by his own standards. Will Whitehorn later told us that for the first time since he founded the airline in 1984, he had stopped writing to his staff for fear that his letters would find their way into the hands of 'Basham's boys'. He was still deeply uncertain whether his strategy for tackling BA was the correct one. Despite a series of newspaper reports detailing some of his allegations, his strategy had yet to bear fruit of any description. The jury was still out. The frustration for Branson was that now there was something that he really wanted to get across to the public, he appeared to lack the credibility required. He no longer needed the acres of uncritical publicity that he had become so accomplished at generating on behalf of Virgin. He was now entering uncharted terrain, and the lights that had guided him until this point could no longer be relied on.

In a sense, Branson was reaping the legacy he had sown in promoting Virgin Atlantic so effectively since 1984, and becoming better known for his ability to generate publicity than for the extraordinary achievements of his Virgin companies. Branson also knew that those within Virgin Atlantic itself who felt he had got the dirty-tricks issue out of proportion, would not have been discouraged in their view by the developments since the open letter to BA.

Branson was certain of one thing – Salomons had still found no serious interest in buying equity in Virgin Atlantic. As long as the battle of words continued to rage, he knew that, in one sense, BA was winning the war. Only his very closest colleagues and his family knew that he had asked John Thornton, the managing director of investment banking at Goldman Sachs, to prepare for the sale of Virgin Music. He certainly didn't tell us. Characteristically, Branson was 'protecting the downside', and the desert morgue bore chilling witness to the ambitions, and the follies, of some of those who had failed to do so.

Branson eventually succumbed to our argument that if Virgin Atlantic intended to make serious accusations against BA, he was the only logical interviewee. We told Branson that Lord King would be invited to put BA's case.

Branson's *This Week* interview took place under the nose-cones of one of the seven BA planes in the Mojave Desert. Perhaps daunted by the physical witness of the shattered dreams of far more powerful barons of the sky than himself, Branson stumbled and hesitated as he groped for the right turn of phrase in response to Richard Lindley's questions. Bringing himself to accuse Lord King and his colleagues of a dirty-tricks campaign against Virgin Atlantic on camera appeared to represent a major psychological hurdle.

'I know a lot of these innuendoes come from Brian Basham who's employed by British Airways, and Brian Basham reports to a man called David Burnside who is the head PR person at British Airways, who then reports to Lord King,' he told Lindley, gasping slightly at the end of his statement, as if he were quite surprised he had managed to say it.

This pronouncement seemed to unblock him. He went on to repeat the allegations of passenger-poaching that he had discovered, and the document-shredding that Peter Fleming had told him about. During the interview Branson confessed that he was reluctant to take legal action against BA:

'I've never sued anyone in court for anything . . . we've probably got a good case to say that someone's tried to damage our business but you know it takes hours of management time. I think our best bet is to get it out into the open and hopefully there'll be people at BA who'll realise it's counterproductive, and that they should not carry on in the future behaving in this sort of way.'

At the end of the interview Branson watched as our cameraman, Frank Haysom, took off in a microlight helicopter to capture the extraordinary desert scene. Branson turned to me, off camera, and remarked:

'It's quite literally like being in a graveyard here, and the truth of the matter is that no small airline has ever survived before. I really believe this is where BA ultimately want our planes to end up so they can get their own back in the air again.'

Before Branson left the USA he flew overnight to New York to pay a brief visit to Virgin Atlantic's North American HQ. The airline's American boss, David Tait, was Laker Airways' manager in Miami when the airline went down in 1982. He was keenly aware of the dangers to small airlines of BA-inspired whispering campaigns. To Tait's dismay, staff at Virgin Atlantic's New York headquarters had begun to pick up gossip that the airline would be out of business by the end of the year. The airline's modest, red-brick office which clings to the River Hudson on the edge of Greenwich Village was alive with rumours. In the States such rumours about a British carrier needed little or no evidence to be believed while two of the major pillars of the American aviation establishment, PanAm and TWA, were crumbling. Tait sensed that morale was being affected. He told Branson he was worried.

'We're obviously annoying the heck out of BA, and the rumours do scare me . . . little stories build into big stories and that's when confidence starts to go.'

After Branson had spent part of the morning chatting to the airline's telephone sales staff, a Virgin limousine took him to New York's Kennedy Airport for his return flight to England. Ronnie Thomas, the boss of the Manhattan International Limousine company, accompanied him. Thomas had alerted Branson to the kerbside passenger-poaching his drivers had witnessed in November, and Branson was keen to get a first-hand account of what appeared to be a particularly virulent breed of barbarian at his New York departure gates.

As the limo cut through the Manhattan traffic, the flamboyant Italian-American explained what had been happening:

'Richard, they are trying to get your customers as we drop them off at the airport, offering them some sort of discount travel coupons . . .'

'You mean they are approaching them as they get out of the limousines after they've started their journey with us?' interjected Branson.

'Exactly that. Right at the kerbside. Identifying themselves, they are in what appears to be British Airways uniform, approaching them right there and then, trying to give them a pass to switch over to British Airways.'

Branson frowned. Thomas's testimony supported the stories he had been told of BA's clandestine activity at Heathrow and Gatwick. At Kennedy the poachers were particularly obvious, because BA has its own terminal and its staff have no reason to be anywhere near the spot where Virgin limos drop passengers.

'Have you said anything to them? Have you told them where to get off?' asked Branson.

'Yes, I approached the BA reps as soon as I found out about it. I spoke to the guy and I told him I didn't want him bothering Virgin's passengers. I said these people wanted just to get out of the limo and get on your plane,' said Thomas with an expansive sweep of his arm in Branson's direction. 'And after trying to reason with him he finally turned around and told me to go fuck myself.'

'Have you ever come across anything like this before?' asked Branson.

'No. Never,' replied the chauffeur boss emphatically. 'I mean, we've dealt with your company since its inception, and before that we've dealt with other companies. Nothing like this has happened before. This is dirty business.'

Branson arrived early for his flight. Spotting some of his staff going about their daily chore of erecting the Virgin Atlantic logos, and unfurling tapes to guide passengers towards the check-in desks, he walked over to give them a hand.

At BA's own terminal several hundred yards away, Concorde taxied for take-off. The pride of Lord King's fleet cruised past a line of BA's 747s. Some of the planes were having vast containers of prepacked food inserted into their sides. Others were disgorging passengers. Minutes later Concorde disappeared over the New York skyline in a cloud of its distinctive, mustard-coloured afterburn.

The sight of Virgin Atlantic's chairman constructing his airline's check-in desk as Concorde took off was an appropriate metaphor for the crisis his airline faced. As Branson knew only too well, the laminated plastic 'Virgin Atlantic' signs could be taken down just as easily as they had been erected.

Back on the West Coast of America, we uncovered new evidence that BA's whispering campaign against Branson and Virgin had taken root in the vast urban sprawl of Los Angeles. Michael Chrisman discovered a small Longbeach travel agency, British Imports Travel, specialising in selling airline tickets to the British expatriate community. The agency's owner, John Healy, told Chrisman that many passengers were cancelling their flights with

Virgin because of rumours that the airline would soon be going bust.

We went to investigate. Healy's office manager, Romel Manalo, showed us a log that he had kept. Scores of passengers had switched from Virgin flights in the previous few weeks. Most had switched to BA, although it would cost them more. The travel agents had also kept a note of the reasons passengers had given. Manalo explained:

'I'd been selling Virgin tickets for about two years and I'd never had a problem with them before, so this was strange.

'Normally most people want to fly with Virgin because it's cheaper and you get a better service on the plane. But suddenly at the end of last year no one wanted to fly with them. About 25% of the calls that would normally have gone to Virgin were going to BA.

'It was becoming a really big trend, so we decided to start the log. People said that they had heard Virgin was going out of business, and that they didn't want to risk flying to London and getting stranded if the airline went down during their trip.

'People said that Branson was having to get money from the Japanese to keep his business going, that he had been caught dealing dope in his nightclubs, that he spends too much money on his balloons and that he's getting eccentric and unreliable'.

The similarities between what Manalo's passengers were saying to him, and what Marshall and Ayling were saying to the British government and what Brian Basham had been taped saying to Chris Hutchins, were unmistakable. With the memory of Laker's demise still fresh among the expatriate community, suggestions that Virgin was about to go the same way were turning into firmly held beliefs.

Richard Lindley then interviewed some of the passengers from Manalo's log who had refused to buy Virgin tickets and changed their bookings to BA.

Cory Quinn bought a return Virgin ticket to London for $455 from British Imports Travel. He needed to go to London to negotiate a contract for the small machine-tool company he had just started working for. When he returned to his company's Longbeach office his boss, Steve Halley, told him to change it immediately.

'I'd seen a lot of negative PR on Virgin Airways,' Halley explained, 'and I didn't want to risk any chance of not getting the venture put together.'

Returning to British Imports, Quinn was booked on a BA flight. It cost Halley $94 more to fly Quinn on BA, but he wasn't prepared to risk his money on Branson's airline.

'It's like PanAm, one day they're here, the next day they're gone.'

Ivan Hilla was another name that appeared in the Manalo log. He was quite categorical when Richard Lindley asked him why he had turned down a $455 Virgin ticket in favour of a $489 BA ticket:

'I didn't want to take the chance of using Virgin Airlines, as I'd heard so many rumours flying around that Virgin was going out of business.'

Hilla is a regular transatlantic traveller. He runs a quaint military memorabilia shop in the lee of the Hollywood Hills, selling a vast array of British military uniforms and medals. Life-size models of Grenadier Guards and stalwart defenders of Rorke's Drift flank the entrance. Half a dozen times a year Hilla flies to London to stock up. His pattern rarely changes. He books early to save money, and when in England he is always pressed for time:

'I'm always on a tough schedule when I go to London. I have to be in certain places at certain times and I have to come back on time.'

Normally a regular Virgin traveller, Hilla decided to fly BA on his forthcoming trip, despite its higher ticket price and hearing from friends in London that Richard Branson had accused Lord King's company of spreading false rumours about Virgin. Hilla had reason to play it safe. In January 1982 he had booked to fly to London with Laker Airways. On 5 February 1982, Laker went under and Hilla was stranded.

'I couldn't use the bloody ticket. I was mad!'

On the East Coast we probed Virgin's allegations that BA's New York office was one of the sources of the anti-Virgin rumours. David Tait gave us details of the most disturbing incident that he had come across. Early in the New Year, Tait's director of interline sales for North America, Patricia

Cunningham, had asked to see him urgently. Cunningham's job is to mastermind liaison between Virgin and other carriers. One of her prime tasks is to organise the exchange of full-fare passengers between Virgin and other airlines and to organise joint promotions with other carriers. Virgin only flies to a restricted number of destinations in America, so Cunningham's department tries to fix onward flights with other carriers for passengers wanting to fly within the USA. The hope is that if other carriers' passengers required transatlantic tickets, they would turn to Virgin. In all airlines, interline sales is a forum for picking up news and gossip about rival carriers.

As Cunningham walked into Tait's office, she burst into tears. Representatives from both South African Airways and KLM had told her that Virgin was on the brink of bankruptcy. The particular cause of Cunningham's distress was that she had just taken on a large mortgage which was based on her continuing to work at Virgin on her current salary.

Tait claimed to have established from South African Airways and KLM that the rumours had emanated from British Airways. At the time KLM was discussing a possible merger with BA and there was a great deal of contact between the two airlines.

Tait quizzed the KLM and the SAA staff who had told Cunningham about the whispers. Both carriers said the rumours were coming from the office of Dick Eberhart, one of BA's vice-presidents. Eberhart worked at BA's Bulova headquarters at Jackson Heights on the outskirts of New York.

Before setting off to confront Eberhart, we made our own checks with South African Airways and KLM. Representatives of both airlines were somewhat startled to hear the unhurried New Jersey tones of Michael Chrisman quizzing them on the dirty-tricks dispute between two rival British carriers from his hotel room at the Grand Hyatt.

Once a pledge of complete anonymity had been given, both contacts confirmed that the stories about Virgin were coming from BA's New York HQ, and confirmed that Eberhart's office was responsible. The KLM manager was particularly keen to remain anonymous. At the beginning of February 1992, BA and KLM appeared to be on the brink of successfully concluding a merger.

We arrived unannounced at BA's Jackson Heights HQ the following day to put Virgin Atlantic's allegations to Dick Eberhart.

Chrisman told the BA receptionist he wanted to see Eberhart on a personal matter and waited for his reply at the BA desk. The rest of us drank coffee and milkshakes in the atrium of the vast office complex.

Eberhart looked stunned when he heard why Chrisman had really come to see him. He refused the opportunity of an off-the-record chat, and immediately sent for the head of BA's press operation in New York, Sandy Gardiner.

'We can't talk about these matters because of American anti-trust laws,' stated Eberhart, and Gardiner added that he would have to consult BA in London for further guidance. During a civil exchange with Chrisman, Eberhart and Gardiner emphasised that it was because of America's tough anti-trust laws that they thought it unlikely that BA London would allow Eberhart to give an interview.

Chrisman was taken aback by the response of the BA men.

'Neither of them challenged the accusation that Eberhart had been spreading the rumours about Virgin. I expected them simply to deny Virgin's allegations and send me on my way. Eberhart sat there looking glassy-eyed, and Gardiner took detailed notes on what looked like a legal notepad. He was very interested in how we knew the allegations originated from BA. Without naming the airlines or the sources, I told him. In the course of my conversation with them Eberhart and Gardiner repeated three times that the anti-trust laws were the reason for not granting an interview.'

At the end of the meeting Gardiner told Chrisman that he would consult London and fax the reply to the Grand Hyatt in the morning. Working on the assumption that, in this context, 'London' meant David Burnside, and the answer would certainly be no, we decided to ambush Eberhart as he left the office later that day.

As he stepped out of the Bulova building into a mild February night, we clambered out of a minibus positioned directly opposite the main exit in a BA parking space. Lindley pursued Eberhart to his car in an attempt to get some sort of answer on camera to the rumour-mongering charges. Eberhart became annoyed and after waving Lindley away, reversed his car at speed out of its space before disappearing onto the Queen's Highway.

The following day, BA's board met in London. High on the agenda was Richard Branson's December letter to the non-executive directors.

As Marshall prepared to report on the public exchange of hostilities with Virgin Atlantic, Mervyn Walker briefed him on the legal implications of Branson's allegations against the company. He advised Marshall that in his view, and the view of BA's external lawyers, Linklaters & Paines, BA had no case to answer in law.

Walker's investigation appears to have been perfunctory. It was never published, and there is no evidence that it was ever written down. Walker told Sir Colin that he had spoken to all the relevant senior members of BA as well as Brian Basham. What Branson described as Basham's 'remarkable conduct' dominated three out of eight pages of Virgin's charges against BA, but the PR man says he was not interviewed by Walker.

'I was rather proud of the first three pages, but I don't remember Mervyn Walker ever talking to me. In any case it wasn't that sort of inquiry, it was an overnight investigation, if it was an investigation. The allegations contained in it [Branson's letter] were not taken terribly seriously by British Airways at the time.'

At the board meeting Marshall referred BA's directors to the robust responses he had issued on behalf of the company since Branson's letter. He went on to reassure the board that there was no legal case to answer on any of Branson's allegations.

Three days after the BA board had accepted Marshall's assurances, Dr James Sorrentino touched down at Gatwick Airport on BA Flight 917 from Frankfurt. The professor was pleased the early evening flight was on time. The previous day's BA flight to Frankfurt had been a disaster. He had got only as far as Cologne and had to complete the journey to Frankfurt in a hire-car. In total the journey took him nearly seven hours. For passengers like Dr Sorrentino, who have to spend a fair proportion of their working lives in the air, such experiences are misery.

Richard Branson launched his 'fun' airline in 1984. BA dubbed him the 'Grinning Pullover'. Lord King later said of him, 'If Richard Branson had worn a pair of steel-rimmed glasses, a double-breasted suit and shaved off his beard, I would have taken him seriously. As it was, I couldn't . . .'

Many found King the man in King the huntsman. 'The bravest fellow I've ever seen in the hunting field' according to his friend, Lord White.

Branson the balloonist leaves Japan in the *Pacific Flyer* to take on the ocean in 1991. Breaking another world record nearly cost him his life when a technical fault caused him accidentally to dump much of the balloon's fuel into the Pacific Ocean.

Freddie Laker and his Skytrain brought cut-price air travel to the people. Five years after its 1977 launch Laker Airways was the fifth largest transatlantic carrier.

Mrs Thatcher used her special relationship with President Reagan to persuade him to cancel his government's criminal investigation into BA's role in the conspiracy to put Laker out of business.

Lord King privatised British Airways in 1987 after the Laker case was settled. Shares went on sale at 125p in 1987.

KING'S MEN ...

David Burnside, the hard-line Ulster Protestant, became known as 'the most powerful in-house PR man in Britain'. Journalists called the right-wing PR chief the 'kneecapper'.

The Ulster Defender

(Published Monthly by Ulster Defence Association—L'derry C...

August, 1975

SPECIAL 12th AUG. ED...

U.D.A.

QUIS SE...

The Voic...

'Communism is a very real threat to the North'

IF THE British Government does not face up to the threat of Communist infiltration in Ulster the people of the Province are in danger of losing their traditional freedoms and liberties destroyed, Vanguard executive member, Mr. David Burnside, warned.

He said: "Ulster cannot afford to sit idly by...

King recruited Colin Marshall as chief executive in 1983 at £88,000 a year, more than twice his own salary. Here Marshall (*above right*) is seen with Sir Freddie Laker while he was working for Avis. In 1985 Marshall met Laker again at BA's HQ to pay him $8 million in compensation for BA's role in his airline's demise. In return Laker agreed to drop his legal suit.

Marshall appointed American Michael Levin (*below*) a marketing consultant at $100,000 a year. He became the third most powerful man in BA, constantly at Marshall's right hand. Levin warned BA that Virgin would have to be tackled 'head-on' in 1988, when Branson had only two planes. Levin's contract with BA was terminated following staff allegations of sexual harassment.

Former civil servant Robert Ayling (*above*) wrote the bill to privatise BA. The former legal director was promoted to head the marketing and operations department while it poached Virgin's passengers in Britain and the USA.

'The Reverend' Jim Callery (*below, far right*), BA's evangelical sales boss. He told staff, 'A good Christian is one who sells a product that has integrity.'

Mike 'Mars Bars' Batt (*below left*), BA's American routes boss. 'There's no difference between selling airline seats and chocolate bars.'

BRANSON'S BOYS ...

Will Whitehorn (*right*). BA described him as 'Branson's boy press officer'.

Gerrard Tyrrell (*below*). Branson's lawyer was first alerted to rumours of dirty tricks in a bar underneath Waterloo station.

Bottom picture: At the height of the dirty-tricks campaign, Branson sold Virgin Music to Colin Southgate's Thorn EMI for £560 million to save Virgin Atlantic. Branson said, 'It was a good way of flicking a V at Lord King and showing him he couldn't mess around with my airline.'

Branson dressed himself up as a pirate, and Lord King's model Concorde as a Virgin plane, to celebrate the launch of his Heathrow services on 1 July 1991. BA lodged an official complaint.

King withdrew BA's annual donation to the Conservative Party in protest at Virgin's entry into Heathrow and the transfer of slots in Japan.

WARWICK CORPORATE LIMITED

Date: 6 March 1991

Invoice Number: BA/91/01

Amount

Project research and consultancy
as agreed

£46,000⁼

Charge Agreed

SIR COLIN MARSHALL
DEPUTY CHAIRMAN AND CHIEF EXECUTIVE

Budget Nr: 88410   Date

Account Nr: X-ref:

Sir Colin Marshall (*above*) paid Brian Basham's Warwick Corporate £46,000 for his 'Operation Barbara' report on Branson and Virgin. At Lord King's suggestion Basham (*right*) incorporated potentially damaging information on Branson's gay nightclub, Heaven.

3.2 Heaven Night Club

Virgin owns this night club, situated under Charing Cross Station. It may have previously been owned by Branson's brother-in-law.

Around the time Virgin took it on, a 'review' was conducted by KAS (a security organisation founded by David Stirling of the SAS). KAS discovered indications (but no hard evidence) of fraud and other problems with the police, bouncers, fire risk, drug dealing, homosexuals and male prostitutes. KAS recommended closing the club and re-opening with new staff. Branson vetoed the move.

There have been suggestions that Westminster Council would not remove rubbish bags from the club on the grounds that they contained infected sharp objects.

'A word in your ear'. Brian Basham (*above*), legendary PR operator and BA consultant, widely known as the 'streetfighter' for his tough PR tactics. Basham told Chris Hutchins of *Today* that one of Virgin's planes would 'fall out of the sky'. He said Branson 'runs a dicky business . . . This is Freddie Laker all over again'. Basham also warned journalists of the 'moral danger' that Heaven nightclub posed for Virgin's chairman. He told the *Sunday Times* that Branson was having to pay cash for his aeroplanes' fuel.

BA's American vice-president, Dick Eberhart (*below left*), refuses to comment to *This Week* on allegations that he had been spreading anti-Virgin rumours in New York.

David Burnside (*below right*) is confronted on the dirty-tricks allegations by *This Week*'s Richard Lindley outside his Chelsea flat.

In November 1991 Marshall's right-hand man, Michael Levin (*above*), spilt the beans on the dirty-tricks campaign. He told Bob Graham of *Today*, 'Lord King and David Burnside are the men you are interested in. Burnside does things that have no place in a company like British Airways . . . some of the things which he is involved in are very unethical. There is not an ethical bone in his body'.

Branson wins *Executive Travel*'s 1992 'Airline of the Year' award and nine other awards – a record. Lord King was absent from the ceremony.

'Helpliner' Sadig Khalifa. The BA group at Gatwick was instructed to access Virgin's computer information during the Gulf crisis. They also impersonated Virgin employees to obtain sensitive data. The Helpliners did the same to Air Europe and Dan Air, BA's other independent British rivals. The Helpliners were told: 'BA doesn't make its money by helping old biddies to the gate'.

The former chairman of Blackpool Football Club, multi-millionaire Owen Oyston, helped to convince Sir Colin Marshall and David Burnside of the fiction that Virgin was mounting an enormous under-cover operation against BA in 1992. Oyston was jailed for six years for rape and indecent assault in 1996.

Branson (*top picture*) names 'The Spirit of Sir Freddie' after his 'hero and inspiration'. Laker joins the celebrations in Virgin overalls. When BA's legal director Mervyn Walker (*right*) accused Branson – in a letter reproduced by David Burnside in *BA News* – of inventing his dirty-tricks allegations for publicity purposes, Laker advised Branson to 'sue the bastards'.

The exposure of Operation Covent Garden in the *Sunday Times* finally caused BA to submit to Branson. The bizarre private detective operation was financed by the BA. The Mastermind was Ian Johnson, the Go-Between, Nick Del Rosso and The Snooper, John Reilly.

Branson emerges victorious from the High Court with £610,000 of damages from BA.

King (*below left*) steps down as BA's chairman to be replaced by Marshall (*centre*). Ayling (*right*) is promoted to become group managing director. Sir Tim Bell (*inset*) is hired to provide the public-relations shield for the subsequent cover-up.

Retired Metropolitan Police officer John Gorman is a BA shareholder, but when he complained about swallowing glass in a drink on a flight to New York, he was branded a 'Virgin stooge' by a BA official. Gorman is now suing BA over what he claims is a three-year dirty-tricks campaign against him.

BA and Harry Goodman (*below*), chairman of Air Europe. BA, through Sir Colin Marshall and David Burnside, hired the New York-based investigators, Kroll, to probe Air Europe's parent group, The International Leisure Group, in 1987, when the Gatwick-based carrier was Britain's second largest scheduled airlane. The payment was made through Brian Basham's then company, Broadstreet Associates.

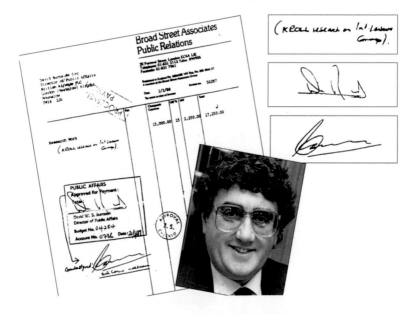

On this occasion Sorrentino, and his travelling companion Dr Young, were both weary and looking forward to flopping into the Gatwick Hilton for a good night's rest. The following day they were both due to fly to New York on Virgin Atlantic.

As Dr Sorrentino hauled himself out of his seat and started collecting his belongings together, a voice on the in-flight speaker system asked the professor and his travelling companion to identify themselves as they left the aircraft.

Sorrentino was concerned. He travels an average of 150,000 air-miles a year but he is rarely paged. His thoughts went at once to his family. Then he thought of a colleague who had not arrived at the meeting in Frankfurt.

Sorrentino was met by one of Ayling's Interliners, Amanda Ritson, as he got off the plane. In their daily scouring of BABS, the Interliners had spotted that Sorrentino and Young were booked to cross the Atlantic on Virgin Atlantic. Ritson asked Sorrentino and Young if they would like to switch their Virgin tickets for BA tickets and take the earlier BA flight to New York. Sorrentino was relieved that he had not been summoned to receive bad news, but dismayed when he found out what the BA rep wanted.

'She started off by saying her job was to "expedite short-time transfer of tickets". I had no idea what that meant. Then she came to the point. She wanted both of us to change our Virgin Atlantic tickets to British Airways.'

Sorrentino and Young told Ritson they weren't interested, and trudged off to reclaim their luggage. Ritson pursued them and pressed her business card upon the weary travellers. Sorrentino recalls that it was only after a sharp exchange of words that Ritson left them alone.

'It was like being vended something you don't want to buy, that you just can't get rid of. I don't think airline travellers should have to put up with that sort of thing.'

Amanda Ritson and her colleagues were behaving so aggressively towards potential switch-sale passengers for a very specific reason. Despite the Reverend Jim Callery and Sue Hollis's exhortations to do everything possible, 'short of breaking arms and legs', to steal other carriers' passengers, the BA sales department's 'revenue gap' on the airline's North Atlantic routes looked as wide as ever as the financial year drew to a close. The mobile switch-selling teams all had a costs-to-revenue ratio that would determine not only their perceived effectiveness, but also whether they continued to exist.

Hollis's apocalyptic address to Ayling's heads of department had filtered rapidly down through the ranks, particularly her dark warning that 'if we don't bring in the revenue in such a crucial environment, we may not have to worry about pressure in the future!'

For those who wished to keep their jobs, the Reverend Jim's despised 'comfort zone' had long been a foreign country. However, since the very promising day in January when Ayling's Interliners had reported grabbing nearly £50,000 of Virgin Atlantic revenue, the going had got much tougher. Both the Interliners at Gatwick and Maude's Marauders at Heathrow started to encounter enormous hostility from some of their BA colleagues as well as the staff of rival airlines. The Interliners were reaching their stiff weekly revenue targets, but the acrimonious atmosphere they were creating was threatening to make their work counter-productive.

Chris Maude wrote a gloomy memo at the end of January:

> Receptivity to anything labelled Mission Atlantic is at best apathetic and at worst hostile. The consequence of which is to make the data-gathering difficult and promotes suspicion. It also raises the question of 'trust' inasmuch as the inquiries that we are making may filter back to competitors . . .
>
> There appears to be a clear infringement of Department of Transport regulations, and BA could be exposing itself to infringement . . .

Despite the elaborate precautions BA had taken to disguise their activities, Maude's Marauders and Ayling's Interliners had been rumbled by some of their competitors.

> Interline sales is suspected of being a cover for switch-selling by many airlines at Heathrow . . . If this campaign links us

with aggressive switch-selling it is not an acceptable trade-off, given our success in gaining acceptance of Interline sales with those airlines.

In other words, losing the rapport that had been built up with rival carriers could potentially cost BA far more than it stood to gain from its switch-selling. On one occasion the police had to be called to separate BA switch-sellers and American Airlines staff as they squared up to each other at a check-in desk.

As the row between BA and Virgin erupted in the press, the Interliners picked up rumours that Branson was collaborating on a television programme about dirty tricks. As a result, Interline leader Denise Fletcher took to deleting almost all references to Virgin Atlantic in her confidential 'Read and Destroy' reports to management.

Fletcher cited legal worries as the reason for her caution. It was one thing to slug it out with American megacarriers whom BA suspected were employing similar tactics on their home ground and at Heathrow, but quite another to be discovered picking on transatlantic passengers from a tiny British rival. In a confidential note to her superiors at Gatwick, Fletcher showed more awareness of the potential legal dangers to BA in the American courts than the Reverend Jim Callery and Robert Ayling's evangelical line-managers.

Apparently aware of Ayling's December warning to staff to adopt his 'rule of thumb test' regarding 'public disclosure', Fletcher sent a confidential memo to the head of Mission Atlantic. She marked it 'Highly Confidential' and stated in a handwritten note at the bottom that there were only two copies in existence. Fletcher started by explaining why Virgin and Branson were hardly mentioned.

'Due to the sensitivity of BA/Virgin anti-trust laws, I have made little reference to VA [Virgin].'

Fletcher did, however, express particular concern about the continued combing of Virgin Atlantic's confidential flight information stored on BA's computer:

I am surprised BA can still access all Virgin flight information through BABS, such as transfer passenger lists, booked and checked-in loads etc. I believe this is because Ogdens [Virgin Atlantic's Gatwick handling agent] use our system for the airlines they handle in the South for load-control purposes. Therefore all the information is fed into BABS Departure Control System.

Ironically, it was the passenger-poachers themselves who were warning their bosses of the danger of continuing to hunt the Poacher's passengers . . .

10

'The Spirit of Sir Freddie'

Passengers hurrying through Gatwick's South Terminal on the evening of 15 February 1992 stopped suddenly when they heard the unexpected roar of a crowd. The roar gave way to applause and foot stamping.

In the Banqueting Suite of the Gatwick Hilton a tanned, seventy-year-old man stepped up on to a makeshift stage. In an attempt to still the crowd he held both arms aloft.

'What can I possibly say?' He paused for effect while the applause died. Then he uttered his catch-phrase. 'What about . . . Hello, mates!'

Sir Freddie Laker was back in England. The old showman was treading the boards at Gatwick again ten years after his airline had gone bust. From the reaction of the hundreds of former Laker staff who had gathered to mark the occasion, the passers-by would have been forgiven for thinking that Sir Freddie had just announced the relaunch of Laker Airways.

On 4 February 1982 Sir Freddie stepped off a Laker Airways flight for the last time. Returning from New York early in the morning, Laker was summoned to see the Midland Bank. He was expecting to see his bankers. Laker had announced a refinancing package before Christmas to enable his airline to survive the aggressive marketing tactics of rival transatlantic carriers, the deepening recession and the plunging value of the pound against the dollar. After tortuous negotiations lasting over a month, Laker was finally able to celebrate the clinching of the deal with some of his bankers and his financial advisors the night before his trip to the States. Sir Freddie swept into London's trendy nightclub, Tramp, and hugged its owner, Johnny Gold. As Laker ordered champagne and bangers and mash for his party, he told Gold, 'I was forty-five minutes away from bankruptcy and these people saved me!'

He explained to Gold that his companions were from the McDonnell Douglas Finance Corporation, and that they had just put together a financial package with the Midland Bank to ensure the survival of Laker Airways. They had told him to go to America and start selling seats for the summer season.

A buoyant Laker left for New York the following day, telling the press that his airline's financial worries were over and that he was flying high again. In New York he recorded an up-beat commercial, 'Are You Ready for Freddie', and his staff noticed that an enormous weight appeared to lift from his shoulders as he told them about the refinancing deal. The Midland phoned him in New York, and asked him to drop in to see them when he returned. To make sure that everything was still in place he phoned David Sedgewick of the McDonnell Douglas Finance Corporation in London. He confirmed that it was. Sedgewick did not tell Laker that at a secret dinner in a London hotel the previous night attended by the CAA, the Midland's chief executive, Dennis Kitching, had announced that the Midland had decided to pull the rug from under Laker Airways. Everyone at the dinner, including Sedgewick, had been sworn to secrecy by Kitching.

Thus, as Laker drove from Gatwick to the Midland Bank's London offices it was with a sense of keen anticipation, and no inkling of what was about to happen. To his surprise he was shown into an empty room when he arrived.

'It was the most non-executive room I've ever been in. It had one small window. It looked more like a prison cell except that it did have carpet on the floor and a table and some chairs. I sat down and people started wandering in. My lawyer came in, and I said, "What are you doing here?" He said, "I don't know." And then other people came in. They didn't look the way I expected them to, and they weren't carrying the documents I expected to sign.

'Finally the Midland manager, George Gillespie, came in. He closed the door and he stood with his back to it. He said, "Good morning. Thank you for coming. We want you to call in the receivers." I couldn't believe it.'

Kitching had decided to call in a loan of £9.2 million in direct contravention of pledges McDonnell Douglas had told Laker the bank had made at the beginning of the week. He had left it to Gillespie to be the executioner. The Midland claimed that the CAA had demanded an unlimited cushion to protect Laker Airways. Laker immediately phoned the CAA, who denied doing so. After a furious meeting with Kitching, Laker started frantic attempts to raise what, in airline terms, is a relatively small amount of money. After phoning contacts through the night, he had to admit defeat and, the following morning, he obeyed the Midland's instruction and called in the receivers.

By the weekend Laker's planes were grounded, his worldwide network of offices had been padlocked, and his 2,300 staff were out of work. Thousands of Laker passengers throughout the world were stranded with unused and unusable Laker Airways tickets. They had to make their way home at their own expense on other carriers, including some who Laker believed had wanted to put him out of business, such as British Airways. After the government had decided not to intervene to save Laker Airways, the chief executive of Lonhro, Tiny Rowland, offered to bail Laker out on the Monday. By then, however, the Midland had stopped listening *and* talking. Dennis Kitching failed to appear for an arranged meeting with Laker and Rowland in his own office, and the airline was already being dismembered by the liquidator.

The 1992 Gatwick reunion, however, was a night to remember Sir Freddie Laker's achievements rather than his airline's demise: to remember the entrepreneur who borrowed £38,000 from a mate in the pub to take on the biggest airlines in the world, the folk hero who had opened up transatlantic travel to the post-war generation, the 'forgotten people', with his £37.50 fare to New York in 1971, the former tea-boy who was eventually knighted in 1978 by a Labour Party that had spent most of the 1970s trying to stop

Skytrain taking off, the showman who had built up the fifth largest transatlantic carrier.

The ex-Laker staff had come to Gatwick that night to pay homage to their past – the pilots, the ground staff, the cabin crews and the engineers. Some of Laker's former stewardesses had taken their old uniforms out of mothballs, and were pleased to show their old friends and colleagues they could still fit into them. The stewardesses' black, pillar-box style hats with their red ribbons and Laker badges recalled the dawn of cheap transatlantic air travel. Some of Sir Freddie's jokes had changed as little as the old uniforms, but each one was still guaranteed a round of applause, and cries of 'Oooh, Sir Freddie!' from those who still found his cracks rather risqué.

As Sir Freddie drew his speech to a close, he asked his audience to greet a surprise guest.

'There have been one or two who have tried to copy us. But let me tell you this is the only worthy successor. Ladies and gentlemen, please welcome Richard Branson!'

To warm applause Branson appeared from the wings. The two entrepreneurs from different generations hugged each other on the stage. After thanking Sir Freddie for inviting him, and the audience for his reception, Branson addressed Laker's veterans.

'I was a fan of yours long before Virgin Atlantic was a little idea in our mind. It's much easier to follow a pioneer than be a pioneer. I think we learnt an awful lot from what you did and what you achieved . . . it's just wonderful to be able to pick up the baton and take it forward. Virgin Atlantic wouldn't have existed if it hadn't been for Laker Airways.'

Branson reminded the anniversary party that shortly before he launched Virgin Atlantic in 1984, he had invited Sir Freddie to lunch on his houseboat to ask his advice on running an airline. To enthusiastic acclaim from all the Laker veterans present, Branson then made a moving dedication.

'We're starting an Orlando route in a couple of months' time, and I would be very happy if Freddie would now accept us calling our plane "The Spirit of Sir Freddie", and hopefully it will be there for ever!' In 1984, Sir Freddie had declined the suggestion. Now, he agreed heartily.

The gathering wallowed in back-slapping and mutual congrat-
ulations long into the night. However, Sir Freddie's first return to
a Laker anniversary party cloaked a more serious mission. Laker
had spent the afternoon with Branson in Holland Park. Branson,
as usual, scribbled in notebooks as Laker ran through a catalogue
of dirty tricks he was convinced BA had pulled against him.

By 1982 Laker's turnover was approaching $300 million. To
British Airways' dismay, he was making deep inroads into its
transatlantic market over which it had previously enjoyed the
British monopoly. One in seven transatlantic passengers were
Laker. By 1981 he had 17% of the New York market and 25% of the
Los Angeles market. Laker argued then, as Branson was doing
now, that he was expanding the market, not stealing BA's share.

Laker's gains were made against fierce competition from British
Airways and he regaled Branson with the variety of tactics the
state-owned national carrier had used against his cut-price airline. Dapper and relaxed in a smart, light grey suit, Laker warmed
to his theme as Branson sat barefoot, his white shirt unbuttoned to
the navel and his knees tucked under his chin.

'They have a name for everything. My code name was "Tudor
King" because I once owned a fleet of Tudor aeroplanes. When
they got me, when they had me really by the jugular, it was
"Tudor King's crash landing". I mean, they behaved like the KGB.
Secret phone calls, secret telexes, secret gatherings.

'They got up to all sorts of things . . . they swamp you, bracket
you, there's the override trick, the bucket-shop trick . . .'

'Hang on a minute, Freddie,' Branson interjected. 'Can we go
through these one by one?'

Branson turned over a new page of his notebook and wrote
'Freddie Laker' with a sub-heading 'BA's dirty tricks'.

'Look at how they have targeted your Miami route – it's a perfect example.' Sir Freddie had flown from Miami to see Branson,
and he had studied the timetables. 'They've bracketed you by
putting their flights on either side of your flight, and swamped
you with too many seats. They say they are losing money and
passengers are hard to come by, but then they double their
frequency and their capacity. That's bracketing and swamping.

'Everyone knows we are in a recession. Airlines normally

tighten their belts in a recession, they don't double the capacity on a route if they're losing money on it. And you'll find they're only doing this sort of thing on your routes.'

This struck a familiar chord with Branson.

'You're right. In the last bi-laterals we were given permission to fly to Washington, Chicago and San Francisco. BA immediately announced that they would be going double-daily on those routes and basically use up all the slots there are at Heathrow, so we don't get the slots, the public don't get the competition, and we don't get up and going.'

Laker detected a long-term problem with BA.

'Basically, BA hasn't got out of the habit of being nationalised. In fact British air transport is now more of a monopoly for British Airways than it was forty-five years ago. There are British airlines in the air but, in terms of the percentage of the air transport cake, British Airways has a bigger percentage today than it did forty-five years ago.'

With his own bitter experience of gaining a measure of justice through the courts only after the death of his airline, Laker was clear what Branson should do.

'You have got to sue the bastards. You've got to sue them out of sight because this won't stop until you do. They'll kill you commercially.

'If I had sued the lot of them under American anti-trust legislation as soon as they slashed their fares, I'd probably still be in the air today!'

Sir Freddie warned Branson that it had taken his lawyer, Bob Beckman, and the liquidator, Christopher Morris, over three years in the US courts to find out some of what was really going on behind on the scenes before Laker Airways crashed. Much of the evidence was never tested in court because President Reagan cancelled the criminal investigation into the price-fixing charges against BA, and the civil suit was settled out of court. However, the conspiracy charge litigation demonstrated to Laker just how determined his larger rivals had been to put him out of business.

Some of the airlines that had targeted Laker's routes with predatory fare-cuts also bombarded McDonnell Douglas (MDC) with threats to withdraw their business when it emerged that the

American aeroplane manufacturer was playing a key role in the refinancing of Laker Airways. Prominent was British Caledonian, whose chairman, Sir Adam Thomson, was said by MDC to be 'incoherent' with anger that the company was supporting Laker, his bitter rival. According to documents which came to light in the American court action, Thomson told MDC that he would 'absolutely forbid any further negotiations with McDonnell Douglas for the DC 9 Super 80s or any other aircraft now and in the future,' if the company helped to rescue Laker Airways, which he described as 'the most disruptive force on the North Atlantic'.

Within hours of Thomson's telex, some of MDC's best customers added their weight to the campaign to stop the refinancing deal. Government-owned European carriers were frightened that if Laker succeeded in extending his cut-price airline to Europe, he would have the same impact on fares as he had done on the transatlantic routes. Sabena's chairman expressed his 'amazement and disappointment that MDC should try and prevent what appeared to be the natural demise of a man who had caused other airlines so many problems'. KLM expressed its 'deep concern', and Swissair warned MDC that its participation in the deal would 'adversely affect our present good business relationship'. Swissair emphasised the 'common position of the European airlines, all of whom are steady long-term and loyal customers of MDC, as to the outcast status of Laker Airways.'

During the anti-trust suit, Laker discovered how that pressure had affected MDC, one of his airline's long-term allies. MDC's London office telexed the company's St Louis headquarters with its assessment of the avalanche of messages they had received simultaneously from Laker's European rivals: 'It is now clear that the vehemence of the opposition to Laker and directed against MDC for our perceived role in creating a potential solution to the Laker financial problem has spread . . . beyond the earlier identified opposition from BCal on an orchestrated basis throughout Europe. The Laker filing of 666 point-to-point routes within Europe which he proposed to serve with the A-300 Airbus fleet, and the ultra-low inclusive tour fares and packages also aimed at the European market – have formed the basis of a violent reaction against MDC now that it has become clear that a potential for Laker survival has been developed by the financial agreement.'

The hostile lobby appeared to offer an explanation for MDC's agreement to remain silent about the Midland's plans to call in the receivers. When the Midland told the vice-president of the McDonnell Douglas Finance Corporation, David Sedgewick, that they were going to put Laker out of business, he agreed to a vow of silence, 'I plead guilty to that,' recalled Sedgewick. 'I'm guilty of not telling Freddie [but] we were told confidentially by his [Midland] bankers what they were going to do and we were asked not to tell him. To me this was a matter between Freddie and his bankers.'

The role of the Midland Bank came under fierce scrutiny in the wake of Laker's collapse. The Midland was also banker to Laker's British rivals, BCal, and Dennis Kitching, the Midland's chief executive who ordered Laker to call in the receivers, had placed Bill Mackie, one of Britain's leading receivers in Laker's team of financial advisers just before the liquidation. Laker himself had no idea he was a receiver, and continued to be reassured until the end by those the Midland paid to advise him that the refinancing was on track. Mackie pulled Laker apart within days of being instructed, and some of the assets, including Laker's main hangar at Gatwick, were sold to BCal.

Laker's collapse was very convenient for BCal, and also for BA, who had started the offensive against Laker within months of Lord King taking over. The removal of its most important transatlantic competitor was sufficiently important for BA to agree to price cuts in 1981 that it had initially described as 'economic suicide' when the American carriers proposed them.

Branson listened very closely to Laker's story, which had also involved BA spreading rumours about Laker's financial troubles throughout the travel industry. As the two men strolled in the winter sunshine in Branson's back garden, he told Laker what he knew of Basham's smear campaign. He told him about the Savoy briefing session in which the *Sunday Times* had been told that Virgin Atlantic was 'paying cash for its fuel'.

'That's an old trick . . . saying you haven't got the money and so on. We had some of that as well.' For Laker, the rumours he had endured about his airline's financial health were particularly galling. 'BA were the ones who were insolvent, not me! The year before they blew me out, they made a huge loss and they were running round saying I was in trouble!'

'Even when you were doing well?' asked Branson.

'Absolutely! We made a profit in 1981. I never defaulted on a loan, and I didn't ever get into a position where people weren't paid.'

'And do you know how they were spreading the rumours, what sort of tricks they were up to?'

'They were going round the travel agents feeding this stuff out. They also have their friends in the press whom they drop a few words to. And, of course, they're big advertisers . . .'

Recalling King's withdrawal of BA's advertising from the *Independent*, Laker's experience sounded more and more familiar to Branson. Even Sir Freddie was surprised, however, by the tactics BA were employing against Virgin Atlantic.

'These people Burnham [sic] or Basham, or whatever their names are, seem to be like character assassins. In the old days, of course, we would have considered that a little un-British but obviously it's fair game now.'

'It's not fair game in most companies in England,' Branson responded. 'That's what is so strange. I mean, you've got British Airways with the image of being BRITISH Airways, our national flag carrier. But behind the scenes it is nothing like that.'

After three years in the American courts, Laker had finally made his peace with BA in 1985, as a wiser and sadder man. As Laker negotiated the final details of his personal settlement with Colin Marshall at BA's HQ, the chief executive frequently left the room for 'consultations'. Although Sir Freddie never met BA's chairman, in retrospect he had no doubt about who had hunted his airline down. 'I think Laker Airways was John King's first victim.' Laker turned to Branson, removed his sunglasses and delivered his parting shot. 'I can tell you that they are the craftiest, most *cunning* experts. Don't ever underestimate the staff of British Airways. They've been around a long time, they're professionals, and they know how to do you and do you well!'

Before Sir Freddie flew back to Florida, he recorded an interview for the *This Week* film in which he repeated his advice to Richard Branson to 'sue the bastards'.

Aviation journalists we phoned during the research phase of the film were unanimous that BA would not participate in a programme on 'dirty tricks'. So, in a bid to elicit a response from BA, our reporter, Richard Lindley, wrote David Burnside a deliberately provocative letter after we returned from the USA. Without revealing what had been discovered in the States, Lindley told Burnside that *This Week* had established '*prima facie* evidence' to support some of Richard Branson's claims.

Burnside responded swiftly. Without committing BA to taking part in the programme, Burnside did agree to meet Richard Lindley and myself at Enserch House on 13 February. Burnside had heard about our ambush of Dick Eberhart in New York and was curious to know what we were up to.

'We've checked out Branson's allegations and they don't hold water,' was Burnside's opening gambit at the Enserch House meeting. Reclining slightly behind a broad ochre desk speckled with phones and briefing papers, Burnside was emphatic. 'We've had our lawyers, and external lawyers, go through everything he's got to say and it simply doesn't stand up.'

I asked him if we could have a look at their report.

'No,' replied Burnside, before my question was complete.

'Will you or Lord King come on the programme and make the point that Virgin Atlantic's claims don't stand up, Mr Burnside?' asked Lindley.

'No,' replied Burnside. There was a short pause. Burnside's deputy, Tony Cocklin, was sitting directly behind Lindley, scribbling notes.

Burnside gave a very frank explanation of why BA would not take part. He said that the airline had received many approaches from TV and radio programmes to debate the dirty-tricks issue and all had been refused. He argued that if BA participated, then Branson would get at least half of any such programme to repeat what Burnside described as his 'rubbish' allegations.

Burnside explained that his policy of not participating had worked with the BBC's *Panorama*. A reporter from the BBC's flagship current affairs show had approached Burnside with a view to making the sort of programme that *This Week* was now proposing, with both sides giving their side of the story. Burnside said that after BA had refused to take part, *Panorama* cancelled the programme. Therefore, he argued, the policy of not participating was working, from BA's point of view.

I told Burnside that *This Week* would be making the programme whatever BA's response, and argued that, in this context, BA would be better off participating than boycotting. If no BA interviewee was forthcoming, we would have to rely on the statements on the dirty-tricks affair that BA had previously issued to the press. Burnside did not appear to be impressed by my argument, but said he would convey our request for an interview to Sir Colin Marshall – but there was no question of either himself or Lord King taking part.

As the discussion became more informal Burnside found it impossible to disguise his intense dislike of Richard Branson. His rich Ulster accent appeared to gain even more texture as he sneered at 'Richard's pullovers' and his 'boy press officer', Will Whitehorn. Burnside claimed that Branson's continuous publicity stunts had cost him the sympathy of the City press. Branson's fundamental problem, he said, was that he hadn't grown up; as a result, businessmen and serious journalists were bored by him.

As we rose to depart, Burnside provided us with an unselfconscious parody of his own image as the toughest PR operator in the business. He smiled, his eyelids drooping menacingly, as he conjured up one of his chairman's *bons mots*:

'As Lord King likes to say: competition is he who bleeds least.'

A few days later I received a fierce letter from BA's legal director, Mervyn Walker, to whom Burnside had referred our request for an interview.

There is nothing new in the allegations. While we have always regarded Mr Branson's claims as unfounded, and in some cases scurrilous, we nevertheless carried out an internal investigation at the end of last year.

. . . that investigation, conducted by me with support from external legal advisers [Linklaters & Paines] confirmed that there is no substance to the accusation that British Airways has engaged in a so-called 'dirty-tricks' campaign against Virgin Atlantic.

Walker accused us of

> falling into the trap of being used as a vehicle for Richard Branson's propaganda, which sets out to contrive controversy with British Airways to create publicity for himself and his company and to inflict serious damage on the reputation of British Airways.
>
> We are not prepared to be provoked into playing Mr Branson's futile game and, therefore, must decline to take part in interviews on this occasion.

Mervyn Walker added that BA 'expressly reserved' its rights, should we repeat Branson's 'unfounded allegations' in our film.

The following week a black Rover sat outside David Burnside's fashionable Chelsea home with its engine running. It was a bright, crisp morning and the exhaust fumes from the idling engine billowed out from the rear of the car before dispersing. Inside the car a British Airways' chauffeur yawned as he flicked through the morning papers. He was waiting to take Burnside to the West End. At 7.15 Burnside emerged from his London *pied à terre*.

As Burnside walked towards the car, Richard Lindley walked towards him with a microphone in his hand. The two men had not spoken to each other since Burnside phoned Lindley the previous week to confirm that BA would not be taking part in the TV programme just before I received Mervyn Walker's letter. We had decided to doorstep the man whom Richard Branson had alleged in his interview was at the centre of the smear campaign against Virgin.

Michael Chrisman had traced Burnside's London address by looking through the company accounts of New Century Communications, one of the Irishman's private companies.

As Lindley confronted Burnside, we filmed their encounter from the other side of the road. Frank Haysom used a telescopic lens to track their progress along the pavement, and Peter Easom monitored the ensuing conversation on a radio microphone. Lindley warned Burnside he was being taped.

'Good morning, Mr Burnside. We are recording this interview for *This Week* . . . Can I ask you why you employ Brian Basham, who's spreading damaging rumours about Virgin Atlantic?'

Burnside put his head down and continued to make for his car as he replied.

'Richard, we had a very good discussion and we made the company's position very clear . . .'

'Why won't you answer our questions?' Lindley interjected.

'It was explained in our legal director's letter to your producer,' Burnside continued as he began to load his briefcase and papers into the back seat of the Rover.

Lindley sensed he wasn't going to get very far with the BA man.

'Why do you have a problem with telling us about British Airways' attitude?'

'We don't have a problem.'

'Why then can't you give us answers to our rather simple questions?'

By now Burnside was sliding into the front seat of the BA car.

'I must go to work. We're trying to make some money in our business.'

With that, BA's director of public affairs was gone. He had given an exemplary performance of how to deal with a TV doorstep. Lindley's reference to Brian Basham, however, had ruffled Burnside. As soon as he got in the car he was on the phone to his friend. He warned him that *This Week* could be about to doorstep him as well.

'David was very flustered,' recalled Brian Basham, who phoned his own chauffeur as soon as he had taken Burnside's call. 'I got him to put my newspapers and my briefcase in the Range Rover and then drive round to the back of the house.'

Burnside guessed correctly. Twenty minutes after Burnside's call, Basham thought he saw the *This Week* team.

'I'm a very keen birdwatcher, so I grabbed my binoculars and scanned the horizon for any sign of a camera. Sure enough, I spotted a group of rather unlikely-looking people sitting in a battered old BMW. I called my wife to take a look. After we chuckled about it, I hopped over the back garden fence and into the Range Rover.'

When Basham's birdwatching glasses picked out the same camera team in a different vehicle the following morning, he successfully repeated his evasive tactics. Our second attempt to doorstep Basham prompted the PR man to move out of his North London home until transmission of the programme on the Thursday evening. Basham took his wife to the North London Holiday Inn, where he spent the early mornings working out in the gym with the Chippendales, who were staying in the same hotel.

When Burnside arrived at his desk at BA, he set to work plucking familiar strings to try and ensure that the programme would get as hostile a response as possible in the media. On the morning of transmission, the *Daily Express*'s chief Whitehall correspondent, Jon Craig, told his readers that Lord King would 'snub the dirty-tricks show' and reminded them that Thames had made the 'notorious "Death on the Rock" programme' – a programme that the staunchly Protestant Burnside particularly disliked. 'Death on the Rock' claimed that members of the SAS had shot three members of the IRA dead in Gibraltar without giving them any warning, and it led to one of the seminal confrontations of the 1980s between broadcasters and Mrs Thatcher.

Although the *Express* repeated the BA line that *This Week* had fallen for Branson's propaganda, Jon Craig saw no need to quote a response from Thames in his report. Neither did David Burnside as he settled down to write the front-page splash of the edition of *BA News* which was due out on Friday 28 February, the day after Thames was due to transmit our programme on the dirty-tricks affair. Burnside based his article very closely on the letter Mervyn Walker had sent to me explaining the reasons for BA's decision not to participate in the programme, and reproduced half a dozen paragraphs from it. The letter had been approved by Sir Colin Marshall before being sent to Thames, so Burnside felt he was on safe ground when he quoted extensively from it. He sent it to Mervyn Walker for legal clearance and then instructed Tony Cocklin to put it on the front page of *BA News* under the headline 'Branson "Dirty Tricks" Claim Unfounded'. As Burnside and Basham sat down to watch the film, 'Violating Virgin?', 50,000 copies of *BA News* were being distributed throughout the world.

The two men watched the programme at Enserch House with Sir Francis Kennedy. After more than twenty years in the diplomatic service, Kennedy had joined the board of British Airways as Lord King's special adviser.

Sitting next to Basham was his wife, Eileen. Watching also was litigation specialist Bill Park of Linklaters & Paines who had led the British government's bid to settle the Laker case. Burnside had asked Park to advise on any legal implications arising from the film before he took press enquiries.

The final pictures of the programme were from the Mojave Desert. They showed the huge hulks of passenger planes that had belonged to bankrupt airlines.

'Perhaps it's time for Richard Branson to put up or shut up – or Virgin Atlantic's planes could end up like Laker's: in the desert sand,' pronounced Lindley.

The credits rolled and the programme's familiar Sibelius 'Karelia Suite' theme tune filled Kennedy's office. Burnside turned to Bill Park for an assessment of the legal implications. Park's old rival in the Laker case, the Washington attorney Bob Beckman, had appeared in the programme saying that in his opinion BA were in danger of breaching American anti-trust laws.

'Well . . . what did you make of it, Bill?' asked Burnside. Both he and Basham were identified by the programme as being responsible for running the smear campaign against Branson, on Lord King's instructions. The lawyer paused for a moment before puffing his chest out slightly and delivering his verdict:

'The cock cannot crow and from his dunghill strut!'

The meaning of Park's Shakespearean quotation eluded his audience. Burnside raised his eyes to the ceiling.

'That's a rather difficult line to put out to the press, Bill.'

Basham also failed to spot the *Henry IV part 1* reference.

'For fuck's sake, speak English for once in your life, Bill!'

'Calm down, dear boy,' intoned Linklaters & Paines' most senior litigation specialist. 'You've got nothing to worry about. Branson's got nothing.'

Basham slumped back into his chair and exhaled an enormous sigh of relief. Watching 'Violating Virgin?' had been a galling

experience for the him. He had no idea prior to watching the programme that Chris Hutchins had taped his briefing session back in
October. 'The worm. The miserable little worm,' muttered Basham
under his breath as he loosened his tie.

Several of the telephones in Burnside's nearby office started
ringing. Basham turned to comfort his wife, who was sobbing quietly into her handkerchief. She felt badly betrayed. Hutchins'
poorly recorded tape of his visit to the Bashams' home was a
centrepiece of the film. The quality was so poor that we had had to
use subtitles to make sure that viewers could understand the
crackly offering.

Eileen had heard her husband telling Hutchins that Branson
'was Freddie Laker all over again', that he ran a 'dicky business . . .
just dicky', and that one of Branson's planes would 'fall out of the
sky'. She had heard her husband asking the gossip columnist to
keep his name, and BA's, out of his newspaper report – all this
because she had tipped off a friend. Park's reassurance that
Branson had no case against her husband was the only comforting
moment of a traumatic evening.

Some of the most dramatic moments in the film were provided
by Peter Fleming. The former BA sales and marketing executive
appeared in silhouette with his voice severely distorted to disguise his identity. He related how BA had set up its anti-Virgin
unit, how Branson had been personally targeted, and how the
mass shredding of evidence occurred when Branson started to
complain about BA's anti-competitive behaviour at the beginning
of 1991.

Branson was then seen in the aeroplane graveyard in the
Californian desert accusing Lord King, David Burnside and Brian
Basham of being responsible for the smear campaign against him
and his airline.

Richard Lindley's ambushes of Burnside and Dick Eberhart as
they climbed into their cars made BA appear furtive. While BA's
director of public affairs had coped capably with his doorstep
encounter, BA's American vice-president had not. Combined with
Lord King and Sir Colin Marshall's refusal to be interviewed by
This Week, the impression left was that BA's hierarchy had something to hide.

Branson put scores of extra telephone operators on Virgin Atlantic's Crawley switchboard for the evening. He didn't know exactly what was going to be in the film, but he did know that when he had appeared on the Des O'Connor show, the Virgin switchboard had registered 36,000 calls.

The vast majority of callers expressed their outrage at what they had just seen. Many said they would never fly with 'The World's Favourite Airline' again. Some simply called with messages of support for Branson himself. At midnight, callers to Virgin Atlantic's Crawley HQ were automatically diverted to the company's New York switchboard. Baffled American bookings clerks had to explain to irate English colonels from the home counties, amongst others, that they had not seen the programme but were sure Mr Branson would reply if they cared to write to him.

The surge of support after *This Week* boosted Branson's morale, but it contained within it something much more important than encouragement. Branson had become so annoyed by BA's kerbside attempts to steal his passengers that he commissioned a pilot commercial on passenger-poaching. Branson's advertising agency, Williams Moira Gaskin O'Malley, came up with one based on the testimony of Ronnie Thomas's limousine drivers in New York, and the experiences of the Virgin passengers BA had tried to poach.

The pilot ad showed an Upper Class passenger emerging from his Virgin limousine at an airport. As the driver handed the passenger his luggage from the boot of the car, an earnest man from 'another airline' is seen accosting the passenger and trying to persuade him to switch his Virgin ticket. The attempt fails and the passenger strides off towards the Virgin check-in.

WMGO shot the pilot advert in grainy, sepia-coloured tones, which made it look as if an amateur video cameraman had chanced upon the attempted switch-sell. Clearly labelling the sequence as a 'Virgin pilot commercial', we included the rough cut of the ad in its entirety in *This Week*.

Of the thousands of callers that night, hundreds said that they had had similar experiences or knew of friends who had. Nearly 200 were prepared to leave their names and contact numbers on the Virgin switchboard. One of the calls was from Yvonne Parsons.

She had watched the programme at home in Sussex. Only three weeks earlier, Parsons had decided that she would never, ever fly with Virgin Atlantic again, even if Richard Branson personally walked through the door of her home and begged her to.

She had been sitting at home on 6 February contemplating her forthcoming trip to New York with Virgin when Branson's reservations office called to say that the flight was overbooked. As she had not yet been issued with a ticket, would she mind changing to a British Airways flight . . .?

Parsons certainly did mind. This was the fourth time in eight months she had been let down by Virgin. Following her two experiences of being messed around by Virgin's New York reservations department in July and September, she had had to endure another charade in the autumn.

Parsons was called by Virgin reservations once again at her New York office. This time the representative, Mary Ann, said that the airline was once again overbooked for her flight on 16 October. To compensate for the inconvenience, Virgin offered to fly her to London the following day on Concorde. Parsons refused. She asked Mary Ann to wait-list her on the flight she had been bounced off, and to confirm her on the following day's Virgin flight out of Newark. Parsons found it difficult to understand why an airline that appeared to value the lucrative custom she brought them had become so slipshod. On average Parsons used Virgin's Upper Class transatlantic service twice a month.

As with 'Bonnie' from Virgin in August, who told her that her flight would be delayed, and 'Larry' from Virgin in September, who couldn't find her a non-smoking seat, 'Mary Ann' failed to call back in October to keep Parsons informed on her waitlisting. And, as with 'Bonnie' and 'Larry', Virgin's New York office denied any knowledge of 'Mary Ann' when Parsons phoned to make her own check. Virgin said there was no problem with her original 16 October booking.

'I went wild,' said Parsons. 'Nobody in the company seemed to have the faintest clue what I was talking about even though one of their own people had phoned me in the first place.'

Parsons flew back on the Virgin flight on 16 October but her patience with Branson's company was at end. She instructed her travel agent not to book her on Virgin Atlantic again. For the rest of the year she flew first class on American and United.

At the beginning of 1992, Parsons decided to give Virgin one last chance. And then she got the fourth call in eight months heralding another Virgin mix-up. Parsons gave Branson's airline up instantly until she watched *This Week*.

'As I watched the programme it suddenly dawned on me that I might have been the victim of an elaborate and disgraceful deception. I remembered that all the callers had offered me flights on British Airways, never another carrier.

'I knew that none of the people was actually from Virgin, so it was logical to assume they might have been British Airways' staff impersonating Branson's people.'

Parsons reached for the diary in which she keeps a detailed list of all the flights she makes. She was becoming more and more convinced that she had been conned by BA. The following morning she phoned Virgin once again and was immediately transferred to Richard Branson's lawyers, Harbottle & Lewis. Branson had instructed Gerrard Tyrrell's team to start investigating every call, every fax and every letter that the airline received.

Richard Branson himself watched *This Week* at home in Holland Park with his family. His pleasure at seeing Basham's activities exposed before a prime-time TV audience was tempered by revelations about the damage his airline was suffering in the USA.

Branson was shocked to see Cory Quinn and Ivan Hilla in Los Angeles explaining that they had switched to BA because they thought Virgin was heading for a crash-landing, and to hear Romel Manalo relate how the rumours surrounding Virgin Atlantic had slashed the airline's trade in John Healy's travel agency by up to a quarter.

The following morning Will Whitehorn arrived at Gatwick Airport from Switzerland. Branson had ordered Whitehorn home from a holiday with his family as the flood of telephone inquiries started. As Whitehorn hurried through London's second airport clutching his baggage, a copy of *BA News* caught his eye. 'Branson "Dirty Tricks" Claim Unfounded' ran the headline. Underneath was Burnside's article about the *This Week* film. Walking swiftly towards the Gatwick Express train terminal while trying to read the article, Whitehorn suddenly dived into a nearby telephone booth.

'Hi, Richard. It's Will. Have you seen *BA News*?'

'No, why?'

'I'm sure it's libellous!'

'What are you talking about, Will?'

As Whitehorn had not seen *This Week*, and Branson had not read *BA News*, one of their less coherent conversations ensued. It only started to make sense when Whitehorn read the whole thing over the phone.

'So BA is basically saying I'm making everything up to get publicity?' Branson asked.

'Precisely,' answered Whitehorn

'Make sure you bring that *BA News* with you,' said Branson as he put the phone down.

Lord King was in a grumpy mood the morning after the programme. Not only had Burnside's press department been inundated with calls from both the media and the general public, he had received personal calls and faxes asking what was going on at The World's Favourite Airline.

'If Branson has got so much information on me, I don't understand why he doesn't sue!' he told one caller.

BA's long-drawn-out negotiations with KLM broke down on the same day, and BA's hope of becoming a megacarrier seemed further away than ever.

Many BA staff were concerned by what they had seen on the programme and pressed senior management for an explanation of the allegations contained in it. Some in the marketing department were concerned about the aggressive public relations strategy Burnside and Basham appeared to be adopting. One member of the marketing and operations department recalls how the head of marketing, Tim Shepherd-Smith, the Reverend Jim Callery's number two, went to see their boss, Robert Ayling, on their behalf.

Shepherd-Smith had chaired the Virgin Project II, under Liam Strong, which had looked at ways that BA could refine its product to counter Branson's. The former Unilever man told his staff he was personally offended by the notion of a company of British Airways' reputation employing PR men to trash the opposition.

'Tim came back and told us that Ayling had assured him that there was no truth in the programme's allegations,' said a member of his staff.

Burnside and Basham launched a counteroffensive in the Sunday papers as they tried desperately to turn the story on its head.

Burnside told the *Sunday Times*: 'Virgin's finger-pointing at BA is the real dirty trick . . . I have been involved in a few rough battles in my time, but I have never experienced this kind of personal attack from anyone.'

With characteristic bravado, Basham told the same newspaper: 'Now I know my job is safe. Branson is starting to drink his own whisky.'

The *Sunday Times* article featured pictures of Branson, Burnside and Basham. However, while the diagonal straps across their portraits read 'Suing, Suing, Suing', in fact both sides were talking, talking, talking.

Despite Tyrrell's advice that the article and Lord King's letter were libellous, Richard Branson remained extremely reluctant to take legal action against BA.

'I still thought that going to court would be a waste of everyone's time, effort and money, particularly mine. I wanted to sort things out with BA and get on with running Virgin Atlantic and a thousand other things I would rather do.'

In the talks Virgin Atlantic was represented by Syd Pennington, the airline's joint managing director, and Colin Howes, a senior partner at Harbottle & Lewis, and Branson's closest legal adviser for many years. BA's two-man team comprised Mervyn Walker and Bill Allen of Linklaters. Branson told Pennington and Howes that his bottom line was a public apology from BA, a pledge that BA would stop smearing him and poaching Virgin's passengers, and the firing of Brian Basham. If they failed to wring these concessions from BA, he would take legal action.

While the peace talks started, Branson was considering his own options very carefully indeed. John Thornton at Goldman Sachs reported a second approach from Thorn EMI, the communications giant, to buy Virgin Music. The previous July, as Virgin launched its Heathrow flights, Branson had been approached by Thorn EMI. Sir Colin Southgate's communications conglomerate wanted to know if he was interested in selling Virgin Music. Southgate received a 'thanks but no thanks' reply. After further approaches to Virgin Music by Warner Brothers and MCA, Branson appointed Thornton to handle inquiries, and Southgate expressed interest again.

'The talks about selling Virgin Music were initially a stopgap, in case Salomons failed to sell the equity we were offering in the airline,' recalls Branson. 'I don't think many people realised the strength of the other parts of the Virgin Group. Certainly not the record company.'

By the spring Thornton was in serious negotiations to bring the sale to fruition. For months the music press had been alive with rumours that Branson was about to sell up. Music-business writers noticed that Virgin Music had recently signed massive deals with the Rolling Stones and Janet Jackson in an apparent attempt to boost its roster of artists to make the company a more attractive proposition. For Branson the decision was anything but clear cut.

'I'd been trying to sign the Rolling Stones since I started Virgin Music twenty years beforehand. Part of me was really unhappy at the idea of selling the company as soon as I had signed them up.'

Branson's involvement in the day-to-day running of Virgin Music had declined as Virgin Atlantic came to dominate his life. He still relished playing the figurehead role, however, intervening personally to help lure artists to Virgin when required. He took Janet Jackson ballooning in the States just before she signed a $40 million deal with Virgin. 'As that didn't put her off, I knew she must be keen to join,' he later joked.

Branson spoke at length to Mick Jagger and Janet Jackson before deciding what to do, and had soul-searching sessions with Peter Gabriel, who had been with Virgin since his days with Genesis. Gabriel had become one of Virgin's most profitable acts, as well as a close personal friend. He was one of several influential voices that advised Branson strongly against abandoning music for flying.

For Branson the clinching factor was one that had guided him through his extraordinary business career: protecting the downside. 'We had to have a fall-back position. If the airline had collapsed it could have taken the record company down with it. It is the thing I find most difficult to explain to people who are not in business. The dividing line between success and failure is so thin.'

Ironically the final shape of the deal between Sir Colin Southgate and John Thornton for the sale of Virgin Music took place on board Concorde somewhere over the Atlantic. The two happened to meet on the pride of BA's fleet just as the two companies entered the final stages of negotiation, and they used the flight to do business. Branson savoured the irony. And the profits. Thorn EMI paid £560 million for Virgin Music. Branson was left with £330 million in his back pocket after Virgin Music's debts had been cleared. At Thorn's request, Branson stayed on as the unsalaried president of the company. The personal sadness he felt at the wrench from the company was mitigated by the strength the deal brought to Virgin Atlantic.

'It was a good way of flicking a V at BA and showing Lord King his silly games were not going to work with our airline. Nonetheless, it was the hardest business decision I have ever had to make.'

Although the sale of Virgin Music gave Branson the money to finance Virgin Atlantic's expansion as well as other Virgin Group projects, he still had to decide what do about BA.

As the talks dragged on with no sign of BA's acceding to Virgin Atlantic's demands, Branson had to admit to himself that the tactics he had adopted since his open letter to the non-executive directors the previous December had failed. Making his allegations public had not worked. BA showed no sign of repenting, apologising or making good the damage to Virgin in any way at all.

The fact that BA stood four square behind Brian Basham was the litmus test for Branson. Even after Basham's role was highlighted in the press, and extracts from the Basham–Hutchins tape were played on *This Week*, Branson knew the PR man was still active amongst journalists and in the City. Branson jotted in his diary: 'Basham out of control!'

The difference was that Basham had become a marked man and it was now easier to monitor his activities. Journalists with no particularly strong links to Virgin were phoning Branson or Whitehorn to tell them when they encountered him. Some, however, still remained under the spell of the 'hidden persuader' and their inquiries often came straight from BA's agenda.

'Joanna Walters from the *Travel Trade Gazette* phoned up with a list of questions that sounded as if she was reading off a BA prompt sheet prepared by Brian Basham,' remembered Branson.

Walters says she had not been briefed by Basham. However, her questions to Branson demonstrated that the agenda Basham had helped to set was firmly in the minds of many journalists who had never met him or read his report.

'It was much more difficult to staunch the flow of rumours than to spot them when they surfaced. Barclays Bank told the airline's managing director, Roy Gardner, that it had heard we were in deep shit, and Citibank told me they had heard the rumours too,' recalls Branson. 'What Basham was trying to do to us was so obviously out of order that I couldn't see why they didn't just sack him, say sorry and we could have started again.'

As BA had known since Branson wrote his 11 December letter to the airline, there was much that Virgin's chairman was still unaware of. Branson, however, remained reluctant to take legal action until the bizarre series of events which started when his airline's marketing director, Chris Moss, arrived, soaking wet, on the doorstep of his Holland Park home. In his pocket was the mysterious tape of the conversation between Marshall and Ayling.

Sitting in Branson's front room surrounded by huge vases filled with fresh flowers, the two men listened intently to the tape. As they did so, Branson was particularly intrigued by their discussion of the *This Week* programme, and the extracts the programme had used from Hutchins' secretly taped conversation with Basham.

Robert Ayling: 'It does appear . . . that Basham did have a pretty specific conversation with that journalist [Hutchins].'

Sir Colin Marshall: 'Oh yes, there's no doubt about it.'

Robert Ayling: . . . clearly very unfortunate that that happened.'

Sir Colin Marshall: 'Yes, it was.'

Robert Ayling: 'Maybe, you know, we can deal with it by
limiting our response to, to, to that?'

The two BA board members moved on to discuss how they should
'limit their response' in reply to the letter Branson had written to
Marshall immediately after the *This Week* programme. Branson
had long since abandoned hope of getting any sense out of Lord
King. Although Marshall appeared to welcome the idea of legal
action against BA, the tape revealed the first signs Branson had
been able to detect of cracks in BA's unity.

Marshall and Ayling discussed the legal action Burnside and
Basham were thinking of taking against Thames TV.

Marshall: 'I gather that there is little doubt that he [Burnside]
had a pretty clear case for defamation . . . and he is very
close to instituting proceedings against the programme.
On a personal basis, of course.'
Ayling: 'Yeah. Well, it has to be. And he has to be represented by people who don't act for us.'
Marshall: 'Yeah. That's right.'

Chris Moss stopped the tape and looked at Branson.
'Maybe someone is trying to embarrass Marshall and Ayling.'
'Maybe someone is trying to embarrass us,' retorted Branson.
Branson told Moss to send the tape to Harbottle & Lewis.
'Get the lawyers to send the tape to BA. I'll do a letter to
Marshall to send with it.'
Two days later, Frank Kane called from the *Sunday Telegraph*
with vivid details of Branson's alleged spying operation on BA,
involving Goldman Sachs and the American investigators, IGI.
Branson interrupted the reporter.
'Stop! This is complete bollocks! And you can quote me on that,'
he said. 'Seriously, if you want a quote for tomorrow's paper, you
can say quite categorically that we have never, ever employed private detectives or bugged anyone. I can't speak for Goldman
Sachs, but I am sure they haven't done that either, certainly not on
our behalf. We don't bug British Airways' phone calls, or anybody
else's for that matter.'

Branson asked for an undertaking that the newspaper would
not publish the accusations. Frank Kane said he would speak to
his editor. Branson thought he sounded disappointed. As Kane
and his colleague, Margareta Pagano, tried to stand up their front-
page splash, they phoned John Thornton. The head of Goldman
Sachs' mergers and acquisitions division was startled by their
inquiries.

'I told them that what they had been told was not true. I'd been
speaking to Richard Branson every day for two months about the
sale of Virgin Music and he'd never asked me to do anything of
the kind. I know Terry Lenzner [head of IGI] very well and I told
the *Sunday Telegraph* that the chances of Richard having hired
Lenzner to work against BA, and neither of them mentioning it to
me, were zero.'

Only after Branson had finished his own conversation with
Frank Kane did he realise how close he had come to telling the
reporter about the anonymous tape. He had no difficulty imagin-
ing how the *Sunday Telegraph* might have run the story:

> The dirty-tricks war between Virgin Atlantic and British
> Airways took a new twist yesterday when it emerged that Sir
> Colin Marshall, BA's chief executive, has been the victim of a
> spying campaign . . .
> . . . A secretly recorded conversation between Marshall
> and another senior BA executive was smuggled to Richard
> Branson, Virgin's chairman. Yesterday Branson confirmed
> he had heard the tape but denied that he had hired private
> detectives to spy on Marshall. A BA spokesman said: 'We are
> alarmed that Mr Branson appears to have got hold of private
> and commercially sensitive material. We have asked him to
> return it and have reported the matter to the police.'

And so on. Jesus! What *was* going on?

Branson spent much of the weekend on the phone to Gerrard
Tyrrell. The urbane lawyer remembers Branson's anger:

'I have known Richard since the mid-1980s, and he rarely gets
angry at all. That weekend he was beside himself. He was taking
the behind-the-scenes talks with BA very seriously, and he was

still hoping they would come up with an apology and get rid of Basham. He told me several times during the talks that he really didn't want to take BA to court. Then suddenly he found himself spending the whole of a Saturday afternoon on the phone denying what he was certain was a BA-inspired fiction about him bugging BA's phones and running a ring of private detectives through John Thornton at Goldman Sachs. Richard was absolutely livid.'

As soon as the *Sunday Telegraph* had assured Tyrrell and Branson that the story would not appear, Branson wrote to Marshall:

Dear Sir Colin,

Last Thursday, even whilst [peace] talks were taking place, a tape was sent anonymously to Virgin Atlantic . . . it contains a recording of a private conversation between yourself and Robert Ayling about Virgin Atlantic and other matters. On Saturday at lunchtime I received a call from a national newspaper. I was told that they were running a major story claiming that Virgin Atlantic had employed a firm of private investigators called IGI, that we have been telephone tapping British Airways for the last six months . . . and so on. If they [the *Sunday Telegraph*] hadn't got hold of me I believe they would have run the story.

I don't know who within British Airways is continuing to supply misinformation about us, but please can we have this stopped once and for all. Someone seems to be playing some mighty dangerous games.

I am enclosing the tape referred to with this letter.

After the tape and the exchange with the *Sunday Telegraph*, Branson decided that this would be his ultimatum. No more negotiations, no more secret talks.

By this letter I am also asking that, no later than close of business on Wednesday 18 March, British Airways formally withdraw the assertion that I have said things which are untrue [and that I said them] for the purpose of obtaining

publicity and apologise to Virgin Atlantic Airways and
myself for having made such an assertion.

I should add that I have not copied this letter to your
colleagues.

Yours sincerely,
   Richard Branson
   Chairman
   Virgin Atlantic Airways Limited.

Branson's deadline passed without any word from British
Airways. On the evening of 18 March, Branson phoned Sir Freddie
Laker in Florida.

'Freddie,' Branson started. 'We're going to sue the bastards!'

11

Operation Covent Garden

'Richard Branson is working through a mole called Robert, and this whole affair is held together by a web of intrigue,' Brian Basham confided to a battery of lawyers hired by British Airways on 26 March 1992.

The arrival of Richard Branson's libel writ at BA took Lord King and Sir Colin Marshall by surprise. Although Branson had been threatening to take BA to court for weeks, King and Marshall became convinced that their rival was engaged in what Burnside and Basham contemptuously referred to as one of his 'piss and wind' exercises.

With the millions raised from the sale of Virgin Music, Branson was now in exactly the position BA had tried so hard to deny him. He could expand his airline if he decided to, and he had the funds to pursue the national carrier through the courts. Sir Colin Marshall and Robert Ayling's strategy of 'emphatic denial' of the dirty-tricks claims would now be tested in the High Court as BA faced its most serious legal challenge since the Laker anti-trust suit. Branson's writ named both Lord King and BA as defendants.

As Branson's writs arrived at Speedbird House, so did the lawyers. John Turnbull headed the Linklaters & Paines delegation. Linklaters were familiar with the issues involved, as they had given BA the all-clear in December when Branson wrote his open letter. John Dickey from BA's American firm of lawyers, Sullivan & Cromwell, had flown over from New York with a brief to assess the airline's possible exposure to anti-trust proceedings. Because the dispute between the two airlines revolved primarily around the transatlantic market, BA was concerned that Branson could take anti-trust action, as Laker had done. *This Week* had demonstrated how Branson's business in the USA was being affected. Ronnie Thomas from Virgin's limousine company described passenger-poaching in New York, and the passengers in Los Angeles who had cancelled their bookings with Virgin showed that rumours very similar to the ones that King, Marshall, Ayling, Burnside, Cocklin and Basham had been spreading about Virgin in London had taken root on the West Coast of the USA. Laker's lawyer, Bob Beckman, said on *This Week*, 'People who spread those rumours for the purpose of destroying competition by Virgin Atlantic are violating the anti-trust laws of the USA, and that's a criminal as well as a civil offence. The whole point is that it's competition between the United States and other countries, and the anti-trust laws apply to anything that involves business to or from the USA.'

In BA's eyes, Beckman was the evil genius behind Laker's anti-trust action, and Branson's announcement that he had hired him caused great concern at Speedbird House. The Washington lawyer appeared to be licking his lips at the prospect of another battle between two British airlines in the American courts.

In the unsuccessful secret talks between BA and Virgin that followed *This Week*, BA's lawyers were allowed to listen to the full version of Chris Hutchins' recording of Brian Basham's briefing. They were not allowed to have a copy or to take notes, but it was clear that Branson's lawyers regarded Basham's activities as the most concrete evidence they had of a smear campaign. When Branson decided to sue after the talks broke down, BA was forced to examine his allegations in proper detail for the first time.

'What happened to the cock who couldn't crow and from his dunghill strut?' Basham asked wryly at the start of his meeting with Turnbull and Dickey's teams.

Basham gave BA's team of external lawyers a sanitised version of his style of 'proactive PR', and described the work he had undertaken on Operation Barbara. He told the lawyers how concerned Robert Ayling had been for him not to admit to the report's authorship. The notes of the meeting prepared by Linklaters & Paines record what Basham said:

> I wanted to admit that I had written it. I was happy to do this. I do it all the time. Ayling told me that I was not allowed to say that I was the author. I was given a prepared script. I was told to say that all my relations with my clients were confidential, that occasionally I did reports for them, but I would certainly not discuss them with the press.

Basham also admitted to the lawyers that he had been encouraged to try and plant stories about Virgin Atlantic he could not substantiate. He recalled Robert Ayling's disappointment the previous July when he had been unable to place a story in the press about Virgin's departure times after BA had secretly accessed them from the computer.

As Basham was being interrogated by the lawyers, Marshall and Ayling were drawing BA's wagons very quickly and very tightly into a defensive circle. The Reverend Jim Callery's switch-selling teams in Ayling's marketing and operations department were instructed to stop trying to poach Virgin passengers instantly. 'Public exposure' of switch-selling, which Ayling had warned his staff about, could be catastrophic to the court action. *BA News* scrapped a second article Burnside and Cocklin had prepared attacking Richard Branson and *This Week*. Burnside's article had already been faxed to Basham for his comments. It dripped with characteristic venom:

> *This Week* is no stranger to controversy in its methods and editorial attitude. [wrote Burnside] This was not gutter journalism – *This Week* sank well below that level.

He went on to allege that the programme contained 'lies, innuendo and outright bias'.

Burnside was peeved at one revelation in particular. In the course of our investigations into Burnside and Basham's business dealings, we discovered an invoice for a £25,000 payment from Basham's Broad Street company to Burnside's New Century Communications company. It was described as an 'introductory fee' for the PR account for the *European* which Basham won from Robert Maxwell. We thought it odd that BA's director of public affairs should be receiving such a large fee from the man he employed as a PR consultant in his own department at BA, particularly as Basham and Maxwell had known each other for years. As a result, we pointed this out.

Burnside was livid and immediately took legal advice. Basham and Burnside both went to the *Sunday Telegraph*'s in-house lawyer, Richard Sykes, and to Patrick Milmo QC. Sykes wrote to Burnside confirming that Milmo took the view that the programme was libellous, judging that the allegation against Burnside's role in the Virgin affair was the more serious.

> It accused you of organising a campaign of false and damaging information, and it accused Brian of implementing your instructions.

Sykes predicted that both men would win damages from Thames TV:

> the result could only restore your reputation and be greatly to the credit of British Airways and the discredit of Branson.

Anticipating that Thames would run a defence of justification, Sykes and Milmo pointed out to Burnside and Basham that there could be difficulties in suing *This Week*. He cited Dick Eberhart's anti-Virgin rumour-mongering against Virgin as an example:

> Assuming for the present purposes that the allegations made against Mr Eberhart are true, you would be faced with the dilemma of either saying that whatever Eberhart got up to was none of your business, or claiming that there was nothing wrong in what he did. A similar dilemma might be raised in deciding how to deal with the accusations of spreading rumours on the American West Coast.

Milmo also observed:

> . . . there will be no question of anybody from British
> Airways, other than yourself, giving evidence . . . which
> might put you in the position of having to fight the British
> Airways battle rather than your own.

This was not a prospect that appealed to British Airways.
Although Marshall and Ayling's involvement in Operation
Barbara had not been revealed, both board members might well
have been called to give evidence when questions were asked
about the funding of the secret report, and the authorisation for
Basham's work.

Ayling told Burnside and Basham that if they wanted to take
legal action against *This Week*, they would have to do it themselves and they would not be permitted to use BA's lawyers. For
the first time, significant divisions were beginning to appear
amongst the leaders of BA's anti-Virgin campaign.

Basham's session with Turnbull's team concluded with the PR
man's analysis of Branson's crusade against British Airways: the
role of 'Robert the mole' was central. He explained that the 'web of
intrigue' that bound the affair together had been spun by Lonhro's
boss, Tiny Rowland. Basham claimed that he had done this partly
as a way of hitting back in revenge for the role he played in helping the Fayed brothers capture Harrods in the 1980s.

Basham was not the only person in the BA camp propounding
intricate conspiracy theory. When Branson sent Marshall the tape
recording of his telephone conversation with Robert Ayling, Ian
Johnson and his team of private detectives in the Covent Garden
operation became convinced that the operation BA suspected
Virgin of running *was* definitely taking place. Johnson reported his
assessment of the tape to BA's security chief, David Hyde, after
The Technician, Jimmy Stokes, had listened to it.

> The conversation was recorded by a third party between C2
> [Marshall] and Ayling. Colin Marshall was talking on his car
> phone from a hotel car park somewhere in Gloucestershire.
> The conversation has been positively identified as having

taken place between 10.00hrs and 10.30hrs on Sunday
1 March 1992.

The tape incident had a profound effect on BA's perceptions of the
forces Branson was mustering against the airline and its key
officers:

> [The] tape was forwarded by Richard Branson, who alleged
> that it had come into his possession through an anonymous
> benefactor. [However] it is inconceivable that it has been
> produced to Branson as an act of charity. If it is a product of
> some interested amateur, it would have been sent directly to
> our client or the media. It is far more likely that this action
> [the sending of the tape] is a 'flexing of muscles' by Richard
> Branson.

The tape appeared to confirm other discoveries that Johnson's
Covent Garden team had made. Johnson believed that Branson
was running a massive operation against BA at a cost of hundreds
of thousands of pounds per week. Covent Garden concluded that
it was being run by John Thornton, the banker who sold Virgin
Music to Thorn EMI.

Covent Garden claimed that Thornton had subcontracted
Branson's work to a variety of undercover outfits. No single
agency knew the full brief. All were working on different aspects
of the investigation.

> We have established that at least five separate investigative
> agencies have been used on this project to date. Two of these
> agencies have been given extensive, well-funded investiga-
> tions and have been told that the projects will continue as
> long as findings continue to be made.

The thirty-page report explains why Richard Branson and John
Thornton suddenly found themselves grilled by the *Sunday
Telegraph* in the middle of March about the ring of private detectives they were supposedly running against BA. With his own
role in the dirty-tricks affair under very intense and very public

scrutiny, David Burnside leaked Covent Garden's findings to the most reliable of the pro-BA papers in the hope of striking back at Branson.

Johnson told Burnside that he believed that the most prominent of the investigative agencies working against BA was IGI. IGI is run by Terry Lenzner, a former District Attorney who had some input into the Watergate investigation. Covent Garden had been probing Branson's American connection by conducting 'pretext' investigations into those suspected of working for Branson. This meant that BA's private detectives approached the target organisations on a false pretext, making out that they were not working for BA, and not acknowledging that they were investigating Virgin or Branson.

> We undertook pretext approaches to Goldman Sachs and IGI. Our investigation of IGI showed that they had received specific instructions from Goldman Sachs to investigate British Airways. An approach was made to a senior manager within Goldman Sachs who reports to John Thornton. He confirmed that their corporate finance section was actively working for Virgin Atlantic/Richard Branson, and had instructed IGI. In tandem with our approach to Goldman Sachs we also conducted a pretext investigation of IGI, which indicated that it was investigating British Airways.

Johnson's most dramatic warning was that Sir Colin Marshall was probably being followed by agents working for IGI. King's security advisor believed it was possible that Branson's agents had actually penetrated BA's executive suites. Burnside told Johnson that he had been tipped off about a mole in his own office. One of Burnside's 'friendly' newspaper sources also told him that Virgin had planted a senior secretary in Enserch House and that she was feeding Branson with information. She had gained access to BA's most valuable commercial and personal data. According to the 'source', Branson activated her at the beginning of the year, and she was passing information to Virgin about Lord King and Brian Basham as well as David Burnside – the three men Branson had publicly identified in his dirty-tricks accusations. Burnside's

'source' said that she was being aided in her work by a receptionist who had recently been hired by BA.

The 'source' warned Burnside that Branson's investigation was
designed to discredit him personally and was probing all aspects of
his personal, private and financial life, including his controversial
past in Northern Ireland. Although neither Finch nor The
Technician turned up any evidence of bugging at BA's HQ during
their 'security audits', Johnson's men made an important find during a similar operation at Burnside's Chelsea flat. According to the
log of Covent Garden's activities kept by the private detectives,
they discovered

> that the distribution point situated externally in the base-
> ment below street level had been left with the cabinet door
> open and the wires hanging loose. Evidence suggests that
> someone had been tampering with it.

Although the *Sunday Telegraph* dropped the IGI–Goldman Sachs
story in the middle of March as there was no evidence to support
Burnside's leak, by the end of the month the information that
Covent Garden was gathering appeared to lend new support to
Johnson's theories. In the giddy days following Branson's writ,
few seemed to notice that there was only one major source of the
information on the campaign against Burnside – BA's director of
public affairs himself. David Hyde believed Burnside was being
targeted because of his pivotal role in the outflow of information
from the airline. BA's apprehension about Richard Branson was
rapidly giving way to paranoia, and two of its first victims were
Lord King and Sir Colin Marshall.

When Hyde first reported Covent Garden's suspicions that
Goldman Sachs was masterminding an undercover operation
against BA, the straightforward option for BA's chief executive was
to pick up the phone and ask John Thornton what he was up to.
Thornton enjoys a formidable reputation in the City and on Wall
Street which Marshall knows is well founded – in 1987 the American
led the British Caledonian team which forced up the price that BA
had to pay for Sir Adam Thomson's airline. Marshall led BA's team.
The implausibility of Thornton being involved in an attempt to

undermine BA's board on behalf of Virgin does not appear to have occurred to the chief executive. Instead, he seems to have been almost unbelievably gullible in accepting the advice that Hyde was feeding through from Johnson's Covent Garden operation.

By late March, Marshall's daily personal and telephone briefings on Covent Garden from his head of security appear to have contributed to his rapidly developing state of paranoia about Branson. On 22 March, for example, Marshall heard strange noises on his private phone during conversations with Lord King. Instead of assuming the obvious – a fault on the line – the chief executive reported the incident to David Hyde, who informed the undercover team.

> C2 [Marshall] reported that his phone went dead during conversations on three separate occasions. All the calls had been diverted automatically from the BA switchboard to his Montpelier Square telephone number. On each occasion he was cut off.

The log continues:

> A conversation was being held between C2 and LK [Lord King] concerning the same subject matter. LK's phone started to screech suddenly, not unlike a fax machine.

Burnside and Basham fuelled suspicion further when they reported a rash of difficulties with *their* phone calls.

On 23 March events appeared to take an even more sinister turn. Lord King's special advisor on the BA board, Sir Francis Kennedy, had his car broken into outside his home in Chester Terrace. It now appeared to the fevered imaginations of those involved in Covent Garden that Branson's men were resorting to Watergate-style break-ins. Kennedy's briefcase was stolen. As Johnson noted, it contained highly sensitive material which could provide the thief with valuable intelligence:

> Inside the case, as well as his personal belongings, was the BA Management UK Directory which lists the names, titles

and house/office telephone numbers of every manager in
the company. In addition, the private residence, car telephone, office, and all ex-directory numbers of every director
and secretary in BA.

The following week fears grew that the chairman himself might be
the target of Branson's campaign when, according to the log,

> Two suspicious characters in their late twenties stopped on a
> private road near to LK's house. The car registration was
> checked by police but nothing adverse was found. The story
> the two gave was later checked and found to be untrue. They
> were both residents in the local area.

A comment in the margin added: 'may have been poachers'. Two
more 'male persons' were sighted near King's Wartnaby estate in
Leicestershire a week later, this time 'driving round LK's house
and village in a grey Rover'.

As King and Marshall weighed up the options they had available to combat Branson, suspicions that Branson's agents had
penetrated the heart of BA resurfaced. Jayne Shiek, a personal
assistant to the BA chairman, suspected that King's kit-form model
of a BA plane had been disturbed. Perhaps the model plane concealed a listening device?

> Jayne reported that a model aircraft on top of a file cabinet
> outside LK's office had been moved. This was unusual, as
> you would need a ladder to get to it and it had not been
> moved for years.

The log also observed: 'There was still dust on top of the file cabinet, so it could not have been the cleaners who moved it.'

Johnson advised that BA's security personnel and office staff
should be especially vigilant while his investigation continued.
He counselled the airline's executives, in particular King and
Marshall, to take every possible precaution:

> It is of paramount importance that our client and its main

officers act to protect themselves. They should be extremely cautious in their use of mobile phones, fax machines and conversations which can be overheard.

Johnson's conclusions were influential as BA decided whether or not to countersue Branson. Writing in a confident, assertive style, Johnson gave the impression that Operation Covent Garden was close to a positive result.

> There is no doubt that a campaign is being waged against our client . . . British Airways has already been the subject of a hostile, Branson-orchestrated *World in Action* programme [this was a reference to the *This Week* programme] and has received an illegal tape recording of a private telephone conversation from Richard Branson, who claimed to have received it anonymously. Our latest findings indicate that it is probable that the tape recording, the television programme and articles in the *Sunday Times* newspaper are part of a well-orchestrated, generously funded, often illegally conducted and ultimately personally controlled exercise by Richard Branson.

On the grounds that he had now proved to BA's satisfaction that Branson was running an undercover operation against BA and some of its key personnel, Johnson asked Marshall and Hyde to authorise an important strategic shift in Operation Covent Garden.

> In line with our instructions, we have conducted a defensive campaign to ascertain who may be investigating our client. We believe that it is now time to alter the approach of our investigation and work from the top down, rather than an ill-defined bottom up. Inquiries should be put in place to ascertain those advisors most closely involved with Richard Branson/Virgin Atlantic, to determine if any of those are involved in the campaign to discredit our clients.

In the fetid atmosphere that had developed in the BA boardroom, no one appeared to attach too much weight to the final paragraph of Johnson's report:

There is strong circumstantial evidence to indicate that
Virgin Atlantic/Richard Branson are the ultimate authors of
the investigation into our client and its senior personnel.
However, there is no direct evidence of this, as yet.

The documents Operation Covent Garden churned out in this
period are heavy with references to 'pretext investigations', 'hostile bids' and the need to 'update' and 'consolidate' existing
findings, but completely devoid of facts. Judgment was awry at
BA, and those employed to bring forensic intelligence to bear upon
problems facing BA appear to have suspended it altogether. One
of the wilder fantasies that began to flourish was that Richard
Branson might be trying to destabilise BA in preparation for a
takeover bid. It was, after all, Lord King who had publicly pointed
out how vulnerable he believed BA potentially was:
    'There is literally no quoted company in Britain that is immune
to the possibility of takeover.'
    By Easter 1992, Operation Covent Garden had the twin objectives
of defeating Branson in the media war by tracking down the leak of
information from BA, and gathering evidence of his undercover
operation which would sink him in the courts. If BA could prove
that Branson himself had been using snoopers and underhand
methods to spy on his main rival after his well-publicised protestations, no jury would find in his favour. It was a high-risk strategy.
    With Sir Colin Marshall's permission, David Hyde removed the
£15,000 cap that had been placed on Operation Covent Garden.
£15,000 now became the average *weekly* budget for the probe into
Branson. BA's security chief was given permission to authorise
any reasonable amount from his budget to get a result. However,
as Operation Covent Garden moved up a gear, a timebomb was
being primed in South-West London.

When Roger Eglin, managing editor of the *Sunday Times*, returned
home in late March, his wife had an extraordinary story to tell
him. As he made himself a pot of tea, his wife explained that the
previous night, while they were asleep, a neighbour had spotted a
man stealing their rubbish. Eglin was incredulous.
    Judith Eglin said that the neighbour who lived opposite had

waited up into the early hours of the morning for her husband to return from a trip abroad. When she heard the sound of an engine running outside the house shortly after midnight, she drew back the curtains in the hope it would be him. Instead, she saw a white Ford transit van parked outside their home. She knew the Eglins didn't have a transit van.

To Judith Eglin's growing astonishment, the neighbour described how she watched as a man got out of the van and started ferrying their rubbish bags towards the vehicle. He appeared to rush his work as the Eglins' dog started barking. Before he drove off she jotted down the van's registration number, EYV 312V, on a doodle pad she kept by the phone.

Roger Eglin had been a newspaper journalist all his life, and reckoned he had heard some strange stories in his time. But why should anyone want to steal his rubbish? He had once written about some fairly hostile commercial battles and hard-fought takeover bids but he never brought his work home. In any case, he was now managing editor, responsible for hiring staff and checking journalists' expenses. Eglin remembers his reaction:

'We puzzled over it for a while and I thought it was fairly suspicious, so I phoned the Teddington police. The sergeant on duty was clearly foxed by what I told him. He hadn't had this sort of crime before.'

The Eglins reasoned that the thief may have been a fraudster looking for discarded credit-card slips or bank statements. He might come back. He might even turn violent if one of the Eglin family encountered him. When the duty sergeant said that he would look into the disappearing bin-bags, Eglin gave him the van's registration number.

Two days later, a bemused John Reilly emerged from Twickenham police station still wondering why Eglin's trash was described as 'sensitive' by Detective Constable Elfed. He knew it was not only private detectives who stole people's garbage. Customs and Excise officials, VAT inspectors and policemen themselves had known been to do 'rubbish runs'.

As soon as he got home, Reilly replayed the message on his answerphone which had commissioned him to steal the trash in the first place.

'If you can pick the stuff up, say, Tuesday morning, what I'll do is contact you Tuesday afternoon when I should be back and I'll arrange to collect it off you, mate, OK?

'I'll try and give you a ring later from where I'm off to, but it's been thrown at me an hour ago and the bloody world's gone mad as usual. Mustn't complain, though. At least it's work. Great stuff. Cheers, mate.'

The voice belonged to Stuart Francis-Love, a fellow private detective whom John Reilly had worked with many times before. Reilly was furious. There was no warning on the tape about the job being sensitive, or who Roger Eglin was. When Reilly had handed over the documents to Francis-Love under the A40 flyover the previous night, he hadn't said anything either; and, the day before his arrest, Francis-Love had left another message on Reilly's answerphone instructing him to steal the Eglins' bin-bags again the following week.

By that evening British Airways' Covent Garden Operation was in turmoil. After a series of hasty telephone conferences between Carratu International and Ian Johnson Associates, the two private detectives, Nick Del Rosso and Tom Crowley, were grounded. The Rover cars Johnson had provided them with were quickly hidden, their pagers and mobile phones were switched off, and Johnson himself took to calling them from a phone box close to his base in Walnut Tree Cottage.

BA's hunt for 'Robert the mole' was in deep trouble.

In February, Johnson had briefed Carratu International's men, Del Rosso and Crowley, on BA's concern that there was a mole inside the airline suspected of leaking confidential information to the press, and possibly to Branson. Johnson gave Carratu a list of likely suspects BA had produced. Some of the names on the list were senior members of BA, others were members of the press suspected of receiving information from the mole. Del Rosso and Crowley were asked to mastermind the hunt.

In familiar undercover fashion, Del Rosso and Tom Crowley organised a series of 'cut-outs' to 'break the circuit' and prevent the operation being traced back to its sponsors in Speedbird House. Each link in the chain would make it more difficult for anyone to trace the ultimate client.

Del Rosso and Crowley contracted Stuart Francis-Love to help them. A former corporal in the territorial SAS, Francis-Love had himself worked for Carratu International. He advertises 'surveillance and discreet investigation' from an address in Connaught Street, London.

The list of journalists Francis-Love was given included Roger Eglin, and Chris Blackhurst, of the *Independent on Sunday*. His task was to steal their rubbish and sort through it for evidence of information that might have been passed to either of them by the BA mole.

Francis-Love established the addresses of Eglin and Blackhurst, and found out when they had their refuse collected by the council. Just before he was due to steal the bin-bags, Francis-Love got another job, so he passed the task one link further down the chain: to John Reilly.

When Reilly was subsequently arrested, British Airways knew immediately that the whole of Operation Covent Garden was in jeopardy.

Forty-eight hours after Reilly's arrest, Roger Eglin put a one-paragraph note in the *Sunday Times* reporting that a private investigator had been arrested for stealing two of his bin-bags. There was no clue as to why the theft had taken place, but the article immediately caused deep concern at the highest level of British Airways. David Hyde discussed the newspaper report with Sir Colin Marshall as he briefed him on Covent Garden the following week. Hyde wrote in his diary for his meeting with Marshall:

Eglin – *Sunday Times* – someone being charged for going through dustbin.

At the top of the page, Hyde scribbled 'CMM 1045 01/04/92', meaning 10.45am on 1 April with Sir Colin Marshall (Sir Colin's middle name is 'Marsh', hence CMM).

The reference to Eglin was brief but highly significant in its context. It revealed that BA staff as senior as Hyde knew as soon as Reilly was arrested that the airline was linked to the theft of the rubbish bags. Why else would Hyde have noted it? At the time, the *Sunday Times* did not link it to the BA–Virgin dispute. No one outside Operation Covent Garden knew that there was a link.

Burnside and Basham quizzed Johnson about the *Sunday Times* report the following day. Then BA started to lay false trails in the media in a bid to steer anyone chasing the story in the wrong direction. In the process they started to give the operation away.

Private Eye reported that Eglin's bins were targeted because of his link to 'Robert the mole', the very same mole that Basham had warned John Turnbull and his team from Linklaters & Paines about only two weeks beforehand.[1] It was the first reference in print to a link between Reilly and the BA–Virgin dispute. Its intention was to mislead, but to those in the know at BA, the leak to *Private Eye* came dangerously close to linking the generals in Speedbird House with the bin-bag foot-soldier. As Hyde discussed the theft with Marshall, Stuart Francis-Love was busy trying to cover his tracks in a working-men's café in South London. He called the unfortunate Reilly to an urgent meeting to find out precisely what he had told the police.

The last time Francis-Love had seen Reilly was the night before his arrest when the two met underneath the A40 flyover.

'Reilly gave me an envelope of papers. I didn't look inside, I just passed it on. I had no idea who was behind this. People ask you to get it or "acquire" it. They don't want me to look inside.

'We had worked together before. I never got paid for that job. When the wheel came off, all the shutters went down.'

Possibly fearing Reilly's wrath, Francis-Love sent an intermediary, Harry Matthews, to meet Reilly on neutral ground at a café just off Clapham Common. As far as Reilly was able to tell, Matthews was nervous. He entered the tea bar with his anorak pulled around his face so tightly that Reilly could see only his eyes peeking out as he sat down. Outside the sky was battleship-grey. The heavens had opened earlier in the afternoon and had refused to close. From within his anorak hood, Matthews spoke in stutters. He exposed his mouth only to sip his tea. Steam began to rise from the green, wet figure.

'All he basically wanted to know was if I had blown Stuart

---

[1] See p. 17 for *Private Eye* report.

Francis-Love's cover,' recalls Reilly. 'I told him I hadn't been charged and that Stuart had nothing to worry about.

'I asked him why he wouldn't take his hood off, as I knew perfectly well who he was and what he looked like. He muttered "counter-surveillance", before dashing off. I wiped some condensation from the café window and watched him running up the street. He zigzagged up the road, constantly looking over his shoulder to see if I started following him. I think he was worried because he knew my speciality is photographic surveillance, and I might have had the place staked out.'

The ghosts of Monty Python and Inspector Clouseau now stalked Operation Covent Garden, and the consequences of the private detectives' blunders began to haunt British Airways.

On 13 April, Reilly was charged with the theft of two of Roger Eglin's bin-bags.

'I felt completely stitched up,' he recalled, ' totally duped.'

The cut-out had been cut adrift. Neither he or Stuart Francis-Love was paid for the mission. The only clue Reilly had as to why he had been charged was the *Private Eye* article. Within Operation Covent Garden, however, the arrest of Reilly brought the tensions between the undercover agents to a head.

Johnson's 'Likely Lads' were inconsolable. The day before Reilly's arrest, they heard from Ian Johnson that British Airways wanted a much bigger operation to start involving the surveillance and counter-surveillance of the entire board. Johnson said the job could be worth up to £250,000. As soon as Reilly was arrested, BA withdrew its new instructions. Although Del Rosso and Crowley told Johnson they had 'controlled' the situation in the wake of Reilly's arrest, they remained grounded until the heat died down.

Del Rosso and Crowley were also furious with Vince Carratu. They accused him of bragging at a dinner-party that he had landed the top-secret BA contract. Somehow word got back to Linklaters & Paines that Carratu International were being employed by their clients. There was much mystification and concern about this revelation at British Airways. BA had no idea that it was employing one of the largest investigation agencies in Britain, or that its highly secret operation was the subject of

dinner-party gossip. The airline was under the impression that
'The Likely Lads' were Johnson's men. After a fierce dispute with
the Carratu family, Del Rosso and Crowley left Carratu International. However, they took the British Airways account with
them and continued to work for Johnson's Covent Garden Operation. Vince Carratu was pleased to see the back of both of them.

'We actually sacked Nick Del Rosso but Tom Crowley left rather
than face up to it. We were working for British Airways and we
discovered that what Nick was doing was totally bloody illegal,
and as soon as we found out we said forget it and that was it . . .
we were out.'

Vince Carratu was not particularly bothered about the bin-bag
operation – 'Everyone does that,' he joked – or the subsequent
arrest of Reilly.

'It was the bugging . . . he was doing under our banner . . . they
will do anything with bugs.'

The investigator also formed the very strong impression that the
assignment had a hidden agenda.

'It was really dirty tricks. One aspect was trying to find the
mole. But they were trying to build up a dossier of dirt on
Branson. They said we will pay you big money, big bucks. And we
said, "Sorry, we don't do that sort of thing. We are not dirt collec-
tors in that sense."'

Perhaps even more pertinently, Carratu International and Ian
Johnson Associates fell out over money. Carratu claimed that Lord
King's security consultant was not paying the bills incurred for the
hire of Del Rosso and Crowley. Carratu claimed Johnson paid
them only £7,444 of the £10,000 they were owed.

'The oldest trick in the book,' said one Carratu insider. 'It wasn't
worth going to court for £2,500.'

At British Airways' headquarters, friction was growing between
David Hyde and Ian Johnson. Hyde had always thought that he
should have been in direct control of Covent Garden, which was
now consuming large slices of his budget. He was also developing
a mistrust of Johnson whom he thought was a bullshitter. Johnson
and his swelling band of undercover men were good at producing
expensive-sounding accounts of what they had been up to with
BA's money, but less good at producing any hard evidence of the

campaign they had convinced BA that Branson was running. It
was difficult to dislodge Johnson, however, as his long-standing
friendship with King gave him an inside track to the chairman.
Hyde suspected that King was getting large dollops of Johnson's
bullshit over backgammon and Scotch at White's.

As BA waited to see if Reilly was charged, Johnson received an
excited phone call from Burnside. Burnside told Johnson he
thought he had made a breakthrough. By chance, he might have
stumbled upon Branson's undercover operation against him. As
voters across Britain made their way to the polls on 9 April 1992,
Burnside had received a call from a friend in the North of England
urging him to attend a discreet rendezvous close to the M60 in
four days' time. The caller was Owen Oyston, the flamboyant
socialist millionaire. Burnside knew Oyston socially and had
developed a friendship with his son through their mutual love of
hunting. Brian Basham also knew Oyston and had recently
worked for him during his battle for control of Transworld.

Oyston explained to Burnside that he had himself been the
subject of intensive investigations by television and newspaper
journalists probing his business empire. To defend himself he had
hired a freelance private investigator, Peter Green, to work undercover for him and to establish who was behind the campaign of
vilification. Green had told Oyston at the beginning of April that
he had received another commission – to probe David Burnside of
British Airways. Green said he was busy producing a report on
BA's director of public affairs for Virgin Atlantic.

Oyston said he had read with great interest Burnside's allegations in the press that he was the target of a Branson-inspired
dirty-tricks campaign, and as soon as Green told him he was
working for Virgin he alerted Burnside. After being hounded by
journalists for years, Oyston said he had no wish to see Burnside
undergo a similar experience. Oyston told Burnside that he
would get Green to bring the report he said he had prepared for
Virgin to the Tickled Trout Hotel, just outside Preston, at 18.00 on
13 April.

The tip-off galvanised Operation Covent Garden. Johnson re-
activated Del Rosso and Crowley for their first operation since
Reilly's arrest in the hope that Virgin had made what the Covent

Garden log refers to as a 'monumental cock-up'. An urgent meeting of the key players in the British Airways' undercover team was convened.

Jimmy 'The Technician' Stokes was instructed to kit Nick Del Rosso and Tom Crowley out with state-of-the-art technology to enable them to sweep the Tickled Trout for bugs before the meeting. They were also equipped to make covert video and audio recordings of the encounter. Johnson said he would recruit extra manpower to ensure that counter-surveillance was in place, so Peter Green could be tailed after leaving his meeting with Burnside. A 'static-surveillance' expert would be on hand to take photographs.

The stakes could not have been higher. The morning after the proposed meeting at the Tickled Trout, Burnside was due to issue a press release announcing that BA was to countersue Richard Branson for libel, on the basis of his 'open' letter of 11 December 1991 to Sir Michael Angus and the non-executive directors. Lord King and Sir Colin Marshall had decided to sue him partly because Johnson and David Hyde were certain that Branson was running his own clandestine operation against BA. If Operation Covent Garden could come up with some hard evidence, Virgin Atlantic's libel case against the national carrier would be fatally undermined.

The Tickled Trout meeting offered not only the prospect of photographs, as well as audio and video recordings, but also the written report that Peter Green claimed to have prepared on David Burnside for Virgin Atlantic – more than enough to counterbalance the Chris Hutchins' tape of Brian Basham trashing Virgin.

The news from Burnside that his friend Owen Oyston had stumbled across a Virgin agent working against BA seemed to fit in precisely with Johnson's view of Branson's changing strategy. Johnson was now convinced that Virgin was using investigative agencies *outside* London because it had discovered that BA was aware of the involvement of IGI. Johnson blamed British Airways' legal team for prematurely alerting Branson's lawyers to the allegation that their client was using IGI. Others blamed Burnside for prematurely leaking the preliminary findings of the operation to the *Sunday Telegraph* when he found himself under pressure in the middle of March. After Frank Kane had briefed Branson on the IGI–Goldman Sachs allegations, Branson informed his lawyers, who raised the matter with BA's legal team.

Whatever the reason, Johnson claimed his source of information on IGI had been compromised and that, as a result, Goldman Sachs had dropped IGI from the case.

Forced to start afresh in his efforts to rumble the undercover team working for Branson, Johnson hoped that Virgin had now blundered.

On 13 April, Del Rosso and Crowley moved through the Tickled Trout hotel with care. Both suspected that counter-surveillance by their opposite numbers from Virgin might already be in place. They noticed immediately that the hotel had a small reception area and an intimate restaurant, 'two factors which make it difficult to maintain prolonged observation without being detected.' They formed the impression that Green had chosen the meeting place with care.

David Burnside arrived on the outskirts of Preston as darkness fell. Before making his way to the modest hotel just off the M6, he was briefed by Del Rosso and Crowley. They warned him about possible counter-surveillance before wiring him up with the bugging device that The Technician had bought, a microphone attached to Burnside's cufflink which he could turn on and off himself.

Burnside entered the Tickled Trout and was greeted by Owen Oyston, who introduced him to a number of people who were drinking with him. There was no sign of Peter Green. Outside the hotel, BA's undercover men recognised the ploy immediately as what they later described as a 'deliberate counter-surveillance' exercise by Virgin; 'surveillance teams can be quickly dissipated by being thrown false leads'.

Eventually Green arrived and joined the group. After a couple more rounds Oyston lured Green to a table for dinner with Burnside. Green then admitted to Burnside that he had been hired by Virgin Atlantic.

Crouched in their nondescript transit van, Del Rosso and Crowley were becoming extremely frustrated. They had waited for hours for Oyston to get Burnside alone with Green. As they peered through the window of the hotel restaurant they could see Burnside talking to Green but couldn't pick up a signal from the bug. It wasn't working. When Green left the Tickled Trout after dinner, BA's undercover photographer took pictures of him. He drove away and two more of Johnson's men followed him.

It was a rather embarrassed 'S1' who emerged from the Tickled Trout. Burnside admitted to Del Rosso and Crowley that he had not been able to turn his bug on. The private detectives' frustration mounted as Burnside explained what Peter Green had told him.

Burnside said that Green claimed he was working for Richard Branson and his task was to investigate his domestic, financial and personal life, looking in particular at all his business dealings. Because of his close links with their mutual contact, Owen Oyston, Green said he would be prepared to show Burnside the report he had prepared for Virgin but he had not brought it with him. Burnside and Green had arranged to meet the following week to see the report.

On 24 April, Burnside flew to Manchester to meet Oyston and Green for a second time. Johnson once again arranged for the meeting to be 'controlled and monitored' – private detective-speak for bugged – by Del Rosso and Crowley.

While Burnside and the Covent Garden team were in Manchester, Johnson called in to see David Hyde at Speedbird House to brief him on the latest developments. Johnson was also watching his own back. He knew Burnside had briefed BA without his knowledge. Before the expedition to the Tickled Trout, Burnside had told Johnson not to tell anyone at BA about the proposed encounter. After the fiasco at the Preston hotel, Johnson wanted to make sure that his paymaster was kept fully informed.

Johnson explained to BA's security chief that a two-pronged strategy had been developed to tackle the Virgin operation against BA. Firstly, Burnside would glean all the information he could from Green, the suspected Virgin agent. Then he would deliberately feed Green with some 'juicy' personal information. It had been agreed that Burnside would tell Green that he was worried that Branson would find out about his, Burnside's, off-shore bank accounts. The Covent Garden team would then monitor where the information about Burnside's bank accounts eventually emerged. The information fed to Green would thus be marked, and act as a form of radioactive trace within Branson's operation.

Burnside made his way to Wilmslow from Manchester Airport for his meeting with Oyston and Green. As the men ate lunch, Del Rosso and Crowley listened in to their conversations. This time Burnside's recording gear worked and the conversations were taped. Green repeated what he had said to Burnside in the Tickled Trout but, once again, he had failed to bring his report with him. He told Burnside he had been asked to dig for further information on his Northern Ireland connections.

A long and boozy lunch was followed by dinner at a Chinese restaurant. Del Rosso and Crowley lost contact with Burnside and an attractive female companion whom Oyston had surprisingly invited to lunch. They mistakenly followed Oyston and Green's taxi, thinking Burnside was in it.

When the group reassembled in the Chinese restaurant more than two hours later, Burnside was disgruntled. He suspected he was being lured into a honey trap by the Virgin agent and possibly by Oyston as well. The girl he had been paired off with was hopelessly drunk and disappeared to the lavatory to be sick. He told Oyston and Green firmly that he needed the report, and quickly. Green said he would bring the report to London and give it to Burnside.

The Covent Garden team's suspicions that Green was acting as a double agent were growing. BA's private detectives began to agree with the director of public affairs that Green's attempts to wheedle information out of Burnside, and his proven ability to access confidential information, indicated a professional approach:

'This, allied to his undoubtedly professional demeanour and a general awareness of surveillance in all its forms, indicates that people with a considerable level of expertise are working against our client.'

When Green stepped off a morning train from Manchester at London's Euston Station on 29 April, BA's undercover men were waiting for him. They watched him cross the concourse of the busy terminal, and shadowed him as he made his way to Burnside's Chelsea flat. The Covent Garden agents used mobile phones and their pagers to guide each other as they took turns to follow Green. Johnson's men hoped that Green's early arrival in London might mean that he was calling in to see Bull & Bull, the firm of solicitors he had claimed were being used by Branson to organise the investigation of British Airways. They were to be disappointed.

> He was observed to arrive in London by train; prior to the meeting, he visited two premises in London, neither of which belonged to Bull & Bull . . . he visited 93a Harley Street and then went to 70 Charlotte Street, London W1, the address of Fuegler and Company, solicitors. He spent approximately one hour at these premises and then hailed a black cab, which took him to . . . his meeting with David Burnside.
>
> He arrived at this meeting an hour early and walked around the vicinity of the meeting, behaving in a manner which strongly indicated that he was undertaking counter-surveillance.

Once in Burnside's Chelsea flat, Green admitted that he had, for the third time, failed to bring the promised report on Burnside. He did, however, provide Burnside and the listening Del Rosso and Crowley with some fascinating information that the two undercover men recorded.

Green alleged that Lord King had been targeted by his, Green's, paymasters, whom he confirmed were Virgin Atlantic. Green also confirmed he was working for Bull & Bull, whom Branson had 'tasked' with the operation. Green said the whole operation was being generously funded, and he described the investigations he had undertaken into Burnside's private affairs. As evidence, he quoted Burnside's ex-directory phone number, the length of time the PR man had lived at his Ebury Street address, and the date he surrendered his American Express card for a British Airways' corporate card.

Burnside was apparently unaware that the details Green was providing him with represented less than an afternoon's work for a commercial inquiry agent, and could have been bought for a couple of hundred pounds.

A summary of the transcript reveals Green's description of 'what he thinks Virgin's next plan of attack will be'. Green states that 'they [Virgin] will not be able to smear Burnside through his obvious contacts. What they needed was something like a list of county court judgments recorded at his London or Northern Ireland residence.'

Burnside responded to Green by saying that 'BA are now aware of the widespread investigation that Virgin is conducting' and went on to tell Green that 'he believes BA is about to put up money in a legal, legitimate and orthodox way for a widespread trawl investigation.'

The number of times Burnside emphasised the words 'legitimate' and 'legal' indicates that he was conscious that the conversation was being recorded, and that there was no watertight guarantee that the tapes would not find their way into 'hostile' hands.

When Johnson listened to the tape, he got the impression that Green was drunk. Notwithstanding the Virgin agent's apparent fondness for the bottle and his inability to concentrate on one topic of conversation for very long, Johnson advised British Airways:

> people with a considerable level of professionalism are working against our client. During the meeting [Green] stated that the ultimate paymasters were Virgin Atlantic. He observed that a great deal of money was being spent on this investigation.

However, Johnson and his team were becoming progressively more convinced that Green, and possibly Oyston, were double agents, actively working for Virgin:

> although throughout his meetings with David Burnside he was apparently offering to assist our clients, our examination of these meetings and the conversations, which took place during them, indicates very strongly that he was using them as an opportunity to gain further information about our client.

As Green left Burnside's flat his trail was picked up by Del Rosso and Crowley. They followed him back to Manchester. From previous surveillance 'The Likely Lads' had identified the car Green was using – a Toyota sports – and as he left Manchester's Piccadilly Station they continued to follow. Apparently realising he was being shadowed, Green turned sharply into a one-way street and drove against the traffic in an attempt to lose his tail. When he reached Sale in Cheshire, he did a U-turn in the middle of the road but, according to their log, Johnson's men managed to stick with him and trail him to his home in Northenden Road.

Green's failure to produce the report greatly annoyed Burnside, but he went ahead with the ploy of setting up offshore bank accounts as planned. By the end of the following week, Burnside had still heard nothing from Green and so he called Owen Oyston. Burnside was now very suspicious of Oyston's role in the affair, and so he taped the call:

'Owen, what's happening on our friend Peter?'

'Well, I don't understand why he hasn't . . . I spoke to him and said, "Give him what you've got and let things take their course,"' replied Oyston.

Burnside confirmed that he had set up new bank accounts as bait for the Virgin agent:

'I went ahead and set up legitimate offshore company banking arrangements . . . which could be legitimately inserted into Peter's report to go back to his clients [Virgin], then we can watch and see where it comes out and I would like to know some idea of timing, when it's going to be done.'

'He's like an eel! . . . Have you given him the information, has he got it for sure?'

'I did that when he came down to London to set it up and he said that he would let me run through to see that it was OK on the report and then he would submit it to his client . . All I need to know is if he's going to put it in the report or not, because we set it up to try to see whether it would flush out the client.'

'Let me talk to him again,' said Oyston before Burnside hung up.

Tensions surfaced within Covent Garden as BA's June rendezvous with Virgin in the High Court drew closer. Knowing that Burnside was in daily contact with Sir Colin Marshall, Ian Johnson phoned the chief executive personally to update him after the Manchester stake-out of the Chinese restaurant. Burnside's unilateral briefings of BA were beginning to grate with Johnson. He noted rather testily in his log on one occasion:

> . . . called into SpHse [Speedbird House] to brief C1 [Sir Colin Marshall] as S1 [Burnside] had done so without prior consultation with me.

Johnson was apparently keen to ensure that the Irishman was not the only person lubricating the wheels of the chief executive's information intake. The security consultant's fees were mounting steadily towards six figures and BA was intending to spend a great deal more. Johnson was also aware that, as the High Court case approached, the results of Operation Covent Garden would come under close scrutiny at British Airways.

Johnson's glossy, thirty-page document included surveillance photos of 'Peter Green' at different locations all over the North-West of England, including his departure from the Tickled Trout in Preston after his meeting with Burnside. It concluded that Owen Oyston had joined the ranks of merchant bankers, private detectives and journalists conspiring with Richard Branson and Virgin against the national carrier. According to the Covent Garden report Oyston had, in fact, been running an operation against Burnside on Richard Branson's instructions,

> the sole purpose of which was to unearth derogatory information on one of our client's employees [David Burnside] and, as a consequence, our client [BA].

Covent Garden concluded that Peter Green was a double agent trying to lure Burnside into revealing details about himself and BA.

And then there was the elusive mole – the second part of Johnson's wide-ranging brief. As his private detectives toiled to try and find the mole, Lord King played for time in the High Court by trying to get the libel cases adjourned until the autumn. The chairman of British Airways declared in an affidavit that one of the reasons he wanted the trial postponed was that he was required to see the Queen off from Heathrow while the case was due to be heard.

In a highly unusual development, during King's preparations to meet the Queen, Johnson's 'private investigators' were permitted by BA to inspect the confidential personnel files of employees the airline suspected of either being the mole, or of being in contact with the mole. None of the names that Johnson was given to investigate yielded anything but further frustration for the undercover team.[1] Nothing was discovered to link any of the names with Virgin or the media, but BA's decision to allow Johnson's team of irregulars into Speedbird House to search the personal files of loyal members of the airline's staff marked a new low in the national carrier's descent into a state of almost desperate paranoia.

Brian Basham remained convinced that the mole held the key to Branson's campaign, as he had told BA's lawyers in March.

'I was concerned with . . . the identity of the mole,' Basham recalled. 'I tried to discover by an analysis of British Airways internal people, the top 150, and those people who knew of those matters which had been discussed. I had conversations with Ian Johnson and with Nick Del Rosso and Tom Crowley about my researches, and about my own theories as to who the mole might be.'

However, Basham's conviction that 'Robert the mole' was at the hub of Branson's campaign was a myth that exploded in the run-up to the High Court confrontation.

The *Independent on Sunday* exposed 'Robert the mole' as Michael John Taylor, a former paint salesman from New Malden whose activities had plagued BA for a decade and a half.

In a colourful career, Taylor traded under the name of 'Robert the mole' or 'Twickenham Pete' after the postmarks his anonymous leaks bore. An obsessive airline buff, with an encyclopaedic

---

[1] The author is aware of some of the names of BA staff who were investigated by Operation Covent Garden but has declined to publish them on the grounds that there is not a shred of evidence to support BA's suspicion that the mole was a serving employee.

knowledge of BA and the airline industry, he claimed to be a former VC 10 test pilot who had once worked for BA. 'Robert' was
lunched by journalists at his favourite restaurants in central
London such as The Upstairs in the Savoy, and the Waldorf Hotel,
and he managed to bamboozle aviation specialists from the trade
press. He succeeded because much of the information he relayed
was very accurate. He chuckled at his double identity: Mike the
paint shop manager by day, 'Robert' the undercover agent by
night. Taylor was apparently able to walk unchallenged into BA's
offices and still pass himself off as an employee. Posting secret
documents provided the thrill of the illicit.

BA first became aware of 'Robert's' activities in 1980, and the
airline's solicitors took out an injunction against him. No charges
were pressed but Taylor gave a written undertaking he would not
enter BA's premises again. There is little doubt that Taylor broke
this undertaking as his list of victims grew to include many
national newspapers and Channel 4 Television, which once featured an interview with the suitably disguised 'mole'. Another of
his 'victims' was Chris Blackhurst, one of the journalists Basham
contacted to ask for their help in trapping and exposing the mole.

'I was working to find out who the mole was by talking to journalists,' Basham said. 'I was in contact with Chris Blackhurst at the
time . . . Blackhurst eventually decided that Taylor had been
deceiving him for years and revealed his identity.'

Blackhurst's exposé of 'Robert' in the *Independent on Sunday*
made good copy and it silenced Taylor. The famous New Malden
phone number, which some journalists habitually dialled after an
aviation scare, was disconnected. There were no more brown
paper envelopes bearing the Twickenham postmark. The
unearthing of Taylor amused some of those who had been conned
by 'Robert' and embarrassed others, but his exposure did nothing
to further BA's case against Branson.

Covent Garden had not turned up anything to support
Basham's contention that Branson was operating through 'Robert',
and neither did the *Independent on Sunday*. Quite the reverse. The
article suggested that David Burnside himself might have been
controlling the mole to leak information to journalists. Blackhurst
related his own experience of arriving early for a briefing on BA

with 'Robert' at the Waldorf. He was startled to bump into David Burnside leaving the hotel. As Blackhurst made his way into the back bar, his suspicions were further aroused when he found 'Robert' sitting there in full view.

There was nothing to link Michael John Taylor to Virgin Atlantic. Nothing Covent Garden or the *Independent on Sunday* revealed bore any relevance to the imminent High Court battle. Perhaps the newspaper's headline provided the most appropriate epitaph for BA's undercover operation: 'The Mole Who Never Was'.

However, as British Airways would discover, Operation Covent Garden would shortly be enjoying life beyond the grave.

12

'The King is Dead! Long Live the Marshall!'

'Are you sure this guy's not winding you up, Gerrard?' asked a mystified Richard Branson.

'I don't know, Richard, but I've asked someone to check him out to see if he's worth taking a statement from,' replied Branson's lawyer, Gerrard Tyrrell.

'Just tell me again what he said to you, Gerrard. Slowly. What was his name?'

Tyrrell drew breath and started reading from his notes again.

'He phoned the airline yesterday. His name is Sadig Khalifa. He has now left BA but when he was working for them he says he accessed Virgin Atlantic's computers in the winter of 1990–91. He was part of a secret team which BA's sales department organised at Gatwick. The team was called the Helpliners. There were more than a dozen of them involved. They had to monitor every Virgin Atlantic flight out of Gatwick and send the details to London. He says it was so secret that everyone involved was instructed not to tell their families or friends . . .'

'Gerrard!' Branson interjected. 'Get someone down there!'

'We're already on our way!' replied the lawyer from his Hanover Square office.

Tyrrell's legal team had already fanned out on both sides of the Atlantic in their search for evidence. Solicitor Frances

Butler-Sloss had been to the West Coast of America to probe the anti-Virgin rumour-mongering, and had flown to Washington to consult Sir Freddie Laker's lawyer, Bob Beckman, on the prospects for Virgin taking anti-trust action against BA. As Branson's team worked its way through the scores of people in Britain who had left their names after the *This Week* programme, many of them emerged as potential witnesses. Sadig Khalifa's call to Virgin Atlantic was but the latest in a series of dramatic developments that had given Tyrrell's team enormous encouragement since serving the writ on Lord King and his airline.

Until Khalifa came forward no one at Virgin Atlantic had a clue that the airline's confidential computer data had been accessed by British Airways. His revelations about the secret activities of BA's Helpliner unit were initially greeted with incredulity. The solicitor on Tyrrell's team responsible for taking Khalifa's statement, Paula Barry, checked Khalifa's background, and the circumstances of his departure from BA, in great detail before taking a formal witness statement from him.

The only other hint that BA might have been accessing Virgin's computer information had come from Peter Fleming. The former BA man confessed in his witness statement that he had analysed Air Europe's computer data through the airline's departure control system in the months before it went bust in 1991. He said he thought some of his colleagues in the marketing and sales department had been doing the same to Virgin Atlantic. Sadig Khalifa's evidence appeared to support Fleming's statement. He also told Virgin's lawyers that the Helpliners were obtaining confidential data on Air Europe and Dan Air.

If Branson had ever had any doubts about the price he had to pay for endlessly promoting his airline, these were the months in which he got his payback. Many of those who came forward did so because of their admiration for Branson and what he was attempting to achieve with Virgin Atlantic. Although Branson had just sold Virgin Music in a deal that made him a dollar billionaire, the image of the tiny airline fighting a monstrous rival was firmly established in the popular imagination. Virgin passengers came forward in droves to do what many saw as their bit to help prevent Virgin Atlantic going the same way as Laker Airways.

Apart from Yvonne Parsons, whose schedule had been badly messed around by the bogus calls, and Geoffrey Luce, whose teenage son had been prevented from switching to a BA flight to Miami because he held a Virgin ticket, few of those who came forward could be described as 'victims' of BA's campaign against Virgin. On the contrary, most of them either benefited or stood to benefit, from the variety of offers that BA made to them in the form of upgrades, free tickets, or more convenient schedules from the national carrier's worldwide network of services. Many of those who emerged took the view that while freebies and upgrades were very pleasant at the time, they would probably not last for very long if BA regained its monopoly on the lucrative long-haul routes they were flying on. Some said they were prompted by Freddie Laker's rousing call to 'sue the bastards'.

Yvonne Parsons' call to Virgin Atlantic the day after *This Week* was now an affidavit. She was able to give Frances Butler-Sloss precise details of the times and the dates of the calls that she received, as well as the names of the people who turned out to be bogus Virgin bookings clerks. Like many of the passengers who came forward, Parsons said she would prefer not to be publicly identified but agreed to take the witness stand if it became necessary. The fury Parsons had directed at Branson's airline over the past nine months now found its expression in a tightly focused legal statement which effectively accused British Airways of trying to con her.

Caroline Mickler made a statement describing how John Danks from BA's Latitudes Club had cold-called her with an offer of two free tickets to Paris if she changed her return trip from Tokyo to London from Virgin to BA. Dr James Sorrentino, in Connecticut, swore an affidavit which described his experience at the hands of Robert Ayling's Interliners at Gatwick Airport. He gave a detailed description of how Amanda Ritson tried to switch-sell him from Virgin to BA. Darren Costin also gave a witness statement describing BA's attempt to get him to switch from Virgin Atlantic at Heathrow.

The importance of these witnesses and their first-hand experiences at the sharp end of Mission Atlantic was considerable. The libel case would hinge not on whether these activities themselves crossed the line between sharp practice and illegality, but on Branson's integrity. The jury would have to believe he had made his allegations in good faith, and that he had evidence to support his charges that BA was running a dirty-tricks campaign against Virgin Atlantic. Effectively Lord King and *BA News* were calling Branson a liar by accusing him of inventing the claims that his passengers were being poached in order to get publicity. Every passenger who signed a statement for Virgin undermined BA's accusations that Branson had invented his claims to 'contrive publicity'. If Branson won his case, then British Airways' libel suit would collapse – the two actions were mutually exclusive.

The other encouraging development from Virgin Atlantic's point of view was that the evidence provided by the new witnesses indicated that there was a pattern to the passenger-poaching activities and the accessing of Virgin's computer information. As well as being exceptionally valuable in their own right, the new informants added colour and detail to what Tyrrell liked to describe as the 'big picture'. They also helped Branson's legal team puncture what they saw as the insufferable arrogance of the phalanx of British Airways' lawyers.

'To begin with, Linklaters gave the impression they were doing us a favour by turning up at all,' recalls Tyrrell. 'By the end of the summer that was beginning to change.'

Sadig Khalifa's allegations made an important contribution to deflating Linklaters. Tyrrell disclosed Khalifa's statement to British Airways' lawyers in July 1992, shortly after Mr Justice Drake granted BA an adjournment of the case. Two months later British Airways gave Virgin's lawyers 'assurances about their employees' future conduct' in respect of extracting information from the computer. In other words they would stop accessing Virgin's computer data which the airline now admitted it had been doing for nearly three years. BA said it would build a 'Chinese wall' into BABS so that Virgin's information could not be accessed by BA operatives. Branson thought BA's timing was revealing. 'Just after the busy summer season had ended!' he remarked with a snort.

Under the process of legal 'discovery' both sides in a libel case are obliged to exchange all documentation that is relevant to the issue. Branson's case against Lord King and *BA News* was quite a narrow one, hinging primarily upon his own integrity, but BA's countersuit against him widened the process of discovery dramatically. As a defendant against BA's charge that he had libelled the company, he also became entitled to ask for all relevant documentation on the matters that BA alleged were libellous.

Thus Tyrrell's legal team probed BA on the matters that Richard Branson had highlighted in his 11 December letter to the non-executive directors – Brian Basham's report, the switch-selling activities of BA's sales teams and the shredding allegations. Under the terms of legal discovery BA were obliged to hand over all relevant documents – or at least the ones that had not been shredded. As a result crateloads of documents were making their way from the City offices of Linklaters to the West End offices of Harbottles. At the height of the legal bonanza twelve lawyers were engaged by BA as the airline took statements from over a hundred of its employees, and was required to surrender thousands of documents.

For BA's lawyers the discovery process was proving a barren and depressing experience. Much of what they found in BA's own files appeared to support Branson's allegations against the airline. The activities of the switch-sellers on both sides of the Atlantic had apparently been carefully documented. One of Linklaters' tactics was to swamp Virgin's much smaller legal team with thousands of documents. While this undoubtedly prolonged the case, it ultimately proved to be counterproductive.

One of the reasons that BA decided to countersue Branson was because of its conviction that Branson was spending hundreds of thousands of pounds orchestrating teams of undercover agents to undermine BA. The problem was that Covent Garden had not established any proof for this theory that BA could confront Virgin with. Nonetheless, BA decided to press Virgin on the issue, as was its right, under the rules of discovery. After a series of meetings involving David Burnside, Brian Basham and David Hyde, as well as Mervyn Walker, British Airways formally requested details of the operation that Ian Johnson and David Hyde had told Sir Colin Marshall they were '100 per cent certain' was taking place. Branson's lawyers were specifically pressed on the role of John Thornton at Goldman Sachs and Terry Lenzner's at IGI.

BA received formal assurances confirming that Virgin had never employed private detectives. When David Burnside leaked the Goldman Sachs–IGI theory to the *Sunday Telegraph* in March, it took two journalists twenty-four hours to knock it flat. After paying Johnson's ring of private detectives tens of thousands of pounds and paying millions in legal fees, BA discovered that its conspiracists' cupboard was bare.

As the rest of Covent Garden's findings came under the legal microscope they, too, dissolved like a vapour trail. Not a single fact in the thirty-page report, complete with its surveillance pictures, would stand up as evidence against Branson in court. Sir Colin Marshall had spent over £100,000 on an operation that had not only induced a state of complete paranoia in members of BA's board, but had also helped to persuade BA to embark upon a disastrous counter-suit against Virgin. Covent Garden's findings had also bolstered Mervyn Walker's advice to BA to counter-sue. As a result Branson's lawyers were now working their way through thousands of BA files they would not otherwise have had access to.

The chief executive and his head of security had allowed themselves to be drawn into the conspiratorial world of Lord King's friend, Ian Johnson, and his team of dodgy ex-customs men and ex-Metropolitan police officers with their sub-military vocabulary and fevered imaginations. Suitably nurtured by tens of thousands of pounds of shareholders' money and large doses of conspiracy theory from Brian Basham and David Burnside, Operation Covent Garden had hijacked BA's navigation system and led the national carrier into thick cloud. At the end of August 1992 Covent Garden flew BA straight into a mountainside, and left its battery of lawyers with a hopeless task as they sifted through the wreckage in a vain search for survivors.

On 30 August the *Sunday Times* splashed a new story on the front page under the headline, 'How BA Spied in Dirty Tricks Campaign'. Inside there were pictures of Johnson 'the mastermind', Nick Del Rosso 'the go-between' and John Reilly 'the snooper' awaiting trial for the theft of Roger Eglin's bin-bags. Although the *Sunday Times* could establish few details about the operation, and was constrained in what it could report by John Reilly's imminent court appearance, the article established the link between the bin-bags and the boardroom.

The story reached the press after BA's private detectives had fallen out badly with each other. The feud between Ian Johnson and Carratu International in the spring turned into a bitter dispute during the summer. Carratu International still hadn't been paid in full by Johnson for its initial work on Covent Garden. What was even worse from Carratu's point of view was that Crowley and Del Rosso had left the company shortly after the row and were now working for Johnson on the lucrative BA account through their own agency CDR – Crowley Del Rosso. Shortly before leaving, Del Rosso had boasted that the BA account could be worth up to £250,000 as Johnson and King were convinced that the leaks to the press were coming from main board members who were to be put under surveillance.

Infuriated by the course that events had taken and having lost two members of staff as well as a valuable account, Vince Carratu went to the *Sunday Times* 'Insight' team with details of what BA were up to.

BA's undercover operation was exposed, and Lord King was in the frame. Any relief that Marshall and Ayling might have felt at not having their names mentioned in the context of the bin-bag operation was mitigated by the knowledge that BA's defence against Branson's allegations was now in tatters.

Branson's reference in his letter to 'activities . . . worthy of an episode of Dick Tracy' had been a stab in the dark inspired by months of unsubstantiated rumours, and Will Whitehorn's and Gerrard Tyrrell's encounter with the private detective, Frank Dobson, underneath Waterloo Station. BA had very publicly rejected his accusations, and the libel cases hinged upon whether Branson was making them up to get publicity.

John Turnbull attempted a damage-limitation exercise. Before publication he had tried to gag the *Sunday Times* by threatening to place the matter in the hands of the Attorney-General. After the article appeared, he phoned John Reilly's solicitor, George Keppe, and suggested he should sue the *Sunday Times* for contempt of court. He helpfully provided a number for the Director of Public

Prosecutions office, and a contact for Keppe to phone. Keppe decided not to take up the suggestion.

At Walnut Tree Cottage, Johnson ordered all records of Operation Covent Garden to be destroyed. For him, the exposure of the undercover operation was the biggest embarrassment of his career.

As soon as the *Sunday Times* story broke, Johnson started his own impersonation of Inspector Clouseau at Walnut Tree Cottage. Convinced that his base was surrounded by hostile agents from the national press, Johnson donned a wig and dark glasses in a bid to change his appearance. Staff were instructed to destroy all records relating to Operation Covent Garden. Certain that the long lenses of the paparazzi were peering through the windows of his unconventional headquarters from the nearby graveyard, Johnson wriggled around on the floor to keep out of sight, while his German-born wife, Jutta, scanned the gravestones with powerful field glasses. When the coast appeared to be clear, BA's bewigged security consultant made his way gingerly out of his secret head-quarters to phone Del Rosso and Crowley from a pay phone in the village. He warned 'The Likely Lads' not to come anywhere near Walnut Tree Cottage as it was surrounded by 'hostile' agents. Del Rosso and Crowley were grounded for the last time, their pagers and mobile telephones recalled to central stores once again.

No amount of 'crisis PR' could retrieve the disaster for BA that Covent Garden now represented. For Turnbull, the exposure of Covent Garden, and the allegation that Reilly was engaged in illegal activity on behalf of BA, compounded the disaster of the discovery process. The crates of material that BA had been obliged to send to Branson confirmed many of Virgin's key allegations against the national carrier and implicated local, middle and senior managers throughout BA, as well as members of the board. As Linklaters ploughed through the documents, and the expanding pile of affidavits that BA's potential witnesses had signed in both Britain and America, the national carrier's defence fell apart like a rotten carpet. The morale of BA's massive legal team plummeted still further as it became clear that many of the private and public denials that BA had made in response to Branson were simply not true.

One of Branson's main allegations in his 11 December letter was that incriminating BA documents about Virgin Atlantic had been shredded. Turnbull was horrified to discover that much of the evidence had indeed been shredded by middle-ranking BA managers in a so-called 'internal audit'. One of the Virgin team remembers how Linklaters reacted:

'Linklaters was shocked when they went into BA for document discovery and discovered that half the stuff had been fucking shredded!'

Branson's key witness on the shredding issue was Peter Fleming. He gave Tyrrell and his team at Harbottles a detailed account of how the mass shredding of information took place at the end of 1990 and the beginning of 1991, when BA heard on the grapevine that Virgin was on the point of submitting its complaint to the European Commission.

BA responded to Fleming's allegations by taking statements from all those whom the former marketing and sales executive had named in his statement as having taken part in the shredding or been aware of it, from the Reverend Jim Callery down to the most humble of his apostles in the secretarial pool. Fleming's former boss, Kevin Hatton, as well as the marketing manager, Martin George, and Fleming's former contemporaries, Peter George and Nigel Bishop, were amongst those whom Mervyn Walker's legal department schooled through their witness statements.

While some whom Fleming identified as taking part in the mass shred said they could simply not recall anything of the sort taking place, others, according to a source who has had access to several of the BA statements, were prepared to admit that they had shredded documents that were 'liable to be misconstrued as anti-competitive,' or that contained 'inappropriate language' which could give 'the misguided impression that BA was acting in an anti-competitive manner.'

Such euphemisms were liberally sprinkled throughout the statements made by the marketing and sales people whom Fleming had named as shredders. Some of the shredders claimed they were acting within BA's document-control policy, others did not sign the catch-all pledge. Some statements gave detailed descriptions of how Kevin Hatton had directed the shredding operation. Others related frenzied discussions as confused members of the sales force quizzed Hatton about what they were required to shred. Others dissembled. Apparently some shredding had taken place 'for environmental reasons', and the bin-bags that Fleming referred to in his statement happened to be lying around the offices to deal with the excess volume of paper generated. A 'paper pillage' day was allegedly held to shred documents.

The statements were a handsome tribute to BA's power of selective memory, and to the fertility of the legal department's imagination. And after the two airlines had exchanged their writs, BA did not encourage dissent.

Immediately after *This Week* was broadcast, BA's popular head of marketing, Tim Shepherd-Smith, went to see his boss, Robert Ayling, on behalf of his staff. He extracted an assurance that the dirty-tricks allegations contained in the programme were untrue. His staff had been shocked by the film's claims, and Shepherd-Smith himself knew nothing of the mass shredding in the sales department at the end of 1990, as he had joined the airline shortly after it had taken place. Even though the marketeers had been placed under enormous pressure to challenge Branson, most had assumed that BA was simply competing vigorously at a very difficult time for the airline, and that dirty tricks were out of the question. Sir Colin Marshall had informed the press, and BA's staff, that this was the case in unequivocal terms. Robert Ayling told Shepherd-Smith that the programme's claims, and Branson's allegations, were totally unfounded. Shepherd-Smith relayed Ayling's reassurances to his marketing staff, who were suitably relieved.

Marketing staff were thus startled two months later when Shepherd-Smith was summarily sacked by his immediate superior, the Reverend Jim Callery, just before the libel trial was first due to have taken place in June.

Shepherd-Smith was fired at 1730 on a Friday evening and told to leave the building. He was told not to return to BA, and not to speak to his staff before leaving Speedbird House. After a blazing row with Callery, Shepherd-Smith marched into his marketing team's offices and explained precisely what had happened.

According to one source, the Reverend Jim told his number two:

'I hope you're going to take this like an adult.'

Shepherd-Smith's reply was reportedly a lot shorter, and he insisted on addressing his staff before clearing his desk. From that moment on, challenging BA's response to Virgin Atlantic's dirty-tricks allegations was not considered to be a wise career move by those who remained.

Those who organised the BA witness statements, Linklaters & Paines and Mervyn Walker, had a special interest in the outcome of the case. Acting on Sir Colin Marshall's orders, Walker conducted BA's initial review of the charges contained in Branson's 11 December letter. He swiftly came to the conclusion that there was no case for BA to answer. As a result Sir Colin issued a string of stinging ripostes to Branson, all of which Walker 'legalled' before they were sent. Sir Colin also satisfied himself that, by the 7 February board meeting, BA was in the clear and informed his fellow executive and non-executive directors of the lawyers' verdict.

Unfortunately for Mervyn Walker, he compounded the inadequacy of his first probe into Branson's allegations by drafting the two letters over which Branson was now suing. The first was the private letter under his own name to me at Thames TV, stating that BA would not take part in the *This Week* programme. David Burnside and Tony Cocklin subsequently plastered it over the front page of *BA News*.

The second letter was drafted by Mervyn Walker for Lord King to reply to viewers who wrote to the airline to complain about BA's tactics as reported in *This Week*. The chairman wrote of Richard Branson that 'he continues to mount a campaign against us through the media. It appears that Mr Branson's motivation is to create publicity for himself and his airline.'

In other words, Branson was claiming he had been libelled by two documents that Mervyn Walker and the BA legal department had drafted and then cleared for publication.

Despite the careful moulding of BA's witness statements, John Turnbull's face fell as he read through the *potage* of contradictory statements that eventually emerged in response to Branson's charges. Not only were key documents missing as a result of the shredding operation, the contradictory accounts of the shredding activities given by those whom Fleming had named revealed the truth of his allegations.

A wit on the Virgin legal team who was familiar with BA's statements dubbed the carrier's tactics as a 'reverse Nuremberg'. Many of the defendants in the Nuremberg War Crimes trials after the Second World War admitted committing atrocities, but defended themselves on the grounds that they were only following orders. According to the suspiciously uniform affidavits from BA, the reverse appeared to be the case at the national carrier: the shredding, the poaching and the smearing appeared to have been carried out by individuals acting entirely on their own initiative.

At BA this became known as 'Operation Distance Marshall'.

Brian Basham was surprised when BA's legal boss, Mervyn Walker, handed him a prepared witness statement to sign. After Basham read it, he burst out laughing:

'You can't seriously expect me to sign that, Mervyn!' he cried.

'Mervyn Walker had produced what looked like a *pro-forma* affidavit which exonerated Colin Marshall and Robert Ayling from all involvement in any of the matters that Branson complained about,' Basham recalled. 'Walker told me if I didn't like his version I should write my own. So I did.'

Basham's encounter with Walker occurred late in the evening on Friday 4 October. BA's legal director said Basham would have to produce his alternative version by the Monday morning, as time was pressing. Alarmed by BA's sudden urgency, Basham went one better. He called his secretaries into his Clerkenwell Green office over the weekend, pulled out his BA files and his business diaries for the past two years, and wrote a lengthy account of his role in the affair.

In the middle of the Sunday afternoon, Basham presented Walker with a thirty-four-page account. He gave it to Walker at the City offices of Linklaters where the BA legal team was also working throughout the weekend. Basham's statement began in an uncompromising fashion.

I was shocked and surprised at Mr Branson's allegation that I was involved in a dirty-tricks campaign to undermine Virgin. Branson in his dealings with BA has won the public

relations battle hands down, but with underhand and unethical methods. He seems to devote his entire life to the
pursuit. He is also a known liar who is quite capable of
standing truth on its head. This is precisely what he has done
in this case.

Having vented his spleen against his tormentor, the remainder of
Basham's statement was a much less emotional account of the life
and death of Operation Barbara.

Basham described how British Airways' growing concern over
Richard Branson's tiny fleet led to the birth of Operation Barbara.
He outlined how Lord King and Sir Colin Marshall commissioned
the report through David Burnside's department, and how he
compiled the report with the help of information from senior managers like Mike Batt and board members, such as finance director
Derek Stevens, before presenting it to Lord King, Sir Colin
Marshall and Robert Ayling. He related how he developed certain
angles in the report in response to the concerns of Lord King –
Heaven nightclub – and Sir Colin – Virgin's weak management
and inadequate capital. He described in great detail how he then
disseminated the report to contacts in the press such as the *Sunday
Telegraph's* Frank Kane, and Lord King's son-in-law, Melvyn
Marckus, on the *Observer*. In unemotive tones he described how he
was taped while briefing Chris Hutchins of *Today* and Nick
Rufford of the *Sunday Times*, and how disgraceful he considered
the two journalists to be. He said that British Airways stopped
him pursuing the two journalists and, subsequently, the *This Week*
programme through the courts.

The head of British Airways' legal department placed Basham's
statement on the desk in front of him. Mervyn Walker looked over
the top of his glasses, and spoke to Basham in deliberate and measured tones:

'Brian, I implore you not to sign this statement.'

'Mervyn Walker was not a happy man,' recalls Basham. 'As he
read through my statement he constantly crossed and uncrossed
his arms and legs. He reminded me of an octopus in a hole.

'I told him I realised that there were tactical considerations
in putting together witness statements, but that my version

accurately described my role and if I appeared in a witness box, that is what I would say.

'He said he would rewrite it to fit in with BA's legal strategy. I wished him good luck and returned to see him the next morning at nine o'clock with my solicitor.'

Basham and his solicitor, the *Sunday Telegraph*'s in-house lawyer, Richard Sykes, studied Walker's new version of the witness statement, which was the third to be produced in four days. Basham's thirty-four-page statement had been boiled down to six pages. The detailed account of the roles played by King, Marshall and Ayling in commissioning, authorising and paying for the report had been almost entirely deleted. Six lines covered the roles of BA's top three executives in Operation Barbara. In Walker's new version of Basham's statement, it was acknowledged that the three had been 'briefed' on the report but no more. Basham was unhappy with Walker's penultimate sentence, 'I have never been instructed by BA to smear Virgin or Mr Branson, nor have I ever attempted to do so.'

A dictionary was sent for as Walker and Basham sought the definitive meaning of the verb 'to smear'. The dictionary revealed that 'smear' could mean 'to (seek to) discredit publicly', which was a reasonably fair description of what Branson alleged that Basham had been doing for the past eighteen months – as Basham and Walker both knew.

Sykes felt there was no danger to his client if he signed the statement on condition that he extracted a categorical assurance from Walker that, if Basham signed, BA would not desert him during the court case.

'We will stand by Brian until the end,' said Walker.

Suitably convinced, Basham signed the revised statement.

At the beginning of November the British Airways main board gathered for its monthly meeting at Enserch House. The atmosphere was already sombre as the directors made their way into the richly carpeted boardroom.

From his customary position at the head of the polished table, Lord King watched as the non-executive directors took their seats. For more than ten years King had counted them in and counted them out. His eyes scanned their movements as they took their papers from heavy leather briefcases. The normal bonhomie that characterises the start of these monthly meetings was noticeably absent.

Flanking King were his executive directors, Sir Colin Marshall and Robert Ayling. Facing him were the non-executive directors. Most senior among them was their chairman, Sir Michael Angus, also the airline's deputy chairman. At sixty-two, Angus is the chairman of Whitbread, a former chairman of Unilever and, at that time, was president of the CBI. His impeccable credentials had prompted speculation that he might eventually succeed King.

Among the other non-executives were Michael Davies, chairman of Calor, King's special advisor, Sir Francis Kennedy, the Hon. Charles Price II, President Reagan's former Ambassador to London, and Lord White of Hull, chairman of Hanson Industries and King's longstanding hunting companion.

After the preliminaries Ayling rose to introduce John Turnbull. The Linklaters lawyer had the delicate and onerous task of explaining to the board what the process of legal discovery had yielded in the Branson case.

As BA's directors listened to Turnbull it became clear that BA would have to settle. The damages would be vast and the costs would be much larger. The harm to BA's reputation would be impossible to calculate.

There was silence.

'No!' cried King slamming his hand down on the table. 'No!' The cantankerous Lord had no desire to submit to Branson, however overwhelming the odds might be.

Sir Michael Angus, famous in the City for his fiery temper, demanded to know who was responsible. Angus's own reputation would be called into question if BA submitted to Branson in court. On the advice of Marshall and Ayling, he had written to Branson the previous year dismissively rejecting the chairman of Virgin Atlantic's request that the non-executives probe his dirty-tricks accusations. He had been told that there was nothing in the charges in December 1991, and he had been further reassured, when Sir Colin Marshall reported to the February 1992 board meeting, that Linklaters & Paines – as well as Mervyn Walker's legal department – had found that Branson's original dirty-tricks letter presented no legal threat to BA.

As the litigation progressed, Angus had continued to accept King and Marshall's assurances that there was no charge to answer. Now it appeared that the board had been misled. BA was being told by the same lawyers who had initially advised BA there was no case to answer that it now had to *surrender* to Branson. Because Angus had expected Virgin to abandon the action as just another publicity stunt, the impact of Turnbull's advice was correspondingly greater.

'We were all shocked as the scale of the defeat sunk in,' said one director. 'We felt betrayed.'

King was still determined to fight on, declaring himself ready and willing to take the witness stand. This was not a prospect that appealed to Angus and the non-executive directors. They tried to cool King down.

Another important factor in the board's debate was the possible damage the Branson case might inflict upon on BA's bid for a stake in USAir.

'We needed Branson off our back so we could get our house in order,' said another director.

After two hours of intense debate, the board broke up with many directors fearing for the future. It was clear to some of them that they had been present at the passing of an era.

'The King is dead! Long live the Marshall!' was how the news was broken to Richard Branson by Michael Davies. Branson at first found it difficult to take in what the long-standing family friend had said. Nearly a year beforehand, when Davies told Branson that his complaints would be like 'an iceberg', neither man had any idea his description would turn into a prediction. The non-executive director now told Branson that the iceberg was now threatening to tear the BA board apart. Davies thought the chairman had been holed below the waterline. He said that he expected the fall-out to be massive, and that he didn't think King could survive the humiliation that would inevitably follow the libel defeat. Marshall was now gearing all his efforts to ensuring that he would succeed King.

Branson was encouraged, but he refused to believe he had won.

'I was delighted but not entirely surprised,' he recalled. 'I didn't see how they could defend themselves, and I was really looking forward to King, Marshall, Ayling, Burnside and Basham being grilled by George Carman in court. It was one thing to hear that King had been told to throw in the towel, it was another for Virgin Atlantic to win.'

Branson had been anything but a passive observer of the litigation he had set in train with his decision to sue BA. When BA started to swamp Virgin's lawyers with thousands of documents, Branson took several crates of the discovery material away to La Residencia, a small hotel he owns in Mallorca, and spent days reading through them. Branson was passionately committed to winning the case. He scribbled hundreds of pages of notes. The more he read, the more he became convinced that his initial allegations against BA *were* but the tip of an iceberg. His frustration was that he was prohibited from speaking about what he read by the rules of the discovery process. Any leaks from either camp would be in contempt of court. Branson knew he was winning and he is the last person to squander the chance of victory.

The press revelations about Covent Garden astounded Branson and he was desperate to find out more about what BA's private detectives had been up to. Although the full extent of BA's operation had yet to be revealed, he felt particularly pleased when Lord King and Sir Colin Marshall were rumbled using undercover operators. He knew that BA was behind the *Sunday Telegraph*'s inquiries in March about the entirely false allegation that Goldman Sachs was using IGI on behalf of Virgin. Now it was clear not only to the lawyers but to the country as a whole that it was BA which indulged in that form of activity.

In the autumn, after the collapse of Covent Garden, Branson's office received a call from someone who said he had been contracted to work for BA against Virgin. He refused to disclose any further details of the operation unless Branson agreed to meet him personally. Virgin's chairman readily agreed.

'By now I really wanted to nail the bastards,' remembers Branson who had himself wired up for the meeting. The prospect of one of BA's snoopers being caught on tape was too good to miss.

Accompanied by an assistant, Branson made his way to the rendezvous. After undergoing the obligatory 'counter-surveillance' techniques that private detectives appear to go in for, Branson settled down with the contact and took dozens of pages of notes in his diary as his tape recorder turned silently underneath his trousers. Leaving nothing to chance, Branson had had himself kitted out with state-of-the-art technology, involving suspending a highly sensitive microphone in the area of his crotch. The contact was extremely helpful and gave Branson an enormous amount of detail on how BA was plotting against him. On condition that Branson never revealed his identity, the former BA undercover man also gave him the complete records of Covent Garden's activities.

As Branson made his way back from his rendezvous, he found himself sitting on his microphone. As he struggled to liberate it from inside his trousers, he turned to his assistant as the bizarre nature of their assignment sunk in.

'This is not quite what I expected when I started an airline!'

Also in the autumn, a mysterious incident at Heaven nightclub which had troubled Branson greatly drew peacefully to a close. In May, just before the libel trial was originally due to begin, one of the bouncers at Heaven had been arrested. He was accused of trying to sell two tablets of the drug 'ecstasy' to members of the public. Within hours the *News of the World* was on to the story.

'I wondered if this was BA's last fling,' recalls Branson. 'Basham had predicted that my downfall would be caused by Heaven, and this looked like a set-up to me.'

And so, it appeared, it was. The case petered out when the bouncer appeared in court and categorically denied the incident had taken place. The Crown Prosecution Service decided to drop all charges against the man, and nothing was ever found to link BA, or Basham, to the incident. The *News of the World* did not print the story.

On 7 December, Gerrard Tyrrell was astonished to hear from John Turnbull at Linklaters that he had just paid £485,000 into court on behalf of British Airways in settlement of Branson's claim, and that BA was prepared to drop its suit against Virgin Atlantic's they alighted from their flights from London – part of BA's bid to give them a positive image of BA's Club Class product.

In early June 1992, Partridge helped to organise a dance at the Regent hotel in Rodeo Drive which was used as the main set in the film *Pretty Woman*, starring Julia Roberts and Richard Gere. During the dance, BA's staff collected business cards from the guests, and shortly afterwards the guests would receive follow-up calls from BA staff seeking to persuade them to fly on BA. Unfortunately for the LA sales operation, this routine, if expensive, marketing effort produced no noticeable increase in passengers.

Internal BA documents provided to Virgin's lawyers by Partridge show that later in the same month the Los Angeles office used information held on the BABS computer to analyse the problem. One memo states: 'We investigated every BABS PNR (Passenger Name Record) which had a booking in South West USA, and for which there was either a "C" [business class] or "J" sector held in BABS on any airline.' The memo, which was copied to David Williams, expresses concern that BA was experiencing a general trend towards American Airlines 'grabbing a substantial market share'. When the sales team's June project (to analyse 'How the Passenger Got to Europe') showed that AA had established a 45% share of the first-class and business-class market and that Virgin was picking up a significant proportion of these premium fares in relation to BA, Partridge recalls that David Williams redirected her efforts:

Shortly after the dance David Williams called me into his office, and told me that from then on I was to access two computer systems, APOLLO and SABRE. I was to get the names and telephone numbers of business-class passengers of other airlines intending to fly between Los Angeles and points in Europe.

I printed vast lists of these contacts and then I was told to contact the passengers, and ask them if they wanted to change to British Airways' Club Class service.

I asked David Williams if we were allowed to use the APOLLO and SABRE systems in this way. He replied, 'No not technically.'

Partridge nevertheless started to access the computers with two
passwords that she was given. The passwords gave her access to
the names and telephone numbers of passengers bound for
Europe as well as their class of travel. Partridge spent long days
printing out lists of passengers planning to travel and attempting
to switch-sell them on the phone before they did. BA approached
Virgin's Upper Class passengers, as well as premium-class passengers from American Airlines, United Airlines, TWA, KLM and
Delta. Partridge remembers:

> My brief was to call the passengers pretending that I did not
> know that they had already bought a ticket with another air-
> line. If the telephone was answered by a travel agent, I had
> specific instructions from David Williams to hang up imme-
> diately and not to enter into any sort of conversation. If I got
> through to the passenger direct, I was instructed to offer a
> free upgrade to a first-class seat on BA to anyone who was
> willing to change from Virgin, or any of the other airlines.

Partridge was also authorised to offer other bribes:

> I could offer them a free limousine service at either end of
> their journey [in direct imitation of Virgin's Upper Class ser-
> vice] or if the passenger lived quite close to San Diego, I
> could offer a free air connection to Los Angeles and back.

Partridge estimated that she succeeded in switching six out of
every ten passengers she approached, having obtained their numbers from the computers. She was employed full-time on
switch-selling for three months until her attachment in Los
Angeles ended in August 1992.

Partridge's account of how the switch-selling was done matches
precisely the interviews I filmed with the Los Angeles travel
agents Romel Manalo and John Healy at British Imports Travel, in
February 1992 and again in February 1993. Partridge was an active
switch-seller in Los Angeles in the summer of 1992. When I
showed him Partridge's written account of her switch-selling
activities, Healy remarked:

What she says in her statement is an exact description of what we experienced here. It's like a script; the upgrades to Club Class, the enticements – it's precisely what they offered us, thinking we were passengers, not travel agents. What we told you when you came to interview us for your *This Week* documentary in 1992, and for your ITN report in 1993 is described here in minute and precise detail. It's also what we told BA when they sent their attorney and their head of North American operations, John Storey.

I tracked David Williams down on the phone to a hotel in Philadelphia where he was attending a sales conference. He still works for BA, but he no longer works in the Los Angeles office. When confronted with Wendy Partridge's allegations Williams denied them: he said that it would be 'immoral' and 'unethical' to misuse confidential computer information. He failed to mention that it is also illegal in the USA.

American Airlines initially told me that accessing the computer data from SABRE in the way that Partridge had described was impossible unless she had been using a stolen computer pass. Partridge was adamant that this was not how she obtained the information, and insisted that she had been given a computer password by BA.

After establishing that the alleged computer abuse had taken place in 1992, however, American Airlines confirmed that Partridge could indeed have extracted the information in just the way that she described in her sworn statement. As a paid-up associate member of SABRE, BA had a computer terminal in its Los Angeles office. This entitled BA to use the full PNR (Passenger Name Record) data for research and marketing purposes but not to attempt to steal passengers from other airlines. The United States Department of Transport published an order in 1988 prohibiting airlines from using the information to 'convert' (i.e. poach) passengers. Because of concerns that certain airlines might ignore the DoT's directive, AA had built 'Chinese walls' into the SABRE computer system in the autumn of 1993 to prevent such abuse occurring. Wendy Partridge says she raided the SABRE PNRs in the summer of 1992 to try and steal the passengers of other airlines.

American Airlines officials insisted on anonymity but a very senior member of its board of management, with personal experience of detailed negotiations with BA, predicted that there would be 'howls of anger' throughout the American airline industry once it was revealed that BA had been misusing confidential computer information in this way.

Ronald Allen, the chairman of Virgin's US partner, Delta Airlines, was astonished to hear that BA had been trying to steal passengers in this manner, and said that he would have no hesitation in taking legal action against BA if he found that BA had tried to steal Delta passengers.

Sir Freddie Laker was also incredulous despite his long and bitter experience of BA's dirty tricks:

> This is dirty tricks with a big 'D'. I would have thought that Virgin would have a massive claim against BA, and possibly against the owners of the computer systems from which the information was being extracted. I wouldn't hesitate to take them to court. People go to prison in the States for this sort of thing and face very, very substantial fines. I'm talking real money, probably several million dollars.

Branson was shocked to read Partridge's confession:

> Our anti-trust case is a civil case, but this is criminal activity in the USA, and I will certainly consider whether or not to start a separate prosecution.
>
> I regard Wendy Partridge's statement as the missing link in our knowledge about BA poaching our passengers. We knew BA had access to our computer information and we knew that it had stolen our passengers in an organised fashion. Partridge's evidence links the two activities together. Furthermore, it appears that BA was trying to steal passengers from American Airlines as well.

Partridge's confessions, and the BA documents she has handed to Virgin, are acutely embarrassing for Sir Tim Bell and Robert Ayling. During their ferocious but unsuccessful campaign to persuade ITN to retract my story on BA's passenger-poaching in Los Angeles, Ayling wrote to ITN: 'The issue is not whether Mr Healy and Mr Manalo were telephoned by people who said they were from British Airways but whether those callers were *in fact* British Airways employees' [Ayling's emphasis]. In a subsequent letter he admitted that BA had, characteristically, failed to find the culprits as he tried to mislead ITN: 'We do not know who was making the calls referred to in your broadcast. They may have been made by a mischief maker who had seen Mr Healy's agency when it featured prominently on the *This Week* programme of 25th February 1992.'

ITN stood firm in the face of Ayling and Bell and their threats of legal action. Now Partridge's sworn statement and documents provide proof of a BA employee in the US illegally accessing computer data on rival airlines. Partridge was employed in BA's marketing and sales department while Robert Ayling was the head of that department. She used confidential computer information to try to steal passengers from other airlines, including Virgin, at the instigation of her immediate boss. The Los Angeles travel agents have been telling the truth and British Airways has not been telling the truth.

Chuck Koob and his team reported by the middle of 1996 that they have made 'very promising' progress during the discovery phase of the anti-trust case. Branson cannot comment on the documents that have been revealed by BA because one of the conditions that BA insisted upon before agreeing to exchange documents was that Branson should not be allowed to see them.

Ayling dramatically raised the stakes in 'World War Three' in the middle of June 1996, when British Airways announced that it intended to form a 'broad alliance' with American Airlines to 'improve aviation services and broaden the reach of both carriers'. From April 1997 BA and AA announced that they would 'co-ordinate their passenger and cargo activities between Europe and the USA, introduce extensive code-sharing across each other's networks and establish full reciprocity between their frequent-flyer programmes. By coordinating their networks, they will offer the widest choice of routings and departure times between almost 36,000 potential city pairings, with seamless connections between the two airlines' services linking destinations throughout Europe, Africa and the Middle and Far East with cities across the USA, Canada, the Caribbean and Latin America'.

Highly secret negotiations to form what would in effect be the largest airline in the world had been going on between BA and AA for the previous eighteen months. After its rocky relationship with USAir which had led to BA writing off £275 million of its investment, BA had been eager to find a functional US partner not already involved in another alliance; and AA viewed BA as the most prized European partner possible.

Rumours had been rife in the industry for many months that BA and AA were attempting to merge. However, Ayling and AA's chief executive, Robert Crandall, only committed their teams to serious talks at the beginning of 1996, in conditions of enormous secrecy, after the two men met in London. Following his very public failure to achieve any sort of relationship with Branson, Ayling was keen to stress that his personal rapport with Crandall was a key factor in moving the negotiations on to their final stages: 'Personally I get on with Crandall very well. If people don't get on, it's difficult to reach an agreement.'

The different stages of negotiation were given codenames: a full-blooded merger was codenamed 'Bermuda' – after the Bermuda 2 aviation treaty; at the other end of the scale was a loose association codenamed 'Hamilton', Bermuda's capital. The final outcome was somewhere between the two, and was codenamed 'Pembroke' – the parish in which Hamilton finds itself. 'Pembroke' nevertheless laid the groundwork for the creation of the biggest airline operation in the world, an alliance of transatlantic giants.

Virgin was quick to characterise the alliance as the 'Aeroflot of the skies', and cited its extraordinary dominance over some of the most lucrative transatlantic routes. The market share figures for the transatlantic routes show that BA/AA has a stranglehold on many of them; in total the two airlines control nearly two thirds of all transatlantic flights between Britain and America. On some of the most lucrative routes the situation is even more markedly tilted in their favour: they have, for example, 100% of the London–Dallas market, 94% of London–Chicago, 76% of London–Miami, 70% of London–JFK (New York), and 60% of

London–Los Angeles. With such a monopoly of key routes, BA/AA stated that their alliance had only been announced 'on the presumption that full anti-trust immunity will be obtained'. This can only be granted by the American government. If granted, immunity would allow the two airlines to function as if they had merged into one, eliminating competition between them. In return, the major concession that BA will be required to make is to persuade the British government to adopt an 'open skies' policy in relation to BA's Heathrow fortress which will allow American carriers to take off and land. This will mean that the protectionist barriers to the UK that are enshrined in the Bermuda 2 agreement between the USA and the UK will have to be significantly amended.

The decisions on both issues will have enormous ramifications for both the airlines involved, and also for their rivals, particularly Virgin Atlantic which is the third biggest carrier over the Atlantic (with 12.3% of the market in June 1996), after British Airways (42.7%) and American Airlines (17.2%). United Airlines had 9.8% over the same period.

When the 'Pembroke' deal was made public, however, it did not receive the Caribbean welcome BA must have been hoping for. Inevitably Branson took the lead in attacking a deal that few seemed to believe would actually lead to increased competition over the Atlantic and the lower fares that BA promised. In an open letter Branson attacked the idea of anti-trust immunity being used as a bargaining counter to obtain 'open skies' agreements:

> Irrespective of the benefit open skies might produce, competition and the associated consumer gains are too important to be traded in this way. Why should open skies be traded for a legalised cartel between the largest (AA) and the third largest (BA) airlines in the world? No other industry would be allowed to operate in this way.

For once Branson was not alone in battling BA: TWA and Delta took the lead in criticising the deal in the USA, and American government officials made it immediately clear that the price of the alliance would be high for both carriers. Patrick V. Murphy Jnr, from the US transport department, spelt out his government's point of view:

> For us to even begin to consider an alliance which includes anti-trust immunity will absolutely require a full 'open-skies' agreement and more. We need not only open markets de facto, but we need them de jure.

In Britain, the President of Board of Trade, Ian Lang, referred the alliance to the Office of Fair Trading, and in Brussels the European Commission said it could investigate the deal under Articles 85 and 86 of the Treaty of Rome. The EC, however, has no power to stop the alliance and, having waited over three years for the EC to act over Branson's 1993 complaint, no one at Virgin was holding their breath.

On the night BA and AA announced their proposed deal, Ayling and Branson made their way to the BBC *Newsnight* studio for a live debate. Unfortunately, no debate took place although the two were seated at the same table; Ayling made it a condition of his appearance that he would not debate the deal with Branson. This has become a familiar tactic with Conservative ministers in recent years, particularly those who are under pressure. Ayling was apparently worried that he might be tackled on the dirty-tricks campaign. As a result, the sober-suited Ayling came across rather like the junior ministers he used to serve and who regularly appear on *Newsnight* – uninspired and sticking to his brief. Branson appeared very nervous and turned in one of his less artic-ulate performances, stumbling over his well-rehearsed arguments as if he had just thought of them.

In an article in the *Independent* the following day headed 'The world's favourite cartel', Branson put his thoughts more coher-ently, arguing that the alliance would create a monopolistic monster in the skies, 'the Aeroflot of the capitalist West', which would increase fares and reduce services. In the USA, the *Wall Street Journal* said that BA and AA were altering the rules of the game: 'Tired of Fighting One-on-One, Carriers Turn Competition into an All-Star Team Sport' ran its headline, while pie-charts and tables illustrated the dominance that the alliance would bring the

new partners. It characterised the transatlantic alliance as a
'Superleague'.

In Britain, BA had to endure a mostly hostile reaction in the
press: 'Atlantic fares fear as air giants join forces' in the *Daily
Telegraph*; 'BA and American fly into flak' in the *Sunday Times*;
and 'Rivals let fly at American deal with BA' in the *Sunday
Telegraph*, as the Branson-led onslaught gained support.

The financial press was particularly savage. *The Economist*
hailed the alliance as 'another twist in the tortuous progress
towards a free aviation market' under the heading 'Right destination, wrong route'. However, it disliked the 'stench of
hypocrisy' caused by BA and AA reversing their positions on key
issues such as code-sharing, 'open skies' and anti-trust immunity
in order to strike their deal. The *Financial Times* amplified this
theme in an article entitled 'A day for eating words'; Michael
Skapinker pointed out just how edible Ayling and Crandall's
words had had to become in order to agree their alliance.
Crandall, for example, had been an arch opponent of code-sharing
deals. As recently as 1995 Crandall had said:

> Code-sharing is profoundly anti-competitive and, in the
> long-term, will inevitably reduce the number of carriers com-
> peting for your business.
>
> When airlines team up and code-share, they are able, by
> means of pretending to be a single carrier, to force other non-
> combined carriers out of the market. When this happens . . .
> consumers lose all the many benefits of competition.

Under the AA/BA deal Crandall was proposing to enter into the
biggest code-sharing deal in airline history. BA and Ayling
showed no more consistency as they defended the deal between
two airlines with a combined turnover of $29 billion and a com-
bined annual profit in 1995 of nearly $500 million.

Until the deal with American, BA had argued that taking an
equity stake in a foreign airline was the way to realise its global
ambitions. BA has a 25% stake in Qantas, and owns nearly 50% of
Deutsche BA and TAT of France in addition to its stake in USAir.
In contrast, the deal with AA makes no provision for an exchange

of equity; Ayling argued that the absence of such an agreement would help the two airlines to get on better with each other.

Another volte-face concerned Bermuda 2 which BA had supported since it was signed in 1977 because it created a fortress for the airline at Heathrow: the single most important factor in BA's post-1987 privatisation success. In 1996 BA still had 164,000 take-off and landing slots at Heathrow Airport – 38% of the total at the world's busiest international airport. (Virgin has less than 1%.) US opponents have always bitterly resented the restrictions it places on US carriers flying into Heathrow. Gerald Greenwald, chief executive of United Airlines, called Bermuda 2 'the worst mistake in the history of US international aviation relations'. Lord King had stopped BA's donations to the Conservative Party partly in protest at the government's decision to tamper with Bermuda 2 and allow United and American (as well as Virgin) to fly from Heathrow in 1991. Less than three months before announcing the deal with American, Robert Ayling was toeing BA's historic line, describing Bermuda 2 as a 'model agreement'.

However, under the deal with AA, BA has agreed to lobby the British government to give the 'necessary regulatory clearances' to make changes to Bermuda 2, 'consistent with industry trends towards open skies'. Precisely how many Heathrow slots BA would be prepared to surrender under its attachment to 'open skies' will be a measure of the significance it attaches to its deal with AA; the American government would require meaningful concessions from BA and, more specifically, the British government, before granting the necessary anti-trust immunity. It is the British government, not BA, that has the power to grant take-off and landing slots. As Malcolm Rifkind was fond of pointing out when he was secretary of state for transport, slots should be correctly regarded as permissions granted by government, not as rights that belong to BA.

Both Crandall and Ayling are veterans of major anti-trust cases, as the first adverts in Virgin's £10 million campaign pointed out:

Lower air fares? Let's see what a boss of American Airlines said.

Reproduced underneath was an extract from a celebrated anti-trust case in which Crandall was being prosecuted by Braniff Airlines. A conversation produced in evidence ran as follows (between Crandall and Howard Putnam who was head of Braniff Airlines):

> Crandall: I have a suggestion for you. Raise your goddamn fares twenty per cent. I'll raise mine the next morning.
> Putnam: Robert, we . . .
> Crandall: You'll make more money and I will too.
> Putnam: We can't talk about pricing.
> Crandall: Oh bullshit, Howard. We can talk about any goddamn thing we want to talk about.

Unfortunately for Crandall he was being recorded by Putnam.
  The Virgin ad concluded with the following text:

> [This transcript] was used in evidence in a prosecution by the Department of Justice of American Airlines and Mr Crandall for breach of the anti-trust laws.
>   British Airways have also had an anti-trust action brought against them.
>   No wonder these two airlines are seeking immunity from US anti-trust law.

Ayling has more experience than any other British airline executive in defending anti-trust actions. As an under-secretary in the DTI he was heavily involved with the British government's negotiations to settle the anti-trust case brought by Laker's liquidators against the state-owned BA, and he masterminded BA's unsuccessful attempts to avoid prosecution by Virgin in the USA under anti-trust laws. Another key player in BA's side of the deal with American Airlines is Roger Maynard, BA's director of investment and joint ventures. As Britain's former air attaché in Washington, he stalked the corridors of power in the American capital as the British government fought Laker's anti-trust action. Like Ayling, Maynard joined BA after the resolution of the Laker case paved the way for privatisation.
  Ayling's experience of anti-trust cases as both mandarin and

senior executive has not led him to a consistent view on the subject. In March 1996 Ayling expressed BA's firm opposition to the strengthening of the alliance between United and Lufthansa after the two airlines had applied for anti-trust immunity so they could work more closely together. Ayling's opposition was clearly stated: 'What Lufthansa wants to do is to reduce the level of competition by relaxing the anti-trust laws,' he said.

Three months later he was literally (at a photo-opportunity with AA president Don Carty) wrapping himself in the stars and stripes of the American flag, and arguing that if the BA/AA deal was granted immunity from anti-trust laws it would actually lead to an increase in competition. Ayling was unable to reconcile these two positions satisfactorily when pressed during his appearance on *Newsnight*. As cynics observed, there is not much point in airlines getting anti-trust immunity if they can't then act anti-competitively.

BA's monopolistic ambitions have remained consistent from the days when BA was owned by the state. Colin Marshall's predecessor as chief executive, Roy Watts, spelt out BA's anti-competitive philosophy shortly before privatisation: 'Competition is about the elimination of competition, not about competition. Business is about eliminating competition. It is the government's job to promote competition.'

After privatisation, BA was forced to pay lip service to the concept of competition from domestic rivals, but it did so from a position of almost complete dominance of the British aviation industry. Lord King took out the following, full-page advertisement in *The Times* in the summer of 1984:

BRITISH AIRWAYS WELCOMES COMPETITION

. . . certain of our local competitors wish to see some of British Airways' routes taken from us and handed to them on a plate. To those airlines we say this.

If they do believe in true competition let them say so and act accordingly. Let the customers decide which airline they prefer on the basis of the service offered to passengers. And may the best one win.

                                                              King

The advert was placed when BA had control of all long-haul over-seas flights from Heathrow. By the start of the 1990s, BA had a problem. Due to its longstanding monopoly of the domestic mar-ket, it had experienced very little competition from British airlines, and it had become clear, within three years of privatisation, that when given the choice, 'the best one' in the eyes of the consumer was Virgin. BA's failure to match Virgin's service, and the gov-ernment's perceived indifference to what BA considered to be its best interests, produced a dangerous and unstable cocktail by the summer of 1991. The worst recession in the history of world avia-tion, and the Gulf War, also contributed to BA's plunging share price and helped to provoke the former national carrier's monop-olistic and anti-competitive tendencies, as it tried to crush its tiny challenger in a market which had effectively been rigged in its favour by Robert Ayling's privatisation legislation.

The high point of BA's dominance of British commercial avia-tion occurred in 1992, five years after privatisation when BA and its subsidiaries carried 87% of all British airline passengers. According to the CAA the figure had risen steadily since 1984 when BA carried only 80% of British airline passengers. Furthermore, the number of people employed in the British airline industry declined by 50,000 over the same period as a series of independent British airlines succumbed to BA's virtual monopoly. The reality of 'enterprise culture' in the British airline industry was that it became one of the last outposts of the command econ-omy, and that the government's commitment to a multi-airline industry had taken a very poor second place to its commitment to ensuring the success of the privatised BA.

Deeply concerned that the effect of the BA/AA deal would be to achieve for BA what the dirty-tricks campaign had narrowly failed to do, and drive Virgin out of business, Branson met transport secretary Sir George Young within hours of the BA/AA announcement. He emerged from his meeting with Young some-what reassured.

'I thought that BA had sewn up the UK government. But I met Sir George Young and he convinced me that this is not the case. He stated very clearly that the government believes in a multi-airline policy which will not allow anything which damages Virgin,' said

Branson after the meeting.

Virgin's chairman was aware, however, that since the government committed itself to developing a second-force carrier to BA
under the multi-airline policy outlined in its 1984 White Paper
Competition in Civil Aviation (the year he founded Virgin Atlantic),
Young's predecessors had said similar things to other airlines: to
British Caledonian shortly before it was swallowed by BA, and to
Air Europe before a combination of factors, including BA's campaign of dirty tricks, had forced it out of business. Both had
become Britain's second-force carrier shortly before they disappeared. The memory of how Laker Airways went out of business
just as it was mounting a serious challenge to BA and the 1980s
transatlantic cartel is indelibly imprinted on Branson's memory
and constantly refreshed by Sir Freddie himself.

Within a week of the announcement of the deal, Branson had
launched a £10 million advertising campaign to denounce it – the
largest advertising campaign in Virgin's history. The Labour Party
described the announcement of the alliance as a 'bombshell', and
called on the CAA to launch an investigation. John Bridgeman, the
director general of Fair Trading, was quoted as saying at the outset that, in his view, the deal constituted a merger. Bridgeman's
investigation will advise Lang on whether the deal should be
referred to the Monopolies and Mergers Commission. Branson
was quick to announce that he 'expected nothing less' than a full
MMC enquiry.

Whitehorn was in his element as he helped Branson organise
Virgin's media counter-offensive against BA and American. As the
press revelled in the spectacle of 'the tie-less one' flying into battle
with BA and American, Whitehorn joined Branson to brief journalists in trendy restaurants in London's Soho, and worked constantly
behind the scenes to ensure that the mighty BA/AA promotion of
the deal was countered. In the hectic days after the deal was
announced, Branson sent Whitehorn to meet the foreign secretary,
Malcolm Rifkind (who had allowed Virgin into Heathrow when
transport secretary), to brief him on the BA/AA deal.

Branson had recognised Whitehorn's importance to Virgin in
April 1996 when he appointed the thirty-five-year-old to the board
of the Virgin Group on a salary of £150,000, and gave him a 0.3%

stake in London Continental which had won the franchise to run the Eurostar train service under the Channel. This could eventually be worth over £200,000 to Whitehorn. 'Almost as much as BA gave Burnside to shut up about the dirty-tricks campaign!' quipped Whitehorn.

The latest member of Virgin's board joined Branson on the inaugural flight to Washington in June 1996 to stake Virgin's presence in the American capital, and to lobby against the BA/AA deal on Capitol Hill in person. They took off from Heathrow in a Virgin plane emblazoned with the slogan 'No Way BA/AA', as the Virgin ad campaign hit its stride: 'BA's biggest dirty trick yet', 'Prepare for rip off', 'Big chief of British Airways speak with forked tongue', and 'The world's least favourite monopoly?' set the tone, with accompanying text setting out Virgin's view that, if approved by the British government, competition in the British airline industry would be completely destroyed.

The irreverent, sometimes insolent and occasionally humorous tone of the Virgin ad campaign brought muffled threats of legal action from BA but no writs. Underlying the bellicose public exchanges, Virgin and BA recognise that the debate is crucial for the future of both airlines. Branson and Ayling encountered each other in the make-up room shortly before their appearance on *Newsnight*. A buoyant Ayling teased Branson with a pointed jibe: 'You took our King. Now we are taking your Queen!'

Ayling is keenly aware of the extent of the danger that his proposed deal with AA represents for Virgin. He feels confident that the British government will not place sufficient restrictions on the deal to block it, and he is banking on the substantial commercial muscle of AA to bring the Clinton administration into line in election year. Politically, Clinton would be delighted to be able to say to America's airlines that he has achieved the 'open skies' over the Atlantic that they have been clammering for, and that an important part of the detested Bermuda 2 agreement had been renegotiated. Clinton would not have to get into the details of exactly how many slots would be available, and to whom, in order to claim a worthwhile political triumph.

Delta Airlines, for example, has never been able to fly into Heathrow; it has only indirect access by buying seats on Virgin and selling them under the code-sharing deal. With 'open skies' Delta would be able to offer direct flights to London and, thus, would have a much reduced incentive to continue its code-sharing deal with Virgin. Delta itself, however, responded in unequivocal fashion to the proposed deal, describing it as 'poison for competition', and warning that, 'Without an open Heathrow [which is not being proposed under the BA/AA deal], open skies will exist in name only'. The Delta statement pointed out that BA controls more than 3,000 take-off and landing slots at Heathrow which could be reallocated to bolster its transatlantic service. (American Airlines has less than 200 slots, and United and Virgin Atlantic, the only two transatlantic rivals currently allowed to fly from Heathrow, have a combined total of less than 300.)

An alternative interpretation of Ayling's 'Now we are taking your Queen' comment to Branson is that he could have meant that, by securing anti-trust immunity, BA would deny Virgin the opportunity to pursue complaints of anti-competitive behaviour by BA and American in the USA in future.

Whichever interpretation of Ayling's comment is accepted, it is clear that neither side is underestimating the importance of the BA/AA deal to the future of both airlines and the relationship between them. The battle will be fought in the political rather than the commercial arena – terrain that traditionally favours Ayling and BA rather than Branson, who is still viewed as an outsider by the current British administration.

One of Branson's nagging concerns is that BA has already got the British government on its side. His discovery that Nick Starling, an assistant secretary in the International Aviation Negotiations division of the British ministry of transport, had been in Washington with BA's negotiators before the deal was made public, has deepened his sense of disquiet despite the reassurances given by Sir George Young. Branson is a gifted if sometimes inarticulate communicator, but he remains ill at ease in the political arena where he has often struggled to make an impact.

Branson did, however, meet Tony Blair at Virgin Atlantic's Crawley headquarters in 1996. According to Branson the Labour leader stressed his party's commitment to fair competition in the airline industry and Blair's then transport spokeswoman, Clare

Short, was quick to insist that the BA/AA deal should be subject to an enquiry as soon as it was announced later in the year. Branson also briefed Peter Mandelson, now one of Blair's most trusted colleagues, on the dirty-tricks campaign in the wake of the libel trial. (Mandelson showed such an interest in the dirty-tricks affair in 1993 that Sir Tim Bell started completely unfounded rumours that the influential Hartlepool MP was trying to get PR work from Branson. An infuriated Mandelson wrote to Sir Colin Marshall to protest.)

Although Branson is constantly wooed by the Conservatives for donations to party coffers, and to lend his name to their campaigns, he has steadfastly refused to accede. In the 1992 General Election Branson threatened the then chairman of the Conservative Party, Chris Patten, with legal action when his name appeared in the national press at the head of a list of 'celebrities' supporting the Tories. The list had been circulated by Conservative Central Office, and Branson had specifically stated that he did not want his name to be used. The determination required to resist Tory blandishments over the past decade should not be underestimated as the government determines how the crucial take-off and landing slots at Heathrow should be allocated.

Although Branson enjoys a higher public profile than any other airline chairman in Britain, and arguably the world, he remains outside the current British political establishment. His consortium was beaten by Carlton in its bid to win the franchise to broadcast TV weekday programmes in the London area, and Branson showed his deep disappointment when Virgin failed to win the National Lottery franchise. A tearful Branson told the press that the failure of his consortium, which had promised to distribute all the profits raised to charity, was the biggest disappointment of his business life. Running the lottery would, perhaps, have finally fulfilled his teenage yearning to 'do something useful'. Two years later, Branson claimed that an attempt to bribe him had been made by GTech, one of the companies in the winning consortium, Camelot, and the two parties are due to meet in court over the alleged libel that this claim represented in the autumn of 1996.

The Conservative philosopher, Edmund Burke, described companies as 'little platoons' in society, linking the state and the individual, and thus helping to define the nature of the state. As Britain became a more sleazy and less accountable society in the 1990s, and revolving doors allowed public service to be rapidly and readily translated into vast private profit, BA appeared to be a typical British platoon.

In 1993, for example, the Friends' Provident Life Office, one of the largest insurance companies in Britain, managing £14 billion of its policy-holders' money, decided to sell its shares in BA after the dirty-tricks campaign against Virgin was publicly exposed in the High Court. The story behind this decision is revealing. During the previous decade Friends' Provident had pioneered the concept of 'ethical investment' through its Stewardship Trusts which invest some £400 million of Friends' Provident money only in companies that meet very high ethical standards. Before the dirty-tricks scandal broke, Friends' Provident had invested in BA despite some objections to the airline's contribution to the 'greenhouse effect'. However, the revelation that BA had gained access to Virgin's computer information, and had used it to poach its passengers, was considered 'unethical behaviour and wholly unsuitable for a stock held by Stewardship'. The final straw for the Friends' Provident Stewardship Trust came after Sir Colin Marshall publicly stated that no more such behaviour would be tolerated at BA; shortly afterwards John Witney, the chairman of the committee of reference which determines the Stewardship's policy, was himself phoned by one of Ayling's passenger-poachers. Witney, a Quaker and former chief executive of the Independent Broadcasting Authority, was offered an upgrade on BA if he switched from his Virgin flight. Appalled at BA's dishonesty and unethical behaviour, the Trust sold its shares.

There were convincing indications in 1996 that even BA's staff do not trust the company. The pilots' union, BALPA, briefly threatened a worldwide strike in the summer over a dispute involving pay and conditions. In the heated debate before the dispute was settled, BALPA leader Chris Darke stressed publicly on several occasions that the major problem from the union side was that 'no one trusts what BA says, or what BA does'. BA management was represented in the talks by David Hyde, who helped to mastermind Operation Covent Garden. According to an opinion survey carried out for BA, and reported in *BA News* in the spring of 1996, only one in three BA employees feel that BA is 'open and honest in its dealings with them'.

The business and political establishment continues to have a higher opinion of Marshall and Ayling than BA's staff: Marshall is the president of the CBI, and Ayling has been appointed to chair the Millennium Commission – a new company charged with distributing lottery funds allocated to the Millennium exhibition. Only three years earlier both men had been identified as having played key roles in the dirty-tricks campaign, and since that time they have continued to mislead the public and BA's shareholders to cover up their involvement.

At the same time the only roles that Branson has in national life outside Virgin are voluntary and self-appointed and he has not received or been offered an honour of any sort. Political 'schmoozing' does not appeal to Branson, who sometimes struggles to remember the names of key politicians. However, while Branson sees individuals in both main British political parties as being sympathetic to what Virgin is trying to achieve, he is aware that BA is attempting to have its deal with American rubber-stamped before the forthcoming British and American general elections and he knows political lobbying will be crucial. The outcome of 'World War Three' could be devastating for the loser.

The stakes in 'World War Three' were raised even higher at the end of June 1996, when the US Justice Department announced that it was launching an anti-trust investigation into 'the competitive implications' of the proposed BA/AA alliance. To Branson's delight, Virgin received a civil investigative demand (the rough equivalent of a subpoena) requiring it to make available all the documents that it had acquired in its New York anti-trust case against BA, to the Department's probe into the proposed BA/AA deal.

By the middle of 1996 Virgin had already obtained nearly a quarter of a million BA documents which its US lawyers claim show a 'deliberate and conscious' attempt by BA to monopolise the transatlantic market. Now the Justice Department will be able to see all of these documents as it considers the BA/AA deal. Airline analysts quoted in the *Wall Street Journal* viewed the Justice

Department's action as an 'unusually aggressive' one which could ultimately block the proposed alliance. Officially the deal is being analysed by the Transportation Department, which is not bound by recommendations from the Justice Department. However, the Justice Department, which brought the price-fixing conspiracy charge against Robert Crandall over the Braniff International affair, retains the power to block the alliance.

BA was aghast to hear that Virgin's anti-trust case had emerged as a potential obstacle to its deal with American, but put a brave face on the development, saying that it showed that the anti-trust authorities were 'putting their foot on the accelerator'. Just over a year after Lowe Bell had managed to produce headlines in the *Financial Times* quoting Ayling's claim that the 'dirty tricks file was closed', BA now had to be satisfied with mildly ironic headlines such as the *Guardian*'s, 'BA welcomes exhumation of its "dirty tricks"'.

Branson was genuinely delighted to hear of the Justice Department's intervention. Its probe brings the two major issues over which BA and Virgin are now fighting into a single focus. The anti-trust case has been brought as a direct result of BA's dirty-tricks campaign against Virgin, and it provides a vivid illustration of why BA requires anti-trust immunity to forge its alliance with American Airlines.

Branson is now more confident that the BA/AA deal can be blocked than when it was first announced. He feels that Virgin has prevailed in most of the intellectual arguments over the deal, and the overwhelming editorial criticism of the proposed alliance in the UK press lends support to his view. And while he sees BA's attempt to 'take his Queen' as the most serious threat to Virgin Atlantic since the dirty-tricks campaign was in full cry, Branson believes that the anti-trust case represents an enormous gamble by Robert Ayling, who missed the opportunity to settle the original dispute for a relatively paltry sum:

'He's gambled BA's future to a large extent, it's a hell of a risk he's taking. For him to settle for anything more than £13 million [Virgin's original demand in the wake of the libel case before Branson started any further legal action] would be a tremendous loss of face. Personally, I think he would have to step down as chief executive. He's taking a hell of a gamble for British Airways shareholders in taking it the whole way.'

The extent of Ayling's gamble was vividly and unexpectedly illustrated at the end of July 1996, when BA's American partner, USAir, sued BA under US anti-trust laws over its proposed alliance with American Airlines. USAir's action took BA completely by surprise as BA holds nearly a quarter of USAir's shares. Ayling and two other BA directors sit on USAir's board and none of them had any hint that Steven Wolf was about to bring an anti-trust suit against BA. To compound the blow to BA, Wolf filed USAir's suit in New York, to Judge Miriam Cedarbaum's court, with a request that the action be linked to Virgin Atlantic's anti-trust action against BA in order to promote 'the just, efficient and economical administration of justice'. Cedarbaum readily agreed to USAir's request, a decision which leaves BA facing a two-pronged anti-trust onslaught in New York by its biggest British rival and its closest American partner. Ayling confessed publicly that he was 'baffled, surprised and mystified' by USAir's move which could kill BA's prospects of an alliance with AA.

USAir's charges against BA paint a devastating picture of anti-competitive behaviour, and detail allegations of how BA has caused 'irreparable injury to USAir' by 'misleading' USAir about its proposed link-up with AA. USAir's action provides a unique insight into a deeply unhappy relationship which started in 1992, days after Branson's libel victory. Wolf accuses BA of using its presence on the board of USAir as a 'listening post', effectively to spy on behalf of its new proposed partner, American Airlines, and deliberately 'enfeebling USAir as an effective competitor', by conducting negotiations that led USAir to believe that their relationship had a future. According to Wolf's document, 'in fact, these "negotiations" were a charade designed to "freeze" USAir by holding out the false promise that the USAir/BA relationship would improve'. USAir's action seeks to force Ayling and BA's other directors on USAir's board to resign and, in a passage that could have been taken from Richard Branson's anti-trust action, USAir claims that, 'Their [BA's and AA's] exclusionary conduct toward USAir is part of their effort to exclude competition from, and keep fares above competitive levels in, the various US/UK markets in which they operate . . . [this] will cause USAir and consumers irreparable harm.'

With the anti-trust court cases still a long way off, Ayling is still revelling in his transition from high-flying civil servant to the head of BA. Before USAir took its anti-trust action against BA, he told one interviewer, 'Lawyers always achieve things through other people. To be able to achieve things for yourself is a rare opportunity.' Ironically for Ayling, his continued enjoyment of the opportunities that running BA affords will depend, to a crucial extent, on the effectiveness of the lawyers he hires to fend off USAir's and Virgin's anti-trust case. His lawyers, in turn, must be hoping that BA is more straightforward in its dealings with them than it was with Linklaters & Paines during the dirty-tricks libel trial.

By the time John Turnbull advised the BA board to abandon its own action and apologise to Branson, many members of Turnbull's legal team felt betrayed by their client. The longer the process of legal discovery went on, the more completely BA's case disintegrated. The lawyers were forced to the conclusion that BA had been lying to them. Branson's switch-selling allegations provided the most telling case in point.

During the course of the litigation, a member of Linklaters had to fly urgently to New York to consult BA's American lawyers on the potential anti-trust implications of a Branson libel victory. The most convenient BA flight was fully booked, so the lawyer reserved a seat on Virgin Atlantic. Shortly before he was due to fly, the lawyer was called by BA and offered an upgrade if he switched his flight to BA. BA's own lawyer had been approached by one of Robert Ayling's passenger-poachers from the switch-selling units BA had assured Linklaters did not exist!

'Do you know who I am?' cried the startled lawyer.

'No,' replied the baffled BA switch-seller.

'*I'M* BA's bloody lawyer,' he screamed, 'and *YOU* are not supposed to be doing this sort of thing!'

16

'The Virgin Stooge'

Enfield, North London. May 1994

'This is what happens when you mess with British Airways!'
screamed a powerfully built black man as he forced John Gorman
to his knees. Gorman was in agony. He had just been blinded.
The man had slammed his head against a wall after spraying a
chemical gas into his eyes and wrestling him to the ground.
Gorman had returned to his flat from a short trip to his garage
when he was attacked by the black man and a white accomplice.
Both were wearing suits. Because he was carrying a suitcase in
each hand, Gorman had left the front door to his apartment open.
When he returned, the two men were waiting for him.

With his head forced against the wall and his eyes being burnt
by the noxious chemical, Gorman could hear the other assailant
ransacking his flat. He heard his telephone answering machine
being ripped from its socket. The second man yelled that he had
got 'the tapes', and then the two thieves fled.

When it was all over, Gorman was left slumped in the entrance
to his home in a state of deep shock. His eyes were stinging, and
he had been badly bruised. He managed to stagger to the phone
and dial 999. Within minutes paramedics from the nearby Chase
Farm Hospital arrived, and they immediately started to bathe
Gorman's eyes. It was an agonising experience. Local police

arrived soon afterwards, and started combing Gorman's flat and
the grounds outside for clues. They interviewed Gorman's neigh-
bours, one of whom said the intruders had tricked her into
allowing them into the block by claiming they had come to read
the electricity meters. A female police officer questioned Gorman
as he recovered with the help of the paramedics.

'Do you smoke, Mr Gorman?'

'No,' replied Gorman, still unable to see the questioner or
understand the relevance of the question.

The officer had found a cigarette packet on the stairs leading to
Gorman's flat. When she opened it, she found a folded business
card. It had been issued by British Airways. The name on the card
was 'Andrew Warman'. Warman works for BA's 'Fraud
Prevention Unit'.

Gorman was taken immediately to hospital for excruciatingly
painful treatment for the chemical burns to his eyes. His eyes were
clamped open as doctors removed the chemical with a solution;
they removed the chemical with what looked to Gorman like a
small strip of emery board. The Enfield police started to investigate the attack, which they treated as 'aggravated burglary' – or
robbery with violence.

John Gorman returned from the hospital several hours later and
phoned to tell me about the attack and the robbery. He was obviously still in shock. We had met less than a month beforehand.
Gorman had written to me after the first edition of *Dirty Tricks* had
been published in March 1994. He said in his letter that he believed
he was the victim of a dirty-tricks campaign similar to the one that
BA had waged against Richard Branson and Virgin Atlantic. I was
naturally curious, but wary that Gorman might be a loony seeking
some of the limelight that Branson's battle against BA had
attracted. The airline industry is a world in which loons abound.

Nonetheless, I had made my way to Gorman's immaculately
kept home in Enfield at the end of May, and I spent the afternoon
and part of the evening with him. We were joined by Peter
Sherman, his twenty-seven-year-old partner who lives with him. I
was astonished by what the two of them had to say.

Gorman is a former detective, and he presented me with a fifty-
page statement which described a catalogue of appalling

experiences that had occurred to him since he complained about the service on board a BA flight to New York at the beginning of 1993. Gorman was flying to New York with Sherman and a mutual friend, Martin Edwards, who works for a leading firm of London solicitors, at the end of January. The party were enjoying their complimentary drinks in BA Club Class when Sherman noticed that Gorman's brandy and Coke appeared to have particles of broken glass nestling in it. Gorman had just sipped the drink and, to his dismay, his mouth started to bleed. He called a member of the cabin crew who swiftly provided him with tissues to help staunch the flow of blood, and water to rinse out his mouth. Gorman told me that the BA crew were sympathetic and professional. The cabin staff advised him where he should seek hospital treatment in New York should he require it. The cabin service director, Keith Fathers, was particularly solicitous. He enquired how Gorman was feeling later in the flight, and advised him to seek hospital treatment in New York and report the matter to BA in New York.

Gorman also made a point of reporting the incident to BA in Manhattan. He did need hospital treatment in New York, and subsequently in London, for the damage caused by the glass in the drink. An endoscopy at the Nuffield Hospital in North London revealed that his gullet had been damaged by the glass, and he had medication prescribed for it. At our meeting in May 1994, Gorman told me that he was still receiving treatment for the injuries, and that his doctors would verify this.

When Gorman returned to Britain at the beginning of February 1993, he reported the 'glass in the drink' incident to BA in London. However, the airline's attitude had by then changed dramatically. BA accused him of being a 'Virgin stooge', and told him to 'go and fly with his friend Richard Branson'. Gorman was flabbergasted. He was no friend of Branson's. The two had never met or spoken, and Gorman had never flown on Virgin Atlantic.

BA was still reeling from the impact of Branson's dirty-tricks libel victory at the time. It appears that the paranoia that had infected the board had spread to the lower echelons of the airline, and many were scared they would lose their jobs because of their involvement in BA's attempts to put Branson out of business; sackings were widely expected to follow Marshall's promise to clean up BA. It was certainly not a good time for Gorman to complain.

Gorman was particularly incensed by BA's reaction because he had always chosen to fly with the national carrier since he was a teenager. As a youngster he had joined BOAC's junior club: 'They gave me a little book and every time I flew they used to stamp it, and the captain always used to sign it. I've still got it. I just enjoyed flying on the national airline.'

Gorman had joined the Metropolitan Police in 1968, and he became a very regular flyer. Many of his large Irish-Italian family come from the East Coast of the United States and, as his career in the police blossomed, he flew BA all over the world trying to track down criminals and terrorists. In nearly twenty years with the police, Gorman won five commendations for outstanding service, including the Commissioner's High Commendation for his bravery in foiling an armed siege. In 1982 the brave young detective joined the Anti-Terrorist Branch.

In 1984 the IRA bombed the Grand Hotel in Brighton during the Conservative Party Conference. With his Anti-Terrorist Branch colleagues, the thirty-seven-year-old Gorman clawed frantically at the rubble of the building with his bare hands in a desperate attempt to find survivors. Gorman unknowingly inhaled brown asbestos as he tried to save the Tory hierarchy, and eighteen months later he was forced to retire on health grounds. When Gorman received substantial compensation from the Criminal Injuries Compensation Board because of his enforced retirement, he decided to spend some of the money on buying shares in BA. He became one of the airline's founding shareholders when it was privatised in 1987. He explained to me that he now lives on a police pension, and a disability allowance. He also showed me a signed photo of Margaret Thatcher that the then Prime Minister had sent to thank him for his heroic efforts in Brighton in 1984. Gorman was touched by the gesture; the photograph had been found in the asbestos-ridden rubble of the Grand Hotel that had cost Gorman his career and his health.

BA flatly denied that the 'glass in the drink' incident had taken place on board one of their flights. Gorman described the BA officials he had to deal with as rude, smug and arrogant, 'light years away from the image in the BA adverts of an airline committed to customer service'. Knowing the importance of evidence, the former detective started sending all his letters to BA by recorded delivery, and taping his telephone calls with air-line officials.

At one stage in the course of increasingly heated exchanges with Gorman, BA claimed he had swallowed the glass in the bar of a New York hotel, and thus he was trying to con BA into paying him compensation. Gorman was incredulous that BA would doubt his word and he was deeply offended that, as one of the airline's founding shareholders and Executive Club members, he was being treated in such a disrespectful fashion. He swiftly produced a letter from the manager of the Essex House Nikko International Hotel in New York confirming that he had passed an uneventful stay there, and stating that they looked forward to welcoming him back.

Gorman was forced to take BA's fantasies very seriously indeed on 14 May 1993. That morning, just before half past nine, he picked up the phone. The caller had a distinctive Ulster accent. He asked Gorman if he needed any of his windows replacing, or was inter-ested in double glazing. Gorman said he did not, and terminated the call. Five minutes later he went downstairs to pick up his mail. He was surprised to see a group of eight large men standing motionless outside the glass doors to his apartment block.

'I was quite scared', remembered Gorman. 'My mind immedi-ately flashed back to my time hunting the IRA when I was in the Anti-Terrorist Branch. A man with an Ulster accent had just called me and I thought they might be terrorists.'

In fact the men were Metropolitan Police officers. When Gorman opened the entrance to them, they swarmed into the com-munal hallway and arrested him. His right arm was thrust behind his back and he was marched upstairs.

'I found it very difficult to take in. There were eight of them and they had all come to arrest one retired police officer! When I asked what I was being arrested for they wouldn't tell me. They wouldn't let me phone my solicitor, and they started rummaging through my files.'

Gorman watched in astonishment as the police started remov-ing many of the records he had been compiling of BA's peculiar behaviour in response to his complaint about the glass in the drink incident. The police sniggered as they examined cards that Gorman and Sherman had sent each other, and managed to break Gorman's expensive Christian Dior watch. They ordered him to remove his Cartier ring and impounded it.

'The officer in charge was DC O'Rourke. He told me that I was being arrested for "conspiracy to defraud British Airways", but he wouldn't tell me what the "conspiracy" was supposed to involve. I did establish that one of his group was the Ulsterman who had phoned me to ask if my windows needed replacing. I recognised his voice. It turned out that he was not a policeman at all. He was a senior member of BA's Investigations Branch, Robin Armstrong. I remember asking the police if they were going to take me away. When they said they were, I asked if it would be Enfield police station. O'Rourke turned to me and said 'No, we're from Heathrow Crime Squad.'

After being locked in a cell at Heathrow police station all day, Gorman was accused by DC O'Rourke of 'conspiring to defraud British Airways' over his 'glass in the drink' claim against BA. Suddenly the raid began to make some sense to Gorman.

'It became obvious from the questioning that BA had put the Heathrow police up to it. They had taken tapes I had made of conversations with officious BA staff, legally privileged correspondence with my solicitor and armfuls of files, as well as personal items.'

Gorman was released on police bail at ten o'clock at night. He had not been charged. Gorman's case was referred to the Crown Prosecution Service (CPS).

The police raid marked the start of an extraordinary campaign of intimidation against John Gorman and Peter Sherman which they proceeded to tell me about in painful detail. The story they told almost defied belief but it was given credibility because they had assiduously logged every phone call and fax that they had made or received, kept every letter and, despite the police raid, had some very interesting calls on tape. The two told me they had read the *Sunday Times'* serialisation of the first edition of this book in March 1994. They then bought the book and, having read it, decided to write to me. They told me that they had also approached the *Sunday Times* Insight team, and the *Observer* journalist David Rose, with their story but that nothing had so far appeared in print. By the time they had finished telling me their story, I could understand why.

The most obvious difficulty from a journalistic perspective was Gorman's partner, Peter Sherman. He used to work for British Airways as a travel consultant in BA's flagship branch on Regent Street. Indeed, Sherman had first met Gorman at his office when he came in to buy a ticket at the beginning of 1992. When BA had started messing Gorman around after he complained about the 'glass in the drink' incident, Sherman made a serious mistake. He used his access to British Airways' computer to credit Gorman's BA Executive Club Card.

'John was a Silver tier member. I thought if I credited him with points from other "J. Gorman"s flying with BA, he would become a Gold tier member and BA would take his complaint seriously.'

BA rumbled Sherman and he was arrested at his desk at BA in full view of his colleagues and members of the public queuing for tickets. Sherman was arrested on the same day that Gorman was seized in their flat.

'I admitted what I had done immediately. I deeply regret it and I apologised to BA.'

Neither man had gained financially from Sherman's misguided attempt to help his partner. The only financial benefit that Gorman would have gained from reaching BA Gold Card status was complimentary travel insurance. In fact, Gorman had just renewed his insurance before Sherman was caught, which provided circumstantial evidence to support his claim that he had no idea what Sherman was up to on his behalf.

BA fired Sherman but not before he had been offered the chance of a reprieve by BA if he framed Gorman. Before the disciplinary hearing to determine his fate, Sherman claimed that a BA supervisor had taken him aside:

'He told me that he had been told by BA management that if I said I had fiddled the computer for John's benefit, at his instigation, I could keep my job. I refused because it wasn't true.'

In the summer of 1993, after Sherman had refused to incriminate Gorman, the two men began to get mysterious telephone calls in the middle of the night: sometimes the caller would just laugh insanely, sometimes there was silence, and sometimes they heard only the sounds of aeroplane engines. Gorman became so worried by the calls that he asked the police to install a tape recorder and a tracing facility on his line. When the calls started to turn nasty, BT's 'nuisance calls bureau' started tracing them with extraordinary results.

In November 1993, for example, the CPS decided that the 'conspiracy to defraud BA' accusation did not hold water and it was dropped. The decision was a massive relief to Gorman who had been tormented for over six months by the prospect of being charged. His joy was immediately cut short, however. The following day an anonymous caller delivered a brutal message when Gorman picked up the phone

'We'll get you next time. You arsehole!'

Gorman had time to activate the tracing facility and BT traced the call to the office of BA's head of security, Ian Jackson, at Heathrow. BA's own telephone log eventually confirmed BT's finding, but the airline claimed Jackson had been abroad at the time. To Gorman's alarm other menacing calls started to come from the Heathrow police station whose officers had arrested him in May.

After the decision by the CPS in November not to charge Gorman with 'conspiracy to defraud BA', his solicitor told him he should go to Heathrow police station and collect the material that had been seized in the raid on his home by the police and BA in May.

When Gorman arrived at Heathrow police station he was met by Detective Chief Inspector Free, the immediate superior to DC O'Rourke who had led the raid on Gorman's home. To Gorman's dismay, DCI Free said that a BA official, James Forster, had asked the police not to return some of his belongings to him. James Forster is the head of British Airways' Investigations Branch. Gorman was astonished that DCI Free had gone along with BA's request. Gorman phoned the Police Complaints Branch at New Scotland Yard from Heathrow police station to complain that he was being denied his right to collect his belongings on instructions from BA. The former police officer then left the Heathrow station without any of the possessions he had come to collect:

'I refused to take any of my belongings unless I could take all of them. Shortly after I got home the phone rang again.'

The caller had apparently been aware of Gorman's complaint:

'If you make any more complaints against the police or British Airways you'll get your heads kicked in,' the caller warned. 'You'll not beat us,' he added, before cutting the line.

Gorman activated his call tracing facility once again. He was later told by Chief Inspector Lovelock that BT's Nuisance Calls Bureau had traced the call to Heathrow police station. In the summer Gorman had filed an official complaint to the Police Complaints Branch about his arrest during the May raid on his home. He defied the advice of friends and his solicitor not to do so, for fear of upsetting the police, and Lovelock had been appointed to head the investigation. Lovelock was also responsible for investigating Gorman's subsequent complaints about the menacing calls, and the mysterious fate of the property seized in the raid. Despite the intimidation that followed, Gorman did not regret his decision to complain about the police

'While I was in the Met I fought against corruption in the police, and the abuse of police powers. I wanted a proper investigation into my complaint to take place. They denied me the right to call my solicitor, they damaged some of my property and they improperly confiscated legally privileged correspondence between me and my solicitor and unopened mail from my solicitor. That is also wrong. None of those things should have happened and, as the CPS eventually decided, there was no case for me to answer.'

It was becoming clear to Gorman that elements in the police were joining in the attempt to intimidate him. After Lovelock started probing the Heathrow police, Gorman's tormentors were keen to let him know that he could not expect any joy from Lovelock's enquiry.

'Any morning now, nice and early we are coming to arrest you, smart arse . . . Lovelock doesn't like you and his sergeant thinks you are a raving poofter . . . You were warned.' Gorman was later informed that BT had traced the call to Heathrow police station.

The day after this call, some of the documents that had been confiscated during the police/BA raid were returned to Gorman in the post. They were sent in a 'Mailsort' envelope advertising the BA Air Miles scheme. Printed on the envelope were the words

'Travel Documents' in bold, BA blue. Inside were some of the documents that DC O'Rourke's team from the Heathrow police station and the BA investigator, Robin Armstrong, had removed from Gorman's flat in their May raid. Included in the package from BA were two American Airlines tickets that the police had confiscated in their May raid: a typed message on BA headed notepaper was enclosed with the tickets. It read, 'Happy holidays arsehole'. BA later conceded that the franked, 'Mailsort' envelope could only have been posted from within the airline.

A further flurry of calls from BA's Heathrow premises heralded a torrid winter for Gorman and Sherman. Just before Christmas 1993 Gorman was woken by the sound of his car alarm going off in the early hours of the morning. He rushed outside. Stuck to the window of his BMW he found a cassette that the police and Robin Armstrong had removed from his flat during their May raid. The label on the cassette read 'BA/Rigg'. Gorman had written the label on the tape of a particularly vituperative call from one of BA's officials, John Rigg. The tape inside the cassette had been removed, leaving only the cassette shell which had been super-glued to the car windscreen. The vandals had caused nearly £500 worth of damage to Gorman's car.

Gorman and Sherman were becoming extremely worried. How could a tape seized in the police raid on their home have been destroyed? And how had the cassette shell reappeared stuck to their car in the middle of the night? Gorman reported the matter to the Enfield police, and brought it to the attention of Chief Inspector Lovelock who was investigating his complaint against the police. A week later, just before the New Year, Gorman got another sinister phone call, this time from a female with a gentle but menacing, Northern Irish voice:

'John, why don't you start off the New Year well? Cancel your complaint against British Airways, because if Mr Armstrong lost his job or other things happened to him you will be very sorry and will live to regret it. So enjoy life, forget it and remember that the police are very friendly with British Airways at London Airport and that they also can cause you a lot of problems in the future. Be sensible and there will be no more calls after today.'

The caller hung up before Gorman could speak but he did

activate his tracing facility. BT traced it to a public phone box in Belfast.

Gorman then decided to take his complaints to the top of BA. He phoned Robert Ayling personally to inform him what was being done to him in BA's name. Ayling wouldn't speak to Gorman and palmed him off with an 'executive assistant' who assured him that he would look into the matter. Shortly afterwards, Gorman was told that Mervyn Walker would carry out an investigation into his complaints against the airline. Walker wrote assuring Gorman that he had launched an internal investigation into his allegations. Gorman was further encouraged by John Parr, the director-general of the Air Users Council. Gorman had written to Parr with details of his complaint against BA. Parr told Gorman that he was confident Walker's investigation would be concluded within a few days.

Days after Gorman received the news of Walker's imminent investigation, the anonymous callers were at work again. One call was traced to a public phone box inside Vanguard House, the Heathrow headquarters of BA's investigation branch. A sneering voice warned, 'Mr Gorman, if you believe that British Airways are going to investigate this matter you are sorely mistaken'. The caller was obviously following developments extremely closely.

Less than a week after Walker started his enquiry, one of his lawyers, Helen Cahill, wrote to inform Gorman that he had been suspended from BA's Executive Club. When Gorman phoned the Executive Club to complain, he was told that he had been blacklisted by BA. Furthermore, staff had been banned from talking to him, the Executive Club travel insurance he had paid for had been cancelled, and he was told to direct all future communications with BA through the legal department. Gorman was extremely offended:

'I was a founding member of BA's Executive Club, and I couldn't understand why BA wanted to throw me out. The CPS had decided that there was no case for me to answer, but BA was treating me as if I was a criminal. And all because I had complained about broken glass in one of their drinks!'

As 1994 opened there was still no word from Mervyn Walker's internal investigation. However, towards the end of January, another anonymous phone call gave Gorman rare hope. Someone who claimed to work for BA Security phoned Gorman with a message of support:

'I know you are having serious problems with British Airways. It is James Forster and Andy Warman who are out to get you along with Robin Armstrong. A cover-up by them is now taking place. They are all frightened for their jobs. They are telling lies hand over fist to management . . . They are all corrupt here. Keep going. Good luck.'

The caller's reference to James Forster reminded Gorman of his clash with the desk sergeant at Heathrow police station in November: the officer had refused to return some of his possessions seized in the May raid on the grounds that Forster had told him not to. The call encouraged Gorman, but BA's insurance branch soon extinguished any hope that his complaint against BA would be satisfactorily dealt with. A letter from BA arrived at the end of January 1994. It finally acknowledged that the 'glass in the drink' incident *had* taken place on board a BA flight, almost a year after it occurred. The letter offered Gorman £500 in final settlement.

'I was utterly insulted,' remembers Gorman. 'There was no explanation of why it had taken BA management a year to admit what the BA crew knew from the start, no hint of an apology, no word about Walker's never-ending internal investigation, and no explanation for the bizarre series of events that had started with my arrest by BA and the police in May. I decided that the only way I would achieve justice was to go to court'.

Gorman served his writ on BA at the end of a dramatic meeting at Speedbird House. Gorman attended the meeting at BA's request, thinking he had been invited to hear news of Walker's enquiry into his complaint. However, he was met with outright hostility and rudeness by Helen Cahill. She was quite straightforward with Gorman. She told him, 'I don't like you, Mr Gorman,' and added, 'You bloody think that this is the only job I have to do. Well, for your information, Mr Gorman, I have other important matters to attend to besides your complaint.'

The fearsome lawyer was accompanied by Keith Kerr from BA's 'internal audit' department. They were unaware that Gorman had a tape recorder hidden in his top pocket which was recording the entire encounter. Cahill and Kerr suspended normal courtesies while Cahill spat out insults at Gorman. They were both served with coffee during the meeting; their visitor was offered nothing. Eventually Gorman requested a glass of water which was reluctantly brought to him by Kerr. At the end of the meeting Gorman served a summons upon Cahill claiming compensation for the 'glass in the drink' incident.

'I sued them for £9,000 over the glass incident, but the money was not important,' Gorman told me. 'I will be out of pocket whatever the outcome of my case. I have spent a small fortune on solicitors' fees, over 120 recorded delivery letters, faxes, phone calls and so on. I wanted to bring out in court what BA, and the police, had been doing to me'.

A fresh wave of intimidation followed Gorman's writ. His tormentors had been monitoring developments very closely indeed.

'Cut your losses now and get out while the going is good,' said the next anonymous caller, 'Don't meet any more officials from BA or the police . . . or you and Peter Sherman will be badly hurt and that's a promise. And don't contact the press in relation to BA!'

Gorman and Sherman were becoming seriously worried about their own safety, as well as the security of the evidence they had compiled against BA and the police. On the advice of his solicitor, Janet White of Howe & Co, Gorman gathered his evidence together to take to her office for copying and safekeeping. He decided to take the evidence to her immediately after attending a meeting with BA which Gorman thought would be a final attempt to resolve the increasingly bitter dispute and to avoid the need to go to court. White confirms that Gorman phoned her at lunchtime on that day, to make sure she would be there in the late afternoon to receive his documents after his meeting at BA. Then he loaded all his evidence into the back of his car, and set off for Heathrow. He told White on the phone that he would drop his evidence in with her after he had met BA at Heathrow. Gorman had made a very serious mistake.

When Gorman arrived at BA's Vanguard House at Heathrow, a BA official took his name and the registration number of his car. He was directed to a parking space, and then taken inside to the boardroom of BA's internal audit department.

After another desultory meeting with Kerr and Chris Agg, BA's 'chief internal auditor', at which BA refused to concede any ground, Gorman trudged back to his BMW in the BA car park, resigned to having to go to court to make BA see sense. As he approached his car, he noticed glass on the ground. Someone had smashed his rear window and broken into it. Gorman ran the remaining yards to the car and found, to his relief that valuables he had left in the car had not been taken. Cash, CDs, the radio cassette all remained. Even an expensive Giorgio Armani overcoat was still there. However, Gorman quickly noticed that the boxes of files and tapes for his case against BA had been stolen. Nothing else had been taken.

Gorman rushed back into Vanguard House and reported the theft and the break-in to Keith Kerr. Kerr responded with blank indifference. He phoned Helen Cahill and told her what had happened. Gorman bit his lip as the two BA officials started joking and laughing over the phone. The Heathrow police arrived shortly afterwards to take details of the robbery. Predictably no one in the BA building had seen anything untoward happening, but Gorman was astonished to be told by BA that the security cameras which scour the Vanguard House car park area are turned off in the afternoons. The former Anti-Terrorist Branch detective was not impressed:

'The break-in to my car occurred a few days after the IRA had bombed Heathrow airport. Hundreds of extra police had been drafted in to meet the terrorist threat, and BA expected me to believe that its own cameras covering a sensitive area immediately outside the high security compound housing Colin Marshall and the BA top brass were turned off. My car was parked only yards away from offices full of BA staff and planes worth hundreds of millions of pounds. The boot could have been packed full of Semtex.'

Fortunately for Gorman, he had copied much of the evidence he had accumulated against BA. The loss of the files was, nonetheless, a blow until some of them were returned to him in the most extraordinary circumstances.

The City solicitors, Beaumont and Son, had been instructed to defend BA against Gorman's legal suit. A young American solicitor working for Beaumont, Dan Soffin, rang Gorman three weeks after the theft to tell him that files bearing his name had been handed into their offices in the City. When Gorman collected them the next day, he recognised them instantly. They were, indeed, some of the files that had been stolen from his car in the BA car park; they still had particles of broken glass lodged between the papers. Soffin said the files had been handed in to a Lloyds bank adjacent to Beaumont's offices in Lloyds Chambers. The bank had handed them on to the solicitors because they were enclosed in a package addressed to Beaumont. Gorman wandered out of Beaumont in a daze. Documents stolen from a car park at BA's headquarters had now been returned to him by lawyers working for BA in the City. Beaumont had not reported the matter to the police, so Gorman did. The Heathrow police declined Gorman's invitation to fingerprint the files.

At this point Gorman and Sherman decided to contact the media. Mervyn Walker had still not completed his 'internal investigation', and the intimidation had become even more intense. When Gorman had entered hospital in the spring for an operation, his car was spray-painted with the words 'No win with BA' in blue paint over his dark red BMW. This time the damage cost over £1,000 to repair. BA denied any responsibility for the vandalism. Gorman was furious, however, to hear that BA had hinted to police investigating the crime that it thought Gorman might have sprayed his own car. Gorman pointed out to the officers that he was under a general anaesthetic at the time.

The two men told me that they had decided to approach the media to get everything out in the open. They said they thought this might halt the dirty tricks. The similarities with Richard Branson's initial reaction to discovering some of BA's dirty tricks were taking place was unmistakable. Listening to them, I could recognise some of the characters they had come across at BA as veterans of the dirty-tricks campaign against Virgin, and I was struck by their own difficulty in believing that BA could stoop to such depths. Sir Freddie Laker, Harry Goodman and Richard Branson had all started off with the same view.

The most difficult question to answer in Gorman's case was that of BA's motivation. It was one thing to wage dirty-tricks campaigns against commercially threatening rival airlines, but what could be its motive to do similar things to one of its own shareholders? The corporate gain for the airline was self-evidently nil, and the financial cost of settling Gorman's action was minute. The whole affair seemed implausible but, I reminded myself, who would have believed the extraordinary escapades that BA sponsored in Operation Covent Garden? As I listened to the dapper couple ploughing through their story, surrounded by their boxes of documentation and carefully labelled tapes, I remembered my first meeting with Branson. He had little in the way of proof of BA's dirty tricks when I first met him, but I did not doubt the sincerity with which he put his case. I got the same feeling with Gorman and Sherman, but their story was even more extraordinary than Branson's had initially seemed.

Two days after meeting Gorman and Sherman I saw the journalist Paul Foot at a *Private Eye* lunch. We had not met socially before, but Foot had enjoyed *Dirty Tricks* and he invited me to lunch. He wrote in his review of *Dirty Tricks* that 'it would be incredible as fiction', so I tried the Gorman story out on him. I also told Foot that I believed him although I hadn't had time to check all the details. Foot roared with laughter when I told him that BA's response to Gorman's complaint about the glass in the drink had been to have him arrested on suspicion of 'conspiring to defraud BA', and that the threatening calls had been traced back to BA by British Telecom. 'Typical of that bloody airline,' Foot scoffed. He immediately said he wanted to write about Gorman in his next column, once he had checked the story out for himself.

Foot had reason to empathise with Gorman. As a journalist on the *Daily Mirror* he had fallen victim to the same sort of bullying that prevailed in King's BA. A year after King's friend Robert Maxwell died suddenly, Foot was hounded out of the paper by the new chief executive, hardline Ulster Protestant David Montgomery. Montgomery is a close friend of David Burnside, who himself worked for Maxwell as well as King.

Foot's subsequent series of articles on the Gorman affair for *Private Eye* had a dramatic and catalytic impact on the course of events. His first report summarised the whole of the former detective's extraordinary experience at the hands of BA and the police under the heading, 'The World's Favourite Dirty Tricks'. The *Eye* article sparked press interest in Gorman, and sent BA's multi-million-pound press operation into retreat. It soon became apparent that under Burnside's successor, Peter Jones, the BA press office was having difficulty establishing any sort of relationship with the truth. It was difficult to blame Jones' staff entirely for the debacle that ensued, as BA's senior management continued to exhibit its traditional distaste for telling the truth about any aspect of any dirty tricks alleged against BA.

As newspapers began to take an interest in Gorman's allegations, the BA press office went 'off the record'. The *Financial Times*, the *Sunday Times* and Paul Foot were told that Gorman and Sherman were dodgy characters who were involved in a host of lost baggage claims against BA. BA subsequently denied it was attempting to insinuate that Gorman and Sherman were involved in a scam, but the tapes of the reporters' calls to the press office tell a different story.

When I approached BA, I was sent a fax implying that Gorman was a professional whinger who had already received £8,500 from BA in compensation for other claims. Gorman flatly denied this: 'I have never received any cash from BA in compensation for anything. I claimed successfully, and uneventfully, on my *own* insurance policies for other incidents, and once received some travel vouchers (worth £3,000) after I found a condom in my BA meal! I have made only one baggage claim against the airline in twenty-six years of flying.'

BA made great play of the criminal charges that Peter Sherman faced for misusing BA's computer. 'The criminal and legal proceedings involving Gorman and Sherman make it difficult to comment . . .' became a standard component in BA's responses.

By the summer of 1994 Sherman faced no less than eight criminal charges and, naturally, this was a consideration when journalists approached the story. *Here and Now*, the BBC's lightweight, current affairs magazine programme even cancelled a preliminary research meeting with Gorman when it heard that Sherman was facing criminal charges.

Mervyn Walker's 'internal investigation' was still in progress in June, nearly six months after both Gorman and the Air Users

Council boss, John Parr, had been assured it would report in 'a few days'. I told Gorman that if Walker's past form was an accurate guide it was highly unlikely that anything significant would emerge from his probe. Gorman knew from reading the first edition of this book that Walker tended not to apply whatever forensic skills he claimed to possess when confronted with the challenge of investigating dirty-tricks allegations against BA. Nonetheless, when Walker did eventually complete his report later in the month, Gorman found it difficult to hide his disappointment.

The report was a pompous and crabby denial of everything that Gorman had alleged, and for which he had been unable to provide incontrovertible evidence to support. In one gem of a conclusion, Walker was forced to admit that the call warning Gorman 'We'll get you next time, arsehole' had, indeed, come from BA. Walker was not breaking new ground here as BT had traced the call to the office of BA's head of security, Ian Jackson, within days of it being made on 3 November 1993. However, Walker's 'investigation' had managed to eliminate everyone who worked in Jackson's office from his enquiries:

> We have established that our then head of security, Mr Ian Jackson, was away from Heathrow at the time . . . We have interviewed Mr Jackson's secretary and we are satisfied that she did not make the call . . .

This did not come as an enormous surprise to Gorman as Jackson's secretary is a woman and the caller was man. Walker had nothing of any interest to say about any of the Gorman's litany of complaints. This is a selection of his statements from a letter that contained no less than twenty-two flat denials of Gorman's claims:

Of the many calls traced by BT to BA premises, Walker wrote, 'We have found no evidence that the call was made by a BA employee.' On listening to a recording of one of the anonymous BA callers: 'Neither we nor the police recognise the caller.' On the theft of Gorman's documents from his car while it was parked in BA's car park: 'We have found no evidence as to the identity of the person who broke into your car.' On the mysterious return of Gorman's documents by BA's City lawyers: 'Neither we nor Beaumont and Son have any idea who delivered the documents to Lloyds Bank'.

In case Gorman had not quite got the message from Walker's eight-page denial of responsibility, the lawyer concluded, 'As you have seen, in many cases BA does not have any information of relevance. I do not feel I can be of any further help . . .'

'Quite frankly, I thought Walker was taking the mickey,' said Gorman after he read the BA lawyer's letter. 'In December 1993 he told me, and John Parr at the Air Users Committee, that his report would be ready within days. Now, over half a year later, he was telling me things I knew before he started his "investigation".'

Walker's unambitious aim appeared to be to limit BA's legal liability to the minimum rather than make a genuine attempt to get to the bottom of Gorman's complaints. As with his 1991 investigation into the Virgin case, Walker had concluded that BA could not be held responsible for anything. The former detective was bitterly disappointed by Walker's response. Until this point Gorman had hoped that BA was genuinely trying to get to the bottom of the matter. He hoped that Walker's delay in reporting back to him earlier was caused by the thoroughness of his interviewing of likely suspects, and the diligence of his investigation.

Gorman had received Walker's flatulent report on his 'investigation' only three days after he had been beaten up and robbed in his home by the thugs who smashed his head against the wall and told him not to 'mess with BA'. When Gorman had recovered sufficiently to reply to BA's legal director he wrote:

Your conclusion that your investigation has been 'thorough' and has, therefore, inevitably taken time is complete nonsense. It is no more than a whitewash dashed out in a desperate, but unsuccessful attempt to shift the blame for your disgraceful behaviour from yourselves.

It could not have been more cursory, biased, self-serving

or utterly incredible. Lame excuses have been copied from one section to the next, including identical spelling mistakes . . .

Your comments are simply not plausible . . . you have failed, once again, to address the main issue which is this: that all the criminal acts committed in the name of British Airways were undertaken, not only for BA's benefit, and BA's benefit alone, but in many cases from within premises to which BA's staff have access, using specialised knowledge only available to British Airways staff.

. . . at the same time, British Airways astonishingly purport that these madmen acted entirely on their own initiative without any instruction from the airline, the only party which stood to benefit from these actions.

Fortunately the courts are not that gullible, and neither are the public. All of these illegal matters with which you are intimately acquainted will be vigorously pursued through the courts.

Gorman copied his letter to Sir Colin Marshall in the hope that, despite his involvement in the dirty-tricks campaign against Virgin Atlantic, BA's chairman would see sense and deal decisively with those members of his staff who were responsible. Gorman also started preparing a final attempt to avoid court action against his favourite airline. He wrote to BA to say that he would be attending the AGM on 12 July. He put the airline's company secretary, Gail Redwood, on notice that he wanted to ask one question: 'Why were my serious complaints against BA not correctly handled?'

Gorman decided to present his dossier of complaints to Michael Davies, the member of BA's board who, Gorman knew, had shown a degree of understanding to Richard Branson. As he sat down to write a covering letter to Davies and bring his lengthy dossier up to date, he was able to include another astonishing incident which appeared to link the dirty-tricks campaign directly to BA's most senior management.

Paul Foot was the only journalist to report the violent robbery at Gorman's home in June. Shortly afterwards, Foot received an anonymous call at his *Private Eye* office. The caller claimed to work for BA's security department, and went on to allege that documents stolen in the raid on Gorman's home had been handed in to Mervyn Walker's office at BA. The caller specified that a document marked 'David Rose' (the *Observer* journalist) was amongst those that had been handed in. The caller also claimed the documents had been handed to Walker by a 'London detective agency', suggesting obvious parallels with BA's Operation Covent Garden against Virgin. Like many other journalists who had attempted to pin BA down on the Gorman affair, Foot had abandoned hope of getting a sensible verbal response from BA's press office, so he faxed his questions to the airline:

> I would not normally bother you with the allegations of anonymous callers but on this occasion I am prompted to do so for two reasons:
>
> a) The fact that the David Rose file was stolen from Mr Gorman's house on the day of the raid had not been published anywhere – no casual mischief maker could have known about it.
>
> b) Material previously stolen from Mr Gorman's car while he was on BA property was eventually handed back, via a rather roundabout route (BA's City lawyers, Beaumont and Son).
>
> Could you please check with Mr Walker and let me know whether the file has been received?'

Foot was not surprised when the BA press office said that Walker could not be found. The following day, however, John Gorman opened his morning mail to find the file he had prepared for the *Observer*'s David Rose, and an accompanying letter from Mervyn Walker:

> In the normal delivery of post to my office this morning I received the enclosed envelope. On opening it I discovered that it contained papers which appear to originate from you. I am therefore returning the papers to you. I have neither read nor made copies of them.

The package had apparently been sent to Walker in BA's internal mail. Gorman was astonished. For the second time, documents stolen from him had been returned by a BA lawyer. Curiously, Walker's letter was dated 6 July, the day before Foot's enquiry, but the recorded letter was posted on 7 July, the day the BA press office said it could not find Walker.

Gorman included an account of this latest incident in his dossier. As he strode into the BA AGM, an hour before it started, on the lookout for Michael Davies, he encountered Robert Ayling. Gorman introduced himself, and Ayling invited him into a private area for a discussion. As the two men exchanged introductory remarks, Ayling told Gorman that he used to work for the DTI under Norman Tebbit. 'I once met Tebbit,' replied Gorman, 'I helped to dig him out of the Grand Hotel after the IRA bombed it!' Ayling's jaw dropped slightly.

BA's group managing director listened intently for half an hour as Gorman outlined the extraordinary catalogue of experiences he had endured since complaining about the glass in his drink. Ayling took delivery of the package Gorman had prepared for Davies. Gorman stressed that it was confidential, and specifically asked Ayling not to pass it on to BA's Investigations Branch as Robin Armstrong and his colleagues were the focus of his complaint.

'I will treat your document as if it were my own,' Ayling assured Gorman.

Gorman was further comforted by Gail Redwood, BA's company secretary. She thanked him for not pressing the question he had tabled to the AGM, thus sparing the board potential embarrassment. Later in the day, Gorman encountered Sir Colin Marshall who shook him warmly by the hand. 'Mr Gorman, welcome to the AGM. Robert has briefed me earlier on the dreadful circumstance that you find yourself in. It is rather bizarre.'

The chairman had already been briefed by Ayling. Gorman stressed to Marshall that he had no desire to discredit BA. Marshall assured Gorman that Ayling would now look into his complaints.

'I will oversee and make sure these matters are dealt with correctly. BA views these incidents with the greatest concern. We regard you as an important person who has travelled with the airline for a very long time, you are a loyal customer and shareholder'.

Gorman's bold move in confronting BA's hierarchy at the AGM initially appeared to have paid off. The day after the AGM, Ayling wrote to say that he had read Gorman's dossier: 'Clearly this is a very odd and disturbing story and it is highly desirable that we get to the bottom of what is happening'.

A week later Gorman and Sherman were invited to Speedbird House to discuss the affair. Their reception could hardly have been in greater contrast to Gorman's previous visits. Mervyn Walker greeted them with a colleague from Linklaters, Michael Bennett. A special parking space had been reserved at Speedbird House. Refreshments were offered as soon as the two arrived and they were told that lunch was being prepared for them. The surprises continued as the meeting got off to a prompt start at 0900. Bennett took detailed, contemporaneous notes upon which this account of the meeting is based.

Gorman and Sherman sat and listened to Walker in astonishment as he opened the meeting by apologising for any rudeness that Gorman had experienced in his dealings with BA staff. He stated that many of the events that Gorman had reported undoubtedly constituted 'criminal activities'. Walker conceded that Gorman's claim over the 'glass in the drink' incident was 'worth thousands', and said that he considered Gorman and Sherman to be allies in his quest to establish precisely who was responsible, and he went further:

'Mr Gorman, we do not challenge what you say and we would not wish to challenge your integrity for one moment. We accept your allegations at face value.'

Gorman could hardly believe that this was the same man who, exactly a month earlier, had written to him in such dismissive terms denying any responsibility for the entire dirty-tricks campaign. 'Clearly Marshall and Ayling had told Walker to get to grips with the situation and stop flapping around,' Gorman remembers. The revelation that he had received stolen documents had obviously shaken BA's legal director badly. Bennett's notes recount what he told Gorman and Sherman at the meeting:

Mervyn's main concern about this incident was that whoever
had sent the papers to him appeared to be attempting to discredit him [Mervyn]. His overriding concern was that this
appeared to be the most overt attempt to set him [Mervyn] up.

Walker informed Gorman that Andrew Warman had been interviewed by police investigating the assault and robbery in his home
and that he had also been spoken to by the officers. Walker also
told Gorman that he had not informed the police that he had
received the stolen documents, which surprised the former detective. Walker said, however, that he was so puzzled by the events
Gorman had recounted that he was thinking of handing the whole
matter over to the police.

This was of very limited comfort to Gorman and Sherman who
were convinced that the police had mounted the campaign of
intimidation against them in conjunction with BA's Investigations
Branch. They were fascinated, however, to hear Walker's theories
on who, at BA, might be responsible. Walker said that if it were
accepted for the sake of the discussion that someone within BA
was responsible, he thought there existed three possibilities.
According to Bennett's notes, Walker described his theory in the
following manner:

'Firstly, that the employee had acted with full authority; secondly, that the employee had acted without authority but had
misguidedly felt he was assisting BA; or thirdly, that the employee
was acting without authority and was attempting to harm BA as
well as John Gorman.'

Walker ruled out the first possibility, felt that the second was
unlikely, and said that the third was the most probable. Gorman
listened with interest. BA's legal director had come a long way in
the course of the past month.

Sherman accompanied Gorman to the meeting partly to provide support and witness, but also because he wanted to apologise
to BA and to make the airline understand why he had abused its
computer.

The night before his trial in June, Sherman had received an
anonymous phone call:

'Sherman, plead guilty tomorrow, or else.'

Sherman went to Isleworth Crown Court with the anonymous threat and the memory of the attack on Gorman still fresh in his mind. He was delighted when the CPS announced that it was dropping all of the eight criminal charges of theft and computer misuse against him.

'I had been desperately worried that with both the police and BA apparently so determined to get at me as a way of discrediting John, I would be put in prison.'

The criminal charges against Sherman, which carried a possible prison sentence, were dropped in return for Sherman's agreement to plead guilty to a minor charge of 'gaining unauthorised access' to BA's computer system. Infused with relief at not having to face jail, and frightened by the anonymous call the night before, Sherman pleaded guilty. He received a conditional discharge for twelve months. After his court appearance, Sherman learnt that the call threatening physical violence against him had been traced by BT to the Heathrow police station.

Sherman had experienced considerable difficulty in getting work after BA fired him and, at the Heathrow meeting, Sherman impressed upon BA's lawyers that he had acted solely to try and get BA to take Gorman's complaints seriously. Walker accepted Sherman's apology and later wrote to confirm this: 'I accept that the apology you gave at our meeting was genuine and sincere.'

Gorman and Sherman left the meeting in high spirits.

'At last we were being treated with proper respect and courtesy. We believed that BA was going to take us seriously,' remembers Gorman. 'Walker said he would write to us very soon having carried out a further probe into the matters we had raised.'

Polite and soothing letters from Walker followed. Walker said he had found the Speedbird House meeting 'useful and productive'. He apologised on behalf of BA for Keith Kerr's 'rude' and 'improper' behaviour. Walker also conceded that, although he had been unable to trace who did it, the Air Miles envelope containing the documents taken from Gorman's flat and the 'happy holiday arsehole' message, had, indeed, been posted through BA's 'Mailsort' system.

Walker said that BA's phone records had revealed that another anonymous call to Gorman had been traced to the BA

Investigations Branch's headquarters in Vanguard House. Gorman remembered it well. The caller had said, 'You two may think that you have made a fool of British Airways at court the other day and British Airways Investigations Branch, but I warn you now the best is yet to come. Beware!'

The caller appeared to have been upset by Gorman's first court appearance in his 'glass in the drink' action. Representing himself, Gorman had successfully appeared before a judge in chambers to defeat a motion from BA to dismiss his action. BA had been ordered to pay the costs of the hearing.

Walker said that his discovery that this call had been made from Investigation Branch's headquarters was 'obviously of concern to us'. He said he was investigating the possibility of installing an alarm system that would immediately go off if Gorman was phoned from a BA number. He also confessed to being sufficiently worried that he was now considering bringing the Metropolitan Police into BA to investigate the matter: 'We are in the process of considering whom we should contact'. In a letter dated 9 August Walker said that he had, at last, reported to Enfield police that he had received documents stolen from Gorman on 6 July.

Gorman and Sherman's feelings of relief at apparently being taken seriously were bolstered by the cessation of the dirty-tricks campaign against them. Every BA official, from Marshall downwards, had denied any knowledge of who was responsible for the extraordinary series of events. However, since the AGM on 12 July, there had been no menacing calls, no more thefts of documents, no physical attacks and Gorman's car had not been broken into or vandalised. Furthermore BA's staff had become uniformly pleasant and receptive. Ayling, for example, began one letter: 'I did not intend any discourtesy in not sending a formal reply . . . On my return from holiday, Mervyn Walker informed me of your long and constructive meeting with him . . .'

Gorman's growing belief that BA was looking for a way out was soon dashed. His solicitor, Janet White, wrote to him with bad news. Beaumont and Son had written on behalf of BA offering to settle the 'glass in the drink' claim:

'[BA] would increase the offer already made to you [from £500] in the campaign against Virgin Atlantic to the BA board, to the public and to the press. Ayling, the lawyer, was particularly keen to extract from Branson a binding agreement that would prevent the dirty tricks from being raised again, in or out of court.

To Branson this was completely unacceptable. His lawyers prepared a press release to announce the breakdown of the talks. It was never issued but it provides an illuminating insight into the perceptions of Virgin's weary negotiators:

> It soon became apparent to Virgin that the directors seemed more interested in stopping Virgin and Richard Branson saying what we knew about the goings on than settling the damage claim. Many clauses were added by BA in an attempt to gag RB and his staff FOR EVER.
>
> They wanted history to be re-written (or, more importantly, never written at all). They asked for a complete destruction of RB's notes, all discovery documents and all of BA's affidavits. They insisted that RB could *nev*er – however old he was – refer to any of these incidents ever again. If he ever wrote an autobiography they wanted blank pages on this issue. No mention of 'computer misuse' of 'Burnside' or 'Basham' or 'shredding' or 'who knew what' could ever, in Richard Branson's lifetime, pass his lips. No passing reference could ever be made in TV interviews, radio interviews, newspaper interviews.

Gerrard Tyrrell advised Branson very strongly against signing the contract BA was proposing. He told him it would severely compromise his scope for further action against BA should it ever become necessary.

'We were being paid off as long as we were willing to be gagged,' recalls Branson. 'BA have also behaved illegally towards other parties. They knew that we knew this. A condition of settling was that we hadn't helped these other parties and, in effect, wouldn't in future due to the gag placed on us and the return (and planned subsequent destruction) of all documents.'

Branson eventually told BA he would accept the money, but flatly refused to sign the gagging clause: 'You might think I'm

mad but I'm not going to give up the right to free speech, even for
£9 million.'

The talks collapsed and the unissued press release, prepared by
his lawyers, eloquently expressed the Virgin team's feelings:

> We have been incredulous at the lengths BA directors have
> gone to to distance themselves and their senior staff from
> events, and paint a picture of only junior staff being
> involved.
>
> BA's senior staff were *very* much involved in the dirty-
> tricks campaign against Virgin Atlantic. On one area alone –
> the illegal accessing and the misuse of our computer infor-
> mation: this carried on for THREE YEARS. At the very
> highest levels of BA people were misusing and abusing our
> computer information.

The collapse of the 'peace' talks presented a dilemma for Marshall
and Ayling. Press reports had it that they were offering Branson £9
million to settle. At the time they were only weeks away from a
potentially hostile AGM at which they faced a grilling over BA's
dirty tricks, and their own role in the campaign. Many shareholders had been appalled by BA's admissions in the High Court and
hundreds had written to the company demanding to know what
had really been going on and who was really responsible. It would
be difficult to explain why BA was offering Branson £9 million if
the dirty tricks really were the 'unconnected incidents' by a small
number of employees' of which Marshall and Ayling 'knew nothing'. Marshall and Ayling had to get themselves off a potentially
difficult hook.

To begin with they denied that they had attempted to gag
Virgin at all. Branson was incredulous. Gerrard Tyrrell had
inspected BA's proposed contract on Branson's behalf. According
to Branson, Tyrrell advised him that it contained the 'most restric-
tive gagging clauses' he had ever seen.

Marshall and Ayling then denied that they had offered Branson
£9 million to settle. *BA News* said that 'reports [BA] was offering or
agreeing to pay £9 million to settle claims made against it by
Virgin Atlantic were not true. Nor was any payment of such

amount under consideration. The airline had made it clear at the outset that the settlement was not worth £9 million . . . or anything like it.' This article appeared in June 1993, the month before the AGM.

Proof that BA was lying about its offer to Virgin emerged at the beginning of 1994 when BA grudgingly conceded defeat in its long-running engineering dispute with Virgin. Just before the matter was due to go to arbitration, BA paid Virgin Atlantic £2,650,000 in damages. It also paid both sides' legal costs. The maintenance dispute had been part of the £9 million offer that Marshall and Ayling had assured the 1993 AGM had never existed.

On settling the engineering dispute BA issued a press release that flatly contradicted its earlier claim that the £9 million offer did not exist. It read, 'Virgin's engineering and other claims were the subject of settlement discussions last March which had resulted in tentative agreement between the two airlines on the basis of which British Airways offered to pay £9 million to Virgin in overall settlement . . . but that settlement was not concluded because of differences as to terms and conditions.'

By this time Richard Branson's conviction that Marshall and Ayling were being 'economical' with the truth had already been dramatically reinforced from an unexpected quarter. As the 'peace' talks were on the point of breakdown, Brian Basham broke ranks and exposed what he described as BA's 'corporate lie'.

For reasons that have never been satisfactorily explained, BA cut Brian Basham adrift completely in the wake of the libel settlement with Virgin. While David Burnside was handsomely rewarded for his silence, Basham was simply paid the £10,000 he was owed for the remainder of his consultancy contract. Basham felt he had been harshly treated. He was extremely annoyed that he had been singled out to take the blame for BA's dirty-tricks campaign, and pointed out that the talks between BA and Virgin were concerned not with compensating Branson for the suffering he experienced at the hands of the PR campaign, but for the excesses of BA's sales and marketing personnel.

In February 1993 Basham heard from a reporter on the *Sunday Telegraph* that Sir Colin Marshall had described his work for BA as 'over-zealous and aggressive' in an interview. Until that moment the PR man's discontent had smouldered. Now it exploded. Not only had he been forced to suffer the indignity of being the only member of the BA team to be named in the High Court settlement, and losing his consultancy contract with BA, he was now being accused of being 'aggressive and over-zealous' by the man he had tried to hold in check during the previous year. In a series of increasingly heated private letters to Marshall, Basham outlined what he saw as the chief executive's treachery.

I went through that report with Lord King and it was presented to you and Robert Ayling. There is nothing in it which could remotely be described as 'over-zealous' or 'aggressive'. Indeed, in the introduction, I went out of my way to knock down your basic misconceptions about Branson.

As a direct instruction from a main board director [King], I was asked to circulate a story that Westminster dustmen were refusing to collect bags of rubbish from Heaven which contained hypodermic needles thought to be infected with AIDS. I flatly refused to do so. Was this over-zealous?

Both you and Robert Ayling were keen to place a story about Virgin's poor punctuality in the first week of their Heathrow operation. Indeed, Robert Ayling said in David's office at Enserch, 'The world's two greatest PR men and they can't even get a story in the press about Virgin's punctuality.' When I asked for substantiation for the story, I was told that I could not have it because: 'The information had been obtained from the computers and we shouldn't have it.'

In his reply Sir Colin Marshall rejected Basham's interpretation of the *Sunday Telegraph*'s article: 'I do not accept that their description of your work for BA as "aggressive" was defamatory. Nor do I consider it untrue or damaging.' He refused to discuss the other matters raised by Basham: 'You well know our position which is as stated in Open Court.'

Marshall's dismissive reply further enraged Basham. The PR man had been told throughout the course of the litigation that there was no truth in Branson's passenger-poaching and shredding allegations:

> I was systematically lied to over a period of years and, therefore, deceived into telling the press that there was no substance to Mr Branson's allegations.
> . . . by your actions in dissembling, if not lying, to the board of British Airways, to the press and to the House of Commons, you have continued the corporate lie which, in the eyes of the world, placed me at the centre of the British Airways 'dirty-tricks' campaign and you have, also, almost certainly disqualified yourself as being a fit and proper person to hold the position of the Chairman of British Airways.

In a final, angry twist Basham wrote to Marshall for the last time at the end of March:

> There are some people you can bugger up and walk away from. There are some you cannot. I hope I am of the latter variety.
> . . . I shall pursue my just cause.

At the end of April, Basham opened his BA files to an edition of *World in Action*, which I was filming for Granada TV. The programme was called 'BA's Virgin Soldiers'. In his first ever television interview Basham revealed the extent of Marshall and Ayling's involvement in the dirty-tricks campaign. In an interview that lasted nearly three hours, Basham told me that he supported Branson's view that Marshall masterminded the dirty-tricks campaign against Virgin, and that Marshall was responsible for engineering the subsequent cover-up.

> I think they thought that by focusing attention on me they would distract attention from the directors, from Colin Marshall in particular . . .
> It's nonsense to say that Colin Marshall would not know and direct and drive all those matters, because Colin Marshall is a control freak. He's a very able manager, and

he's a man who has his finger on the pulse of everything that goes on in British Airways.

He works insanely hard and was clearly obsessed by Branson himself.

That obsession fathered a concerted campaign which involved a wide range of departments, computers, marketing, sales, ticketing, engineering possibly, and a public relations campaign. It's nonsense to suggest that the chief executive and senior director of BA was not aware of it.

Marshall certainly didn't want to go into the witness box, he couldn't have stood up to cross-examination. It's very convenient to have said it was some wild man going off doing things without instructions, which wasn't true.

What I did was what is normally done in the course of the sort of trade in which I'm employed, and British Airways' attempt to put me at the centre of this affair was a pretty rotten thing to do.

Basham is contemptuous of BA's claims that there was no 'concerted campaign' against Virgin:

I think that tens of thousands of pounds of lawyers' fees were spent on that word 'concerted'. British Airways sheltered behind it. It's a weasel word and counts for nothing. The fact is there was a campaign. It was orchestrated from the very top of British Airways and . . . the people who ordered the campaign are now running British Airways.

BA declined an invitation to put up an interviewee to answer either Brian Basham's or Richard Branson's charges. BA was also unwilling to answer charges made in *World in Action* that it had employed Kroll to probe Air Europe and Harry Goodman in 1987–8. When confronted with the invoice that his Broad Street company sent British Airways for the Kroll investigation, Basham admitted that BA did use Kroll to probe Air Europe. Sir Colin Marshall and David Burnside had both signed the invoice to authorise payment but neither would elaborate on why BA was using the American-based private detective agency. At BA's final-results press conference in May, shortly after *World in Action* was transmitted, Marshall said publicly that he knew nothing of the Kroll report for which he had paid £17,500.

In fact, Kroll's task for BA was at least partly to establish the foreign shareholdings of the airline's parent company, the International Leisure Group, in an apparent bid to establish whether BA could challenge Air Europe's status as a British carrier. The report established that 53% of the voting shares were controlled by a Hong Kong-based company. Harry Goodman himself does not believe that this was Kroll's only task.

'Why pay all that money to find out something BA's own people could have done themselves by going to Companies' House?'

Goodman suspects that the 'hostile and discreditable' press stories which he suffered, and which BA admitted planting in the press about Branson, could have sprung from the Kroll probe. What is certain is that the Gatwick Helpliners, and the BA sales and marketing department, accessed Air Europe's computers, as the statements of Sadig Khalifa and Peter Fleming make clear. Richard Branson is in no doubt that BA undermined Air Europe:

'I'm absolutely certain that a contributing factor in Air Europe's demise was the accessing of computer information.'

Further details of BA's campaign against Air Europe emerged in a subsequent investigation Michael Chrisman and I undertook for the *Guardian*. In the wake of the Virgin libel case former BA and Air Europe employees spoke for the first time about BA's campaign to destabilise its smaller rival, and we established remarkable similarities between BA's campaign against Virgin and its campaign against Air Europe. One former BA departmental chief told us that Michael Levin had been working on Air Europe as well as Virgin in the late 1980s: 'Levin asked me what I knew about Goodman. When I started to reply with an analysis of Air Europe's operation, Levin told me he wasn't interested in that. He wanted to know what the dirt was on Goodman. I had at least two of these sessions with Levin.'

Witnesses to the rumour campaign against Air Europe that Peter Smith and Harry Goodman had become so concerned about in 1989 spoke for the first time. Their evidence was supported by affidavits that they had signed at the time detailing how they had traced the damaging gossip back to BA. In subsequent interviews, the former Air Europe employees confirmed that they thought the exposure of BA's campaign against Virgin revealed striking parallels with their own experiences. As well as accessing Air Europe's computer information, BA had used private detectives to probe the airline and Harry Goodman. Using Brian Basham's Broad Street company to launder the Kroll payment gave BA the 'plausible deniability' that it sought, and exercised, in the Virgin affair by contracting out Operation Barbara and Operation Covent Garden.

When BBC News tried to follow up on BA's dirty tricks against Air Europe on the day that Chrisman and I revealed our new evidence in the *Guardian*, the corporation ran into a fierce Lowe Bell offensive. One of the BBC's business correspondents, Peter Morgan, had to endure a tirade of abuse from Terry Collis, the managing director of Lowe Bell Financial, as he compiled his report, 'Without doubt the most hostile verbal assault of my career,' Morgan recalled after Collis's tirades interrupted his attempts to prepare a report for the BBC's news bulletins.

Collis is Bell's number two at Lowe Bell Financial, and the Air Europe story was evidently embarrassing for the PR men. They appeared unconcerned about representing both BA and the BBC, as an enraged Collis tried to persuade the BBC not to run the story about BA.

I had been invited to the BBC to be interviewed about my article on BA's dirty tricks against Air Europe in that morning's *Guardian*. As I waited to be interviewed, listening to Collis screaming at Morgan on the phone, I was fascinated to witness one of the BBC's own reporters, transport correspondent, Christopher Wain, also attempting to undermine our report. At the time Wain was working in BBC radio, and he spoke to Morgan on the phone from Broadcasting House to tell him that the Kroll invoice might have been a forgery. He suggested that the words 'Kroll research into ILG' might have been added to the receipt after Marshall had signed it. It was a baffling performance by Wain. He declined to cover the Air Europe story for BBC radio, and opted not to talk to me directly about the sources of my story. The document had appeared on *World in Action* two weeks earlier, and in the *Guardian* that morning. Unbeknown to Wain, BA had confirmed that the document was authentic.

Despite the pressures from Wain, and a BBC lawyer who was initially concerned by Wain's reservations about the Kroll invoice, Morgan broadcast the story on the *Six O'Clock News*. His report included a call from John Prescott, who was then the Labour Party's transport spokesman, for the 'conspiracy of silence' between BA and the government to be broken over the allegations that BA had been undermining Virgin Atlantic and Air Europe. BA had lied to the Labour politician as well:

> I, myself, was personally assured by Sir Colin Marshall that there was no truth in Virgin's allegations and that he was not involved in any dirty-tricks campaign. The latest evidence exposes such assurances as worthless.
>
> It is left to newspapers and television programmes to inform us of the extent of the anti-competitive, immoral and illegal activities perpetrated by British Airways in the name of competition.
>
> Neither the government nor the CAA will launch an investigation, and the longer this conspiracy goes on, the more damage is done to Britain's aviation interests.

Although the government predictably failed to respond to John Prescott's broadside, the revelations galvanised Harry Goodman and his lawyers. Goodman was immediately struck by the similarities between BA's campaign and that which we had revealed to have been waged against Air Europe:

> The similarities with the Virgin case are uncanny. I knew about the smears at the time although I had no idea that Levin was on my case or, indeed, that he was Marshall's personal guru. The revelations that BA was nicking our computer information and employing private detectives are highly significant. Perhaps *I* should have sued the bastards at the time!

Goodman startled the aviation industry in the spring of 1994 when he started legal proceedings against BA. A slim-line, alcohol-free, sun-tanned Goodman told a packed press conference in the City of London that he would sue BA alleging 'conspiracy to injure', 'wrongful interference' with his business, 'malicious falsehood' and 'a breach of Article 86 of the Treaty of Rome 1960', which is designed to prevent anti-competitive abuse in the European Community. Goodman's writ listed a cast of characters that was almost identical to those who ran the dirty-tricks campaign against Virgin Atlantic: Lord King, Sir Colin Marshall, Robert Ayling, Kevin Hatton, the 'Reverend' Jim Callery, David Burnside, Brian Basham and Kroll Associates. Goodman's lawyer, Stuart McInnes of Pannone, Pritchard, Englefield said the central charge that Goodman would seek to prove in court was that 'the actions of the defendants in orchestrating a dirty-tricks campaign which seriously affected his business led to a climate in which its financial backers withdrew their support, resulting in the collapse of the business in March 1991. Following this some 6,000 employees of International Leisure Group lost their jobs.'

In the autumn of 1994 Goodman announced he had been granted legal aid to fund his case, but this announcement proved to be the high-point of his legal action. Goodman's lawyers subsequently found insurmountable difficulties getting access to the evidence they required to prosecute the case. McInnes and his legal team required the backing of Air Europe's creditors to gain access to such evidence. Inevitably, the creditors' committee included some companies that do important, ongoing business with British Airways, such as Rolls Royce, and the committee showed no appetite for assisting Goodman's action. It was not in their interests to assist a probe into BA's responsibility for the collapse of its largest British rival. Harry Goodman remembers an enormous box of material containing specific information about dirty tricks that could not be found when his lawyers approached Air Europe's receivers. Shortly after starting legal proceedings against BA, Goodman accepted a lucrative job which would have made him ineligible for legal aid. Thus the absence of legal aid for Goodman, and the difficulties with obtaining the necessary evidence, spelt the end of Goodman's bid to get to the bottom of BA's role in the downfall of Air Europe.

British Airways took some satisfaction from seeing the back of Harry Goodman and Air Europe, and even more from the conclusion of Virgin Atlantic's legal suit for the abuse of its computer information in the spring of 1995.

Branson had started fresh legal action in May 1993 after the 'peace' talks which started in his Holland Park home had collapsed. The talking had ended after Branson had refused to sign BA's 'gagging order' in return for £9 million. Before suing BA for a second time Branson had appealed to Sir Michael Angus to intervene on behalf of the non-executive directors, after he had despaired of striking a deal with the BA team. Branson later likened Ayling to a 'Dickensian schoolmaster' during the negotiations, one of the rare occasions that Branson has publicly resorted to personal invective against his BA opponents: 'I found his whole negotiating tactic incredibly tiring and boring and drawn out. That's how I imagine a Dickensian schoolmaster to be. Not my sort of person at all.'

Branson had written to Angus because the BA board had appointed him to head a three-man team charged with 'monitoring all actions in connection with the recent litigation involving Richard Branson and Virgin Atlantic'. The board was specifically concerned to 'avoid any similar situation arising in the future'.

When Branson had first written to Angus in December 1991, the chairman of BA's non-executives had said 'it would be inappropriate' for him to investigate the matter. He had passed the matter over to Sir Colin Marshall, Robert Ayling and Mervyn Walker with disastrous consequences for BA. Branson had hoped that Angus would now seize the last chance to impose his authority following BA's High Court humiliation.

When pressed on his own position, as Branson threatened to engage BA in a further round of potentially damaging litigation, Sir Michael Angus told him haughtily:

'. . . it is impractical for the Directors of British Airways to review "all available documentation" themselves. The board relies on reports and summaries prepared internally and by external advisers.'

In other words, Angus was prepared to rely upon reports prepared by Mervyn Walker, who had written and sanctioned the original libels against Richard Branson, and Linklaters & Paines who, with Walker, had advised the board of BA that Branson had no case against the company in February 1992.

Angus knew by the spring of 1993 that if he had received accurate legal advice when Branson first wrote to the company in 1991, King and Marshall's obsession with Richard Branson could have been brought to heel, and the non-executives would have had the opportunity to curtail the commercial dirty tricks in Ayling's marketing and operations department. 'Discovering' the dirty tricks in the course of the litigation cost BA millions of pounds, and incalculable damage to its reputation throughout the world. Branson had hoped that, on this occasion, Angus would intervene on behalf of the shareholders and bring 'independent judgement to bear' on the dispute as the Cadbury report had recommended. Branson was bitterly disappointed when Angus once again rebuffed his appeal, and announced that he was starting legal action for breach of copyright with 'sadness and regret'.

Virgin was confident that it would win the case: during the libel litigation BA staff had admitted to having improperly accessed Virgin's computer information. BA had even given an undertaking that it had built a 'Chinese wall' into the BABS computer system to ensure that unauthorised staff could not access information on Virgin in the future. Furthermore Virgin had sworn witness statements from the former Gatwick Helpliner, Sadig Khalifa, and the former marketing executive, Peter Fleming, to back up its case if the board decided to backtrack. The fact that BA had accessed Virgin's computer information was not in dispute – BA had admitted it in the agreed statement in the High Court. What was at stake was the extent of their actions and the amount of damages BA was prepared to pay in compensation. Gerrard Tyrrell had warned Branson that, for breach of copyright, damages would be very limited.

At a very early stage in the litigation, in early 1994, BA made a payment into court of £265,000. Such a move is a familiar legal tactic; it challenged Virgin to attempt to get higher damages in court. If the trial took place and the judge awarded Virgin lower damages, then Virgin would be liable to pay the costs of the trial for both sides. Inevitably this would amount to far more than BA had paid into court.

Branson recalls that Gerrard Tyrrell advised settlement, on the grounds that Virgin was most unlikely to get substantially more from the British courts:

> BA admitted that they had done what we were alleging that they had done, they had paid money into court, and on that day we decided that we would not get any more money than the amount they had paid into court and we decided to accept the money.

Branson did not, however, accept his lawyers' advice and settle with BA because he was determined to see Marshall, Ayling and their key managers in court to answer for themselves in the most public forum of all. Branson had just started major legal proceedings against BA in the USA under the USA's fierce anti-trust (anti-monopoly) legislation. When BA paid into court in Britain, Virgin's case was before the Federal court in New York but the judge had still to decide if the court had jurisdiction over the matters raised by Virgin. Branson recalls the dilemma:

> We were told that if we took BA's money out of court in Britain, and then we weren't allowed to pursue the American case, we wouldn't be able to get them into court. So just to make sure that these people did see their day in court, we decided to delay taking the money out of court until we knew whether or not the American case would be allowed to go ahead.

Branson's position came under pressure in November 1994 when the computer abuse case in Britain was set down for trial in early 1995. Furthermore, the judge decided to deal with the issues of liability and quantum at the same time; Virgin was thus required to put a figure on the amount of damage it estimated had been caused by BA's abuse of its computer information. The figure of £29 million emerged from a process which Virgin now admits was 'highly speculative'.

Two critical things then occurred: the court in America decided that Virgin's anti-trust case could be heard in the USA, at the same time as the English court made a ruling that precluded Virgin from bringing part of its case. At this point Branson finally decided, despite his desire to see BA's computer hackers and their bosses in a British court, to accept a payment of £265,000 from BA plus a £100,000 contribution to Virgin's costs. Because Branson had made his decision at the very last possible minute allowed by the court, Virgin was required to pay BA's legal costs which BA initially estimated at £750,000 and which eventually turned out to be £400,000.

A furious public scrap ensued in which both sides claimed victory – Branson on the grounds that BA had admitted to underhand, dirty tricks against his airline, BA on the basis that Virgin was ultimately having to pay the greater proportion of the costs, and that the settlement payment of £265,000 bore no relation to the £29 million Virgin was at one stage claiming.

For once BA's PR operation triumphed over Branson and Whitehorn. Lowe Bell phoned news desks very late in the afternoon to alert them to a breaking story in the court case, but did not tell them what it would be. Just before seven o'clock, news desks were sent a BA press release portraying the settlement as a victory for BA, on the basis that BA was claiming that Virgin was having to pay greater costs than it was.

BA had caught Virgin cold. Branson had authorised the settlement, but he and Whitehorn were at 36,000 feet somewhere over the Atlantic returning from Atlanta when Lowe Bell broke the news. As a result newspapers were, unusually, obliged to report that there was 'no immediate comment' from Virgin, while Ayling was given space to revel in the outcome. The *Financial Times* carried the following comments from BA's managing director:

> I am pleased it has been resolved. We offered to pay a modest sum to Virgin in 1993 or to go to arbitration . . . We have always said these claims are worth very little and this result proves it.

With no balancing comments from Virgin, Branson and Whitehorn read the headlines with dismay as they landed in London. Ayling was widely quoted claiming credit for 'putting in place a less confrontational relationship between the two airlines'. Most infuriatingly of all, from Branson's point of view, was Ayling's claim that the settlement 'closes the so-called "dirty tricks" file'. Branson reflects:

> We handled the end of the computer case very badly indeed – it was a cock-up. We allowed them to dictate the terms of the press release; we should have had our press release ready but we were actually partying in Atlanta with Delta Airlines!

The computer misuse case represented a rare example of Virgin snatching defeat from the jaws of victory in its battles with BA and, due to an equally rare lack of coordination between Virgin's legal and PR wings, an unusual triumph in the press for Lowe Bell. It was caused because Branson was torn between a burning desire to see BA answer for its misdeeds in a British court and the advice of his lawyers to settle. He was prepared to pay for the privilege of seeing Marshall, Ayling *et al* roasted in court – a pleasure that the libel trial settlement had denied him – but his late decision to heed his lawyers' advice meant that Virgin paid more than BA in costs and that BA escaped the ordeal of the witness box.

And there was a greater price to pay than a solely financial one. Will Whitehorn worked furiously hard to turn the coverage of the case round as soon as he returned from Atlanta, and he achieved some success in undermining the impression given by Lowe Bell that the dirty-tricks dispute between the two airlines had ended in a victory for BA. However, the genie had escaped. It was not surprising that *BA News* carried the headline 'Virgin climbdown in dirty tricks', with a series of quotes from a very smug Ayling drawn from the Lowe Bell press release. It was, however, worrying for Virgin to read headlines such as 'BA says settlement closes dirty tricks file' in the *Financial Times*, which also quoted the largely unexpurgated Lowe Bell press release at great length. Such coverage led many in the airline industry to believe that there was no substance to Branson's further claims against BA. Sir Michael Bishop, the chairman of Britain's other main independent airline,

British Midland, was one who felt that the computer case damaged the credibility of Branson's other claims against BA.

Despite BA's PR victory in the computer misuse case, the most important legal chapter in the dispute between the two airlines sparked by BA's dirty-tricks campaign had yet to start. The computer misuse case illustrated to Branson that British law is not capable of dealing with the competition issues at stake raised by BA's dirty-tricks campaign. It could be that the European Commission will eventually decide to investigate the complaint that Virgin lodged with it in 1993, but by the middle of 1996 nothing had officially been heard of its deliberations. As a senior Virgin legal source put it, 'They keep on saying they are going to do something but they haven't said what, and they certainly haven't done anything yet!'

In this context, it is unsurprising that Branson is pinning his hopes on gaining legal redress in the USA under anti-trust laws. Writing in the wake of the 1993 libel trial, the *Financial Times* contemplated the prospects of Virgin bringing such action against BA in the USA. Not a paper renowned for hyperbole, the *FT* predicted that it would be the international airline industry's equivalent of 'World War Three'.

15

'World War Three'

'I call the case of Virgin Atlantic versus British Airways,' declared Judge Miriam Cedarbaum in New York in April 1994. In fact, Cedarbaum was convening her court to consider a motion from British Airways to dismiss Branson's $325 million anti-trust suit. BA left its appeal to its lawyers; no one from the airline attended court, but Branson turned up with some of his most senior lieutenants.

British Airways' lawyers, led by Sullivan & Cromwell's John Dickey, had stood in line behind the Virgin delegation and hundreds of New Yorkers queueing to hear proceedings in the Federal District courts. A grey-suited, tie-less Virgin chairman waited in the fresh spring sunshine with the new head of his airline's legal department, Frances Farrow, the director of his American operation, David Tait, and his American press chief, Lori Levin.

In the autumn of 1993, Virgin Atlantic had filed its massive anti-trust suit against BA. Virgin claimed $325 million in damages from BA on the grounds that BA is continuing to abuse its monopoly power in the marketplace, and that the airline had used this power to try and destroy Virgin Atlantic with a series of dirty tricks.

British Airways had announced it was moving to have Virgin's complaint struck out as soon as the suit was filed. BA's defence begins, 'This a quintessentially English dispute, misguidedly brought before this United States District Court.' At Judge Cedarbaum's invitation, John Dickey rose to put BA's case. A grizzled, middle-aged man with short grey stubble covering his chin and his scalp in roughly equal proportions, Dickey is a tubby and persuasive advocate. In a twenty-minute address, Dickey opened BA's case by claiming that the case should not properly be tried in the USA.

Dickey pointed out alleged inconsistencies in Virgin's arguments but avoided referring to BA's High Court admissions of 'disreputable business activities', or responding to any of the other substantive points made in Virgin's suit. He argued that it was structurally impossible to achieve the monopoly of which Virgin was complaining in such a highly regulated industry. Governments fix the ground rules, he argued, and thus BA could not have breached the anti-trust laws. He referred the judge to the Bermuda 2 agreement governing flights between the USA and Britain which was in the process of being revised in inter-governmental talks. When Cedarbaum questioned Dickey about how prices were controlled under such agreements, he had to confess that he did not know.

Cedarbaum is a striking, middle-aged woman who exercised calm, firm control of her court. Her side-parted, shoulder-length, black and grey hair was swept behind her ears and she wore red lipstick. She sucked her glasses as Dickey referred her to Virgin's case against BA in Britain concerning computer abuse which was then pending. 'This is how such cases should be decided,' he argued, 'They should not be brought here'. Dickey continued by claiming that the accessing of computer information does not represent a breach of anti-trust law. Cedarbaum smiled as she asked Dickey, 'Is that not predatory behaviour?' On another occasion she interrupted and told Dickey to concentrate on Virgin's allegation that BA was attempting to monopolise the market. 'Focus on that,' she told the podgy attorney.

An air of unreality prevailed as some of America's most expensive lawyers performed the opening scene in a courtroom drama which could see Britain's two best-known airlines slugging it out in court until the end of the twentieth century. In the public gallery sat legal assistants, clerks and members of the press, who were anxiously glancing at their pagers for messages from their news desks confirming the expected death of a former President. Richard Nixon's dirty tricks in the Watergate building against his Democratic opponents twenty years earlier had led to his downfall, and now 'Tricky Dicky' lay on his deathbed.

Branson sat amongst the ranks of lawyers and press as they watched Judge Cedarbaum preside over several minor cases before she called BA's motion to dismiss Virgin's anti-trust case. In one case a defendant emerged from the cells to try and dismiss his lawyer. The man was handcuffed to a policeman, and his head was shaved to leave only a Mohican-style tuft. Branson turned to his colleagues and whispered loudly, 'I wasn't expecting Colin Marshall to turn up today!'

The stakes for BA are extremely high. The Conservative government remains committed to the success of British Airways, but it is difficult to imagine Prime Minister Major campaigning on BA's behalf against the anti-trust suit in the way that Margaret Thatcher did on behalf of Lord King in her desperation to see BA privatised. If BA fails to halt Virgin's action before it comes to court, the whole of the competitive terrain on which British Airways does battle with its tiny British rival will be examined in the most minute detail in the American courts. When it was first served, Robert Ayling had described Virgin's suit as 'a fifty-page litany of old grievances' about aviation policy regulation. Ayling is right in the sense that Virgin's complaints go to the heart of the competitive relationship between British Airways' inheritance and Virgin's challenge. The anti-trust case will place the issues of privatisation, competition and consumer choice under the microscope for years in a country which sees competition as a cornerstone of its belief in economic liberalism.

At the heart of Branson's anti-trust suit is the claim that Virgin is 'being denied the opportunity to compete against BA on the merits of their competing flight services on a route by route basis, and customers are being denied the opportunity to choose freely which competing airline passenger service to purchase.' Citing BA's conspiracy against Laker Airways as a precedent, Virgin's suit alleges that:

as a . . . result of the conduct of defendant BA, the public at
large has been and will continue to be injured, in that defendant BA has deprived consumers of the opportunity to
purchase the best possible transatlantic flight service at the
lowest possible prices established by supply and demand in
a freely competitive market.

As he rose to fire Virgin's opening salvo, Chuck Koob started by
defining very precisely the market that his client claimed BA was
trying to monopolise. Whereas Dickey had taken a broad, wide-
angled perspective, the slim, youthful-looking Koob tried to
persuade Cedarbaum that a tightly focused view of the issues
between the two airlines was more appropriate. Koob spoke of the
transatlantic market being defined in terms of 'City pairs' – a limited number of routes from London to New York, Miami, Los
Angeles, and Orlando on which BA and Virgin compete. He said
that Virgin would focus on BA's marketing activities and its
attempt to leverage its monopoly.

'So your claim is against BA's activities against British competition?' asked Cedarbaum.

'Precisely,' responded Koob. He claimed that BA enjoyed a 52%
share of the Heathrow to New York market. He emphasised that
BA's dirty-tricks campaign against Virgin provided evidence of
motivation: 'We are very conscious of BA's intent to do Virgin in'.
He stressed, however, that Virgin's anti-trust case did not depend
solely upon the exposure of BA's dirty tricks.

Branson's suit includes allegations that BA is operating corporate travel deals designed to exclude Virgin from competing and
special commissions to travel agents. Freddie Laker described this
ploy to Branson as 'the discount over-ride trick'. The suit alleges
that BA is using its 'grandfather rights' at Heathrow to exclude
Virgin from flying on routes it wants to fly on. Because BA was the
only long-haul international British airline permitted to operate
from Heathrow when it was nationalised, it retained its 'grandfather rights' to its take-off and landing slots when it was privatised.
Branson alleges that BA is abusing these 'grandfather rights' to
block Virgin. For example, in 1991 BA cancelled its service to
Ireland and used over 5,000 slots that were thus liberated at

Heathrow to increase its flights to Newark and Los Angeles – Virgin destinations – and to San Francisco, Chicago and Washington – routes that Virgin had won licences to fly on, but was still waiting for slots to be able to start services.

Chuck Koob will highlight what he describes as the 'structural part' of BA's conduct:

> We are talking about the corporate deals, the deals with travel agents, the way that British Airways unfairly uses its route structure, its dominance and its position at Heathrow to gather to itself a significant share of corporate customers and travel agent business. These are shares that they would not in our view otherwise have if we were competing on a route by route basis. Richard Branson has demonstrated that he can knock the socks off BA in route by route competition, and all we are trying to do is to establish a level playing field where we can compete on a route by route basis, where we're not competing with a route system that was given to British Airways by the British government.

Koob believes that Robert Ayling is wrong to claim that the anti-trust case has nothing to do with the dirty-tricks campaign:

> It is clear that Judge Cedarbaum dismissed several of our causes of action which were based on the dirty tricks, but she also noted in her judgment that the same conduct forms an integral part of our anti-trust case, and it does.
>
> We intend to pursue the dirty-tricks aspect of this case because it shows a pattern of intent. When you are claiming an abusive monopoly, intent is a very important part of the case, and we think the dirty-tricks campaign orchestrated by BA is conclusive evidence of an intent, of a focused, concentrated attack on Virgin, and we think that evidence is very, very relevant to the question of proving intent which we have taken on the burden of proving in our anti-trust case.
>
> So while we're not going to recover under the common law for those dirty tricks, they remain part of the anti-trust case and the judge has already found that.

Branson feels that he has been forced to seek redress under US anti-trust laws because British law does not protect competition adequately. Even after BA's admission of anti-competitive activities in the High Court, the government showed no inclination to take up Branson's frequently repeated calls for a strong regulator to protect competition in the airline industry. Branson argues that such a post should at least be on a par with watchdogs in other privatised industries such as telecommunications (Oftel), gas (Ofgas) and water (Ofwat).

> The real issues are the lack of take-off and landing slots at Heathrow that are stopping us running new services to North America, Africa, Singapore and Australia.
>   Laker, British Caledonian, Air Europe and Dan Air did not fail because they were inefficient. They all had lower costs than BA and charged lower fares. They failed because British competition policy failed them.

Branson's determination to heed Sir Freddie Laker's advice and continue 'suing the bastards' symbolises the change in Virgin Atlantic's chairman, the reluctant litigant of early 1992. BA's dirty-tricks campaign has transformed the misty-eyed Corinthian who had launched his 'fun' airline on an unsuspecting airline industry in 1984, into a battle-hardened veteran fighting to keep his airline flying. Branson had discovered, to his dismay, that the airline game is not only a question of how good you are, or the quality of the service you provide, but how you play the game.

Branson also knows that the net result of British 'competition policy' in the aviation industry is that, with the exception of Virgin Atlantic, most airlines that attempted to compete against British Airways in the 1980s were either beaten or bought. Laker Airways was brought down by a combination of predatory international carriers and Mrs Thatcher's determination to privatise BA. Laker's fate was particularly ironic given the high esteem in which Mrs Thatcher held the Kentish entrepreneur.

Sir Freddie Laker had appeared to epitomise the enterprise culture that Thatcher was so keen to nurture in Britain. To warm applause at the Conservative Party conference in 1981, she hailed the 'spur of competition' that Laker had provided to the state-owned British Airways.

'It's thanks to Freddie Laker that you can cross the Atlantic for so much less than you could in the 1970s. Competition works!'

As she spoke, her transport minister, Iain Sproat, was authorising BA's predatory fare cuts that were to kill Laker Airways, substantially reduce competition in the airline industry, and thus prepare the way for BA's privatisation. Immediately after Laker went down, three months after the cartel's fare cuts, Sproat appealed to the chief executive of Lonrho, Tiny Rowland. 'You must help me! You must help Freddie!' Sproat implored Rowland as the airborne symbol of Thatcher's enterprise culture crashed to earth. Sproat urged Rowland to put up the money to bail Laker Airways out after Sir Freddie had been forced to call the receiver in. 'I have Freddie Laker's blood on my hands,' Sproat told Rowland.

In fact, Laker's demise served both BA and the Conservative government very well. Although BA's privatisation was substantially delayed by the legal action taken by Laker's liquidators in the USA, the millions raised by the sale were used by the Chancellor, Nigel Lawson, to finance tax cuts before the 1987 general election.

Five years after Laker's demise Lord King paid substantially over the odds to swallow British Caledonian, which was the second largest domestic carrier. Air Europe then briefly became Britain's second largest carrier before a combination of BA's dirty tricks and the impact of the recession and the Gulf War forced it out of business in 1991, months after Mrs Thatcher herself had been ousted from Downing Street. A similar fate awaited Dan Air in 1992, after it, too, had become Britain's second largest carrier.

Branson survived BA's onslaught at least in part because of the strength of the other companies in the Virgin Group. When Brian Basham wrote his report on Virgin and Branson for Sir Colin Marshall, he observed that the rate of Branson's business activity at that time would 'make ICI's hair stand on end'. Having defeated BA's attempt to ground his airline, Branson started expanding and diversifying the Virgin Group at a frenetic pace even by the standards that had impressed Basham.

The emphasis of Virgin's development in the years that followed its dirty-tricks libel victory was on Virgin Atlantic and the group's transport interests; Virgin was part of the eight-company consortium, London and Continental, that won the Channel Tunnel rail link; in the summer of 1996 Branson was offering return fares to Paris and Brussels for less than £50, as the first part of a strategy to build up the number of passengers using Eurostar to 30 million by the turn of the century.

Branson continued to profit from rocking and rolling as well as flying. Shortly after the libel case, Virgin 1215 became Britain's first national commercial rock music station, later becoming Virgin FM. Branson is currently considering whether to float the radio station on the Stock Market, grappling with his own reservations about taking the company public: 'I'm not very keen on public life in company terms, but there are those at the radio station who are asking me to do it.'

Virgin Retail became the largest record retailer in Britain when it bought the Our Price chain of record stores in the UK and Ireland. Although he has sold Virgin Music, Branson remains the unpaid chairman of Virgin Music and he started another independent music company – V2 – as soon as he was able to:

> We had an agreement with Thorn EMI that I should not return to the music business. That lasted three years and, now it's over, I'm going straight back into it. We're currently plotting and planning our re-entry and I hope the first releases will be at the beginning of 1997.
>
> We will be breaking new bands, and if there are big names to be signed, you can be sure that we will be trying to sign them.

Virgin still owns the highly profitable worldwide Virgin Megastore chain and, in 1994, Virgin Megastores (Hong Kong) was established to develop the 'megastore home entertainment concept' with Wheelock Pacific in Hong Kong, Taiwan and the People's Republic of China. In Korea, Virgin teamed up with Saehan Media in a 50/50 joint venture called Virgin Megastores (Korea).

Virgin also targeted other areas of the leisure market in 1994; Virgin Games was renamed Virgin Interactive Entertainment plc. Before the year was over, Hasbro Inc., the world's largest toymaker, acquired a 15% stake and Blockbuster Entertainment bought 20%; both companies thus became strategic minority shareholders.

The Virgin Hotels Group was formed and it acquired a string of prestigious hotels, as well as London's County Hall which it has promised to develop into the British capital's 'premier family hotel and leisure complex'. Once again this project will be a joint venture, on this occasion with the Japanese company Shirayama Shokusan.

Virgin, in alliance with the US investment fund, TPG Partners, acquired Britain's largest cinema operator, MGM cinemas, and announced ambitious plans to expand the chain over the ensuing five years. Virgin Television Mexico City opened, and Rushes in London and 525 in Los Angeles opened post-production services.

Branson also sought to exploit the growing strength of the Virgin brand name in new areas never before associated with Virgin: Virgin Vodka heralded Branson's first venture into the alcoholic drinks market, and Virgin Cola his first venture into the international soft drinks market. For the first time Branson was moving Virgin away from service-related industries and into products. However, he insists that his business philosophy remains consistent:

> We are known for taking on the large conglomerates who are overcharging the consumer and we are trying to give them a run for their money. We are not simply selling the products on the Virgin brand name. Our new projects are joint ventures, with Virgin putting in at least 50% of the money.
>
> Take Coca Cola. It's unbelievable when you think that they are the richest company in the world, the best-known brand name in the world with one of the biggest turnovers of any company in the world, and yet they've only got one competitor (Pepsi) and they've managed to keep it that way for a hundred years. We're already coming across very similar business practices that we have had to contend with with

British Airways and we are considering whether to take
them to court in Europe . . .

In March 1995 Virgin Direct Personal Financial Services was
launched as a joint venture with the Norwich Union. As with so
many of Virgin's diversifications after the libel trial, this move
had the Branson image stamped all over it. Adverts in the national
press feature Branson asking, 'People ask us: "Why are you getting
into life insurance? It's a dreary, discredited business." And we
say: "Yup, that's why."' In the accompanying photograph,
Branson is pictured in the charateristic pose that annoyed Lord
King so much in the late 1980s: still grinning and still in a pullover.

Branson is particularly proud of the impact that Virgin has had
in the financial service industry in a very short space of time:

> It's been a fascinating year and a half. Billions of pounds, and
> I mean billions, have switched from the City to the con-
> sumer, since Virgin started competing. Prices have come
> right down, and all sorts of ways that the existing market
> was ripping off the consumer have disappeared.

Ironically, BA's ham-fisted attempts to destroy Branson's reputation only served to enhance it, and Branson regularly rates highly
in an wide range of opinion polls. In 1994, NOP conducted a poll
for *PR Week* magazine which found that Branson's high profile
boosted sales of Virgin's products and services. Of those interviewed, 34% said that their personal opinion of Branson made
them more likely to buy Virgin products, and only 2% were put off
by his image. *PR Week* described the finding as 'astonishing'.

Many of the ideas for expanding the Virgin Group have come
from Branson's 'new projects teams' which develop ideas in his
Holland Park house. The teams work on their ideas for a maximum of three months before Branson decides whether to proceed.

Virgin Atlantic, however, remains very much Branson's project. He confirmed in 1996 that he is more committed to the
airline's survival and prosperity than anything else in the vast
Virgin empire when he announced that he intends to pump £3 billion into Virgin Atlantic. This will expand the size of the Virgin

fleet from sixteen to forty planes, in a worldwide operation that will be based at Gatwick; Branson has been denied the slots he needs to base his expansion at Heathrow. A proud Branson declared:

> This will make us the fourth largest long-haul airline in the world after British Airways, Singapore Airlines and Cathay Pacific. We shall fund the expansion from our own internal resources . . . Taking on BA has become the inevitable next step. BA is worth about £4 billion on the Stock Market: we intend to overtake it.

This vast investment in the airline marks the most important shift in the airline's strategy since it was founded. For years Branson had expounded his 'small is beautiful' philosophy, and insisted that he had no intention to restrict Virgin's growth to his original goal of flying on the twelve most profitable routes in the world. A speech to the Athens chamber of commerce in 1993 was typical: 'The humble ant survived but the dinosaur is long extinct . . . small is beautiful.' At that time he was trying simply to survive in the airline business; the entire Virgin group was reeling from the impact of BA's dirty-tricks campaign. When a Greek businessman asked him to give his personal advice on how to become a millionaire, Branson replied ruefully: 'Become a billionaire and then start up a small airline!'

Since the failure of BA's dirty-tricks campaign the fortunes of the airline have undergone a dramatic up-turn which saw Virgin Atlantic declare 1995 pre-tax profits of £35.5 million for the ten months ending 31 August 1995. Branson confidently predicts profits of '£80/90 million' for 1996.

A number of factors have helped Virgin Atlantic to recover so spectacularly, in addition to the exposure of BA's attempts to put the company out of business. The airline industry has recovered from the world-wide slump of the early 1990s and the crises that the Gulf War represented. Virgin has now got ten A340s, and will shortly have six Boeing 747-400s, making the Virgin fleet the most modern and thus the most efficient in the world – a far cry from the small collection of second-hand jumbos that so annoyed Lord

King when Virgin Atlantic started. Branson is now reaping the benefits of being prepared to gamble in the depths of the recession. He tells an extraordinary story of how he ended up buying his new fleet because he wanted to make sure all Virgin passengers had seat-back videos:

> It was just when BA was starting its dirty-tricks campaign. I wanted to get seat-back videos on all economy-class seats well before any of the other airlines. The cost of this was about $18 million so I said, 'Okay, fine, let's buy them.' Steve Ridgeway, our director of customer services, came to me and said, 'Richard, we can't get credit for the $18 million, so we can't go ahead.' Confidence in the airline was very low because of all the lies BA were telling about us at the time, and because of the press campaign against us. So I phoned up Phil Condit, the chairman of Boeing, and I said, 'If we buy brand-new 747-400s from you, will you include a seat-back video in the price?' and he said, 'Of course, no problem, Richard.' Then I phoned up Jean Pierson from Airbus, and I said, 'Look, if we buy a brand-new Airbus A340 from you, will you include seat-back videos in the price?' and Jean said, 'No problem, Richard.' So we ended up ordering $5 billion worth of equipment to get $18 million worth of seat-back videos! But, of course, because that was in the depths of the recession, we got the planes for fantastic prices.

Another reason for Branson's confidence in the airline by the mid-1990s was Virgin Atlantic's highly successful 'code-sharing' deal with Delta Airlines, the biggest airline in the world. The vast American carrier, which carries nearly 90 million passengers to over 200 destinations in 563 planes, announced a formal link-up with Virgin in 1994. At the time Branson's airline was carrying approximately 1.5 million passengers to 11 destinations in 12 planes.

The 'code-sharing' arrangement means that a passenger in Britain can buy a ticket to any of the destinations that Delta flies to in the USA from Virgin, and can then automatically transfer to a Delta flight after the Virgin transatlantic flight: the passenger's ticket has a joint Virgin/Delta code. The deal enormously enhances Virgin Atlantic's appeal, as British airlines are not allowed to fly within the States. The deal also allows for a 'blocked space' arrangement between the two partners: every year Delta purchases a third of the total number of seats on Virgin transatlantic seats and then prices, sells and markets them independently. Thus Delta in America can advertise flights to Heathrow for the first time, and Virgin is secure in the knowledge that a third of all its seats are sold before the start of each financial year.

The ground-breaking agreement was hailed widely on both sides of the Atlantic. The *Financial Times* welcomed the agreement as an 'imaginative commercial solution to a regulatory problem'. After approval from the British and American governments, the Delta/Virgin code-share deal came into operation in April 1995 with festivities in New York and Atlanta. Delta's chairman, Ronald W. Allen, hailed the agreement as 'pro-competitive, pro-consumer and fully in the interests of the travelling public'. Branson said that the agreement marked an important milestone in Virgin's history, and that 'it will enable us to remain independent and competitive in the face of an increasing number of global alliances'. In a full year of the Delta/Virgin alliance, Branson reckons that the deal would generate £25 to £30 million 'on the bottom line' from an extra 300,000 passengers.

Virgin successfully launched a series of new routes in the wake of its High Court triumph. In 1993 a holiday route to Greece was launched in association with South East European Airways of Greece, and the Virgin City Jet service between Dublin and London City Airport was also started. In 1995 the airline launched what it described as a 'unique partnership' agreement with Malaysian Airlines, to launch a double daily scheduled service from Heathrow to Kuala Lumpur with an onward connection to Australia. Transatlantic expansion continued with new services to San Francisco (1995) and Washington (1996) and, to the East, Virgin launched a daily service to Hong Kong (1994).

The inaugural flight to Hong Kong was particularly poignant, as Branson invited Sir Freddie Laker and his wife Jackie to be his guests of honour. Scores of journalists joined the Lakers and three generations of the Branson family, including his ninety-six-year-old grandmother, on the flight. The guests were flown to the Far East on one of Virgin Atlantic's new fleet of A340 planes; the sixteen-channel interactive seat-back videos had been installed for each passenger as Jean Pierson had promised they would be, and guests were invited to sample Virgin's new in-flight gambling service.

In his speech at the inaugural ceremony in Hong Kong, attended by Governor Chris Patten, Branson hailed Laker in front of thousands of guests. Branson repeated his belief that 'it's much easier to follow a pioneer than to be a pioneer', and Laker nodded in acknowledgement as he received a warm round of applause.

Later, bobbing around in a junk in Hong Kong harbour for the benefit of the BBC's *Forty Minutes* camera, Branson told Laker that his legal battles with BA and the British government in the States in the 1980s had helped the credibility of Virgin's dirty-tricks claims in the 1990s: 'I think we've been helped by your experience. I think people wouldn't have believed you whereas they'll believe us because of what happened to you. So, in a strange sort of way, you've actually helped us.'

'It's a pity my case didn't go to trial,' replied Laker, 'because I'm sure I would have won, and they obviously thought so too or they wouldn't have settled out of court.'

Laker insisted that he has got over his anger at the role played by BA and the government in driving him out of business in 1982: 'Life is too short to be bitter about taking a hiding in business.' He does, however, express surprise at the revolving doors that linked government and commerce in Thatcher's Britain. Laker had met Robert Ayling at a travel awards ceremony in London in 1993. He remembered him well from the marathon anti-trust litigation ten years earlier but they had subsequently not been in touch. Although Ayling's job had been to advise the cabinet on how to torpedo Laker's anti-trust case, Sir Freddie retained fond memories of the personable civil servant. Laker had heard that Ayling had gone on to mastermind the legislation enabling the government to privatise BA.

'I said, "Nice to see you, Robert, what are you doing now?" He told me he was now the group managing director of British Airways. I couldn't believe it!' exclaimed Laker, 'I thought he was the civil servant in charge of privatising the bloody airline! I don't think that sort of thing would be allowed in the States!'

The final meeting of the creditors of Laker's Skytrain eventually took place in November 1995. Only two creditors were present as Touche Ross's Christopher Morris finally wound up a project that had taken thirteen years to complete. Within a week of the end of the liquidation proceedings, Sir Freddie announced that Laker Airways would once again fly the Atlantic. Laker Airways (Bahamas) had been running profitably with just three planes for several years, flying holiday-makers and gamblers to the Caribbean from the south of the USA, but the final settlement of the Skytrain liquidation proceedings meant that Laker could fly the Atlantic once again. Laker's combative PR style was very much in evidence as he launched his new services.

'What happened to me in 1982 could never happen again,' he told the press. 'If anyone thinks they're doing it for a second time, they have another think coming!'

The likelihood of BA or any of the large airlines picking on Laker Airways' holiday flights is, however, remote. Sir Freddie's new airline is based in America and has just three DC10 planes. It will offer 75,000 seats per year as part of a three-year contract with Transatlantic Vacations. Laker Vacations is offering 20,000 US holidays. The veteran pioneer savoured the symbolic and emotional significance of Laker Airways' return to the transatlantic routes fourteen years after British Airways thought it had seen the last of him: 'I don't know what Lord King is doing now. I suspect if he's playing golf he's taking air shots!'

If Laker's marketing pitch – 'a club-class service at economy prices' – has a familiar ring to Virgin Atlantic, then so do his routes to Orlando from Gatwick and Manchester: by the summer of 1996 Virgin Atlantic was also flying to Orlando from Manchester as well as Gatwick.

'We'll compete hard during the day and have a drink in the evenings. That's how it should be!' said Branson, welcoming the competition from his hero's new airline and apparently unperturbed that Laker Airways was undercutting Virgin Atlantic by £50 on a return flight from Gatwick to Orlando in the summer of 1996.

The two entrepreneurs can still be heard singing each others praises in print and on the air whenever the opportunity arises. Laker has asked Branson if he can christen one of his planes 'The Spirit of Richard Branson', to reciprocate Branson's decision to name a Virgin plane 'The Spirit of Sir Freddie'.

Laker's ambitions now stretch no further than establishing his airline in the transatlantic holiday niche of the market. Eventually he wants to hand over a thriving airline to his son, Freddie Jnr, who came of age in 1996. Branson, however, has continued to move out of the niche in the market that led David Burnside and the BA press operation to brand him a 'cherry picker' – flying only on the high volume, high profit, 'gravy plane' routes. Virgin is now, quite literally, taking on the world.

The scope of Branson's flying ambitions has changed dramatically, but he insists that his approach remains the same:

> We have identified many long-distance routes where the established airlines are keeping fares artificially high and standards too low. We intend to shake them up. But we will do it in the Virgin style. I remember the tremendous camaraderie of the initial two hundred people who set up Virgin, who knew each other well, their weaknesses and their strengths. That will be my management model – breaking down the airline into smaller teams.

Branson will break the airline down into its constituent parts, establishing Virgin Africa and Virgin Pacific, in addition to Virgin Atlantic and the recently founded European airline, Virgin Express: 'We bought a little airline called European Belgian Airlines, a good, profitable airline. We are using it to get our European operation started – it's now called Virgin Express.'

EBA had very quickly made a profit after it was founded in 1994 on Laker principles; it offered no-frills, half-price scheduled flights to Rome, Vienna and Barcelona. After Madrid and Milan were added to its route network, it declared a profit of £4.5 million in 1995. Now Virgin Express, it currently has twelve Boeing 737s, and Branson says he will expand it to eighteen or twenty planes. One of the first new Virgin Express routes linked Rome with

Madrid at prices which Branson claimed were 50% less than the lowest fares available on other carriers:

> I have long wanted to attack artificially inflated European air fares, and as soon as we started our routes, our competitors were forced to bring their fares down by over 50%. We've definitely got the majors rattled, and some of them have approached us to find out if there is a way of working together. We will see.

Outside Europe, Virgin has set its sights to include Las Vegas, Beijing, Bombay, Bangkok, Moscow, Buenos Aires, Cape Town, Mexico City, Chicago, Nairobi, Abu Dhabi, Seoul, Osaka and Shanghai. Branson's 1995 deal with Malaysian Airlines has already given Virgin the ability to exploit the Far East market by expanding its route network to cover Australia and the Pacific Rim via Kuala Lumpur.

Virgin's current annual passenger load has been boosted to 2.5 million as the airline's network of routes has increased and the deal with Delta has taken effect. Branson hopes to boost this figure to 10 million by the turn of the century. British Airways currently carries 35 million passengers a year.

Branson believes that the anti-trust case against BA is crucial to Virgin Atlantic's plans to expand. At the beginning of 1995 Judge Cedarbaum announced that, having deliberated for over eight months, she had dismissed BA's motion to strike out Virgin's anti-trust case. It was crucial decision for Virgin and for Branson, who declared jubilantly, 'We are determined to go all the way with the anti-trust case and get proper recompense from BA. Hopefully the action will set a new competitive scene in British commercial aviation'.

Chuck Koob continues to insist that Virgin's anti-trust case is only partly based upon the dirty-tricks campaign. However, it is clear that had it not been for the campaign, which continues to incense Branson, there would be no Virgin anti-trust action.

Robert Ayling told the press after Cedarbaum's decision: 'Virgin did make claims for damage based on alleged "dirty tricks" but these claims have been thrown out by the US court . . .'.

Ayling can avoid detailed scrutiny of such statements in the

British press, sections of which remain pliant to his press office and to Lowe Bell, but life could be much more difficult for him once the US court case starts. Although the details of her remarks were scarcely reported in Britain, Judge Cedarbaum was very critical of BA's attempt to strike out Virgin's anti-trust case. She criticised BA's 'hyperbole', and stated that Virgin had 'easily met' the criteria required to bring the case to court. She went on to dismiss BA's arguments as 'misplaced', and accused it of deliberately 'misconstruing' Virgin's case. Cedarbaum threw out five of the eight issues on which Virgin wanted to challenge BA, but decided to hear Virgin's central charge under the Sherman Act: that BA has tried to monopolise the transatlantic passenger market through anti-competitive activities, and that it has abused its positions at Gatwick and Heathrow Airports in order to do this.

The cost of attempting to create this 'new scene' through the American courts is proving to be very considerable. Virgin has spent $3.5 million on a computer software system alone; its function is to cope with an estimated 1 million documents that BA is required to hand over during the anti-trust case. Branson calculated in the middle of 1996 that the weekly cost to both airlines of legal and associated fees could be as high as $1 million per week. Branson hopes to recover Virgin's costs if he wins the case, but for BA, as the defendant, these costs can never be recovered. BA has already paid out much more in legal fees alone than it would have cost the airline to pay Branson the £13.1 million he was asking for in 1993 to settle the dirty-tricks issues arising from the libel case.

From a financial perspective, simply paying these costs will not prove to be a problem for British Airways: results steadily improved in the first half of the 1990s and, in 1996, the airline once again declared record profits. In 1995/6 BA declared record after-tax profits of £473 million, up by 89.2% on the 1994/5 figure of £250 million. This provided for a dividend of 13.65 pence per share for the tax year ending 31 March 1996.

At the 1994 AGM Sir Colin Marshall claimed that Virgin's actions had had a 'quite minimal effect on BA'. The 1996 annual accounts note: '. . . legal claims have been made against the Company by Virgin Atlantic Airways Limited. Having regard to the legal advice received . . . the Directors are of the opinion that these claims will not give rise to liabilities which will in the aggregate have a material effect on these accounts'. Nevertheless the accounts also record that BA continued to make a £22 million provision for litigation for 1996/7.

BA's excellent results gave Marshall and Ayling a cushion to defend themselves in the courts against Branson, but not all members of BA's hierarchy were impressed with their manoeuvres. It was widely thought at the time of the boardroom crisis that followed BA's High Court humiliation that the company secretary, Gail Redwood, had handed in her resignation. Apparently she handed it to Marshall after the board meeting in which he and Ayling absolved themselves of all responsibility for the dirty-tricks campaign against Virgin. She was said to be appalled at their failure to own up to their own misdemeanours. Marshall refused to accept her resignation, and apparently persuaded her to withdraw it. The resignation of the company secretary at that time could have proved fatal to the cover-up operation. Redwood is highly respected at BA, and thought of as a woman of great integrity. She is also married to the Conservative MP John Redwood who, at the time, was a minister at the Department of Trade and Industry, and who subsequently challenged John Major for the leadership of the Conservative Party. Current speculation is that Gail Redwood will leave BA before the American jury is sworn in to hear Virgin's anti-trust case.

In 1994 BA admitted that no one had been sacked or disciplined by BA for participating in the dirty-tricks campaign against Virgin despite Marshall's 1993 pledge to clean up BA and institute a new code of ethics. So there now exists an extraordinary situation whereby BA claims there 'never was' a campaign against Virgin, and the directors who ran it now say they played no part in it, and knew nothing about it. Furthermore, the airline says that no one has been sacked for the 'disreputable business practices' which cost BA £5 million in damages and costs, and which Ayling and Marshall offered Branson a further £9 million to settle if he would sign a gagging clause.

In this somewhat unreal context, it is hardly surprising that BA has continued to refuse all my requests to interview any member of the board or senior management, or indeed any member of staff, on the subject of 'dirty tricks'. To the best of my knowledge neither Marshall nor Ayling has ever submitted themselves to an interview on the subject. This is even more telling if one accepts BA's own argument that the dirty-tricks campaign was no more than a series of disconnected examples of 'disreputable business practices'. Why should there be a problem doing interviews about such an insignificant matter, particularly in the context of Marshall's commitment to introduce a new code of ethics?

Inevitably the subject of dirty tricks has cropped up in passing, and the standard BA response has been: 'We will defend ourselves in court, not in the media'. This is an extremely convenient reply for the two most senior individuals at BA as neither of Branson's UK cases has been heard in court, and the US anti-trust case is still some way off. It does, however, create some problems for those who are trying to improve the airline's image. 'The major problem we've got,' one senior PR man told me, 'is that after the dirty-tricks libel case, everyone assumes we're guilty until we prove ourselves innocent!' With Marshall and Ayling in charge at BA, this seemed likely to continue to be the case.

In November 1995, however, BA took the City and British commercial aviation by surprise when it announced that Marshall was standing down as chief executive in favour of Robert Ayling. It had long been assumed that Ayling would eventually succeed Marshall, but not when Marshall had spent only eighteen months in the position that he had coveted for so long and overcome so many obstacles to reach. Marshall became the non-executive chairman of BA, so although he will continue to be involved with BA, power at 'The World's Favourite Airline' is now in the hands of Robert Ayling, the man who framed and drafted the legislation to privatise BA while he was a civil servant. BA's share prices climbed when the City heard the news.

The rehabilitation of both men from their parlous positions in the turbulent days of 1993 has been made possible by BA's increasingly impressive financial performance and, no less importantly, by the black arts of Sir Tim Bell's PR machine.

The *Sunday Telegraph* admired the 'elegance' with which Marshall passed on the BA succession while creating a new career for himself. BA will not reveal how much Marshall now earns as non-executive chairman, but Marshall's 'new career' includes the deputy chairmanship of BT (annual salary £34,000) and the chairmanship of Inchcape, the motor distributor and marketing group, for which he will receive £200,000 a year for working one and a half days a week. Most remarkably of all, Marshall's new career will include the presidency of the CBI. He was appointed to the post in the autumn of 1995 shortly before he went non-executive at BA. The CBI hailed Marshall's 'distinguished career in international business' when it appointed him and, of course, made no mention of his substantial misjudgements during the dirty-tricks campaign against Virgin, such as his financing of Brian Basham's work and Operation Covent Garden, or his decision to use Kroll to probe Air Europe, or his victory in the fratricidal boardroom battles at BA which permitted him to flout the Cadbury committee's guidelines and combine the roles of chairman and chief executive.

Unsurprisingly Richard Branson did not share the CBI's enthusiasm for Marshall:

It's a bit like the situation in China after Tiananmen Square. If you bully it out and you crush the opposition, you survive and you're still in power, people will want to deal with you. It's not a particularly good moral to teach the next generation. If you're chucked out you'll obviously be quickly forgotten. That battle in the BA boardroom was absolutely and utterly critical to those people's careers. On the one hand Marshall was going to be nothing but, having survived the battle, he ended up chairman of BA and then of the CBI.

Ayling's meteoric rise to the top of BA also owes much to the airbrushing of his image by Lowe Bell's PR effort. Branson found Ayling impossible to do business with and is particularly unimpressed by him: 'There's no way a man like that should be running BA.' He was particularly offended by Ayling's failure to honour his promise: 'He shook me by the hand in my own home and promised to settle the damages quickly, and then tried to slap a gagging clause on myself and Virgin.'

However, within three years of the Virgin libel case the public image of the steely lawyer unfamiliar with the give-and-take required in business had begun to change. In carefully placed interviews with selected journalists in management magazines and on City pages, Robert ('call me Bob') Ayling emerged as a modest, genial, 'boyishly charming' executive apparently surprised by his own success. None of these profile articles examined Ayling's role in the dirty-tricks campaign in any detail, or subjected his record to any critical scrutiny.

Ayling's advice to the British Cabinet on the Laker anti-trust case ('Laker has no case') had been wrong when he was an undersecretary in the DTI; his opinion on Branson's dirty-tricks libel case had been wrong, and his view on Virgin getting its anti-trust case to court had also been wrong. His view on its likely outcome – 'there is no basis on which it can be said there is any liability' – should be judged in the light of his record in these matters. However, there has never been any doubt that Ayling's 'modesty' cloaks a fierce ambition. When *Management Today* asked Ayling in October 1995 if he expected to become chairman of BA, he affected modesty and surprise: 'Oh, good heavens! I think I am a bit too young to think of being chairman of anything.' The following month Ayling replaced Marshall as chief executive of BA.

The rehabilitation of Marshall and Ayling represented a typically 1990s achievement – a decade that witnessed the erosion of accountability in British politics and business. Marshall, Ayling and Angus showed no more willingness to take responsibility for their actions (or lack of action in the case of Angus) than Cabinet ministers did in the Matrix Churchill affair. The government appointed Lord Justice Scott to investigate who in government should take reponsibility for the 'arms to Iraq' scandal that broke shortly after John Major's Conservatives scrambled to victory in the 1992 election. The Scott enquiry killed the 'arms to Iraq' scandal for three years, and when the damning Scott report was published, the government used ruthless parliamentary tactics and spin doctors to kill its political impact. No one was prepared to take responsibility and no one resigned.

When asked by a shareholder at the 1994 AGM whether there was an anti-Virgin dirty-tricks unit in BA, Robert Ayling replied with circumspection worthy of a politician before the Scott enquiry: 'Not to the best of my knowledge.' Protestations of incomplete knowledge by the airline's directors might be acceptable to shareholders, but the reaction of those who had inadvertently been caught up or implicated in BA's dirty tricks is less charitable. When I gave John Thornton of Goldman Sachs details of BA's suspicion that he had run an undercover operation against the airline on behalf of Virgin with a weekly budget of up to £400,000, he was completely mystified. 'This is unreal,' exclaimed the American banker, 'I find this information staggering, quite amazing.'

Roger Eglin was equally amazed when he found out that BA had organised the theft of his bin-bags. The veteran aviation journalist and author believes BA deserved the fate that befell the airline in the High Court:

Once the top people at British Airways start to hire private detectives who run around the landscape, they shouldn't be surprised if it gets out of control, and turns into a cross between the Keystone Cops and the SAS at work. But it's not the sort of thing that you expect from a reputable multinational company.

The top people at British Airways have got to look deep into their consciences and say 'Was I responsible?' and 'What should I do now?'

The board of British Airways has looked into its collective conscience and has apparently emerged with the answer that it should do absolutely nothing. Essential to the process of making this decision acceptable to the public and to the City has been Sir Tim Bell, who was first sighted in BA colours as he stood next to Marshall and Ayling while Lord King was being fed to the wolves on the steps of Enserch House in February 1993. Because of the continuing stain on BA's reputation that the dirty-tricks affair has caused, Lowe Bell has now been retained by BA for three years; initially it was hired on a three-month contract. Journalists seeking information on any aspect of BA's dirty-tricks campaign against Virgin are automatically directed to Lowe Bell, whose primary objective is to kill any coverage, and to steer Marshall and Ayling away from any form of interview on the subject.

Lowe Bell's objective is made considerably easier by the extraordinary lengths that some journalists will go to on both sides of the Atlantic to ingratiate themselves with 'The World's Favourite Airline'. The BBC's Christopher Wain and the former *Sunday Telegraph* duo Frank Kane and John Jay (both now with the *Sunday Times*) have been identified as leading BA admirers elsewhere in this book, but the top prize for uncritical admiration to BA must go to Henry Dormann. Dormann is the former president and editor-in-chief of the New York business magazine *Leaders*. It appears that he used to clear articles about BA with Marshall before he published them. On one such occasion an article was accompanied by the following letter:

> Dear Sir Colin,
> Enclosed is a highly confidential document [a forthcoming article about Marshall and BA]. I would appreciate it if you could keep it such but, in view of the fact we have such a close relationship with BA, and because I consider myself president of your fan club, I thought you should see it in case you have some suggestions or changes, or if you think we should perhaps not run the article at all. I'll await your thoughts.

Even Marshall was embarrassed by such sycophantic behaviour and he wrote back to Dormann politely telling him to use his 'good judgement'. It seems unlikely, however, that many *Leaders* articles will require the attentions of Sir Tim Bell. Once Virgin's anti-trust case gets underway in New York, however, Bell will do well to emulate David Burnside's performance during the Laker anti-trust case. Although Laker's case delayed the privatisation of BA by up to two years, it received scant coverage in Britain, particularly on television and radio. At the beginning of the 1980s, Laker was a hero of Thatcher's economic revolution; by the middle of the decade he was in exile in the USA fighting a lone battle for compensation against the state airline and the British government. In the Virgin anti-trust case, Bell will have to take on an expanding airline as well as Branson and Whitehorn in full cry. And as Lord King can testify, Ayling and Bell will underestimate Virgin at their peril.

Some of Lord King's associates now describe him as a rather sad figure, although he remains life president of BA. King also moved from the chairmanship to the presidency of Babcock International in 1995, and he remains a non-executive director of the *Telegraph* group. The owner of the *Daily Telegraph*, Conrad Black, tried to console him immediately after the humiliation of the libel defeat with a seat on the board of the *Spectator* magazine. Black's move backfired, however, when the publisher André Deutsch resigned as soon as he heard that King had been invited to join the board; he said he found King's behaviour towards Virgin disgusting.

The fate of the PR men whom Lord King gathered in his office in the spring of 1991 to send into battle against Virgin has been chequered. King himself was one of the principal guests at London's Savoy hotel in the spring of 1993 at the launch of David Burnside Associates, the company that Burnside launched after BA sacked him. King immediately placed Babcock International's PR account with DBA, and although Burnside no longer represents Babcock, the two men's loyalty to each other has endured their humiliating departure from BA.

More surprisingly, BA's former director of public affairs and Owen Oyston retained their links after the demise of BA's Operation Covent Garden. It was reported in 1993 that Burnside was one of the former Maxwell aides helping Oyston to raise £150 million for an 'International Colosseum' in Blackpool. The company of Owen Oyston proved dangerous for Burnside during Operation Covent Garden, and led him into more trouble in 1994 when he was convicted of drunken driving. Burnside was found unconscious in his car on a country road the morning after a spectacular drinking bout with Oyston. The car's engine was still running and the headlights were still on, although Burnside had been found in broad daylight. The policeman who discovered the slumbering PR man told Lancaster magistrates, 'It took several minutes to wake Burnside. He kept putting his finger to his lips and going "shhh". When he finally did awake his behaviour led me to believe that he was very drunk.' Burnside was so drunk that he was banned from driving and fined £1,000.

Oyston himself came to grief in May 1996, when he was jailed for six years after being found guilty of raping and indecently assaulting a sixteen-year-old model. Oyston spent £1.5 million on his defence, but was still found guilty. The judge described his offences as 'horrendous'.

Peter Martin was tried for rape in the same trial as Oyston but was found not guilty. Martin was the private detective who, using the name Peter 'Green', had been introduced to David Burnside in the 'Tickled Trout', and whose information had subsequently been so instrumental in persuading Burnside and Marshall of the fiction that Virgin was conducting a vast undercover operation against the airline. In June 1996 Martin, a former policeman, was accused of raping and abusing young girls for more than thirteen years after duping the girls and their parents with the prospect of modelling careers with his 'Model Team International' agency. In court Manchester police said they had found secretly filmed videotapes of 500 girls undressing. The jury was shown a video which the prosecution said 'shows girls lying as if drugged, their legs akimbo – and a camera zooms in on their private parts'. It was alleged that some of the drugged girls, many of whom were virgins, were forced to submit to violent sex; their hair was pulled and they were bound and gagged while the former policeman raped them. The result of the trial is not known at the time of writing.

One of David Burnside's new PR accounts is with British Mediterranean Airways which flies a daily service between London and Beirut. Owned by Lord Hesketh, the former Conservative chief whip, the airline hopes to profit from the end of the civil war in the Lebanon. Ironically, one of Burnside's first challenges was to advise Hesketh how to defeat a bid by British Airways to grab some of its new services to Beirut. Burnside argued that BA was trying to wreck the expansion plans of British Mediterranean which, at the time, had five of the seven flights available to British carriers. BA argued that all it wanted was an equal opportunity to compete in order to meet demand but, after a hearing and a subsequent appeal by BA, the CAA upheld British Mediterranean's permission to fly five times a week to the Lebanese capital.

Burnside's new business was initially funded by his very generous severance deal from BA. The PR man once fabled for his ability to use the power of silence also knew the price for his own silence. Burnside's gag was reported to last for three years but, even after its expiry, he has shown no sign of breaking it. There are even rumours that his gag has been extended by BA, as the airline's hierarchy remains haunted by its dirty-tricks past and the last thing it needs is Burnside divulging to a journalist or to Virgin what he knows about the involvement of BA's board. It is difficult to check this as both Burnside and BA refuse to comment on the arrangements they struck when Burnside was fired. The impression given is that the former head of BA's PR department wants to put as much distance as possible between his current work and the lowest point of his career.

Burnside remains a fiercely committed Ulster Protestant, active in support of David Trimble's Ulster Unionist Party. He was widely rumoured to be behind the leak of the highly sensitive Ulster framework document to *The Times* in late 1994 which caused a political uproar at a highly significant time in the Northern Ireland peace process. Burnside denied any involvement in the leak, and it appears that the Tory hierarchy felt inclined to believe him; when the Conservative Party's PR chief Hugh Colver quit in 1995, Burnside's name was mentioned as a potential successor. Although these rumours proved to be without foundation, it was widely reported that the Conservative Party chairman, fellow Ulsterman Dr Brian Mawhinney, is an admirer of Burnside's.

Burnside still drinks in the Savoy with Ian Watson, the former *Telegraph* journalist who played the key role in steering Burnside away from the Conservative Party and towards BA in the 1980s. Suggestions that the tiny David Burnside Associates bears the same relationship to the big City PR firms as Virgin's PR operation bears to the one he used to run at BA can produce a wry smile, but not a word about dirty tricks. When I asked him for an interview he restricted himself to the following comment:

'BA will say very nice things about me and I will say very nice things about BA'.

The PR industry is no longer saying such nice things about Burnside, however. *PR Week* described his fall from his post at BA as 'spectacular' in its 1994 round-up of the previous ten years, but it still placed him at number eight in its top forty most influential PR people of the decade. His former colleague, Brian Basham, was placed one rung below at number 9; the magazine described him as a 'fallen hero . . . no longer a main player in the business'. The magazine concluded that as a result of Basham's role in the dirty-tricks campaign against Virgin, 'it is difficult to see how Basham can recover his previously formidable reputation as a ruthless and effective public relations man'.

Basham himself can be spotted commuting regularly to the Savoy from his Clerkenwell Green offices in his chauffeur-driven Mercedes, opting now for a spiky, Vietnam vet-style haircut. His office is adorned by trophies from a bitter past, and it is warmed by his redeeming sense of humour. Framed writs reminding him of narrow escapes from the legal clutches of Tiny Rowland and Ernest Saunders jostle for position on the walls with cartoons celebrating a colourful and now notorious career. In one, Lord King is seen piloting a bomber over 'Virgin territory'. 'Aren't we taking Branson just a little bit seriously?' asks a co-pilot who just might be Brian Basham.

An unopened bottle of Scotch whisky on the bookshelf has an unusual but appropriate name for the man credited with inventing crisis PR, 'Auld Acrimony'. The founder and most distinguished practitioner of the art of negative PR was finally nailed – by his own side. A posse of assistants and secretaries tend him as he sits, sometimes rather grumpily, doing business from a sofa. He still fiercely defends his role in BA's campaign against Branson, claiming he had no part in the dirty-tricks campaign. He has proudly framed an extract from Branson's diary that came into his possession. It reads, 'Basham out of control'. At his side is a small shredder into which sensitive documents are immediately fed after he has read them.

British Airways, like the Fayed brothers, is having to deal with the legacy of employing 'negative PR'; eventually the black art of this form of public relations became less of a strategy and more a way of life. Ever since Basham was fired, Sir Tim Bell and his henchmen, 'hidden persuaders' from the same school, have seamlessly carried on where the 'Streetfighter' and the 'Kneecapper' left off.

It would, however, be entirely wrong to see BA's humiliation at Branson's hands simply as a public relations debacle. Burnside, Basham and Bell have not built their extremely well-paid careers by setting their own agendas. All are paid to be highly sensitive to their clients' priorities, and their agendas. 'Negative PR' can only flourish at the behest of their clients – King, Marshall and Ayling all wanted Branson's airline out of the way, and told its in-house PR department, and its most prominent external consultant, to do their worst. And when they got caught they hired Bell to mount the cover-up to protect their positions.

Basham flourished when he worked for the Fayeds because the Egyptian brothers' loathing of Tiny Rowland knew no limits and they were prepared to fund attempts to 'fuck Tiny' by fair means or foul. So obsessed was Fayed with Tiny Rowland that, at one stage, he commissioned toilet seats that bore the inscription, 'I shit on Tiny Rowland' around the rim. Fayed tried to amuse visitors to his Park Lane offices by showing them the seats which had a peculiar marble finish. King and Marshall hired Basham to do similar things to Branson and, like Fayed, suggested ploys that Basham found unacceptable. Basham now laughs dismissively when he recalls the puerile aspects of both Fayed and King's behaviour.

BA's former PR man kept a low profile in the autumn of 1994 as a tide of sleaze swept several Conservative ministers from office following Fayed's claims to have paid some of them to ask questions in the House of Commons. Documents reproduced in the *Guardian* showed that Basham had been responsible for passing on the Fayed-sponsored questions to the press. The ministers were forced to resign after Fayed decided to reveal details of Conservative MPs' links with his campaign to win control of Harrods. One, Tim Smith, admitted to receiving payment from Fayed and resigned on the spot; another, Neil Hamilton, the minister for business probity at the DTI, had to be levered from office after Fayed revealed he had enjoyed hospitality at the Ritz in Paris worth thousands of pounds. The minister had failed to declare it in the register of members' interests. A third minister, Jonathan Aitken, stepped down from his post at the Treasury during a government reshuffle in order to fight a libel case against the *Guardian* and *World in Action*. All three ministers had enjoyed hospitality from Fayed very similar to that which Basham arranged for key journalists during the time he worked for the phoney pharaoh.

By the mid-1990s both Fayed and his former PR man had turned into whistle-blowers: Fayed blew the whistle on Tory MPs who had allowed him to take over Harrods but whose government had crossed him by allowing the DTI inspectors to publish a report portraying him as a conman, and Basham blew the whistle on those at BA who had commissioned him to carry out their dirty work, and then singled him out for blame when they got caught.

Basham is still angry with BA's decision to abandon him. He told me several times in the course of being interviewed for the hardback edition of this book that he badly wanted to sue some-one connected with the dirty-tricks saga in order to redeem his reputation in court, having failed to do so in the 1993 libel trial. His motive, he said, would be to expose the involvement of the BA board in the dirty-tricks campaign. He said that BA had stopped him suing my *This Week* film 'Violating Virgin?', and that the most likely target would be the *Today* newspaper because of its post-libel trial article which used large extracts from the tape of his conversation with Chris Hutchins.

It came as a considerable surprise, therefore, when Basham sued myself and Little, Brown, the publisher of the hardback edition of this book, in September 1994. Basham had been a welcome guest at the launch of the book in March 1994, turning up in good spir-its and signing several copies. He appeared in a Sky TV broadcast about the book to say, 'Gregory has actually found out a tremen-dous amount that nobody knew, that was kept very secret.' Although Basham wrote an article in the *Sunday Times*, after that paper had run a three-week serialisation of *Dirty Tricks*, which indi-cated he didn't like parts of the book very much, he agreed to be interviewed by me about BA for a BBC *Newsnight* programme in August 1994. Then, in September 1994, without warning, he started his legal action, alleging that I had libelled him. I must leave my comments on his action to the next edition of this book when the trial will be over if, indeed, it takes place. All I can say now is that Basham's action will, as my publisher's lawyers would put it, 'be vigorously contested' by myself and Little, Brown. Basham's libel case is due to start in the High Court on 25 November 1996.

In the meantime, Basham has had some success in rehabilitating himself. He has emerged as a supporter of Britain's embryonic Republican movement, founding a 'discussion group' which meets once a month in London's fashionable L'Etoile restaurant. Basham also stresses his support for the Labour Party and says he has remained a socialist despite making millions from financial

PR. At one stage, he was involved in an unsuccessful bid to buy the *New Statesman*, the ailing left-wing weekly.

Basham's PR work has diversified. He has worked for the British Legion, many of whose members fought against Hitler, and also for Dr Hastings Banda, the nonagenarian former Malawian dictator. In 1996 Warwick Corporate was hired by the International Meat Association after the BSE scare blighted Britain's beef industry; for a man who made his name in 'crisis PR' this account could present Basham with his ultimate challenge.

Basham has always maintained that he had no knowledge of, and was not involved in, BA's damaging commercial dirty tricks against Virgin; that he had no knowledge of the matters that are currently being contested by the two airlines in the Federal Court in New York. Thus he considers that he has nothing to do with the anti-trust case. Although Branson blames Basham for some of the disinformation that was being spread about Virgin, he shares Basham's view of his own demise: 'they were trying to scapegoat one member of their tribe,' says Virgin's chairman.

Branson has now turned his attention to some sensational new evidence of BA's attempts to poach Virgin passengers that his lawyers unearthed in the course of putting together their anti-trust case against BA. A former British BA employee has made a sworn statement admitting that she extracted confidential computer data on passengers from Virgin Atlantic, and other rival airlines, and used the information to try and poach passengers. Branson describes the statement as 'the missing link' in the passenger-poaching episode of the dirty-tricks campaign.

Wendy Partridge[1] left British Airways in extraordinary circumstances at the beginning of 1994. She had risen to the position of senior customer relations executive after nearly ten years with the airline. Having just returned to Britain after a temporary posting with BA in California, she decided that she would explore other career opportunities in the airline industry. Partridge made initial calls to Swiss Air, KLM, Air Canada and Virgin Atlantic to establish if they had any vacancies for someone with her experience.

---

[1] 'Wendy Partridge' is not her real name as she wishes not to court publicity.

Shortly after her conversation with Virgin she was called in to see her manager in BA customer relations, Charles Weiser:

> I thought Weiser had called me in because a cheque I had recently tried to cash at BA had bounced. This was due to a mistake by my bank, but I had a letter from the bank apologising for its mistake, so I wasn't particularly bothered.
>
> When I entered Weiser's office I was astonished when he produced a tape recorder, and played me a tape of the conversation I had had with Virgin Atlantic asking if there was any chance of a job. I had no idea that BA taped its employees' phone calls, but I had to admit to him that I was looking for another job. He told me that he did not want me working for BA if I really wanted to work for Virgin Atlantic.

Partridge was then given a stark choice: resign or be sacked. Weiser said he would use the 'bounced' cheque incident to sack her; he warned Partridge that if she forced BA to sack her she would not get a reference.

After considering her position on a holiday in Africa, Partridge returned to Britain and resigned from BA. She subsequently spent a short period of time at Virgin before moving on to a job in the telecommunications industry. When she became aware of Branson's legal battles with BA she came forward with a sworn statement about her passenger-poaching activities in Los Angeles.

Wendy Partridge told Virgin's lawyers that after she had been with BA for seven years she told her bosses that she would like the chance to work abroad. The young executive was highly thought of within the customer relations department and, within weeks, she was posted to the Los Angeles sales office for six months in the summer of 1992. Her boss in the States was David Williams, the head of sales in Southern California.

Williams told Partridge when she arrived in LA that he was particularly concerned about BA's Club Class performance between London and LA, and that he would like her to become part of his team's efforts to improve it. Initially Partridge's activities were routine: she helped to 'meet and greet' passengers as chairman. BA would also pay both sides' legal costs, estimated at over £4 million.

The payment put the ball into Branson's court. He had to decide whether a jury would award him more money after a trial than BA had paid into court. He also had to decide if he wanted to spend three months in the High Court watching George Carman humiliating King, Marshall and Ayling, and scores of other BA staff who had been involved in the dirty tricks. It was a prospect that appealed to him immensely.

However, the impulse to get everything out in the open, which had driven Branson to write to Sir Michael Angus exactly a year beforehand, could prove costly in the High Court. If the jury awarded Branson less than the sum BA had paid into court, Branson would not only have had to pay legal costs, he could also forfeit public sympathy and be accused of wasting three months of the court's time.

'In some ways there was something in me that wanted just to go ahead with the case and get it out in the open, but my lawyers advised me against it.'

Over the next two very tense weeks, the two airlines' legal teams hammered out a settlement acceptable to their clients. Virgin's QC, George Carman, negotiated directly with BA's, Christopher Clarke, as the two teams of exhausted solicitors finally took a back seat. At the height of the negotiations, Linklaters and Harbottles exchanged correspondence twelve times a day.

'Having Carman on our side was thirty per cent of the reason we won,' enthused Branson later. Jonathan Crystal had urged him to hire the diminutive QC, and when Branson asked his solicitors, Gerrard Tyrrell and Colin Howes, whom he should most fear BA hiring to cross-question *him*, they replied in unison: 'George Carman'.

'Then hire him!' replied Branson.

During the negotiations BA increased its offer to £610,000 – £500,000 to Richard Branson personally, and £110,000 to Virgin Atlantic – plus costs reliably estimated to be in the region of £4.5 million, approximately two-thirds of which were BA's. It would be the largest libel payment ever in British history. The wife of the Yorkshire Ripper, Sonia Sutcliffe, and Elton John had been awarded more in previous actions but were eventually paid less after appeals by the defendants.

More difficult to agree was BA's apology, which Branson insisted must be read out in open court.

'I took George Carman's advice on the wisdom of settling rather than going ahead with the trial, but I wanted the statement in court to make it crystal clear what BA had tried to do to us.'

Several drafts of the proposed settlement made their way between Linklaters and Harbottle before Branson read the words he had wanted to hear for nearly a year.

> Both British Airways and Lord King apologise unreservedly for the injury caused to the reputation and the feelings of Richard Branson and Virgin Atlantic by the articles [*BA News*] and the letters [Lord King's] which they published. In particular, they wish to apologise for having attacked the good faith and integrity of Richard Branson.

In the rest of the seven-page statement, BA admitted that Brian Basham had attempted to place 'hostile and discreditable stories' in the press. It admitted that Basham's work, as well as the accessing of information about Virgin held on computer, the shredding and the switch-selling organised by the marketing and operations department, gave Richard Branson

> grounds for serious concern about the activities of a number of British Airways employees and of Mr Basham, and their potential effect on the business interests and reputation of Virgin Atlantic and Richard Branson.

At Virgin Atlantic's insistence Brian Basham was named in the agreed statement.

'Game, set and match,' recalls a delighted Branson who left for a three-week Christmas break on Necker Island in very high spirits indeed. 'It was one of the happiest holidays of my life!'

Both sides agreed to keep the deal secret until the day of the High Court action on 11 January. Premature disclosure of the statement would constitute a contempt of court.

Mervyn Walker and BA's legal department kept both David Burnside and Brian Basham in the dark about the libel endgame. On 21 December Brian Basham and his solicitor, Richard Sykes, arrived slightly early for a meeting with BA's QC, Christopher Clarke. There was no sign of anyone at Clarke's chambers. Ten minutes after the meeting was supposed to have started, Basham tried his own office to see if Clarke had phoned to cancel the meeting. His secretary read him a fax from BA that had been lying on the machine when she arrived at work. It said that the meeting with Christopher Clarke had been cancelled.

'When was it sent?' asked Basham.

'At seven-thirty on Friday night.'

Basham put the phone down slowly and stared at the back of the booth for a few moments. Before his hand left the receiver, the Streetfighter knew that he had been nailed – by his own side. He knew in that moment that Mervyn Walker had broken his promise to stand by him 'to the end'. His lower lip trembled slightly as he turned to Sykes.

'We're out of the loop.'

Basham's chauffeur whisked him back to Clerkenwell Green. As he hurried through the doors of his office, his secretary had the *Sunday Express* holding for him on the telephone. The reporter said that rumours were sweeping the paper's offices that the 'mother of all libel battles' had been settled. Apparently Lord King's office had phoned to reinstate a lunch date with the editor of the *Sunday Express*. BA's chairman had previously cancelled it, as he was due to be in the High Court. Basham suggested that 'pretext enquiries' to the chambers of the barristers hired by BA would establish how they were planning to spend the next few weeks.

After a morning of frenzied consultation with David Burnside and furious phone-bashing, Basham confirmed his worst fears. For the last time Lord King's PR double act swung into action. This time they were both fighting for their professional lives, not their clients' reputations.

In a desperate final throw of the dice, they decided to leak the story to the press in the hope that by seeping the news out over the Christmas period, it would reduce the impact and the news value of the story when it broke on 11 January. It was just possible they might be able to clamber out of the wreckage, and that Lord King might be spared. Without King neither Burnside nor Basham would survive. Neither man had been allowed to see the statement agreed between the two sides.

Over a desultory pre-Christmas lunch, Burnside briefed Frank Kane on what he had been able to establish about the deal that had been struck. Kane was by now working for the *Guardian* and his story appeared on 24 December under the headline 'Virgin and BA to bury hatchet'. Kane reported that 'peace was about to break out in the so-called mother of all libel battles', and that the 'peace' was a result of 'shuttle-diplomacy' between BA and Virgin. The settlement, according to Kane, was to be in the region of £1 million. For Kane and Burnside, it was to be their last tango. BA had misled Kane for the last time.

By sheer coincidence John Reilly was convicted of stealing Roger Eglin's bin-bags on the same day as Burnside briefed Kane on the 'peace settlement'. The private investigator was fined £150. The judge explained to Reilly that he was only imposing a modest fine because he believed that Reilly was 'clearly part of a much greater scheme of things'. At the same time, Scotland Yard disclosed that it had started a criminal investigation into Operation Covent Garden.

Any hopes that British Airways entertained of a short, sharp end to the dirty-tricks affair disappeared well before Mr Justice Drake opened proceedings at the High Court on 11 January. For days, the papers had previewed the humiliating climbdown that BA was about to perform in court. The *Sun* provided the most succinct forecast of the outcome: 'Virgin Screws BA'. Only the *Sunday Telegraph* was prepared to whistle long after darkness had fallen on BA. It declared that its own investigation had been unable to detect 'even a whiff of dirty tricks' in BA's approach to Virgin.

13

Virgin's Victory

Richard Branson emerged from a black cab outside the High Court with his father, Ted. The two Bransons were immediately engulfed by a sea of newspaper reporters, photographers and television teams from all over the world. Still refusing to comment on what he knew would be an historic victory, Branson smiled as he eased his way silently through the scrum. Flanking him were Will Whitehorn and Gerrard Tyrrell. For Branson's two most senior aides, the dirty-tricks affair had started nearly two years beforehand with their encounter with the private detective in a smoky bar below Waterloo Station.

Richard Branson stopped at the steps of the High Court to wait for his silver-haired father. The former barrister's path to the court was impeded by the jostling news crews following his son. The last time Ted Branson had been anywhere near a court with his son was when the teenage journalist was convicted of poaching. At the entrance, the poacher and his father walked proudly together into the Royal Courts of Justice to claim the hunter's pelt. Unusually, Richard Branson was dressed in a suit and tie.

As Mr Justice Drake brought the court to order, there was no sign of Lord King or Sir Colin Marshall – or Brian Basham. Three days earlier, the PR consultant fled to Malawi on a BA flight having been pursued to the Heathrow departure lounge by reporters.

Basham had taken out his own legal action against British Airways and Virgin Atlantic in a bid to get himself struck out of the action and to clear his name.

Patrick Milmo QC rose on behalf of Brian Basham to attempt to get the references to his client deleted from the agreement between BA and Virgin. In an affidavit which bore very close similarity to the one Mervyn Walker had implored Basham *not* to sign, the PR man stated: 'At no time did I act without the knowledge or approval of the British Airways Board.' Basham went on to stress that he had tried to 'discourage BA from disseminating disparaging and unsubstantiated rumours' about Richard Branson and Virgin.

Milmo declared to the court that Basham did not accept the references to him in the statement as 'an accurate summary of his actions on behalf of BA', but his bid to get his client 'struck out' failed. It was too late even for the 'Streetfighter' to escape. The two airlines had filed their legal flight-paths in December, and BA had agreed to sacrifice Basham.

When George Carman QC rose on behalf of Richard Branson and Virgin Atlantic to read the statement that the two airlines had agreed the previous month, it became publicly clear that BA had decided to distance itself from Basham and the public relations campaign against Virgin Atlantic. The statement agreed that 'Brian Basham was conducting a campaign aimed at both Richard Branson and the Virgin companies by attempting to plant hostile and discreditable stories about Virgin and Richard Branson in the press.'

As had also been agreed, BA accepted that accessing Virgin's computer information, shredding documents about Virgin and switch-selling had given Branson 'grounds for serious concern'. The airline also apologised 'In particular . . . for having attacked the good faith and integrity of Richard Branson and Virgin Atlantic'.

When Christopher Clarke QC responded on behalf of BA, his statement stressed that 'the directors of British Airways were not party to any concerted campaign against Richard Branson and Virgin Atlantic'. Thus Basham, the airline's external PR consultant, was the only person held to be personally responsible in the High

Court by BA for any of the range of activities that had galvanised departments throughout the national carrier, and had been directed, financed and controlled by members of BA's board, members of its board of management and some its most senior managers.

As Branson and his party made their way from the High Court into the January night, traffic in the Strand was brought to a halt as reporters fought to interview him. Branson described the settlement as 'a complete and total vindication', adding: 'It is a shame that Lord King and Sir Colin Marshall were not in court. That would have made it a more genuine apology.'

Branson's only regret as he was whisked off for a round of television interviews was that George Carman had not had the opportunity to grill BA's board and its senior managers. The QC had planned a sarcastic opening address:

'The world's favourite airline has a favourite occupation . . . shredding documents that are liable to be misconstrued!'

In preparation for its High Court climbdown, British Airways attempted to soften the impact of the story by indulging in another of its favourite occupations: providing chosen members of the press with a timely freebie.

In addition to leaking the High Court verdict in advance, BA worked its press contacts hard in the run-up to the court verdict, in a bid to dissipate the impact of the libel verdict. The week before the court case King, Marshall and Burnside led the press on a flight out of Heathrow. A plane full of selected journalists was taken to Brussels and lavishly entertained at BA's expense for two days. Ironically for an airline about to admit to a series of anti-competitive activities against a tiny rival, the ostensible purpose of the trip was to introduce the accompanying journalists to the European Commission's new Competition Commissioner at a champagne reception.

As the storm clouds gathered, Burnside weeded out potentially hostile members of the press in advance. Nonetheless, all that the accompanying posse really wanted to know about were the terms of BA's climbdown and the likely fallout within the airline. King, Marshall and Burnside all remained tightlipped about the outcome of the case, but their mood was glum. ITN's Julian Manyon –

one of the journalists Burnside prevented from joining the free-bie – flew to Brussels at ITN's expense to attempt to interview Lord King. Manyon described King's proud Protestant minder as a 'broken reed'. Burnside nevertheless had the energy to wrestle Lord King out of Manyon's reach as the ITN man bore down upon the embattled chairman of BA with a camera team.

British Airways' PR efforts had no impact whatsoever on the avalanche of negative coverage that engulfed the carrier as Richard Branson walked triumphantly from the High Court with his arms held high above his head and his fists clenched. The image of Branson triumphant dominated the news coverage for the next twenty-four hours. The BBC and ITN led their main bul-letins with the dirty-tricks verdict. Some of the star witnesses in the trial that BA had paid nearly £5 million to avoid dominated ITN's coverage. On *News at Ten*, Sadig Khalifa revealed how the Helpliners had ferreted out Virgin Atlantic's confidentially stored flight information from BA's computers, and admitted he had impersonated Richard Branson's staff on behalf of BA. He revealed how the airline had been engaged in similar activities against Air Europe and Dan Air. Yvonne Parsons detailed how she had become the victim of hoax calls. Caroline Mickler appeared on *Channel 4 News* describing the offer of two free tickets to Paris that BA's telephone switch-sellers had made to her. She agreed to switch to BA but the tickets never materialised.

Branson watched the extensive coverage of Virgin's victory at home in Holland Park with Will Whitehorn and a small group of friends he had invited in for a celebratory drink. Though it had at one stage resembled a bunker, it was an appropriate venue for the low-key get-together. At the height of BA's press campaign against Virgin, every other phone call seemed to put the future of the airline and the Virgin group into question. Now Branson's phone lines were jammed with messages of congratulation from supporters as well as journalists wanting to apologise for doubt-ing him in the first place. Branson's fax machines chattered busily as messages made their electronic way to Holland Park. 'Got the Old Sod at last!' read one, which Branson particularly cherished.

Despite his recent holiday, Branson was exhausted. BA's two-year campaign had taken its toll. One Virgin executive estimated that fighting BA's dirty-tricks campaign had consumed two thirds of Branson's time for nearly two years. It was only in victory that Branson realised the magnitude of the forces that BA had thrown against him. One of the first things he did was to draft a letter to all his staff thanking them for their support.

> British Airways' activities have affected everyone who works at Virgin . . . Therefore I feel it is only fair that the £500,000 paid to myself personally should be distributed as a thank you to all staff . . .
>
> Thank you all for your help in our defence. After all, a Virgin's honour is her most prized possession!
>
> I'd like to congratulate you (as always) on the wonderful job you are doing.

Each member of Virgin Atlantic received £166. The payment became known as the 'BA bonus'. Branson put the £110,000 Virgin Atlantic was awarded in the High Court into 'a fighting fund to continue the campaign for fairer competition'.

In his hour of victory, Richard Branson did not forget the man who had urged him to 'sue the bastards' in the first place.

'Freddie, this court victory is more for you than anyone,' he exclaimed in a celebratory phone call. Laker replied, 'I am absolutely delighted you beat the bastards!'

For Branson, the most important objective had been achieved – his credibility in the airline business had been established. The chairman of 'The World's Favourite Airline' had called him a liar; Branson had taken him on and beaten him.

Will Whitehorn's Scottish accent thickens in drink and, occasionally, under extreme pressure. At Holland Park on 11 January, his accent was as thick as a Scottish mist. And for the first time in many months he wasn't under pressure. When he phoned his mother in Edinburgh to tell her what had happened in the High Court, Richard Branson grabbed the phone and told her:

'He's saved Virgin! He's saved the airline! He's saved the whole bloody Virgin group!'

It's not entirely certain that Mrs Whitehorn knew what her son's boss was talking about, but Branson was in no doubt of the role the young Scot had played in Virgin's triumph. Later in the year, Whitehorn's role in defeating BA's campaign against Virgin was recognised by the PR industry. The *PR Week* magazine awarded the man David Burnside had dubbed Branson's 'boy press officer' its prestigious 'Outstanding Individual Contribution' accolade at its annual ceremony.

It was Whitehorn who helped Branson craft his press strategy in an area in which, despite his enormous success in establishing the Virgin brand, Branson had no previous experience. In the face of a hostile campaign organised by two of the PR world's acknowledged masters of the art, Burnside and Basham, and supported by BA's worldwide network of contacts and influence, it was Whitehorn who established many of the crucial connections between the different elements of the dirty-tricks campaign. What appears clear in retrospect was distinctly murky at the time, especially as BA had contracted out both Operation Barbara and Operation Covent Garden, and officially denied contact with either. Perhaps the quality Branson appreciated most was Whitehorn's faith in his conviction that dirty tricks were in progress when older, but, as it turned out, no wiser heads doubted him.

'He took on BA's army of PR men and renowned "kneecappers" and beat them,' recalls Branson. 'I wouldn't have swapped him for all of them. He's young, he has great integrity and he's great fun as well.'

Branson and Whitehorn were particularly amused by the BBC's coverage of the High Court verdict. Only in victory did the BBC take any of Branson's claims seriously. The corporation effectively boycotted the dirty-tricks story when it first broke in the newspapers – *Panorama* wouldn't cover it after David Burnside told the programme that BA wouldn't take part, and its news programmes had shown little interest. On the night of 11 January, however, the BBC was unable to avoid reporting the largest libel payment in British history. Branson watched its *Nine O'Clock News* bulletin with enormous pleasure. The sight of transport correspondent, Christopher Wain, having to explain Lord King's misdemeanours in an extended address to camera outside the High Court afforded a moment of sublime pleasure. Wain had revelled in what he describes as his 'professional and friendly' relationship with King for years.

The following morning Branson's hangover was soothed by the arrival of the morning papers which heralded Virgin's triumph, as well as the start of open season on British Airways. The 'editorial support' Burnside, Cocklin and Basham had so assiduously cultivated for Mrs Thatcher's favourite Lord and his airline melted instantly in the heat of violent criticism of BA. Much of it was written by journalists who felt they had been badly misled by BA from the start of the dirty-tricks affair. In particular, City and aviation journalists felt betrayed as they had been assured for so long by BA that Branson was running an extended publicity stunt against it.

Withering denunciations of BA followed in the editorial columns. The *Financial Times*, reflecting on the worldwide damage that had been inflicted on BA's reputation, wrote, 'dirty tricks have a price of their own', under the heading 'Dirty Dogfighting'. The *Independent* called for Lord King's immediate resignation:

> Such behaviour would be barely tolerated in the back streets of the second-hand car business. In a major corporation that in some degree represents the nation, it is a disgrace.

The *Daily Mail* found the climbdown, 'A delicious moment and one to be savoured', noting that Lord King had made 'a hearty breakfast of rivals for as long as most of us can remember. He polished off Laker and finished up the remains of British Caledonian with scarcely a commercial burp. For one dish, however, he has never had much of an appetite: humble pie. But yesterday it was on his menu with a vengeance.'

The tabloids savoured every moment of the 'take-'em-all-on' tycoon's triumph. 'There surely hasn't been a bigger humiliation anywhere since Saddam lost his knickers in the Gulf', wrote the *Star*. For the *Sun*, 'Branson proves that the little man CAN win against overwhelming odds', and its editorial got to the heart of the issue in two sentences:

> His pioneering Virgin Atlantic airline, which made the dream of cheap travel to America a reality for so many, was seen as a real threat by mighty BA. But they couldn't take fair competition.

Whitehorn had shrewdly slipped the *Sun* a copy of Sadig Khalifa's affidavit the previous day and the former Helpliner's account of how he accessed Virgin's computers for BA provided the paper with its front-page story under the headline, 'How I Shopped BA'.

BA's protestation's that there had been no 'concerted campaign' convinced none of the papers. The *Daily Telegraph* judged that 'Favourite Airline behaves like [a] spoiled brat' and the *Guardian* bemoaned: 'Competition British-Airways style seems to include personalised attacks, systematic campaigns of denigration and even abusing commercial privacy – not what the enterprise culture was supposed to mean.' The *Scotsman* developed the theme:

> BA stands condemned for the abuse of monopoly or near-monopoly power. Most people would say that it has behaved unethically. Individuals who treat each other that way would be censured and shunned by their fellow men and women. Unfortunately there is no such thing as a code of business ethics.

The *Independent* called for a DTI inquiry, not only into the Virgin affair, but also into Sadig Khalifa and Peter Fleming's claims that Air Europe and Dan Air had been undermined in a similar fashion.

Less than a year beforehand, Richard Branson jotted 'Lord of the Lies' into his private diary after Lord King had claimed Virgin's entry into Heathrow would cost BA £250 million. *Today* now used exactly the same phrase for its banner headline. In the wake of the verdict, the paper also finally summoned the courage to print

extracts from Chris Hutchins' tape of his meeting with Brian
Basham. All the papers led with Branson's triumph, apart from the
Daily Mirror, which relegated the story to page seven. At the time,
the Mirror Group's chief executive was David Montgomery, a
close friend of David Burnside's and a fellow Ulster Protestant.

It was richly ironic that one of the libels that caused Lord King's
case to collapse so dramatically included an attack on 'Richard
Branson's propaganda which sets out to contrive controversy with
British Airways to create publicity for himself and his
company . . .'. BA's climbdown handed to Branson the best publicity and press coverage even he had ever enjoyed. Two phone
calls made the real meaning of the libel victory clear to him. The
first was from Toulouse. Jean Pierson, the president of Airbus,
called with a simple message: 'Let's talk planes!'

During the dirty-tricks affair the French aeroplane manufacturer had picked up what it described as the 'bad vibes'
surrounding Virgin Atlantic from the City pages of the British
press. As a result the company had put plans to do business with
Branson on the back burner. When Jean Pierson heard the news of
Virgin's victory he seized the moment:

'Virgin thought we were reluctant to do business with them
but, in fact, we noticed that they were more cautious than usual
during the legal proceedings. When Branson won, I thought, let's
get down to business.'

The second call was from Seattle. Phil Condit, the president of
Boeing, called with a very similar message and, by the end of the
week, Branson had offers to commit on nearly $2 billion of aero-
planes. Branson was massively relieved:

We had been trying to find partners for Virgin Atlantic for
over eighteen months, but we simply couldn't do deals with
the BA thing going on. First, potential partners and investors
were put off by BA's smear campaign, and then they were
put off by the litigation. After all, BA was suing us, and as far
as the outside world was concerned, BA might have won.
Even banks that were helping us with other Virgin projects
wouldn't invest in the airline while the dirty-tricks affair was
unresolved.

Virgin Atlantic had a surge of new bookings as many people switched from BA in protest. The outcome of the dirty-tricks affair touched a chord that took Branson himself by surprise. Radio phone-ins were inundated with callers expressing disgust over what BA had tried to do to Virgin, and many recalled the millions in compensation that BA had paid to Freddie Laker.

Many of BA's own staff shared the public outrage. One BA worker photocopied his staff pass and wrote a letter of apology to Branson saying how ashamed he felt of his own airline; others complained bitterly and publicly in the columns of *BA News*. Derek Porter, a priority spares controller, wrote to say that he hoped 'the perpetrators of this obscene episode are brought to justice.' Pilot Peter Jenkinson argued that he found it 'difficult to believe' that the directors of BA did not know what was going on. Jenkinson recalled a previous instance when a director stepped down after accepting responsibility for events of which he had no knowledge at the time. 'Surely the same rules apply today, and the responsible parties must accept their grave mistakes and take the consequences.' Product development coordinator, Gary Moore, added his voice to those who hoped that 'heads would roll' amongst those who planned the malpractice and had tried to cover it up.

In response, Sir Colin Marshall announced that BA was taking 'fair but effective action' to ensure there would be no repetition of the 'regrettable conduct'. He announced a new 'code of conduct' and attempted to reassure staff in a statement:

> The overwhelming majority of you have had no involvement whatsoever in the [regrettable] incidents to which I have referred.

Most members of BA staff were *fully* aware that they had not been involved in the dirty-tricks campaign. What many wanted to know was precisely who had been, especially in bizarre escapades such as Covent Garden.

Operation Covent Garden was one of the most damaging of all the anti-Virgin activities but, because the full details were revealed when it was too late for them to be considered for inclusion in the

High Court statement, it was not included as one of the 'disreputable activities.' It is, however, difficult to think of anything that occurred during the dirty-tricks campaign that reflected more badly on the judgment of Lord King and Sir Colin Marshall than the activities of Ian Johnson and his band of bungling irregulars.

At a very early stage in Covent Garden's life, David Burnside leaked Johnson's 'preliminary findings' to the *Sunday Telegraph*. In the absence of any proof whatsoever from BA, and point blank denials from Branson and John Thornton, reinforced with Gerrard Tyrrell's threats of immediate legal action, the paper dropped the story.

It took Lord King and Sir Colin Marshall's lavishly funded extravaganza several more months of extremely 'disreputable' activity to reach the same conclusion. Covent Garden employed agents to steal journalists' trash, probe the background of loyal members of BA staff, sweep the executive and management offices on a weekly basis, and obtain the details of bank accounts and telephone records of members of the public in the hunt for the alleged 'mole'. Covent Garden's contribution to the humiliation of 'The World's Favourite Airline' was enormous. The only people within BA who knew about the small army of private detectives were the members of the main board – King, Marshall and Ayling – and members of the board of management – Hyde, Burnside and Walker. By definition, BA's workforce knew nothing of what was going on, as the operation had been contracted out, and the undercover operatives were instructed to work secretly and never to acknowledge that BA was the client.

The official BA version of events emerged within ten days of the libel verdict. The 'disreputable business activities' BA had admitted to in court had become 'regrettable conduct', and the airline stressed that this had been 'confined to a relatively small number of unconnected incidents involving a very small number of employees'.

In a message to BA's staff, Marshall said: 'There are many challenges ahead of us and in facing them you must not be distracted by publicity about this matter.'

Much can be laid at Sir Colin's door over the dirty-tricks affair, but in its aftermath, he cannot be accused of failing to concentrate on the personal challenge that lay ahead of him.

At the end of January, the *New York Times* reported that
Marshall had been busy tunnelling an escape route out of BA
altogether as the clouds gathered over BA. The authoritative
American paper reported that Marshall had been offered the chief
executive's job at American Express. The *New York Times* reported
that when the BA scandal broke, AmEx withdrew its offer.
Unconvinced by BA's routine denials of the story, British newspapers also carried it. BA's chief executive was said to be
'devastated' by American Express's decision. It left him with only
one option – to push for the summit at BA.

As King, Marshall and Angus manoeuvred for position, and
for allies, Marshall's relationship with his old friend, Michael
Levin, returned to haunt him. Brian Basham discovered in the
course of his own unsuccessful action to try and clear his name in
the High Court that Levin had played an important role in setting himself and Burnside up, and he became convinced that
Marshall knew about his activities. Because Basham took his own
action, he was entitled to obtain some of the documents Branson
was required to produce on discovery, including the Virgin
chairman's diary.

Basham was astounded to read the note that Branson wrote about
his conversation with Bob Graham after the *Today* reporter had spoken to Levin at the beginning of November 1991. Branson wrote:

> The [anti-Virgin] group was set up at King's instigation.
> Burnside ran it. No boundaries set – legal or not . . . Levin
> [was] told that Basham was part of plan . . . Levin will go on
> affidavit.

Basham had no idea until he read Branson's diary on the eve of
BA's climbdown that Levin had continued to meddle in BA's
affairs up until his death, and neither, according to Basham, did
Lord King. He was amazed, however, that Sir Colin did not warn
him or Burnside that Levin was still involved in 'consultancy
work' for BA, or that he had been speaking to the press. Furious
that BA had abandoned him, Basham started briefing journalists
on Levin's role in the Virgin affair. Before long, lurid headlines
such as 'CIA-Linked American Waged BA War on Virgin' and

accounts of the 'shadowy' BA figure started to appear in the press. Ironically for Sir Colin Marshall, who signed £46,000 away for Operation Barbara as he sent him 'back to the brickwork' in 1991, Basham was now guiding the press back to the genesis of BA's campaign against Virgin which predated his own work.

For British Airways, Basham's attempt to pin the blame for the dirty-tricks affair on the dead American was rather convenient, until it was revealed that Levin had kept copious notes which were now in the hands of his son, Chris, in Manhattan. In an interview with William Lewis of the *Mail on Sunday*, Chris Levin revealed that his philandering father 'loved women, but he liked filing more'. He confirmed that Marshall's guru had kept detailed records of his entire career at British Airways.

When Michael Levin died, still engaged in consultancy work for Marshall, BA made strenuous efforts to persuade the family to return his files to BA. When his father died, shortly after his breakfast meeting with Marshall, Chris Levin called to tell him that his old friend was dead. He was startled when his call was returned not by Marshall but by BA's lawyers.

'I got a call from BA's attorneys before I got a call from Colin. They asked if they could pack up my father's BA stuff and take it home with them.

'They wanted it straightaway, so the first thing I did the next morning was to pack the stuff and move it out to my house on Long Island.'

When the *Mail on Sunday* reported in January 1992 that Chris Levin was putting his father's papers up for sale in the wake of the High Court verdict, Marshall and BA's interest in Levin's papers was very swiftly rekindled. In by now familiar BA fashion, Marshall contracted out the dirty work. BA's chief executive phoned Chris Levin himself and told him that he would find it 'unhelpful' if the crates of files and documents found their way into the public arena. Simultaneously BA's lawyers threatened to start a massive lawsuit against Levin junior if he sold the papers or divulged their contents to myself or any other journalist. BA warned Chris Levin that it would seek to reclaim all the money BA paid his father – approximately $800,000 – and that the case itself would cost him personally at least $200,000. The intermediary also warned Levin that anybody publishing any of the documents would also be sued.

Although Chris Levin is a wealthy man in his own right, he has no appetite for a lengthy and expensive encounter with BA in the courts and he has, therefore, refused to reveal the contents of his father's files. It is understood, however, that there are key papers on Virgin Atlantic and Air Europe in the collection, as well as on United Airlines. The importance of the papers is perhaps best judged by the efforts BA is prepared to put into preventing their being published. Chris Levin felt that BA had awarded him a walk-on part in the dirty-tricks affair when he noticed someone was taking his garbage away every night: 'I'm sure it wasn't the refuse collector!'

A further obstacle to Marshall's ambitions then loomed into view : the Cadbury Report. The long-awaited report on corporate governance was published at the beginning of December 1992. Sir Adrian Cadbury's report was British business's response to the corporate scandals that had rocked Britain in the previous years. Cadbury advocated a system of checks and balances designed to prevent the recurrence of the Maxwell and Polly Peck scandals. In both those affairs, the boards were dominated by extremely powerful men who combined the posts of chairman and chief executive, and abused their omnipotence. Top of Cadbury's 'code of best practice' was the recommendation that

> there should be a clearly accepted division of responsibilities at the head of the company which will ensure a balance of power and authority . . . Where the Chairman is also the Chief Executive it is essential that there should be a strong and independent element on the board with a recognised senior member.

The Cadbury Report was widely welcomed throughout Britain's boardrooms and also by the president of the CBI, Sir Michael Angus, the chairman of BA's non-executive directors. The BA dirty-tricks scandal provided Angus with an early test in both of his elevated capacities. The eyes of the City and influential sections of the press were upon him as he approached the challenge of cleaning up 'The World's Favourite Airline'.

The *Independent* had called for DTI inspectors to be sent in to investigate BA's dirty tricks, and *The Times* declared that, 'the non-executive directors should use this unpleasant incident to put paid to any prospect of Sir Colin seizing the jobs of both chairman and chief executive'.

Angus himself had long been unhappy with the prospect of Marshall taking both jobs and the backwash from the Virgin libel action threatened to expose all BA's dirty linen.

'Mike [Angus] was obsessed with checks and balances,' said a colleague. 'He was determined to turn BA into a shop window for Cadbury.'

The solution Angus wanted was for the two top posts to be held by different men. With Sir Francis Kennedy, Angus arranged for the non-executives to meet privately the night before the next board meeting. On the evening of 20 January, nine days after BA's High Court apology, Angus gathered his fellow non-executive directors at the Orangery, a discreet and luxurious dining room at Claridge's.

Around the table sat Charles Price, just in from the States, Michael Davies, and Kennedy and Angus. They were joined by Bill Knight, a senior partner with the law firm Simmonds & Simmonds. In the most turbulent days since BA's privatisation, the non-executive directors had hired Simmonds & Simmonds to represent their interests. They were concerned that the High Court apology might leave them open to further legal action. The Virgin affair had also thrown up a number of unresolved legal issues. They included the Scotland Yard inquiry and the question of whether BA had breached the Data Protection Act by accessing confidential computer information on Virgin passengers and flights.

The legal advice from Bill Knight was that all ten directors of BA, including King and Marshall, should be required to sign a written undertaking that they had neither known about nor sanctioned any 'disreputable practices', a phrase that had by now secured its place in BA's expanding lexicon of euphemisms for activities that most people outside the airline termed 'dirty tricks'. Further assurances would be extracted from each executive director of the airline that he had not lied to the board when discussing the February 1992 report prepared for the board by Mervyn Walker and Linklaters & Paines which perfunctorily dismissed Branson's charges.

Over claret and entrées, the group then went on to discuss a second Linklaters report which John Turnbull and his massive team of lawyers put together while unsuccessfully attempting to defend BA against Branson's libel charge. Effectively, Linklaters had been investigating its own failure to detect the dirty-tricks campaign when Branson first raised the issue. This report recommended that David Burnside and the mastermind of Operation Covent Garden, Ian Johnson, should be dismissed.

The board meeting at Speedbird House the following morning was the most dramatic since BA's privatisation. Angus and the non-executives angrily confronted the four executive directors of the airline: King, Marshall, Ayling and Derek Stevens, the finance director.

As Angus and his colleagues had agreed over dinner, the four would be forced to sign a pledge before the board could move on to discuss how BA could extricate itself from the increasingly deep hole it was digging for itself.

According to the confidential minutes of the board meeting, each member had to sign a confirmation that

> He had not implemented or authorised any of the disreputable business activities complained of by Mr Branson and Virgin Atlantic or any press campaign or other improper action against Virgin Atlantic Airways or Mr Branson.

Derek Stevens signed his pledge and so, without blushing, did King, Marshall and Ayling. All three men had lied to the BA board.

King and Marshall had authorised Burnside and Basham's press campaign against Branson and Virgin, and, with Ayling, they had egged the PR men on in different ways. King authorised the Basham report, and had tried to persuade the PR man to spread untrue stories about Branson's gay Heaven nightclub, including the false rumour about AIDS-infected needles. Marshall had authorised the Basham report and signed the cheque for the £46,000 Basham charged BA for it. The directors were aware that BA had obtained Branson's September 1991 letter to his staff which Burnside, Cocklin and Basham used so freely in their press briefings. Marshall and Ayling had played their parts in trying to spread false stories about Virgin's finances to the press, to the City and to the 'greater Whitehall'. Ayling had told Basham to keep quiet about the authorship of his report on Branson and Virgin. While he was BA's legal director, Ayling had encouraged Basham to place a story in the press about Virgin's departure times on the basis of information BA had improperly extracted from its computer.

In the agreed statement in open court, BA acknowledged that

> In the course of preparation for trial . . . [it was] revealed that some British Airways employees had obtained access to information relating to Virgin Atlantic flights.

Marshall and Ayling were two of those employees, and the 'revelation' had nothing to do with the preparation for the trial. One of the first things Marshall did when King exploded at Branson's Gulf exploits in 1990 was to get his marketing men to obtain information for him held on the computer relating to Virgin flights. Since September 1991, Robert Ayling had been in charge of the department from which Maude's Marauders, the Interliners and the telemarketing teams had all been working to steal Branson's passengers in Britain and America. These hit squads combined two of the activities that BA admitted in court were 'disreputable' and gave Branson 'reasonable grounds for concern'.

The grilling of Robert Ayling was the most tense moment of a very fraught board meeting. Branson had ultimately been more concerned about the impact of the dirty-tricks campaign on Virgin Atlantic's business than on his personal image, and Ayling's massive marketing and operations department was responsible for the *commercial* dirty tricks about which Virgin had complained. Ayling pleaded ignorance. According to the minutes, the man whose department ran switch-selling squads on both sides of the Atlantic told the board he was unaware that

> unacceptable means had been adopted by a very small number of staff in order to persuade other airlines' passengers to fly on the company's services.

The former legal director of BA also claimed that the shredding of documents was authorised by BA's document-control policy. This appeared to contradict the view of Linklaters & Paines, who found that shredding had taken place outside the policy.

Even more remarkable was the sight of the three men signing the second half of the pledge that

> On 7 February 1992 when an assurance was given to the board that there was no substance whatsoever in the accusation that the company had engaged in any campaign against Virgin Atlantic Airways other than through normal marketing and promotional effort, he had no knowledge to the contrary.

Given the activities that BA had agreed in the High Court were 'disreputable', it appeared that all three men were exercising prodigious 'economy with the truth'. King, Marshall and Ayling attempted to huddle behind half a sentence at the end of the agreed statement in Open Court: '. . . the directors of British Airways were not party to any concerted campaign against Richard Branson and Virgin Atlantic.'

Once the three had prolonged their own careers at BA by signing the pledges, they joined the non-executive directors in a discussion of who should be fired. The most senior victim under discussion was David Burnside. Since the High Court climbdown, Burnside's position had been under enormous pressure, and there had been much press speculation that he would be sacked. Burnside had no intention of departing without a fight. He wrote a passionate defence of his own role, and his department's, which he sent to each board member before the meeting. He savaged BA's legal and marketing departments, and the scores of lawyers who had been employed to defend BA. 'The refusal of the company to be open and up-front on our public affairs activities and the handcuffing of the public affairs department by legal advisors, whose record of competence on this whole affair is certainly open to question, has resulted in a PR disaster affecting the whole corporate image and reputation of the company . . .' Burnside told the board that he had no intention of resigning, and stressed that he wanted to continue working for BA.

In defeat, open warfare had broken out between the factions involved in trying to undermine Branson, and Burnside was in no doubt where the blame lay for BA's predicament. 'There has been a trail of errors and mistakes, including the advice given to the board, and what appears to have been at worst illegal, and at best unethical and improper, practices within the marketing department. By the failure to uncover those practices in earlier investigations, either through negligent management or because people were trying to cover up their activities, the company continues to suffer by not publicly dealing with the problems.'

Burnside summoned his proud seven year-record in his defence, citing the string of PR awards and commendations the public affairs department had received in Britain and throughout the world: 'My department . . . is one of the best, if not *the* best, PR operations in the world.' Burnside invited members of the board to ask journalists and prominent Conservative politicians if 'I, or my department, acted without authority, improperly, unethically or illegally'. The lengthy list included an impressive selection of newspaper editors, political correspondents, television journalists and senior Conservative Lords and MPs. Amongst those Burnside claimed would vouch for his work were Sir Nicholas Lloyd, the editor of the *Daily Express*, Stewart Steven, editor of the *Evening Standard,* David Montgomery, chief executive of the Mirror Group, Charles Moore, editor of the *Sunday Telegraph,* John Jay, City editor of the same paper, Martyn Lewis and Christopher Wain of the BBC, the Lords Tebbit, Parkinson and Amery, his old friend Ian Watson of the *Sunday Telegraph* and Frank Kane, now of the *Guardian*.

Burnside emphasised, 'I have always carried out, as I said in my witness statement on the Branson case, my duties with normal and constant liaison with Sir Colin and Lord King.'

The board studied Burnside's testimony in silence. The phrases 'cover-up', 'illegal activities', 'negligent management' leapt from the page. The letter was a barely disguised attack upon Ayling and the activities of his marketing department, and the leadership of Marshall. Mervyn Walker was implicated but, as senior board members, it was Ayling and Marshall who were the targets of Burnside's attack.

After a discussion of the findings of Linklaters' second report, and consideration of Burnside's letter, the board fired its director of public affairs. The botched operations – Barbara and Covent Garden – had proved terminal for Burnside. The board declined Burnside's offer to provide 'full and comprehensive' information about his department's activities during the 'Branson affair'. The dry minutes record:

> It was clear from the findings of the [Linklaters & Paines] report that David Burnside could not remain with the company . . .

The board meeting also agreed that Ian Johnson's contract should be terminated.

Michael Angus demanded a list of employees to be disciplined, the appointment of a special committee of non-executives to monitor future relationships with Virgin Atlantic, a new code of conduct for the airline, and less aggressive public relations.

As the board started to discuss Angus' suggestions, Lord King fell silent. David Burnside, Brian Basham and Ian Johnson had all been close allies. Now all were gone, and their departures were shattering blows for him.

'John King went very quiet after that meeting,' said a colleague. 'I had not seen him so depressed since the mid-1980s, when Nicholas Ridley threatened to suspend the airline's privatisation. He looked waxen and bereft, as if all his years had caught up with him in a morning.'

King admitted he had completely misjudged his adversary.

'If Richard Branson had worn a pair of steel-rimmed glasses, a double-breasted suit and shaved off his beard, I would have taken him seriously. As it was, I couldn't . . . I underestimated him.'

Ever since the libel verdict King had been contemplating resignation, an unthinkable prospect before BA's court climbdown. He had planned to step down formally as chairman in July, after bidding his final farewell at the summer's Annual General Meeting. The prospect of facing BA shareholders was no longer so enticing. In July 1992, King's role at BA had already changed to non-executive chairman. So it was only a short step to resigning the post altogether.

The board agreed not to publish the findings of Linklaters' second report, and Angus pushed head with his plan to impose the Cadbury rules on BA. Shortly after the board meeting dispersed, Angus also started promoting the idea that he should become chairman of BA. Over the following week, he canvassed support for the idea amongst the airline's City fund managers and financial advisors, including Lazards and N.M. Rothschild.

'Angus wanted to know whether the City would accept him as a *pro tem* chairman while Marshall was "run in" as managing director for a few months,' said one.

On 28 January, Angus confronted Lord King in his office. Angus proposed he should take over as temporary chairman for long enough to assure the City that the necessary checks and balances were in place as recommended on the Cadbury Report.

Furthermore, he hinted that the non-executives might be reluctant to deliver the presidency to King unless he stepped down early, according to a close friend of King. 'The word ultimatum did not do it justice,' said one of those present. However, other BA sources deny this was a cold-blooded attempt by Angus to seize control. 'Mike didn't want to do it at all,' said one. 'After all, he had his hands full as head of the CBI and Whitbread. I think he simply thought it was what the institutions wanted. He felt he was only doing his duty.'

King swiftly countered Angus' challenge. Flanked by Sir Colin Marshall and Sir Francis Kennedy, he agreed to go straightaway, but on his own terms. 'John said it was fine,' recalled a senior BA source. Sir Michael Angus later confirmed this version of events.

'The initiative [to step down] was John King's and he was right to take it. I guess he didn't think it was worth going on for six months.'

However, the veteran boardroom campaigner had one last trick up his sleeve.

'He was happy to step down early but Angus had to understand one thing. It was Colin who was going to be chairman.'

Behind the scenes King and Marshall made a Faustian pact. King would back Marshall for the joint post he had craved for so long if Marshall would back King for the presidency. In this way Sir Michael Angus would be thwarted.

Angus realised he had little choice but to accept. Support drained away from his bid for power over the following weekend when BA's institutional shareholders considered his plan to be temporary chairman. They did not like it. On 1 February, representatives from Warburgs, Phillips & Drew and Lazards met the non-executive directors in Angus' boardroom at Whitbread. Led by David Verey, Lazards' chairman, they warned Angus that a temporary takeover could exaggerate the impact of Branson's victory and create instability within the company.

Four days later, the BA board met to confirm King's accession to the presidency. Marshall would be appointed chairman and Robert Ayling would become group managing director. An exhausted King staggered out of Enserch House with Marshall and Ayling to face the dozens of reporters who had laid siege to BA's West End headquarters.

'Good morning, Christopher!' cried King, singling out the BBC's BA-friendly transport correspondent, Christopher Wain, as he emerged to face a sea of hostile microphones and cameras. King announced the board changes to an incredulous press, and immediately launched into a speech about his achievements since he joined BA 'When you and I first stood here ten years ago . . .' he said to Wain.

The scrum of reporters grew restless, and tried to interrupt King's soliloquy. They all wanted to interview him about why he had resigned.

'If you want to make what is a very happy, proper occasion for the board into something else, then go ahead', King snapped, inadvertently revealing the strain of the dramatic wheeling and dealing that had engulfed the board for nearly a month.

King turned back to Wain and continued saying something about 'the crowning achievement of my working life'. At this point ITN's Joan Thirkettle interjected with the question that was on the lips of all the reporters present.

'Lord King, have you resigned because of the dirty tricks?'

In a final, imperious, gesture King rounded on Thirkettle. Stabbing his finger in her direction, he barked:

'No!' A slight pause as he fought to control has anger. 'Madam.'

When a reporter from the back of the crowd cried 'Why not?', King had to be hustled inside by his minders.

'Fuck 'em all,' cried King as he stormed back into Enserch House.

That afternoon, David Burnside cleared his desk following the board's confirmation that, in the light of Linklaters' second dirty-tricks report, the combative Ulsterman had to go.

Burnside had been his master's voice for nearly a decade. With King on his way back to Wartnaby, the 'most powerful PR man in Britain' had to endure the indignity of waiting in Enserch House while a courier brought his severance cheque by tube from a bank in the City. The only grim satisfaction he could take was the accuracy of his prediction that caving in to Branson would lead to a BA public relations disaster.

Burnside's settlement with BA was staggered over three years. The mastermind of the anti-Virgin media offensive had to sign a pledge not to discuss his work for 'The World's Favourite Airline'. Press estimates of the size of his settlement range between £300,000 and £500,000, plus free first-class travel on BA for three years.

The tensions in BA's board were revealed by King's old friend and Yorkshire hunting companion, Lord Hanson, as BA's chairman made his undignified departure. One of King's staunchest non-executive allies on the BA board, Lord White, had been unable to attend the crucial January caucus in Claridge's and the subsequent BA board meetings at which King's fate was decided. White runs Lord Hanson's North American operation, and had had to stay in the States because of ill health. He was consulted by fax. When the news reached White and Hanson that King had been forced out, Lord Hanson took up his old friend's cause. In an interview with the *Daily Telegraph* that had trumpeted the achievements of the three Lords so loudly for so long, Hanson was savagely critical of Michael Angus and the non-executive directors whom he accused of waffling and letting King down. Angus, said Lord Hanson, had 'confused the issue' and weakened the management's position with his public statements.

'They have behaved terribly. They haven't had the guts and inspiration to back him up, and when it came to the crunch they didn't publicly support him.

'It is a tragedy that John King has gone in this fashion because he was one of the most outstanding businessmen of the century. He is a fighter. He has displayed leadership and he has great determination.'

When the Princess of Wales learnt of Branson's High Court triumph in January, she had sent him a handwritten note from Kensington Palace which read simply, 'Hurray!' When Branson phoned to thank her, they agreed a date to play tennis. Appropriately, they were on court when the news of the demise of the Lord who so craved royal patronage was brought to Branson. The Princess, whom Lord King was once proud to be on cheek-kissing terms with, now shared the news of his demise with his tormentor.

Disappointing those who expected Branson to gloat at the demise of his rival, Virgin Atlantic's chairman paid warm tribute to the contribution Lord King had made to BA as soon as he heard the news. He wished King well in his retirement. Although Branson knew that Lord King had been one of the prime movers in the campaign against him, he also knew that others bore more responsibility and he felt that they should have resigned from the airline altogether.

King's premature departure also represented a triumph for his replacement, Sir Colin Marshall, and his ally Robert Ayling.

Despite the angry noises from the leaping Lords, King's men couldn't put the former chairman together again, and Marshall and Ayling moved swiftly to make sure they didn't take the new chairman apart. King's seat was still warm as Marshall slipped into it after the decisive 5 February board meeting and, with Robert Ayling, started a very rapid reorganisation of BA's management structure.

Levin was dead. Basham and Johnson were gone. Burnside was gone and gagged. There were, however, still many in BA who knew in which cupboards the numerous skeletons of the dirty-tricks campaign were hanging.

Marshall and Ayling quickly broke up the old marketing and operations department, which had provided Ayling himself with his springboard to the top of BA and which had perpetrated many of the dirty tricks against Virgin. Announcing the changes in *BA News*, Ayling commended the system of 'devolved accountability that has served us so well in recent years'. While cynics in the airline scoffed at Ayling's description of the process by which he and other senior members of BA had managed to 'devolve' responsibility for the dirty-tricks campaign, the new order was in place within ten days of King's departure. And it looked very much like the old order.

The Reverend Jim Callery, the inspiration and the driving force behind BA's aggressive switch-sellers, retained his job as head of world sales, responsible for BA's global sales and marketing. Callery's UK sales manager, Kevin Hatton, who supervised the accessing of Virgin's and Air Europe's computer information, the shredding of documents relating to Virgin, and who managed the switch-selling teams, was promoted to become managing director of world cargo.

Mike 'Mars Bars' Batt, who played a central role in formulating Mission Atlantic's strategy to deal with Virgin and passed on key information to Brian Basham and David Burnside about Virgin's allegedly 'dangerous' planes, was promoted to become the new director of marketing – the most powerful marketing post in BA.

To the surprise of many, Mervyn Walker survived. There had been much speculation that the young lawyer would be fired. He probably owed his survival to the fact that he is the protégé of fellow lawyer, Robert Ayling. He checked all the major mistakes he made with Ayling, his immediate predecessor as legal director, before he made them. Following Walker's initial, completely ineffective 'investigation' into Branson's claims at the end of 1991, he wrote both of the libelous statements over which Branson sued BA, and approved each for publication beforehand. According to the log kept by the Covent Garden detectives, Walker held meetings with them in Speedbird House, and then masterminded BA's doomed legal offensive against Branson which totally undermined the libel defence he was attempting to mount on BA's behalf. Falling on swords was not, however, a popular pastime at BA following King's resignation and Burnside's lavishly funded sacking.

David Hyde, the link man between the BA board and the small army of private detectives that stole rubbish on behalf of BA and launched the probes into BA's own staff, also kept his job as head of security. More than £100,000 came from his 'security' budget to finance Operation Covent Garden, and the extraordinary activities of Ian Johnson and his oddball team of private detectives.

Sir Colin Marshall took personal control of David Burnside's public affairs directorate and immediately split it into two, appointing Peter Jones to head the public relations effort and promoting Burnside's number two, Tony Cocklin, to become head of communications. In practice, Cocklin is Marshall's personal assistant. The former BCal press chief is a survivor. It was Cocklin who gave Brian Basham the figures on Virgin Atlantic's late departure times from the computer. He also organised the leaking of Branson's private letter to his staff to the press, and told Basham that Virgin was having to pay cash for its fuel – the rumour that undid the smear campaign after Basham was taped passing it on to the *Sunday Times*.

BA never published any details of disciplinary action against those who had participated in the 'disreputable business activities', and the airline eventually admitted that no one had been disciplined or sacked. This was predictable, as the most disreputable of the business activities were organised at such a senior level and, according to the minutes of a 1993 board meeting, there was 'very slight evidence' against the remainder of staff, and the board felt severe punishment was not 'merited'.

Thus the only information BA has made available about post-dirty tricks staff changes, indicates that all the staff who were most deeply involved in the 'disreputable' anti-Virgin activities have subsequently been promoted. The list of promotions technically includes Lord King who was relieved of the chairmanship, but 'promoted' to become BA's first president.

However, King returned to Wartnaby in February 1993 as a fallen Lord. On his Leicestershire estate he was still lord of all he surveyed, but the newspaper headlines proclaimed his disgrace.

'Thatcher's Icarus Falls to Earth', was *The Times* front-page headline; and inside its leader provided a succinct summary of King's reign at BA:

[He] has done a fine job of turning a loss-making nationalised industry into a highly competitive and profitable
private airline. But under his chairmanship, there seems to
have sprung up a bullying subculture that endorses almost
any tactic to harm a competitor . . . BA has to learn that, in
the private sector, battles should be fought purely on the
quality of the product. The commercial war cannot be won
by smear and innuendo.

Arriving home, King sat slumped in an armchair in front of a blazing log fire. As he leafed slowly through the dozens of cards which
well-wishers had sent him, the telephone rang. A member of his
household recalls that he shuffled to the sideboard to answer it.
Wartnaby pretended to be the butler as an elderly woman started
to speak. She said she was calling from America and that there
was no point in Lord King's pretending he was the butler.

'John, I just wanted to tell you, you were the greatest achievement of my years in office.'

'Thank you, Margaret,' replied Lord King, his voice choking
with emotion.

14

BA: Gags and Cover-ups

BA's 1993 Annual General Meeting was a humiliating experience
for Mrs Thatcher's 'proudest achievement'. As thousands of shareholders filed in to London's Barbican Hall, they noticed that Lord
King was absent from the platform for the first time since the airline was privatised. No place could be found on the platform for
the fallen Lord, even though BA had stressed that King had been
elevated to the post of life president. He had also been compensated with a generous pay-off. In his final year as chairman, King's
salary of £407,650 was supplemented with a performance-related
bonus of £220,000. As president of BA he receives an annual salary
of £220,000 for his 'ceremonial duties'. In addition he enjoys free
first-class travel on BA for himself and his family, and a generous
package of benefits which includes an office, a secretary, a limousine and a chauffeur.

Because of the Faustian pact that King and Marshall had made
to ensure that they were not both forced out of the airline, the
AGM represented a bitter reminder to King of his failure to deny
Marshall the chairmanship of BA. According to a biography of
Lord Hanson, written by Alex Brummer and Roger Cowe, King
had been actively plotting to ensure Marshall did not succeed him
before he was forced to deal with his deputy. King had apparently
attempted to persuade Hanson to launch a takeover bid for BA as

he prepared for his retirement from the airline. Brummer and Cowe's account of Hanson's move has been disputed, but they relate how King's motive was to deny Marshall control of BA. According to them, Lord White warned Hanson not to bid after King had approached him. White was on the BA board at the time, and he told Hanson that BA would be an 'expensive, controversial and risky' investment for him.

King's plan had failed. Now he had to watch Sir Colin Marshall and Robert Ayling presiding over the AGM while he sat amongst the shareholders. Many of them had come to the Barbican specifically to quiz the board over the dirty-tricks revelations which had led BA to concede defeat to Richard Branson and Virgin Atlantic in the High Court.

After a sycophantic tribute to King by Marshall that some present thought reeked of insincerity, given King's absence from the platform, BA's new chief executive made a statement on the dirty-tricks affair on behalf of the board. Marshall stuck closely to the script that he and Ayling had used to persuade BA's board not to fire them: he emphasised that he and Robert Ayling had been in ignorance of the 'unconnected incidents . . . [of] . . . disreputable activities' that BA had admitted to in court:

> These activities were not authorised by the board of directors of British Airways, nor by any member of the board. Each member of the board has given written assurance to that effect. For my part, I repeat the assurance to you here today and state further, without qualification, that I did not direct, authorise or implement any improper activities against Virgin or its chairman. I did not know about them at the time they occurred. I did not – and do not – condone any such activities.

Marshall is not a natural or a gifted orator, and he worked himself into quite a lather as he attempted to persuade shareholders that the voluminous television and newspaper reports outlining BA's dirty tricks were, in fact, incorrect:

> Virgin Atlantic, in effect, alleged that British Airways had

engaged in a wide-ranging, centrally-orchestrated campaign to damage Virgin. We denied that claim and continue to deny it. There never was such a campaign

From Virgin Atlantic's point of view, this was the formal stage of BA's operation to cover up the board's involvement in the campaign. An admission of involvement or knowledge by any senior member of BA in the commercial dirty tricks against Virgin would have led to the elaborate cover-up operation unravelling.

Anticipating that Marshall and Ayling would use the 1993 AGM to cover their own involvement in the dirty tricks, Branson produced a sharp reminder to BA's shareholders that he would not buy the whitewash. Branson instructed his lawyers to file a complaint against BA to the European Commission, under Articles 85 and 86 of the Treaty of Rome, alleging continued anti-competitive activity. The announcement was a blow to Marshall and Ayling, as it confirmed that Branson was determined to keep the issue of compensation for the dirty-tricks campaign alive in the courts of Britain and Europe. This was precisely what Marshall and Ayling appeared to have been working so hard in the first half of 1993 to avoid.

In the middle of January, shortly after the libel case, BA's two most senior officials had arrived on Richard Branson's doorstep in Holland Park, for much publicised 'peace talks' which, it had been widely assumed, would bring an end to the lengthy conflict between the two airlines. Branson had made it publicly clear that he was prepared to pursue legal actions against BA in Britain, Europe and the USA if no agreement was struck. However, BA did not believe at the beginning of 1993 that Branson possessed the will or the resources to do this, and Marshall had orchestrated a series of press releases in which BA indicated that it wanted to settle the outstanding issues.

It had, nonetheless, been an awkward moment for Marshall and Ayling as they walked through the hallway of Branson's Holland Park home. On a typical day, Branson's hallway would be strewn with his children's bikes and toys. For BA's visit the elegant passage had been cleared; the contrast with the entrance to BA's Heathrow or Central London offices, however, could not have been greater.

For Branson there was irony to savour. His front room had resembled a bunker at the height of BA's dirty-tricks campaign; it was here that Branson had agonised for hours with Will Whitehorn over how to respond to, and then counter, BA's dirty tricks; it was here that he and Whitehorn had first listened to the tape of Brian Basham trashing Virgin Atlantic to a tabloid gossip columnist; and it was here that Branson had wired himself up before travelling to meet one of BA's private detectives who was to confess to the illegal and underhand activities that BA had sponsored in Operation Covent Garden. Now Branson hoped that Marshall and Ayling had come to eat large slices of humble pie.

Marshall and Ayling eased their way rather awkwardly onto Branson's peach-coloured sofas, and found themselves staring at a mantelpiece laden with awards and trophies won by Virgin Atlantic. The rival teams began probing each other as members of Branson's staff brought them tea and biscuits. The managing director of Virgin Travel, Trevor Abbott, accompanied his chairman. Marshall and Ayling could still not be entirely sure how much Branson knew about their own involvement in the dirty-tricks campaign: neither knew that, having studied every one of the thousands of documents that Gerrard Tyrrell's team had unearthed in the process of legal discovery, Branson held the two men personally responsible for orchestrating the campaign to destroy his airline. Both sides were acutely aware, however, in the stormy days that followed Virgin's libel victory that the only matters resolved in the High Court were the libels perpetrated by Lord King and *BA News*. BA had paid Virgin nothing to compensate for the commercial damage caused by the dirty-tricks campaign.

By the time Branson and Marshall emerged for a ceremonial handshake for the benefit of the sea of cameras engulfing the doorstep, the agenda for the talks had been set. Branson wanted millions of pounds in compensation for BA's abuse of the information it had accessed from its computers about Virgin, and for the passengers its poachers had stolen. Virgin's chairman also wanted the dispute over the long-running engineering allegations to be taken into account, as well as a commitment from BA that it would not resort to dirty tricks in the future. According to Branson, Ayling shook his hand privately before the group emerged for a photo-opportunity handshake on the doorstep, and promised him that the relevant damages would be paid promptly.

The optimism that was publicly apparent at the photo-opportunity dissolved almost as soon as the talks started. In meetings with the BA team at Enserch House and at the City offices of Linklaters & Paines, the Virgin team very quickly got the impression that Ayling and Turnbull were only interested in finding out how much Virgin really knew about what had gone on.

'For me it was a case of the old broom being unable to sweep the stable clean. Marshall and Ayling seemed far more interested in grinding us into submission rather than negotiating. It was obvious that BA essentially wanted to buy our silence rather than compensate us for trying to put us out of business,' Branson remembered.

In tactics reminiscent of those it adopted during the libel battle, British Airways summoned a vast army of lawyers in an apparent attempt to square-bash the smaller airline into submission. In addition to Mervyn Walker's legal department, which had to approve any final deal on behalf of BA, the airline was represented by three different sets of lawyers. Linklaters & Paines were joined by BA's New York lawyers, Sullivan & Cromwell, and, because trust on the BA board had broken down almost completely, Simmons and Simmons represented the interests of Sir Michael Angus and the non-executive directors.

Marshall and Branson delegated the talks that followed their Holland Park meeting to their senior colleagues: Robert Ayling and Linklaters' John Turnbull led for BA, and Trevor Abbott and Gerrard Tyrrell for Virgin. The Virgin team was supplemented by Colin Howes, one of Harbottle and Lewis's senior partners, but the relatively compact Virgin contingent struggled to keep awake during some of the sessions as it was confronted by up to twenty BA lawyers and negotiators. The BA team developed a shift system that kept one session going for more than twenty-four hours without a break.

Branson had been peeved when King, Marshall and Ayling signed their pledges in front of the BA board disclaiming responsibility for the dirty-tricks campaign. Branson knew that this was not true. It was widely reported at the time that it had been Sir Michael Angus' idea to make them sign the undertaking that they did not 'implement or authorise' any of the 'regrettable business activities' complained of by Branson. To Branson, Angus appeared to have become a willing accomplice to the cover-up when he emerged from the board meeting and claimed, in an interview with the *Observer*, that

> [Sir Colin Marshall] had nothing to do with, or knew anything about, what was going on.

Without pausing to refer to his own lawyers, Branson had written Angus a furious letter:

> Your personal statement . . . adds injury to insult. Even from your own discovery documents it is clear that some directors knew exactly what was going on and in fact were actively involved in it. Trying to give the impression that this was carried out by a few junior members of staff was to perpetuate a gross misconception as to where in BA responsibility for these activities lay.

Virgin's chairman was particularly angry that the board members had all denied that they had authorised the accessing of Virgin's computers.

> There was hardly a department in BA that was not in some way misusing this information – from senior directors right through to the marketing, sales, accounts, tele-sales and press departments.

Allegations of bad faith further plagued the negotiations from the outset. On one occasion BA accused Virgin of leaking its latest offer to the press. Branson hotly denied it, and pointed out that he had not received the offer that had been leaked. A shamefaced Marshall wrote a letter of apology a few days later. BA had discovered that a draft of the offer had been leaked before it left Speedbird House.

Dear Richard,

. . . I am truly sorry that our draft letter was leaked to the press. It is particularly embarrassing to us because it was an early draft of the letter which was finally delivered to you and it was accompanied by a letter from our solicitors which you can imagine we would rather had been kept confidential.

. . . We are continuing to investigate the matter internally.

BA was a very divided company in the aftermath of the libel settlement, and the leaks to the press actually came from feuding board members.

The following week BA was forced to launch another massive internal investigation when it was revealed that its American operation was continuing to attempt to switch-sell Virgin passengers in Los Angeles. Michael Chrisman and I discovered in the middle of February, in the course of researching an article on America's anti-trust laws for the *Independent*, that John Healy and Romel Manalo at British Imports Travel in Long Beach, California, were continuing to get unsolicited calls from BA representatives seeking to switch Virgin passengers to BA. We had phoned Healy and Manalo because they had appeared in the *This Week* film, and they had proved to be extremely reliable witnesses. We were particularly impressed by their evidence, because they did more business with BA than with Virgin Atlantic. When we phoned them in February 1993, we asked them how badly they felt Virgin's trade had been damaged by the smear campaign the previous year. They told us that Virgin's trade was still being damaged, *not* by the rumour campaign, but by continuing switch-selling by BA. We found this difficult to believe, and grilled them very closely.

Manalo had taken details of the calls and noted precisely when they occurred in a log. He explained how he had been cold-called more than a dozen times in the previous two months by BA reps. When Manalo sells a ticket he puts his own name, and the contact number of British Imports Travel, in his computer rather than that of the passenger, as travel agents normally do.

'I do this with many of my customers to help them out if there are changes in their flights. It's all part of our service, and it is popular with people who buy tickets from us.'

As a result of this unusual service to his clients, Manalo had found that he had received dozens of calls from BA switch-sellers in the previous two months, as the BA reps had apparently mistaken Manalo for a Virgin passenger.

'The BA representative always offers an upgrade to business class if I switch my tickets from Virgin to BA. When the BA callers realise I'm the agent and not the customer, they get really embarrassed and slam the phone down.' Some of the BA reps were more persistent. 'Occasionally they stay on the line and try to persuade me to switch my passengers to BA. They offer me a financial inducement to do this by selling the tickets at a discount rate.' Manalo was extremely surprised by the calls. 'I'm totally baffled as to how BA can access the information about Virgin passengers that I put into my computer.'

Manalo's boss, John Healy, had also detected another mysterious strain of calls from agents claiming to work for Virgin.

'We were asked for the telephone numbers of their ticketed passengers to update their flight details.

'We've been dealing with Virgin for about four years, and we've never had this type of request before. We eventually decided to contact Virgin directly in Los Angeles and New York, and they told us that this was not their policy.'

Healy suspected that the 'Virgin' callers were actually BA switch-sellers once again getting up to the tricks that he had first experienced in 1992.

I was freelancing for ITN as well as for the *Independent* when we discovered that BA was still trying to steal Virgin's passengers. ITN's foreign editor, Michael Jermey, promptly dispatched myself and reporter Paul Davies to interview the two travel agents. They confirmed their story on camera and gave us details of some of the passengers who had been cold-called. One passenger was a professor at the University of Southern California who had been called at home by BA on 25 January, and offered an upgrade if he transferred to BA. On the condition that he remained anonymous, the professor related the details of BA's approach which he said was confirmed by BA officials at Los Angeles airport when he arrived to catch his Virgin flight.

When Davies and I returned to London we invited BA and Virgin

Atlantic to come to ITN and watch the interviews we had recorded
in LA. Their responses were illuminating. Richard Branson and
Will Whitehorn turned up at ITN's Grays Inn studios within an
hour and, having watched the tape, Branson accused BA of 'bla-
tantly disregarding' the apology it had made in the High Court:

'They promised the dirty tricks would stop and they clearly
haven't. Sir Freddie Laker said that British Airways was a leopard
that couldn't change its spots. But I still find it amazing that only
a month after admitting it in court, they are at it again.'

As we recorded Branson's comments, our call to the BA press
office was returned by Mrs Thatcher's former advertising guru, Sir
Tim Bell. In the wake of BA's High Court climbdown, Bell had
been drafted in by the BA board to replace his old rival, Brian
Basham, as BA's main external PR consultant. Initially hired on a
three-month contract, the only task Bell's agency, Lowe Bell
Communications, was given by the BA board was to cope with the
fallout from the dirty-tricks affair; in other words, to provide a PR
shield for BA's cover-up of Marshall and Ayling's involvement in
the dirty-tricks campaign, and to prevent any more damaging revelations being broadcast or published.

Bell had made his first appearance as part of BA's cover-up
team on the day that Lord King was forced to quit the chairmanship. As the nation's press watched Lord King floundering
embarrassingly outside Enserch House, the hirsute, greying figure
of Bell emerged from the shadows and eased King back into
Enserch House. Some asked why so seasoned an operator as Bell
had allowed his Lordship to be thrown to the media's wolves in
the first place, and thus suffer an indignity to which he had no
response but an earthy expletive. Perhaps the smug expressions
on the faces of the new chairman of British Airways and his new
group managing director as King was being humiliated gave a
clue. Marshall and Ayling had just recommended to the board
that Sir Tim be hired at an annual fee of £360,000 to defend them
both from further probes into the dirty-tricks affair, and Lord King
was now, very visibly, the former chairman of British Airways.

Lowe Bell Communications had, by the 1990s, become something of a refuge for those who had prospered, as Bell himself had
done, in the Thatcher decade. As plain Tim Bell, he had played a

key role in moulding Mrs Thatcher's early image while he worked with the Saatchi brothers. In the 1987 election it was Tim Bell who appeared as the cavalry over the hill to Mrs Thatcher when she became worried that Neil Kinnock's resurgent Labour Party appeared to be closing the gap in the week before polling day. Bell was credited with rewriting the Tory advertising, and steering his mistress through what became known as her 'wobbly Wednesday'.

After Bell had been knighted for his efforts by Mrs Thatcher, he transferred his talents from advertising to public relations in 1989. His close links with Thatcher bestowed upon Bell a credibility and an authority that his rivals envied. After Thatcher had been forced to resign, Bell's agency, Lowe Bell Communications, became something of a last chance saloon for Thatcherite fellow-travellers who had outlasted their leader but who were struggling to make their way into the 1990s. Even Sir Tim Bell couldn't prevent one of his clients, cabinet minister David Mellor, from being cast into the political wilderness. It was Bell who persuaded Mellor to parade three generations of his family for the picture-hungry paparazzi in a last-ditch attempt to convince the public that he was happily married. However, revelations about the minister's penchant for having his toe sucked as part of his extra-marital activities with Antonia de Sancha while allegedly wearing the colours of Chelsea FC put Mellor beyond Bell's help.

The PR man did, however, help to salvage the career of another of his clients, the BBC's director general, John Birt. Appointed by a board of governors stacked with Thatcher appointees, Birt's BBC career was progressing promisingly until his Schedule 'D' tax status was revealed – the BBC's boss was not, it turned out, a member of staff. After a couple of days of behind-the-scenes contact-making and lobbying by Bell, the calls for Birt's removal were transformed into a clamour for the resignation of his boss, BBC chairman Marmaduke Hussey, for allowing Birt to enjoy Schedule 'D' tax status in the first place. Birt obviously appreciated Bell's work and this helped the PR man to retain his BBC contract while many of Birt's senior colleagues were questioning the wisdom of paying a third of a million pounds a year to someone who shared Mrs Thatcher's intense dislike of the BBC, and the public service ethic it represents.

The BBC said that Bell's brief was to advise on 'corporate communications' as it sought the renewal of its charter. However, senior BBC executives were alarmed to hear reliable reports, in the early days of John Major's incumbency, that Bell had heavily criticised the BBC at a dinner-party with the Prime Minister. At the time the BBC was particularly keen to create a favourable impression upon the new Prime Minister, and to build on the admiration for the BBC's coverage of the Gulf War that Major expressed in the House of Commons. At that particularly crucial phase in the corporation's history, with its future in the balance, the BBC's top PR man tore into the BBC, describing it as 'out of touch' and in need of privatisation. It was a strange interpretation of the role for which the BBC pays the 'hidden persuader' over a third of a million pounds of its licence fees every year. Ironically, the Prime Minister was so alarmed to hear Bell's tirade that he leapt to the BBC's defence. When the story filtered back to the BBC, senior members of the corporation suggested that the fees the BBC was spending on Bell's services might be better spent on making programmes. What precisely was it, they asked, that the BBC got for its money? Journalists throughout the corporation were delighted when the BBC announced in 1996 that Sir Tim Bell's contract with the BBC had been terminated. When it was heard that the PR man had departed because of a possible conflict of interest, no one was very surprised as many thought it inappropriate that he should work for the BBC while actively trying to stifle media coverage of BA's dirty tricks. However, it turned out that Bell had ended his BBC account not because of his work for BA, but because he had been signed by Rupert Murdoch's satellite channel, BSkyB, one of the BBC's direct rivals. A BBC spokeswoman said, 'He could probably pay more than we could.'

Bell appeared to be an appropriate signing for BA as he specialised in helping those who had been accused of dirty tricks or fraud, particularly those who, like BA, had a record of generous donations to the Conservative Party. As many of the icons of Thatcher's market-driven enterprise culture tumbled after her departure from Downing Street, Bell was on hand to try to shield them from hostile coverage as they awaited trial or fled the country before they had to face justice. Octav Botnar, for example, hired the ubiquitous PR man after he had fled Britain. The former head of Nissan UK had been a major donor to Mrs Thatcher's Tory Party, but stood accused of conspiring to defraud the British government of nearly £100 million. Bell also worked for the Reichman brothers, the owners of Olympia and York, during the Canary Wharf collapse.

1994 provided an usually vivid kaleidoscope of Bell's activities and one in which he plumbed uncharted depths. In the spring, during the first free elections in South Africa, Bell was hired as an adviser by the National Party. As the architects of apartheid watched the racist system they had built being dismantled, Bell advised them on how to grapple with the unfamiliar experience of submitting themselves to the electorate's verdict, and how best they could defeat Nelson Mandela's ANC. Selling such advice was profitable for Bell, but it had little impact on the ANC's landslide victory.

In the summer Bell committed his most notorious gaffe when he became indelibly associated with spam fritters. The government paid Bell over £60,000 of taxpayers' money to think up ideas as to how the 50th anniversary of D-Day should be celebrated. Over lunch at the Savoy, Bell dreamed up the unlikely idea of challenging people to create the best war-time menu they could from Second World War rations while 'celebrating' D-Day with street parties: hence spam fritters. Bell's preposterous proposals achieved the improbable feat of driving a wedge between the Conservative government, and Britain's Second World War veterans. With the support of the forces' sweetheart, Dame Vera Lynn, the veterans united to oppose Bell's laughable ideas, showing the same determination to defeat Bell that had been so valuable in driving Hitler from the beaches of France. Under such enormous pressure from veterans' organisations, the government eventually abandoned Bell's proposals, but his agency still collected its fee, amid cries in the press of 'Give it back!' and 'Cough up Sir Tim!'.

In the autumn of 1994 the *Sunday Times* reported that Mark Thatcher had pocketed £12 million for his middle-man role in the largest arms deal in British history. The massive Al Yamamah arms deal with Saudi Arabia had been signed by his mother. It was little surprise to find that Thatcher junior had called upon the services of his mother's former guru to attempt to dispel such slurs on the family's name. Bell told the press to ignore 'the rubbish about arms dealing and the rest of it'.

When Bell phoned ITN on 22 February 1993 he immediately insisted on knowing what would be in the *News at Ten* report. We repeated our invitation to Sir Colin Marshall or his nominee to view the LA interviews at ITN, but we refused to divulge the details of our interviews to BA's PR consultant. For the rest of the evening we were treated to a display of Bell's version of 'crisis PR' which would have had David Burnside and Brian Basham blushing. He started by telling me, 'You have no idea how much corporate damage this story could do to British Airways'. I told him that, as a journalist, my proper concern was for the accuracy of the story, and corporate considerations would have to remain his concern. After I made it clear that we would not reveal the names of those who had made the allegations against BA before transmission unless one of the airline's representatives came to ITN, Bell tried other tactics. He tracked down a jet-lagged Paul Davies in the cutting room and told him that, if the story was broadcast, his reputation would be ruined. Davies, who had been awarded the OBE by the Queen the previous month, ignored the PR man's threats. Undeterred, Bell contacted ITN's associate editor, Dame Sue Tinson, who had also been recommended for her honour by Mrs Thatcher. Tinson checked the story with Davies and myself, and then told Bell it would run because she was satisfied it was true. In a final flurry of calls from his office, his car phone and his home, Bell tried unsuccessfully to contact ITN's editor-in-chief Stuart Purvis in a last bid to stop the story being broadcast. Bell's efforts were in vain. The story led the *News at Ten*, and provided the *Independent*'s front page splash the next day. Scores of regional newspapers, and radio and television stations, followed up the ITN story.

Having failed to prevent ITN broadcasting the passenger-poaching story, Lowe Bell masterminded an urgent damage-limitation exercise on behalf of BA. Robert Ayling followed up Bell's threats to ITN by threatening to sue the company unless it retracted the story and apologised on the *News at Ten* the following night. As the former head of BA's passenger-poaching department, Ayling was apparently worried that further exposures of an area of the dirty-tricks campaign for which he was personally responsible might undermine his new position as group managing director.

While he attempted to bully ITN into making a retraction in London, Ayling also dispatched the head of BA's North American operation, John Storey, from New York to Los Angeles the following day. Storey flew to the West Coast with an attorney in an apparent attempt to find flaws in our report. The BA delegation left Los Angeles empty-handed; John Healy and Romel Manalo told the BA men precisely what they had told us about the continued poaching of Virgin's passengers.

After David Mannion, ITN's editor of programmes, had refused to bow to Ayling's demands for an on-air retraction, Sir Tim Bell plied his contacts in the press with disinformation about the passenger-poaching allegations. Despite John Storey's findings, Bell claimed that the story had been fed to the late Joan Thirkettle, one of ITN's most senior reporters, by Richard Branson. I knew this was not true, and Thirkettle and Branson confirmed that it was not true. Bell told journalists who pursued the story from other newspapers that the professor in California whom BA had tried to poach had recanted, and had denied the story. This was also untrue. The professor was so annoyed when he heard that BA's representatives were misrepresenting him in London that he refused to have any contact with BA whatsoever when the airline later launched an investigation into the matter.

Bell phoned me at ITN the morning after transmission to chastise me for not 'trading' information with him. He told me that BA had issued a worldwide directive on 22 January to halt the poaching of Virgin's passengers. He argued that our story was, therefore, out of date. This also proved to be untrue. When BA was subsequently pressed by Virgin's lawyers on the 22 January instruction the airline could not produce it. The professor's call from BA had, in any case, been received on 25 January.

The saga eventually petered out at the beginning of May when Robert Ayling informed David Mannion that BA had decided to let the matter drop following a personal visit to ITN's headquarters in Grays Inn Road. Mannion was not surprised that BA had been unable to refute the story because it was true, but it was a relief to ITN's management that BA would not be taking action. Bell had been telling his contacts that BA had decided to sue.

The impact of such meddling by Lowe Bell should not be underestimated. With the benefit of hindsight, the untruthful elements in Bell's statements can be spotted and dissected. However, as a story breaks and reporters throughout the media fight tight deadlines as they try to chase the story, and editors are deciding whether or not to run the story at all, the impact of Bell's dissembling can be enormous. As with his efforts to sabotage our ITN report, Bell and his henchmen went straight for newspaper managements and their editors the following day, rather than the journalists working on the story. Newspaper hierarchies were advised by Lowe Bell that 'ITN is considering an apology' and that 'BA's lawyers are preparing to take legal action against ITN'. Bell told *The Times* and the *Daily Express* that BA had 'turned' the professor – in other words he was now retracting his story of being poached in LA. Some of these claims bore an extremely limited relationship to the truth (ITN was, indeed, reading BA's letter asking for an apology; it was not considering making one) and some of them were false and not designed to stand up to informed scrutiny. They were deterrents to newspaper and television managements as their journalists attempted to follow up the passenger-poaching story, and were designed to have the effect of dampening the story down. This is one way Lowe Bell earns its fee from BA – crisis management and damage limitation with no obligation to adhere to the truth in any given situation. The PR company has no role at BA other than to deal with stories related to the dirty-tricks campaign.

A second, equally important objective is to dissuade broadcasters and newspapers from pursuing the dirty-tricks issue any further. In this sense Ayling and Bell's tactics did have some effect at ITN. Nothing that Bell told ITN at the time, and nothing that Ayling said subsequently convinced anyone at ITN that there was anything wrong with our report from LA. However, BA's three-month period of pressure on ITN's management over what, in news terms, was a very straightforward and well-sourced report acted as a deterrent to ITN to pursue the subject any further.

When *World in Action* provided documentary evidence about the role of Marshall and Ayling in the dirty-tricks campaign in the spring of 1993, the revelations were reported on the front page of the *Guardian* and were subsequently followed up by newspapers on both sides of the Atlantic. ITN, however, declined to cover the story on the night *World In Action* was broadcast despite being offered the story exclusively in advance of transmission. That decision was made while Ayling was still threatening to sue. ITN has subsequently broken no new ground on the dirty-tricks dispute between Britain's two leading airlines, and it has barely covered subsequent events as they have unfolded. Ayling and Bell lost the battle over the Los Angeles passenger-poaching story, but they won their war to deter ITN from investigating the dirty-tricks campaign any further.

Initially, Lowe Bell's stewardship of BA's public relations did little to repair the damage that the libel verdict had caused the airline's public image. The *Presswatch Quarterly*, which monitors and evaluates press coverage of British companies, charted a dramatic decline in BA's fortunes which coincided with Lowe Bell Communications taking over from Warwick Corporate as BA's external PR consultants. In the last quarter of 1992 – the final period of the Burnside/Basham regime – BA was riding high in the chart. For the first quarter of 1993 BA recorded the lowest rating – minus 3,653 – ever achieved by a British company, placing it comfortably bottom of the Presswatch league table in 641st place. Virgin came top with +1002. BA's indignity was compounded when the SFB agency placed the airline third in its 1993 'clumsy communicators' awards. David Mellor was first, and the BBC was fourth, giving Bell the dubious distinction of representing three out of the top four 'clumsy communicators'.

Despite the acrimonious exchanges, and Branson's fury over BA's continuing determination to steal his passengers, it appeared by the end of February 1993 that a compromise was in sight. Branson said he would settle for between £12.5 million and £13 million to compensate for the passenger-poaching, and the accessing of Virgin's computer information. BA offered £9 million. Both packages were to include approximately £3 million for the engineering dispute. The remainder was in compensation for the dirty-tricks campaign.

Branson was personally very keen to settle during this period, and the financial incentive for him to accept what he described as the 'token' compensation on offer was quite strong. The airline managed to make a profit of £6.1 million in the year to October 1991, withstanding the effects of the Gulf War and the recession comparatively well. However, in the financial year ending October 1992, the year in which BA's dirty-tricks campaign had been at its height, Virgin Travel Group reported a loss of £14.5 million. The annual accounts attribute this loss to the recession, the introduction of the new 'Mid Class' service on all flights, and the costs of building the airline's new lounge at Heathrow and launching the Orlando service. Unable to attract new investment to replenish the ageing fleet with new planes, Virgin's maintenance costs had soared, and many of its passengers were stolen by BA.

Branson, however, remained as reluctant to take further action against BA as he had been to start proceedings a year beforehand. The strain that the legal battle had placed upon himself and the compact management structure of his tiny airline had been immense, and he yearned to be able to devote his energy to building 'the best airline in the world'. Branson was finding it increasingly hard, however, to accept Marshall and Ayling as bona fide negotiators. His conviction that they had both played key roles in orchestrating the dirty-tricks campaign grew stronger as BA's motives were revealed in the negotiations.

In March 1993, BA finally showed Branson its true hand. It produced a draft contract for Branson to sign. BA agreed to pay Virgin Atlantic £9 million in compensation, but only if it would agree to return to BA all the documents that had been handed over during the process of discovery in the libel case. In addition, Branson and his senior colleagues would have to agree to sign a strict gagging clause prohibiting them from ever speaking about the dirty-tricks campaign again. Marshall and Ayling were particularly keen to ensure that Branson kept quiet about their attempts to put him out of business. Both had given misleading accounts of their own roles to £1,000 but this must be subject to a gagging clause in respect of the settlement'.

Gorman was furious.

'I have never been so insulted,' says Gorman. 'These people had ruined my life for the past eighteen months, and then they offered me this paltry sum if I accepted a "gagging clause". Talking to the media was the least of my considerations. I thought they wanted me to join the quest to find the perpetrators of the acts of criminal violence, vandalism, theft and intimidation.'

As it had tried to do with Branson and Virgin, BA was attempting to gag Gorman. As with Branson, BA was completely unsuccessful. Bitterly upset by BA's response, Gorman readily agreed to my proposal to approach the BBC's *Newsnight* programme with a view to making a film about his experiences. One of the programme's senior producers, Sian Kevill, and the then deputy editor, Richard Clemmow, immediately saw the potential of the story. Within days of my call, Peter Horrocks, *Newsnight*'s editor, had commissioned the film.

As *Newsnight* producer Dee McIntosh, cameraman/journalist Ian Pritchard and I started our investigation, the press officers at BA and the relevant Metropolitan Police forces went into their shells. Neither organisation would put up any interviewees, and both confined themselves to uninformative and bland press releases. However, we gleaned interesting 'off the record' information from police officers involved in the case. I spoke to one officer who had been involved in the Enfield police investigation into the attack on Gorman in his home, and the anonymous calls that warned him it would happen. He told me that once the calls were traced to BA and to Heathrow police station, he was instructed to discontinue his enquiries. The officer said that he had been told, 'We wouldn't have got anything out of them, so what was the point in trying?'

A fax from the police did, however, reveal that Chief Inspector Lovelock of the Complaints Branch had sent his report on Gorman's complaint to the Crown Prosecution Service. It said it would then be sent to the Police Complaints Authority. The *Newsnight* investigation appeared to dispel the lethargy that had surrounded the Enfield investigation. As we interviewed Gorman in his flat we heard a succession of officers leaving messages on his answerphone asking him to contact them urgently.

'I haven't heard anything from them for weeks,' commented Gorman, as he listened to the officers leaving their direct lines and pager numbers on his machine, 'but now the BBC has started an investigation they appear to have woken up. I was attacked on 17 June, but they still haven't taken a statement from me about the call I got a few days before that warned me it would happen'.

The police appeared to be keeping a very close eye on the *Newsnight* investigation itself. Dee McIntosh had invited the paramedics from Chase Farm Hospital to participate in her reconstruction of the attack on Gorman in his home. The paramedics had played an important role in saving Gorman's sight by arriving quickly and acting professionally. She explained to their press office that their work would be shown briefly and in a wholly positive light. Chase Farm readily agreed, but on the eve of filming they pulled their staff out of the reconstruction. Their fax said they had done so 'on the advice of the Metropolitan Police'. The paramedics were replaced by actors.

BA's press office was appalled that the BBC was intending to make its first-ever film on its dirty tricks. 'No-one we have spoken to seems to think this is really a *Newsnight* topic,' was the best its pressmen could come up with when we asked BA for a response to Gorman's allegations. Marshall, Ayling and Walker all refused invitations to be interviewed, in line with the policy David Burnside established when I first started to enquire about Branson's allegations of a dirty-tricks campaign against Virgin.

After *Newsnight* insisted that the film would go ahead without its participation, BA assembled many of the most prominent remaining members of its dirty-tricks team at Speedbird House to consider how to respond. *Newsnight* had intended to transmit the film on Friday 26 August. BA had promised a press release on the Gorman allegations before transmission. Under Ayling's chairmanship the most expensive minds of the post-Burnside and Basham era were gathered together. Tony Cocklin represented Sir Colin Marshall, departmental heads Peter Jones and Mervyn Walker represented the public affairs and legal departments, and the meeting welcomed Lowe Bell's Terry Collis to advise on the finer points of tactics and strategy. Eventually, two weeks after *Newsnight* had first approached BA, and in response to a list of twelve questions, BA faxed a four-paragraph response to *Newsnight*'s editor, Peter Horrocks, three hours before the scheduled transmission. In fact, the film was delayed until the following week for a variety of editorial, technical and logistical reasons.

BA's 26 August response to Horrocks started with a disingenuous claim. Peter Jones repeated BA's claim that 'the Gorman matter is in the hands of the police, with whom British Airways has co-operated from the beginning'. This directly contradicted a 9 August letter from Robert Ayling to Gorman in which he wrote, 'We are collating the information we need to put to the police and we are considering whom we should contact. As soon as we have decided, Mervyn will let you know our decision.' As British Airways were well aware, Gorman's complaint against BA started in January 1993, and the police became involved in May 1993 when they joined BA to arrest Gorman in his home.

Peter Jones' curt, defensive reply dismissed most of *Newsnight*'s questions as 'irrelevant', and specifically refused to answer our detailed questions about Mervyn Walker's role in the affair. We had, for example, asked:

> When did Mr Walker realise that he had been the recipient of stolen documents, and when did he report the matter to the police? Dates, times and the identity of the police officers who dealt with the matter would be appreciated, as well as any supporting documentation you care to provide us with.

No reply was forthcoming to the detailed points we raised, simply a re-hash of the letter Walker had sent to Gorman on the matter when he returned the documents in July. The suspicion thus lingered that Walker had not reported to the police at the earliest opportunity that he had received stolen documents. Jones' press release claimed that 'there was nothing to suggest that the documents had been stolen'. Once again this was a disingenuous claim, as Paul Foot's fax had alerted BA, and Walker, to the fact that they had been stolen on the day Walker posted the documents back to Gorman.

Walker's bungling of the Virgin and Gorman dirty-tricks allegations had made him an extremely vulnerable member of BA's
top team, particularly with Branson's impending anti-trust action
casting a shadow over the future of BA's most senior management. Ayling decided to deal with Walker in characteristic fashion.
He was promoted. As Ayling and his PR men huddled in
Speedbird House preparing BA's response for *Newsnight*, they
emitted another short press release, announcing Walker's eleva-
tion to the post of Director of Purchasing and Supply. The release
stated that the career lawyer, who had hitherto not had any experience of management, would henceforth be occupying this 'key
post' in BA with a budget of £1.8 billion and a staff of 260.

The news of Walker's promotion, and the appointment of his
successor, Ken Walder, BP's former group legal adviser, made a
few lines in London's *Evening Standard* but was otherwise lost over
the August bank holiday. The discrete announcement was, however, the only shrewd PR stroke that BA pulled during the Gorman
affair. The following week, as the BA press office was besieged
with enquiries about Walker's sudden transfer after *Newsnight* had
highlighted his role in the Gorman affair, BA was able to point to
the small article in the *Standard* to indicate that the announcement
had been made before the *Newsnight* film had been transmitted.

BA became extremely agitated over suggestions from television
and newspaper journalists that Walker's move might in any way
be connected to his botched handling of the Gorman affair. Ayling
faxed stern statements, not to the reporters chasing the story, but
to the directors and editors of their organisations, stating that
Walker was a 'trusted and respected senior employee'.
Suggestions that he had been involuntarily moved could not be
'further from the truth'. Walker had indeed been promoted,
Ayling insisted, and any attempt to link his 'promotion' to the
Gorman affair would be to 'seriously misrepresent the truth'. As in
the case of ITN's passenger-poaching story eighteen months earlier, Sir Tim Bell was called in for his part of the double act with
Ayling. This time Bell's role was to bully the journalists he thought
might be working on the story based on his rather hazy knowledge of the BBC's editorial and journalistic structures. Soon the
Newsnight team's endeavours to set up a programme to consider

the implications of the IRA ceasefire were interrupted by a call to the producer of that night's programme, Jim Gray, 'It's Sir Timothy Bell here,' barked BA's PR man. 'Mervyn Walker has not been sacked . . .'

'Who is Mervyn Walker, anyway?' wondered Gray, who had not been involved in the Gorman investigation. Although baffled by Bell's abrupt and unwanted interruption, Gray and his team felt a frisson of excitement at getting a call from the fabled Bell. They knew BA must be taking the story very seriously to devote such heavyweight and expensive PR to getting their point of view across.

The Ayling/Bell combination was once again unsuccessful in suppressing negative coverage of Walker's unexpected move. The *Mail on Sunday* reported his move on the front page of its City section. Its headline read, 'BA gives key job to 'dirty tricks' lawyer – fourth anti-Virgin campaigner rewarded with promotion.'

The *Newsnight* film on Gorman on 31 August was preceded by a report on the *Nine O'Clock News*, and a lengthy article I wrote for the *Guardian*'s 'Inside Story' section the same morning.

'British Airways had claimed to have cleaned up its act [after the Virgin dirty-tricks campaign],' intoned *Newsnight*'s presenter, Jeremy Paxman, as he introduced our film on Gorman. 'But *Newsnight* has evidence of another dirty-tricks campaign, this time involving harassment, vandalism, theft and physical assault. The target this time wasn't one of its competitors but one of the airline's own shareholders.'

We condensed Gorman's odyssey into a report lasting just over twenty minutes. Gorman came across in the film exactly as he does in real life – honest, articulate and extremely miffed. BA also came across exactly as it does in real life when questioned about dirty tricks of any description – pompous and deceitful. In the absence of a BA representative to interview we were reduced to summarising BA's position in a graphic. Viewers were left to draw their own conclusions. We also carried the Metropolitan Police's statement that a file on Gorman's complaints against the police was being sent to the Crown Prosecution Service and then to the Police Complaints Authority. Much had to be left out of the film but condensing the story and reconstructing some of the appalling things that had happened to Gorman, such as the attack in his home and the threatening phone calls, demonstrated his plight vividly on Britain's leading daily news and current affairs television programme.

The effect of the BBC coverage was, nonetheless, extraordinary. Despite the imminence of the IRA ceasefire, three national newspapers put the Gorman story on their front pages the following morning. The *Today* front page screamed, 'British Airways' "bullies" accused of hate vendetta', the *Express* caught the mood with 'Ordeal of BA "hate" victim' and the *Sun* chimed in with 'Vendetta on ex-cop over glass in BA drink'. The broadsheets gave the *Newsnight* story prominent coverage as well. *The Times* reported 'Passenger "target of violent campaign by BA"' and the *Telegraph* decided to place the emphasis on the police role in the campaign against Gorman, 'Police accused of "dirty tricks" war on BA passenger'. The *Mirror* devoted a whole page to Gorman's trials under the heading 'Flight from hell ruined my life', shamelessly stealing the picture of Gorman and my article from the *Guardian* without acknowledgement or reference to Gorman, the *Guardian* or myself. The Press Association watched *Newsnight* and immediately made Gorman lead with the story, 'Probe into ex-detective's "BA staff attacked me", claim', which ensured that Gorman's allegations reached news desks throughout the country.

Gorman read the headlines as he sat in LBC's studios waiting to be interviewed on the morning news show, *Prime Time*. The programme's editor, Peter Kimber, had been startled by the *Newsnight* film, and had invited Gorman to appear the following morning. Kimber watched the *Newsnight* report with his mother, who is also a BA shareholder. He said she had watched the *Newsnight* film and that she was 'levitating' by the end of it as she was so angry with BA. Gorman was inundated with requests for television and newspaper interviews. He was heard on coast-to-coast radio in Canada; American and Australian television channels had put in bids to do documentaries about him; and the *Sunday Times* of South Africa featured his plight.

BA's response was entirely predictable. According to Tony Cocklin, Marshall, Ayling and Walker had viewed a tape of the *Newsnight* film together in Speedbird House the morning after it was shown on the BBC. They immediately instructed the press office to continue to refuse what had by now become an avalanche of requests for interviews. With the Gorman genie now out of its bottle, the press office was reduced to faxing ever less informative statements to journalists chasing the story. BA's tactics did not impress the papers. 'BA silent over "harassment" saga' ran the *Financial Times* headline, and an exasperated correspondent from the German news magazine, *Der Spiegel*, exclaimed, 'I can't speak to bits of paper! I want to speak to a real person from BA!'

Gorman's persistence in pursuing his claim, in refusing to be fobbed off by BA's dissembling, doggedly carrying on his attempt to seek justice, when many others would have given up, had reduced the board and the senior management of one of the most powerful companies in Britain to evading questions, and using its press department to shield it from legitimate press enquiries from all over the world. The Gorman affair also torpedoed Marshall's attempts to restore his own image.

For the eighteen months after the dirty-tricks court case Marshall had been vulnerable to the charge that he either knew what was going on during the dirty-tricks campaign and had, therefore, lied to BA's board, its shareholders, Parliament and the press, or that he did not know what had been going on and was, thus, incompetent. On 25 August 1994 BA paid for a twenty-four-page insert in *The Times* to mark the airline's '75th anniversary'. A series of articles lauded the achievements of BA's leaders. Marshall was fêted in an article entitled 'Leading right from the front' by the paper's aviation correspondent, Harvey Elliott. *The Times* reported that the chairman and chief executive 'takes delight in keeping close tabs on every department in the vast BA empire'. Marshall apparently felt that a sufficient period of time had elapsed from the dark days when he paraded as the chief executive who knew nothing about the 'disreputable activities' BA had admitted to in court, and it was now safe to attempt a re-emergence as the man in control of BA. Within a week the Gorman affair shattered Marshall's attempts to re-cast his image. Happy to claim credit for the BA's rising profits in 1994, and to accept a salary of £788,000 as a reward, Marshall had nothing to say on Gorman's complaints against the company.

Marshall had assured Gorman at BA's AGM that he would personally oversee Walker's investigation into his allegations. Now he was, once again, denying all knowledge of a dirty-tricks campaign, and refusing to be interviewed by journalists asking legitimate questions. Once again Marshall was organising another PR cover-up with Sir Tim Bell to try and avoid further embarrassment in the press for British Airways. And the whole affair had arisen, on this occasion, because one of BA's shareholders had complained about the service on a BA plane.

Robert Ayling's nadir in the Gorman affair was still to come. Shortly after the *Newsnight* film was shown, Marshall's right-hand man, Tony Cocklin, phoned Gorman at home and invited him to Speedbird House for a confidential meeting with Robert Ayling. He asked Gorman, who was by now receiving regular enquiries from the world's media, not to tell anyone about the meeting. Gorman agreed.

Tony Cocklin welcomed Gorman to Speedbird House and chatted amiably with the disgruntled shareholder for half an hour before the meeting with the group managing director began. Ayling was accompanied by Mervyn Walker's replacement, Ken Walder, who sat quietly throughout the meeting possibly wondering what sort of company he had joined.

'Mr Gorman,' began Ayling, 'did you find the *Newsnight* film an accurate account of your complaints against BA?'

'Hundred per cent,' replied Gorman.

According to Gorman, Ayling looked briefly crestfallen, but the meeting got under way in a relaxed and friendly atmosphere with copious refreshments on hand.

'Mr Gorman ' said Ayling. 'What we need is your help'.

The discussion went on in similar vein for nearly two hours. Ayling re-emphasised that BA accepted what Gorman was saying in good faith, that the airline accepted that he was not trying to discredit it. He said that, as group managing director, he, too, was interested in rooting out the culprits responsible for disfiguring Gorman's life for the past eighteen months.

Gorman had brought to the meeting a list of areas that he felt aggrieved about, in addition to the 'glass in the drink' incident. He stressed to the BA team that he had come to Speedbird House, at their request, not to seek financial compensation, but to accept BA's invitation to join it in getting to the bottom of the affair. To demonstrate his good faith he told them that he had turned down a TV interview that morning so he could attend the meeting.

After a friendly and, Gorman thought, constructive meeting, Ayling appeared to be on the brink of making Gorman an offer to settle the dispute. Instead he leant forward and told Gorman, 'I need hours to think about this.'

'Well, I'll pop back and see you after I've had a bite to eat, then,' replied Gorman, noticing that it was nearly lunchtime.

'No, Mr Gorman. I'll need a little longer than that,' replied Ayling. 'Tony Cocklin will keep us in touch and I'll write to you tomorrow.'

Gorman drove back to Enfield feeling that, after eighteen months, his extraordinary odyssey was nearly over. Tony Cocklin had told him that he thought his evidence was 'irrefutable', and had even said he hoped they could meet socially for a pint of beer when the saga was over. He had got the firm impression from Ayling that he wanted to settle the matter. Ayling had appeared to think this would be good for BA and good for Gorman. As he made his way back to Enfield along the M25, he allowed himself to envisage the final curtain falling on the affair, possibly a 'picture-opportunity' outside Speedbird House with Sir Colin Marshall apologising on behalf of BA. Gorman longed for his conflict with BA to be over, and to be able to return to his normal, very private life. His struggle with BA had created enormous strains on his relationship with Peter. After eighteen months of searching for a full-time job, however, Sherman had just been hired as a senior travel consultant with Phoenix Travel. The firm had watched the *Newsnight* film and read the *Guardian* article, and it had decided to ignore the malicious references from BA that had dogged Sherman since he was fired. Gorman allowed himself to imagine that a new chapter in their lives might be on the point of opening for them.

Gorman and Sherman had agonised for months over whether to try and alert the media to BA's dirty-tricks campaign against them. Both had known that their private lives would become very public, and that base elements in BA and the Metropolitan Police would seek to exploit this. The Gorman and Sherman families had been closely consulted before John and Peter approached journalists. Both families had supported their decision, and had continued to offer encouragement and love throughout their ordeal. The accumulated stress of the struggle to obtain justice was by now affecting Gorman's health. He was on medication to counter the stress, and was still being treated for the damage to his gullet caused by swallowing the broken glass. His doctor had told me that his condition was being aggravated by the strain that the dispute with BA had placed on him. Now it appeared to Gorman that there was real hope that BA would propose an honourable settlement.

Ayling did not write to Gorman the next day, but Cocklin phoned to assure him that his reply would not long be delayed. As he waited, Gorman continued to keep his pledge to BA and gave no further media interviews. Ayling's reply, however, never came. Instead Gorman received a letter from Ken Walder. BA's new legal director wrote to inform Gorman that he saw no further point in correspondence or discussion. Walder said that if he intended to carry out his threat to sue BA, Linklaters & Paines would accept his writ on BA's behalf.

Gorman was beyond surprise but he had no intention of giving up. The media interest had boosted his confidence, and restored to him some of the dignity that BA's campaign against him had robbed him of. The following day he appeared on LBC's morning news programme again and announced that he would be suing BA for its entire campaign against him. Gorman lodged his fresh legal action against BA at Uxbridge County Court. The particulars of Gorman's claim against BA lists the malicious and threatening phone calls he received from BA, the theft of documents from his flat during the violent attack on him, the theft of further documents from his car in the BA car park, and the repeated slander by the BA press office.

After the secret negotiations with Ayling broke down, the dirty-tricks team, which had been inoperative since Gorman confronted Marshall and Ayling at the AGM, swung into action again.

At the end of September the threatening calls started again; an anonymous man rang to tell Gorman, 'Your remarks in the media have caused immense damage to British Airways. Unless you desist from this action you will receive a further visit to remind you how you should behave'.

Ayling had asked Gorman if he still recorded his calls at their Speedbird House meeting earlier in the month. Gorman replied that he no longer had to as the calls had ceased after the BA AGM. Gorman did, however, retain the BT tracing facility, and he activated it during the call. He was depressed but not surprised to hear from the police several days later that the call had, once again, been to traced to BA. This time the call had been traced to BA premises in central London.

The BA press office also went on the offensive against Gorman again, after its almost mute performance during August and early September. It implied to journalists from the *Daily Telegraph* and *The Times* that Gorman was attempting to blackmail BA by threatening media exposure if he did not receive compensation from BA. This was quite untrue. Gorman had pointedly refused to discuss a sum of money at his meeting with Ayling. He simply said that he wanted the matter settled. The journalists found BA's line quite implausible, particularly as Gorman had only just received acres of publicity that could hardly have portrayed BA in a worse light, and they omitted BA's insinuations in their reports.

Other journalists had no qualms, however, in rubbishing Gorman in a way that would have made even the BA press office blush. *Skyport*, an airport free-sheet that claims a circulation of 80,000, published an ugly article about Gorman the week after the *Newsnight* report. Gorman immediately issued a libel writ against it. It is not possible to discuss the content of the libel here, and I would not want to give the *Skyport* smears any further currency. It is possible to record, however, that *Skyport* journalists are frequent visitors to Speedbird House, and that BA is one of the paper's main advertisers. *Skyport* has also acknowledged that the Metropolitan Police was a source for the story that it published. The *Skyport* story was riddled with inaccuracies and innuendo. Had the journalists who wrote it bothered to check their facts with Gorman before they published it, they would have discovered this. Unfortunately for Gorman, and ultimately for them, they did not.

As Gorman set about taking the BA and the Metropolitan Police to court, he knew that he faced an extraordinarily difficult and possibly dangerous task. Whoever is persecuting Gorman resumed their activities shortly after BA's bosses challenged Gorman to take them to court. On 10 November 1994, Gorman and Sherman arrived at Heathrow to fly BA to Rio for a short holiday. Gorman had been reinstated in BA's Executive Club shortly after his meeting with Marshall and Ayling in the summer, and so they waited in the Club lounge in Terminal 4. Shortly before the flight Gorman heard his name called on the tannoy. He went to the desk and collected an envelope which was addressed to him. On a single side of BA-headed notepaper, he read the following:

> Mr John Gorman
> Mr Peter Sherman
>
> I want to you inform you that you are both not welcome aboard this flight today to Rio . . . It is suggested you use a different carrier.
>   . . . Both of you still persist in trying to discredit the good name of British Airways with your insipid and menacing allegations. Senior management have decided that the only way to deal with you both is by instructing Linklaters & Paines to defend any action that you bring against this airline.

The typewritten script continued with increasing menace:

> The consequences for you both can be quite devastating. It is intended by Linklaters acting on our instructions to make application for your property, motor vehicles and assets to be sequestrated when you fail to substantiate your allegations.

Their tormentor appeared not to have shaken BA's original, mistaken belief that Gorman was a 'Virgin stooge':

> We are now in possession of evidence, that links both of you with Richard Branson of Virgin Atlantic. It has been further established that both of you have had meetings with him and sums of money were handed to you.
>   It is the determined belief of B.A. management that you both accepted this cash in an effort to destroy the reputation

of British Airways for the benefit of Virgin Atlantic.

None of this is true. Gorman and Branson have never met or spoken, and Gorman has never received any money from Virgin. The author of the letter was either fantasising or relying on sources of information that were as flawed as those used by BA's private detectives in Operation Covent Garden. Apparently the widespread publicity that the *Newsnight* film had provoked had upset the author:

> You have also allowed yourself to be used by a gutter television program [sic], together with so called professional journalists and the newspapers that employ them, to destroy B.A. . . .
> *You will not succeed.*

Finally there was yet another threat of physical violence:

> Consider your position very carefully, before further serious damage is contemplated against you both . . .

Gorman and Sherman were extremely distressed by the letter. The BA staff that had unknowingly handed Gorman the threatening letter were also upset when he showed it to them. They willingly signed the envelope to indicate that it had, indeed, been delivered to Gorman by them in the Executive Club lounge. Cabin crew comforted the distressed pair on the flight to Brazil, and told them how appalled they had been by the accounts they had read of their ordeal in the press.

At the end of November a sensational leaked fax from Aviation Defence arrived at *Private Eye*. It was sent anonymously to Paul Foot, apparently by a source who objected to the harsh treatment that Gorman was continuing to get from BA. Foot was an obvious choice for the leak. Since his first article in June, he had established a reputation for ignoring the mischief-makers in BA's press department, and he had defiantly published a series of extraordinary revelations about BA's appalling treatment of Gorman in the *Eye*. The fax is a copy of a memo. It could possibly have come from the same BA source who phoned Gorman himself at the beginning of 1994 to encourage him, claiming that 'they're all corrupt here . . . they are telling lies hand over fist to management'; or perhaps the source who phoned Foot in the middle of the year to tell him that the documents stolen in the violent robbery had been handed in to Mervyn Walker's office.

The memo is addressed to Keith Kerr in the 'Internal Audit' department. Gorman had been particularly angry with the way Kerr had conducted himself throughout his 'investigation' into his claims, finding him arrogant and rude. Mervyn Walker had apologised to Gorman for Kerr's oafish behaviour. The memo was signed and sent by Peter Goodenough, who is identified on the headed 'Aviation Defence International' notepaper as a 'Cabin Services Manager'. It is marked 'DIRECT FAX/STRICTLY CONFIDENTIAL'. Goodenough tells Kerr in the memo that:

> the letter we discussed will be deposited one hour prior to departure, at the reception desk outside the first class lounge at Terminal 4, this should avoid any identification of the person delivering it.

The memo is dated 7 November. Gorman collected the threatening letter before he boarded his flight to Brazil on 10 November. It had been deposited at the First Class lounge, as the Goodenough/Kerr memo said it would be, and it was then brought down to the reception desk in the Executive Club lounge by BA staff who were as shocked to read it as Gorman was when he opened it. The memo from Goodenough also contained some extraordinary admissions about other aspects of Gorman's appalling treatment:

> In answer to your questions, the remainder of the GORMAN/DAVID ROSE file have [sic] now been destroyed, also the GORMAN taped conversation with officials Walker/Cahill including several of yourself.

Aviation Defence thus admitted that the file and the tapes stolen in the violent robbery on Gorman had not only been received but also destroyed. There were further crucial references in the memo to Kerr about his fellow BA 'investigators'. The name of Andrew Warman, one of Kerr's colleagues in the 'Internal Audit' department, was found on a calling card dropped by one of the thugs as he fled from Gorman's flat, having beaten him up and robbed him. Goodenough was able to reassure Kerr on that score:

> The calling card accidentally left at Gorman's flat is not an official B.A. card of Warman, so he will be in the clear.

This information could only have come either from the Enfield police who found the card after the robbery, or from one of the two thugs who dropped it. Gorman himself has never seen the card.

It appears from the memo that Aviation Defence International is trying very hard to cover the tracks of Robin Armstrong, Gorman's chief tormentor:

> In relation to Armstrong the relevant documents have been removed and some minor alterations to others have been carried out.

Shredding potentially damaging documents is, of course, accepted practice at BA, and amongst those they employ in a 'security' capacity, particularly when court cases loom. It will be interesting, however, to see how BA explains the removal of documents relating to Armstrong, and the destruction of the property stolen from Gorman, when his cases come to court in 1996.

Goodenough was satisfied that the police had made no progress in their investigations into the violent attack on Gorman:

> We have it on good authority that the Enfield Police are handling the case badly, and that no progress is anticipated and it is not conceivable for them to make any connection with B.A. without the evidence.

Goodenough thus confirmed what the source at Enfield police station had told me when I was preparing my *Newsnight* report.

In one of the most damning sentences, Goodenough tells Kerr that no more threatening calls should be made to Gorman:

> Our source at Heathrow Police Station has advised that no further action should be taken against GORMAN and SHERMAN. In particular it was stressed that no further telephone calls should be made from B.A. premises as the tracing facility is still effective.

The letter provided Gorman with a smoking gun for his court case against BA. It is as damning as the operational log kept by Covent Garden's sinister fanatasists in their undercover operation to bring Branson down.

BA admitted that Goodenough was working on a BA contract at Heathrow, and acknowledged that the fax number from which the memo was sent is located at Terminal 1. Predictably, however, BA said that despite 'considerable efforts' it had not been able to establish who sent the fax, and that neither Kerr nor Goodenough knew anything about it. Every detail in Goodenough's memo, however, checks out with known facts, every individual named is familiar to Gorman, and it could only have been written by someone with an intimate knowledge of the lengthy affair.

By the middle of 1996, Gorman had fled Britain and was living in Tenerife, effectively in exile, pending the start of his court cases against BA and the Metropolitan Police. The first one, against British Airways over the 'glass in the drink' incident, is due to come to court in November 1996. Gorman and Peter Sherman had quit Britain in the winter of 1995 on the advice of Gorman's doctors and lawyers as the campaign against them reached a crescendo following a sea-change in BA's attitude towards Gorman's complaint about the 'glass in the drink' incident.

In the summer of 1994, according to BA's record of their meeting, Mervyn Walker told Gorman: 'British Airways accepts what you are saying at face value. We do not challenge your version of events . . . Your claim is worth thousands . . . It is clear that serious criminal matters have occurred.' By the summer of 1995, BA not only denied being responsible for the campaign of harassment against Gorman, it had also reversed its position on the 'glass in the drink' incident. Its defence documents state: 'It is not admitted that Mr Gorman suffered the injury alleged.'

Furthermore, BA has lined up members of the cabin crew to challenge Gorman's account of the 'glass in the drink' incident, and it has asked the Uxbridge County Court to reserve three weeks for the hearing. Quite how the airline intends to square this position with the offer it authorised Beaumont and Son to make to Gorman (of £1,750 in compensation if he signed a gagging clause) will no doubt be revealed in court.

BA's decision to fight Gorman's claims through its lawyers, Linklaters & Paines, has been accompanied by a fierce PR offensive conducted through its press office and Lowe Bell to discredit Gorman and restrict media coverage of the saga. It is clear that BA intends to launch a massive attack on Gorman's credibility in court. In preparation for this assault, Lowe Bell has been operating behind the scenes to try to discredit Gorman and to prevent any further media coverage of the case in the interim period.

Journalists at *The Times*, the *Observer* and the *Daily Telegraph* have all been subjected to Lowe Bell's familiar tactics. Nowhere has this pressure been more noticeable that at the BBC, which BA appears to fear more than any other media outlet. Although BA later stated that it was incensed by the original Gorman reports, which were transmitted on the *Nine O'Clock News* and *Newsnight* in August 1994, it made no official complaint to the BBC.

The BBC asked me to make a follow-up report in February 1995, after Dee McIntosh had been alerted to further intimidation aimed at Gorman. The second Gorman film was originally pencilled in by *Newsnight* to be shown on 12 April 1995. However, partly as a result of both written and oral objections to the film from BA and Lowe Bell, the BBC has still to decide whether it will transmit the film. BA and its PR men have succeeded in delaying transmission substantially. The Gorman film was sent up to the BBC hierarchy by Peter Horrocks, the editor of *Newsnight*, in the autumn of 1995 after a series of lengthy meetings with senior BA officials. As I write these words in July 1996, the hierarchy has yet to bestow its approval upon the film. The first Gorman film took twenty-eight days to make, from the start of production to transmission; the BBC hierarchy has been considering the second Gorman film for over nine months, following an eight-month production period.

Our second film reveals another extraordinary series of events that befell Gorman after BA declared that it would 'see him in court', which eventually drove him into exile in the Canary Islands.

The menacing calls recommenced shortly after his direct negotiations with Robert Ayling and Tony Cocklin collapsed. One caller warned Gorman: 'Your remarks in the national media have caused immense damage to BA. Unless you desist from this course of action you will receive a further visit to remind you how you should behave.' This call was traced by BT to BA's Central London office in Buckingham Palace Road. The police told Gorman that the call had been traced to a senior manager's office; several BA personnel were interviewed, but no one was arrested or charged. Gorman logged all the calls in his normal fastidious manner, and BT traced some of them to BA premises and others to the Metropolitan Police at Heathrow. In September 1995, shortly before he decided to quit Britain, Gorman recorded the following call: '. . . you were warned not to go to the AGM and now you are going to pay the price. By the way your latest complaints are going nowhere.' The voice was quiet, uneducated and menacing.

The BT nuisance calls bureau traced the number from which the call was made – 0171 730 1136 – to British Airways' Buckingham Palace Road office. BA later admitted that the call had been made from its premises, but said that it could not establish who had made it. The caller was referring to Gorman's appearance at BA's AGM in July 1995 which afforded some moments of light relief in the dark saga, but also provided confirmation that BA was hardening its attitude towards its discontented shareholder.

Gorman had defied another threat to attend the AGM at

London's Barbican Centre on 11 July. The disgruntled shareholder had received a sinister fax the day before the AGM. Gorman was abroad until the evening before the AGM. He returned home to find the following fax had been sent at 10.30 that morning: 'Conditions for peace of mind . . . No 11 July 1995'. The warning, sent on a BA fax sheet, had been faxed to Gorman after *The Times* had reported in its 10 July edition that Gorman was intending to go to the AGM.

At the 1994 AGM Marshall and Ayling had both listened intently to Gorman in private meetings away from the floor of the AGM. They had both assured him that his complaints would be taken seriously; those conversations heralded a three-month lull in the hostilities against Gorman.

At the 1995 AGM Gorman immediately found himself surrounded by BA security men who followed him everywhere he went:

'They were large men with square heads and wires coming out of their ears. They didn't impress me a great deal as I've obviously known the real thing in the Anti-Terrorist Branch, but they had clearly been told to shadow me. When I went for a pee, one of them appeared at each shoulder and neither of them were having a pee!'

Gorman spotted Ayling as soon as he arrived; he tried to confront him with the fax which had warned him not to attend the AGM: 'Ayling read the fax and then disappeared saying he had more important matters to deal with . . .' Gorman did manage a brief conversation with Ken Walder, who was also wearing an ear-piece. 'Walder was very friendly,' recalls Gorman. 'He said he was "sorry this sort of thing is continuing", and told me that trying to find who was responsible was "like trying to find a needle in a haystack".'

Gorman managed to evade his minders briefly on the floor of the AGM itself and slipped into a seat next to Lord King, while Lady King was absent from it. Horrified security men surrounded Gorman and BA's president, but not before Gorman had been allowed to ask a question. Marshall was on the platform and, presumably unable to identify the hand waving next to Lord King as Gorman's, invited him to ask a question:

I asked Marshall why the dirty-tricks department is allowed to continue to operate in BA, and I asked him what he had to say about the flood of adverse publicity that BA was suffering as a result. Marshall was really annoyed and replied angrily that there was no dirty-tricks department in BA and that there never had been one. So then I asked him who had sent me the threatening fax on the eve of the AGM and I read it out. Marshall didn't answer directly but said that the matter would be dealt with in the courts.

As soon as he had asked his question Gorman was immediately surrounded by BA security men who prevented him continuing his conversation with Lord King, 'just as it was beginning to get interesting,' recalls Gorman.

It must have been clear to Gorman's tormentors, whether they were present at the AGM or whether they read the subsequent press coverage, that there was no longer any chance of BA seeking an out of court settlement with Gorman. Soon the threats became even more sinister.

The most dramatic was a note sent to Gorman and Sherman with a bottle of BA champagne. It was crudely stencilled in capital letters on Metropolitan Police memo paper:

IF THESE MATTERS EVER REACH COURT BOTH OF YOU ARE DEAD GAYS. HAVE THE CHAMPAGNE ON US. IT'S YOUR LAST?? REMEMBER NO WIN – NOBODY.

The homophobic theme continued in a cluster of obscene, semi-literate letters, written on BA stationery which was left on the windscreen of Gorman's BMW. The car had been vandalised at the same time; the words 'No win with BA' had once again been etched on the boot, and every panel of the car had been scratched with a sharp instrument. The cost of repairing the damage was £2,000.

In April 1995, Gorman travelled to visit his family in New York en route to Hawaii for a holiday, in a bid to escape the relentless pressure of the campaign against him. He made a point of booking with American Airlines, as he had experienced so many mishaps on BA. When he arrived at Heathrow, however, an American official told him that someone claiming to be from BA had been trying to find out about his flight plans. The AA computer log read under Gorman's entry:

> AS PER LONBA REF JAMES HANON/CALLED TO CFM IF PAX ON FLT AS CERTAIN DOCUMENTS LEFT BEHIND BY PASSENGER IN NYC WILL BE DELIVERED TO HIM IN NYC

– which meant 'James Hanon from BA in London called to confirm if the passenger was on the flight as certain documents left behind by the passenger in New York will be delivered to him in New York.'

No one called 'James Hanon' works for either BA or ADI. As the surname suggests, the name is a fiction. The message was also a fiction as Gorman had been nowhere near New York for a long time, nor left any documents there. AA officials were convinced that the caller was from BA, however, and thus entered the message in their computer.

The caller's name was fictitious, but the message contained a truthful prediction. As Gorman boarded his plane for Hawaii in New York, he did receive a document. As he took his seat on board the plane, an American Airlines official presented him with an envelope with his name on it. Gorman opened it as the plane took off. The letter inside was written on headed notepaper indicating that it came from BA's New York office. It read:

'Welcome to New York Mr Gorman. Your interference will not be tolerated any longer. You are aware of the devastation we can inflict on people's lives. So far you've gotten off lightly.' The letter ended with a threat to Gorman and his New York-based family. 'Your continued involvement in this lawsuit will have very serious implications to both you and your family. Once again, you have been warned.'

Gorman was devastated as he flew west to Hawaii via Los Angeles. Bob Crandall, American Airlines' chief executive, was sufficiently concerned to set up an enquiry into the incident to look at how someone, claiming to be from BA, had found out about Gorman's flight details, and how his staff had unwittingly delivered a threatening letter to Gorman on board one of his airline's flights. BA said it had no idea who could have written the letter, and stated that the BA notepaper used is readily available to its staff in New York.

The American Airlines incident came shortly after Gorman had vowed to avoid BA flights wherever possible, following a chilling sequence of events when he flew to Israel on a short break in February 1995. As he set off for Heathrow Airport, Gorman suspected that he was being followed. As a former member of the Anti-Terrorist Branch, he was used to studying his rear-view mirror carefully, and to employing counter-surveillance techniques. He moved from lane to lane on the M25 as he drove towards Heathrow from Enfield. The car was still there. Gorman eventually drove off the motorway at the South Mimms exit and shook the car off. He took the car's number as it passed him. He then continued to Heathrow, parked his car at the Heathrow Hilton and took his flight to Israel.

Gorman had just begun to relax in Israel when two messages delivered to him by the Tel Aviv Hilton message service ruined his holiday. According to the typed messages from the hotel message-takers, both callers were from 'ADI in London'. The first message read: 'You are advised to contact your lawyers in London to withdraw court action against BA.' The second message, timed just one minute later by the hotel's computer log, read: 'Your car parked at Hilton Heathrow. Message. No win with BA. Regards ADI Heathrow airport.'

Gorman was alarmed. Surely his car had not been vandalised again. He went straight to the British consul, Mr John Fielder, whose office is situated opposite the Tel Aviv Hilton. Fielder called the Metropolitan Police at Heathrow, and asked them to check Gorman's car. Within half an hour the police phoned back to tell Fielder that there was no damage to the car. A relieved Gorman returned to his hotel.

However, shortly after he returned to his room, William Costley, a manager from the Hilton in London, phoned to say that his car had been daubed with the words 'No Win BA'. The following day, Costley faxed Gorman a photograph of the graffiti.

Gorman was incredulous. The British consul had been assured by the Metropolitan Police that there was no damage to his car.

Gorman's return to London was further marred by another mysterious letter which arrived for him at his hotel shortly before he left for home. It arrived in a British Airways envelope, at the Hilton's reception desk. On the back someone had written 'from British Airways Ben-Goryon [sic] Airport 9/2/95'. Inside was a familiar message: 'British Airways, Gorman. No win BA'. The words had been cut out of newspapers and magazines.

Gorman was met by William Costley and a police officer when he returned to Heathrow, and they took him to retrieve his car. Gorman took it to his garage once again to be repaired. Soon after his return the menacing calls started again: 'Did you like the free re-spray Gorman? No win with BA. More to come. Withdraw your action now.' Gorman has a BT Caller Display Unit. It revealed that the call came from 0181 759 7555. This is the main number of Aviation Defence International.

Gorman gave the police and *Newsnight* the number of the car he claimed had tried to followed him to Heathrow as he set off on his holiday to Israel in February 1995. Eight weeks later a secretary on *Newsnight* took a call from an anonymous caller who claimed to be a police officer. He said that there was an enormous cover-up going on at Heathrow police station, and that the car that had been used to follow Gorman in February was parked in a space reserved for a BA security manager at Heathrow. We followed up the lead immediately, and filmed a car bearing the number that Gorman had given us parked exactly where the caller had described. When we asked BA about this, we were told that the owner of the car is a highly respected member of staff.

ADI's name had started to appear with increasing frequency in the threats against Gorman since the memo which appeared to come from Peter Goodenough had been leaked to *Private Eye*. I wondered if it was possible that BA had been contracting out dirty tricks against Gorman to ADI. Operation Covent Garden provided a clear precedent for such a pattern of activity. In BA's campaign against Branson and Virgin, BA had used Carratu International and Ian Johnson's band of motley irregulars, partly because of their 'specialists skills', and partly as a way of giving BA 'plausible deniability' if anyone was caught. Unfortunately for BA, those charged with doing its dirty work on that occasion exhibited few skills and committed the ultimate crime of getting caught.

ADI's managing director, Trevor Warburton, repeated his denial that the author of the fax to Keith Kerr was his employee, Peter Goodenough, and said that ADI's computer telephone log showed no record of a call to Gorman's home or to the Tel Aviv Hilton. Furthermore he said that if any ADI employee was discovered to have been involved in any of the incidents that I put to him, the person would be sacked.

As John Gorman and Peter Sherman prepared to leave Britain to escape the relentless pressure on them, Gorman admitted to *The Times* newspaper that he had been paid $5,000 in 1991 to settle a similar incident in America. Gorman claimed on this occasion that he cut his mouth when he swallowed shards of glass in some ice cream he was eating on board a Delta Airlines flight. Dobbs International Services, the catering company that supplied Delta with its in-flight food, paid Gorman the money after he received hospital treatment following the flight.

Gorman's belated disclosure of the Delta incident damaged the credibility of his claim against British Airways significantly. The possibility of such an incident occurring once is remote; the chances of it happening twice is too small to calculate. If one adds to that another incident on board BA in April 1990 when Gorman found an unused condom in his meal, for which BA paid him £3,000 compensation in ticket vouchers, it is not difficult to see why so many people have been sceptical of his claims. It is also the case that Gorman did not disclose the Delta incident to *The Times* until he knew that British Airways had discovered it while preparing to defend itself against his action.

Gorman points out that since the condom incident and June 1996 he made 178 flights on seventeen different airlines and thus he was much more likely to experience problems than an occasional flyer:

'I just thought that no one would believe me at all if I had volunteered information about the Delta incident in the first place. My experience at the hands of British Airways was difficult enough to believe anyway, without introducing another element that people would find incredible. But I swear that both incidents did happen, and I have the evidence to prove it. In the condom case the BA cabin crew witnessed it, and I was swiftly compensated with no fuss. In the Delta case, Dobbs settled quickly and politely when I complained and provided the evidence.'

Delta confirmed the facts of the 1991 incident but declined to comment further. While saying little publicly, British Airways leapt on the revelation about the Delta incident, and tried to place stories in the quality press to drive home the rare advantage that the Delta story had handed them. Peter Jones's press office hawked stories about previous complaints made by Gorman around news desks before finding a sympathetic ear at the *Sunday Times*. Two of 'Basham's boys' from the era of the dirty-tricks campaign against Virgin now work there. John Jay is the City editor and, remarkably, Frank Kane is the head of the paper's much reduced 'Insight' team, which once had a reputation as an investigative unit of some note.

'BA case man in five earlier complaints' cried the *Sunday Times* headline as BA smacked its lips gratefully. Unfortunately for the story's authors, Frank Kane and Mark Franchetti, neither the headline nor the story were accurate. Gorman had no hesitation in taking the *Sunday Times* to the Press Complaints Commission, and is confidently awaiting the outcome as I conclude my account of this extraordinary saga in July 1996.

The Gorman case has already caused the Metropolitan Police enormous embarrassment, as it has Aviation Defence International. As a former member of the Anti-Terrorist Branch, and a veteran of twenty years in the Met himself, Gorman was well aware of the close relationship between BA and the Met before he lodged his initial complaint against the police. He knows that the two organisations have always had many areas of genuine mutual concern, from attempting to safeguard BA, its property and its passengers from terrorist attack, to detecting international ticket fraud and smuggling. Because of these close connections, Gorman has always been concerned about the objectivity of the Heathrow police.

Gorman had initially complained to the Police Complaints Branch at New Scotland Yard about the May 1993 raid on his home by BA investigator Robin Armstrong and officers from Heathrow; Gorman had been arrested on suspicion of 'conspiracy to defraud BA'. Chief Inspector Lovelock was appointed to head the investigation into Gorman's complaints. His investigation also handled Gorman's subsequent complaints, including those about the threatening phone calls which BT traced to Heathrow police station. When Lovelock had failed to complete his report into Gorman's complaints against the Heathrow police more than a year later, Gorman wrote to Peter Winship, the Assistant Commissioner at New Scotland Yard in charge of inspection and review. He complained that Lovelock's investigation appeared to be stalled and that the Enfield police investigation into the raid on his home – described by officers as 'aggravated burglary' – had got nowhere.

At the end of October 1994, Winship's office wrote to Gorman to say that two senior DCIs (one at Heathrow and one at Enfield) had been verbally admonished as a result of Gorman's complaints. Gorman had been told that if he agreed to an informal resolution of the action against the two DCIs, it would help Lovelock's enquiry concentrate on the main issues raised by his complaint. When Gorman agreed on an informal resolution, which avoided the need for formal disciplinary action, the Assistant Commissioner wrote to thank Gorman for his 'much appreciated' assistance.

Lovelock handed his report to the office of Barbara Mills, the Director of Public Prosecutions, who eventually decided that there was not enough evidence, 'beyond reasonable doubt', to warrant a prosecution. The report was then passed on to the Police Complaints Authority, the body set up by Parliament independently to investigate complaints against police by members of the public.

The PCA laboured for over two years over its investigation into Gorman's complaints before deciding that there was 'insufficient evidence on which to base a formal disciplinary charge' against any of the officers that Gorman complained about. In a letter to Gorman summarising the PCA's findings, a Mrs Cawsey wrote:

The evidence emphasises that some of the calls were made from police establishments, but unfortunately, despite the Investigating Officer's stringent efforts, the identity of the culprit(s) has not been verified (although it should be noted that no personnel were interviewed twice in connection with the calls) . . . the Deputy Assistant Commissioner accepts that these calls were probably made by Metropolitan police personnel. The Authority concur with his view, and I have relayed my concerns to the Force regarding the unsatisfactory outcome of this aspect of your complaint.

Gorman himself was not interviewed or spoken to during the PCA's investigation, and he was incensed at the PCA's conclusion, spotting many errors and omissions in Cawsey's letter summarising the Authority's conclusions. He was particularly angry that the PCA appeared to have accepted DC O'Rourke's account of the 1993 raid on his home, and his consequent detention at Heathrow police station. As a former police officer himself, Gorman is a stickler for procedure; he knew that O'Rourke had acted unlawfully in taking privileged correspondence between himself and his solicitor in the raid. When Gorman had confronted him at the time, he claims that O'Rourke responded by saying, 'I'm in charge and I'll take exactly what I want.'

Despite his angry and articulate letters of protest to the PCA, Gorman assumed that this was the end of the PCA's probe into his complaints, until an announcement at the end of May 1996 took him, and everyone else, by surprise. The PCA announced that a new enquiry was being launched by a very senior police officer into the Gorman complaint after a bundle of documents, relevant to the original PCA probe but not disclosed to the PCA during its two-year enquiry, had been discovered in the solicitor's office at New Scotland Yard.

At the beginning of July 1996, Detective Chief Superintendent Fred Ashmore, accompanied by Detective Inspector John May, landed at Tenerife Airport and made their way to Gorman's apartment. Ashmore is the head of Thames Valley's complaints department and his appointment by the PCA to probe the Gorman affair was in itself significant; his enquiry marked the first time since the massive Operation Countryman enquiry into corruption in the Metropolitan Police that a member of another force had been asked to probe alleged wrong-doing in the Met.

Ashmore informed Gorman and Sherman that two bundles of documents had been discovered in the Metropolitan solicitor's office at New Scotland Yard. The bundles contained ninety-nine documents that had been seized by the police when they arrested Gorman in May 1993. Approximately a third of the documents were legally privileged items of correspondence between Gorman and his solicitor relating to his complaint against BA. What made the documents particularly significant was the fact that the officers who conducted the raid on Gorman's home with the BA investigator, Robin Armstrong, had specifically denied seizing any of them when quizzed by the original PCA enquiry. The most telling discovery in the two bundles was DC O'Rourke's working exhibit notes on the Gorman case. Although O'Rourke had consistently denied to Gorman, and to the PCA enquiry, that his posse of police officers had seized two American Airlines tickets, his own notes revealed that he had seized them. These were the tickets that were returned to Gorman with the message 'Happy Holiday Arsehole!' several months after their expiry date. Even more significantly, the insulting note was written on BA headed notepaper, and Mervyn Walker had written to John Gorman two years earlier to confirm that the envelope containing the tickets had, indeed, been posted through the BA mail sort system.

Gorman had good reason to feel vindicated. Also discovered in the bundles at New Scotland Yard were photocopies indicating that the police had seized Gorman's and Sherman's private diaries:

'We didn't even know the police had taken them!' Gorman exclaimed. 'We both thought we must have lost them. The new evidence also shows that they also took the deeds to my house in Enfield, my nephew's passport and other personal documents that were of no conceivable use to the police or BA.'

That Ashmore's probe took place at all was a victory for Gorman's relentless pursuit of the Heathrow police, and his energetic and detailed criticism of the PCA's conclusions. It was also a victory for Paul Foot, who had written more than a dozen *Private Eye* articles on the unfolding Gorman saga. He had persisted where other journalists had faltered and, according to Ashmore, it was Foot's highly critical articles of the PCA's enquiry into the

Gorman affair (one was entitled 'Police Cover-up Authority') that had created the pressure on the PCA to request the Metropolitan Police to re-check the available documentation on the affair. In the course of reviewing the documents, a young detective, DS Kyte, came across the bundles in the solicitor's office on New Scotland Yard that had not been made available to the original PCA enquiry.

Gorman is not by nature a conspiracy theorist. He is a decent former police officer who believes that he now has considerable evidence to prove that elements within BA and the Metropolitan Police have collaborated to victimise him and deny him justice:

'It is remarkable to think that documents crucial to my case against BA have now been found on no less than three occasions in solicitors' offices. First my car was broken into in BA's highly secure car park at Heathrow and some of the documents stolen were returned to Beaumont and Son, BA's City solicitors. Then documents stolen from my flat when I was beaten up appear on Mervyn Walker's desk at Speedbird House, and, finally, documents seized by the police in their 1993 raid on my home turn up in the solicitor's office of New Scotland Yard after the Heathrow police denied for over three years that they had even taken them. I think I am entitled to ask what is going on!'

Further evidence of BA's close links with the police came in one of the letters that Robert Ayling wrote to the BBC as he tried to prevent it broadcasting our second *Newsnight* report on the Gorman affair. Although BA was furious at the first *Newsnight* report, it made no formal complaint until seven months later when we alerted it to our second investigation; we invited BA to take part in the film. At this point Robert Ayling wrote to Tony Hall, the BBC's managing director of News and Current Affairs. In an attempt to undermine the second *Newsnight* probe, Ayling made a number of criticisms of our first report. All of these were easily dispatched by Hall as our report was completely accurate and based strictly on the evidence that we had uncovered and checked out, but there was one criticism we were unable to respond to.

Ayling took particular exception to *Newsnight*'s reconstruction of the attack on Gorman in his home. We had depicted the police finding a BA business card. The police had told Gorman and,

much later, *Newsnight* that Andrew Warman's name had been
scribbled on it. We had not reported this latter detail. Neither had
we reported the fact that Warman was interviewed but not
charged by police investigating the attack. Ayling wrote to Hall:

> The suggestion made by the programme, which was cer-
> tainly not confirmed by us, was that Mr Gorman's assailant
> dropped a business card in the course of the attack and that
> this linked the Company with the attack. This did not hap-
> pen. The police confirmed that it did not happen. The only
> evidence that exists in relation to this aspect of the affair – the
> baggage tag – proves nothing as such as tags are freely avail-
> able and it is, of course, very simple for anyone to write
> anything they like on one.

The fascinating thing about this claim from Ayling is the obvious
question it raises: where did Ayling get his information from? The
police had not told *Newsnight* that they had found a baggage tag as
opposed to a business card, and they had most certainly not told
Gorman or his solicitor; both had been told by the Enfield police
that a business card had been found. Gorman was shocked to discover that the information had come from BA's group managing
director. How did Ayling know that the card dropped was not a
business card, and that it was a baggage tag? If the police informed
Ayling, the managing director of the company under suspicion of
instigating the attack, why didn't they inform Gorman, the victim
of the crime, or his solicitor?

I have not encountered anyone who can supply a satisfactory
explanation as to how a minor passenger complaint has been
allowed to mushroom into an affair of such epic proportions. In a
sense everyone is losing: British Airways has reaped another
whirlwind of 'dirty tricks' publicity as it has utterly failed to come
to terms with its disgruntled shareholder; the Metropolitan Police
at Heathrow have laid themselves open to charges of complicity in
the campaign against Gorman, and, after the ineffective police
complaints investigation, officers are now being interviewed for a
second time to discover why key documents were not made available to the PCA in the first place; certain journalists, broadcasters

and newspapers have confirmed that BA's expensive and highly influential PR operation continues to carry disproportionate weight despite its humiliation and subsequent exposure in the Virgin dirty-tricks affair; and Gorman's life has been ruined for the past three years by the pressures and the strain of mounting his one-man campaign for justice.

Gorman has a great deal of evidence to support his legal actions against BA and the Met, but it will be a remarkable achievement if he wins them. Both organisations are fighting his actions with the vast resources at their disposal. 'The World's Favourite Airline' is devoting a minute fraction of its record 1996 profits to fending off a retired ex-policeman who lives on a disability pension. It is not an edifying spectacle.

Picture Credits

The author and publisher are grateful to the following sources for pictures reproduced in the book:

T. Boccon-Gibod (Richard Branson, p.1*; Richard Branson, p.2); Camera Press (Richard Branson, p.1; Sir Freddie Laker, p.3); Jim Meads (Lord King, p.2); the Press Association (Reagan and Thatcher, p.3; Robert Ayling, p.6; Sir Colin Marshall, p.9; Popperfoto (Richard Branson, p.1; Lord King, p.3); *Travel Trade Gazette* (David Burnside, p.4); Phil Sayer/*Management Today* (Mike Batt, p.6); Virgin Group (Will Whitehorn, p.7; Richard Branson p.8; Sir Freddie Laker and Richard Branson, p.13); *Legal Business* (Gerrard Tyrrell, p.7); Express Newspapers (Richard Branson and Sir Colin Southgate, p.7); Times Newspapers Ltd (Lord King, p.8; press cutting, p.14; John Gorman, p.16); Granada Television/*World in Action* (Brian Basham, pp.9 & 10); Thames Television (Dick Eberhart, p.10; David Burnside, p.10); *Executive Travel* (Richard Branson, p.11); Abigail Sharp (Sadig Khalifa, p.12); *Euromoney* (Mervyn Walker, p.13); Rex Features (Owen Oyston, p.12; Richard Branson, p.14; Sir Tim Bell, Lord King and Sir Colin Marshall, p.15); Ashley Ashwood/Camera Press (Harry Goodman, p.16) Graham Turner/The *Guardian* (John Gorman, p.16).

(* all page numbers refer to the two picture sections)

Index